LIZZIE

EDWARD RAND

BloodChuckles Press

Lizzie

This is for Jordan.

Always.

"If not for the beast within us we would be castrated angels."

—Herman Hesse

"Love doesn't just sit there, like a stone; it has to be made, like bread, re-made all the time, made new."

—Ursula K. Le Guin

Book I

Animosity

The Price You Pay

THE BEDROOM door crashed open. A shadow reached out and stopped the shuddering door from rebounding, then stepped into the room. Dan sat up fast, top sheet and comforter sliding down his chest.

"Wha—Beth? Is that you?"

The shape didn't respond, but for the moment Dan only pressed his temples with both forefingers. *Goddamn wine.* Beth had been in charge of his party favors, thus the wine and not a tasty dark beer; Dan didn't mind the cheap Italian Merlot she enjoyed, but the vino always gave him the *worst* damn hangovers.

Speaking of his lovely wife…

When he was almost positive his head would stay attached, Dan regarded the silent form outlined in the doorway.

"That wasn't funny, dearest."

The figure stood there.

"Beth?"

Nothing.

That had to be Beth. Didn't it? The height was right, short, and it was obviously a woman, with a female's curvy silhouette, so it had to be…wild locks flowed across this woman's shoulders, with curls spilling to her slender waist.

Beth's dark hair barely brushed her shoulders.

"Um, hello?"

She didn't reply; she only watched him from the shadows.

Was he dreaming? Dan glanced across their king-sized bed at the alarm clock perched on Beth's nightstand—the square red numbers told him 5:27—then scrubbed his face. He'd suffered vivid dreams as a kid, and some had been nightmares that had woken him screaming, not to mention his parents and older brother, but he'd only experienced a handful of those bad boys as an adult, thank God.

Dan held still; birds chirped outside. He dug his fingers into his eyeballs; he could also taste the inside of his own mouth.

Gaak.

He lowered his hands and looked toward the shadowed doorway, but the woman continued to just…stand there. Who was she? What did she want? Beth wasn't in bed with him; had she let this person in? Why? *It's five o'clock in the fucking morning, for God's sake.* Maybe that was her in a wig, playing some kind of wacky birthday prank.

"Beth?"

Whoever she was, she took that as an invitation, swaying forward with clumping steps before stopping on the hardwood near their mirrored dresser.

Dan blinked.

The bedroom was stuck in predawn gloom, but now a silvery luminescence bathed her and her alone, as if she were slowly being lit from below by stage lights. *What the hell?*

And then he gasped. He knew that glowing face; heart-shaped, with a pert and lightly freckled nose, full lips knotted in a hateful smirk; his mother's blue eyes, full of spite.

It was Dan's daughter.

"Lizzie?"

She shared her mother's dark-brown hair, but now it sported a new decoration, a streak of silver: not white or gray, but pure and gleaming silver. The streak started at her right temple and flowed behind her ear and down her back, widening as it went so that almost a third of her curls had that bizarre, metallic luster.

Then Dan forgot all about the hair.

The emergent light had revealed her clothing: knee-high, high-heeled, white-leather boots; skin-tight, white-leather miniskirt; a matching sleeveless vest with no undershirt. The vest's black laces barely kept her full breasts from spilling out.

So it *was* a dream. It had to be a goddamn dream because Dan would never let her out of the house dressed like that in a zillion fucking years. Besides, Lizzie was only four; this woman was in her mid-twenties.

And then she spoke:

"Hello, *Daddy.*"

That word, normally so sweet and treasured from her lips…hearing her say it like that made the agony in his skull less than nothing. Then she made a grasping, clawing motion, and invisible steel bands seized him around the middle. The sheets and comforter slid away, and he found himself dangling above the mattress in his "Football Happens" tee-shirt and plaid boxers with his jaw resting on his chest.

Lizzie clenched her fist.

Dan's ribs snapped, crushing his scream; he threw his head back, writhing as what felt like four giant fingers and a thumb met at his spine. He jerked spasmodically, blood jetting from his mouth and splashing the tray ceiling. Part of his fading consciousness watched in disbelief as an errant crimson streamer curled through the air parallel to the hardwood. Lizzie stood awaiting it with eager mouth open, fist raised and clenched. Dan tried to scream again, hitching at his ruined lungs; he could feel shards of ribs ripping through them.

Across the room, his daughter lapped at his blood like a dog at a water hose.

Dan gasped and sat up. He shot a frantic look at the door to the hallway, discovered it was closed, then sucked in a relieved draught of sweet, painless air. *A dream. Only a dream.* He felt at his wonderfully intact ribs, then dropped his face into his hands.

"Jesus Christ." His voice echoed in his cupped palms; his breath smelled worse than it tasted. "Could've done without that."

The latch clicked, and the bedroom door swung open. Dan gaped at it, then sighed and flopped back on his pillow.

Lizzie stood in the doorway. One little hand held her Dora the Explorer blanket over her shoulder; most of the orange and blue bedspread trailed into the hall. The other hand was planted firmly in face, thumb stuck in her mouth. In the crook of that arm rested Mr. Fred, her stuffed giraffe. Owlish blue eyes hung sleepily in Beth's face three feet from the ground; pillow-tousled dark hair stuck up in back.

Dan said, "Hey baby." *Four again. Still. Thank you, God.* The most terrible part had been the thought that Lizzie had grown up and he'd somehow missed it. What a fucking nightmare; worse than the ones about being back in high school, and he always woke sweating from…

The silence made Dan glance toward the doorway again; Lizzie's eyes were glazed blue marbles on either side of her small fist.

Christ on a cracker, not this shit again. Dan propped himself on his elbow. "Lizzie?"

Nada, zip, zilch; she stared into space, or at the paint on the walls, or at something floating in the air he couldn't see.

"Lizzie."

Nothing.

"Elizabeth."

Eerie silence.

"Elizabeth Ann!"

Her eyes swam into focus. She saw him. He held out his arms, and she responded as if under water, shuffling toward the bed on bare feet, Dora sliding face-first across the planks in her wake. He lifted her and tucked the blanket around her as she settled onto his chest, thumb still planted.

After a minute of feeling his head pound and listening to his daughter breathe and hoping she would drift back to sleep, Lizzie dashed those hopes by pulling her thumb out with a wet pop and greeting him officially:

"Good morning, Daddy." Back went the thumb.

"Good morning, pumpkin." He smoothed her silken hair and kissed the top of her head; her Elmo shampoo smelled of green apples. She hadn't sounded a bit sleepy; no trace of vagueness haunted her piping voice, either. *Vagueness.* It wasn't the right word, but it was close enough. He and Beth called it graying-out. Lizzie sometimes slipped off into her own little world—grayed-out—after one of her nightmares, horrible episodes that began tormenting her when she was two.

Bad dreams must be catching this morning, he thought guiltily.

The vivid dreams were something Dan feared she'd inherited from him—if dreams could be hereditary. Genetic or not, she had them, but they'd stopped when they'd moved into the castle seven months ago, giving them hope that the nightmares as well as the gray-outs were over.

So much for that idea.

Dan scowled, reminded of that waste-of-oxygen Dr. Lewiston, the three-hundred-dollar-an-hour Nashville therapist Beth had insisted they take their then three-year-old to see. At first, Lewiston had wanted Lizzie to talk about the dreams—as if having the damn things in the first place wasn't bad enough, he'd wanted her to rehash what went on during the things that woke her with the screaming heebie-jeebies. The esteemed Dr. Lewiston then diagnosed the graying-out episodes as—how did he put it?—"Elizabeth's conscious mind rationalizing the images that her unconscious mind fomented in the dreaming state", or some gobbledygook. And *then* he'd recommended starting Lizzie on an oral medication. For dreams. *A three-year-old!* The pharmaceutical mega-corporation that held the patent on *that* particular snake oil had likely paid for all the fishing trips that had netted the stuffed exotic fish mounted on Lewiston's paneled walls—where the fucker could fit them between his sheepskins, at least. Corrupt, arrogant, asshole; they were well rid of the good Dr. Lewiston.

Nobody ever asked me to talk about my dreams, and I turned out just fine. Well, mostly.

The thumb popped out again and Lizzie raised her head from a foot away and grinned at him; she'd knocked out both top front baby teeth earlier that summer after falling off her pink, training-wheeled Barbie bike while practicing her riding in the castle's circular driveway (and what an apocalyptic commotion *that* had caused); she now possessed the cutest, gummiest grin on planet Earth.

Dan grinned back.

A sound began, and they cocked their heads to listen; the jingle of chains and the *whump* of something hard striking something soft, followed by the "Kiah!" of exploding breath; these energetic noises were wafting from the backyard.

"Mommy's working out," Lizzie told him, solemn as a little preacher.

Thus proclaimed, the thumb went back in, the head went back to chest, and she squirmed to get comfortable; Dan found himself the recipient of a face-full of stuffed giraffe. He gave himself some breathing room. *Phew.* It was time for Mr. Fred's bath in the washing machine.

Dan braced himself, then swung her down and sat up on the side of the mattress and paused there to see if his brain would ooze out of his ear and flop around on the floor; when it didn't, he said, "Want to help Daddy make coffee?" *And find the goddamn painkillers?*

She nodded behind her fist. Dan picked her up and headed downstairs, leaving Dora pooled on the hardwood.

He tromped down the staircase gingerly while frowning sideways at that thumb; they had worked to break the habit since last year, when her pediatric dentist, Dr. Chubby (that still made Beth giggle) informed them it would eventually deform the shape of her permanent teeth. Well, they couldn't have that, and until this morning Dan would've said they had it whipped. Oh, she backslid sometimes, usually while she was sitting on the couch watching the tube, but nothing like this.

As he curved down the stairs, the banisters curving with him, Dan gave a mental shrug and cut her some slack; hungover birthday mornings were tailor-made for the cutting of slack.

They hit bottom and crossed the open foyer and entered the kitchen's green-tiled expanse. Dan's wife liked green. A lot. He put his daughter down and rooted in some cabinets and a few drawers and finally located the generic ibuprofen, then struggled to remove the child-proof cap. Muttering swear words under his breath (so Lizzie wouldn't parrot them to her mother—or worse, at daycare), he twisted it open and ran a glass of water and downed about three times the recommended dosage, then assembled the coffee and clicked the little orange switch, making it glow, and looked around; Lizzie was pressed up against the French doors, thumb finally out, hands splayed as she peered into the backyard; Mr. Fred's lone remaining goggle eye squeaked against a pane.

Dan waited a painful eon for the thing to piddle enough java to make it worth his while, then filled his favorite mug, the green one that labeled him "Mommy's Little Helper". He took a scalding sip, ahh, then motivated his old and throbbing head over in front of the sink so he could watch, too.

"Kiah!"

The seventy-pound bag folded over Beth's right leg, and she backed off and circled, fierce brown eyes fixed on her opponent; one-two-one-two-left-jab-right-cross, left leg flashing in a round kick that stopped her adversary cold; then, almost too quick to follow, her right heel rocked the bag where a tall man's sinew would bind his jaw to his ear; the chains holding the unfortunate bag off the ground jingled as it spun in a new direction.

"Good kick, Mommy!"

Dan jumped, hot coffee spilling down his chin. Lizzie bounced, gummy smile beaming as she watched her mother beat the shit out of the bag; kid wouldn't know a spinning hook kick from Houdini, but she knew a good one when she saw one.

He snatched a handful of paper towels and dabbed as Beth wiped sweat-soaked hair from her forehead and waved at Lizzie, then caught sight of him in the window above the sink. She bowed mockingly. Dan raised his half-empty mug in reply: *"Let's-drink-some-wine-for-your-birthday" my ass.* He would eat his favorite 3-wood if she'd had over two glasses; no wonder he felt like hell.

Beth whopped the bag one last good one, reminding it who was boss, then the gloves and wraps went into the aluminum storage shed set against the privacy fence. She carried the step stool back and placed it below the crosspiece, climbed up, and lifted the bag and its chain off of the gallows. Beth then carried the chain and the seventy-pound bag *and* the stool over and stowed them in the shed with only a slight grimace.

Dan shook his aching noggin in admiration: *My Tigress.* She outweighed that bag by about thirty pounds. "Tigress" was Dan's nickname for her, a nickname which he'd made the mistake of uttering out loud once and once only; she didn't like it, but Beth *was* a tigress, complete with teeth to bite and claws to rake.

His beloved finished toweling off as she opened the French door. Wisps of fog followed her in as she scooped Lizzie up and rained kisses; their daughter squealed with laughter while informing her mother that ooh she smelled. Beth glanced at him, then whispered something and put her down.

Lizzie launched at Dan. "Happy Birthday, Daddy!" She crashed into his right leg, enveloping it in a fierce hug, and he winced; maybe his brain really *would* ooze out of his ear.

"Thank you, sweet pea."

He disengaged from the tattered giraffe known as Mr. Fred, whose fuzzy face was pressed into his crotch. Seeing that, Beth covered her mouth and moved around the corner; muffled giggles and snorts issued from the castle's empty dining room.

"Wanna go watch cartoons while Daddy cooks breakfast?"

Lizzie beamed up at him. "Okay!"

She pounded toward the living room, his new special friend Mr. Fred in tow, bare feet slapping tile, then going silent as she raced onto the living room carpet. Seconds later came the blare of their small flat screen; after a moment, the volume decreased. Dan's bright little girl could operate the remote just about as well as he could; she even knew the numbers for the most important channels: Nickelodeon and the Cartoon Channel and ESPN.

Beth poked a twinkling russet eye around the door frame, then followed with the rest of her, which was still smiling. Dan opened the cabinet below the left-hand sink and pointed at the two empty wine bottles resting on top of the refuse filling the can.

"Weren't you supposed to help me with those?"

"Didn't I open the second one for you?"

Beth laughed at his expression, and he winced. She came over and took the mug out of his trembling hand and put it on the green counter, then wrapped her arms around his waist. Dan laid his cheek on her sweaty hair; her cheek was on his chest, and her not-quite-small, not-really medium, but perfect-to-him breasts pressed into his stomach.

After a minute, he tipped her face up by the handle of her chin. "Conniving wench. Ye got me soused and took advantage of me."

"Didn't you like your birthday present?"

"One of the best I ever got," he said truthfully.

Beth separated them by an arm's length. "*One* of the best?" She looked at where her hand rested, then pulled his "Football Happens" shirt out for examination; a happy-trail of coffee darkened it from neckline to bellybutton. "Poor old guy. Rough morning?"

"A bit."

"Mm, mm, mm."

She led Dan to the small, round table ensconced in the castle's breakfast nook that fit their little family so much better than the big dining room. Beth seemed to have forgotten his slip, or at least put it aside, but he wasn't fooled; there would be a reckoning sooner or later. Such was the price you paid when you opted to mate with a tigress.

Beth slid his chair out: "I'll make breakfast after I take a quick shower." She kissed him on the forehead and ruffled his hair like he was ten. "Can't have old men puttering around in the kitchen. Might leave something on the stove and burn the castle down. You just sit here and suffer—I mean recuperate."

She walked past the island, heading for the foyer and the stairs, but Dan noted she took the long way through the dining room; he sipped his coffee and watched her, wondering why.

Beth paused in the archway and glanced toward the living room, where the raucous sounds of Pokemon or Digimon or some other godforsaken jittery Japanese cartoon was busy sucking their daughter's soul. When she seemed reassured that Lizzie was fully engaged, Dan got his answer; she pulled her soaked white tee-shirt over her head and dropped it on the hardwood.

The mug froze halfway to his mouth.

The gray cotton shorts went next, and Beth kicked them over to join the shirt. She toed off the sneakers. The black sports bra joined the pile. With a saucy curve to her full lips, Beth turned her back and removed her white granny-panties, shaking her hips and bending all the way over, sliding them down her legs and lifting her feet out one at a time.

She faced him with one hand full of pantie and the other cocked on her hip; her strategically placed yellow-rose tattoo stood out, and so did the mysterious ridge of livid scars that crisscrossed her belly and left hip, wrapping around to her left buttock. She refused to talk about those scars, so as usual Dan pretended he didn't see them; his tigress was tan in all the right places and pale in all the other right places.

Beth twirled the panties on one finger. "Happy birthday, love."

Dan groaned, and she laughed, then blew him a kiss and snatched her shoes and the rest and dashed to the staircase. He couldn't see from where he sat, but listening to (and picturing) her running up the stairs naked did nothing for the throbbing. His head hurt a lot, too.

Dan sipped his cooling coffee, thinking and letting his blood pressure inch back to normal, waiting for the ibuprofen to work its magic; he was thinking of prices, and that you always had to pay.

Then he smiled.

Some prices are worth it.

Oatmeal, Ad Infinitum

Beth fixed them bacon and waffles. It was yet another birthday present. Normally breakfast was a regimen of plain oatmeal with various fruits; strawberries were his favorite. Dan admitted it was a healthy way to eat, but it was no fucking bacon and waffles. Not even close.

"Bacon!" Lizzie bounced in from the living room. "Mommy, can I have waffles too?"

"We're all having bacon and waffles for Daddy's birthday." Beth patted Lizzie's chair. "It's almost ready."

"Yay!"

She climbed up and plopped Mr. Fred on the table; the toy promptly folded over and rested its ragged head on the wood. Dan sympathized; Lizzie was a harsh taskmistress. He opened his mouth, but Beth beat him to it.

"Elizabeth Ann, you know better. On the floor." The first batch of waffles *ka-chunked*, and she plated them.

"But Mommy, I *love* Mr. Fred! He's my favorite in the *whole world*, and I—"

"Do as your mother says." Lizzie was strident if not always elegant when she had the bit in her teeth.

Her face screwed up, so Dan cut the brewing storm off: "Lizzie." He held up three fingers. "I want you to do three things for me. Three *very important* things."

She eyed him and his fingers, deflating visibly as curiosity got the best of her. "What are they, Daddy?"

"First is go put Mr. Fred in your room, so he doesn't get sticky. Okay?"

"Okay!" She was out of the chair in a flash, Mr. Fred clutched in one fist.

"Number two!" Lizzie skidded to a halt beside the island. "Number two, come here." She did. "Give me your foot." She raised it to his waiting hand with a giggle. Dan felt his daughter's small, smooth foot; her toes were icy. "Grab your slippers out of the closet and put them on while you're up there." He tickled before letting go, eliciting another giggle.

"What's number three?"

He lowered his face inches from hers and crossed his eyes: "Gimme smooches!"

She giggled harder, then planted a wet-one on him and tore off toward the foyer.

"Lizzie!" She stopped next to the fridge and looked back. Dan patted his distended stomach and smacked his lips: "Better hurry, Daddy's hungry. If you take too long, there might not be any bacon left!"

She scowled. "Don't eat my bacon, Daddy!"

Dan pointed past her. "*Mmmmm, hungry!*" He patted his inflated stomach again.

"Don't eat my bacon!" She dashed out of the kitchen. "Don't eat my bacon, Daddy!" She thumped upstairs; seconds later a muffled "Don't…bacon…!" floated across the castle.

Beth sat the platter of said bacon down. "You're rotten." She went for the waffles, opening the fridge and grabbing the pretend butter and the almost syrup on the way back.

"I know." He snagged a piece just before Beth.

"…bacon, Daddy!"

They ate bacon and sipped their coffee and listened to their daughter thump around in her closet, and then Beth nodded sideways toward the thumps.

"What got the rugrat up so early?"

Dan gave her a nonchalant shrug; he wasn't going to open *that* can of worms, thank you very much, sure as hell not on his birthday. "Heck if I know. She just climbed into bed with me. Maybe she wasn't that tired."

Her eyes narrowed, making Dan squirm. Since they'd moved into the castle, Lizzie had become infamous, at least in their little family, for being a slug-head. Fortunately, that's when the slug-head reappeared, saving him further lies.

"Mommy, don't let Daddy eat my bacon!" She shot into the kitchen with the slap of slippers on tile.

Beth gave him a last, lingering squint. "I made sure he didn't eat it."

Lizzie jammed her fists onto her hips in a frightening mother-daughter doppelgänger moment as she stared suspiciously from Dan to the platter and back. He leaned away and raised his hands, palm out. Mollified, she climbed back up and Beth served them.

Dan watched his wife shovel waffle for a bit, then said, "Where's your oatmeal?"

She gave him arch. "We're celebrating, remember? And don't worry, old man. Oatmeal's back on the menu tomorrow, and for all eternity thereafter."

Fuck. He hated oatmeal, even with strawberries. "I'll shut up now."

"Wise."

Despite the infinity of oatmeal awaiting him, Dan was feeling particularly fine this morning: the ibuprofen was doing its thing, he was having breakfast with his two most favoritest gorgeous ladies in the entire universe, it was his birthday, and he had the day off.

Wait—it was Saturday, and he was off work.

Uh oh.

"So, are you girls going shopping this morning?" Dan took a bite of waffle.

Beth stopped chewing and gave him the squint. Lizzie chomped enthusiastically; it seemed he wasn't the only one tired of oatmeal.

His wife said, "I thought *all* of us were going."

Dan opened his mouth, but she forestalled him with an upraised hand, half-eaten bacon dangling between thumb and elegant forefinger: "Birthday veto?"

"You betcha."

"I should have known." She added the frown to the squint and hit him with both barrels.

Dan concentrated on his food; gloating would only piss his tigress off more. They had a standing agreement about their birthdays, as well as Mother's and Father's Day: Twice a year they each got to do exactly what they wanted, with no arguments allowed—supposedly. Beth did pretty much what she wanted any day of the fucking year, but now wasn't the time to bring that up because while today was his birthday, to her it was also a summer Saturday; it was yard-sale day. Dan hated yard sales more than he hated oatmeal.

Yard sales were a true sore spot because Beth was a Yard-Sailor 1st Class, and loved driving around and searching out bargains—which, in retrospect, Dan supposed was a good thing. When they'd moved from their apartment to the castle, they'd been woefully under-furnished, and the big house had seemed to echo. It still did sometimes, but Beth had been slowly putting a dent in the empty. Dan admitted she was good; his wife would search through piles of other people's crap and find stuff they needed, cleaning and repairing the "treasure" herself. Unfortunately, she also liked to have him along as a pack mule, although she cloaked it by saying she valued his "opinion". *Right*. Well, today she could get along without his opinion *and* his back. In fact, if his head kept feeling better—and if the fog ever let up—Dan thought he might go for a birthday bike ride.

Beth shifted the frown and the squint from him to Lizzie; alarm bells rang in Dan's head, but they were way too late.

"How come you're up so early, baby? Did you have another bad dream?"

The fork with the last bite of Lizzie's second waffle stuck on the end clattered on the plate, and the thumb went back into her syrup-sticky mouth. The equally sticky fingers of her other hand grasped her earlobe and worked and pinched. Her little face scrunched, and a tear slid down a sticky-smooth cheek.

Dan and Beth exchanged stunned looks. His wife picked Lizzie up, settling her into her lap, murmuring reassurances that it was only a dream, that it wasn't real. Their breakfast sat on the table, cooling and forgotten; after a bit, Lizzie began to settle, but then Beth asked the goddamn fucking idiotic question that Dan had *known* she would:

"Do you want to tell Mommy and Daddy about it?" She immediately stared a challenge at him over their daughter's head, and in the manner of married couples across the planet, an entire conversation complete with hurtful nuance took place inside that look; they had both laughed off the ridiculously horrifying idea of medicating their then three-year-old for dreams, but Beth had taken Dr. Lewiston's suggestion of talking about the nightmares as providence.

Dan broke her gaze with a sour grunt and picked up his last piece of bacon.

Beth turned her attention back to Lizzie, who had not answered her mother's well-meaning but dumb question. His wife gently tried again:

"Baby, do you want to talk about it?"

Dan chewed his bacon and stared out the window at the pall of gray that had enveloped the castle. When Lizzie still didn't answer, Dan looked at her; she sat there with thumb jammed in sticky face, reluctance to revisit the nightmare clear in every cute little line of her. Couldn't Beth and the goddamn worthless therapist understand that it was best to forget?

It was just a stupid *dream*, for Christ's sake!

Beth said, "You don't have to talk about it if you don't—"

Lizzie sat up and yanked her thumb out. "A *bad man* wanted to hurt you, Mommy!" The thumb went back in, but she didn't slouch and bury her face in Beth's shirt again; she now sat rigid, blue eyes glaring at something beyond her fist. She seemed a touch bewildered as well, as if wondering why anyone would want to hurt her mommy.

Dan threw back his head and laughed.

His ladies stared at him, Lizzie going so far as to pop the thumb out. He stood and plucked his daughter out of her mother's lap, then gave her a big hug and stood her on his knee and looked into her eyes from six-inches away:

"I would *never* let anyone hurt your Mommy. I promise."

"And *I* would never let anyone hurt me, either." Beth's voice was firm with confidence. They looked at her; she was smiling with that ripe mouth, but her eyes held a deadly promise.

Yeah, Dan thought, *there is that.* His tigress was one tough little lady.

"Hey," he said. Lizzie looked at him again. "It was just a dream. Okay?"

"Okay."

"It wasn't real. Okay?"

"Okay."

"No one will hurt your Mommy because *we* won't let them. Okay?"

"Okay."

"I'm going to eat the rest of the bacon on your plate. Okay?"

Lizzie gaped at him.

Dan smiled. "Okay?"

"No Daddy!" She scrambled off his lap and into her chair, snatching her three remaining pieces of bacon, syrup oozing between her fingers. Dan and Beth laughed.

Lizzie appeared surprised, then she laughed with them and shyly held out a piece of dripping bacon. He took the sacred offering with a grave thank you. She gave the next piece to Beth, who repeated the courtesy; the last of the bacon began to disappear in comfortable silence, silly bad dream forgotten.

Dan caught his wife's attention and gave her a salute with his soggy bacon. She rolled her eyes and gave him a *whatever* salute back, but when her gorgeous brown lamps rested on him again, he could feel the love shining from them like heat shimmering from a tropical sun.

Dan would happily slit his wrists ten times a day for that look.

Or eat oatmeal.

The Call

D AN FLASHED hand signals by rote as he braked at the three-way junction of Barron Road and McFarlane Farms Road—even though there was no one around to see. *Good habits die hard.*

His head throbbed as he put his sneakers on the pavement and reached under the crossbar and freed the road bottle filled with vitamin-and-mineral infused mango-flavored "water" he'd snagged out of the refrigerator. He took a swig and grimaced; ghastly stuff, but he should've known, really. Beth had bought them over a month ago, and the five-that-used-to-be-a-six-pack had sat moldering behind the pitcher of grape Kool-Aid ever since. Dan took another drink; it was what he had.

Disgusting hydration and lingering hangover aside, he was in fine spirits as he sat on his 21-speed Mongoose at the cross of the T, smiling and looking around.

What a beautiful goddamn day.

The local weather weenie had gushed about what a spectacular Saturday it would be, and—miracle of miracles—he'd been right. It was twenty degrees cooler than it should have been on the first day of August, a true blessing, and the fog had burned off except for a low-lying field or three where misty humps still clung, glowing in the sun, while the pale-blue morning sky soared overhead without a wisp of pesky cloud to mar it.

And it wasn't just the weather; the rich, rolling Nashville Basin stretched before him, fences and farms and rugged tree-lined ridges. Summer colors and smells assaulted Dan from all sides, including the omnipresent reek of cow shit, although these days he barely noticed it; seven months living amongst cow-swarms would do that. The two-lane blacktop he was pointed down, McFarlane Farms Road, dwindled to a hazy point on the southern horizon, deserted except for him. At his feet, Barron Road intersected McFarlane Farms coming west; equally empty, it lifted and vanished over a steep ridge about a mile and a half to the east.

Dan studied that crest with mild interest; his normal route was a 12.8 mile loop comprising lonely blacktop and deserted dirt roads and no big dogs—a loop he tried to beat his best time on at least once a month. He wasn't in any hurry today, not with a hangover, and Dan could've ridden anywhere his birthday-boy heart desired, but when he'd rolled out of the castle's driveway he'd followed his usual route out of pure, dumb habit.

Over the past seven months, Dan had noted that imposing ridgeline almost every time he'd blasted through this intersection because it was the same crinkle of earth that ran to the east of their house, but here it was a lot higher and a hell of a lot more foreboding. Dan took another shot of otter sputum, swished it around, then leaned and spit and wiped his mouth with a forearm. *Jesus.* He capped the bottle and hooked it back under, still staring up at that looming ridge.

He admitted he was a tad curious to see what was up there, not to mention discover what was on the other side, and it was no doubt a grand view—but he wasn't *that* curious. Dan had no particular urge to sweat even more than he already did just for what were likely more cows and more farms and more ridges; he already had a nice, dry view of those out his living room window.

A woman singing caught his ear. Dan looked around, but couldn't pinpoint where that incredible voice was coming from; one of his scattered neighbors must have their windows open and the volume seriously cranked for him to hear it way the hell out on the road.

The voice faded.

The mass of Black-eyed Susan crowding the ditch nodded to him in genial yellow waves as the breeze freshened, bringing the sweet scents of clover and diesel tractor fumes and manure. Dan unfastened the strap below his chin and removed his helmet and hung it on the brake handle, then scrubbed fingerless-gloved hands through sweaty hair.

I wonder where the girls are. They could still be perusing yard sales, although by this time Beth had likely found what she was looking for—whatever the hell that was—and had started on her other errands. She was still pissed at him for using a birthday veto to wiggle out of pack-mule duty and had let him know so when leaving. At least Lizzie had given him hugs and smooches before—

The woman's voice came again, fading in and out, tickling the back of his mind; there were words he couldn't quite catch. *Someone needs to turn their fucking stereo down.*

What had he been thinking about? Oh yeah, Beth. Dan scowled. Beth. He didn't know why she was so grouchy; it was *his* birthday, and he'd cleaned the castle before he'd taken off, just like she'd "asked" him to, so she didn't have any reason to be such a b—

The lilting voice surged. Dan sat rock-still on the 'Goose, listening open-mouthed.

After a time, the song faded, and he blinked hard and looked around. *Christ.* Dan kneaded his forehead. *Someone is really rocking out.* He shook off the woozy that had stolen over him and backed the bike around until he was facing east down Barron Road; its unlined black asphalt rose gently at first, and then sharply before flying over the jagged ridge in the distance.

"Screw it," Dan announced. "Let's go exploring." It felt like the exact right thing to say, not to mention do—and why shouldn't it? Might as well wander off the beaten path; it was a gorgeous Saturday, perfect for wandering.

The half-dozen yearling steers grazing closest to the barbed-wire fence across the ditch raised their long faces from the grass, regarding him with what passed for bovine curiosity as he strapped his helmet back on and took off. Halfway up the slope got serious about things, and he down-shifted and stood on the pedals, puffing. Dan coasted to a stop on the crest and wiped his face with a sleeve before looking around.

He whistled.

I was right, quite the view.

Ahead, Barron Road fell into a deep, foggy cut before climbing out the other side and continuing to plumb darkest Rutherford County. To the north, the murky ravine broadened into an ocean of treetops sticking out of the fog like a host of leafy ships-masts; a knotty hill thrust out of the forest about a mile away, its top obscured by thick waves of white.

Dan whistled again, louder and longer this time: Four miles long, maybe five; two and a half across at its widest point, just beyond the ugly hill…640 acres per square mile…math sucked…son of a bitch, there were *thousands* of acres of prime timberland down there! *And I had no damn clue!* That pricked his pride; real estate was how he put waffles on the table, although Dan was a residential stud, not a rec or an ag guy.

Still…

He peered back to the northwest, taking in the long vista: "I can see my house from here," he mumbled; the castle's half-barrel roof tiles glinted red-orange in the sun, though other details were iffy at this distance.

Dan looked out over the primal valley again, then pedaled forward and dropped into the mist.

He tapped the back brake as the road and everything else disappeared; only the thrumming of his tires reassured him that the solid world was still down there. A big head of steam later, Dan tapped the brake again (he didn't dare use the front brake) and this time the tire locked on the damp pavement. He cursed and over-corrected and the bike wobbled as he geared down and down, screw the fucking brake, and then he flew out of the fog at the bottom, glimpsing a blacktop lane that branched off Barron Road as he zipped past before shooting up the opposite slope. Gravity and gears were his pals; he used them to slow and turn around.

Heart lub-lubing, Dan coasted to a stop, then rapped his helmet. *Whap-whap!* He always wore it; no exceptions and no excuses. It looked stupid, and it made his head sweat, but sweaty hair and looking dumb were insignificant prices to pay to avoid slumping in a wheelchair for the rest of his life. Dan had much-too-much to do for all that mess; he had his girls to take care of.

He glanced up. A roof of vapor swirled just above his head; it was cold down here, too, though right then he didn't feel it through the blood-rush of adrenaline. He looked to his right. A paved lane ran straight between the trunks and disappeared into the fog, leading deeper into the valley. Dan looked to his left and saw a narrow metal notice bolted to a fencepost; he was edge-wise to it, so he rolled the 'Goose forward, craning his neck to read. The bolt holding the small sign to the post was loose, and the rust-spotted arrow that was supposed to point down the lane instead canted toward the leaves. Beneath the tilted arrow were two faded words; rust streaks dripped from their letters like dark tears:

BARRON CEMETERY

Dan backed the bike around and faced the lane that arrowed through the trees before vanishing into the fog. He rolled his shoulders. A cemetery. Dan didn't like cemeteries. Who did? Shivering, he rubbed his arms.

Well, what now, Dan-o me boy?

He looked to the left and right; uphill each way. He looked back down the fog-enshrouded path that led into the dark and scary woods and dead-ended at a cemetery—pun very much intended.

Am I reeeealy doing this? Dan shook his head. *No. No, I don't think—*

The woman's voice came again, floating through the fog, gentle, almost teasing, once more filled with words that hovered on the edge of understanding.

Dan sat for a long time, letting the song flow through him, and then he glanced around in alarm as a new sound intruded: the throaty swell of an engine. A car had topped the ridge and was dropping into the cut. The vapor confused him about which direction it was coming from, but there was no doubt it was coming.

Dan put his feet to the pedals and surged into the trees.

The blacktop slanted down and down and then leveled off, and even though he couldn't see ten feet, he maintained a fair clip, tires thrumming, cold mist swirling past his face. *This is fun*, he thought. *Creepy, but fun.* Suddenly the shrouded tunnel he was cruising through lit up pink and orange and violet, like God Himself had flipped a giant pastel switch.

Dan braked and stood there gaping. Then he laughed; the sun had risen over the valley's high northeastern rim and turned the blanket of fog into a stunning light show. He stared around, entranced, as the glow spread through the trunks; what had seemed dark and threatening a moment before was now a thing of pink-tinted wonder.

Grinning, Dan pushed the bike deeper into the shining woods.

Soon the rosy fog thinned and disappeared, and the forest came to life; red squirrels barked, tails undulating as they bounded through branches laced overhead. Hundreds, maybe thousands of birds called to each other as they flitted through the high canopy, shadows flickering past his feet when he crossed the rare beam of sunlight. Rank upon rank of broad trunks marched away on both sides, fading into verdant shadows. Dan's dad had taught him and Will how to distinguish an oak from a walnut from a hickory while out feral-hog hunting, but that was all the tree-lore he possessed; those species were well-represented, along with two-dozen he didn't know. His tigress would probably know; she'd been a big hiker before Dan and Lizzie had come along.

Now that I think about it, Beth would love this place.

He picked up a leaf that had drifted to the blacktop; an oak, it was still firm and green, with only a thin band of yellow death marring its spiny edge; the thing was at least fourteen inches across. Dan let it see-saw back to the pavement.

"I'm in fucking Narnia."

The lane dipped for another stretch and turned into an arched wooden bridge spanning a busy stream—*crick*. *This ain't Ohio, son.* They were livin' large in Dixie now, and 'roun these parts it was a crick. The bridge was stoutly constructed for vehicle traffic, though it only had one lane, and it didn't possess any handrails, just a low wooden barrier on each side; to keep some overenthusiastic hearse-jockey from accidentally dumping the dearly departed into the crick, he supposed.

Dan walked the bike to the top of the arch; a blue trough in the canopy mirrored the crick, letting in a major dose of broken sunshine; even so, wisps of fog still drifted above the water. He peered over the edge. *That there crick must be cold.* Probably spring-fed. Dozens of squat willows lined its banks, ropey arms trailing and bobbing in the swift course. The blacktop on the other side climbed briskly up the knob he'd spotted earlier; high above, a hole of light beckoned in the gloom.

He stared up at that opening, swallowed, then scowled and pushed the 'Goose forward and off the bridge.

"Fuck it. *Let's go exploring!* What a good idea."

A few minutes of pushing uphill later, he stepped out into full sunlight that seemed extraordinarily bright after the twiggy tunnel; he shaded his eyes and stared.

Dan had found the cemetery.

The Keeper of Roses

SOMEONE, DAN decided, liked roses.

Barron Cemetery loomed above him—or at least he assumed it did. Dan couldn't see any graves because a high, oval hedge obstructed his view. Over that, some sort of black pillar poked into the sky like a crooked ebony finger.

He hardly noticed any of that strange crap though, because below the waxy hedge were roses, and not just a bush or three; *thousands* of roses spread across the hill. In front of him, the blacktop ended at a small, empty parking lot. To his left, a concrete sidewalk bulled through the roses as it curved from the lot and around the north slope and out of sight.

Dan parked the 'Goose in the closest space and hung his helmet on the handlebar, then walked to the edge of the lot opposite the footpath; as far as he could tell, waves of flowers stretched all the way around and covered the slope from the hedge to the forest.

Yep, it's official, somebody likes roses. And not just any ol' rose; someone liked *red* roses, because no matter where Dan looked, red roses looked back at him. They were all shades of red, too; the flowers bunched on the steep slant between the hedge and the lot were orange-red; they were also a shape Dan wouldn't have called a rose, but he was pretty sure were, anyway. He didn't know much about roses—or rather, he knew what every other guy on the planet knew, that women loved to get them on Valentine's Day and that they miraculously quintupled in price around the first of February.

To his right and a little uphill, a patch of bushes sported nearly pink roses, though they never left the spectrum of red, just pushed the boundary. The climbing roses entwined in the hedge above him were the rich, burgundy shade Dan associated with roses. The shape was right as well; they resembled what he'd wasted his hard-earned cash on in the years before he'd met his wife. Speaking of Beth, when you lumped these flowers in with the forest straight from Middle Earth, it was a sure bet she would love this place, dead people or no dead people. He decided to surprise her by bringing her out here; it would put a smile on her face, and Dan was all for anything that would do that.

He tugged his riding gloves off as he walked back across the lot and up the concrete footpath; it roamed around and then took a ninety-degree turn and shot up the slope, parting the roses like Moses. At the turn, Dan stopped and dug his cell phone out and checked the time: 10:32. His ladies weren't due back to the castle until noon, so he still had plenty of time.

Dan put the phone away, then froze in terror.

Bees were flying around the roses. *Millions* of them. Okay, maybe not millions, but it seemed to Dan's mildly panicked eye that every flower had its own bee. Moving only his eyeballs, he watched one zoom its way to a rose somewhere on his left, and he relaxed; he doubted they would pay much attention to him unless he did something stupid or morphed into a giant flower.

At least I fucking hope not.

Dan continued up the path, eyes jumping, tracking his closest hill-mates; some were smaller—honeybees, he supposed—but most were those big black-and-yellow bastards like the one that had flown across the walk; they made the little ones resemble fighter jets maneuvering around a flight of B-52 bombers.

Dan kept walking; at least they weren't wasps.

There had been a regrettable incident involving a yellow-jacket nest when he and William had been kids, but that travesty didn't bear rehashing so Dan just kept motivating up the path. *Not wasps, only bees.* Bees were necessary, pollination of the fruits and veggies and planet and all that crap. He was sure wasps had some vital function in the biosphere, but Dan didn't give a flying—

He halted in his tracks; he'd reached the entrance to the cemetery.

He'd also found a different colored flower.

A wrought-iron lichgate spanned a gap in the evergreen hedge wide enough for four grown men to enter abreast—or a coffin and its pallbearers. Climbing roses snaked up each side and mingled on the lower half of a tall, arcing sign: WELCOME TO BARRON CEMETERY curved above him in ornate wrought-iron letters. The roses hanging off the outside of this perky greeting were red, but those festooning the inside were white. Dan peered through the arch and his breath caught; the climbing roses weren't the only whites.

Every flower inside the hedge was white.

Dan stepped beneath the lichgate and entered Barron Cemetery.

White roses everywhere was his first impression—well, white roses and dead people. The twin distractions of roses and bees had granted him temporary amnesia about what kind of place he was exploring, but the even rows of black, rectangular headstones poking out of the mass of bushes to either side were a stark reminder. The paved path he was standing on cut straight through to the pinnacle where the twisted ebony stone shoved into the blue sky; pale blooms obscured its base.

"Weird."

Dan's feet took him toward the tall stone, and he kept his gaze pinned on its darkness and tried not to look around; there seemed to be twice as many bees inside the hedge as out, but maybe that was the contrast of their black-and-yellow bodies against the white. *Forget the goddamn stingers, there are enough to just carry my ass off.* Dan tried to stop thinking about that as he reached the summit and stopped.

Four paved paths met and merged into an oval walkway surrounding the stone; from this elevation he could see a narrow walkway just inside the hedge, running all the way around the bone yard. The course that branched to his immediate left fed down the hill to a rose-blanketed wrought-iron gate just wide enough and tall enough for one person. Black gravestones and white roses filled the four lopsided pie wedges between the walkways. And bees.

Dan turned and discovered the crooked stone wasn't truly black; viewed up close, patches of gray faded to a grimy white and then morphed to brown and then charcoal and then jet, all in the space of a few inches. He stepped back for a better view and it turned midnight again, just that quick. *Huh.* Dan took another step back and looked it up and down; about twenty feet tall, and nearly six feet wide at the point where the roses swallowed it. It narrowed and thinned toward the top, but only by maybe half. The tip was bulbous and skewed, as if some unimaginable force had come along and partially melted it. The ugly thing was even more distorted than he'd first thought; the side he was facing at the bottom wasn't the side he was facing at the top. Dan didn't know what kind of rock it was, but it wasn't chalky or pitted or chipped; it looked as smooth as a baby's butt, though a lot harder.

He stepped forward again, hesitated, then reached out and touched it.

Dan jerked his hand back and wiped his fingers on his shorts; the stone had a greasy, unpleasant texture. He grimaced at his fingers, then looked the thing up and down once more.

Somebody needs to take a hose to it. Yuck.

Peering at the stone, he saw it was all one piece. *So, it's a monolith.* Or maybe it was a megalith. *Whatever.* It'd been a fair lick since Ohio State, but he seemed to recall that these babies were called monoliths or megaliths if they comprised a single stone.

Something caught his eye, and he leaned closer; there were symbols carved into it. Dan leaned closer yet, and, careful not to touch it again, used one hand to shield his eyes from the sun and the other to shade the stone.

"The hell?"

The symbols were a fraction of an inch tall, harsh slashes spaced by elegant swirls with a plethora of dots. The whole mess flowed in bizarre geometrical patterns up and down and around the entire stone; nary a centimeter of greasy rock was free of the bizarre etchings.

A B-52 buzzed him and he jerked back, then squinted at the symbols from a safe distance; they looked familiar somehow. Dan searched his cranium, and then he had it; they resembled the flowing script Al Jazeera put on the bottom of the screen whenever Al-Qaeda issued a proclamation in the name of their bloodthirsty god, usually after slaughtering a batch of innocent people; otherwise known as Arabic, he supposed. This writing looked a helluva lot like that. Sort of.

Eyeing the flowers closest to him—excellent ambush spots for B-52s—Dan leaned in again. *So what the hell is Arabic or whatever that is doing on a big, ugly rock in the middle of Tennessee, not to mention smack dab in the heart of a cemetery?*

"Ssssay dere! I think ssomebody wants to talk to ya! I wonder who it is? Hoo hoo hoo hoooo!"

Dan cursed and stumbled back. Tigger lisped again from Dan's shorts: "Ssssay dere! I think ssomebody wants to talk to ya! I wonder who it is? Hoo hoo hoo hoooo!"

He pulled his iPhone out with a slight tremble. "Jesus, Tigger. Scared the shit out of me." He had a voicemail. Dan frowned; the damn thing hadn't rung. Not even a missed call. He checked the display and noted no bars. He peered out over the hedge and considered the tree-covered slopes and rocky ridges that stretched into the pale sky all around him; he'd damn near forgotten he was stuck down in a valley. Dan tried to listen to his message but the call wouldn't go through; a text would likely have the same result. Assuming that had been Beth, he'd just have to hope she wasn't calling to say they would be home early. Dan slid the phone back into his pocket. He needed to stop screwing off and finish his birthday ride; both he and the day weren't getting any younger.

Instead of leaving, he considered the tall, repulsive stone and its odd carvings, then squatted and parted the bushes. Maybe there was some good old-fashioned English on the base; these things had to have a base or a foundation or whatever. *They'd fall over ker-smash if they didn't.*

Dan hunched closer, putting his head right into the thorns, and stared in amazement.

There was no foundation. The stupid piebald-one-moment, jet-black-the-next goddamn rock ran *right into the fucking dirt*, along with the weird etchings, as if the whole shebang had grown out of the ground like an ugly ass rock-tree or something.

"What the fuck?"

"The reception is poor down here," a woman said, "even on this prominence. You might get a call to go through once in a blue moon, but I wouldn't count on it."

Dan jumped backwards and fell over and then scrambled to his feet and was facing her by the time she'd mentioned moons. She was thirty feet downslope to his right, her lower half obscured by a bush crawling with white roses. She was wide, not tall, although she was taller than Beth—not that that was hard to accomplish. She wore a long-sleeved plaid shirt and a floppy manila sun hat tied under her chins with white ribbon; more white ribbon laced her gray-streaked strawberry ponytail. Vivid green eyes shone out at him from the shade cast by that cavernous hat brim; Dan put her at late forties or early fifties.

"Christ! I didn't know anyone else was out here!" He issued a depreciating laugh, but let it trail off; those eyes could be beautiful, he decided, but right then they held nothing but flat consideration. "I'm Dan Sims." No reply. "I was out riding my bike and I found this place." Nada. "I live over on Daisy Road." Zilch. Was she hiding behind that bush and watching him the entire time? *Fuck me, she had to have been.* "My wife would love these roses." Dan was babbling and knew it but couldn't seem to stop. "We have a yard now so she grows her own. Or tries, anyway. She's only gotten a few to bloom. She likes yellow best."

Dan clicked his teeth together, hard, and swallowed; they stared at each other as the bees buzzed back and forth.

Turning away abruptly, the woman raised turtle-head clippers and detached a bloom from a bush. *Snip.* She wore leather work-gloves, and she guided the truncated blossom to a wicker basket she bent and picked up; it was filled with white roses. The clippers flashed again:

Snip.

"This is a private cemetery, Mr. Sims." Surprisingly, she didn't have a Tennessee drawl; there was a tinge of…something, some accent Dan didn't quite recognize, though if pressed he would say Eastern Europe. Whatever it was, it was dusty; she'd been Tennessee-bound for a good stretch. *Snip.* "I am the Keeper here," she continued, and Dan sensed the capital.

And then she moved, fast, up the hill and closer to Dan. *Snip.* Another bloom tumbled into the woven basket.

Dan edged back. "Of the roses?" The question was inane—she'd meant the cemetery—but she made him nervous, and it had popped out before he could get it back.

Green eyes flashed at him from the darkness under the floppy brim. Her smile was a hard slash. "Yes." *Snip.* "Among other obligations."

She moved closer.

Dan backed down the walk and then stopped when he realized what he was doing. The woman stepped out onto the path between him and the stone, then made a point of examining him from toenails to eyelashes; by her face, Dan was merchandise she had once considered purchasing but was now having second thoughts; faded jeans and steel-toed work boots matched the checkered shirt. The basket hung in her left hand; this close, Dan could see a layer of crimson below the white. The turtle-head clippers nestled in her right hand were fucking enormous.

She finished her inspection and then considered him for a silent eternity with those cold, shining eyes. Dan wanted to back up more, but his feet felt rooted to the path. He wasn't even sure he was breathing. Time stretched. Bees buzzed. The stone loomed above her head, a chunk of twisted darkness cut out of the blue.

"You are strong," she suddenly pronounced, making Dan jump. "Stronger than I had believed possible. Stronger than I had dared hope. But are you strong enough to do what needs to be done when the Time of Choice is upon you? That will be the true test."

Dan blinked. "Excuse me?"

She didn't reply, or say any more about how strong he was, or tests, or choices, or anything else. She…watched him, eyes gleaming beneath the hat. Dan thought she looked hungry.

He pried his feet loose and backed down the hill. "Yeah, thanks, that's me, strong. I, ah, I have to be going, um, ma'am." She hadn't offered a name, and he quashed the wild urge to call her Ms. Keeper. "But if you don't mind, I'd still like to bring my wife to see your roses. I wasn't kidding when I said she'd love them."

The Keeper shrugged, amused. "That would be fine with *me…*"

She spun and took swift, thick strides up to the megalith, circled it for some reason, then moved down the walk that led to the small wrought-iron gate, still carrying her basket of beheaded roses. Dan stopped backing up to better watch her go. The white ribbon woven into her strawberry ponytail dangled and swayed across her wide back. When she reached the gate, she looked at him over her shoulder; that slash of smile was back.

"Thank you for appreciating my roses, Dan Sims, but as stated, this is a private cemetery. On your way out, please do not disturb those who rest here." She opened the small gate, stepped through, and closed it behind her with a muffled clang.

Dan scowled. *What, does she think I'll pull a folding shovel out of my pocket and have at it?* He scratched his cheek. Maybe they'd had kids messing around out here, or vandals, or even grave robbers; that would explain her comment, and her spying on him, and her attitude, of which she'd possessed an overabundance.

And strong enough? He shook his head. *Maybe she keeps her marbles in that basket.*

Dan twitched when a motor cranked and caught; the unseen engine revved, and gears clanked in a gearbox. He hesitated, then sprinted up the hill and edged by the nasty stone and took the path down to the side gate and poked one eye around, peering through the wrought-iron bars between dangling flowers.

The Keeper sat on a camouflaged Polaris four-wheeler just on the other side of the gate. A steel-mesh trailer was hooked to it; inside were tools and bags of Rose Feed, the brand Beth used. The basket of cannibalized rose heads rested between her meaty thighs as she motored away down a worn dirt track chopped through the red roses; the trees on this side were closer to the hedge, and bigger. Back under the eaves, Dan spotted an imposing steel gate with KEEP OUT and PRIVATE PROPERTY posted. Beyond the gate, ruts with a strip of grass between led deeper into the woods.

She stopped before the gate and unlocked a hefty padlock and unwound a gleaming chain; Dan heard it rattle. She swung the gate out and motored through, then re-swung and re-chained and re-locked.

Then she stood there, looking up at the cemetery.

Dan quit breathing.

Ten seconds; thirty seconds: *Christ, can she see me?* The wide hat shaded her face, although Dan fancied he could still see the glowing green sparks that were her eyes.

I gotta be imagining that shit. Gotta be. She's too far away. It sure as hell fucking *felt* like she was looking at him. Dan resisted the urge to hide behind the hedge; she might catch the movement.

Shit, she's staring right at me!

Dan couldn't take it anymore; he started to edge back.

The Keeper turned and mounted the four-wheeler, settled the basket in front of her again, then puttered away and melted into the shadows.

THE METS FAN

AND THERE *she goes. Thank God.*

Had she hunkered behind a bush and watched him that whole time? The thought freaked Dan out more than a little, but he'd glimpsed no movement, heard no clippers; the Keeper hadn't shown herself until he'd poked his…

Dan turned and raised his gaze to the megalith: *Until I nosed around that.* And now that he thought about it, she'd deliberately interposed herself between him and it, there at the end.

But why? And why bury a big ugly rock smack dab in the center of your neighborhood bone yard—with paths leading straight to the thing, no less—if you didn't want anyone screwing with it?

He shook his head, then turned back and peered through the side gate; the runnels the Keeper had used wound off between massive trunks and vanished under leafy shadows. Where the heck did *those* lead? Dan couldn't see any buildings, just more trees, but they had to go somewhere—somewhere important enough to justify the ominous postings, not to mention the gate and the big-ass chain and the monster padlock.

He backed up a dozen graves or so to where he could see over the hedge and spotted a clearing about two miles away, near the center of the valley. It was a big sucker, too; fog still clung to it with the sun riding high. Dan strained, but couldn't see any buildings—the mist, and he didn't have the angle—but that had to be where the Keeper scurried off to; those ruts led—

Dan whipped around, heart stuttering.

White roses and black headstones greeted him, them and that lopsided thing dirtying the sky; nothing else besides bees. For a second there, though, Dan could have *sworn* there were people standing tall up on the crest behind him. They'd been clustered around the stone, watching him.

"Oookaay," he whispered, eyeballs bugged and darting.

His feet carried him back down to the small gate and then they hurried him along the walk that hugged the hedge. Dan wasn't afraid. He had things to do, that's all, and those things just happened to be elsewhere. *Shit to do, that's it, not scared at all.* And he wasn't avoiding passing by that nasty rock, he was just taking the fastest way out. *Efficient, that's me.* He kept his eyes pointed straight ahead as he neared the lichgate with its wrought-iron message welcoming everyone to the fun of Barron Cemetery and then passed under and out.

Feet still doing their thing, Dan glanced over his shoulder:

WELCOME TO BARRON CEMETERY

You bet.

He not-quite ran down the hill and made the turn and booked it through the reds to the parking lot and climbed aboard the 'Goose and strapped his helmet to his noggin and tugged on his gloves. Dan backed out of the spot, stopped, then reluctantly looked up; the top few feet of the standing stone thrust over Barron Cemetery's hedge, a black thumb hitchhiking in the sky; giant goosebumps had broken out all over his arms.

He felt watched.

Screw this noise. Dan stood on the pedals and shot into the leafy tunnel.

Watched? Ridiculous. Trunks whizzed by as he picked up steam. Hanging out in a cemetery had given him a major case of the willies, Dan could admit that, but *watched?* Stupid. And his attack of the heebie-jeebies hadn't been helped *at all* by the unfriendly Creepy Keeper Lady; it was her fault he was so jumpy.

Strong?

I'll show that bitch strong.

He blew across the bridge with a thrumming rattle of wooden planks, then drove hard up the long incline and hit the flat stretch and then the shorter, steeper incline and skidded to a stop at Barron Road, checking both ways: clear. Dan resisted the urge to turn and look down the woodsy tunnel stretching behind him to see if anybody (or anything) was following—*there isn't!*—and turned right and powered up the side of the gorge.

Blowing and pumping, forgotten vino hangover returning to pound his head, Dan made it to the top and freed the road bottle and took several gulps, not even noticing the taste, then found a gap in the weathered outcroppings and wind-gnarled trees and gazed out over the woods to the north. Without the fog, the cemetery's knoll swelled above the forest, but he avoided looking at it and spotted the wide glen he'd glimpsed earlier; a layer of smoky vapor still floated inside, hiding the contents, if any.

And then Dan blinked in astonishment.

The clearing was circular.

This place just gets weirder and weirder. From this height, he also noted that the crick looped around the cemetery's hill and emptied into that circle. *Maybe it's a lake. That would explain the mist.*

Dan squinted at the far rim of the valley; a sun-on-metal glint had caught his eye. He counted half-a-dozen buildings and did some quick navigational calculations and decided that had to be the backside of John McFarlane's farm, their neighbor. On clear days, Dan and Beth could gaze out their bedroom window and see the front of that sprawling ranch shining up on this same ridge, although there it was lower and less craggy.

Does McFarlane own this place? It wouldn't surprise him, seeing as how the vale was just about the old man's backyard—and also seeing as how Mr. McFarlane owned most of the terra firma around these parts, including the fields on three sides of the castle. Before the housing crash, when Murfreesboro had been one of the hottest markets in America and subdivisions had been inexorably spreading this way, McFarlane had stood to make a killing. Not now, not with everything still in the toilet, but once the economy ramped back up and the damn banks loosened their grubby fists on the loan money and construction restarted…yeah, the old man would be golden again—or in McFarlane's case, platinum.

Lucky bastard. Must be nice to be filthy stinking rich.

Dan searched for a better vantage on the circle; he wanted to know if it really was a lake, or if not, see if he could spot any structures down there. He couldn't find a clear spot before Barron Road fell off the ridge, however, so he parked the bike on the shoulder and scrambled up and clung to a scrub pine angling out of a crack between two giant limestone slabs.

"Well, shit."

Dan now had the desired view, but it did him no damn good; fog filled the circle, obscuring everything inside, water or otherwise.

Motion turned his head; from this rocky perch he enjoyed a breathtaking panorama, but what had seized his attention was closer: below him, a tiny white pickup barreled south down McFarlane Farms. As Dan watched, it turned with no signal and sped up Barron Road, climbing closer and then closer still; it was a Dodge Ram dually, he saw, and not a clean one; dried mud crusted the bumpers and wheel wells. The driver wore a blue baseball cap and black sunglasses and talked on a cell phone.

Dan scrambled off the rocks; for some reason, he didn't want to be observed snooping on the valley. *Stupid, but there you go.* He ran to the bike and had just planted his narrow ass on the seat when the Dodge topped the crest with the rattle of a diesel engine. Blue cap spotted Dan sitting on the side of the road and said something into the phone and lowered it into his lap.

Then he screeched to a stop.

Dan's scalp tingled as they stared at each other; finally, blue cap let off the brakes and clattered closer. Dan waved, just to be sociable, but the guy didn't wave back. *Prick.* The blue cap had an orange N and Y, with the Y hanging out of the N.

Huh, he's a Mets fan. Didn't encounter many of that ilk in Tennessee, that's for sure.

The Mets fan slowly rattled past, staring hard. *Take a picture, asshole.* Tufts of white-blond hair jutted around the edge of the cap and matching pale fuzz lurked on his lip and chin; an intricate tattoo sheathed his left forearm. He was maybe ten years younger than Dan; early twenties, just a kid.

Kid or not, he was a big bastard; not fat, but tall, with long arms and huge hands that white-knuckled the steering wheel as he stared at Dan with no expression behind the sunglasses.

Then the rattle jumped to a clattering roar as the kid sped away; they watched each other watch each other in the wide wing mirror until the pickup dropped into the cut.

Dan coughed and waved away diesel fumes. "Alrighty then."

He put his puppies to the pedals and dropped off the ridge in the opposite direction, glancing back every three rotations, but no white truck had appeared behind him by the time he reached the junction. *What the hell had THAT been about?* That big, unfriendly fucker had seemed to bear Dan a grudge, and in the normal course of events that wouldn't bother Dan because Dan was perfectly capable of bearing a grudge right back.

The problem was, he'd never seen that kid before in his life.

I like to know the people I hate.

Dan laughed and pulled his phone out. *Probably can't stand sharing the road with bicyclists.* A whole heap of people felt that way, 'specially 'roun these here parts.

He checked his voicemail, and sure enough it'd been Beth who'd called while he was in the cemetery. The girls had finished up at the junk sales, and his wife had dropped by her restaurant to eat lunch with Lizzie and knock out some paperwork and ride herd on the troops before she ran her remaining errands: point was, Dan was on his lonesome for lunch. Beth finished up by saying they would be home by one, one-thirty at the latest, and that he better have a good reason for ignoring her calls.

One or one-thirty; Dan still had plenty of time to get in a full circuit if he wanted, but he wasn't sure he wanted one anymore; not after the cemetery and its oh-so-lovely Keeper, not to mention the affable Mets fan.

Speaking of that asshole…

Dan glanced over his shoulder and nearly fell off the bike in shock. The white Dodge dually was rolling down the long slope of Barron Road behind him, rolling fast.

Shit.

He froze for a second, then for lack of a better idea pointed the 'Goose toward the castle; home sounded pretty fucking wonderful right about then. Dan looked back in time to see the pickup slam to a stop at the intersection and then surge onto McFarlane Farms, coming after him.

Shit!

Maybe the kid had forgotten something and was only going back to get it. *Sure.* The Dodge rattled up behind him and then slowed. Dan moved to the far right and waited for it to pass, but it stayed on his butt. Irritated now, he waved for it to go around, and then there was a clattering bellow and the reek of diesel fumes and the pickup bumped him.

"Fuck!"

Dan wobbled and lost it and went down, bashing his hip on the pavement, smashing his elbow, tingling pains shooting in his fingers as he jumped to his feet and picked the 'Goose up and flung it into the Black-eyed Susan. The kid was laughing, hands side-by-side on top of the steering wheel, knuckles ridged like ivory mountains.

Dan punched the hood just behind the chrome ram's head with the spooky red eyes; a deep and extremely satisfying dent appeared.

The kid quit laughing.

"Ya like that, motherfucker?" Dan spread his arms. "What's your goddamn problem?"

The Mets fan rolled his knuckles on the wheel and snarled as the engine roared, hot wind blowing over Dan's shins, big truck rocking from the torque, and then Dan's survival instinct kicked in and he threw himself to the side as the bumper caught his already sore hip and spun him into the ditch, wing mirror just missing taking his head off. He tripped over the 'Goose and fell across it, jagged pedal digging into his side.

Dan scrambled up in time to watch as the pickup roared over a small rise, diesel clatter fading into the distance.

"Son of a *bitch!*"

He grabbed up the 'Goose, but aside from a scratch on one pedal, he couldn't find any damage. He pushed it out and pulled stems and blooms from spokes and brake cables and tossed them into the road, then stared incredulously at the horizon where the white truck had vanished.

That fuck-nut tried to kill me.

Dan fumbled for his phone, an alarming thought making the fumbling urgent, but when he pulled it from his pocket, it was whole and sound. *Whew.* Dan dialed 911, hesitated over the last 1, thinking, then grimaced and shoved the phone back; he hadn't had the chance to get a tag, but he could describe the Mets fan and his truck, oh yes he could.

But then what?

It would be Dan's word against his, that's what. The kid would lie, probably even say Dan had started it, and then there that big ol' dent in the Dodge's hood would be—a dent that just happened to match Dan's fist.

Shit.

He held his right hand out palm-down and watched it do the post-adrenaline boogie, then swiveled his hip, wincing. He checked his elbow and found a bleeding scrape, but the tingle-fingers had already faded. Not too bad, considering; he'd gotten worse screwing around on his own.

Dan climbed on the 'Goose and pedaled for home, keeping both eyes and both ears peeled for the Dodge.

Happy fucking birthday to me.

Weapons and Scars

ETH SCOWLED into her rear-view mirror.

The pickup filled the Nissan's back glass, looming over Lizzie's sleeping head. Beth punched the accelerator, creating a safe cushion, and the white truck raced to catch up, sticking to her again as they passed Helen's house.

And I thought Columbus drivers were morons.

The castle appeared, and she hit the blinker and slowed to turn, but the guy in the blue baseball cap didn't wait and whipped into the left lane and zoomed around her with horn blaring.

"Jerk."

She checked to make sure the horn hadn't disturbed Lizzie and saw she was still comatose, head fallen to the side, hair fanned across her face. Charming everyone at the garage sales and playing the darling at Slo Eddie's had worn her out; add being tormented by another nightmare, and it was no wonder the kid was zonked.

Beth pulled around the driveway and bumped up into her spot next to Daniel's mountain bike, which was down off its hooks, which explained why he couldn't be bothered to answer his phone—or call or text her back!—but it didn't excuse it. Lizzie didn't stir when she unbuckled and lifted her out of the car seat, so Beth tucked Mr. Fred under an armpit and shut the back door with her hip and went inside. She left the garage door up.

Bacon scent still drifted through the castle, now mingled with lemon cleanser, and Beth smiled; her Daniel, though extraordinary in many ways, was like most men in that he would find any excuse not to do something he didn't want to do; also like most men, he would do it if prodded, even if he did pout and mope his way through it.

Jingling and thumping reached her ear; Beth's heavy bag was getting worked over, and it wasn't her hitting it. Curious, she carried Lizzie through the sun-drenched foyer past the sunken living room and entered the kitchen and set her purse on the island, then crept through the dining room to the French doors and peeked into the backyard.

Daniel panted in front of her swaying bag, sweating with his shirt off; most men dismissed him because of how skinny he was, but Beth knew—none better— that he was strong. His right elbow was bleeding, and he was talking to himself again, angry words she couldn't make out—swears, knowing him. Then he went at the bag once more; her husband was favoring his right side.

Beth shifted Lizzie to the other shoulder; he'd never shown an interest in her bag, even though he'd built the gallows for her. "Her thing", he called it, lumping it with her blade-work, her meditation, her yoga, and her training with Takamatsu Sensei. "His thing" was riding his bike. She knew Daniel's dad had taught him and his older brother William to box when they were kids, though, so Beth studied his footwork: he was rusty. True power came from the ground, not the arm, channeled with proper stance and timing and body-torque up *through* the fist; he wasn't moving his feet with the right timing, which meant he was throwing arm-punches.

As if Beth was transmitting thoughts to her husband, Daniel's footwork smoothed, and he relaxed his shoulders; two quick hooks to the kidneys, then a left jab. That jab was fast but lacked pop. Then her eyes widened as the right cross thundered in.

He found a rhythm: jab-cross-jab-cross-hook-hook-jab-cross. The other punches were serviceable, but each right cross was a beauty, delivered with speed, power, and timing; if one of those landed on the point of a chin, the fight would be over.

Daniel seemed to feel the same thing. He backed away at guard, then lowered his hands with a satisfied smile.

Beth rapped her fingernail against a pane.

Daniel whirled, glaring, then beheld them behind the glass and relaxed. *My my.* She twitched her head at Lizzie and put a finger to her lips. He nodded and pantomimed her shush, and Beth discovered more rust; the wraps were coming loose, tag-ends hanging; he hadn't worn her gloves, of course, those being much too small for him.

Beth pointed to her bag and arched a questioning eyebrow. He looked at it, then suddenly danced around it, landing punch after punch, then stopped it with both hands, faced her, and bowed, fingers tented, face solemn.

"Ahh so," he said.

Beth shoved the door open an inch and whispered, "Smart ass!", then shut it and carried Lizzie to the staircase. His laughter followed her up the curve, and she paused at the top and cocked one ear when the thump and jingle started again. Lizzie blew soft peppermint snores into the other ear; the lunch hostess had snuck her a mint that Beth had pretended not to see.

She listened to her husband spend his anger on the bag for several seconds more, then shrugged and let it go—for now. Beth would get it out of him eventually, even if she had to tie him down and interrogate him.

Her lips twitched. *That could be fun.*

She carried Lizzie into the pastel riot that was her daughter's bedroom and tucked Mr. Fred in next to her. Lizzie rolled over and murmured something in her small voice, clutching the stuffed giraffe; Daniel's blue eyes opened, muzzy with sleep, then slipped shut.

Wonder, gratitude, and a fierce love filled Beth as she gazed down at her sleeping daughter; an Ohio foster kid, she'd been alone from her earliest memories, with no one to count on or count for but herself. Now here she was, a mother and a wife, with a great (on most days) job. They'd even bought a gorgeous home in the countryside; the castle was expensive, true, and too much house for them, also true, but they'd gotten it for a steal, and when the market rebounded, they would sell it and make a killing—or so said her husband. Beth had no reason to doubt him.

The silence caught her attention, and she moved to the window and opened the blinds and looked down into the backyard; the fingers of her free hand lifted the edge of her tee-shirt and toyed with the scars ridging her lower abdomen while below, the bag swayed, but for some reason Daniel was now peeking through a crack in the fence. He straightened and said something, then laughed and limped to their patio table and donned his favorite OSU tee-shirt; with its fresh rip and bloodstain, it was a match for the rest of him.

Beth tried to spot what he'd been looking at; the giant field beyond their back fence held multitudes of splotchy red-and-white cows and a dusty green tractor with a guy in a dark-colored baseball cap sitting high in the driver's seat; just as she looked, the tractor trundled over a fold in the ground and disappeared. There was nothing else.

She frowned and rolled the blinds closed, then realized what she was doing with her other hand and put it firmly down by her leg; Beth didn't need to play with her scars. She could remember how she'd gotten them like it was yesterday. *Five minutes ago.* On occasion, her Daniel would trace those livid ridges with his fingers, curiosity in his beautiful eyes, but he never asked how she'd come by them.

Beth sometimes thought she loved him the most for those unvoiced questions.

She took a deep, calming breath into her *itten*, her center, and whispered the mantra she lived by every day—or tried too:

"The past is gone, the time is now, and I am here."

Beth slid out of her daughter's room, pulled the door almost shut, and flowed downstairs; here and now, she needed to work out and stretch; she hadn't sat Zazen yet, either. Daniel's birthday had *seriously* disrupted her routine. Her lips quirked; perhaps she should make him pay. She moved into the kitchen and went to the sink and ran a glass of water. They might as well take advantage of Lizzie's nap while they—

Two booming thuds, loud in the still house, made Beth turn back toward the foyer and the staircase; those had come from upstairs—or at least she thought so. She set her glass on the counter and walked over and looked out the French doors; Daniel had returned her bag and its chain to the storage shed, and now he peered through *another* crack in the fence, this time along a different section.

Beth rolled her eyes, then walked over and stood at the bottom of the stairs and listened; a car passed out on Daisy, but no more booms and thuds. The patio door opened then, and her husband came in and shut it behind him.

Then he just stood there and stared at her.

"Really?" She spread her hands, indicating his disheveled state. "You're going to make me ask?"

"It's…a long story." He touched his hip, winced, then pointed past her up the stairs. "Do you mind if I take a shower first?"

Like that, is it? Beth flapped her fingers under her nose. "By all means."

He laughed and limped by her; midway up, he stopped and looked back. His eyes were very blue in the muted sunlight filling the castle.

"Love ya, beautiful. Know that?"

Beth fluttered her eyelashes. "Yes."

Daniel's wry chuckle followed him up and into their bedroom, and Beth forced herself to stop grinding her teeth; she let an evil smile leak out when she heard the shower start.

He would *beg* to tell her what was going on!

Beth recalled the thumps then and walked back into the kitchen and opened the farthest drawer from the sink, the rag drawer, and reached under the fragrant pile and pulled out the chrome length of a crescent wrench; she'd wrapped the handle with duct tape to improve grip, and one tine had broken off during some past task, making it useless for its original purpose but just right for hers; it gave the big wrench a wicked look.

Beth listened again; the shower and another passing vehicle was all she heard.

She hefted the wrench, testing its feel; a claw hammer lurked in the junk drawer on the other side of the double oven and a hatchet with a rusty notch waited under a pile of work gloves on a shelf in the closet below the stairs. Beth had tucked another hammer beneath a stack of Daniel's baseball caps on a shelf in the foyer closet, just behind the castle's double front doors; various other weapons were concealed throughout the big house, including a razor-sharp eight-inch stainless-steel chef's knife she kept stuffed between the mattress and box spring on her side of the bed.

Beth also had her Kit Carson designed CRKT M-16 folder hooked inside her shorts; she shifted her weight and felt it press beneath her right hipbone. She had all her clothes altered to carry it concealed, even the few dresses she bought. That raised eyebrows at the tailor, but Beth couldn't have cared less. Her M-16 was black on black, with a three-inch, single-edged blade and a flipper for quick deployment. She loved Carson's designs, especially the M-16, and this one was her fourth in ten years; she kept them clean and oiled and sharp without fail, but she wore them out practicing her blade-work.

Daniel knew about the Carson, of course, and he'd found some of her weapons hidden around their apartment that first year of marriage and dubbed them her "weapons cache". He liked to tease, but she could tell it all made him a little uneasy. Beth didn't know if he knew about the chef's knife under their mattress—her Daniel was good about cleaning the kitchen and bathrooms, but making the bed or doing laundry never seemed to cross his idiot male mind—but she didn't care if they made him nervous; long ago, she had made a promise to herself:

She would never be helpless or defenseless again.

Beth intended to keep that promise.

Then she snorted and shoved the wrench back and ran the drawer shut with a bang; she could handle upstairs mystery thumps—but she would check everything out *downstairs* first, just in case; vigilance was the first line of defense.

She started with the garage; nothing seemed amiss, so she walked under the rolled-up door and stood in the sunshine and glanced around the front yard and grimaced; she needed to tend her roses and trim the hedges. Daniel also needed to mow in a bad way; all the rain had put the grass on steroids.

Beth popped her trunk and retrieved the antique umbrella stand and parked it on a shelf until she could get around to refurbishing it; intricate rose buds covered the waist-high wooden stand, and once she had it sanded and re-stained it would look great in their otherwise-empty foyer; lonely, but great. It would be difficult to restore without ruining those carvings, and Beth was looking forward to the challenge.

She went back in, punched the button and lowered the door, then walked into the laundry room, which was larger than the bedrooms in their old apartment. Combined. *It's bigger than that whole crummy place I had when I was nineteen.* The overflowing green basket made her growl—*Would it kill him to throw a load in?*—but nothing here would have made those loud thumps.

Beth went through the rest of the bottom floor and flowed upstairs and checked Lizzie's bedroom and bathroom, listening to the Lizmonster snore and ignoring the master bedroom and bath for now, then looked in the spare bedrooms one by one; when she opened the door furthest from hers, Beth found the source of the thumps.

The empty window threw a rhomboid of hot light across thick blue carpeting that still held that chemical yet somehow pleasant new-carpet smell, and she left clear footprints as she crossed to her boxes of books stacked against the wall; Beth had over five hundred titles, marked fiction and nonfiction, the extent of her organizational system. Two of the fiction boxes from the top row had fallen, spilling hardbacks and much-loved paperbacks across the blue carpet. Lizzie had likely crept in here (even though Mommy's books were OFF LIMITS) and climbed on the boxes and pushed the stacks out of alignment; gravity had eventually done the rest.

That kid gets into everything.

Beth folded into half-lotus at the edge of the sunlight and began re-boxing books, hands and smile lingering over old friends she no longer had time to visit; she also needed to organize these better, but again, who had the time?

She had just filled the first box when she sensed someone behind her and felt the touch.

Beth spun up into a fighting crouch and flicked her Carson open, eyes darting.

The spare bedroom was empty.

She straightened, then pressed her palm on the back of her neck, where the fingers had stroked. Beth brought her hand back around and looked at her own slim, trembling fingers, then clenched them into a fist.

That mocking touch…not to mention the hostile presence standing right be-hind her…it had been so *clear*. She looked around the sunlit room again; she even looked down at the fresh carpet, but there were no tracks but her own.

Beth slowly folded the Carson and put it away.

"Stress," she told the empty room.

Slo Eddie's had ran into the red last month, the first time since Beth's watch began, not to mention the whole saga with her kitchen manager and onetime friend, Mark. And Lizzie's daycare was going up. Again. And don't forget their satellite bill! She hadn't told Daniel about *that* travesty yet; no wonder she'd had a stress freak-out. She sat back down and finished boxing and re-stacking and left the spare bedroom, closing the door behind her.

Beth paused there and breathed deep into her *itten*; she'd wound herself up. She needed to relax. She needed to meditate. Then Beth heard the shower cut off and with a grin decided what else she needed and followed the polished banister around, trailing her fingers along it; to her left, the foyer's chandelier hung sparkling out in space. She poked her nose into the Lizmonster's room and found her sprawled on her back, rasping snores with the covers thrown off. *Good*. Beth pulled the door to a crack again and walked to her own door and reached for the handle.

Multiple rumbling thumps boomed through the castle.

Beth whipped around and stared at the far bedroom door.

Behind her, Daniel muttered to himself as he got fresh clothes from the dresser; other than him and Lizzie's faint rasps, the house was now silent. Beth followed the banister back around, eyes never leaving that door. When she stood in front of it again she hesitated, then turned the handle and threw it open; it rebounded from the doorstop, and she caught it with her palm.

Beth stared at the spray of books and boxes on the blue carpet; she must've got-ten distracted by her stress freak-out and re-stacked the boxes off kilter. Takamatsu Sensei would be disappointed; infusing every moment with focused awareness was the heart of her training: *Here and Now!* Beth could almost hear him shout it at her; here and now were all that mattered.

She boxed her old friends again and squared the stacks firmly against the wall, then stepped back and nodded in satisfaction; it would take a six-point earthquake to budge them now.

When she got back to her room, she glanced over her shoulder at the far bed-room…then snatched the handle and waited, listening, tense. When no thumps came, Beth shook her head at her own foolishness and entered.

Daniel sat on the edge of their bed, tying his sneakers. He looked up when she came in; his hair had turned dark gold from the shower.

"Did you hear—" He saw her face. "What's wrong?"

"Nothing." Beth composed her features. "Nothing at all." She shut and locked the door, then kicked her sandals off and pulled her shirt over her head. Her bra went next. Daniel seemed to have forgotten all about tying his shoes. Her shorts and panties dropped, and then she knelt and took his shoes off, starting with the unlaced left one.

When Beth finished Daniel reached for her, but she slipped away and swayed toward the bathroom. Steam still fogged the air as she stopped in the archway and smiled over her shoulder; he lifted his eyes back to her face.

Beth said, "So, Birthday Boy, we have a situation: your daughter is asleep, and I am a dirty, *dirty* girl."

She walked into the bathroom.

He didn't answer—speech seemed beyond him by that point—but the speed with which he shed his clothes and followed was eloquent enough.

Beth kissed her husband and, hands busy, shut the damp door with her foot.

The Fate of Dick and George

B YE MOO cows!" Lizzie waved her stuffed giraffe at the indifferent bovines sprinkling the field next to the castle.

They completed the ritual in tandem: "Bye moo cows."

Daniel's voice was dry. Beth's sounded tired; it was Saturday, and craziness was bound to rear its ugly head tonight despite her best efforts.

She straightened her spine against the seat-back; she was lucky to even *have* a job in these tough times—and considering her lack of a degree, she was fortunate to have *her* job. General manager of a restaurant the size of Slo Eddie's usually required a degree. Beth scowled. That was *Mark's* belief, anyway. Mark Ingram, her current kitchen manager and onetime friend, had a *master's* degree; two, in fact.

Beth glared at her husband. He'd explained the cuts and bruises, but she had a strong suspicion he wasn't telling her everything, and unfortunately for him, that suspicion ticked her seething irritation a notch toward critical.

"You should have called the police."

Daniel gave her a wary look before putting his gaze back on the road. "What would I have told them? Like I said, the guy spaced out and ran me off the road. And then instead of being cool about it, he was a complete..." He glanced in the rear-view at Lizzie, who had both little ears perked: "jerk face." Lizzie giggled. "So instead of kicking the..." Glance in the mirror, "crud out of him like I reeeeealy wanted to, I rode home and took it out on your bag." He shrugged. "No big deal."

No big deal? Her husband almost getting flattened by some inattentive yahoo was *no big deal?* As if she didn't have enough to worry about! Beth narrowed her eyes; that feeling she wasn't being told everything still dug at her.

Then Daniel made a face. "Wonderful."

Beth turned and spotted Helen standing at the end of her driveway, waving for them to stop, something small and black clutched in her multi-ringed fingers. The other bejeweled hand gripped her cane. Beth had never seen her with it outside; her hip must be bad today.

The engine revved, and the automatic transmission down-shifted as the Nissan sped up.

"Daniel..."

"Kidding. I'm kidding."

He wasn't, but she let it slide as he turned into Helen's driveway. Beth rolled her window down as Helen hobbled over and beamed through the side glass at Lizzie.

"Hey, Lizzie girl!"

"Hey, Ms. Helen!"

Beth and Daniel shared a resigned glance; Lizzie had just duplicated Helen's rich Tennessee twang. Most of the time their daughter talked like them, normal, but lately they'd noticed a drawl after she'd spent a few hours at daycare. Or around Helen. It was inevitable, Beth told herself; Lizzie had been born in Nashville and was growing up here. She still didn't like it, but she didn't know what the heck to do about it.

"Woman, what are these blasted things good for if ya don't answer 'em when they tootle?" Helen waggled her cell phone in Beth's face and then planted fists on ample hips. She wasn't truly mad, though, her grin and manner as cheerful as ever. Leaning down, Helen peered inside the car; her voice dropped twenty degrees. "Hello, Daniel."

"Helen."

He didn't look at her, only stared bemusedly at the jumble of statuary and windmills and birdbaths and handmade cardboard signs quoting scripture that cluttered Helen's front yard; the two had never gotten along, which didn't bother Beth. For her, visiting with Helen was a treasured escape, and, as much as she loved him, that most assuredly included from her husband.

"I'm sorry, Helen. I left my purse in the car. Why did you call?"

Beth flushed at the lie; her phone was in her purse, true, but her purse had been inside, and she'd ignored the phone on purpose, but that purpose hadn't been to avoid Helen. Today her friend had on a garish combination of canary yellow pant suit with a blue vest. Red sandals matched the eye-popping red straw hat perched on her head, and the bright yellow ribbon tied around it trailed across her left shoulder; its yellow didn't quite match the yellow of the suit.

Beth shuddered; she'd always wanted to ask Helen if she was color blind but treasured the friendship too much.

"That's okay, honey. And the reason I called is I wanted to tell you that *that woman* called, and I get Jacob for the whole afternoon tomorrow!" She peered into the back seat again. "Lizzie darlin', do you want to come on over and have a visit with me and Jacob?"

That woman was Maria—or at least Beth thought that was her name; it was uttered so rarely she couldn't be sure. Whatever her name was, *that woman* had gotten pregnant and married Helen's oldest son, Paul, five years ago. On his third deployment to Iraq, *that woman* had left her son for another man, taking Jacob with her; now Helen only got to see her grandson once a month, and she treasured it.

Helen's youngest son, Ryan, wasn't discussed.

"Can I go see Jacob, Mommy? Please! Can I, Daddy? Please, please, *puhlllleee-aaase!*"

They looked at each other, and Daniel shrugged.

Beth said, "Of course you can, baby."

"Yay!"

"Good!" Helen said. "We'll have us a grand ol' time! We'll play with Pickle, and I'll get the Slip 'N Slide out and hose 'er down!" Lizzie cheered again as Helen turned back to Beth. "Those two *love* that silly thing! I set it up in the front yard—"

"*Where* in the front yard?" Daniel muttered. Beth slapped him on the thigh without turning.

"—and they just go go go! I can kick back in the shade and relax, don't have to do a thang!" She winked at Beth. "Wears 'em out nice'n good for a nap, too!"

"Ms. Helen?" Lizzie piped.

"Yes, dear?"

"Can we feed Butterball and Skipper, too?"

"Why, it just so happens I have a pile of old carrots just waitin' to be fed to some lucky horses!"

"Yay!"

Helen turned back to Beth, lowering her voice. "Lord knows the poor things need the attention; they just about fly to the fence when they see those little ones." Beth gave her a questioning look, and Helen lowered her voice another notch. "They're not *hungry*. Frank feeds 'em, he just don't have much to do with 'em. They were Isabel's, you see." Beth nodded. Isabel White had passed about six months ago, not long after they'd moved into the castle.

Helen then glowered; Helen, Beth reflected, could glower with the best. "That's no excuse, though. Man's gonna own horses, he oughta do right by 'em! Why, they're gittin' shaggy! They need curryin'; any fool can see that, includin' this one. And their hooves need trimmin', and probably a dozen other things I don't know about!" She shifted her weight, taking more of it onto her cane. "Never rode a horse in my life and don't plan ta start, Heaven forfend, but I know animals. My Harold and I raised cattle and pigs back in our day, so you *betcha* I know 'em! Why, we farmed near two hundred acres of—"

"Helen." Beth had grown fond of the eccentric old woman, but she *did* love to talk.

"Oh, don't mind me! You need to git, I know." Helen peered into the back seat. "I'll see you tomorrow, Lizzie girl! Bye!"

"Byeee, Ms. Helen!"

Beth said, "What time do you want her?"

"Oh, let's say 'round twelve-thirty?"

"Twelve-thirty would be f—"

"*That woman* wanted to bring Jacob early in the mornin', but I had to set 'er straight! Sunday's God's day! More to the point, it's the day He expects His due!"

"Helen—"

"I *told* Paul, back when he first brought her across my doorstep, I *told* him that hussy was no good! She's no church goin', God-fearin' woman, or she would know…"

Helen trailed off; her seamed face had acquired an anxious look.

Beth smiled. Helen believed she'd talk them into attending her church if she kept trying, and keep trying she did, but offering a backhanded insult (at least on accident) was not her way. "It's all right," she said, still smiling. Her friend smiled back, grateful. Then Daniel cleared his throat, and Beth felt the car shift into reverse; she smacked him on the thigh again. "We'll see you tomorrow at twelve-thirty. Bye."

"Bye, dear. Don't let 'em work ya to hard! Bye, Ms. Lizzie!" Daniel, she ignored. Helen hobbled back up her driveway. Beth could hear Pickle barking in the house.

Daniel was glancing both ways for traffic when a thought struck her. "Wait. Pull back in."

He gave her a look, and when she only stared back, he grimaced and did as she asked. Helen paused and turned to gaze a question at them as Beth rolled her window back down.

"Helen…" Now that she was about to ask, she felt silly. But she was curious. "How did you know we'd be driving by?" She gestured at the end of the driveway. "How did you know when to wait for us?" It was fifteen after three, but Beth wasn't supposed to be at work until five; unfortunately for her, lately it had been necessary to go in early to make sure everything had been prepped right, especially after Mark had been in charge during lunch.

Helen gave her a strange look, then limped back to the car; by the time she got there, amusement had replaced that fleeting expression, gone as if it had never been.

"Honey, it's Saturday."

"Right…"

Helen rolled her expressive gray eyes. "Since you been havin' trouble with that coworker of yours, you been goin' in early nearly every night, 'specially on the weekends. When you couldn't be bothered to answer, I just came on out here 'bout three o'clock and waited." She shrugged padded canary-yellow shoulders. "Not like I have much on my plate anyhow." She suddenly turned and yelled at the house: "Be quiet, you! You done been outside already!" Helen turned back, and up at the house Pickle stopped barking for all of two seconds, then started up again.

"I'm sorry, I forgot I told you about Mark. It's been so *long* since I visited you! Maybe tomorrow when I bring Lizzie we can sit and talk."

"Don't think a thing about it, hon." Helen tapped the brim of her unbelievably red hat. "The gear up here still works just fine, unlike everythin' else. Yes, we'll chat tomorrow. Bye!" She caned up toward her house, yelling something unintelligible at Pickle.

Daniel gave her an are-you-done look that almost got him smacked again. Then they drove off, and Beth reluctantly pulled her phone out; besides three calls from Helen, there were two texts, one with a pic attached.

Beth smiled grimly; her spy at work. But a part of her had been hoping that there wouldn't *be* any pictures.

She read the texts and looked at the pic and by the time she did her smile was long gone. *Has it truly come to this?* Beth took measured breaths into her *itten* until she'd grasped a tenuous calm by her fingernails. Mark had been her friend—he was *still* her friend, at least to her face—but now things were coming to a head. Worse, he had to think she was too stupid or too weak to do anything about it. Or both!

Beth practiced her belly breathing, placing the tip of her tongue on the roof of her mouth. Calm. She was calm. She was CALM! She breathed and looked out the window, not seeing the picturesque countryside slide by and then not seeing Centerville as Daniel drove through town toward the interstate. What if it came to firing him? The man had a family. She'd eaten dinner with his wife, at his house, and Lizzie went to his kids' birthday parties. But she couldn't put up with this crap any longer.

Beth sighed, then forwarded the photo to her boss, Clint Jennings, as instructed; they had named the chain after Eddie because he was the famous big-shot world-champion pool player, but everybody knew who was really in charge, including Eddie. Clint was the one who had offered Beth the floor manager's position at the new Murfreesboro store almost six years ago. By that time she had been working in the Columbus Slo Eddie's since she was nineteen and had busted her butt to climb from lunch hostess all the way to kitchen manager. Beth recalled what an amazing week that had been for them; she and Daniel had just celebrated their one-year anniversary, and they had also just told everyone they were seven weeks pregnant.

So Beth had been overjoyed by Clint's offer, but she'd also been shocked; she had only been management for five months. There were fourteen Slo Eddie's by that point, and although managers were swapped between stores regularly (to keep the blood fresh, as Clint was fond of saying), normal policy was to factor seniority heavily during consideration for promotions. That meant there were at least two dozen managers in the queue ahead of Beth, but Clint had offered a position at the brand new Tennessee store to *her*.

When she'd bluntly asked him why, Clint only smiled and said he'd had his eye on Beth for some time and that she'd impressed him and that he thought she would do well at the new store. He told her to talk it over with her husband and let him know by the end of the week. So she had, and her Daniel had been lukewarm on the idea until he'd done a search and discovered that Murfreesboro was the sixth fastest-growing municipality in the country; needless to say, he'd been on-board after that.

The pic finally went through, and she settled lower into her seat with another sigh.

It was done.

"Does she still have Dick and George up?"

Beth took a moment to shift gears; Daniel had sounded amused.

He certainly *looked* amused. "Yes. At least I think so. I haven't been in her backyard in some time. Why?"

He shrugged. "Just thinking about your…" He glanced in the mirror. "*Unusual* friend." He looked at her, blue eyes twinkling. "I can't believe the Secret Service didn't make her take them down."

"They said they didn't want to spoil all her hard work. They did make her take them out of the front yard." Helen had sewn the dummies herself, not to mention stapling the pictures on the heads and hanging them up. "She said they even got some target practice in before they left."

The Nissan sped up the ramp, and he merged into the northbound I-24 traffic. "Do you believe that?" He put the car in the left lane and pushed it up to eighty.

"Does it matter? It makes a good story." Helen liked to tell stories, true, but Beth didn't think she'd make up something like that.

Daniel snorted laughter. "Makes me wonder what happened to Rumsfeld. Probably buried him under one of those Jesus statues." And then he made the mistake of muttering, "Crazy old bat."

Beth sat up and poked her husband in the shoulder, hard. "How would *you* feel, Daniel Terrance Sims, if you lost one of *your* sons in a useless war? And not only a *useless* war, but an *illegal* war, begun on false pretenses!" She folded her arms under her breasts and glared at him. "And all for people who couldn't care less about him! If it wasn't just for *oil!* You would do a lot worse than shoot BB guns at the effigies of two foolish politicians!"

Suddenly Beth blushed; she was on edge and taking it out on her family, something she'd vowed never to do. She glanced in the back seat; Lizzie sat wide-eyed and still, watching them. "I'm sorry, baby. I shouldn't have yelled at Daddy."

"It's okay, Mommy."

"No, it's not." Her husband stared out the windshield with a knotted jaw. Beth touched the shoulder she'd jabbed. "I'm sorry, I'm just…" She put her hand in her lap. "I'm sorry."

Daniel took her left hand in his right, stroking the fine bones with his big thumb, then squeezed gently and held it over the console. "This thing with Mark has you wound tight, doesn't it?"

She squeezed back. "Yes."

"Then you have to do something about it." He looked at her then; his eyes were blue stones. "Tonight."

"He has a family, Daniel."

He put his attention back on the surrounding traffic.

"So do you," he said.

Lizzie began clamoring for the Disney Channel, so they drove the rest of the way listening to their daughter warble along off-key with Justin Bieber.

They didn't speak again, but they held hands the entire way.

Daniel parked beneath the green-canvas awning that sheltered the front doors of Slo Eddie's. It was only twenty until four, but Beth watched a family with tow-headed twin boys leave as a larger, less duplicated family entered.

Daniel said, "Sure you don't want us to pick you up tonight?"

"I gave Jen forty bucks for gas this week. Might as well make her use it."

"All right."

She unbuckled her seatbelt and climbed between the seats, straining puckered lips toward her daughter. Lizzie did the same, and Beth was certain they looked like two baby birds working on the same worm from opposite ends, but she didn't care. Then they kissed, and Beth smoothed her hair back and cupped her chin, looking into those eyes.

"You guys have fun tonight. Be good for Daddy."

"I will, Mommy."

Beth then leaned and kissed her husband, free hand doing interesting things out of view of the back seat. She opened the door and got out.

"That wasn't fair." His accusation was a tad breathless.

"Sure it was. Pop the trunk, please." He did, and she got her cue case and shut the lid and slung the case's leather strap over her shoulder and walked back and shut the car door, then bent over to look through the window he'd rolled down. "I love you guys. See you later."

She stood up and Daniel said, "Hey." She looked back in the window. "I almost forgot. There's something I want to show you tomorrow, while the Lizmonster's at Helen's."

"I've seen it."

He fought a grin and lost. "Not that. It's something I found on my ride today, before all the fun with rednecks began. It's a surprise."

"Okay…"

"You'll like it. I promise."

"All right then, it's a date. Love you, gotta go to work."

"Love you, Mommy!"

"Love you too, baby."

She walked toward the glass double-doors; from inside came a muffled crack, the distinct sound of a rack of pool balls being broken.

"Daddy, can we get McDonald's?"

"No, we've got good food at home."

"But I want McDonald's!"

"I said no."

Her daughter's protesting wail cut short as the window rolled up, and she turned to watch the silent argument continue as her husband pulled out of the parking lot and drove away.

Beth sighed, then adjusted the case strap on her shoulder and opened the right-hand door and walked inside.

Seizing Chaos

BETH DREW her cue back smoothly while keeping the tip lined up on the bottom half of the gleaming white ball; it rested near the center of the nine-foot Olhausen, and she was stretched out, one leg kicked back for balance. *Nine-foot pool tables were NOT designed with five-foot people in mind.* Families and couples occupying the booths surrounding the House Table were silent; only the distant throb of dance music and the hushed voice of one girl asking if someone wanted a refill on that pitcher could be heard.

Beth stroked the ball, the tip of her Pechauer bending almost to the emerald felt, and it shot forward and hit the eight with a crack; the black ball disappeared into the far corner pocket. The cue ball hesitated and then reversed toward the opposite corner and the yellow-and-white nine-ball. It slowed, and Beth held her breath; she could've ended the game with two easy shots, but this was supposed to be entertaining.

The creeping white ball nudged the nine, and it hung on the lip for an agonizing moment, then dropped into the webbed pocket with a click.

Cheers and applause exploded, with some whistling in the mix. Beth stood her cue out to the side and bowed, then pulled her headset up from around her neck and clicked it on. She walked toward her incredulous opponent with her hand out.

"Good game, sir." Her amplified voice boomed above the music and clinking dishes and conversation. "Thanks for playing Beat the House Shark." They shook, and she propped her cue in the crook of her elbow and clapped. "Give him a hand, folks! He played well, but I'm afraid the Shark eats tonight!" They laughed and applauded as Beth smiled at the man whose name she couldn't remember; he looked a little lost, as if not quite aware that he was done, or why or how.

He shook his head, and then, despite the gold band on her finger (not to mention the one on his, and the statuesque blonde waiting for him at forty-one), gave Beth a measured once-over.

"You're good."

Beth turned from his dark-eyed smile; a handsome face had long ago ceased to impress her. "If you think *I'm* good, you should play him."

She pointed up at one of the sixty-inch flat-screens hanging in the rafters; it was showing Eddie on his way to winning a Trick-Shot Championship; '03, she thought. Beth watched her boss set up, taking his own sweet, trademark time. This trick involved an open long-neck bottle with an eight-ball placed on top. She knew he nailed the amazing jump shot, just as she knew he toasted his opponent before downing the unspilt beer.

Whatshisname smiled ruefully. "No thanks." He dug for his wallet. "Let's do that again." He sounded determined.

She brought his attention to the brass bell in the Pit's corner, knotted rope hanging low. "The Shark welcomes all comers, sir, but we must give others a chance. If no one has rung that bell in ten minutes, then you can try again."

"Good." His pretty brown eyes held a degree of heat; Beth had noticed getting beat by a woman brought that reaction from more than a few men. "I'm warmed up, now."

Beth turned to the watching patrons with a grin that hid her flaring irritation. "Oooooh! He's warmed up now, people!" She turned back to whatshisface. "In that case, I must give you a *real* challenge and play right-handed."

Amid the laughter, he stiffly walked over and rammed his house cue into the wall rack. Beth watched him stalk out of the Pit and back around to forty-one with only a tinge of regret. She shouldn't have taunted him, but she was seething, and despite his ego, the guy couldn't shoot his way out of a wet paper bag. Beth dismissed him from her mind and turned back to the crowd.

"Remember, anyone can challenge the House Shark!" She pointed to the white-board below the bell: "The rules are posted down here, and in our lobby near the host stand. A ten-dollar donation gets you one game of eight-ball with the Shark, and if you win you get a twenty-five dollar gift certificate to Slo Eddie's, good for one year and redeemable at any time!" She turned, playing the crowd. "Any time we're open, that is!" That got a few laughs, but not everyone was still paying attention; good customers, they were old hands at this speech, and had dialed her out.

"There are more options, all the way up to a donation of fifty dollars!" She kept turning, meeting as many eyes as she could. The ones still watching her were mostly men, and that didn't surprise Beth; there were reasons and reasons she was out here sharking, and the fact that she could play was only one. "Fifty bucks gets you a best-of-three nine-ball match, and if you win, you'll receive a two-hundred-and-fifty-dollar gift certificate to Slo Eddie's!" Not that she would let that happen; give away too much of Clint and Eddie's money, and you were likely to be handed your walking papers forthwith; murmurs as that dollar figure got a reaction. "And folks, you can feed a lot of people with two hundred and fifty dollars—or have way too much fun by yourself!" That got more laughs.

"And don't forget, during August and September all donations go to The Sunshine House. If you can't give cash, or if you're scared of the Shark," Beth put one hand on her waist and cocked her hip, which got more laughs, "you can donate items in the Big Box by the host stand." Her tone turned serious. "These women and children have had a rough go of it, so they'd appreciate anything you can give, especially kids' clothes, all sizes, and toiletries. Ladies, if you have any makeup you don't want or are about to throw away, don't. Put it in the box."

Most of the faces looking down at her had turned somber; a few even showed a touch of irritation. Beth ignored those. Some people needed a reminder that not everyone could afford a cold beer and a twenty-dollar steak; if she had ruined the flavor of their appetizers, that was just too bad.

"A quick note before I go." She pointed up at the big flat-screen, where Eddie was polishing off his beer while being congratulated by his challenger. "My boss, Slo Eddie himself, will play on the House Table the third week of November, the 17th through the 24th, so if you want to measure your game against a pro, that'll be your chance. We are taking reservations now for the booths around the Pit, so save your seat and come challenge a pro!" They were almost booked solid already; it would be a wild week, and one she wasn't particularly looking forward to. "I'll see you marvelous people again, just as soon as the next bait offers itself to the Shark!" That got more laughs, lightening the mood.

She clicked off her headset and was breaking down her cue when one of the girls came down the steps and into the Pit, ticket book in hand and a printed receipt clutched in the other.

"Um, Beth, could you help me?" Stacy tucked a stray strand of ash-blonde hair behind her ear and smiled in a way she probably thought was winning.

Beth grabbed double-handfuls of patience and shouldered her case and moved up the steps and out of the Pit; the blonde had to scramble to keep up.

"What is it, Stacey?"

The pretty server blanched at her tone; only two weeks into the job, Stacey was slow to learn and mistake-prone. Not her fault, really, just the way it was; some girls learned quickly, and some didn't. Beth glanced sideways at the long legs stretching below the fringe of tight cut-offs, knowing she wasn't the only one doing so, and was reminded that Stacey's strong suit wasn't her brains.

"Well? Spit it out!"

"Ah, sixty-four ordered the Combo Nachos starter *with* jalapenos, I *swear* they did, but when I brought it out, they said they didn't want jalapenos, but they would try to eat them anyway because they were hungry…" Beth weaved through server traffic near the bar and handed her cue to Mike, who was shaking a drink one-handed. He took the case without looking and put it in its cubbyhole without breaking stride. Beth turned to Stacey and raised an eyebrow. "And, uh, well, they don't want to pay for it. And they want to talk to a manager."

Beth snatched the ticket. "Where's Jen? She's on the floor tonight—or at least she's *supposed* to be."

"She's with the hostesses. The new one screwed up the seating. She told me to find you."

Splendid. "Did they eat it?" Beth took the order in with a glance. "Did their Steak Fajita Platter come out? It should have."

The light of remembrance shone from Stacey's face. "Um, yeah, they ate most of it." The girl shifted like she had ants in her panties. "Would you talk to sixty-four? Thanks, Beth!"

Stacey's tan giraffe legs carried her off toward the kitchen; while glaring at her back, Beth caught sight of a four-top of guys—one looked barely old enough for that half-empty beer pitcher; she'd have to remind Carla to double-check for fake IDs—watching Stacey's legs go by. Once again reminded that the blonde server's brains weren't her primary asset, Beth grumpily turned to the computer station at the end of the bar and swiped her card.

She gave sixty-four half off their appetizer; if they ate it, the jalapenos couldn't have bothered them *that* much. She checked the times from the kitchen; steaks were taking *nine minutes* longer than they should! They were packed, true, with a line of not-so-patient people stretching from under the green awning and into the parking lot, but despite the name of the place, slow steaks were unacceptable!

With a small, evil smile, Beth decided to do something about it—after she charmed sixty-four, that is.

They were an older couple; definitely not Slo Eddie's usual demographic. They were also well-dressed and looking primly about, especially at the girls in their tight Slo Eddie's tee-shirts and Daisy Dukes. The lady's disapproval was genuine, though Beth doubted the gentleman's; the gleam in his eye betrayed him. Even so, she left them satisfied, and actually pried out a laugh or two, although the woman was still miffed about not getting free nachos.

Leaving them, Beth decided to go on a quick tour; she'd wait until the end of her circuit to rain hell on the kitchen.

As she made her way to the Pool Room, one of Takamatsu Sensei's lessons played in the back of her mind; she often thought about it while doing her job. That day at the dojo it had been just them, as it so often was back then, and they'd sat facing each other knee to knee in seiza, the traditional way of sitting in Japan.

Beth pushed through the heavy doors, and the din of laughing conversation and the crack of breaking balls nearly overcame the blare of music. She moved aside as two young couples with drinks in their hands headed the other way, red light blinking from their pager. Beth walked over and stood in the shadows by the wall at the end of the bar.

His lesson had been simple:

"YOU WILL DIE!"

He had tried to get her attention, and it had worked. She'd sat entranced as the perpetually happy old man calmly explained (after screaming in her face) about the exercise randori, which meant "seizing chaos".

During randori, multiple opponents attack you from all sides, and the purpose is not to win; no one wins randori. The attackers keep coming, and no matter how hard or skillfully you fight, eventually you end up at the bottom of the pile. Randori's purpose is to demonstrate how you keep your mind free yet focused, how you use your attacker's momentum and intent to foil them, and how your techniques hold up once you become exhausted from attack after attack after attack after attack.

No, in randori you could not win.

Randori was to show how well you died.

"Life," Takamatsu Sensei *had stated softly, staring into Beth's eyes, "is* randori. *You cannot win. In* life, *as in* randori, *the attacks never cease."*

Beth could still remember her chill at the old man's gentle words.

"A non-warrior," Sensei *continued, his sunny smile never faltering, "does not know this, or if she knows, does not accept it, and lives her life with a mind full of falseness. The warrior accepts this, here,"* her teacher thumped himself over his heart, age-spotted hand moving almost too quick to see, *"and fights on regardless, never quitting. You are not a warrior yet if you have not accepted this truth in your heart: life is seizing chaos."*

"Hey boss!"

Beth turned. Javier held three frosted mugs in one meaty fist, tilting them under the Bud Light tap one after the other, leaving just the right amount of head. "You dozin' off over there?"

She smiled and walked to the end of the bar, but didn't go behind because Javy and the skinny new guy, Tim, were hopping and she didn't want to get in their way.

"Nah, just working my manager magic."

"What, doin' the heavy looking?"

"You know it."

Javy laughed and handed the beers to Stephanie at the servers' slot; Stef was on the eight-foot tables tonight. The printer hummed and Javy grabbed the ticket and reached into the well and pulled out two long-necks and used the bottle opener in his back pocket on them, then glanced around in a terrible skulking-spy parody and slunk down the bar closer to her. Beth wanted to groan.

"You get my text?"

He'd lowered his voice and put his broad back to Tim, who was watching and trying to pretend he wasn't. Tim probably thought she was there to check on him since this was his first weekend shift, but Beth was there to check on many things, of which Tim was only one. Besides, if he couldn't hack it on a Saturday night, Javy would let her know.

"Yes."

Javier stood there looking at her, condensation dripping on his fists. "Well?" he finally said. "What you gon' do about it?"

"I haven't decided yet."

He shrugged, not offended by her tone, and rumbled back down the bar. "Okay boss, you da man!" Javier's laughter boomed while Tim eyed them nervously, sure they were talking about him.

At five-two in his non-skid work shoes, Beth didn't get a cramp in her neck when she talked to Javy—one of the many things she liked about him. Javier was short, no doubt about it, but he was nearly as wide as he was tall; she watched Javy and Tim weave a delicate dance in the narrow confines behind the bar, Javy rolling around Tim like a boulder around a sapling, Tim swaying and bending to get out of his way. Arms as big as her legs poured beer and shots, and Javy motivated about on thighs she swore were thicker than the distance across her shoulders. He didn't have any martial training (or at least he didn't admit to any), but he competed in the local power-lifting circuit. Javy could also do just about any job in the restaurant—she'd been grooming him for management for the last six months—but she always scheduled him in the Pool Room on weekends.

"Everything running smoothly back here tonight, Javy?"

"Smooth as my Ali's bare bottom, boss!"

Beth suppressed a laugh at Tim's shocked glance. Alejandra was Javier's newest daughter, less than four-months old. Javy and his wife, Marta, who was the same height and weight as her husband, had been blessed with five daughters—if blessed was the word. Another thing she liked about Javy was that he was always happy to be at work; he was fond of saying that coming to work was his vacation, and Beth believed him.

"Oh, a little while ago, two fools over there," he nodded toward the semi-crowded dance floor, thick hands busy pouring beer, "decided they wanted to hurt each other." He shook his head, sad; sad about what, Beth didn't know. The general foolishness of fools, she supposed. Javy's voice went flat. "I talked them out of it. They been good ever since, boss."

Beth smiled. It was best to be good when Javier wished you to be good, that's for certain. "Okay then, I'll leave you to it. I'm heading to the kitchen to kick some—"

"*There* you are!"

Trisha pushed the rest of the way through the swinging doors that separated the bars and stopped and glared at Beth. She wasn't supposed to be back there, but Trisha thought most rules didn't apply to Trisha—inside the restaurant and in life. The girl was also firmly in Mark's camp. The fact that there *were* camps only ramped up Beth's anger, which was heating nicely, helped by the way Tim was eying the striking girl. Even Javier was watching her out of the corner of his eye, and he was the most married man on the planet besides her Daniel.

"Hello, Trisha. What can I do for you?"

Beth didn't want to hate the girl, but she was afraid she fell well short of that goal; after one look, most women decided to hate Trisha on general principal.

"I've been looking all over for you! They said you were sharking, and then Jen said she thought you went back to your office, and then *Mark* said—"

"Get out from behind that bar. You know better." The girl opened her mouth to argue, cat-green eyes widening in outrage. "Shut it. I don't want to hear it." Motioning sharply for the midnight-haired server to follow, Beth walked over against the wall where she'd stood before. She kept the volume down, but everything else turned up; after a minute, Trisha was in tears, shocked that someone would actually speak to her in such a manner. Tim went pale and walked to the other end of the bar. Javy watched openly, a huge grin splitting his dark face.

"Do you understand me?"

"Yes, ma'am." The girl hiccoughed into the neck of her Slo Eddie's tee-shirt, smearing eyeliner. Beth felt a flash of pity; Trisha was young, not yet twenty-two; a good-looking, foolish puppy.

"Now, why were you looking for me?"

"The dirtbags at thirty-seven want—" Trisha caught her expression. She swallowed. "I mean, the two *customers* sitting at thirty-seven want to talk to you."

Beth sighed; you could only do so much. "What's the problem?" The thirties through the fifties were the Pit booths.

"I don't know, there was nothing wrong with their order. They just told me they wanted…" Trisha eyed her and then continued; brave girl. "That they wanted to talk to the 'little shark'."

Beth motioned Trisha away. "All right, you told me, now back to work. And Trisha? Remember what we discussed."

The sultry girl nodded and left, most definitely *not* going back behind the bar. Beth used that highway herself, pushing through the swinging doors, leaving the music and noise and reentering the relative quiet of a packed restaurant. She slid behind Mike and used his computer to check the times and found that they'd slowed even more.

Not disappointed by that in the least, she stole a glance toward thirty-seven and saw two men sharing a pitcher of amber beer. The older one sported a close-cropped dark beard and had made the dubious decision to dress in camouflage from cap to boot; the other was a tall, young guy with longish white-blonde hair. Something struck Beth as familiar about the young one, but he'd probably been in here before; Slo Eddie's was popular with that age-bracket.

Little shark?

The dirtbags at thirty-seven could wait.

Beth left the bar and walked into the kitchen. It was her favorite part of the restaurant; the wonderful smells and the choreographed pandemonium were things she was comfortable with, having worked in the kitchen at Slo Eddie's Columbus for years.

She let no trace of pleasure leak into her voice, however.

"Orders are taking *eleven minutes* longer than they should!" The cooks and helpers under the hoods of the great open kitchen could hear her, but the customers a few dozen strides away would have to strain to make out details; that there was someone yelling, there could be no doubt. "*Pick it up!* You people are holding up this entire restaurant!" Beth prowled from one end of the line to the other. "Do I have to cook these nice people's food myself?"

No one answered, and stiff, worried faces were kept carefully turned away. Beth came back down the line and stopped behind Mark. She could *feel* his jaw clench even though she couldn't see it; he didn't acknowledge her beyond that.

And then, suddenly, Beth had had enough.

She'd endured this man's duplicity for weeks, *months*, doing nothing while he smiled to her face and sabotaged her efforts behind her back. She'd planned to let him work tonight, partly because she needed him but mostly because she wanted to confront him with the pictures in private and see if they could work things out, but now Beth's instincts were telling her to attack.

She donned a pair of gloves from the dispenser and snatched tongs from the rack and flipped a chicken breast, turning it so the grill marks crossed each other at a thirty-degree angle. Mark eyed her sideways, then inched over to make room. They filled platters with meat and sent them down the line, and Beth was content to wait; her enemy would move and give her an opening. They always did.

After a minute, her patience paid off. Mark waved toward the dining area with his tongs. "How's it going out there?" His deep voice was even and cool.

"Good. How much did you get for those steaks?" She checked the monitor and plated a rare Fillet Mignon and passed it to Sue, who was closest.

Mark barely hesitated, but it was enough. "What steaks are those?"

"The three boxes of rib-eyes you put in your truck this afternoon, right after Metro came. Did you sell them, or did you take them home and put them in that freezer in your garage?"

This time the silence stretched. "I have no idea what you're talking about," he finally said.

Beth turned to him. "You don't? So if I pull the invoice and check the deep freeze, everything will be there that's supposed to be there?"

"Gee, Beth, I wouldn't know. I suppose *someone* could've taken something they weren't supposed to. Employee graft is a sad fact in this business, in case you haven't learned that yet." He flipped a T-Bone, almost slamming it back down, then thrust his tongs down the line. "A dozen of us have been in and out of that freezer all afternoon. Why don't you ask them?"

Fury writhed like mating snakes just under her skin, but she forced it down and spoke calmly; her enemy had overextended, and it was time for the killing blow.

"Because I don't have pictures of them stealing the boxes of steaks, that's why."

Mark faced her for the first time, and the kitchen rippled to a halt as everyone turned to watch; she had to end this quickly.

He mulled that over, then said, "There are no cameras back there. You're bluffing." He looked a lot less certain than he sounded, though.

Beth smiled up at him. "True, there are no security cameras where you park your truck. But there *was* a camera in Javier's hands, just across the fence in the Walgreens' lot."

Outrage did unpleasant things to Mark's face. "Javier! I should've known! What, are you fucking him, too?" He stepped closer, looming, and leveled a finger in her face. Mark was taller than Daniel, and wide with it, but Beth didn't back away. She also saw three ways to break him now that he'd stepped closer, but she had to win this battle with words.

"*I* should've been promoted to GM after Joe got canned, and *you* know it!" He thumped his chest with two fingers. "*I* have degrees in business administration and finance!" He pointed at her crotch. "What do *you* got? That!"

Despite everything, Beth was shocked. Did he actually think she'd *slept* her way to a GMs job? Mark foolishly kept talking: "*I* bust my balls for this place, and what do *you* do? Spread your legs and whore—"

Beth stepped forward as the snakes came leaping out of her eyes, but then she got a fingernail's hold on her temper and stopped. Mark took a wary step back; the drunk that had grabbed her in the Pool Room two summers ago had been twice her size, too, and everyone knew what had happened to him; ironically, Mark had vouched for her side of the story with the cops that night.

"You're fired, Mark. Get out."

He sneered, but kept a careful distance; smart man. "Clint told me he wanted me in the Santa Monica store when it opens, so we'll just see how *fired* I am, bitch." Mark untied his apron and let it fall, then snatched off his chef's beret and slung it down. He pointed at her again, and Beth told herself that snapping that finger would be wrong. "You're going to regret this!" Mark stalked out of the kitchen and slammed through the double doors that led to the back of the house.

Beth sighed softly. *I already do.* Clint had seen the photos; there would be no Santa Monica store, not for Mark, not in this company. But he would find that out soon enough.

She looked around. Mike gaped at her from behind the bar, and several girls had stopped to stare. The kitchen behind her was at a standstill. She glanced out into the sea of customers; several four-tops, those closest to the kitchen, were watching.

Beth cracked her hands together. "Show's over, people! Back to work!"

They surged into motion as if they'd all been sitting at a red light. Beth faced the grill and filled orders for a minute, thinking, then put the tongs down and snapped off her gloves.

"Sue? Come here, please." The hefty woman stopped what she was doing and came to fidget by Beth; the rest of the kitchen worked feverishly, not looking her way. "Hold on a second," Beth told her. "Mike!" Several people jumped, Mike included. He handed a pitcher of frozen strawberry margaritas off, cleaned up the spill, then walked into the kitchen, now wiping his hands on the bar towel hanging from his back pocket.

"Ma'am?"

"Go make sure Mark leaves without taking anything else, and that he's not in my office." Mike looked at her uncertainly; he was as tall as Mark, but only about a third as wide. "If he gives you even *this* much of a problem," she held up a forefinger and thumb with a tiny space between, "you take out your phone and call the cops. Understood?"

Mike nodded, confidence restored now that reinforcements were only three little numbers away. He pushed through the double doors, and Beth looked at Sue and motioned toward the grill. "Take over here." The big woman did, and Beth lowered her voice. "You're in charge of the kitchen tonight."

Sue glanced at her in surprise. "But I don't—"

"I have confidence in you." Beth gestured down the line. "You can make anything on the menu, am I right?" Sue closed her mouth and nodded. "You've been here since we opened this place five years ago, right?" Sue nodded again, looking less uncertain, and Beth squeezed her arm. "I *know* you can do it. I can't promise you Mark's job, but I can promise you're in consideration. Do a good job tonight and we'll talk more."

Sue's smile lit up all of Slo Eddie's, bar side included. "Yes, *ma'am.*"

Beth then went down the line, doling out compliments and praise, leaving a much more relaxed kitchen in her wake.

Mike came back through the swinging doors just as she reached them. "He's gone." At her impatient eyebrow, he said: "He didn't take anything, not that I could see, but when I first went back he was walking out of your office." Mike shrugged. "It just looked like he was carrying his stuff, but I couldn't really tell. You might want to check."

"I'll do that. And thank you."

He nodded, smiling and preening. Beth pointed to the bar where three girls stood holding trays and looking everywhere but at her. "Your drinks are backing up."

"Uh, yes, ma'am." Mike scooted off to do his job, and Beth looked out over the restaurant. She drew a deep, slow breath, then blew it out.

I did it. Then she grimaced. *I could've handled it better.* Causing all that drama in the middle of a Saturday rush...*not* the plan; right or wrong, though, it was done.

She turned to go see what Mark had taken when a server at the bar tripped and dropped her tray; a full pitcher and four frosty mugs crashed almost at Beth's feet. Several tables clapped and cheered. The girl—it was Stacey—took one look at Beth's face and burst into tears.

She soothed her as best she could and then sent her back to Mike to get her order filled again, then collared a busboy and set him to sweeping glass and mopping up the mess while she put the yellow "Wet Floor: Caution" signs out.

Beth set the last one down and turned to find one of the girls working the Pool Room waiting to be noticed.

"What is it, Lisa?"

The brunette cleared her throat. "Uh, Javy's computer froze up again." At that moment, the challenge bell rang, then clanged again, as if the idiot yanking on the rope thought no one could hear it the first time.

Beth smiled at Lisa. She had her long, curly hair cinched into a ponytail tonight; it looked nice that way.

"Randori."

Lisa's smooth brow creased. "What?"

"Never mind." Beth took her case from Mike, who handed it over the bar without being asked. "Tell Javy to unplug it, wait a couple minutes, then plug it back in and turn it back on." That had fixed it the last time, although Beth had no clue why. *Stupid computers.* "You girls will have to write your drink orders out by hand until the software reboots. You'll have to do the same with food orders and run them to the kitchen yourselves, so remind everyone to write *legibly.*"

Lisa nodded and scurried off and Beth flowed toward the Pit, relaxed and still smiling; she had some overenthusiastic bell-ringing bait to dispatch, and then she would visit the dirtbags at thirty-seven, who could wait a bit longer for the little shark.

Centered and focused, senses scanning the packed restaurant, Beth waited for the next attack.

Birthday Wishes

THEY WERE watching *Star Wars*. Again.

Dan was reminded of that old saw about good intentions; when he'd introduced Lizzie to the movie three months ago, it had been a desperate attempt at getting out of watching another *Dora* episode, or the *Lion King*, or *Finding Nemo* (great, *great* movie, but after the gamillionth time, even *Nemo* got old), or *Shrek*, or—God forbid—*Shark Tales*. He'd ignored Beth's protests that Lizzie wasn't old enough for *Star Wars* and his own misgivings about whether she would even like it.

Twenty-five screenings later, Dan was confident their fears had been unfounded.

The crackling hum of a lightsaber pulled his attention to the flat-screen, and Dan watched Luke whine his way through another session with the training remote. He stole a glance at Lizzie, where she sat on the far end of the couch, and beheld open-mouthed delight.

Dan sagged deeper into his corner and sighed.

What would he give to recapture that enthusiasm for *Star Wars*? What *wouldn't* he? Dan remembered watching it for the first time with Will when he was…nine? Ten? *That's* what he wanted for his birthday: a *Star Wars* Memory Wipe. They could do it to Threepio, so why not him? Every time his ass hit the couch and someone pressed play, that part of his brain which retained Luke and Han and Chewie and Artoo and the rest of the gang just got wiped out. Zap. Then he could watch with renewed wonder, awe, and enthusiasm as the *Star Wars* saga unfolded.

Dan stared at the wall beyond the television as Obi-Wan got gas when a billion poor bastards on Alderaan were vaporized. Again. He dreaded the day Lizzie figured out there were more movies in the series.

Jar Jar Binks.

God give me strength.

Inspiration struck. He dug the remote from between the cushions and hit pause. Lizzie frowned at him.

"Hey kiddo, I've got an idea."

"What?"

"Let's go surprise Mommy at work. We'll get some strawberry ice cream and a banana pudding." Slo Eddie's served a righteous banana pudding.

Lizzie's face scrunched. "Me and Mommy ate lunch at her work *already*. I wanna watch *Star Wars*." She plucked the remote from his hand and pressed play.

Dan stared at her. *Oh yeah*. Shit. Still, the mention of strawberry ice cream should've had her scrambling into the car by now. She must not be hungry. A smile spread across his face. She just needed to be sold, that's all. Dan had been selling one thing or another since seventeen: cars, boats, houses, even a regrettable and forgettable stint selling insurance. Dan shuddered. *Too goddamn depressing.*

Sell ice cream to a four-year-old?

Please.

He took the remote from her and pressed pause again, which earned him another frown. "I know that," he said, "but when we go tonight, it will be *special.* It's my birthday, and you and I are going on an Ice Cream Birthday Date!"

Instead of jumping up and down on the couch and yelling "yay", Lizzie folded her arms across her retro Powerpuff Girls tee-shirt and stuck her nose in the air.

"I can't go on a date with *you*, Daddy! You're my *Daddy.* And I have a boyfriend. I don't want him to get mad."

"You have a what?"

"A boyfriend."

A boyfriend. "You do?"

"Yes."

"Who?"

Lizzie gave him shy. "Jacob."

"Oh."

Jacob. Dan groped around and found his bearings again; Helen's grandson was a stout little boy with carrot hair, skinned-up knees, and more often than not he had something smeared on his face. He seemed to love Lizzie, though, so Dan supposed she could do worse. He also doubted Jacob knew of his promotion: that seemed to be how the system worked, from four to a hundred and four; the female of the species decided such things, and the male was just happy to reap the benefits.

Lizzie was looking at him like she expected something other than "Oh". Dan cleared his throat: "He's a good boy. I'm happy for you both." She beamed, the gap where her front teeth used to be a gummy, pink M. "But," Dan continued, thinking fast, "this won't be a *real* date, it'll be a Father-Daughter Birthday Date." He scooted closer and dropped his voice: "Just think, Lizzie. You can put on one of your pretty dresses, and I'll wear something nice." What he had on now, if Dan had any say in it. "We'll go surprise Mommy and have some strawberry ice cream and maybe a banana pudding." Thank God Slo Eddie's didn't do that singing-at-the-table-for-birthdays shit. That was fucking unbearable, even with Grade A eye candy doing the singing. "It'll be special, just you and me. Mommy will be glad to see us, too."

"I can wear any dress I want?"

Hooked. "Sure."

She bit her lower lip. "But…"

She wasn't in the boat yet, so Dan took her small hand in both of his and brought it dramatically to his chest; it was time to close the deal. "Elizabeth Ann Sims, would you be so kind as to accompany your father on an Ice Cream Birthday Date?"

Lizzie giggled and then stood and flung her arms around his neck; holy crap, she was strong for such a little thing.

"Yes, I'll go!" She scrambled down, trampling him. "I know what dress I'm going to wear!" She shot out of the living room and pounded up the stairs.

Dan followed slowly; his hip hadn't enjoyed being stepped on, but he limped up after her with a smile.

Sold.

It turned out Dan didn't have much say in what he wore; in between changing dresses four times before settling on a dark-green with white flowers embroidered on the hem, Lizzie informed him he looked "yucky" in his khaki shorts and sandals and "Got Football?" tee-shirt.

Yucky?

He ended up wearing what he wore to work every day, dark slacks and dress shoes and a button-down Polo, but sans tie. Lizzie vetoed the first three shirts, finally stamping into their closet and picking out a green that matched her dress; Dan endured the second mother-daughter doppelgänger installment of the day with some reservation.

He offered to brush her hair, and they went into the bathroom and Dan stood her bare-footed on the counter between the sinks and dug around in the drawers on Beth's side and found her brush and began. Lizzie stood still for him, hands folded primly at her waist; this had been a daily ritual when she was younger, but they'd fallen out of the habit. He hadn't realized how much he'd missed it.

Out of nowhere, primal panic welled in Dan's heart, and he fought to keep the emotion from his face and the strokes steady; Lizzie was watching him in the mirror. *God, she's growing up so fast.* She seemed years older with her hands folded like that and wearing her big-girl dress; a small vision of the stunning woman she would become. Dan didn't slow the brush as he wiped his eyes with his sleeve, moving behind her to hide his tears. Maybe it was the whole boyfriend thing; she was only four, true, but someday Dan would turn around and she'd be fifteen and have a real boyfriend, and all that went with it. *God help me.*

He'd overheard two coworkers talking once, years before, fathers lamenting on how fast kids grew. He'd been single back then, wasting time chasing one woman or another; Dan didn't remember who, but no doubt he'd thought her important. The last thing those men said had stuck with him, though he hadn't understood, not really:

Time is different for parents.

Dan got it now.

Time was penciled marks notched higher and higher on the laundry room door jamb, old toys and full coloring books, boxes of clothes you kept meaning to donate but never did, dusty homemade Christmas ornaments, and pictures. God, the *pictures!* Digital photography was swell and all, but now photographs never went away; they just lurked in your hard drive, ready to yank out nostalgic tears whenever summoned to haunt the monitor. Dan almost missed that old Polaroid Instamatic his parents had been gaga for; at least you could lose those, and they mercifully faded with time.

But the worst part, the absolute *worst*, was that parents got to stand around and watch, both hopefully and helplessly, as the tiny people who needed them so much grew into adults that walked away with few backward glances—and that's if the parents were lucky.

What a raw fucking deal.

It went by so fast. So goddamn fast. Dan flashed to Lizzie, wearing only a diaper, lying on her back in her crib, kicking her feet and waving her pudgy arms, smiling a gummy smile as he made faces at her. Her squeal still resounded in his head, and the absolute joy in her eyes…he could still *see* that, could still *feel* that in his heart.

Why does it have to go by so fast?

Dan fought the wild urge to snatch her up and run, somehow pressing the Big Pause Button on life, keeping them thirty-three and four, both still young; stopping time when Lizzie still needed him and still wanted to hang out with him.

He composed himself, then put Beth's brush away and grabbed a handful of the gewgaws his girls liked to stick in their hair: bands, scrunches, butterfly clips, whatnot. They were tangled together, so Dan held the mass up for her inspection.

"Wanna put your hair up?"

"No," she piped. "I like it down." Dan shut the drawer and Lizzie held her arms out; he started to pick her up, but she jumped and he caught her and she hugged him fiercely with all her limbs. Dan hugged her back, watching in the mirror, wishing hard for that Big Button. Then she squirmed, so he set her down; her legs were already pumping before she touched the tiles, and she shot out of the bathroom, half-running and half-skipping in that way only kids could without breaking their spines.

"Thank you, Daddy!"

"You're welcome! Get your socks and shoes on, we'll be ready to go in a minute!"

"Yes, sir!"

Dan hustled back downstairs to find his phone and wallet and keys; he'd wished for a *Star Wars* Memory Wipe and a Big Life Pause Button, but he'd take a night out with his girls and a banana pudding and call himself a lucky man because that wasn't settling in his book, not even close.

SHADOWS

DAN STOPPED at the bottom of the stairs: phone-wallet-keys. He'd left the phone upstairs on the dresser, that's right, but his wallet and keys should be…on the computer desk?

He walked into the kitchen and spotted them, bing, then strolled through the breakfast nook and snatched them up; now back upstairs, grab the phone and the kid, go have strawberry ice cream and a banana pudding, and spend time with his wife. A man should be with his wife on his birthday.

Dan's hip gave a strong twinge, so he detoured to dig the ibuprofen out of the cabinet and went to the sink and washed the pills down, not bothering with dirtying a glass. He turned the faucet off, and as he stood up and wiped his chin, he glanced through the little square window over the sink and froze in shock.

There was someone in his backyard.

Dan squinted and leaned over the sink, unsure if he was seeing what he thought he was seeing; the outdoor floods were off, and only crosshatched squares of dim illumination lit the yard. And then he was sure; the outline of a human figure was standing by his fence.

What's more, the way they stood, they had to be looking right at him.

He jerked back and down, out of view.

"Shit!"

Phone. Call 911. Phone was upstairs. House phone. Fuck, no land line. They only had cells to save money. Dan crouched on the green tiles, heart racing. Gun. No gun. Beth didn't like guns. They needed to have a *serious* talk about that. Wife. Weapons! He duck-walked over and snatched the junk drawer open, the contents sloshing, and yanked out a hammer; the foam-rubber grip felt good in his shaking hand.

Who was out there? What did they want? Could it be that asshole in the Dodge? No, no, he didn't know Dan from Adam; he'd only had some fun with a random bike rider and then went on his angry little asshole way. But *someone* was out there.

Floodlights!

He ran in a crouch to the switch by the French doors and slapped it up.

Stark white light surged into the backyard. Dan jerked open the door and stepped into the muggy night, hammer at the ready. He saw Beth's bag gallows, the storage shed by the fence, their patio furniture, his covered $300 combination grill/smoker he used maybe twice a year, and Lizzie's swing set; razor-edged shadows from the patio furniture stretched onto the green grass in front of him.

He hefted the hammer and stared at the spot by storage shed, where he'd seen someone standing.

Nobody home.

"Hello?"

His voice filled the space between the fences and died; only a moist cow-shit-scented breeze answered him, a sharp contrast to the cold and expensive air flowing out of the open door at his back. But he had seen someone, he was sure of it, and there was only one place to hide with the yard lit up.

Dan strode onto the grass and peeked around the side of the storage shed, hammer raised.

Nada.

He looked over his shoulder at the window above the sink, then eyed the eight-foot fence beside him; unless it had been a professional gymnast or fucking Spider Man, there was no way they could've gotten over that, not that quickly. Dan looked at the gate that led to the side yard and the paving stones that curved around to the front of the castle. He would've heard someone go through there; the gate handle didn't set flush and made a grinding racket.

Dan considered the fence again, and a cold prickle went down his arms; he was judging the situation by his own current thirty-three-year-old abilities; it would take him more than a few seconds now, sure, but when he'd been a snot-nosed teenager…

Yeah, someone young and spry enough could've gone over, and fast.

Then Dan's eyes widened.

He'd left the garage door *wide open*.

"Shit!"

He raced inside, then scanned the backyard again as he slipped the bolt home in the flimsy and glass-filled French door; it was better than nothing. *I hope.* Dan then sprinted through the house, going from switch to switch and flicking on all the outside floods; they normally left those off because they ate a lot of juice, and he could almost feel the meter outside wanting to helicopter away, but right then he didn't care. Dan glanced out each window as he blew past but saw no one and reached the door to the garage and jerked it open and hit the switch for the over-head light, hammer at the ready.

Their Nissan and his Kubota riding mower sat quietly under the light. He stepped down and sidled over and looked in the blind spot where someone could hide behind the car.

Empty.

Dan stepped back up and hit the button and listened to the door chug down, thinking, tapping the head of the hammer against his palm. Then he went back through the house, flipping the floods off, putting everything back the way it had been, and walked over to the French doors and stood and looked for a long time, face pressed to a square pane, before hitting the switch.

Night flowed into the backyard. He tiptoed over in front of the sink and leaned and peered outside.

The crosshatched squares were nothing compared to the floods, but Dan could clearly see the top half of a human figure looming against the fence; he raised his hand and waved, and the shadow waved back.

Dan snorted, then shoved the hammer in the junk drawer. *Jumping at my own fucking shadow. Beth will get a kick out of this.*

"Lizzie!"

He could hear her run out of her room and stand at the top of the stairs.

"Yes, sir?"

"Did you put your socks and shoes on?"

A distinct pause, and then she pounded back into her room. "I'm putting them on!"

Dan walked to the middle of the empty dining room and yelled up the stairs: "Hurry, it's getting late!"

She yelled something back, sounding like she was deep in her closet. Dan would probably have to remind her again; four-year-olds, he'd noticed, weren't big on attention span. He glanced out into the backyard through the dining room's triple-bay window; the blinds were open, and the horizontal wooden slats threw stripes of muted light onto the grass. One of Lizzie's horses sat in the alcove beneath the window.

Dan picked it up; the little guy was dark brown with three white socks, frozen eternally in mid-gallop, black mane streaming in a plastic wind. This waist-high alcove was Lizzie's favorite place to play, and it was a constant battle to remind her not to leave her toys on the ledge. Dan walked toward the bottom of the staircase and opened his mouth, intending to shout for her to come get her horse…and then he slowly turned to face the bay window.

Velvet night crawled across the panes, oozing and probing like it was seeking a way past the fragile glass. Dan could no longer see the backyard. Dan could no longer see anything but heaving, writhing darkness. Worse, there was something looking in at him, something within that darkness. He couldn't see it, but he knew it was there, just as he knew his feet were there without looking down because he could *feel* them.

Okay, then.

The front door was behind him, past the stairs and through the foyer, and then he would be *so* gone. It would smash through the glass with a coughing roar, oozing darkness coming for him, but he would have a step on it, and that's all he needed, one step…

Lizzie.

It would be in the house with Lizzie.

Not gonna happen.

"Fuck you," Dan told that boiling mass. Did it lighten? Just a little? He took three lunging steps and slapped up the switch by the door, turning on the floods, then pushed off the wall, plastic horse raised like a weapon, his other fist cocked. The backyard brightened, but the panes stayed in shadow for a second, two seconds, three seconds, ebon darkness swirling, dissipating, and then the glass cleared.

"Jesus Christ!"

Dan put his hand on the wall above the switch and leaned, letting it keep him off the floor since his legs didn't seem to want the job any longer. His other hand cramped, and he released his death-grip on Lizzie's horse. It tumbled to the hardwood. Shaking his hand, he peered down at it; the hooves didn't all gallop in the same direction anymore. He straightened and looked outside at his green backyard and then he looked around at his beautiful house and then Dan considered the possibility he was losing his goddamn mind.

It happened, he knew, although normally people didn't imagine…whatever the fuck that had been; they freaked out and quit their jobs and hijacked their family to Arkansas to milk goats and grow kale; or maybe they pulled out a pistol and wasted a few people before turning the gun on themselves; just another sad, psycho blurb on the nightly news radar.

That's how people lost it.

So what the hell was that?

Dan shivered; he'd sweated his shirt through in patches, the dark green darker where the damp spots clung. He could smell himself, too. He picked up the horse and tried to straighten its legs with little success, then carried it into the kitchen and put it on the counter by the sink where it promptly fell over. He splashed lukewarm water on his face, then stared out the little window; it was lit up out there like an airport runway.

"A panic attack. I had a fucking panic attack."

Dan dried off with paper towels. He'd never had a panic attack before. He'd heard of *other* people having them, even seen some pithily named drug advertised to prevent them—which, he remembered thinking, was a huge waste of money because a twelve-pack of Shiner would get you the same thing; now Dan knew what all the fuss was about.

He had to admit he didn't care for it.

"Daddy?"

Lizzie sounded like she was standing at the top of the stairs; he hadn't heard her come out of her room.

"Coming." Dan splashed water on his shirt and grabbed more paper towels and dabbed as he walked. "I spilled something, so I gotta change real quick and then we're out of here, kiddo." Somehow he managed to *not* look out the triple-bay window as he passed through the dining room, but only just. He reached the bottom of the stairs and smiled up at his daughter.

The smile faded.

Lizzie's eyes were blank, her face pointed into space somewhere to the left of the chandelier.

Dan glanced up there, then back at her.

"Lizzie?"

No answer.

Dan went up. "Baby?" Nothing. He picked her up and smoothed her hair. "Sweet pea, are you all right?" No look at him or answer, but she rested her head on his shoulder. "I'm sorry I spilled something on the nice shirt you picked out. Can you help me choose another one?" After a second, Lizzie nodded against his neck, and Dan breathed a little easier; she seemed to be coming out of the fog. He carried her toward the master bedroom with a big frown; this was the first time she'd grayed-out without a nightmare, at least that he had seen, and he didn't like it one goddamn bit.

He stopped in front of their walk-in closet and looked down at her brunette head. What did *he* know? Maybe all kids zonked out sometimes, their little brains taking a timeout as they processed this crazy world.

Maybe that's why adults like to zonk out, too.

Dan snorted, then set her on the hardwood and went in the closet; children should come with a fucking owner's manual. "C'mon, pick me out another good one." He stripped off his shirt and dumped it into the hamper behind the door, then thumbed through the hangers, grabbing a dark-blue Hugo Boss. He held it up and turned around. "What do you—?"

Lizzie was gone.

He stepped out and looked around; she was in front of the window, looking down through the blinds at something. Dan watched her for a few seconds, then tossed the shirt onto the bed and went in the bathroom and used the deodorant and the cologne. Back in the room, he buttoned and tucked while watching his daughter; she never moved. She didn't even *twitch*. Dan finished and walked over to stand beside her and followed her gaze.

The backyard was verdant in the strong white floods, and the sharp shadows cast from the bag gallows, patio furniture, and Lizzie's swing set stretched long from this vantage. There was nothing else to see. Dan glanced at his daughter again; she stood unblinking, looking down through the blinds. He scanned the yard again. There was nothing down there. Nothing. Just like there'd been all night.

Not a goddamn thing.

"Lizzie." No response. "Elizabeth Ann!" She blanched, and then finally looked up at him, but her eyes didn't quite focus on his face. He squatted in front of her. "Are you ready to go, sweetheart?" He turned the rod, shutting the blinds, and held out his arms.

She came to him as if sleepwalking and he picked her up and grabbed his phone from the dresser and carried her out of the bedroom and down the stairs. Her head was back on his shoulder, and her entire body was limp; along for the ride.

Dan halted on the bottom step and gently shook her. "Hey."

She sat up and looked at him—*really* looked at him, he was glad to see.

"I need your help," Dan told her. Then he shouted, "Come on!" and took off. Lizzie gave a small shriek and threw her arms around his neck. She was giggling by the time they reached the first switch.

"Turn it on." She looked a question at him, and he said, "Hurry! Hurry!" so she flipped it up, and he took off again, Lizzie laughing as they raced through the house while turning on every outside light and all the inside, too.

He was panting by the time they stopped in front of a living room window, the one closest to the fireplace. Lizzie hugged Dan's neck and kissed his ear, then turned his chin so he had to look at her.

"You're *silly*, Daddy."

"Yeah."

They stood that way for a comfortable time, peering into the dark beyond the floods.

"Let's go surprise Mommy," Dan said at last.

"Okay."

They left all the lights on.

Good Men and Bad

ETH LOWERED her fingertips between the orange four and the green six, thumb arced over the four and rock-steady under the Pechauer; committing a foul would mean losing at this juncture. With a sharp stroke, she brought the leather tip into contact with the cue ball and it spun forward, curving around the maroon seven to strike the cushion where it jumped off and sped toward the corner pocket; with a solid click, it knocked the black ball into the webbing.

She straightened to whoops and whistles, though her opponent thump-thumped the butt of her cue on the floor:

"*Fine* shot, girl! *Fine* shot!"

Beth held out her hand. "Thank you, Janet. Good game."

The taller woman glanced at the hand and said, "Oh, pooh," then enveloped Beth in a hug with their cues crossed between them. Janet held her at arm's length and said, mock-fiercely, "I'm gonna beat you yet!"

"I believe you. You misplayed that last safety and left me an opening, but other than that you shot great."

"Do you think I'm getting better?"

"Much better." Unlike whatshisname, Beth hadn't dared play Janet left-handed.

The dignified graying woman pulled her in for another hug, and Beth stepped away and clicked the headset on: "Give Janet a hand, folks! She almost had shark-fin soup for dinner!"

That got a few laughs, and the requested applause; the loudest by far came from Janet's husband, Bill, who whistled as he clapped, bald head gleaming as he beamed down at his wife; people in the surrounding booths turned to eye him as his baritone rolled over the din:

"That's my girl!"

Beth broke her cue down while Janet blew him kisses; she hoped she and Daniel were still that affectionate after twenty years. She slid her cue in the case and zipped it closed and then looked around.

The girls were moving briskly, but not at the frenetic pace of before; Beth couldn't see the host stand from the Pit, but she was sure the line no longer stretched out under the green awning. She glanced at her watch. They had over two hours until the restaurant side closed; the Pool Room stayed open till one. She shouldered her case; it was time to check on Sue, and she also needed to see how Javier was getting along with the bar computers…and then she remembered.

Beth turned and looked at the two men sitting at thirty-seven.

The older one with the close-cropped dark beard had just tilted back his mug, emptying the glass. He had a camouflage ball cap on with dark sunglasses perched on the brim; a camouflage tee-shirt tightened across thick shoulders as he grasped the pitcher handle for a refill. He wiped his mouth with a furry arm and said something to his friend, who glanced up before resuming playing with his smart phone; that one looked almost too young for the beer sitting in front of him.

If Trisha didn't card him, I really will fire her.

Beth studied the young man's profile with a frown; pale-blue eyes and white-blonde hair, tall…he still seemed familiar somehow…he had to have been in Slo Eddie's before. She shifted her attention back to the older man and found herself studied in turn. He smiled in a friendly way and lifted his mug to her, saying something to his friend, who turned to look.

Beth nodded to them, then walked across the Pit to where Janet stood discussing the match with the people at forty-nine.

If nothing is wrong, what the heck do they want?

Janet introduced Beth to forty-nine, friends from her church. "Jeremy here wants to know if a kid can challenge the Shark." A gawky boy, twelve or thirteen, watched Beth with eager eyes; a leather cue case rested in the booth next to him.

"With his folks' permission, you bet he can; but if you don't mind, I need to take care of some things real quick. Give me twenty minutes?" She looked at the boy's parents, who nodded graciously.

The father said, "That was a nice shot, Mrs. Sims."

"Beth, please."

"Beth, then; a *very* nice shot." He pointed across the table at his son. "I bet Jeremy gives you a run for your money, though." The boy swelled, bony chest puffing. "I taught him to play when he was four." He shook his head, rueful: "Now he's better than I ever was." Behind him, his wife rolled her eyes and gave Beth a long-suffering look.

She fought off a smile as she peered at Jeremy: "That good, huh?"

"Yes, ma'am." She thought pride would seep out of the boy's pores and splash on the seat.

"Practice a lot?"

"Every chance I get."

"Good. That's what it takes."

"Yes, ma'am."

Beth turned back to the parents. "It was nice meeting you."

"You too, Beth."

She then looked at Jeremy with a challenge in her eye: "I'll be back in twenty minutes. We'll see what you've got."

He grinned as Beth turned to Janet, who appeared amused. "I'll escort you to Bill. He looks lonely." She hooked her elbow in Janet's as the older woman made her goodbyes, and they stepped up and out of the Pit arm and arm, cases slung over their shoulders. Bill watched them come with a toothy grin, face even redder than usual.

"Good game, ladies!" He saluted them with his mug, drained it, then glanced around; Trisha was coming down the aisle carrying a tray of steaming platters. Bill grasped the handle of the empty pitcher and waggled it at her. Trisha scowled as she went by, and Bill's eyes pulled the rest of his head around, tracking the striking server until Beth thought his thick neck would crack.

He finally turned back around and announced, "Damn fine figure of a woman, that, *damn* fine, but a cold fish, I think. Tumble 'er inta bed, and she'd only worry about mussin' that hair."

"*Bill Younger!*" Janet glared daggers at her husband as she slid into her side of the booth, then glanced up at Beth, embarrassed. "We're celebrating tonight."

"I see that." Beth wasn't offended; most men watched Trisha, even those who should be old enough to know better. Besides, Bill's take on the girl was dead-on, in her opinion. "What are you celebrating?"

Bill belched, fluttering his mustache. "The Grand Opening of Younger's West, is what!"

Janet gave him a resigned look before explaining: "We just opened another repair center, Younger's West, on the other side of Murfreesboro. Over on Syc-amore?" Beth nodded, although she didn't know where that was; most days she wore a groove between Slo Eddie's and the dojo and the grocery store and Lizzie's daycare and the castle, with little daylight left to explore. "We can service everything now," Janet continued. "Why, the new place even has a bay just for paint jobs! We'll generate three times the business." Janet reached across the table and took Bill's meaty hand in both of hers.

His snort turned heads two booths away. "Three times the work and twice the debt, you mean, but if we're lucky, four times the money for the grandkids to piss away."

"*Bill!*"

"Don't bark at me, woman. Nothin' but the goddamn truth."

Beth laughed. "Congratulations, you guys. Let me buy you that next pitcher." It was the least she could do; Bill and Janet had been frequenting Slo Eddie's since they'd opened, sometimes multiple times a week; more importantly, they'd become friends. They even babysat Lizzie on occasion, and she always had a great time.

Janet opened her mouth to protest, but Bill beat her to the punch. "Thank you, sweet thang." Janet sighed, but she patted her husband's hand.

Bill suddenly jabbed a sausage finger in Beth's general direction. "You're lucky I'm in my cups tonight, or I'd go down there and show you how to play that beau-tiful game."

"I know you would, Bill." It was nothing but the truth; Bill had been shooting pool since before Beth was born—a fact he never let her forget. She winked at Janet. "You've been putting your wife through shooting drills, haven't you?"

"She's gettin' better, ain't she?"

"She is." Beth laughed again as Janet blushed. "I gotta get back to work, guys. Tell Trisha that next pitcher's on me." She bent to hug Janet and whisper a question: "You've got the keys?"

"Of course, dear."

Beth straightened. "I'll try to visit again before you leave, but I've got things to take care of and a young shark to teach, so I might not have time. Congratulations again, Bill."

He tipped his mug. "Thank ya, darlin'."

On impulse, Beth then did something she'd never done before. She hugged Bill. He stiffened, and then a knotted arm went around her and a slab hand patted her on the back.

Unexpectedly, Beth had to fight her own reaction; Bill smelled like Aqua Velva. She stood back up and let nothing of her struggle show, but Bill's neck above his collar had turned redder that his face. She shared a smile with Janet, but inside Beth was roiling as she walked around the Pit toward thirty-seven.

Janet was lucky to have found Bill; good men were few and far between. Look how long it had taken Beth to find her Daniel.

She repeated it to herself firmly:

Bill is a good man. It wasn't his fault he wore the same aftershave as a monster.

She stopped at booth thirty-seven. "How can I help you gentlemen?"

Both men looked up. This close, Beth could see pale whiskers spotting the blonde man's lip and chin; the muted light hanging over the table also revealed he was going bald. Even so, he was handsome enough—he had pretty blue eyes, for one thing, which had always been her weakness. An intricate tattoo sheathed his left forearm, and he was even taller than she'd thought, all arms and legs. His hands were enormous; that sense of recognition tickled Beth again.

"Well," the burly older man pronounced in a deep cracker voice. "We'd heard the view 'round this place was better than the service, and now we know it's true." He gave a chuckle and winked at his partner.

Beth's smile remained, held up at the corners by pure will: "Is there something I can do for you?"

"There sure is, sweetheart." He waved a hairy paw at the Pit. "You shoot a mean stick. I wouldn't mind playin' with ya m'self." His sly grin confirmed the double entendre.

Beth pulled a slow breath deep into her *itten* as she framed a response; his innuendo was crude, but nothing she hadn't dealt with before. *Sweetheart?*

Suddenly, the blond, who'd been watching Beth, issued a grating laugh and began typing with his thumbs, banana fingers enveloping the phone as he held it over the table.

Beth found her voice: "If you would like to play, sir, there's a young man ahead of you, but we're open until eleven so there's still plenty of time. The rules are posted below the bell," she pointed, "and up by the host stand. All donations go to charity—"

Camouflage Boy held out a hand; his phone, sitting on the table by the pitcher of amber beer, was buzzing: "Hold that thought, little darlin'." He read, then laughed and put it back down. "I think you're right," he told his friend.

Then they both pinned nasty smiles on her.

So. These.

Men of this stripe were inevitable in Beth's line of work. *Customers.* They were just customers, people who made money for the restaurant and by extension her family; they were only customers, no matter how repugnant: "As I was saying," she continued brightly, "there's a young man ahead of you, but if you'd like to play the Shark, I'll be free after that." *I will trounce you all over the table, big boy. I may even embarrass you a little.*

"Nah, got bigger fish ta fry. But I wanted ta ask ya 'bout this *charity* you're donatin' all this money to, this…Sunshine House? That right?"

Nonplussed, Beth took a second to answer. "Yes, the Sunshine House for Women and Children. For the next two months, all donations will help abused women and children get back on their feet; Beat the Shark donations go to various causes. In September, Slo Eddie's will—"

"'Abused women and children'? Faithless whores and ungrateful brats is what I'd call 'em. Won't do what a man tells 'em, like the Good Book sez. Forget that shit. I gotta better charity for yer money."

The blond, who still hadn't said a word, barked another laugh and set to typing with his giant thumbs again.

Customers. "Oh? And what's that?"

"We got us a huntin' club. You donate them sharkin' funds to us for a coupla months, we'll take the poor mites out and learn 'em how to kill and dress-out a deer. Little shits can feed themselves after that." He laughed and picked up his vibrating phone, looked at it, then grinned across the table. "Whachoo say? Better'n givin' some fickle bitch an excuse to split a God-fearin' family apart." He took another drink, watching her over the rim with dark and dancing eyes.

Beth slid forward and leaned a hip against the table; she could feel her Carson pressing into her leg. The blond looked her up and down, tongue darting to wet his lips.

Customers.

"That's a wonderful idea, sir, but we're committed for the next several months. Perhaps this time next year?" Camouflage Boy's grin faltered as Beth placed both palms on the table and leaned toward him: "In the meantime, I'm delivering some much-needed supplies to those women and children tomorrow. Would you like me to take a message to your wife and kids? I know you want to yourself, but the judge wouldn't like it if you violated that pesky restraining order."

Beth leaned back and crossed her arms under her breasts and waited.

Camo Boy's mouth worked, and then the blond kid began laughing. Camo Boy turned his glare on *him*, and into all that stepped Trisha, cat-eyes curious as she picked up the vibe.

"Um, Beth?"

"What?"

"Your family is here."

Trisha pointed, and Beth looked up by the host stand and saw Jen just putting Lizzie down from a big hug. Daniel stood watching them with a smile. Lizzie wore one of her big-girl dresses, the dark green with the tiger-lily embroidery. She also had on her Dora the Explorer sneakers; the bright orange and blue clashed horribly with the green dress.

Beth's delighted smile turned wry; you couldn't expect a four-year-old to think of such things. She shifted her eyes; husbands either, for that matter. Daniel looked nice. Beth was glad they'd come; she hadn't realized how much she was missing them.

She was just opening her mouth to tell Trisha to put them in the next available Pit booth when there was a soft drawl at her back:

"Excuse me, ma'am."

Beth turned around and then backed up fast as the young man unfolded out of the booth; she'd *had* to move fast, or he would've bowled her over! She glared up and up at all six-four, maybe six-five of him; he loomed, their eyes met and held, and Beth changed her mind; they were blue, true, but much too full of cold arrogance to be called pretty.

She also recognized something else in those eyes.

He broke their gaze. "Restroom's this way?" He strode off without waiting for an answer, swaggering even as he slouched; he hadn't even so much as *glanced* at Trisha. Beth supposed he liked older women.

Dream on, junior.

Beth didn't inform him he was going the wrong way. *Let him piss himself.* She gave Trisha instructions and then turned back to her other beloved customer, but found he didn't wish to play anymore. Camo Boy gave her one heated glower, then began typing furiously on his phone, so Beth went about her business, glad to be shed of them; the moment they crawled back to whatever puss-hole of ignorant darkness spawned them would be a wonderful moment indeed.

Beth checked on Javier and found that the balky bar computers had rebooted on the second go and the girls didn't have to scrawl their food orders anymore—much to the kitchen's relief. Speaking of the kitchen…she did a time check; they were *still* behind, but catching up fast. While there, Beth noticed Ricardo shooting both her and Sue disgruntled scowls, and it wasn't hard to understand why: Ricardo had also helped to open Slo Eddie's five years ago, and he thought he should be the one to replace Mark. He had a legitimate point, but Clint would make that decision—based on her recommendation, of course. Until then, she would have to let them take turns. She'd been grooming Javy for promotion next, but now wasn't the time to show favoritism, and she hoped he understood his time would come; Beth had to knit this place back together and have it running like a well-oiled and money-making machine again, or Clint would replace her without hesitation or remorse, and sooner rather than later.

She then went looking for her family and found them standing at Bill and Janet's table. Trisha was behind them, holding two menus and scowling. Beth halted before anyone spotted her and watched Bill and Daniel shake hands and Lizzie hop into Janet's arms for a hug.

"Nonsense!" Janet proclaimed to something Daniel had said. "You'll sit here with us. Put those down, honey." Trisha complied with even more than her usual attitude. Beth was about to join them when the girl spotted her and stalked over.

"Thirty-seven ditched me! The tall one never came back, and the big one bailed right after! They didn't even leave a tip!"

Beth hesitated only a second. "I'll cover it."

"*You'll* cover it?"

"Yes. Don't let it happen again, though." She'd had healthier conversations with customers, and Trisha shouldn't have to pay for Beth's temper.

"Um, thank you."

The girl's stunned bewilderment was almost worth it. "You're welcome. Remember what I said about not letting it happen again."

"Yes, ma'am."

Beth walked past Trisha and up to the booth that held her friends and family. "Hi, guys."

Beth's husband gave her his usual insufferable grin, but grin or no grin, she could immediately tell something was wrong. "Hey, beautiful. Surprise."

Before Beth could reply, Lizzie, who was standing in the booth and talking to Janet, turned around. "Hi, Mommy!" She gathered her little arms in and hunched over, then flung out her hands. "*Surprise!*"

People all across the restaurant turned to look.

The grownups laughed as Beth gathered her energetic four-year-old for hugs and smooches. "Shh, don't yell, I can hear you."

Small hands on Beth's shoulders, Lizzie stared at her seriously from a foot away. "Were you surprised, Mommy?"

"I was very surprised."

"Good, 'cause we wanted to surprise you. And me and Daddy are on a Ice Cream Birthday Date!"

"Oh you are?"

"Yeah, but it's not a *real* date, 'cause he's my daddy, and you can't go on a real date with your daddy, so I hope Jacob doesn't get mad, 'cause he's my boyfriend, and I'm s'posed to go on dates with him. It's okay if Jacob's my boyfriend, isn't it, Mommy?"

Beth laughed and kissed her. "Of course it is, baby." It had to happen sooner or later. *Helen will be delighted.*

Daniel spoke to Bill, but staged to carry: "I notice she didn't ask *me* if it was okay."

Beth smirked. "Better get used to that."

They all laughed, even Lizzie, though she appeared uncertain about why. Beth set her back in the booth. "Ice Cream Birthday Date, hmm? So I guess you want strawberry ice cream?"

"Yeah!"

Beth turned to her husband. "And what does the birthday boy desire?" She held up a hand. "That's on the menu?"

He smiled as Bill and Janet laughed, but she could still tell there was something bothering him. "Well, in that case…a banana pudding?"

"One strawberry ice cream and one banana pudding, coming up."

Janet said, "Happy birthday, Daniel. How old are you?"

"Thank you. I'm thirty-three."

"Thirty-three! I remember thirty-three." Bill took a swallow from his mug; he looked wistful, and drunk: "Enjoy it while it lasts. Thirty-three turns inta fifty 'fore ya know it."

Beth's husband nodded somberly as she tugged on his sleeve while telling Lizzie, "You be good for Ms. Janet and Mr. Bill. I need to talk to your daddy for a minute."

"Okay, Mommy."

Daniel followed her, and when they had a bit of privacy between two empty four-tops in the sixties, she reached up to adjust his shirt collar, though it didn't need it.

"What's wrong? What happened?"

He glanced toward the kitchen. "How's it going with Mark?"

"I fired him, that's how it's going, and don't change the subject. What happened?"

Something moved across his face, then; something she didn't like: "Nothing happened." At the look on *her* face, he cleared his throat: "Nothing happened, Beth, really. Well, I have to sit on an open house for Steve tomorrow to pay him back for covering for me today, so there goes family Sunday. The bastard's playing Pine Ridge without me."

"You said he'd cash that chip. Big surprise he did it already?" He shook his head. "Then what is it?"

He hesitated, then grimaced: "Lizzie grayed-out without the nightmare. Just… blam, out of nowhere. It scared the hell out of me."

Beth frowned over her shoulder; their daughter was busy talking Ms. Janet and Mr. Bill's collective ears off. "She seems fine now." Trisha went by with a full pitcher and a set of frosty mugs; she quickly looked away when she saw Beth watching. If Lizzie was going to start having the nightmares again *and* gray-out without them, maybe they needed to make another appointment with Dr. Lewiston.

Daniel won't like that at all.

"Oh, she's fine, all right," he said. "Sang me her ABC's the whole way here—the *whole* way, mind you."

He smiled, and Beth smiled back in relief; whatever these spells meant or were, they were only temporary. Still, seeing Dr. Lewiston again would be an excellent idea; she would have to convince her husband, just not tonight; twenty minutes had passed five minutes ago, and Jeremy would soon yank on the bell rope.

Beth opened her mouth, then shut it as Daniel continued with a strange expression, his blue eyes far away: "And I…" He shook his head and looked down at her. "I think I had a panic attack."

"You *think?*"

He shrugged. "Never had one before, just heard about them. You ever had one?"

"No…" She'd dealt with a lot of bad stuff in her time, but Beth was sure she'd never had a panic attack; the memory of the spare bedroom pricked, but that had been stress. She looked him over. "You seem fine, now."

"Oh, I'm *just* fine." He cleared his throat, then sang, loudly and off-key: "AB-CDEFG…!" Heads turned, including Trisha's as she walked by again, this time carrying spent mugs.

Beth speared two fingers into his liver, and he winced.

He also—thankfully—stopped singing.

"Smart ass."

"At your service." He rubbed his chest. "That hurt. But seriously, it was…" That strange, almost fearful cast crept back over his features. "Well, it was fucking *weird*, is what it was. I—"

The Pit bell clanged, and then again. *Everybody thinks you have to yank the stupid rope twice!* Beth would have to do something about that. "Back to work. We'll talk later, okay?"

"Okay. Knock 'em dead, beautiful."

Beth blew him a kiss, then went to the bar and retrieved her cue and walked down into the Pit and flipped her headset on and introduced Jeremy to the crowd after he told her his parents had shelled out fifty for a best-of-three nine-ball match.

As she spun her cue together and chalked up, Beth reflected on men.

The world was stuffed full of men (as she well knew), some good and some bad, but most a concoction of both; the lad she was about to play appeared to be growing into one weighted toward the former—but really, what did she know? They lagged for the break and Jeremy won. Beth stood back as he lined up on the right side, taking a steep angle on the one-ball.

She'd thought Mark was a good man, but being mistaken about men was nothing new to Beth; when she was seven, she'd found out the hard way that there were bad men in the world, and when she'd met her Daniel, she'd discovered there were wonderful ones, too. Jeremy broke but sank nothing, and she moved around the table, studying the layout, planning her attack.

Good men and bad.

The trick, Beth knew, was figuring out which was which before it was too late.

Surprise Me

I CAN'T STAND it anymore.

Beth rolled her window down and unbuckled her seatbelt, then gripped the "oh shit" (as her husband called it) handle at the top of the frame and lifted her head and torso out and rested her butt on the door.

Daniel said, "What the hell are you doing?"

The Nissan slowed as he let off the gas. Beth hung her head and shoulders out in space and sucked air through her nose, taking in the valley's earthy scents.

"Jesus, be careful."

"I'm fine, just drive."

Beth felt him grip her ankle as she strained for a glimpse of the canopy high above, but she caught only sun-bright flashes through a lacework of limbs. They had just rattled across a wooden bridge spanning a brook lined with willows, and now a woodsy tunnel carried them up a hill. The August humidity was stifling, and there were giant mosquitoes trying to feast on her, but the opportunity to pull that green scent deep into her lungs—the fragrance of life itself—was worth some sweat and a few bug bites. Beth had felt strangely energized since they'd crested the ridge and dropped into this vale; more *alive* somehow. It must be all the oxygen these trees were emitting.

"This place is amazing," she yelled. "I can't believe it's so close and I never even knew it was here!"

"You ain't seen nothin' yet, babe!"

Beth wiggled her foot for him to let go, then swung back in and rolled up her window. She brushed hair out of her eyes and looked across the console at him. "You keep saying that, but what could be so special about an old cemetery out in the middle of—"

They exited the tunnel then, and mid-afternoon sunlight blasted into the car.

Her eyes widened.

"Oh," she said.

He slid into the first space in a tiny parking lot cut out of the side of the hill. She was aware of her husband watching her with a grin.

"Well? What do you think?"

Beth said the only thing she *could* say.

"All red?"

Still staring, she groped her shades from her purse and slipped them on, then climbed out; the smell that radiated from the mass of red flowers hit her like heat from a bonfire. Beth loved that scent, but this was a trifle much.

Daniel turned the car off and got out. Beth followed the red wave up the hill with her eyes and found the oval evergreen hedge—and then she saw what loomed above it.

"What on earth is *that?*"

"You'll see." He banged the door shut, then plucked his powder-blue button-down Polo out with two fingers and blew down his front. "Christ. It was a helluva lot nicer out here yesterday." He started up a concrete footpath that parted the roses before winding around the hill and out of sight.

Beth stood rooted where she was and frowned up at the tall, bulbous, crooked rock thrusting from the crown of the hill; it was terribly black. Maybe it was volcanic rock, though Beth had always thought igneous stone was shiny; sunshine blasted the surrounding hilltop, but the stone seemed to absorb light, not reflect it. Whatever it was made of, the thing was some sort of standing stone, unless she missed her guess. She'd read a book about them years ago, and she thought she remembered it stating that most standing stones were scattered across Ireland and Scotland and England and northern Europe. Beth didn't remember it saying any of them had been hewn from volcanic stone, either, but maybe she hadn't read the right book; she definitely remembered it stating that there were few stones in North America, and those confined to the northeastern states.

So what was this dark, twisted lump doing in the middle of Tennessee?

Daniel stopped and pulled his shirt out and blew down his front again: "Are you coming or not? It's hot as fuck out here. I want to show you this and then get back in the goddamn air conditioning."

She pulled her gaze from the warped stone—it was hard to look away from, for some reason—and rested the weight of her regard upon her husband.

He saw that look and sighed. "Waiting patiently, dear."

Beth eyed him dangerously; he'd come home straight from Steve's open house and insisted on dragging her out here to show her this "surprise" that she'd mercifully forgotten about—*insisted*, even though she was sweaty and gross from practicing for her upcoming sandan test; if *he* wasn't smart enough to change out of his stuffy work clothes first, it wasn't *her* fault.

She slowly—*slowly*—walked across the lot and moved past him up the path. "Are you coming or not?"

He grimaced and followed, but wisely kept silent.

As she walked, Beth let her gaze drift across the hillside; at least there were different *kinds* of red, though she only recognized a few; she was no rosarian, far from it, but she loved her yellow Celebrity's and her orange Just Joey's. She'd found the Joey's at a small garden center outside of Nashville three years ago and raised them for their wonderful scent; most importantly for her, both hybrid teas were easy to grow and maintain—well, easi*er*.

It's so nice to have a yard now and not have to grow roses in a pot!

Beth stopped and fingered a velvety petal on what she thought was a Mister Lincoln; a beautiful specimen with good hue, the fully double petals had nice substance and perfect exhibition form—better than she could manage, that's for sure. Further up the path, she thought she spied some Chrysler Imperials and a few Crimson Glories, but couldn't be sure; red roses weren't her thing. Away from the concrete walk, bushes of Grandifloras vied for space with clusters of Floribundas; she didn't know what any of them were. Above her, below the oval hedge, spread masses of low-growing Polyanthas, their single-petal formations a pleasant interlude in the complex flowers. Beth also like the burgundy climbers scattered through the hedge; the dark green was a nice contrast.

Most of the teas were near or above the walkway, with the rest spreading down the hill; whoever designed this place—and she used that term loosely—must've chosen varieties that flowered from spring to fall, because she saw no break in the blooms; there weren't any maintenance paths, either, only waves of red flowers and the walk she was standing on.

How does whoever takes care of these get out there to take care of them?

Daniel halted next to her and eyed her scowl. "You don't like them?"

He sounded almost offended! Beth smoothed her face and tried; for him, she tried. "I like them." *Sort of.* "It's just so much…*red.*"

"Let me guess. You want to plant a few yellows."

"Yes." Beth went back to studying the hillside. "All red? It's…strange, Daniel."

He continued up the path, motioning her to follow. "They're not *all* red." He grinned mischievously when she looked at him, then suddenly cursed and ducked a large bee.

She followed, fingering petals and sniffing two or three exquisite specimens; she also amused herself watching her husband gyrate to avoid bees; Beth ignored those that buzzed her.

The walk turned up the hill, and she got a look at the entry; she stared, then hurried to catch up and stood under the lichgate.

"All white inside?"

She glanced at her husband when he didn't answer; he had left the path and was peering behind a bush chock-full of white, semi-double blooms. Beth had no idea what they were.

"Daniel?"

He peeked behind another bush.

"Daniel!"

He jumped, then put a finger to his lips. "Shhhh!"

Beth raised an eyebrow. "And why should I be quiet?" She motioned to the nearest headstone. "I don't think he'll mind." She looked closer and realized it was a woman: **Allison Jean Reaves 1927-1966** was carved into the simple upright granite headstone—black, of course. "What are you looking for?"

"Would you be quiet?" He whispered. "I'm looking for the Keeper."

"The what?"

"The who, actually. The Keeper; she was here yesterday."

Beth made a point of peering about the empty cemetery. "I see no one but us," she told him.

"That don't mean anything, believe me."

He peeked behind another bush with single white blooms; Beth had no clue what they were, besides white roses. She looked up; the red and white climbers mingling and dangling from the wrought-iron were quite lovely. *Too bad whoever "planned" this place hadn't taken the hint.* Beth backed out and craned her neck to read:

WELCOME TO BARRON CEMETERY.

Shaking her head, she rejoined her husband. *And I thought all red was bad.* This unbroken white was ghastly. Beth observed as Daniel snuck up on another bush, then checked her watch; she had to babysit Jen and Sue tonight, and she still needed to shower and change; firing Mark had been the right thing to do, but she'd created extra work for herself until she got the others trained.

"Dear." Daniel glanced up from the shrub he was stalking. "If you don't tell me what's going on, I'm going to kick you."

He stepped back onto the path, noticeably keeping his distance. "There was someone here yesterday, a lady." He waved for her to follow as he walked to the top; Beth went reluctantly, using her tee-shirt to wipe away the sweat. *Good thing I hadn't put makeup on yet.* Her only consolation was that he looked even more miserable. She roamed around the crooked stone and listened to his encounter with this "Keeper" while she fingered petals, turned over leaves, and inspected stems, shaking her head at what she found.

Daniel wound down, and Beth straightened. "'Strong enough'? Strong enough for *what?*"

"No clue, babe. She mentioned something about tests and choices, too."

Beth scowled. *Tests and choices?* "Did you ask her what the heck she was talking about?"

Her husband chuckled, but she noted it was an uneasy effort. "I thought about it, but by that point she was…well, truth is she was freaking me out a little. I wasn't really up for a Q and A session. I was just ready to vamoose the fuck back to Dodge." Beth gave him a look, and he spread his hands. "What? She wasn't exactly what you'd call cordial, beautiful—although she said yes when I asked if I could bring you out here, so I guess she wasn't all bad."

"True." *Strong enough? Tests? Choices?* Beth gave a mental shrug and let it go; Daniel had probably misheard this "Keeper" while she was busy "freaking him out". She took in the secluded cemetery from this high vantage: "Maybe they've had teenagers screwing around out here, or even grave robbers. That would explain why she hid and watched you, and her mindset." She absently reached out and turned back a spotted leaf, shaking her head again.

"I had the same thought." He watched her for a few seconds, then: "Check this out." He moved to the stone, and she walked over next to him and looked where he pointed. "See the writing? Fucking *weird*, huh?"

Beth blinked in astonishment; the stone wasn't truly black. Up close, it was a mix of dirty white, gray, brown, and black, like a nasty species of marble. She brushed a thumb over the miniscule carvings that looped and swirled up and down and across the mottled stone; the top of the cemetery's knoll was a rose-scented open-air oven, but somehow the stone was cool, almost cold, beneath her fingers.

She made a face and wiped her hand on her shirt; not only was the thing chilly, it had a strange, oily texture. "It needs a bath."

"I noticed." Daniel squatted, knees crackling, and carefully parted the thorns. "Something else weird; the whole kit and caboodle goes *into* the ground, writing, too; this is only the top twenty or so feet sticking out. I wonder how big it really is."

Beth bent over and looked, then backed away—it turned black as midnight again, just that quick; must be a trick of the light—and frowned from the twisted, bulbous tip, to where it widened and disappeared into the soil.

She said, "Not only does it need a bath, it's about the ugliest thing I've ever seen."

"No argument here."

Heat shimmered above the white blooms, and out over the valley. There was zero breeze; the bees buzzing around them were loud in the hush. Beth wiped more sweat away and grimaced; the overpowering fragrance of roses was grating on her nerves—and she *liked* that smell.

Daniel dusted his hands and stood up. "Well? What do you think?"

Her eyes dropped to slits. "You didn't drag me out here to look at flowers. You wanted to see what I thought about that." She pointed at the stone, then spread her arms, taking in Barron Cemetery on its hill and the wooded vale beyond. "About *all* of this. Am I right?"

He shrugged. "Probably a bit of both. So what *do* you think?"

She lowered herself in front of a polished black tombstone, brushing aside white blooms to read: **Jeffery Dale Cartwright 1915-1938**; only twenty-three, just a kid. "It's not like any cemetery I've ever seen, that's for certain, but that's not exactly a crime."

"No, but I wonder what language that is." He hiked his thumb at the stone hulking beside him. "It sure as fuck ain't English."

"If you want to know so bad, darling, take a picture and Google it." She moved to the next tombstone; it was so overgrown she had to part the thorns and squint into deep green shadows: **Annabel Louise May 1856-1902**.

The silence made her glance at him; Daniel smacked himself on the forehead. "Take a picture. Google it. I knew I married you for your brains."

"Wish I could say the same."

He said, "Mmmm," and pulled his phone from the carrier on his hip, pointed the back at the stone, and pushed a button:

A cheerful female electronic voice commanded, "Say cheese!"

Beth stood up and spotted the small gate this supposed Keeper had left by; it was at the end of another path. There were four that met at the stone, like spokes in a lopsided wheel.

"Say Cheese! Say Cheese! Say Cheese! Say Cheese!"

Beth walked down to the wrought-iron gate; white climbers wreathed it inside and red climbers outside. She looked out toward the woods and saw the barrier he'd described. *Forbidding, with those unfriendly signs and that chain and padlock.* Beyond the gate, wheel ruts with a strip of grass between vanished into sun-dappled darkness; she spied some awesome red oaks lining those ruts, their spreading branches covering an enormous quantity of ground; they gave Beth the itch to go exploring.

This valley is incredible. What else would she discover if she plumbed its depths? Beth reversed until she could see the layer of mist obscuring that circular opening he'd pointed out to her up on the ridge.

Daniel came up behind her. She said, "You're right, I think those tracks lead to that glen. Or lake. Or whatever it is."

"Of course I'm right, but what the hell's out there that needs gates and locks? Not to mention 'Keep Out' signs?"

"I don't know. Are you sure that's where this so-called Keeper went?"

"I'm not *sure* sure, but she took off that way on her four-wheeler."

Beth faced him. "And she didn't tell you her name? Just 'The Keeper'?"

Daniel wiped sweat from his face, then tugged his shirt out and unbuttoned it. "*Jesus*, it's fucking hot out here. Yes, dear, that's it, 'The Keeper'. You know, you still haven't told me what you think about all this."

Beth stared at her husband; with his shirt undone to his stomach, blond hair, sunglasses, and trim, muscular build, he looked like a model in some absurd magazine clothing ad, though the red face and sweat spoiled it somewhat.

"Come here." Beth led him to a bush with white, semi-double flowers and moved two blooms aside and pointed. "See those?"

He leaned down. "Bugs?"

"Those are aphids. They eat roses." She turned back a leaf. "See this?"

"You mean those spots?"

"That's called Rust Disease; no bueno for roses." She stood up. "I saw Japanese Beetles earlier; they eat roses, too. And some Black Spot, and some mildew that needs to be sprayed for…" Beth looked at him. "What I *think* is that these plants need to be cared for properly."

Daniel was watching her with his most infuriating smile.

"*What?*"

"Maybe she doesn't do things like you'd do them." He spread his hands and turned full circle. "Or maybe she doesn't have time for all, you know, *this.*"

"It's not just bugs and a few spots." Beth indicated the bush beside him. "Beautiful, aren't they? Lots of blooms? Pretty flowers?"

"Sure, I guess."

"See these?" Beth showed him several shriveled blooms, petals brown and drooping. "These old flowers need to be deadheaded. That focuses the energy of the plant into making fresh flowers."

"Deadheaded?"

She shot him a look. "Yes, *deadheaded.* Why?"

"Nothing. Just fits this place, that's all. The Keeper was doing some of that, but I think she got it backwards. She was cutting fresh blooms; she had a basket full of red *and* white."

Beth grimaced in confusion, then shrugged it off: each to their own. "Well, these still need to be deadheaded. And the *pruning!* I could spend *days* pruning. Weeks! You think there are a lot of flowers now? I promise you, a boat-load of pruning and some TLC, this place would be stunning." Daniel opened his mouth, and she raised a hand. "I know, I know, different strokes. It's just..."

"What?"

"It's like whoever planted these wanted roses, but doesn't really care *about* roses. Does that make sense?"

He nodded slowly. "I see what you mean."

"And then you have these headstones." Beth knelt in front of one that was relatively clear; she only had to move three flowers and two thorny branches: **Donald Lee Wright 1823—1863**. Don was probably a Civil War vet, not that his stone gave any indication besides the year he'd passed.

"What about them?"

"They're so...*impersonal*, Daniel; only names and birth-and-death years. Normally there are all sorts of..." Beth stared up at her husband.

"What? Why are you looking at me like that?"

"You didn't notice the graves?"

"I noticed them!" Then he shrugged, uncomfortable: "I didn't really *look* at them, I guess." A note of defiance crept into his voice. "Hey, it's not like I know anybody here."

Beth blanked her face. *He visits a cemetery, but doesn't acknowledge the dead?* She pushed to her feet and glanced at her watch; past time to be done with this foolishness.

"You want to know what I think? I think this is the strangest fucking cemetery I've ever seen."

His startled look was laughable; Beth cursed so rarely it always took him by surprise—which was the idea; swear words were wonderful ways to add emphasis with minimal effort. Using them all the time diluted their power, a concept her husband didn't grasp.

Daniel took a knee on the other side of the walkway. "Guess I see what you mean." Beth read over his shoulder while he gingerly parted blooms and thorns: **Carroll Suzanne Walters 1804-1878**. "There are no little sayings...what do you call 'em?"

"Epitaphs."

"Epitaphs. There's nowhere to leave offerings, either." He looked around, frowning. "I don't see any side-by-sides, like Mom and Dad's, or family plots. Do you?"

"No. Just singles, and only these identical upright slabs for markers; usually there are all kinds of headstones in a cemetery. Not this one."

"You're right. It *is* impersonal. Cold. This old gal could've been the best lay in the county." He hopped up and brushed at his pants. "Or the knitting champ at the fair every year." He shrugged. "Or both; hard to tell with just names and dates."

Beth gave him a disgusted look. "Grow up."

"I'm a full-grown boy, ma'am. I'm just pointing out the facts."

"Please. Who still had *Star Wars* sheets the first time we did it in his apartment?"

"Hey, you were the one face-down on the Millennium Falcon, and I don't remember any complaints."

They shared a smile. It was true; Beth had noticed the ridiculous bed linen and pillowcases, but she'd been much, *much* too busy to comment.

She turned slowly, surveying the entirety of Barron Cemetery; there was something about it she didn't like, which was stupid: it was just a cemetery, no matter how strange; a place for the dead to rest; a place where the turbulence of life didn't intrude; her opinion didn't matter one whit to the inhabitants or their loved ones. Still, Beth found herself detesting the place, and it was more than just the weirdo megalith or the chaotic landscaping or the impersonal headstones.

It was...

Memories flooded back, of a cemetery long ago in Chester, Ohio. Beth didn't remember much about Chester, or the school they had forced her to attend, or even the fosters she'd lived with. It had only been a place the state had put her after... after. Nothing more. But she remembered the cemetery. She couldn't dredge up the name, though, and that vexed her because eleven-year-old Beth had retreated there whenever she could to read or do homework or just sit under a big elm and watch fat white clouds scud by. She could still see it: the manicured green grass, the spreading trees, the silent stones and monuments; the somber people who came to pay their respects, and who often came to weep.

A red-brick wall surrounded it, with traffic and bustling sidewalks crowding three sides; on the fourth there had been a park with playgrounds and baseball diamonds and soccer fields and yelling, laughing kids and mothers pushing strollers. Even with all that, inside those red-brick walls, that nameless cemetery had been a place of peace, of rest.

The hushed, hot stillness pressed in on her as Beth peered over the tall hedge; wooded slopes marched up to a cloudless, steel-blue sky in all directions except to the north, where the valley broadened and deepened around that enormous, mist-shrouded, circular clearing; with its remote location, Barron Cemetery should have been a haven of serenity.

Instead, it felt...vibrant. There was no peace or rest here. It was—

...no peace...no rest...

Her breath caught. She glanced around; Daniel was watching her.

"What's wrong?"

"Nothing."

Beth wiped her face with the hem of her shirt; for the first time in her life, the smell of roses was making her nauseated. She pressed knuckles to her temples and rubbed. *The heat. Must be the heat.* Daniel raised his sunglasses to the top of his head and squinted at her with a deep frown.

"This so-called Keeper woman," she said abruptly. "She told you this was a private cemetery?"

"That's what she said." He moved closer. "Are you okay? You don't look so good."

"I'm *fine!* I'm just hot." Beth hadn't meant to snap; she smiled to take the sting away. "If this is a 'members only' kind of place, I'm glad we're not in the club."

"That makes two of us, beautiful." He took her hand and led her down the walk and out under the lichgate. "Let's find you some shade and a cool drink."

"Good idea." They cleared the roses and got back into the car. Daniel started the engine, and she sat with three vents blowing on her as he fished under his seat and came up with a half-full bottle of red Gatorade.

"I bought it this morning. It's warm, but it's liquid."

Beth drank and immediately felt better; she'd overheated out there, in more ways than one. *Hearing voices, of all things.* She screwed the lid on and handed it back, then stared at the mass of red roses and the tall, oval hedge; over it, the twisted black stone intruded on the sweltering, steel-blue summer sky.

What a strange place.

Beth had meant it: she was glad they weren't members, because she would never, *ever* want to be buried here—not that there was any chance of that; they'd both specified cremation in their will. Even so, she frowned at the vehemence of her feelings: what did it matter where you were buried? The dead were beyond caring about such things; as the great Bob Hope had told his wife, Delores, when she asked where he wanted to be interred:

"Surprise me."

Beth became aware of her husband watching her thoughtfully; meeting his eyes was difficult for some reason, so she checked the time on the dash.

"Let's head back. If I have to babysit tonight, I need to shower and change."

"All right." He got the car turned around, and they drove into the darkness under the trees.

Beth fought the urge to look back at the cemetery and won.

A Little Girl's Voice

THEY WERE silent as they rolled down the hill, cold, blessed AC blowing in their faces; then they rattled across the bridge and through its wedge of sparkling glory rays and Daniel took her hand.

"I'm sorry you didn't like the flowers."

Guilt stabbed; she had to offer him something. "I do like these woods. The old trees are incredible." Beth squeezed his fingers. "It was a wonderful surprise."

He squeezed back. "Good."

They rode like that to Barron Road, where Daniel stopped and looked both ways, then pulled out and punched the accelerator until they were up and out of the gorge. Beth instantly felt her energy level drop, which was strange; the oxygen concentration shouldn't have affected her *that* much. Maybe she was more worn out from her test practice than she'd realized.

He slowed to lean and point past her shoulder: "You can see John McFarlane's farm up there on the ridge. This valley's gotta be his; it's practically his backyard."

Beth craned around; there was the cemetery on its hill. It was almost beautiful from up here, shining red and green and white in the sun; the only blemish was that warped and lightless thing on the crown. Beyond the cemetery was the mist-shrouded circular clearing, and above that, on the far rim, the glimmer of sun on metal: buildings. Then they were rolling again, and lichen-scarred limestone and stunted pines filled her vision until they zoomed off the crest.

It's a shame, really. That cemetery ruined a spectacular natural environment. Beth wondered if she could get permission from Mr. McFarlane to go hiking in his valley; she would lose herself beneath those marvelous red oaks—while avoiding the cemetery, of course—and just breathe and breathe and breathe…

Her phone beeped, and she grimaced; exploring would have to wait until she had time—like when Lizzie went off to college. Then Beth read the text and was tempted to curse for the second time that year. She settled for a big sigh.

"What? Who was that?"

"Jen wants to know how to season the black beans for the fajitas." Beth couldn't help but laugh. "She's made a batch before! I've *seen* her!"

"She's just nervous."

"I know." Beth checked the time: 4:11. They'd only been gone about an hour, but for some reason it felt like ten. She opened the glove box and slung her phone on top of the registration and proof of insurance and slammed the little door shut. Jenifer—and the stupid black beans!—would just have to wait until Beth got there.

"I'll only stay for the dinner rush," she told him. "They need the practice closing, especially Sue, so we'll still have *some* family time tonight."

"Do what you gotta do, babe. The Lizmonster and I will be fine 'till you get back."

He stopped at the stop sign and then turned right on McFarlane Farm's Road. Four minutes later they turned left on Daisy and then a minute after that they pulled around the castle's driveway. The garage door gaped open; they'd forgotten to put it down, as usual.

A thought struck her, and Beth reached across the console and gripped his wrist. "Wait." He stopped the car and looked at her. "You'll have to pick Lizzie up."

"And?"

"And I promised Helen I'd stay for a visit when *I* picked Lizzie up! I begged off earlier. I said I had house to clean and laundry to do, but what I really wanted was a little me-time. It's been over a month since I've sat and talked to her, Daniel. She'll be so mad at me."

"Yeah." He lifted his foot off the brake, and they bumped up into the garage. "But she'll forgive you. She loves you almost as much as she loves Lizzie."

"True." Another thought: "I told Helen six o'clock. She insisted Lizzie stay for supper, but by then those kids will have worn her to a frazzle. Don't be late, okay?"

He shut the Nissan down and pulled the key out of the ignition; the engine ticked as he pursed his lips.

Suddenly she understood his hesitation.

"The car will be with—"

"But I'll have the—"

They shared a quiet laugh. "But I'll have the car," Beth finished.

Daniel got out. She followed on her side.

"No big thang, beautiful." His cheer seemed only a bit forced as he walked out under the door and peered toward Helen's. "I'll hike; it's only half a mile. We'll pick some of those little blue and purple wildflowers crowding the ditch on the way back. We'll make it an adventure. Lizzie will love it."

Beth joined him, scowling at the unlined country blacktop that was Daisy Road; it was posted 40 mph, but that meant nothing to the local cross-eyed bumpkins: "*Or*," she suggested, sugar-sweet, "you could have Helen give you guys a ride back."

Daniel gave her a narrow, sidelong look. "I'd rather walk, thanks." Then he grimaced around at their ankle-high grass. "Shit. I've got to get changed and mow before we're living in a fucking jungle."

"Do you miss your truck?"

It just popped out; Daniel had sold his custom four-wheel-drive seven months ago, consolidating them into one car; when they had been buying the castle, the math didn't work, even with the great deal they'd gotten from the bank, so Beth's husband had given up his beloved Yukon. Being a one-car family was tough, but considering his job, and the fact they lived twenty miles from town now, she sometimes wondered how they made it work.

"You know I do." He searched her face with those eyes. "What's bothering you, beautiful?"

So Beth took a deep breath and told him.

"—of the economy combined with the crap Mark pulled the managers won't get bonuses this quarter. And I checked the satellite bill online: it's over three hundred dollars." He blinked. "Yeah. I guess we've been buying too many movies." *Way* too many movies. "And Lizzie's daycare is going up."

"*Again?* Fuck."

"Yes, and now we won't have Sunday family-nights until I can get everybody trained. My test's coming up, but I've been to the dojo a whole five times in three months, and two of those were just in the last week to teach class while Sensei is in Japan." Beth looked up at their beautiful house: their gorgeous, *expensive* house. She swiped a tear from her cheek. "Is all this worth it, Daniel?"

He turned and looked at the castle with her, draping an arm over her shoulders. She snuggled into the side of his chest; although she hadn't mentioned it, Beth had also gotten word that their medical would take a bigger hit out of her check starting in October. And things had *really* slowed for him; combine that with no bonus, and Beth didn't know how they would pull this off.

"We'll make it."

The steel in his voice lifted her head. He met her eyes: "We'll make it." She opened her mouth, and he put a finger to her lips. "I *promise* you we'll make it, beautiful. You still want to go to college, right?"

Beth nodded and scrubbed more tears away with his sleeve; she *so* wanted to take college courses: online, community, whatever, Beth didn't care; she both envied and was frustrated by the MTSU students working part-time at the restaurant; most didn't appreciate the opportunity they had, and some pissed it away, partying instead of studying. Beth wanted to smack sense into the lot of them.

"I have plans for that equity too," Daniel continued quietly while gazing up at the castle. "It may take a few years, but the market'll rebound one day, and when it does, we'll sell this place to some rich asshole and find a little three-bed crackerjack on a quiet cul-de-sac somewhere." He looked down at her again, now with a gleam in his eye: "Or maybe four bedroom."

Beth smiled up at him. He was right: they *would* make it, somehow, despite the odds stacked against them; his determination had rekindled hers. And as for a reasonable four-bedroom…

Daniel wanted a son. Beth wanted one as well, so much, with her brown eyes and his father's blonde hair, running around and terrorizing his big sister…but not right now. They couldn't afford it, for one thing; and she certainly couldn't go through her third-degree black-belt test gravid.

But after she'd passed, and once their finances stabilized…

Yes. A little brother for Lizzie would be just right.

Her nipples stiffened as their tongues swirled in a deep, slow kiss. Beth felt the swell of him against her stomach and pulled away, glancing up and down Daisy;

there was only Mr. White's horses in the pasture across the road, heads down and tails flicking, but this was too exposed for her.

He chuckled and tried to pull her back. "Nobody's watching."

Beth stroked the long, lovely bulge in his dress slacks, then seized his hand and pulled him through the garage and into the castle and down the hall; they crossed beneath the chandelier and hit the curved stairway and started up. "We have to be fast," she told him.

"Fast? I can do that."

"Funny."

Beth was above him on the stairs; she turned to add something smart, maybe something about how he needed to learn when to keep his mouth shut—but then a man wearing a brown ski mask stepped out of her kitchen. He was tall and wore faded jeans, scuffed work boots, a gray tee-shirt, and black driving gloves. A six-inch lock-blade knife gleamed in his right hand; in his left, a short-barreled revolver was leveled at Daniel's back. A colorful tattoo on that forearm glinted in the sunlight shining through the kitchen windows. Icy blue eyes peered up at her from the holes in the mask.

Beth recognized him at once.

Daniel saw her face and spun—and apparently so did he.

"*You!*" He stepped down towards the masked man, as if he couldn't see the pistol now pointed at his chest. "Get out of our house!"

"Shut up." The revolver's barrel twitched toward the bottom of the stairs. "Down here. Now."

"Take what you want and get out!"

Those cold eyes swiveled back to her, and Beth's breath congealed in her lungs; this was no simple robbery.

Somewhere in the depths of her mind, a little girl's voice murmured: *No, no.*

"I said shut up." He backed up then, long legs putting the island at his back; he was quick for such a big man. "Down here. *Now.* Move slowly, hands where I can see them."

After a second of hesitation, they both did it; the man in the ski mask suddenly pointed the gun straight at her.

"Not you," he said. "You stay right there." He chuckled. "None of that Jackie Chan bullshit, not today. I know about you." Those frozen eyes pierced her and drank her in; Beth couldn't look away. "I know *all* about you," he said, almost a purr, then shifted the gun back to Daniel. "Come down here!"

Her husband walked slowly to the bottom of the stairs, crossed the strip of foyer between the staircase and the kitchen, then stopped next to their refrigerator. "Listen," he said. "I'm sorry about that thing yesterday. I shouldn't have punched your truck."

The man in the mask studied Daniel; Beth had seen a snake watch a mouse that had dropped into its aquarium just the same way. Then he reached up with the knife hand and dragged the ski mask off, tossing it behind him; it slid off the island and puddled on her tile.

"You're *sorry*, huh?" The tall kid from table thirty-seven grinned like a wolf; his thinning white-blonde hair stuck up in back, roughened from the mask. He jabbed his blade at the floor near his feet, keeping the pistol up and the short barrel rock-steady on Daniel's chest. "Lay face-down and grab your ankles behind your back." Daniel didn't move. "Do it!" He pointed the gun at Beth again, where she stood halfway up the staircase. "Do it now, or she gets it."

Daniel turned and looked up at her.

He knows.

Despite his words, Beth's husband knew this wasn't a robbery; his beautiful eyes were sick with terror—terror for her.

They stared at each other for a heartbeat…

…two heartbeats, three, four…

They moved at the same time.

Daniel lunged and seized the bigger man's wrists, forcing the knife to the side and the pistol toward the ceiling as Beth put her left hand out and vaulted over the railing to the hardwood, hitting and rolling back to her feet. The pistol boomed, making her ears whine as the chandelier tinkled and swayed overhead. Glass shards shattered all around as she flicked her Carson open and darted past the newel post, but then she stopped; the men were surging in the entryway to the kitchen, Daniel's hands still locked on the intruder's wrists, both men snarling and cursing and panting with the effort.

Beth saw an opening and darted for the arm with the gun—the important one. She didn't need to stab him; she knew a good shoulder lock, and if she got him into that, it wouldn't matter how big he was; together they could take this guy down, subdue him, and call the cops.

Daniel managed to shoot her a glare. "RUN, goddamnit!"

Beth ignored him and closed, but then with an incredible display of strength the intruder heaved Daniel at her. She jerked her knife up to keep from stabbing her husband in the back and his butt knocked her sideways, where she tripped over a black gym bag she hadn't seen sitting on the shady side of the island. She fell, slamming her shoulder and elbow; her Carson skittered across the tiles and disappeared into the living room.

Beth popped back up in time to see her husband push the bigger man into the island and raise his arms and slam his fists into her floating cabinets; there was a crash followed by a shower of glass, and the lock-blade tumbled to the tiles. The big man heaved, throwing Daniel off, and his other hand came down bloody but minus the gun; it was stuck up there with her fine China.

She lunged for the knife block sitting in the island's center, stretched, snatched, and metal gleamed in both fists as she started back around. The men squared off. Daniel feinted with his left, and the kid fell for it, swaying to his left, and then the right slammed into the intruder's nose with a *crack*; he slumped back against the island.

Beth shot forward, knives raised.

They had him!

But again the bigger man showed terrible stamina and strength; he seized Daniel's wrist and slammed an elbow into her husband's forehead. *Thock!* He dropped, boneless.

"No!"

Their attacker shot a look of terror at her upraised knives and fell over Daniel in his haste to get away, then dragged him across the floor, putting him between them as he pawed desperately and came up with his knife and shoved its point against the side of her husband's neck.

Beth froze. Less than five feet separated them. He glared up at her as blood ran from his nose and into his pathetic excuse of a mustache, staining his teeth.

He bared those bloody teeth at her, panting, "Throw theb abay, back ub, and sid down against dad wall."

Beth stayed where she was.

"Now!" He pressed the knife against Daniel's carotid artery. "Or he'll die ride in frund of you."

She could end it: one fast step, and Beth could plunge her knives into him over and over and over…but inside that step, her Daniel would die.

No! No! Not again!

Glass crunched under her shoe. She glanced over her shoulder at the floating cabinets; Beth was now closer to the pistol than him.

He pressed the knife against Daniel's throat. Blood flowed. His broken-nosed mumble was soft, taunting: "Go ahead, sweetheard. Go ged dad gun."

And then with a grunt Daniel grabbed the hand with the knife, wrestling it away from his throat:

"Do it! Kill him!"

Beth lunged as the man jerked his arm away from Daniel's weakened grip and reversed the knife, slamming the hilt into the spot just over her husband's right ear. Daniel dropped flat on his face as she slashed, but their attacker kicked at her, forcing her back, and then scrambled just out of reach, dragging Daniel with him again; in an instant, the knife was back at her motionless husband's throat.

No!

"Now," he said, breathing heavily, "you bitch. One more fuging dimb: Throw dem abay and back ub ober by dat wall. You do anyding else, *anyding else*, he dies ride fuging now."

He meant it.

Beth shuddered as she dropped one knife and flung the other into the dining room, frustrated tears streaming; the second knife clattered to a stop below the triple-bay window.

NO!

He nodded at the one by her foot. "Kig id abay." Blood dripped from his chin into Daniel's hair, mingling with her husband's blood.

Beth hesitated, and he pressed the gleaming blade closer in a wordless promise; the knife spun across the bloody green tiles before vanishing under the fridge.

NOOOO!

"Bag ub." She did. "On your knees and cross your ankgles and lace your fingers behind your head, elbows oud." He watched as she complied. "Good girl."

"Don't hurt him!"

"Shud ub." He swiped delicately at his nose with a forearm, smearing blood on the tattoo. "Fuger broge my nose." He snarled and seized Daniel's hair, putting his mouth next to his ear and whispering, "You're gonna pay large for dat, son."

The intruder surged to his feet but kept the knife at Daniel's jugular, watching her warily, then dragged her husband to the island and reached up and grabbed the pistol, dislodging more glass. He dropped Daniel like a sack of meat and stood over him and pointed the gun at his back, then raised a long thumb and pulled the hammer back with a loud *clack;* the cylinder rotated, and Beth spotted gray stubs waiting in the holes.

"Stand ub and walk ober here." Beth complied. "Ged back on your knees, same position wid your hands." She hesitated, glaring pure hate; he was within her reach, now. "Try id." He twitched the revolver, finger tight on the trigger. "You mighd make id, but luber boy here wond. Eben ib he lives, he'll neber walk again. Ib got this cannon poinded ride ad his spine."

She sank to her knees at his feet, crossing her ankles and lacing her fingers behind her head. Beth would turn thirty-six in less than eight months, but inside she was seven again:

No. No. No.

The monster seized her hair, cranking her head back, and she could feel his overwhelming strength for the first time; strong or not, his hand, wrist, and shoulder were now locked against her, and Beth could do any number of things with that advantage; the problem was the finger on his other hand, which was tight on the trigger of the gun pointed at her Daniel's back.

She couldn't reach that.

"What do you want?" Beth whispered, but she knew.

"Whad do I wand?" Soft, mocking; his wintry predator's eyes seared into hers. "I'm gonna *show* you whad I wand, bitch. You and me, we're gonna hab us a real good dime."

No! The little girl cried.

No. Please.

A FEW PIECES OF PAPER

A SHARP STING on his cheek lifted Dan out of the black. He groaned; his head felt like it would split in half, so he tried to massage his temples but his arms wouldn't—

His head rocked to the side as someone full-arm slapped him. His brain throbbed, and he thought he would puke, but he managed to swallow it back and open his eyes.

A face loomed, saying something, but his gaze slid away and focused on Beth. She was lying on their bed, on top of the green-and-white diamond-patterned comforter. Her ankles were duct-taped together, and her mouth was covered in silvery tape. Duct tape was wrapped around her head as well, bunching her beautiful dark hair on the back of her skull. Her arms had been pulled behind her and taped together at the wrists.

She was nude.

Their eyes met, and Dan's soul recoiled from what he saw there.

Oh God. Oh God, no.

"Wakey wakey hands off snakey!"

Dan shifted his gaze back to the face hovering in front of him—a face full of horrible good cheer; icy blue eyes regarded him critically and then moved back and up as the man stood. Two red cotton balls poked from his nostrils; seeing that, grim satisfaction filled Dan.

"Glad ya could join the party, sport. Wouldn't be the same without ya." Noticing what Dan looked at, the man used his right hand to pluck the red balls out and toss them to the hardwood, where they joined several other crimson balls, sodden and spent; the snub-nosed revolver was in his left hand, held down low by his leg. It was a Smith and Wesson five-shot .38. Long ago, Dan's dad had taught him and Will how to break down, clean, and care for his numerous pistols and rifles; this one looked oiled up and ready for action.

"I think you broke my nose," the man said conversationally, voice off but understandable, and then he switched the gun to his right and a huge fist slammed into Dan's face. A second later agony filled his world as the back of his head crashed into the hardwood; fingers tangled in his hair and he was jerked up and off the floor and set upright again.

Dan fought to focus his mind and remain conscious:

The asshole's a southpaw. I'm tied to a fucking chair. We're up in our bedroom. Beth is...

Oh God, Beth.

Tears streamed out of his eyes, and he could barely see. Worse, something covered his mouth, and air didn't want to pass by the blood and mucus filling what was left of his nose.

I can't breathe. I can't breathe!

That terrible, jolly face thrust into his again.

"Havin' problems there, pard?"

Snot and blood formed bubbles at the end of Dan's nose and then were sucked back up as he fought for air. The guy watched this avidly, then seized Dan's nose between two knuckles and shook it back and forth. Dan screamed, or tried to, and that's when he realized his mouth was taped like Beth's.

The man grimaced at his fingers in disgust, then wiped them on Dan's shirt and stood up.

"Now we're even."

He watched Dan's life-or-death struggle for air with a thin, cruel smile. "I'm gonna take the tape off so you can breathe," he finally said after six ice ages, then raised the pistol, showing it to him. "No yellin' for help, now—not that anyone can hear jack shit way out here. I just don't like yellin'. I'm delicate that way." He leaned down again, filling Dan's blurry world. "One sound above a whisper, and…" He pointed that crooked smile at Beth, who watched them with big brown eyes, nostrils flaring above her tape. The man turned back to Dan, who was nodding franticly, desperately.

He watched him, smiling, for another eon, then ripped the tape off.

Sweet, glorious air; lungful after lungful of beautiful, wondrous air; the man moved away as Dan hung his head, panting, and that's when he realized he'd been fastened to his daughter's chair; blood drip-dripped between his legs, covering scrape marks from Lizzie's old booster seat. It'd only been a few months since she'd announced that she didn't want to use the seat anymore; they were for babies, and she was a big girl. So they'd put it away and sat eating dinner with their daughter's head just poking over the side of the table, arms stretching to reach her plate. She'd grown since then; she no longer had to strain to reach her food.

It was amazing how you didn't notice such things until it was too late.

Dan lifted his head slowly and looked at his wife; she turned her face away and squeezed her eyelids shut. Tears leaked from beneath those long lashes and dripped from her lightly freckled nose. Beth hated those freckles, but Dan loved them; she trembled so hard their comforter twitched.

Oh God, please not this.

He strained around, head throbbing; his wrists were taped together behind the ladder-back; braided white Nylon cord bound his ankles to the chair legs and crisscrossed his chest and stomach and thighs, fastening him tight; unused lengths played out in bright Zs on the planks behind him.

Running water jerked Dan's head back around, and the pain almost blinded him. *The fucker is using our bathroom!* Somehow, that made things worse. He flexed, hard, and then *jerked* his wrists apart, ignoring the flare of pain in his shoulder; Dan thought he felt a tiny space open, but maybe that was just hope. Beth was watching him again, and she began to flex and jerk, testing her own tape.

If the shit-bag stays in the John for just a few more minutes…

The water cut off and Dan went still, aware of Beth doing the same; the prick appeared in the doorway, using one of Beth's flower-print washcloths to clean the last of the blood from his face while watching them shrewdly, that thin little heartless smile playing across his asshole face.

They watched him back, breathing hard.

He dropped the wet cloth on the hardwood without looking and strode forward, boots thumping, and stopped beside their bed and traced Beth's yellow-rose tattoo with a giant finger, then brushed his knuckles across her scars,…and then his hand slipped lower.

She stiffened and closed her eyes.

"Don't touch her!"

"Ya think yer gonna get loose?"

"Get away from her, you motherfucker!"

"I think ya do," he said, voice gentle, fingers moving rhythmically; a horrible swelling had appeared in the front of his faded jeans; he used the other hand to rub and pat it.

Dan wanted to staple his eyelids closed. *This can't be fucking happening!*

The man straightened and sniffed his fingers, then tasted one: "Mmmm, nice," he told her. "But first, I think hubby-pooh here needs a lesson in cooperation."

He went to a black gym bag that lay at the foot of their bed and unzipped it; something clanked inside, metal on metal.

"Listen," Dan began; a desperate idea had come to him: "Let her go, and then—"

"Shut up."

"—I'll give you all the—"

The guy yanked something from the bag and then a pair of vice grips floated two inches from the end of Dan's nose; streaks of dirty grease or old oil coated them.

"I. Said. Shut. Up." The tool closed with a click, then opened with a *ta-chunk.*

Click. *Ta-chunk.* Click. *Ta-chunk.*

"Gonna shut up now?"

Dan nodded.

"Maybe yer not as dumb as ya look." He stepped back, staring at the greasy vice grips in his hand as if they were the only thing in the world. Click. *Ta-chunk.* "I expect ya to do what I say, when I say it." Click. *Ta-chunk.* "*I'm* in charge, here."

He turned toward Beth. Click. *Ta-chunk.* That thin, crooked smile came nowhere near his lifeless eyes.

Oh dear fucking God no. "I have forty thousand dollars. Don't hurt her, let her go, and you can have it."

The big bastard looked at Dan. Beth opened her eyes and looked at him too, but they didn't have time to deal with that shit right now. The silence stretched as they stared at him, the man with a knowing smirk, Beth busy boring holes into Dan's head.

"Forty thousand dollars?"

"Yes, cash, and you can have it. Just let her go, and then we can—"

"*Forty* thousand? Are you sure?"

Was he sure? *Of course I'm fucking sure, you stupid piece of shit.* "Yes. Let her go, and—"

"Where is it?" He suddenly leveled the vice grips at Dan. "Don't lie again." Ominous.

"I'm not lying. It's in a safe deposit box in a bank in Nashville, the River—"

"Wait!" The fucker shouted, then set the vice grips on the hardwood with a clank and used both giant hands to dig through the bag, grinning like a big, evil kid on Christmas morning; he stood up with a legal envelope, standard 8x11, and straightened the prongs and pulled out several sheets of paper.

"Wait!" He proclaimed again, as if someone had been about to interrupt a grand performance; he shuffled through the papers, shaking his head when he didn't find whatever he was looking for. They were lined pages, Dan saw, like back in school, with the three holes on the left; most were white, but here and there a yellow peeked out.

"Here we go." The fucker jabbed a long finger at a spot on a yellow: "River Valley Bank and Trust, Nashville branch."

Dan stared at him.

"And it's not forty thousand, it's…" He consulted the paper: "Thirty-eight thousand, one hundred and eighty-four dollars. You *lied* to me. Big mistake."

The man bent and placed the envelope and papers on the hardwood and then reached into the bag once more.

"No, wait—"

He shot to Dan's side and seized his hair and yanked his head back; Dan's eyes followed the head of the claw hammer as it sailed toward the tray ceiling like a silvery moon.

The moon paused, hanging:

"Say yer sorry fer lyin'."

Oh God Lizzie, I'm so glad you're not here, Daddy loves you—

"Say yer sorry, ya lyin' fuck!"

The moon began to drop.

"I'm sorry, I'm sorry!"

His head was yanked sideways, and then they were eye-to-eye; stale cigarettes wafted from the man's mouth, and Dan found himself incredibly, almost hilariously, craving a smoke.

"I should make ya choke on those purty white, lyin' teeth! Smash 'em right down yer goddamn throat!" He snarled, displaying his own not-so-purty whites; the silvery moon twitched.

A last twist and yank on Dan's hair, and then he stepped back, lowering the hammer. "But I won't." That thin little smile reappeared. "Not yet, anyway."

He shoved the hammer and the vice grips back in the bag, producing more clanks, then gathered the envelope and the papers from the floor and squared them off neatly before standing up; late-afternoon sunlight blazed through the window, highlighting the blond-wood grip of the .38 sticking out of his back pocket. "I might miss those lyin' teeth," he told Dan, "and then you'd be in no condition to enjoy the show." He stepped to the bed, smiling that smile down at Beth. "And that'd be a real shame, sport, because it's gonna be quite the show."

"I forgot that I took some out, okay? It's still a lot of money, and you can have it. Don't hurt her, let her go, and then you and I can—"

He whipped around. "You think this is 'bout *money?*"

Dan shook his head, dazed. "No. No, of course not, but—"

The man lunged and seized his jaw, bending his head back until he thought his neck would crack; Lizzie's chair creaked and popped beneath him. "Think yer better'n me, don't ya, Dan. By the by, can I call ya Dan, Dan?"

"No—I mean, yeah, you can call me Dan, but I don't think I'm—"

"Yeah ya do."

"No, I—" Dan choked off as the powerful fingers dropped to his throat and squeezed.

"Say ya think yer better'n me."

Dan jerked his head side to side, trying to speak; trying to breathe.

"Say it!" He released Dan's throat and pulled the pistol out of his back pocket, cocked the hammer, and gently pressed the stub barrel to the top of Dan's right knee.

"Say it." Soft.

"I—" Dan swallowed painfully. *Oh God.* "I think I'm better than you." He winced in anticipation of his knee disappearing.

"Yer not," he growled. "Got me, bucko?"

Dan nodded eagerly; he wasn't better than this walking smear of dog shit, not in the least little fucking bit.

The psycho stared at him, unblinking, for a few centuries, then lifted the revolver from Dan's knee, easing the hammer before returning it to his back pocket. "See ya remember it." He straightened then, stretching to his full height, and looked around their bedroom as if seeing it for the first time. "Whew! Need me a cig." He set the pages and legal envelope on their dresser and then bent and rooted in the gym bag again and soon stood with a pack of generic cigarettes; his eyes held Dan's as he packed them *whap whap* against his pancake-palm and then knocked one out and fitted it to his lips. "You still think yer better'n me, I can tell." He pulled a shiny Zippo out of his front pocket, flipped it open with a practiced *clink*, and lit the smoke. He took a long drag and then blew a cloud over the bed that hovered and swirled above Beth in the slanting sunlight.

Dan had never wanted a cigarette so badly in his fucking life.

"I don't think I'm better than—"

"*Shut up.*"

Dan shut up.

"Yes you do, with yer biiiig, fancy house and yer hot little wife." He flipped the Zippo closed and stuffed it back in his pocket. "But yer *not*. I know." He turned to the dresser and picked up the legal envelope and the lined pages and presented them with a flourish. "It's all right here." He stepped over and waved them in Dan's face; this close, Dan could see that loopy cursive script covered them in blue ink; little hearts dotted the I's, like a sixth-grade girl's handwriting.

What in the hell?

The puke took a drag and blew it out: "I haven't thanked you yet, have I."

"Thanked me for what?" Dan asked cautiously.

The fucker blew more smoke and looked at Dan like he'd never come across anything like him. "You really don't know, do ya? The cemetery, man!" Seeing Dan's expression, he laughed. "Fuck, I was wrong! You *are* as dumb as ya look!" He shook his head, mock-sad. "Should've never messed with that place, bro. Bad idea…fer you. *Real* good fer me."

Dan's hope, already small, began to shrivel and die. *Christ, this guy's nuttier than a squirrel's lunch.* He twitched his eyes toward his naked, bound wife, then spoke carefully: "You can have the thirty-eight grand, just please don't hurt her. Let her go, and you and I will drive to—"

The big, crazy fuck didn't even seem to hear. He moved to the side of their bed and stood over Beth again. "I tool by and I see this sexy little thang out waterin' her flowers, struttin' 'round in those cutoffs, bendin' over just as I go by, smiiilin'… but can I do anythin' 'bout it?" He snorted. "'Too close', the man says. 'It'll draw too much attention', he says." He glanced over his shoulder at Dan. "But that's all changed now, thanks to yer little field trips, champ. He gave me the green light. *Fine*ly." He turned back and lowered his voice, speaking to Beth almost lovingly; Dan's skin crawled. "I saw how you was lookin' back at me that day I honked. You want this as bad as me, don't deny it."

Beth shook her head, glaring utter revulsion up at the whack job looming over her.

Oh shit. Dan tried to distract him. "Thirty-eight thousand, man, all yours, just—"

"Shut *up*." To Beth, harder: "You knew I was lookin'. You'd bend over on purpose, just as I rolled by…"

She shook her head sharply, oozing waves of contempt as only she could.

Oh God.

"Lyin' bitch!" He grabbed her upper arm in a huge fist and jerked; she came to her knees facing him, breasts bobbling. He lowered his face until it was inches from hers. "I honked that one day, and you turned 'round and smiled! I *know* you want me…"

Beth's eyes were bright with distaste; she said—spat—something unintelligible behind the tape; the meaning was crystal, however.

Oh. My. God.

"*Bitch!*" His slap sent her bouncing, and she would've slid over the side but he grabbed her calf and dragged her back. The envelope and papers spilled to the hardwood as he hit her again and again and again, heavy, openhanded blows that reddened her face.

"Stop! Stop goddamn you you son of a bitch! *Stop hitting her!*"

He stood with a curse, then pulled the pistol and looked around wildly. "Shut up!" He ripped the tape away from her mouth, unwinding it violently from her head; more than a few dark hairs trailed from the mass as he slung it into the corner. Beth panted, teeth bared in a snarl. Then he stepped to Dan's side and something hard jammed behind his ear.

The clack of the hammer going back filled Dan's universe.

"Say you want me." Beth said nothing; hate *glowed* from her features: "Say ya knew I was watchin', and that you want me! *Say it!*" A shove with the pistol: "Say it now, bitch, or hubby's brains will decorate that wall. They don't need him, only you. They said I can do whatever I want with him."

Dan rolled his eyes, trying to see the crazy bastard; first it was the cemetery, and then it was "he" giving this vile shit some sort of insane permission to attack them, and now it was "they" didn't need him, but "they" needed her?

Jesus, this nutbag really is *a nutbag. God help us.*

"SAY IT!"

Beth shifted her eyes to meet Dan's, and then she seemed to deflate as she turned her head away; fresh, clear tears leaked across that smattering of freckles. "I...I knew you were watching." Her voice, normally so clear and feminine, so strong, was hoarse: "I want you."

Dan's heart broke a little.

"I knew ya did. I *always* knew." The hard barrel vanished from behind Dan's ear as he sauntered back over to Beth. "And I'm gonna show this fuck what a *real* man can do with ya." He flicked ash on her head from the cigarette he'd somehow retained through all of that; fine gray powder drifted through a slant of sunlight, speckling her dark hair.

Something shifted and coiled in Dan's gut, and red wires shot through his limbs; vague thoughts of getting free somehow and subduing this whack job and calling the police so they could haul him to the loony bin where he belonged disappeared:

I will murder this cocksucker.

A phone suddenly rang, a standard *brrp-brrp* tone that to Dan sounded like it came from another dimension—a sane one, far, far away.

They all looked at the black gym bag.

"You gotta be fuckin' kiddin' me." The dead man stamped over and pulled out a phone that'd been high-tech five years ago, checked the number, scowled, then flipped it open and put his back to them.

"*What?* I'm busy here."

Dan flexed his arms, then gave a tremendous yank; he winced as something burned in his right shoulder, but a fierce satisfaction blew through the rest of him as he felt play between his wrists.

Kill you, motherfucker.

"Don't rush me, I'll be done when I'm done." The dead man leered at Beth before turning back around; it sounded like a man on the other end. Who was he? Whoever he was, he seemed to both know and approve what this sick fuck was doing to them. Dan flexed and gave another yank; the chair creaked and popped, and the waste-of-oxygen looked around suspiciously. Dan froze.

"I know, I know, I'll get 'em. Wha…? Yeah? Well, fuck you. The man *said* I could, so stay out of it." He hung up. "Goddamn nosy sonsabitches." He chunked the flip phone back into the bag and dropped his cigarette and put it out with a twist of his boot, then walked out through the open bedroom door.

Dan felt a surge of hope. *If he's leaving us alone, we might have a chance…* but then he heard the dead man immediately clomp back in, and Beth's eyes widened.

A second later, he understood why; their unwanted guest carried Dan's mower gas can to the foot of their bed and shook it, listening to the slosh.

"That's plenty," he said.

Dan sat perfectly still.

"That meddlesome fuckwad did remind me of some 'bizness we gotta take care of." He pulled the Zippo from his pocket and held it and the red plastic container up for them to inspect. "I need the pictures."

"What pictures?"

"Don't play dumb, Dan. Yer a natural, but I ain't got the time. The pictures you took out at that place. They want 'em." At his expression, the fucker laughed and shook his head almost fondly, like Dan was a slow-but-beloved pupil. "I *told* ya it was a bad idea to fuck 'round out there."

Dan looked at Beth and then back at the man. "The pictures we took at the cemetery?"

"Ding ding ding! Give the man a prize!" And then Dan flinched violently, almost tipping over sideways as the crazy fuck screwed the yellow cap off and splashed gasoline on his feet and legs and lap.

"Stop!" Beth shouted, twisting on the bed.

"Shut it, cunt." He screwed the cap back on and set the can down and then flipped open the Zippo.

Clink.

Dan quit breathing.

"Pictures."

"They're, uh…" Where *was* his fucking phone? The freak put his ginormous thumb on the striking wheel. "Wait! They're—"

Beth said, "They're on my phone, but I left it in my purse."

They both looked at her.

"Where's yer purse?"

"In the car, in the garage."

Beth held Dan's eyes. *What is she doing?* The pics were on *his* phone. And her phone wasn't even in her purse; it was in the glove box. But then he got it; knowing her, there was a knife or four in her purse; his Tigress was trying to give them a chance.

"Good girl. We'll get 'em when we're done havin' our fun."

The psycho flipped the lighter closed and stuffed it back in his pocket and then moseyed over and cupped her breast, tweaking her nipple; his other hand rubbed the horrid swelling that had reappeared at the front of his jeans.

"You 'bout ready for me, sweetheart?"

Dan flexed and *yanked*, gaining a little more space between his wrists. *Kill you!* The gas fumes made his eyes water even worse. *Keep him talking.* "How do you know about the money?" Dan thought three of four more good yanks would free one of his hands, and then they would see, oh yeah, then they would see!

The dead man turned to look at Dan with narrowed eyes. "I don't know nuthin'. Don't care to, neither. It's *them*. *They* know. And they know lots, Dan, like you bet the pigskin to get that pile of scratch, and that wifey here didn't have a clue."

At that, they both looked at Beth; it was an even toss which of them was getting the worst of those eyes. The wacko laughed. "Looks like yer in the doghouse, son!"

Dan didn't bother to look at her again. *She can divorce me if we live.* "How do you know about that?"

"I told ya, ya numb shit, don't ya fuckin' listen? I-don't-know-and-couldn't-care-less! But *they* sure do." He bent and gathered the scattered papers and the legal envelope, then presented them almost proudly: "It's all right here. *All* of it." That last was said with a sly glance at Beth, for some reason.

Dan was flexing his wrists while trying to keep his motions unnoticed. *Kill you.* Keep him talking. "Yes, but *how* do y—do they know all this?"

The dead man didn't answer as he backed up against the wall beside their dresser. He smiled a promise at Beth, then faced Dan.

"We'll start with you."

Start with me? Dan flexed and yanked, not caring that the puss-bag was watching; he felt tape stretching.

Just let me get one hand free...

"First off, you killed yer parents."

Dan went still on his daughter's chair.

"Got busted in high school, let's see…fer toilet-paperin' a *house?*" He snorted. "Petty-ante bullshit, gimme a fuckin' break…and then Mommy and Daddy had to rush to the po-leeece station to rescue their precious baaaby booooy…"

Dan's struggle to free his wrists was forgotten; Beth's stare burned like a hot iron on the side of his face, but he couldn't look at her.

The dead man continued to read gleefully: "And then they missed a curve and flipped the car into a big ol' ditch!" He looked up at Dan then, eyes hellishly alight. "Daddy broke his neck, but Mommy took 'er sweet time and drowned in a rain-swollen culvert. How's that feel, son? To know you offed Mommy and Daddy?"

"It was an accident."

A harsh laugh: "Sure, an accident, but they wouldn't a been out there 'cept for you." He grinned, an expression devoid of humanity. "You killed 'em, pard, sure as stink on shit."

No.

Yes.

Dan squeezed his eyes shut as the old guilt washed through him; late Friday night, and Mom would've been on her third or fourth Bombay rocks (or seventh or eighth), so Dad would've had to drive, but Dad couldn't see so well at night. It had stormed most of the two days before, and the culvert had been full of runoff… Mom's body had washed a hundred and fifty yards downhill; they'd found her stuck headfirst in a drainage pipe.

From far away, Dan heard hateful laughter.

I killed my parents.

Will knew it. Dan and his older brother had never been close again; he'd lost his entire family in one night.

And it's my fault.

The psycho fucker was still reading from those goddamn girly notes: "…partied the insurance money away…bet on football…" He whistled. "And everythin' else! Did a little dealin', I see—weed, coke, ecstasy. Did ya ever go to *class* while you were at that big, fancy college?" He hooted laughter.

The answer was pretty much no. Dan had wasted his college years chasing pussy and dealing, thinking he was some sort of player. He'd dropped out his junior year to sell boats. But how did this puke *know* that? Dan had told no one about those years, especially Beth.

Oh God, Beth.

Dan could *feel* his wife's eyes on the side of his head; not a scalding iron now, but a nest of rabid hornets. He knew her history with drugs—or at least what she'd told him—and he'd never told her about dealing because…well, because he wasn't dumb. She knew about the partying and the gambling—some of it, anyway. Dan wanted to look at her, but it scared him to think about what he would see in her face. Instead, he asked the dead man a question:

"How can you know all this?" *Nobody knows all this!*

"I told ya, dumb ass, *they* know." He shook the pages at Dan, making them pop. "Don't listen so good, do ya college boy?"

"But *how* do they know? And who's 'they'? And what's a fucking cemetery got to do with—" A sudden thought gripped him: "*She* sent you for the pictures, didn't she? The Keeper." She hadn't liked Dan messing with that weird rock, and apparently she didn't like people taking photographs of it, either. *Wait, she said I could bring Beth by to look at her roses. Why would she do that if…?* Dan shook his head. *No, that was before I took the pics. She must've been hiding out there again, watching us, and she…*

Dan noticed how still it had become in the bedroom and looked up. The dead man standing beside their dresser with his back to the wall was no longer even faintly amused; he was breathing hard and staring at Dan with a mix of rage and fear.

He knows her, Dan realized, *and the psycho fuck is even more scared of her than I am.* "Am I right? Did The Keeper send you?"

He snatched the gun from his back pocket and pointed it, trembling, at Dan. "Shut yer hole. I don't have nothin' ta do with that bitch, which means she don't have anythin' ta do with me, and that's just the way I like it." Stark terror was in his cold eyes, now. "I don't even like *talkin'* 'bout her. I answer to—" His face went blank, and then his blue eyes narrowed dangerously. When he spoke again, his voice was soft: "I'm not here to answer questions, fuck face, so you'd be wise to shut yer yap. Understood?"

"Understood."

"And you'll just have to take my word for it when I say *they know*." That hooked little slash of a smile again: "Oh, they don't know everythin', which is a damn good thing. Had me some fun with that uppity bitch up in Smithville last year. Cunt thought she was too good, but I taught 'er different. Boy *did* I. She was beggin' for it by the end. They don't know 'bout that, and wouldn't be happy if they did…ya know, *unsanctioned* as it was. Numb-nuts cops don't know shit either. Pulled me in, but didn't have jack and had to cut me loose." The sick fuck laughed uproariously at that. "Stupid fuckin' pigs. They'll never find 'er neither, cuz I put what was left of 'er in the lake. She's a fish-food memory, now." He shook his head slowly, holding Dan's eyes. "No, they don't know everythin', Dan, but they can find out anythin'."

He turned toward Beth.

"Anythin' 'bout anybody. There's a lot hubby-pooh here don't know, idn't there?" He consulted the pages.

"Leave her alone!"

"Shut up." Reading: "A foster kid, huh? Mommy and Daddy didn't want ya?"

"Goddamnit, *leave her alone!*"

"Kicked from place to place, then fin'ly got 'dopted when you were five…"

"Goddamn you—!"

"New Daddy broke ya in right, I see." He whistled: "Might try some of this later; relive old times, so ta speak."

"LEAVE HER ALONE!"

The twisted fuck was still reading; suddenly he laughed and gave Beth an admiring glance. "Dropped a *truck* on New Daddy. Nice." He flipped the page: "Let's see…back in the system…a dropout at fifteen…hooked on smack…" He looked up with a grin from hell. "I know how ya got them purty scars…"

Beth was shaking her head so hard her hair whipped back and forth across her face.

A whisper: "Became a prostitute…"

Dan's world slowed to a crawl and then stopped, the sunshine slashing through the window breaking into individual motes that illuminated nothing, the room around the motes squeezed by red-tinged darkness.

The world lurched into motion again: "*Bullshit!* That's my wife you're talking about, you fucking lying sack of shit!" He gave a tremendous jerk and his shoulder flared, but he felt at least an inch of space open between his wrists: "If you ever say anything like that again, I'll fucking kill you, you—!"

She was watching him. Her eyes searched his face fearfully. Her mouth opened, closed, and then those eyes cracked and she slumped and turned her head away; she seemed to become even smaller than she was, withering where she lay.

No.

The only sound was Beth's bitter sobs.

No.

A rich, rolling belly laugh turned Dan's head; their unwelcome guest was bent over, grasping his knees; he coughed, then stood and drew a deep breath, a beatific smile scoring his angular features.

"Ah, me, they were right. Helluva lot more fun than a plain ol' hump 'n dump." He quick-scanned a white page, flipped to another, then addressed Beth again while still reading: "Got the names of yer birth parents here. If yer real, *real* good, maybe I'll tell 'em to ya later."

Beth quit sobbing and rolled back over to look at him, eyes wild; birds twittered outside the window; a cow lowed in the distance.

Then the dead man threw the pages to the side; some hit the hardwood on edge with a click, and others see-sawed through the slant of smoky sunlight. He grinned at Dan, eyes glowing: "Time fer the show!" He hurried around to the side of the bed opposite Dan and then flicked out his knife; the gun was back in his left hand.

"Let's see what tricks yer little whore remembers."

Dan's mind stood right on the edge of sanity, staring into the black gulf: *This is a dream*, it announced, like a clerk paging someone in a department store. *It's only a dream, and I will wake up. It's time to wake up, Dan-o, because I've had enough of this fucking dream. It's only a dream—*

The dead man was talking to Beth: "Look at me. Look at me! That's better. I'm gonna cut yer hands free, and yer gonna show us what you know, little girl, but if I feel one tooth—*one, single, tooth…*" He leveled the pistol at Dan's chest. "Hubby there gets it. Understand?" Beth nodded, hair falling forward to hide her face. Then he cut her hands free, and she stripped the tape from her wrists and wadded it and threw it onto the floor, then reached up and undid his jeans, pulling out what he had for her.

As his wife's head began to bob, what was left of Dan's mind dove headfirst down the slide and into the dark.

Kill you, motherfucker! I'll fucking KILL you!

"How ya think yer gonna do that, numb nuts? Oh! Yeah, baby. Like that. Yeah." A dank, hellish grin at Dan: "I think she likes it."

Fucking KILL you! Dan ripped his wrists apart, tape ends trailing as he brought his hands around, and the dead man's eyes widened; the pistol that had started to waver now pointed rock-solid at Dan's chest. He ignored it and ripped white cord from his torso and lap.

"Uh uh, sit still! Make a move ta get out o' that chair…" The dead man lowered the stub barrel to Beth's temple. He froze, but his wife didn't seem to notice; if anything, her head bobbed faster. Dan frothed, helpless, and then the rapist shit-bag moaned; the pistol lowered from Beth's head to point at the mattress. He worked at the cord again.

"Oh yeah, like that, yeah." He suddenly reached down and smoothed Beth's hair back. "Name's Scott, by the by. My friends call me Scotty."

Beth paused, rolling her eyes up to look at him.

I'm gonna fucking KILL you, Scotty! I'm gonna get all your little toys outta your bag there and I'm gonna shove each one up your ass, you rapist piece of fucking dog shit! You're gonna wish you never—

The revolver was pointing at Dan again. "Yeah? Think so? I'd like to see ya try it, that's what *I'd* like—" A gasp. "Oh, baby, that's it."

Scotty the rapist threw his head back and closed his eyes; the pistol drifted to the side—

And the bedroom exploded.

Something zipped past Dan's ear, sounding like the world's biggest supersonic wasp, and the muzzle flash made him see spots. And then Scotty the would-be rapist convulsed, screaming like an animal being butchered. He fell backward, tangled in the faded jeans around his knees; the pistol boomed again and Dan's ears whined as their dresser mirror shattered.

Beth spit something red onto the floor.

Dan ripped the last cord from his lap and stood, but his legs were still bound to the chair so he lost his balance and fell over as she swung taped legs off the bed and lunged, disappearing from view. Shrill screams, and the revolver fired again, making Dan's ears pulse. "*Beth!*" The chair clung to him like a live thing. "Beth!" He dragged himself up using the coverlet, looking frantically on the other side.

"BETH!"

They surged to their feet, locked together, hopping about and leaning on each other because of their bound legs. She had the wrist with the pistol gripped in both bloody hands as he stabbed her with the knife, gashing her shoulder. Blood flowed down her arm.

"*Oh God you bitch you RUINED me oh God oh God you bitch!*"

"Beth!"

She suddenly spun under his arm, and then she was standing behind him, still with the gun wrist in her hands; his elbow now pointed at the ceiling. Screaming, back arched, what was left of his manhood sent a hot rope of blood splashing over their pillows and comforter and Dan's face. He gagged and spit and cursed and wiped his eyes in time to see the tendon in that elbow give, and then the pistol dropped from Scotty's limp hand and thumped on the floor. He tried to stab her across his body, missed, dropped the knife, and grabbed a handful of hair and pulled her down; they disappeared on the other side of the bed a second time.

"Beth!"

Dan kicked at the chair, punched it, and then froze in amazement as she reappeared and hopped-lunged toward him and plunged her hands between the mattress and box spring so hard the bloody bed rocked and bopped him in the chin.

What the hell?

Behind her, Scotty had found his knife again. He sat up and slashed wildly, still screaming that he was ruined.

"Look out!"

She turned, but now she had a big, gleaming knife of her own. Beth let loose a garbled screech and pounced. Scotty had time for one last scream.

"Beth!"

Big hands rose into Dan's view, trying to fend her off. The knife stabbed; the hands dropped away.

"Won't let you—"

Stab.

"—do this—"

Stab.

"—to me—"

Stab.

"—*again!*"

Stab.

"Beth," Dan whispered.

She came to her knees then, knife raised above her head in both small hands. Blood slicked her hair to her skull, ran crimson from her teeth and down her chin, and coated her breasts and belly. Her features were twisted, unrecognizable; a queen of red rage. She shrieked, and then the knife plunged faster and faster and faster; a warm rain began to fall, dotting the comforter, his arms, his face, the floor, the walls, the tray ceiling.

Dan watched from far away as the late-afternoon sun streamed through their bedroom window, shining on the scarlet knife as it rose and fell, rose and fell, rose and fell.

Book II

The First Rule

A Warning

Bᴜᴛ I feel fine," Dan lied.

Nurse Stefanie wasn't buying, however; she stopped her waddle toward the door and turned, planting fists on ample hips. "Forty-eight hours observation is what Dr. Williams ordered," she said. "And forty-eight hours is what you gonna get."

Dan gave her his best smile. "But they scanned my cat yesterday, and everything turned out hunky dory, no brain bleeding."

She snorted, and not delicately; there wasn't much delicate about Nurse Stephanie. "You know very well you're showin' other concussion symptoms." She squinted at him knowingly. "How's that headache?" She didn't wait for an answer before pulling a sample pack out of her scrubs' pocket and shaking it; two oblong pink-and-purple pills rattled in their individual blisters. "Dr. Williams told me to give these to you if you changed your mind; better than Tylenol, I can tell you *that*." She pointed to his nightstand where the bottle of Extra Strength Tylenol he'd requested sat taking up space. "And I know he'll write you a prescription if you ask." She shook the little pills again, sculpted eyebrows twitching.

Dan refused to look. "I told you, I'm fine, no headache. My vision's not even blurry anymore." *Not much, anyhow.*

"Uh huh." Nurse Stefanie rolled her eyes and then vanished through the open door, taking the goodies with her. *Maybe just a couple, to take the edge off?* Dan scowled at the useless Tylenol and looked away. It didn't matter if his head felt like it would split open and fall off his shoulders; he had way too much shit to do to go traipsing off to la-la land. He also had way too much to do to be lying around in this fucking hospital torture rack for another goddamn day! Dan glared at the clock hanging on the wall. It wasn't even eight yet! He hadn't made it here until around seven Sunday night, so he had another eleven plus hours to stew in this antiseptic hell. *Fuck!*

Nurse Stefanie suddenly waddled back in. "You're s'posed to get your walkin' papers tonight, but if you're a good boy today, I *miiiight* just *maaaaybe* be able to expedite you outta here sooner, say around five?" Dan perked up. She raised a cautionary purple-glitter nail. "*If* you're a good boy."

Dan batted his eyes, giving her all the good he could scrape together, but she only laughed and came back across the room to fluff his granite pillow, pat him on the shoulder, and ease him back in the rack; she smelled like cinnamon and hand sanitizer, with something exotic lurking underneath.

"You're gonna have to do better than that," she told him. "Dr. Williams is scheduled to reexamine you sometime early this afternoon, so we'll see how that goes. You'll just have to be patient in the meantime." Her big eyes twinkled. "Now I think a *good* little boy should close those pretty blue eyes of his and take him a nap. It'll make the time go by." She headed for the hallway, hips rolling. "Might help with that headache too, Mr. Sims."

"Please, Nurse Stefanie, call me Dan."

"Only if you quit on this 'Nurse Stefanie' bizness! It's just plain ol' Stefanie, Mr. Sims."

"Yes, Nurse Stefanie."

She cackled as she squeaked out into the hall again. Dan's grin lasted until he glanced back up at the clock; that little distraction had bled all of three minutes from his sentence.

Shit.

Dan frowned suspiciously at that clock; a circle of sterile black numbers and black marks and black, ticking hands over a plain white face. It looked just like the one he used to watch crawl toward recess in the fifth grade. *For all I know, it's the same fucking clock.*

Dan made himself quit staring at the hateful thing and looked at the TV remote sitting next to the Tylenol and then away; he wasn't going to make *that* mistake twice. He needed something else to kill time besides stare at the clock or watch the tube or think; he'd done all his thinking yesterday between CT scans and the doc poking and prodding him and Steve bringing him some spare clothes that he'd picked up from Beth, staying only a little while to chat awkwardly.

Dan was done thinking, and now he wanted to get up and *do* something, goddamn it—and he knew exactly what needed to be done.

During all that thinking yesterday, he had worked out "The Plan".

Dan looked at the clock again; it was finally eight. Only eleven more hours to go, nine if Nurse Stefanie came through. He ground his teeth, which only made his head throb harder, so he quit it. *Whenever* they struck his chains, he would have to turn his iPhone back on and call a cab. They hadn't talked about it, but Dan knew Beth expected him to call her sometime this afternoon so she would know when to pick him up, but that wasn't going to happen. It wasn't in "The Plan", for one thing, and for another…no. Dan had places to go, things to do, and things to buy before he went home and faced his…wife.

He unclenched his jaw and glanced back up at the clock; two minutes after eight. *Shit!* Beth didn't know about "The Plan". They'd talked about two things during their one conversation since Sunday and two things only:

One, what she'd told Lizzie, and two, what to do about the media.

The answers were simple (or at least they sounded simple); one, lie, and two, ignore them. Lizzie knew her daddy was in the hospital, but she thought he'd fallen down the stairs. Dan hated to lie to her, but it worked a helluva lot better than the truth.

A fuckin' men.

And as for their fifteen minutes, they were willing to wait it out; something would happen in this crazy world to shift the focus from them—somebody would kill another batch of innocent people for no discernible reason, or some crook stockbroker would steal another billion from trusting retirees—something. Dan couldn't quite bring himself to wish for those awful things to occur, but he'd be grateful when the spotlight shifted.

And as for Beth, their conversation yesterday had been so cold there could've been a freak August blizzard blowing on the cell tower connecting them.

Dan had that strange feeling again, the one that'd been with him since he'd woken up in here yesterday morning—a sentiment he couldn't for the life of him ever remember having before. It seemed to make this bizarre situation even worse.

I don't want to go home.

Not in the least little fucking *bit* did he want to go home. He wanted to see Lizzie, of course, but as to the rest…

Beth.

Shit. Beth.

Dan winced at the bolt of white-hot pain that shot through his cranium and he unclenched his jaw yet again and snatched the Tylenol and shook a few onto his palm; he was disobeying the little bottle about dosage, but fuck the little bottle. His shoulder gave a twinge when he set the bottle down, and his lower back gave a shout, but he ignored them as well; he felt like he'd been in a fucking car wreck. He washed the pills down with the cup of water Nurse Stefanie had left on his nightstand and then carefully fingered the shaved spot and seven staples above his right ear; a nice little present from Scott the Dead Rapist; Scotty to his friends.

Scotty's full name was—had been—Scott Duane Rison, and he really *had* been a kid, only twenty-two. Dan eased back on his freshly quarried pillow, trying to get comfortable; twenty-fucking-two years old; way too goddamn young to have that much evil stewing in him.

But he'd sure as fuck had it, hadn't he?

Dan had learned all this when he'd made the mistake of turning on the television yesterday morning. The first thing he saw was a blonde reporter from one of the Nashville network affiliates standing in the ditch across the road from his house, the castle framed squarely in the shot past her shapely shoulder as she yammered on about the "terrible home-invasion attack" that had unfolded in the residence behind her Sunday afternoon. Then a cut to previously recorded footage showed the reporter ringing Helen's front bell, and then her brief conversation with the Sims' "family spokesman".

Helen stood in her doorway with a red bandanna holding back her hair and emerald earrings brushing the shoulder pads of her lime-green pantsuit and said they had no statement to make and that the reporter needed to leave these good people alone and go find some crank heads or Muslim heathens to bother. Someone had interrupted the disjointed rant, someone behind her and out of view; Beth. Helen had glanced over her shoulder and then signed off by telling the bemused reporter she ought to be ashamed of herself and then the front door had slammed. Helen managed to call the blonde reporter honey three times in the span of five sentences.

Then a face that Dan would never forget popped onto the screen. The sharp features were younger, the white-blonde hair was shorter, and the facial scruff was missing, but those same cold eyes shone out of that same arrogant face: Scott Duane Rison, rapist.

Scotty to his friends.

While the face from hell hovered obscenely on the screen, the blonde informed him in a voice-over that Scott Rison, who had been employed as a farmhand by McFarlane Farms for the past two years, had a juvenile record that was, of course, sealed, but a source within the Rutherford County Juvenile Justice Authority had confirmed to this reporter that Rison had been convicted of multiple sexual assaults. Despite that fun little fact, Rison hadn't been forced to register as a sex offender when he'd aged out of the system at eighteen—which was raising eyebrows, to say the least. He had no record as an adult, not even a traffic violation, but this reporter had also learned that Rison had been questioned in Decalb County concerning the disappearance of Lisa Rene Stalls in November 2009. Lack of evidence had led to no charges being filed. Questions from this reporter about why Rison had not been required to register as a sex offender had gone unanswered. Questions from this reporter about why the Decalb County Sheriff's Department had divers searching Center Hill Lake since dawn Monday morning, and whether it had anything to do with the disappearance of Lisa Rene Stalls or information gleaned from the death investigation of Scott Duane Rison, had also gone unanswered. Blondie concluded by saying that the Rutherford County Sheriff's office was treating the death of Scott Duane Rison as an open investigation and had no further comment at this time.

At that, Dan had turned the TV off, mashing the power button on the remote so hard that it wouldn't work anymore; Nurse Stefanie had to go scrounge him a new one.

Open investigation? Seemed like a pretty goddamn simple open-and-shut case to Dan. *Why are they still investigating?*

The national news had soon picked up and then ran with the story, and Dan's phone hadn't stopped ringing since; Beth's as well. He'd returned calls to friends and coworkers, but not reporters—and there were all *kinds* of fucking reporters calling him; print and television, radio, Internet, true-crime bloggers (whatever the fuck those were), even a producer for the Nancy Grace Show. That worthy had offered them a tidy sum for the first interview, and all they had to do was appear on national television and spread their terror and pain around for all and sundry to feed upon.

No thanks.

He and Beth had been in agreement about that, at least. They were also now operating with cell phones turned off. Dan didn't mind, not really, but it was driving Beth crazy.

Beth.

No, he didn't want to think about Beth.

Dan glanced at the clock: 8:09.

Fuuuuck!

Seemingly on its own, his hand reached out and picked up his new remote. A stranger's finger pressed the power button, and the set up in the corner came on with a static pop.

Matt Lauer smiled at Dan while sitting on a pale couch in far-away New York City, looking dapper in charcoal pinstripes and a yellow-silk tie. His long face filled the small screen; Matt had his glasses on this morning.

"…turn to new developments out of Tennessee concerning that horrific home invasion in Rutherford County. We now go live to Meredith Blake with our NBC affiliate WSMV in Nashville. Meredith, I understand that the investigation has taken a new twist. What can you tell us?"

Yet another hot reporter appeared, this one with chestnut curls brushing her shoulders and intelligent dark eyes. She waited for the delay in the satellite feed and then nodded in response to Matt. She was standing on deep stone steps, the faux Greek columns fronting an official-looking building rising behind her.

"Yes, Matt, thank you. As you know, Sunday night word of a terrible home invasion shattered the peace of Centerville, a rural community of less than four thousand souls located twenty-one miles southeast of Murfreesboro. As has been reported, Daniel and Elizabeth Sims were the victims of an assault in the sanctity of their own home. Their attacker, a man that has now been identified as Scott Duane Rison, was killed by Elizabeth Sims after she had broken free of her restraints. Cause of death for the suspect was multiple stab wounds. Daniel Sims, who was hospitalized to treat injuries sustained during the assault, is scheduled to be released from Middle Tennessee Medical Center later this evening. However, we—"

Shit.

"—have learned that the Rutherford County Sheriff's Office is keeping the investigation open due to new information that has come to light about the circumstances—"

"Yes," Matt said, and the screen switched to show him leaning forward on the couch, the New York traffic, pedestrian and vehicle, flowing outside the window over his shoulder; a handful of tourists had their faces pressed to the glass. "What new information can you tell us?"

The camera switched back and showed the reporter with mouth still open while unsuccessfully hiding her irritation at being interrupted as she waited for the delay. She cleared her throat. "Ah, yes, Matt, as I was saying, our source, while unable to comment officially, is now telling us that authorities have questions about the suspect's manner of death. While initial reports were of multiple stab wounds, we're now learning he may have been stabbed upwards of *forty-five* times. Also, unconfirmed reports that Scott Rison had genital mutilation combined with drugs found at and seized from the residence have authorities speculating that this could have been a sex game gone horribly wrong, not a home invasion."

"Wow," Matt said, the television again flashing to the pristine studios in New York as he issued his intelligent summary. It switched back to the reporter on the courthouse steps and she said something else, but Dan had quit listening.

Son of a bitch.

He tried to focus past the blood pounding in his ears. "…again stated their investigation was ongoing, and couldn't comment. They did reveal that they are planning on interviewing Daniel and Elizabeth Sims again, who obviously have some new questions to answer. Back to you, Matt."

"All right, thank you, Meredith. That was Meredith Blake with our NBC affiliate WSMV, coming to you live from the courthouse steps in Murfreesboro, Tennessee." Matt turned on the couch to face Dan's favorite, Natalie Morales. "It sounds like there's a lot more of this story to come, Natalie."

"I think you're right, Matt," Natalie said, with a twitch of those lips. She faced the camera, amber eyes calm. "And now to The Disaster in the Gulf. The sea-floor gusher has finally been capped, but the massive response that has been mobilized to protect beaches, wetlands, estuaries, and the wildlife that call them home has only begun to—"

"Son of a motherfucking BITCH!"

A hesitant knock whipped Dan's head around, and he gripped the bed rails until the room stopped spinning. When he could focus again, he saw Nurse Stefanie standing in the doorway with a stranger who looked sort of like Howie Long; he had the ex-lineman's build and shovel jaw and buzz cut, but he was about Dan's height, a little over six feet; not as tall as the ex-Raider (if there was such a thing as an ex-Raider). L'il Howie wore an off-the-rack charcoal suit and a cheaper tie and he might as well have had COP tattooed on his shiny forehead.

Nurse Stefanie spoke to her white-on-white sneakers.

"You have a visitor, Mr. Sims."

She'd heard the news, all right. Dan was sure that *everybody* had heard by now.

That's it.

"Fuck this," he growled, and then put the rail down and swung his legs out and stood up, swaying until he found his balance. Nurse Stephanie scowled and opened her mouth. "I'm leaving, Stefanie." She met his eyes and then clicked her teeth back together; the game was over. Dan waved toward the TV. "You heard…" She hesitated and then nodded. He stumbled toward the bathroom, grabbing the bag Steve had brought, the bag that Dan's…wife…had packed.

"I'll go get the doctor," Stephanie said. Her shoes squeaked hurriedly away.

"You do that!" What were they going to do, force him to stay? To tell the truth, though, Stefanie could probably hold him in that bed with one hand.

Dan studied himself in the bathroom mirror; as if the shaved spot in his hair and the staples weren't bad enough, he had a huge purple knot in the middle of his forehead from Scotty the rapist's elbow. He also sported two swaths of purple around each eye, and his nose no longer went straight down his face. All in all, Dan thought he looked like a clumsy raccoon that moonlighted as an MMA fighter. He fingered what was left of his nose. Doc Williams had straightened it—and boy, had *that* process been fun—saying that in his "opinion" it wouldn't require surgery; but just in case, Dan needed a follow-up consultation with an Ear-Nose-Throat specialist.

Dan snorted. Gently.

He changed clothes and then eased his butt down on the cold-ass-motherfucking toilet lid and put his socks and sneakers on. Of *course* he would need a follow-up; that was how these bastards took care of each other, wasn't it? Referring you here and referring you there until they milked you dry or your insurance dropped your broke ass, whichever came first. Sonsabitches. It was a goddamn scam!

Dan stood up, anger propelling him past the pain and the dizziness like rocket fuel, and stepped out of the bathroom. L'il Howie was waiting for him. Dan locked eyes with the man, and any remaining doubts he was law enforcement jumped out the window; he had those weighing and measuring cop-eyes. Dan had seen enough of those Sunday night to last him a fucking lifetime.

"You can forget about me answering any more fucking questions," Dan told him. "You'll have to arrest me if you want—"

The man used a weight lifter's arm to raise a weight lifter's hand, palm out. "There seems to be a misunderstanding, Mr. Sims. I'm—"

"We'll have to hire a fucking lawyer! I *hate* lawyers!" He shoved the rest of his stuff into the bag, then snatched the worthless Tylenol from the nightstand and threw it in; a sudden vision of the pink-and-purple capsules disappearing into Nurse Stefanie's pocket didn't improve Dan's temper. He stepped past the goddamn cop and headed toward the goddamn hallway. "You can shove your questions up your—"

"MR. SIMS!"

Dan stopped.

"My name is Jeff Scandlin. I'm a Special Agent Criminal Investigator with the Tennessee Bureau of Investigation. I'll be upfront with you; I'm not part of the inquiry into Scott Rison's death, or his assault on you and your wife. I'm here on my own, and if you want my job and what's left of my career, you can pick up a phone and call my superiors right now and have it. I have questions, but you're under no obligation to answer them. Would you do me the courtesy of answering a few questions, Mr. Sims?"

Dan studied the Special Agent; his hands were folded calmly at his waist, but that shovel jaw rippled, showing what the pretty speech had cost. Hard hazel eyes stared at Dan; weighing, measuring: waiting.

Here on his own? Why? Wait—Tennessee Bureau of Investigation? There had been a TBI Agent at the house—what had his name been? Trying to remember details from Sunday night was like trying to see through one of those kaleidoscope tubes he and Will used to play with—everything was fractured and mostly blood-red.

"TBI?" Dan said. "There was a TBI man there Sunday night. I can't remember his name." But Dan remembered what he looked like; tall, with a paunch and a shock of graying black hair; his cynical gaze had taken in everything and given nothing back.

"Bobby Scarborough," Scandlin supplied, voice and face neutral. "Special Agent Bob Scarborough. Yes, he was there."

"I answered *his* questions." *Most of them.* "Why do you need more?"

The nostrils flared, and that jaw squared, the shovel ready to dig. Dan supposed the good Special Agent was used to having his questions answered post-haste.

"As I've stated, Mr. Sims, I'm not officially part of the investigation." Dan watched as Scandlin furthered his polite request through gritted teeth; must be a skill they taught at Special Agent School. "If you'd so kindly—"

"I'll answer as many questions as you want if you'll first answer one for me."

"If I can." Cautious.

"Why?" Dan jabbed a finger toward the television in the corner where Matt Lauer was blathering about something that hopefully wasn't Dan's family. "Why are they doing this? *He* broke into *our* house! *He raped my wife!*" Faces stopped and turned to look from the hall, and Dan choked back to a furious whisper. "Why would they keep the investigation open? That piece of shit got what he deserved! And what do they plan on charging us with? Defending ourselves? And *drugs?* What fucking drugs? We don't do drugs, and there weren't any in our house to find! And a sex game gone *wrong!?* That's a buncha crap! There's not a goddamn jury in America that would convict us for…for…!" Dan couldn't even think of anything. "Just tell me *why*, Special Agent."

Scandlin had regained his calm even as Dan lost his, and he stared at Dan for over a minute with those cop-eyes while the fifth-grade clock ticked and shoes squeaked in the hallway before he finally answered:

"It's a warning."

Dan gaped. "A *warning?* From *who?* For *what?* We didn't—"

Motion at the door made them turn. Dr. Williams stood there dissecting each of them over the wire-rimmed glasses perched on the end of his sharp nose. Dan had never seen the man look through the things. That dark, penetrating gaze settled on him.

"Dan, I'm told you'll be leaving us. I don't think I can condone that, considering—"

"I'm outta here, Doc, sorry. Thanks for the nose." *And do they make electric hand warmers, Doc? How much do they cost? Can I buy ya a pair?* "But I'm not gonna lie around here all day again. You said yourself that my CT scan came back negative, and I've got things to do."

The silver-haired man peered over his glasses at Dan, eyes flicking toward Scandlin before he raised his index and middle fingers. "I'll release you on two conditions."

Dan ground his teeth and then stopped when his head throbbed. He *could* and *should* just walk right past the bossy ass doctor and away from this fucking cop; he'd had his fill of both species, and now it looked like they would have to hire a fucking lawyer!

Lawyers and doctors and cops, oh my!

"What are they?" Dan grated.

"I talked with Dr. Gertsteiner, an ENT friend of mine. Gert's got a clinic over on Maple. You have an appointment with him Thursday, at eleven. You will be there to have him look at that nose." The middle finger went down.

"Fine. What else?" *Sure, Doc, I'll help "Gert" make his fucking Mercedes payment. You bet.*

"Swing by after and let me examine you. I'll take those staples out while you're here, if they're ready to come out. I may need to replace them with stitches. Also, your headache should clear by then, but if it hasn't, we'll need to take steps. Bad concussions are nothing to fool around with. Your—"

"My head's great, Doc."

"—subdural hematoma should fade in a couple weeks," the old man continued, ignoring him, "but if you experience further dizziness or blurred vision, trouble concentrating or sleeping, I want you to come see me immediately; your word on it."

Dan stared at him. *Shit, I hate being bullied.* "You've got my word, Doc."

Dr. Williams dropped the last finger and nodded. "I understand, son. I'd be doing the same thing if I were in your shoes. Go take care of your family."

"I will, Doctor. Thank you."

"Just make sure you take care of yourself while you're at it." With a last, searching look at Scandlin, he left. Cop-eyes had nothing on doctors'.

The room spun and then settled as Dan set his bag on the floor and lowered his butt on the edge of the bed; he wasn't dizzy, he just needed to rest for a second, that's all.

"Why would someone send us a 'warning'? That doesn't make any fucking sense, Scandlin."

The man considered him, and then his eyes flickered toward the open door before he said, "What do you know about this county, Mr. Sims?"

"What the hell does *that* have to do with anything?"

"Because Scott Rison is, was, related to Sheriff Jacobson; distantly, but related." Dan blinked. "Even more importantly, they're both related to Henry Donaghey."

Dan frowned; that name sounded familiar.

Special Agent Scandlin helped him out: "Rutherford County District Attorney General, Hank Donaghey."

Fuck me. "That shouldn't matter, though, right? I mean, the guy assaulted *us.*"

"This is the South, Mr. Sims; family and clan come first." Taking in Dan's flabbergasted stare, he shrugged. "They have nothing to charge you or your wife with; the circumstances are pretty clear-cut. They know that. Unless I'm way off base, I think the case will be quietly closed within the next few days. As I said, all that," he waved toward the television, "was just a shot across the bow. A warning."

"But *why* would—?"

"Do you mind if *I* ask a question, Mr. Sims?"

Dan flushed. "Fine. What?"

The Special Agent moved to the open door. Dan expected him to close it but instead he stuck his head out, glancing both ways. Scandlin then turned back around, but he stood where he could keep an eye on the hallway.

"Did Scott Rison brag about…other activities? Specifically, did he name any other women he'd assaulted, or that he knew had been assaulted?"

Scandlin's eyes burned for such a quiet question.

Dan repeated what the dead rapist piece of dog shit had said about "that stuck-up bitch" in Smithville, the one he'd killed and put in the lake. Scandlin listened, not interrupting, hands stuffed in his pockets. Dan finished and then added, "I told all this to Scarborough Sunday night. So did Beth." He let the obvious question hang.

The Special Agent ignored it. "Nothing else? Rison didn't mention any other women?"

"That was it." Scandlin's face didn't change, but the lineman's shoulders slumped. "Why? Do you k—?"

"What do you know about John McFarlane, Mr. Sims?"

Dan blinked harder. "The farmer? My neighbor? The guy that rapist trash worked for? He's a farmer, and my neighbor, and the guy that rapist trash worked for. I've also heard he's loaded, but I don't know about that for sure, not really. I know McFarlane owns a bunch of land." Dan eyed the muscular Special Agent. "Why? What else should I know about him?"

Again Scandlin ignored him while asking yet another question, and this one almost made Dan fall off the bed:

"What did you and your wife burn in the fireplace?"

"I don't know what you're talking about."

Dan got a full dose of the cop-eyes, and then Scandlin nodded as if he'd answered with a complete written essay. The Special Agent pulled his hand out of his pocket and held out a card tweased between two thick fingers. Dan didn't deign to look at it.

"When the first-responders arrived, smoke was all over your house. You have a gas-log fireplace, but paper had recently been burned inside. Before you called 911?" Dan didn't answer. Scandlin shook the card as if he couldn't see it. Dan still didn't take it. "Everyone wants to know what was burned, and why, including me." He waggled the card again; Dan ignored it again. Shrugging, Scandlin tossed it on the bed. "That has my cell. We need to talk, Mr. Sims. Not here."

"I thought you were out of the loop."

"I know people. Things get out."

Dan stood up. When the room stopped spinning he said, "I believe I'm done answering questions, Special Agent Scandlin."

The cop-eyes bored into Dan's. "I hope we didn't get off on the wrong foot here today, Mr. Sims. For your family's sake, I hope that."

"Oh? And why's that?"

"Because I may be the only friend you have in this whole mess." The Special Agent pointed at his card lying on the white sheet. "If you're smart, you'll call me, and soon." He walked out.

Dan looked around at his soon-to-be-empty hospital room. "I don't need this shit right now," he told it. The room didn't respond. *Mr. McFarlane?* Why the hell would Scandlin ask about his neighbor? Rison had worked for the old farmer, true, but he was just some old farmer.

Wasn't he?

Dan rubbed his temples. Gently. He didn't need some crazy cop's crazy questions right now; he had things to do, things to buy, and his own crazy questions to answer.

Dan looked at the card and then picked it up and stuffed it into his wallet.

Just in case.

He grabbed his bag and focused his splitting brain on The Plan. First, turn his phone on and call a cab, then head over to the office to retrieve his laptop. Shit, Irene would be there, along with everyone else…oh well, he'd deal. Then on to the bank in Nashville, and then it would be time to go shopping!

And then he would go home and hug his daughter and deal with his lovely… wife.

Dan limped out of the room, but it was a determined limp.

He had shit to do.

MOUTHWASH

THEY WERE back.

Beth stood by the fireplace, peeking out the window at the competing news crews setting up at the edge of the weedy ditch on the other side of Daisy. She'd just sent Helen out to chase off the crew that had mistakenly thought it could park in her driveway; she would've done it herself, but the last thing Beth wanted was to be on camera.

She was careful not to disturb the curtains as she set the bucket of dirty water down to give her arm a rest. The stitches in her shoulder itched, but she didn't scratch them; Beth had had stitches before. Her swollen lip had gone down, but she still sported a light shiner where…that man…had hit her. The small mouse under her eye didn't bother her though; Beth had received worse at the dojo.

That man…

She knew his full name now, as of yesterday, but she didn't want to think about it.

There were a lot of things Beth didn't want to think about.

She pooched her bottom lip and blew a strand of sweaty hair out of her eyes; she'd been cleaning all morning. The cops that had tromped throughout her house Sunday afternoon, evening, night, most of early Monday morning—and, she presumed, *all* of yesterday—hadn't worried about dirty boots. They *certainly* hadn't concerned themselves with her floors; she was doing what she could to rectify the situation today, even though she would eventually have to hire a carpet-cleaning service, but no matter how much she or anyone else cleaned downstairs, what truly needed to be cleaned was upstairs.

Beth could still smell the blood, and the gasoline.

They'd taken…that man's…body away, but the blood remained, splashed all over their bedroom; *so* much blood. What was the procedure to remove congealed blood from real walnut flooring? Would it stain no matter what they did? And what would gas do to a hardwood floor? Would they have to rip up and replace the entire thing? She needed to talk to her husband and decide whether they would hire someone to clean it or do it themselves so they could find out—but would a cleaning service even *touch* something like that? Beth knew there were businesses that specialized in cleansing crime scenes, but she didn't know if there were any in Tennessee: L.A., sure; New York City, of course; but Tennessee? Still, crime happened everywhere, so maybe they could find one in Nashville. It wouldn't be cheap, however.

The news teams were only a few feet apart now that she'd evicted the one from her driveway; they eyed each other like strange jackals hunkered over a carcass. Beth had thought—hoped—that everyone would leave them alone from here on out since they'd issued no statements besides a wish for privacy.

I should've known better.

Beth and Lizzie and Helen were at the castle today because Special Agent Scarborough had stopped by Helen's late last night to tell her that the investigation was winding down, and that he'd removed all the crime scene tape; in short, they could go home. Beth had wanted to ask him about the phone call…that man… had taken in their bedroom: they had recovered the phone, but had they traced the number yet? Had they found out who…that man's…accomplice was? If not, she could suggest a certain burly, camouflage-loving cracker…

Beth had kept her swollen lip zipped, though, and for a simple reason: Special Agent Scarborough had asked Beth many questions Sunday night, most of which he'd gotten an answer to; most, but not all, so if *she* questioned *him*, Beth had no doubt he would retaliate with a renewed slew of his own.

Beth grimaced at the fireplace beside her; she couldn't *believe* she'd been dumb enough to leave the flue closed! But she'd never owned a house with a fireplace before—she'd never even owned a *house* before!—so how was she supposed to know you closed the smoke hole in the spring and summer to keep out birds and wasps? By the time she'd realized her mistake, smoke was filling the castle even as the sirens wailed closer and closer. Daniel hadn't bothered to inform her either, and he had called 911 just as she'd lit the gas and then promptly passed out on their love-seat; the smell of burnt paper filled the house, the sirens converged, the EMT's and cops came swarming in, and then the questions started.

It'd been at her insistence they burn those horrid notes before they called 911. Whose handwriting had that been? A girlfriend's? Beth couldn't imagine *that man* having a girlfriend. And how had all that information about her gotten on there? She'd told no one in her new life about her past, and all those people in her old life, the ones that already knew, were dead!

So how?

Beth massaged her temples as she eyed the impossible ashes lurking behind the screen; too many questions. She was getting a headache. Besides, she had enough on her plate as it was.

She turned away from the fireplace and the ashes that couldn't be but were and sniffed and then scowled in frustration; she had been airing out the castle all morning, but it wasn't doing much good. If Beth didn't get the smell of burnt paper and gasoline and blood out of here soon, she was going to be sick.

Motion at her side turned out to be Helen peering out a different crack in the curtains; the combination of lavender slacks and bright-red blouse was especially jarring today. Enormous silver-hoop earrings swayed as she sniffed.

"Vultures! Can't they let good people be?" Helen's phone suddenly sang a gospel hymn from the depths of her purse. "That'll be Jessie. I'd better take it." She gimped deeper into the living room while digging for the phone and answered, then glanced at Beth and turned her back and whispered something to Jessie.

Beth peeked out at the reporters again, now with a sour twist to her lips. Helen had become point-woman for a cadre of ladies from her church, and her phone hadn't stopped singing for two days; the old woman was at ground zero of the most exciting thing to happen in these parts in ten years, maybe longer, and was the envy of all her friends.

The "visits" had begun late yesterday morning: Oh, they were just stopping by to chat, of course, and what a terrible thing to happen, wasn't it? How are you and the little one holding up, dear? And your poor husband! Helen was such a good Christian woman to put them up in their time of need, wasn't she? And that young scalawag! How could he have gone and done such a terrible thing? Most if not all the ladies had seemed to know…that man…and not a one had seemed surprised at his bad end, either, but oh, what a *devil!* How could he have done…that?

Every single one of the old biddies had been dying—*dying!*—for the details; Beth could see the eager curiosity swimming in their rheumy eyes, but she had remained silent. Only three people knew what had really happened up in that bedroom, and one of those would never tell anyone anything ever again. Neither of the two left were talking, and it would stay that way; she and Daniel had agreed—on that subject, at least.

Daniel.

No, Beth didn't want to think about him. *Especially* him! He'd been *lying* to her about betting on football! And he'd been a *drug dealer!* She *hated* drug dealers! To Beth, drug dealers were only a rung above pederasts on the slime-ball scale. And her husband had been one!

Her *husband!*

Taking deep breaths into her *itten,* she fought for calm. That'd been years before she'd met him, but still—

A terrified hollow opened behind Beth's navel.

If *she* was busy judging *him…*

He'd been so short with her on the phone yesterday, so cold and angry, that she couldn't help but mirror him; they'd hung up without even saying goodbye. He was being released from the hospital tonight, but he hadn't asked her to pick him up. Would he get Steve to drive him home?

Will he even come home?

Beth dismissed that thought immediately; Daniel would come home because of Lizzie, she knew that, but the real question was, what then? They had so much to talk about, to decide, but he didn't even seem to want to speak to her.

How could they decide anything if he wouldn't talk to her?

How would or could they ever sleep in that room again—let alone do anything else!—even after they cleaned it? How?

How could *anything* ever be the same between them?

Beth wiped fresh tears away as bright lights bathed both pretty reporters; those unflattering white lights would bring out every flaw. No wonder they wore makeup. Beth turned her face away, tired of watching, tired of *thinking*, and picked up her bucket. Back to cleaning, no thinking; she would talk to her husband tonight.

He'd BETTER talk to me tonight!

When Beth turned all the way around she found Lizzie standing in her blind spot, Mr. Fred clutched to her chest; she was supposed to be playing horsies up in her room.

"Is my Daddy home?"

Beth set her bucket back down and knelt, holding her arms out. "No, baby, not yet. He'll be home tonight, like I told you." Those eyes searched her face somberly, and then Lizzie came for the offered hug. After a moment she freed herself and walked over to look out the crack in the curtains, adopting Beth's furtive pose. She looked up.

"Why are those people taking pictures of our house?"

Beth searched for a lie, found one: "They think it's pretty, and they wanted some photos of it."

"Oh." Lizzie turned back to the crack. Beth looked at Helen and found the old woman still on the phone but regarding her sadly.

Interpreting Beth's silent plea, her friend cleared her throat: "Jessie? I have to go. What? Yes, yes, I promise, bye." Helen hung up and dropped the phone back into her giant purse. "Lizzie, dear?"

"Yes, Ms. Helen?"

Although her daughter had turned and promptly answered, Beth's heart ached at the listlessness in her little voice and posture; the only time she'd seemed herself the past two days was when she'd been giggling and chasing poor Pickle through Helen's backyard.

The old lady limped over and put on a grin. "A little fly told me you have some bee*you*taful horses up in that room of yours! That true, Ms. Lizzie?"

Lizzie gaped at her, big eyes as wide as they would go: "Flies can *talk?*"

Helen winked at Beth and guided Lizzie out of the sunken living room and across the foyer. "Why of course they can, dear! But only a few special people can hear 'em, like me. How do you think I know so much?" Lizzie stared open-mouthed at Helen, stumbling, Mr. Fred dangling forgotten in her hand. Beth watched them with the first true smile she'd managed in days—and then they reached the bottom of the staircase and stopped.

Beth moved toward them, saying, "She can bring them down here, you don't have to—"

"Oh, foo!" Helen said, waving her away. "No dang staircase is gonna beat *this* old broad! Hold this." She thrust her cane at Beth, who took it. "Now watch and learn." She climbed slowly while using the handrail, a grimace of pain warring with determination. Lizzie went in front, also going slowly and using the rail; she had her own reasons. Those stairs had hurt her Mommy and Daddy—or so she'd been told.

Since they'd been home, Beth had noticed that Lizzie now eyed those steps warily, like an otherwise-friendly dog that she'd found out would bite. It broke Beth's heart.

How many lies have I told my daughter in the past two days? She was losing track.

She followed them up, carrying Helen's cane; being a parent was a lot more complicated than she'd ever dreamed.

Everything was a lot more complicated.

Beth's sour thoughts were interrupted as their little procession reached the top. Freed from the dangerous stairs, Lizzie ran ahead.

"C'mon, Ms. Helen!" She darted into her room, but Lizzie didn't know she'd lost her audience. Helen's head had turned to the left, and her gaze was now fixed avidly on Beth and Daniel's bedroom door. Helen's eyes fell to the bottom of the door where Beth had stuffed the biggest, fluffiest towel she could find in the downstairs bathroom into the crack; there was a bloody boot-print on the beige carpet just in front of the rolled-up towel, tread pointing out; it had dried a crusty black.

Beth cleared her throat, and the old woman jumped, head snapping forward. Still gripping the banister with one hand, Helen reached out silently for her cane. Beth gave it to her; she couldn't see Helen's face, but there was a scarlet flush on her neck below the gray bun.

"Thank you, dear," she whispered, then limped forward quickly, not looking at the door again, or Beth. Lizzie's little voice came from her room and Helen answered, "Coming, Ms. Lizzie, coming!" She vanished inside, and Beth heard her exclaim over something and Lizzie's answer.

Their voices faded to a buzz as Beth slowly turned and looked at her bedroom door…and then she fled back down the stairs and retreated into the kitchen; she'd put Helen's mouthwash next to the sink first thing this morning. Her own mouthwash was trapped in her bathroom, beyond the bloody bedroom. She poured a cap-full of the minty-green liquid and swished it around before spitting into the sink. She repeated the process, and then again. It did no good. It had done no good for the last two days, but she couldn't seem to stop.

Beth could not only smell blood, she could still taste blood.

She could still taste *him*.

She couldn't even say his name in her head!

Am I turning into a coward?

NEVER!

Scott Duane Rison.

There, she'd said it: the name of the man she'd killed—the name of the twenty-two-year-old *kid* she'd killed. Beth could still see the terror in Rison's boyish face as she plunged the knife into his chest, feel the jolt and her hand slip on the slick handle as the blade hit bone before slipping deeper, hear the burble and hiss as his punctured lung collapsed. Beth watched the light fade from those terrible eyes as she kept stabbing, over and over and over and over and over. She could still feel his blood slicking her hands and arms, the handle of the knife, her breasts and belly and legs.

Beth poured and gargled and spit.

It did no good. She could still taste him.

Scott Duane Rison.

And I know other names now, don't I?

Beth hadn't been able to stop herself; she'd held that hateful orange envelope over the hissing flames and hesitated. Daniel had looked at her, then. He'd spent the surreal few minutes after…after *not* looking at her, but he'd looked at her then, waiting with his iPhone in his hand to call 911. Then she'd given in and opened it, scanning through blood-splattered reams of damning knowledge, the looping handwriting unquestionably a woman's. And then she found them, the names of her birth-mother and father:

Riley Ann Washburn and Thomas Danbury; no middle name for her father.

Beth stared out the window over the sink as the late-morning sun shone on the bag gallows that her husband had built for her seven months ago; a lifetime ago.

Riley. What a pretty name; her mother's name. *Danbury. I'm a Danbury.*

No. Beth poured and gargled and spat. She *wasn't* a Danbury. Riley and Thomas had made their choice. Three names; her birth parents, and the man she'd killed. Three names she hadn't known two days ago, but now those three names were written across Beth's brain in lines of blood and fire.

Why did they give me away?

It was the old question—the oldest question. *Why?* Were they just not ready? Had Riley been pregnant and on her own, scared? *No.* Beth wiped her eyes. She would *not* do this to herself! The hard truth was there were no good answers, and there never had been. When she was little, she'd made up fantasies about them, imagining a Prince and Princess coming back and scooping her into their arms, saying it was all a big mistake and that they were sorry, or that they'd been kidnapped by an evil King but now they'd escaped and they would all go live in their castle far away and be a happy family.

Those fantasies had faded as she grown older and they didn't appear, but the question never went away: Why? And then, when Beth had been adopted by the Morrisseys, the question retreated as she experienced what it was like to be a part of a family. She'd been happy, loved…for a time.

And then—

And then she'd been back in the system, older, and she'd thought about looking for her birth parents, but she hadn't. Both scared and scarred by her experience, young Beth had decided she could make it on her own; she didn't *need* a family.

Beth smiled sadly, remembering that headstrong eleven-year-old girl. She'd thought she'd been through it all, seen everything, and had life figured out. At eleven!

Little did I know what was coming down the pipe…

Beth raised a hand toward the mouthwash; her fingers trembled, and she clenched them into a fist.

Names! She was thinking about *names*, not—

NAMES! Riley and Thomas. Danbury. Had she ever met a Danbury? She didn't think so. Scott Duane Rison. Gargle. Spit. Morrissey: despite everything, Beth had kept it because they'd adopted her. It had been her maiden name when she'd married Daniel.

Sims.

That one, Beth had planned on keeping forever.

How long will I keep Sims now?

Beth's whisper filled her huge, gorgeous, and uncaring kitchen:

"Oh, I am one messed-up chick."

From upstairs came yet another gospel tune, and then Helen's muffled voice as she stepped out of Lizzie's room to answer. Beth knew what Helen was staring at as she stood in the upstairs hallway and whispered.

She ground her teeth; Beth truly didn't know what they would've done without the kind old woman, but this rumor-mongering switchboard was getting on her last nerve. It was time for Helen to go home. She just had to tell her. Somehow.

"Beth?"

She spun the cap back on the mouthwash and went to the bottom of the stairs and looked up. Her friend peered down at her, and Beth didn't like her expression.

"What is it? What's wrong?"

"Oh, honey…" Lizzie came up behind her, a horsie in each hand. Glancing at her meaningfully, Helen looked back down at Beth. "I need to speak to you."

"Lizzie, go play in your room. Ms. Helen and I need to talk for a minute."

"Okay!" Lizzie skipped away.

Helen started down the stairs, awkwardly carrying her cane under one arm as she held the curving banister in both hands.

Beth started up. "Let me—"

"Don't you dare!"

Beth stayed where she was, admiring her friend's pluck. When Helen finally got to the bottom she looked at Beth, breathing hard. She opened her mouth and then closed it again.

"What's going on?"

"Oh, honey, you, um, you need to turn on the news. There's, ah…that was Penelope. She's *such* an old busybody, but she said…you need to turn on the television, or get on the Internets," she waved a vague hand toward the computer desk, "'cause there's news…" Helen was looking everywhere but at Beth.

"Helen, tell me."

"Oh darlin', I don't…"

"*Just tell me.*"

So Helen did.

Twenty minutes later Beth was finally taken off hold at Middle Tennessee Medical Center; she was surprised the green tiles under her sneakers weren't bubbling. She listened, and then they *were* bubbling:

"What do you mean, he left?"

"I mean I was told he was released over two hours ago."

"He was supposed to be under observation for forty-eight hours for a severe concussion! Why was he released early?"

"I don't know, Mrs. Sims, I don't work on that floor. But I can transfer you up there. I think Stefanie was his nurse. Let me—"

"I want to speak to Dr. Williams."

Two hours ago. *Over* two hours ago. He hadn't called her.

"Dr. Williams is with a patient, ma'am. I'm sure Stefanie can tell you—"

"*Dr. Williams* was my husband's doctor, not the stupid nurse! I want to speak to *him*, and I want to know why my husband was released early!"

And I want to know where he is!

"I realize that, ma'am, but I can't—"

"Go to hell. Oh, and thank you so much for your help."

Beth hung up and then tried to call her husband again. He didn't answer, and the call went to voicemail. Again. His phone wasn't turned off anymore—he was just ignoring her! *Where is he? What is he doing?* Beth carefully set her phone on the kitchen island and stalked the other way; slamming it on the tiles and watching it disintegrate would solve nothing, no matter how gratifying it would be. It would only cost fifty bucks to replace, too. She had insurance.

He was *ignoring* her!

Beth stopped pacing and unclenched her fists and took several deep breaths and blew them out, then glanced over at the two people who shared the kitchen with her. Lizzie had come downstairs to see what all the yelling was about, and Beth hadn't had the heart to order her back to her room. She stood holding hands with Helen, watching Beth with big eyes; Helen stared at the tiles between her orthopedic shoes.

Beth opened her mouth to say something—she wasn't quite sure what—when Helen's phone began to sing, and she had to clamp her molars together to stifle a shriek.

"I'd better get that," Helen whispered. She avoided Beth's eye as she limped into the foyer to take the call.

Beth was at the point where she could put what hymn went with which biddy: "Praise to Thee". *Say hello to Adele for me, Helen!* She looked at Lizzie. "Baby, go back up in your room and play. I need to talk to Ms. Helen again."

"I don't want to."

She eyed her daughter carefully; Beth was in a quiet place. She was calm. She was serene.

"Ms. Helen is about to go home, and you and I will finish cleaning, and then we'll watch a movie or whatever you want to do, but for now I need to talk to her alone. You can tell her goodbye when—"

"I don't *want* Ms. Helen to go home!" Bright blue eyes glared defiance up at Beth, and Lizzie looked so much like her father in that moment it made Beth's heart hurt even as it raised her temper a notch toward critical.

"Do as I say, young lady, or you're going to lie down for a nap." She pointed toward the stairs. "*Now*, missy!"

"No!" Lizzie flew out of the kitchen and then up and around without using the banister. "I don't *want* to take a nap! I want my *Daddy!* I want my *DADDY* to come *HOME!*" Beth heard her door slam. Muffled crying floated down the curving staircase; something thumped against a wall. Beth massaged her throbbing temples with the tips of her index fingers. She became aware of Helen watching her; the call with Adele must've ended sometime during the commotion.

Beth dropped her hands and faced her friend. "Helen…thank you so much for everything you've done, we really appreciate it…"

How oh *how* to do this gently?

And then Helen said, "You hush, girl." She limped over and enveloped Beth in a hug, enormous bosom pressing against hers, then pulled away and held her at arm's length. "I know when water's wet: you've got that young one to take care of, and chores to do before that man of yours comes home…besides, I could use some peace and quiet m'self. Haven't had this much hubbub about in a month of Sundays! I'll git out of your hair and git on home to Pickle, maybe git my own chores done, though right now I feel a snooze callin'—speakin' o' naps."

"Thank you, Helen. You've been so good to us, I don't know what we'd have done without you. You know you're welcome here anytime, it's just…I…" Beth could feel the dam cracking. "I…" The tears came, and she couldn't stop them.

"Oh, honey." Helen pulled her in again. After a minute, Beth pushed back and wiped her eyes and took a breath that seemed to start somewhere out beyond the end of her big toes.

"Helen, about what happened…you heard?" The old woman hesitated and then nodded. "I *had* to. He was going to…I didn't have a choice." *Forty-five plus times?* "We—"

"Stop. Stop it right there. You don't have to explain anything to me."

"I know, but all that terrible stuff they're saying about us isn't—"

"Hush." She gripped Beth's shoulders with surprising strength. "*You did what you had to do*, for you *and* your family. Am I right?"

Beth nodded, not trusting herself to speak.

"Then you did good. And don't you let nobody tell you different. Ever."

Beth smiled. "Yes, ma'am."

"Good." Helen let her go and turned and gimped toward the front door, hooking her cane over one bicep and digging in her cruise-ship purse. "That *boy!* I knew he'd come to no account, but *this!* Lord Christ A'mighty!"

Beth watched as Helen paused below the shot-up chandelier to dig harder and then retrieve her keys from the depths. She'd known Rison? It hadn't occurred to

Beth to ask, what with everything else going on, but it stood to reason; all those other ladies had.

"Did…did you know him well, Helen?"

The old lady turned and studied Beth sharply, and then that piercing gaze softened and she sighed, nodding. "I did. I'm related to his whole family—distantly, but related." She shook her head. "I'm just glad his momma isn't around to see how he turned out; it would break her heart. Louise was a good girl, but she didn't have the sense God gave a goose, 'specially when it came to that boy's father. Now *there* was a rascal, and no mistake."

"Helen, I'm so sorry, I didn't know." The thought of that monster as someone's son put a whole new face on the situation—a human face. It was a face Beth wasn't sure she was up to examining further.

Helen waved her cane dismissively. "Don't fret about it, honey; he was trash, plain and simple. I hate to say that about my own kin, distant as he was, but it's the truth, and God knows the truth is the truth." Her laugh was harsh. "I'd give you that old saw about bad apples on every tree, but it's more like a tree five fields over in our case, praise the Lord." She turned and put a hand on the knob. "If you need anything, dear, you know where I am. Don't hesitate to drop by."

"I won't. And thank you again. Thank you so much."

"You're welcome. Kiss that precious little one for me."

"I will."

Helen tugged the door open and then peered out suspiciously, muttering about vultures, then turned and winked at her and went out, shutting the heavy door with a thump.

Beth listened; Lizzie had quieted upstairs, but she heard Helen yell something at the news people, then the rumble as she fired her Silverado up and drove around and out of the driveway. Beth went to the window in time to watch her shake her fist at the reporters, and then with a squeal of tires she roared down Daisy toward her house. The news people watched her go with bemused expressions.

Smiling, Beth stepped away from the window before the vultures spotted her; she had acquired her first gray hair riding to town with Helen, and Daniel liked to say the old lady had missed her calling as a stock-car driver.

Beth's smile faded.

Daniel.

Where was he? What was he doing? She would *not* call him again. She wouldn't! *Screening* her calls, *ignoring* her; he would be lucky if she answered when he called back!

Where *was* he? What the heck was he doing? She wandered back into the kitchen, listening; still no sound from upstairs. Beth glanced down at her phone, and then before she could stop herself she picked it up and hit the quick-dial button assigned to her husband's cell number:

It went straight to voicemail.

Beth slowly placed her iPhone back on the island and stared at it. He'd turned his phone off again. What on *earth* was he doing? When was her husband coming home?

What if he's not *coming home?*

The doorbell bonged.

Beth jumped. Lizzie pounded out of her room and yelled from the top of the stairs: "Is that my Daddy?"

It was likely a reporter trying to cage an interview; they wouldn't give up. Beth walked out of the kitchen and looked up at her daughter. "I don't think your daddy would ring the doorbell, sweetie." Lizzie's face fell. "It's probably more people who want to take pictures of our house."

"Oh."

Beth's heart hurt at seeing that look, so she held her arms out and Lizzie came down the steps slowly as the doorbell rang again, multiple chimes filling the castle. Beth picked her up and kissed and hugged her, then put her down on the bottom step. "You stay here while I see who it is. I don't think it's your daddy, but you never know."

"Okay."

Beth walked through the foyer, glancing back once: Lizzie stood with her hands folded at her waist, ladylike; bare feet and the lime-green Dora the Explorer tee-shirt didn't spoil it. Two sets of big eyes watched Beth, Dora's brown hovering below Lizzie's blue; the hope on her daughter's face was hard to take.

Beth crept to the foyer closet and retrieved the thick phone book Daniel had placed in there for her. She put it down in front of the door and stepped up and went on tip-toe and looked through the peep hole.

The fish-eye view revealed two strangers standing on her red-brick porch; a round man with round glasses and a short, graying beard faced her, and behind him a thin woman with ash-blonde hair pulled into a ponytail frowned off to the side at something, clipboard and pen clutched to her chest. Beth saw no microphones or cameras, but that meant nothing. The round man reached for the bell again so Beth shouted through the door:

"Can I help you?"

The blonde turned, her frown deepening to a scowl as the man answered in a raised baritone: "Are you Mrs. Elizabeth Sims?"

For now. "This is she. What can I do for you?"

"We'd like to come in and speak with you, Mrs. Sims."

"I'm not saying anything to reporters. Talk to the police if you—"

"We're not reporters, ma'am!" The severe blonde stepped aggressively toward the door, the clipboard and pen still clutched to her flat chest: "We're with Rutherford County Child Services! There have been concerns raised about the safety and wellbeing of one Elizabeth Ann Sims, age four! Is the child home with you now? If so, we would like to come in and speak with her!"

Beth's heels thumped on the phone book.

"Shit," she whispered.

"Mommy, you said a bad word."

Beth looked over her shoulder. "I'm sorry, baby."

Sudden fury surged through her, and she had to unclench her jaw and both fists. *Damn you, Daniel, where are you? DAMN YOU for leaving me to face this by myself!* She took a deep breath to compose herself, and then another for good measure, and then one to grow on.

"Ma'am?"

"Just a second!" Beth plastered a smile on her face, threw back the deadbolt, kicked the phone book to the side, and opened the front door.

"Please come in."

HOMECOMING

I T WAS just past eight-thirty on Tuesday night when Dan cruised through downtown Centerville; it didn't take long. He then journeyed east, using the two-lane highway that would eventually dwindle and become Daisy Road. He powered up his phone and dialed Beth's cell from memory. She picked up on the second ring.

Silence.

"Hello?"

"Hi."

What did *she* have to be pissed off about? "Hi. I'm about five minutes away. I'll pick you guys up from Helen's and then we'll head home. I don't care if the goddamn crime-scene tape is still up, I'll rip it down. I've got some—"

"Agent Scarborough already did that, right before he told me the investigation was closed. And we're not at Helen's. We're home."

"Oh." *Closed?* Son of a bitch, Scandlin had been right! In the background he heard Lizzie's little voice asking if that was her daddy. Dan smiled and said, "Put her on."

More silence. Then: "We're waiting for you."

The line went dead.

Dan held the phone out and stared at it, then threw it into the passenger seat and clenched the steering wheel with both hands.

That's how she wanted to play?

So fucking be it.

Four minutes later Dan topped a small rise and the lights from Helen's house appeared on the right, but he only had eyes for the big house further down on the left; the sun had set just minutes before, and pink and orange and red chased each other across the sky in his mirrors even as early stars floated in the purple creeping above the castle's red-brick chimney and the high ridgeline beyond.

A strange notion suddenly struck Dan: his house didn't look the same; he couldn't put his finger on how, really—it was all still there—but something about home had definitely changed.

Home.

That word sure didn't *feel* the same, either.

Dan shoved these glum thoughts aside as he hit the blinker and turned in; as he drove the pickup past the front porch, the light came on. He could see two faces peering out of a window and he waved at the one closest to the floor. Dan parked in front of the closed garage on the far right side and the motion-sensor light came on, blinding him. He flipped the sun shade down and let the truck idle for a few seconds, then turned the ignition off. He leaned back with the keys in his lap and blew out a long, long breath.

The castle's front door opened and Lizzie stepped out, barefoot in bright-blue shorts and pale-green Dora tee-shirt; she peered uncertainly at the new truck. Dan opened the pickup's door and got out slowly; he'd stiffened up during the endless drive back from Knoxville. He stretched, then snatched off the ball cap he'd bought to hide his bald spot and staples and tossed it back on the seat and shut the door.

Dan squatted, winced, and then held his arms out to his daughter. "C'mere, baby."

She eyed him, hesitating, and Dan's heart clenched, but then she walked down the steps and across the driveway to him, her gaze first on his battered features and then on the truck behind him. She stopped just out of reach.

"Daddy…" Tears welled in her eyes and then spilled down those round cheeks. "Your *face*…"

Dan scooped her up and clutched her to him, and she hugged his neck as he wiped his leaky eyes carefully with a forearm. Beth was standing on the porch now, watching them.

He turned away.

"It's okay, sweet pea, they're just bruises. See?" He moved one of her small hands to his cheek; after a second she nodded tentatively. "Just bruises. The doctor said they'll go away soon, and then I'll be back to my old, ugly self."

She sniffled, and a smile peaked out, then her eyes went back to the pickup. "Is that our new truck?"

"It sure is."

"It's pretty. Can we go for a ride in it?"

"Not tonight, baby, but I promise you and I will go for a ride tomorrow, okay?"

"Can Mommy come too?"

"Mommy can come if she wants," Dan answered smoothly. He set Lizzie on her feet. "But first I have a surprise; it's in the back of the truck. I'll give you three guesses what it is."

She opened her mouth, but then a sharp bark widened her eyes as far as they would go, and the dawning understanding and wonder and joy on her face made up for everything…well, *almost* everything. Dan reached over the bed rail and pulled the pet taxi out and set it on the driveway; a short-haired, big-eared creature squirmed behind the crosshatched gate.

"Oh," Lizzie whispered.

The little dog issued another bark, whining eagerly as he stared at his new mistress. Then Lizzie's face clouded over. "But won't his hair make you sick?" She bent and peered into the taxi. "Is he a boy?"

Dan laughed and kissed the top of her head. "Yes, he's a boy." He wanted his daughter to have a dog—and for them to have a living, breathing warning system in case more of Scotty Rison's ilk popped by for a visit—but the *last* thing he wanted was a whole pack of the little bastards running around. "And check this out." He opened the Toyota's door and grabbed a small bottle out of the console and shook it; pills rattled. "Allergy medicine. This will keep me happy with all the dog hair." Dan then knelt painfully next to her and pointed at the little guy in the cage. "And besides, he's a special breed called a Chihuahua. They're from Mexico. They don't shed much, so their hair is easy for people like me to get along with. I may get the sniffles or cough a little, but we'll keep his hair vacuumed and give him baths to keep him clean. With the medicine and all those things, I'll be fine. Don't worry about me, pumpkin."

She smiled then, and Dan knew he would never forget it; it was that kind of smile.

"Okay!" She looked at her new dog. "What's his name?"

"I don't know, that's up to you to decide, sweetie. You'll have to think of a good one." Dan swung the taxi door open and their new family member bolted out and into Lizzie with tongue leading the charge. She fell over with a small shriek and mountains of giggles. It was love at first lick. Then Lizzie yelled and stood up, peering down at herself.

"Yuck! He peed on me!"

Dan laughed and petted the little guy; the big-eared dog squirmed, butt leading back and forth as he licked a hand that was longer and wider than he was. "He doesn't know us yet, baby, and we're so big to him."

Lizzie made over her new dog, who reveled in the attention, only a few sprinkles appearing on the cement before they stopped; her grin was about to split her head in half. Suddenly she raced onto the front yard.

"C'mon!" The small dog whined as he watched her, trembling with one paw in the air. Lizzie stopped and turned and patted her knees. "C'mon!" He barked and bounded toward her, and she turned and fled laughing with him in hot pursuit.

Dan stood up painfully and watched with a grin rivaling Lizzie's. The pair moved in and out of the rectangles of light cast from the living-room windows, and her legs pumped as she circled the elm saplings Beth had planted that past spring; the grass was above the dog's head in places but he plowed through gamely, looking like a big-eared Velociraptor knifing through the elephant grass in one of those terrible-but-somehow-entertaining dinosaur movies Hollywood kept churning out.

I'll never understand why those morons keep going back to those fucking islands…

Dan's wife was standing on the front porch with her arms crossed. She was watching him; not Lizzie and her new pal—*him*. He opened the truck again and pulled something else out of the console, then turned back, lit a cigarette, took a deep drag, and blew smoke at the stars. He hooked an arm over the bed rail and looked at her for the first time since he'd gotten home.

"Yo quiero Taco Bell."

She went back inside. The front door exploded shut, and he grinned around his Marlboro.

If she's pissed now, just wait 'till she gets a load of what else *I bought.*

Dan unloaded his new truck while listening to the glad sounds of his daughter laughing.

He carried everything in as Beth called Lizzie and the dog inside; by the time he finished they were in the backyard, wearing each other out under the bright floods. Beth, meanwhile, was silently and energetically cleaning the spotless kitchen.

Dan looted the stack of recyclables for some old newspapers and spread them on the living-room carpet. He put the Smith & Wesson Model 686 with the six-inch barrel on the paper next to the Mossberg 500 ZMB pump 12-gage, setting the cleaning kit, soft cloths, gun oil, and boxes of shells on the coffee table. He surveyed his workspace and decided he was missing something important and went back out to the truck and grabbed his seven-pack of Shiner Bock. It used to be a twelve. On the way back in Dan snatched his smallest cooler from the garage shelf and headed to the kitchen for ice; he eyed the gray gym bag with the bright-white Nike swoosh, the one he'd stuffed onto a shelf a few minutes before, but didn't pick it up.

It wasn't time yet.

Beth was gone from the kitchen, but the ice-maker was right where it was supposed to be so he was perfectly happy with that. He opened a beer and took a drink; cold enough. He filled the cooler with the remaining six-pack and ice and rumbled back into the living room and found her standing at the edge of the newspapers with her arms crossed again; she was looking down at what was on the newspapers with a face of granite.

Dan put the cooler on the floor and eased himself cross-legged onto the paper. He cleaned the Smith first. She watched. He had it reassembled and was reaching for the box of .357 Magnums when she spoke:

"You know I don't like guns."

He thumbed the Magnums into the cylinder one by one and then snapped it in and sighted down the barrel at the flat-screen, then slipped the Smith into its black Nylon clip-holster and set it aside and picked up his beer, finished it, and clinked the bottle on the coffee table. He then liberated a fresh soldier from the cooler. When he'd twisted the cap off and washed a cold mouthful down, Dan looked up at her.

"Yeah," he said. "Me either."

God, she was beautiful, even with that mouse under her eye. He jerked his eyeballs away and set the beer on the table and broke down the shotgun.

Beth went back into the kitchen.

Dan finished with the zombie gun and loaded it with 00 Buck, leaving the chamber empty. He set it beside the 686 and then reached into his back pocket and pulled out the little single-action, five-shot American Eagle .22 and cleaned and loaded it with .22 Magnum hollow-points. When he was done, Dan picked up his Shiner and savored it for a minute, then cleared his throat; this would be rough, but he had to give it a shot:

"Beth?"

She appeared, arms crossed, and Michelangelo would've been proud to call her face his latest masterpiece.

Dan held out the tiny pistol. "Here. This is for you."

"I knew you were hurt, Daniel. I didn't know you were deaf. I don't like guns."

"Fine."

Well, I tried. She liked knives, anyway; really, *really* liked knives. Dan wondered if all the knives in the knife block were accounted for; he wondered if he would ever stop wondering that, or if he could watch Beth dice an onion without remembering…

Probably not.

The castle spun, and he almost fell before he made it to his feet. Shit, it'd been a long day, and there was a drum-happy Zulu tribe living in his skull, but he still had things to do. Important things. He slipped the Eagle into its miniature holster and stuffed it into his back pocket and lurched toward the garage. Dan had two more presents to give his wife. She probably wouldn't like those either, but he didn't give a shit. He was going to give them to her anyway.

"Are you just going to leave these here? What about our daughter? Have you thought about her? Loaded guns in the house with a *child?*"

Dan stopped, staggered, and then turned; her face was still a sculptor's dream, but those eyes—like two dark suns about to go supernova. He wondered if she had her little black folding-knife hidden in her jeans. *Of course she does.* He glanced at the loaded guns. She was right. Shit.

He raised his beer to his lips and took a drink.

"Why you are so correct, dear. I'll take care of that right this very instant." He limped into the kitchen, giving her a wide berth; his fucking back was *killing* him. Dan counted the knives in the block as he went past; all there. Good. He jerked open the French door and poked his face out.

"Lizzie!"

The laughter and barking cut off, and then his daughter appeared at the edge of the light, her new friend panting at her heels.

"Yes, sir?"

"I need to talk to you. Come inside." It was getting late anyway. Dan peered into the dark over the fence. Anyone could be out there. Anyone at all. *Are they watching?* It wouldn't be difficult to set up with binoculars a little way off in the dark and see everything going on in the big house. They would never even know someone was out there—not until it was too late, at any rate. That reminded him of his other new toys. It would soon be time to play with them.

"Yes, sir."

Lizzie was subdued as she came in, studying his face before slipping by him. The dog trotted at her heels, and then twisted and cringed as he neared Dan, so they went through the whole petting-and-peeing ritual again; when the sprinkles stopped, he shooed the mutt inside and shut the door and turned around and found everyone staring at him; Beth with her arms crossed, Lizzie with big eyes, and Mr. Sprinkles with tongue hanging.

"First things first; your dog looks thirsty. Let's get him some water."

"Okay!"

Dan downed the rest of his Shiner and set the empty on the island with a clink and opened the cabinet and got two small plastic bowls they never used from the bottom of the bowl pile. He picked up Lizzie and helped her fill one from the faucet (the whole time wondering why the fuck there was a half-empty bottle of green mouthwash sitting by the sink) and then chose a corner of the kitchen tiles far away from the hardwood and set them down. "We'll keep his food and water here on the tile, never over there on the wood, okay?"

"Okay." She looked at the empty food bowl as the tiny dog lapped greedily. "Can we feed him a grape Popsicle?"

"No, no Popsicles. I've got a small bag of puppy food in the truck. And dogs don't like grape Popsicles." They probably did, but this one wasn't getting any. "We'll go get it in a minute, but first we've got to have a talk. C'mon." He led her into the living room.

They passed Beth on the way; arms still crossed, waiting for that sculptor.

"Hi Mommy!"

"Hi, baby."

Dan walked to the edge of the newspaper and pointed. "Do you know what these are?"

She looked at the weapons uncertainly, then said, "Guns?"

He squatted next to her and almost fell over, catching his balance with a hand on the coffee table. "Yes, these are guns." He looked deep into her eyes. "*Real* guns, baby, not pretend guns, like they have on television. Those can't hurt you 'cause they're pretend. These *can* hurt you, or me, or your Mommy, or your dog, or anybody, and they're not for little girls. Understand?" She nodded. He took her by the shoulders. "I mean it, Lizzie. These are *not for little kids*. Someday I'll teach you how to shoot them safely, but you'll have to be older, about ten or so. That's when your grandpa taught me. Until then, I don't want you to ever, ever, *ever* touch them, for any reason. Do you understand me?"

She nodded, a little frightened. That was good. "I want you to promise me. I want to hear you say it."

"I promise not to touch the guns. I promise, Daddy." A glistening tear ran down her smooth cheek.

Dan picked her up and hugged her. "It's okay, sweet pea." Maybe he'd been too gruff. "I'm sorry. I just want you to understand how dangerous guns are. They're only for grownups, not little girls. I just don't want you to get hurt, okay?" She nodded into his shoulder and he saw that their newest family member had joined them and now stood trembling at Beth's feet, watching with a dripping chin.

Dan turned away from the expression on his wife's face. "C'mon, let's go get his food." Unnamed followed them to the garage while sniffing his new surroundings six ways at once. Beth stayed where she was, arms crossed; her eyes were like two brown drill-bits boring into Dan's back.

They went out through the garage and to the Tundra and Dan set Lizzie down and grabbed the dog food out of the bed. Then he remembered Lizzie's other surprise.

"Hey." She looked up from cooing over Unnamed, who'd tumbled down the garage steps to follow them outside. "I got something else for you."

She grinned; the gap in her upper teeth was big and dark and happy. "What is it?"

Dan opened the door and reached into the plastic Walmart sack in the back seat and pulled something out with a flourish. "It's a new *Star Wars* movie!"

Her face turned into an O of surprise. "A *new Star Wars* movie?"

Dan handed her the Blu-Ray case. "Remember how Luke blows up the Death Star at the end?"

"Mmh hmmh." She flipped it over to check out the back.

"Well, remember also how Darth Vader got away?"

"Yeah." Her face crinkled; she didn't like Darth Vader.

"This is about what happens after that. It's called *The Empire Strikes Back*, and it's just about my favorite one. There's lots of cool stuff—"

"Who's *that?*" She was pointing to a screen-capture of Yoda; the swamps of Dagobah oozed in the background.

Dan told her, and she giggled. "That's a funny name. He's got ears just like—" She glanced up at her dog, who, Dan noted, had just finished pissing on his front tire. "*Yoda!*" Lizzie jumped up and down. "We'll name him Mr. Yoda!" She ran back in the house with the movie. "C'mon, Mr. Yoda!"

Dan watched the newly minted Mr. Yoda struggle up concrete steps that were taller than he was and disappear inside after Lizzie. Dan could hear her talking excitedly to Beth as he shut the truck door, and then he about fell over when he bent to pick up the dog food. *Shit.* He locked the truck with the remote, lowered the garage door, grabbed the gray Nike bag off the shelf, and gimped inside.

Everyone was in the living room so Dan went through the kitchen. He set the Nike bag on the island where Beth couldn't miss it and then counted the knives in the block; still all there. Fantabulous. He filled Yoda's bowl and then found an empty spot in the cabinets to store the dog food. He joined everyone in the living room and Lizzie cut off the patter waterfall and turned to him.

"Can we watch my new *Star Wars* movie, Daddy? Please?"

"Not tonight, baby, it's getting late. It's almost your bedtime. Tomorrow night, I promise."

"No! I don't wanna go to bed! I wanna watch my new *Star Wars* movie!"

"I said no. It's too late to watch movies. Tomorrow is soon enough." She crossed her arms in imitation of her mother, who stood watching him, eyes slashing and cutting and burning. "If I get any more lip," he warned his daughter, "you'll brush your teeth and go to bed right now. Understand me, miss?"

She scowled and pouted but then gave in. "Yes, sir."

"All right, I put food in Yoda's bowl. See if he's hungry and then go get your rabbit jammers on. You can play with him in your room until bedtime."

"It's *Mr.* Yoda, Daddy."

"Oh. Sorry. *Mr.* Yoda."

She nodded primly, satisfied, then turned and patted her knees. "C'mon, Mr. Yoda! Are you hungry!" Pat-pat. "C'mon!" He gamboled to her from where he'd been sniffing around the fireplace. Dan saw a new dark spot on the carpet over there. Great. Lizzie led the little shit into the kitchen.

Dan got another beer and took a mighty pull; when he lowered the Shiner, his wife was still staring at him. She opened her mouth, and he knew what she would say before she said it.

"We need to talk."

He took another drink and then sighed. *It sucks being right all the time.* "I guess we do."

"Are you going to do anything with these?" She freed one arm to point at the guns. "Or are you just going to leave them on the floor for your daughter to play with?"

"I'll put them up when she goes upstairs. You don't want her to know where they're kept, do you?"

"Of course not." She hesitated. "Where *are* you going to put them?"

"Why do you care?" He took another swallow of Shiner. Damn, that was good. "You don't like guns, remember?"

The look on her face made Dan glad he'd counted the knives. Beth turned and stalked back into the kitchen. He was getting another beer from the cooler when Lizzie yelled over the sounds of crunching: "He's hungry, Daddy!"

"All right, now let him eat and then go get in your pajamas."

"Okay!"

Dan sat (fell) on the couch; the Zulus had evidently brought out the sacrifice because the drums were going nuts. *Fuck me, I left the worthless Tylenol in the truck.* He didn't bother to get up for it. He was glad his daughter was happy; at least *some* good had come out of this fucked-up situation. He could hear Lizzie cooing to Mr. Yoda.

Beth's silence was thunderous.

Dan sat on his couch and drank beer.

The mutt eventually got his fill, and then it was time to go upstairs. Dan levered up painfully to watch, walking to the edge of the foyer and peeking around. Lizzie stood on the fifth or sixth step, patting her knees, trying to coax the dog; Mr. Yoda stood at the bottom with one front paw dangling in the air, trembling. He jumped onto the first step and then tried to put his front feet on the next, coming up short. That staircase had to look like Mt. Everest to Mr. Yoda, but he was still game; the little guy had stones; tiny stones, but stones nonetheless.

Dan was at the point of saying something about picking him up, but Beth beat him to it.

"You'll have to carry him, baby. I think he's tired."

Dan's wife stepped from the kitchen and moved lithely into view; barefooted, with bright-orange toenail polish she needed to touch up, she had on her favorite pair of faded jeans with the ragged holes that showed her kneecaps and an old Buckeyes tee-shirt of Dan's that hung down to mid-thigh on her and no makeup and she was drop-dead gorgeous; now that *he* was out of her sight, a smile lit her face. She scooped up Mr. Yoda, who licked her hand and wagged his tail and didn't pee a drop. Dan watched her show Lizzie how to carry him, and then his daughter climbed the steps while cradling the tiny dog like an egg. Dan watched Beth watch Lizzie and Mr. Yoda ascend, and then he turned away.

He liberated a fresh soldier, carefully wiping tears from his sore cheeks before opening it. Guns. Think about guns—where *was* he going to put the shotgun? The Smith was going everywhere *he* went, no fucking question about *that*, but he hadn't considered the Mossberg. He thought for a second and then put his beer down and picked up the 12-gauge and its box of shells and carried them to the foyer and stared at the closet behind the front door. No—too far away if he needed it fast. He wandered deeper into the house…somewhere more centrally located…

When he passed the kitchen, he saw Beth standing by the island; she was staring at the gray Nike bag, its bright-white swoosh shining under the fluorescents; pale marble had replaced her smile, and her arms were crossed beneath those breasts again. She glanced up and their eyes met and he looked away, and then Dan found it.

There was a small closet below the curve of the staircase; he opened it and found their winter coats and gloves and the snow shovel and some rubber boots he'd forgotten he owned and not much else. He went back and got the shotgun's case and zipped it in and then propped it in a dark corner, shifting the coats to hide it. He put the shells on the shelf and then closed the door.

Dan nodded. That would work.

"What if she finds it in there, Daniel? You know how she gets into everything."

If he had been any less tired, he would've leapt straight up in the fucking air and bonked his head on the goddamn chandelier; her soft voice had come from right beside his shoulder; sometimes Dan forgot how quietly she could move.

He didn't look at her, but she was right. *Shit.* He jerked open the closet door and collected the shotgun and the shells. "I'll find somewhere else."

He left the closet open as he went back through the foyer to the living room for his beer; after a few seconds, he heard her shut it. Other than that, the silence was so thick he could reach out and mold a fucking ashtray from it like he'd done in fourth-grade art class.

Dan was trying to kill that beer so he could get another one when she appeared from the kitchen side, arms crossed, staring at him. *She's fucking stalking me.* Those dark eyes bored. Shit. He downed the Shiner and then peered into the cooler—only two left. He should've picked up *two* twelve-packs. He grabbed the holstered 626 and picked up the shotgun case by its handle and carried his beer past her into the kitchen.

"You ready to have that talk now? I'll find someplace to put the shotgun later."
As he passed the Nike bag, he nodded sideways at it. "Grab that, would you?" He
opened the French doors and stepped into the night; the contrast between the
warm humidity and the conditioned air was stark. He looked back when she didn't
follow and found her standing by the island with the bag in her hand.

"Why are we going outside?" She hefted the bag, testing its weight. "And what's
in here?"

"I'll tell you out here. C'mon."

She crossed her arms again with the bag's strap still in her hand. "Why can't
we talk in *here*, Daniel? Tell me that."

Dan hesitated. From upstairs he heard Lizzie's voice and a small bark; he didn't
have a concrete reason, really, just a suspicion. Finally he shrugged; he was too
goddamn tired to argue with her.

"I need to sit down. If you want to talk, I'll be out here." He walked to their
second-hand patio furniture and put the shotgun on the cross-hatched metal table
and fell into one of the matching chairs with a sigh. A few seconds passed, and then
he heard the door shut and Beth slid gracefully into the chair opposite him…and
then she slammed the bag on the table, crossed her arms again, and glared at him.

Dan winced. There was some expensive equipment in that bag. He drank beer
as the silence pooled, and when it started to run, he turned to her.

"So," he said brightly. "What do ya wanna talk about?"

A Missing Light

BETH STARED at her husband and then looked away.

She'd seen this side of his personality a few times, but never this bad, and *never* directed towards her. Beth watched him out of the corner of her eye as he lit a cigarette; she knew he smoked sometimes when he played golf with Steve because she could smell it on him when he got home, but he knew better than to smoke around her—or at least he used to. Bugs swarmed them, and she slapped at a moth on her arm.

"Hold on." Daniel got up, staggered, and then limped inside; the lights cut off, washing the patio in darkness. He came back and sat with a pain-filled grunt.

"You should've stayed in the hospital."

The cherry on the end of his cigarette lit the eggplant bruises around his eyes like a red-orange strobe, and he tilted his head back and blew a stream of smoke at the stars before he bothered to answer.

"Yeah, well, I had things to do."

He sat and smoked, and when Beth realized he intended to just sit there and let her carry this conversation, her well of pity dried up; he was judging her, but he didn't know the whole story. Should she tell him?

The icy hand of fear gripped the base of her spine; she'd never told *anyone* her whole story.

Beth pushed the fear aside and tried to focus on what they needed to talk about right now; at that thought, she almost wanted to laugh, but held back because she was afraid it would just manifest as sobs. *Where to even start?* She had to decide nothing less than the fate of this marriage—though Daniel didn't seem to know it, or care much if he did.

Beth gathered patience with everything from teeth to toenails and opened her mouth, and then a string of barks punctuated by laughter sounded up behind Lizzie's window. They both turned and looked at the softly glowing rectangle. She smiled. Mr. Yoda. It was a good name. The smile faded as she turned back around; now, if she left, she'd have to find a place that took pets. Had Daniel thought of that? Maybe, maybe not…and how could he have made such a big decision without even *mentioning* it to her, let alone discussing it?

Beth tamped her anger down; it would just get in the way. And that truck! She knew where he'd gotten the money for *that!* No. She would be calm, in control; that did remind her of some minor questions she had to go along with all the important ones.

Might as well start small; avalanches start small. She'd read that somewhere. "What kind of Chihuahua is Mr. Yoda? He's so small. Is he a teacup?"

"No, he's just the runt. There's no such thing as a teacup Chihuahua."

"There's not?"

Her husband grunted. "Trust me." He reached out past the edge of the patio and flicked ashes onto the grass. Beth scowled but kept her peace. *Calm.* "I made the mistake of asking the breeder the same thing and got a ten-minute lecture on Chihuahua's." He sat up straight and assumed a pedantic tone. "Mr. Yoda is a short-haired, deer-headed Chihuahua with a hypoallergenic fawn coat that is perfect for people who suffer from allergic reactions to dog dander." He blew more smoke and flicked more ashes and then slouched back in the chair. "The little shit wasn't fucking cheap, either."

"Well, that's good, I guess." He looked at her. "I mean about your allergies." A little dog was also much less expensive than a big one, not to mention the cleaning-up-after-it factor. She said as much, and he snorted.

"There's a reason I didn't bring home a fucking St. Bernard, you know. And I'm not sure it matters how 'hypoallergenic' he is. I've interacted with some dogs over the years and didn't get sick, and others that set me off, and the ones that did were mostly outside dogs. I'm not even sure I'm allergic to dog dander. I may just be reacting to the stuff caught in their fur, you know, pollen or whatever. I think Mom just told us I was allergic so she wouldn't have to take care of two boys, my dad, *and* a dog; she never did have me tested." His laugh was low and bitter; he flicked more ashes. "Yeah," he said. "That sounds like Mom."

"Oh," Beth said, watching him out of the corner of her eye. He hardly ever talked about his parents, especially his mother; she was beginning to understand why. "Has Mr. Yoda had his shots?"

"Some. I'll make an appointment tomorrow to get him updated." He leaned back and stretched with a small groan. "Is *this* what you wanted to talk about? The goddamn dog?"

Beth gripped the arms of her chair. *Calm!* "We had visitors today."

"Yeah? I had one this morning, in the hospital."

She waited for him to continue but he just sat there, so she told him about hers. She didn't mention how he'd left her here to face them alone; she didn't bring up how furious she was with him. Beth let him draw his own conclusions.

"Son of a bitch," he breathed, staring at her in shock.

"The police didn't find any drugs in this house, Daniel, so why would they say that? What are we going to do? Should we hire a lawyer?" Not that they could afford one, but they might not have a choice; she would *not* let her daughter be taken from her, not for *any* reason. She'd said exactly that to that skinny blonde bitch today. "Those two had the good-cop-bad-cop routine down pat. The man was nice; Lizzie even took him upstairs to show him her horsies. The woman, well, not so much."

That might be the understatement of the century. Ms. Jenifer Hayden's attitude had rubbed up against Beth's temper like flint against the knife, nearly sparking a conflagration. Ms. Hayden, Rutherford County Child Services' Senior Case Worker and Bureaucrat from Hell, seemed to harbor a personal enmity towards Beth, even though they'd never met before today; stalking around the castle while making snide comments about its size and their taste in furniture; scratching ominous little notes on that form on her clipboard—even flat-out asking where they hid the drugs!

"Beth? Earth to Beth, come in Beth."

She stopped kneading her temples with an effort and folded her hands in her lap. "I'm sorry, what?"

"I saaaiiid, what grounds do you think they'd have to take her away? You dealt with the system growing up, so…" He cleared his throat. "I mean, what can they *do*, really? We haven't been charged with anything; she's happy, clean, well fed. She's not abused, and the house isn't nasty. They can interview all our friends and coworkers and the people at Lizzie's daycare, and they can search the house and drug test us all they want and they're not gonna find dick. So what *can* they do? Nothing, is what I think. Fuck them."

"I don't really know," Beth answered slowly. "That was different: foster kids in foster homes…even when they took me away from my adopted parents, it was different." A silence you could knead filled the table between them. She breathed deep and pressed on. "I just don't know, Daniel. They've heard things in the news, I guess, or maybe some well-meaning busybody called social services. They would have to investigate under those circumstances."

He grunted and sat up and put one hand on the Nike bag. "If they come back, we'll hire some smart, nasty lawyer and run them off. Right now we've got other stuff to worry about." He patted the bag. "There're a couple of things I want to show you and one thing I want to give you, but first I need to tell you about an interesting chat I had today. It may clear a few things up." He paused, and then his laugh came, wild and grim in the dark. "Or maybe not."

Beth listened, and by the time he'd finished so many protests and questions had piled up behind her teeth they'd bunched like horses tangled at the starting gate; eventually, something spluttered out. "A *warning?* That doesn't make any *sense*, Daniel! Why would the police send us a warning by lying to the media about us?"

"You heard me. Rison was distantly related to Sheriff Jacobson, the Sheriff of Rutherford County, not to mention this District Attorney General muckety-muck whose name I can't remember."

"So what does that matter? *Rison attacked us!*"

"I know that, dearest, but evidently we live in the South now, and clan and family come first—or so says Special Agent Scandlin."

"You're missing my point, *dearest*. What is the 'warning' about? Is it a warning to *do* something or *not* do something? To *say* something? *Not* say something?" Beth snorted and crossed her arms under her breasts. "This is ridiculous."

He scowled and took another drag before answering. "I don't know. I tried to ask, but Scandlin decided he was done fielding my questions and asked if Rison had bragged about killing any other women besides that one he put in the lake, and then he asked me if I knew anything about old man McFarlane, just like I told you. Then he gave me his card and vamoosed, saying we needed to talk more, but not there."

"He didn't want to talk at the hospital? Why? Who did he think would hear, the nurses?" Beth's eyes narrowed as a dark suspicion solidified into black certainty; she glanced at the house glowing at their backs and then leaned over the table and lowered her voice. "Tell me why we're talking outside, Daniel."

He just looked at her, and then he unzipped the bag and pulled out a small, square plastic something about the size of her hand and set it on the table; it had a darkened LCD screen and some buttons and dials.

"Because I think the castle's bugged, that's why." He tapped the gadget. "This is an EM meter; it picks up electronic frequencies. One of the things you can do with it is find hidden listening devices. I found it on E-Bay and drove to some guy's house fifty miles east of Nashville to pick it up, which was okay because I was heading over to Knoxville to meet the man who had the guns for sale in any case." Beth groaned and dropped her face into her hands, but her idiot husband didn't seem to notice—or at least he pretended he didn't. "I'll sweep the house top to bottom with it tomorrow, see what I can find."

Face still buried in her palms, Beth tried to control her sudden fear. *I didn't even consider this possibility.* The shock of being attacked, of seeing what...what he'd seen, along with the head trauma and concussion...not to mention some stupid cop showing up and reinforcing the paranoia...

Beth lifted her face out of her hands and gathered herself. She had to talk him down from this madness; the situation was bad enough with a husband whose marbles were still cinched in the bag.

"Daniel..." She searched for the right words.

He read her tone perfectly. "Goddamnit, Beth, I'm not crazy!" He surged to his feet, leaning over the table. "Think about it!" He glanced warily at the house and sat down again. "Think about it," he whispered, and then ticked off points on his free hand, cigarette tracing glowing lines in the dark. "I did some calling around today. Know what I found out? This house sat empty for over a year before we bought it; anyone could've been in there doing God knows what. Believe me, it happens."

"Daniel..."

"You *know* he didn't do this by himself. Remember the phone call? And the handwriting? You think that was *his* fucking handwriting? And let's not forget the pictures! How the hell did he even know there *were* pictures?" He leaned closer and spoke so softly that she could barely hear: "*They*, Beth? Remember *they?*" He leaned back. "Then there's what Scandlin told me." He took a fierce drag and blew it out. "And if the house isn't bugged, tell me how all that stuff about us got on those fucking pages you burned, Beth. Explain it to me."

"We never talked about any of that."

"Yeah, I'm aware." Beth could see him scowling over the fence as he smoked. "But there's got to be some goddamn explanation for how it all got on those pieces of paper. I'll scan for bugs, and if I don't find any at least I can move on from there with a little peace of mind." His sudden laugh was bleak. "About *that*, anyhow."

He was looking for an explanation, and Beth already had the answer: "Daniel, Rison was on drugs." He opened his mouth, but she rode right over him; she'd been thinking about this for two days, and she knew she was right. "And when you're spun out, you believe and say things you think are true, are *real*, but they're not. Trust me, I know." She sniffed. "And old Mr. McFarlane? Are you *listening* to yourself? So what if Rison worked for him? He's just a farmer."

Scott Rison strung out on drugs was the only explanation that made sense to Beth; and when you combined drugs with being a psychopath…no wonder Rison had sounded crazy. Still, she couldn't explain the phone call, or the pictures…and why *would* someone care if they took pictures of a stupid, ugly rock? But what really bothered her was the information on those pieces of paper, forget the handwriting. Rison must have researched them on the Internet. But her past wasn't in any database—or at least she hadn't thought it was.

No, it didn't matter how he found out: Rison was dead, and Beth had to deal with the fact her husband knew a twisted version of her history.

That's all that matters now.

Daniel wasn't giving up. "It still doesn't add up, Beth. He turned around to follow me after I went to the cemetery that first time, on Saturday morning. He was talking on a cell phone, saw me, and then drove off and turned around and came back."

"Daniel…" She had to be careful here. "I know what he said about 'they', and about the cemetery, but that had to be the drugs talking. I mean, do you really think he attacked us because we went to some stupid cemetery? *Really?*"

He hesitated, but when he spoke his voice was as firm as she'd ever heard it. "I know what it sounds like, but that doesn't change the fact that some things aren't right about this, Beth—a whole fucking *lot* of things."

"You think I don't know that? You saw what I had to do to save us. You don't think that bothers me?" Beth suppressed the urge to spit.

"That's not all." He cast a furtive glance at the castle and lowered his voice again. "I've been doing a lot of thinking about that cemetery, and not just what Rison said. Remember those gravestones, and how they were missing everything but names and dates?"

"Of course I remember, but what does—"

"I finally realized what else they were missing." He waited, watching her across the table.

Beth sighed at the theatrics, and then bit. "What?"

"Crosses."

She stared at her husband, and then slowly dropped her face into her hands again.

It's worse than I thought.

He said, "What?" She didn't reply. "Don't you think it's strange we didn't see a single cross on that entire hill?"

"Daniel—"

"Have you *ever* seen a cemetery that didn't have a single cross? *I* sure as fuck haven't."

Beth's temper frayed, but she gathered the threads and held on tight. "How many gravestones did we look at Daniel? Seven or eight? There has to be a hundred we didn't, maybe more. One of them has to have a cross; in fact, there are probably *dozens* of crosses scattered under those bushes."

"Oh come the fuck on, Beth! You saw that place! You can't tell me you actually think there are any crosses in a cemetery like that!"

"Don't you *dare* take that tone with—"

"And I saw how you reacted! You can't *stand* it out there—and now you can't sit there and tell me you don't think there's something wrong with that place!"

"Okay, *fine*, I didn't like it! So what? *It's just a cemetery!* It doesn't matter if I like it or not!"

He shot an uneasy look toward the house. "Shh, don't yell."

"I'll yell if I *want* to yell, because *there's nobody listening!* And *crosses?* Seriously? Can you *hear* yourself? Do you know what you *sound* like? You're scaring me, Daniel."

"Beth—"

"So I didn't like it, and so it's *weird,* and so there are no crosses within ten stinking *miles* of the place? *SO WHAT!?* Where exactly are you going with this?"

"Rison said—"

"*I don't care what Rison said!* He was on drugs or deranged or both, and now he's *dead!*" Beth squeezed her eyelids closed and breathed deep until she found calm again. Daniel didn't say anything—for once. She opened her eyes and looked at her husband across the little round table and spoke calmly. "It's just a cemetery, Daniel."

"Beth—"

"*It's just a stupid cemetery!*" Calm. "It's just a cemetery, and I don't want to hear another word about it. We have more important things to talk about. *Real* issues."

They glared at each other for a minute, breathing hard, and then he turned away and lit another cigarette. "Fine," he growled. And then his voice deepened, and he finished in a tone that, unfortunately, she knew all too well. "I don't care what you believe. There's something hinky about that place, and I *will* find out what it is—and why."

Beth rubbed her temples again; she had a splitting headache, and it was sitting across the table from her, smoking. She also fought the urge to stand up and kick him in the side of his moronic head. What she needed to do was divert him from this insanity somehow, and Beth thought she saw a way:

"He followed me, too," she said.

"*What?*" He lurched around in the chair. "Who, Rison?"

"Yes."

"When?"

"Saturday, after lunch, when we were on our way back from the yard sales. Lizzie was asleep. He was in a white truck. He and his buddy showed up at Slo Eddie's that night as well. They wanted to talk to me, but I thought it was just—"

"WHAT? *What* buddy?"

"Let me finish! There was a guy with him at the restaurant. I didn't get any names." She paused, frowned: "I told all this to the cops Sunday, don't you remember?" Even as she said it, though, Beth recalled they had transported him to the hospital by then; she'd refused to go and had been stitched up right here at the castle.

I was probably a little dazed myself by that point.

"No," he said, sullen.

"I think that's who called him during…anyway, I told Special Agent Scarborough about the buddy, and about how Rison had been playing with a new smart phone in the booth at Slo Eddie's but he'd been using that cheap disposable when he took that call in our room. He said they would try to trace the number, but I don't know if they had any luck; whoever they were, they were probably using a disposable, too. Scarborough said it would be a long shot."

"Goddamn bastards," he breathed. "Scandlin was right! They know all about this asshole and the phone call, but they won't do shit about it! They've closed the case already! *Fuck!*" He stood up and paced, lighting another cigarette and waving his arms around as he yelled; he seemed to have forgotten all about someone supposedly bugging them. "Don't you see? This proves my point! There's something—!"

"No, it proves *my* point!" Beth was on her feet now, too. "Don't *you* see? Rison was stalking us! Both of us! *Just like he said he did!*"

He stopped and stared at her. Beth sat back down and composed herself. "He was stalking us, Daniel—and yes, maybe he had help, but this crazy talk about 'they', and a cemetery, and now this paranoid cop showing up—!" Calm, centered, serene; she was getting a lot of breathing practice tonight; Sensei would be happy. "A psychopath targeted us, a rapist who watched us and found out all about us somehow—using the Internet, probably—and then he attacked us in our own home. But it doesn't matter."

"It doesn't *matter?*"

"It doesn't matter because it's *over.*" Deep breath. "Rison was going to do unspeakable things to me—to us—but I stopped him. *I* saved us, Daniel, and now it's over." Beth could feel his glower, but she pressed on; if the truth hurt his feelings, so be it. He still needed to hear it. "All this other stuff, bugs in the house and the stupid cemetery with no crosses…I think you're just compensating now because you were helpless then."

Beth winced. His glare was a palpable thing as a charged silence filled the backyard. She searched for something to say, something mollifying, anything, but before she could find it there was a rap at the glass. They both turned.

Lizzie stood behind the French doors, the new puppy at her side; she had her hands behind her back, hiding something. She'd put her rabbit jammers on, and a hesitant smile shined out at them, eyes flicking between her parents. Mr. Yoda barked.

"Come on out, baby." Daniel snuffed his cigarette on the concrete, waved the smoke away—as if *that* would help—and then sat down.

Lizzie wrestled one-handed with the door until she put what she was hiding down on the floor to tackle the knob with two; it was one of her books, Beth saw. The door swung open, and Lizzie retrieved her book and stepped out, again with that cautious smile. The book was *Yertle the Turtle*, Dr. Seuss's allegory about Hitler and Nazi Germany. Lizzie didn't know that, of course, but it was her favorite. Beth did, and it was her favorite as well.

And then Mr. Yoda started barking and growling as if he'd never seen the adults before. Beth frowned at him; *little turd.*

Lizzie said, "Be quiet, Mr. Yoda. That's just my Mommy and Daddy." With a blurring wag and an adoring look, Mr. Yoda did as he was told.

Despite everything, Beth smiled; the dog had already picked up on who was truly in charge around here.

Then Lizzie made a face. "He pooped in my room," she said. "It's gross."

Daniel laughed. "It's all right, pumpkin. I'll come up in a few minutes and we'll clean it up. And tomorrow we'll start teaching him to go outside."

"Okay."

Beth eyed *Yertle.* "You want to read a story, baby?"

Lizzie looked at her. "Yes." She looked at Daniel. "Daddy, can we read *Yertle the Turtle?*"

A shocking flash of jealousy washed through Beth—and was that *satisfaction* on his face? Beth looked back at Lizzie, trying to keep her voice smooth. "Your Daddy and I need to talk for a while longer, sweetheart. Go back up to your room. He'll be up when we're done." Surely she didn't feel jealous of her husband's relationship with their daughter.

What's wrong with me?

Lizzie hesitated, looking at Daniel.

"Do as your mother says. I'll be up in a few minutes."

"Yes, sir." She eyed them both before shutting the door and continued to watch them as she walked out of the kitchen. Beth's heart ached at that tentative expression; Lizzie wasn't gathering flies, despite the fact they could talk. Mr. Yoda followed without a backward glance.

Silence settled between them as a bevy of crickets creaked and peeped on the other side of the fence; he lit another cigarette. Beth massaged her temples and tried to order her thoughts. *And to think I'd planned on bringing up Lizzie's dream!* She'd wanted to know whether Daniel thought their daughter really had dreamed of Rison's attack before it happened. Beth had been obsessing about Lizzie's "bad man" dream off and on for two days, but considering her husband's current mental state, there was no *way* she was broaching the subject now. He'd apparently forgotten about it anyway, and no telling how he would react if reminded.

Besides (as he would say), it was just a stupid fucking dream.

It has to be a coincidence. Beth ignored the uneasy feeling in her gut as she pushed Lizzie's probable precognizant dream aside; she had *real* issues to deal with. Beth had to make her stubborn idiot of a husband see reason, but how?

Then he reached into the bag again and set something bulky on her side of the table. "I got these for us, too."

She picked whatever it was up. "What are they?"

"A pair of night-vision goggles, Army surplus." He chuckled. "I think a few of those boys coming back from the desert have been making some off-the-books requisitions; they were a helluva lot cheaper than I thought they'd be."

Beth almost threw them back down. "And why on *earth* do we need night-vision goggles?"

"Because it'll be hard to see without them when we sneak back into that cemetery at night. I'm sure as hell not going in waving a flashlight around."

Calm. SERENE! "And why would we be dumb enough to do such an idiotic thing?"

He flicked ashes in the grass. "You heard me. There's something going on out there, and even if I'm just *compensating*, I'm going to find out what the fuck it is. Someone was spying on us Sunday afternoon, so this time the plan is to go in at night."

Beth stared at her husband; this was way worse than she'd thought. Calm. "I will not be a part of your…" She'd almost said madness: "fantasy, Daniel. If you want to traipse around the woods at night and stare at graves, you can go by yourself."

"That's perfectly all right by me, beloved."

"Good."

He picked up his stupid night-vision goggles—night-vision goggles!—and bug detector, but didn't put them back in the Nike bag. Instead, he shoved the bag across the table at her. "Here's your present."

Present? She held up the bag; it was still heavy, even with all the ridiculous crap already taken out. "What's in here?"

"Open it and find out. I need to email these pictures." With that, he picked up the big holstered revolver and the shotgun and his beer and carried everything inside.

"Email the pictures? To who?" She threw the bag back on the patio table and got up to follow him.

"Don't forget your present," he said, then put the guns and his other useless crap on the kitchen island and sat down at their computer, jiggling the mouse to wake it up. Beth tried to glare a hole through the back of his head, and when that didn't work she grabbed the bag and stamped inside and slammed the French door so hard the glass rattled. She threw the bag on the island next to his stupid toys and crossed her arms under her breasts, trapping her hands in her armpits; she did it for his safety.

"Daniel, tell me what you think you're doing."

He was attaching his phone to a USB cord he'd plugged into their desktop tower. "I looked up the name of a professor over at MTSU today, the guy who teaches Arabic. I want to see if he can translate that gibberish on the stone. It looked like Arabic to me, but if he can't help, I'll find someone who can."

"What good is *that* going to do? What does it *MATTER?*"

"Aren't you going to open your present?"

Beth snatched the bag and unzipped it and stuck her hand inside, not knowing what to expect: her eyes widened, and she pulled her hand out and unzipped it further and looked inside. Stacks and stacks of cash; most of the bills had a picture of Benjamin Franklin.

Daniel had swiveled around in the chair to watch.

"It's yours."

She shoved it across the island. "I don't want it. Gambling money. *Football* money. You won it, so you do what you want with it."

"I am. I'm giving it to you."

"I'm not touching money you won betting on football." The pain of that betrayal was still fresh even though it'd been pushed aside in the face of so many other issues. "You promised me you'd stop, Daniel. How long have you been lying?"

A guilty expression flickered beneath the bruises, but then he sneered at her. Sneered! He spun back around to face the monitor.

When he spoke, it was a gut-punch:

"Yeah, well, I guess I'm not *perfect,* like you."

Except for his fingers clacking on the keyboard and the click of the mouse, silence filled the castle.

And there it is.

"We need to talk about this."

"Did I miss something? Haven't we been enjoying a lovely conversation?" He leaned closer to the screen, muttered something, then began clicking and dragging the mouse.

"You know what I'm talking about!"

He kept his back to her. "Yeah, I know what you're talking about, and I don't want to fucking talk about it. What's the point? I killed my parents, and I used to deal drugs, but I don't anymore, and you're not a…" Deathly silence. Then, softly: "We're not who we were, Beth. We're different people now. We're Lizzie's parents. We're a family. The past doesn't mean shit, right? Isn't that what you're going to say?" Her husband swiveled to look at her then, and she flinched. When she didn't respond, he swung back around.

Beth gathered her courage and spoke; it was the hardest thing she'd ever done. "You don't know what really happened, no one does, but I want to tell you so you—"

Daniel whipped back around violently. "I DON'T WANT TO FUCKING KNOW, BETH! *I don't want to know!*" He glared at her with those awful eyes: empty eyes, when they used to be so full; the agony spread from Beth's heart and filled her. He turned back to the computer, his tired words somehow worse than the shouting. "I just want to forget the past and keep moving forward, okay? Is that too much to ask?"

Silence except for mouse clicks.

And then the tears came because now Beth knew the answer to her question: It was no.

Things would never be the same between them. She'd known it the moment he'd turned and looked at her, because the light in his eyes was missing.

Beth remembered the day she'd first seen that light. It was a sunny Sunday afternoon at the restaurant-league softball game. He'd kept looking at her, even when that blonde bit of bartender fluff he'd shown up with got jealous and spread her glares around; that light had never faded over the years, even when he was mad or frustrated with her. Other men looked at Beth, sure, but none had ever looked like her Daniel.

That light said she was on a shelf above the others. That light said she was special.

That light was gone.

The pain of what she'd lost wracked her, and she sobbed; through a blur of tears she saw his back stiffen, but he didn't turn around.

He receded from her. Neither had moved; Beth still stood ten feet behind him, but she now viewed him across a chasm that made the Grand Canyon look like a drainage ditch.

Can I live without that light, live with him in this house, pretending everything is the same?
Beth knew the answer.

She gathered herself to say the words that had floated in her heart, words she'd dreaded and tried to ignore for two days—words that would change everything— when the titanium bridge that still spanned the abyss stepped into the kitchen, carrying her dog.

Lizzie took one look at Beth and her little face scrunched and she began crying.

Beth wiped her face and went over and scooped them up. Mr. Yoda trembled, picking up on the emotions swirling through his new family; a small tongue rasped Beth's cheek. She felt the hard corners of Lizzie's Dr. Seuss book, and then she understood: Lizzie had heard them and snuck downstairs and lurked and listened. The computer chair creaked as Daniel got up and came to stand beside them. One shared glance, and Beth knew he also understood.

Beth said, "Shh, it's okay, baby. It's okay."

"Here, sweet pea, let me take Mr. Yoda. He's getting squished." Her husband's knuckles brushed her breasts, and it was the first time they'd touched in over two days. Daniel put Mr. Yoda on the floor.

Lizzie raised her face from Beth's damp shoulder. "Mommy, are you mad at Daddy?"

Beth decided that she'd had enough of lying to her daughter. "Yes, a little, but it's all right, we're just having an argument. You know grownups argue sometimes, right?" Lizzie nodded uncertainly.

"That's right, just a little argument, no big deal, pumpkin." Daniel eyed the thin green book pressed against Beth's chest. "You still wanna read *Yertle?*"

Lizzie rubbed her eyes with a small fist and then nodded and held out her arms. Beth let her go, moving out of the way as they came together. Lizzie's head went to her father's shoulder. He started to leave the kitchen, then stopped next to the fridge and turned to look at her—or rather, somewhere over her head.

"I sent the pictures, and what's in that bag is still yours."

"I don't want it, Daniel. I'm not touching it."

"Okay then, I guess we'll make little green airplanes out of it and fly them around the backyard."

"Fine."

"Fine."

He turned toward the stairs and Beth followed, standing at the edge of the foyer and watching; as he put his foot on the bottom step, he spoke to the air again: "By the way, the locksmith and the alarm guys are coming tomorrow. I'll be mowing, so let them in and—"

"I'm taking Lizzie to daycare tomorrow. She needs a break, and I have things to do."

He stopped, waiting for her to elaborate, but that's all she had to say for now. Lizzie's eyes peeked at Beth over his shoulder.

Locksmith? Alarm?

He hadn't even bothered to *consult* her!

Beth kept her face smooth with an effort; those eyes.

"Do what you have to do," he finally said—coldly—and continued to the top. "After I read her the story, I'm hitting the sack. It's been a long day."

"Where will you sleep?"

He stopped dead and then turned and looked at their bedroom door. His silence confirmed what she already knew; he hadn't given one single thought to the state of their bedroom. Beth expected to be angry—she'd worried about it for two days!—but now she just felt a leaden nothing.

"Shit."

"You said a bad word, Daddy."

"Sorry, pumpkin." Beth's husband turned and looked down at her. "I didn't think about…I mean…" He closed his eyes and swayed, gripping the banister with his free hand; he looked so beat-up and worn-out and plain pathetic that despite everything, Beth felt a flash of compassion—a *small* one. "I'll clean it tomorrow," he said. "After I mow the yard. And after the locksmith and the alarm guys leave. You don't have to go in there." He opened his eyes and looked at her, then; *really* looked at her, maybe for the first time since he'd gotten home. "I'll take care of it."

"Well, *one* of us will have to go in there tonight and get our clothes, and our toiletries. The clothes I sent with Steve came out of the laundry room, and I had to practically beg Special Agent Scarborough to let me in the castle long enough to get them."

He sighed. "I'll do it after *Yertle*. I don't want you in there."

That was all well and good, but he still wasn't thinking everything through. "What about the mattress? It's ruined."

He glanced at the closed door again, the memory of what had happened behind it stark in his eyes. "I guess you're right," he said. Then he flashed her his most infuriating smile! "Maybe, since you don't want it, we'll use some of the money to get a new one."

"We'll see. Go read her the story. And I'll sleep with Lizzie tonight. I'll get you the sleeping bag from the garage, and you can sleep…wherever."

His face hardened again. "That's fine with me."

"Good."

They disappeared upstairs. Beth squeezed her eyes shut and turned the plain gold band on the ring finger of her left hand around and around; it had suddenly become a hot lead weight dragging at her finger. She heard a conversation begin above:

"What's wrong with your room, Daddy? Is Mommy going to sleep with me?"

"Yes she is, and our room, ah, got something broke in it, and, uh, something spilled. We'll have to clean it before we can sleep in there again."

"Oh."

"Let's read that story. Daddy's tired."

"Are you mad at Mommy?"

"Yes, a little, but that's okay because grownups argue sometimes. C'mon, let's read your book. I've got a lot to do tomorrow."

Beth crept up the risers about midway to the top and then sat facing the kitchen, twisting her wedding ring faster and faster.

"You can sleep in here with us if you want."

"I don't think that would be a good idea, kiddo."

"Why not?"

"It's complicated…tell ya what." Beth heard a thump. "I'll put my sleeping bag down in the room right on the other side of this wall, so we'll be real close to each other. Okay?"

"Okay." Beth could tell Lizzie still didn't understand but was accepting the situation.

She turned the hot gold ring faster.

They loved each other so much.

How can I ever split them apart?

"C'mere, pumpkin, let's read—"

"Daddy, do you still love Mommy?"

Silence.

Beth's heart clenched; she stopped twisting her ring and waited.

And then Daniel's voice, so soft that she could barely make it out: "Yes, baby, I still love your Mommy. Very much. We're just arguing right now. And we both love *you* very much, too. Okay?"

Beth cried and rocked on the step, chest hugged to her knees. Mr. Yoda sat on the hardwood at the bottom of the stairs, watching her; he cocked his head and whined.

"Okay!"

Beth smiled through her tears; she could hear the happy grin in Lizzie's voice.

Daniel said, "All right, let's—whoa!"

"Don't sit there, Daddy, that's the poop."

"I see that. Here, go get a wad of toilet paper and we'll pick it up and flush it."

"Okay. Daddy?"

"What?"

"Can we take Mr. Yoda over to Ms. Helen's tomorrow to play with Pickle? I think they'd like each other."

"Not tomorrow, but we will soon."

"When?"

"Soon, Lizzie. Go get the toilet paper, a big wad. That's a lot of poop for such a little guy."

Lizzie giggled. Beth heard another question, but got up and crept downstairs before she could hear his answer, or the story of how a plain turtle named Mack who wanted to be free brought the mighty King Yertle down. She'd gotten what she needed.

Mr. Yoda stood up and wagged his tail when she reached the bottom. "Bad dog," Beth told him, smiling. His stub tail blurred, namesake ears perked.

So. He still loved her. That was good. That was very, *very* good, but it didn't change the fact Beth was still furious with him.

He wants to forget the past, to pretend everything is a-okay, and just go on?

In other words, he *loved* her, but he didn't want to know *about* her?

No. It wasn't going to work like that. Beth had spent her whole adult life fighting to get over what had happened to her when she was a teenager, to be a different person, and then to forget it—which was why she'd never told him. But now that it was finally out, she wanted him to know the truth, not that half-truth garbage Rison had spouted.

And as for the missing light, Beth would make it come back, or she would leave. She refused to live without it. She couldn't.

But for now, she needed leverage to move the stubborn idiot boulder of a man she'd married. Beth tapped her lips, thinking, and then smiled grimly as she headed out to the garage to get him the sleeping bag. Mr. Yoda padded at her heels.

Tonight, when her daughter was sound asleep and her husband was slumbering in the spare bedroom, she would get up and quietly fetch her and Lizzie's suitcases from the upstairs hall closet and get them packed and ready.

You WILL listen, Daniel Terrance Sims.

Beth flung open the door and stepped down into the garage.

You will listen to me or else.

HOPE

Professor Aarif Hameed leaned forward and squinted at the picture filling the monitor, then leaned back and removed his glasses and opened the bottom left-hand drawer of his desk and took out the cleaning spray and the special soft cloth and carefully wiped the lenses. He put everything back and ran the drawer shut with a bang and placed the wire rims on his thin nose and hooked the earpieces behind his ears and leaned forward and studied the photograph again.

Motion drew his attention to the hallway; two pretty coeds strolled by, full backpacks slung over shoulders. They glanced through the open door at him and then continued chattering their way down the hall.

Aarif jerked his gaze away from the heart-shaped bottom of the one on the right. He was twice her age, for Allah's sake, and married besides—at least for now. He took his glasses off again and put them on his desk and rubbed his face with both hands.

Aleena.

What am I going to do about Aleena?

His cell vibrated on his desk; he'd forgotten to turn it up after his eight o'clock. He replaced his glasses and picked it up hoping that it was his wife and that she was calling to apologize for this morning, but it wasn't Aleena. Aleena didn't call him while she was working, and Aleena didn't apologize. Not anymore.

Aarif's eyes narrowed when he saw the face on the screen. It was Chad. He glanced at the photo on his monitor, then let the call go to voicemail; as he suspected it would, the phone immediately vibrated in his hand again, his friend demanding to be answered.

Aarif nodded to himself and set the phone back on the desk and let it buzz.

I get it.

The mysterious email was yet another practical joke by his unlikely friend, Chadwick Dean Hottson, Professor of Mathematics Extraordinaire—or Professor Hot, as he was known to hordes of female undergrads (and to more than a few of their colleagues). Chad's golden-blonde hair and green eyes assured the nickname, not to mention the many hours the man spent in the gym obsessively perfecting his body. Aarif looked at the improbable photograph filling his monitor and shook his head in grudging admiration.

Professor Hot strikes again.

His phone buzzed a third time. Aarif ignored it as he shrank the first pic and then opened the rest, saving them to his hard drive absently as he lined them up.

There were eight total; four close-up shots of each side of what appeared to be a strange, twisted megalith, the other four seemingly of the same side, but at a distance to include the whole length. Aarif judged the stone at least twenty feet tall; it had a slightly lopsided, somewhat bulbous, and almost phallic tip. All in all, he thought it was the most unpleasant example of a standing stone he'd ever seen.

And the shape wasn't the only culprit. The four close-ups showed the lith to be composed of an odd, multicolored stone, but through some trick of the light the mineral appeared jet black in the four pictures taken from only a few feet away. The photo quality was poor, obviously taken by a layperson with a cell phone, so perhaps that explained the discrepancy.

Every photo included multitudes of tangled white roses in the background, of all things, and in one, a small woman in a gray tee-shirt and black shorts and white and pink tennis shoes with no socks—*a teenager?*—knelt beyond the twisted megalith, hands on her thighs as she looked at something out of the frame. She had dark hair pulled into a ponytail, and a large white bloom obscured her face.

But those things were unimportant. What fascinated Aarif were the minute sunken-relief etchings that covered every centimeter of the unsightly lith.

He leaned closer, almost smudging the screen with his nose.

Aarif had never seen anything like them.

Or have I?

He pawed through desk drawers until he found his magnifying glass; better, but the glass couldn't improve photo quality. He leaned back, considering. He had Photoshop at home; he could put the files on a stick, and…he chuckled and put the glass down. Professor Hot had roped him in; even so, Aarif's eyes were drawn to the characters once more, and he frowned.

If this is a prank, it's a cut above his usual.

He could admit (now) that the last gag had been funny. The man had managed to palm Aarif's car keys from his office and then return them, stopping by twice on some pretext that Aarif couldn't remember, but the end result had been his total ignorance of anything wrong until he tried to leave on the last day of classes before spring break, only to find a white poster-board staked on the swath of grass beside his parking spot. The sign was as wide as a football player's shoulders and just as tall, and proclaimed in big-block maroon letters, with a huge red arrow pointing toward his Camry: RIDES TO STUDENT UNION AND DORMS $1; below that in smaller print: ALL OTHER SERVICES NEGOTIABLE.

There were laughing students posing for cell-phone pictures in front of the sign, and in front of his car, which had the blow-up doll sitting in the driver's seat, inflated hands gripping the steering wheel, her mass of flaming red hair shining in the sun and wide blue eyes staring out the windshield, mouth a permanent O of surprise. It had made the front page of *Sidelines*, MTSU's student-run newspaper, with the caption "Hope you had a great Spring Break!"

The phone vibrated again; Chad again. Aarif picked the glass up and raised it to study a photograph again. Those symbols tickled the back of his brain, but the language was indecipherable; he was no epigrapher. Aarif was interested in modern Arabic and how to bridge the gap between the myriad dialects so understanding could bloom; after September eleventh, he had been energized by a new purpose: teaching Arabic to his fellow Americans had seemed the best way to dispel the fog of hate and fear that had roiled his country like a thunder cloud.

Such a youthful fool I was.

Despite his best efforts—and thousands of moderate Shia Muslims like him—that hate-cloud had only hardened into something more deadly than any storm.

He leaned closer. Not an epigrapher, he decided; judging by how weathered (and therefore ancient) that standing stone appeared, it would take a paleographer to decipher the symbols. Aarif was neither. He spent his days teaching Modern Standard Arabic to college kids who couldn't tell the difference between Shia and Sunni Muslims and couldn't care less, let alone bridge any gap of understanding. Most had signed up for Arabic because they were bored by the Spanish and French they'd already learned in high school. Over half dropped out when they realized it would be no cakewalk; there were exceptions, of course, and Aarif was grateful—those exceptions and their enthusiasm for his beautiful language kept him going, especially lately.

He blinked and scowled and leaned away again. *I'm being sucked in.* He put the magnifying glass down firmly and grabbed the mouse and closed the pics and the email from this supposed Dan Sims; a nice touch, that. He checked the time: 9:46. Aarif wanted to fine-tune his review lecture for his two o'clock; the few hardy remaining souls would need all the help they could get. The final was Friday, in two days, and Aarif was sure that half of them wouldn't pass, not without him practically giving it away. That he would not do, but he would help them as much as he could.

Instead of working, however, Aarif rocked back in his chair and laced his fingers behind his head, his struggling summer-semester Introduction to Arabic students the furthest thing from his troubled mind.

Aleena.

What in Allah's holy name was he going to do about his wife?

Theirs was an arranged marriage, a fact that still shocked most Americans, particularly the ones from here. He was as American as any of them, of course, although quite a few didn't see it that way; Aarif was second generation off the boat, his parents having been born shortly after his grandparents emigrated from Syria. Aleena's parents came from Egypt carrying her in the womb. Their families belonged to a loose enclave of Shia Muslims in the San Francisco Bay Area that had clung to the old ways almost desperately in the face of the overwhelming tide of American culture—thus the arranged marriage. Aarif had been opposed to it at first, stridently so, but after one look at Aleena, he had changed his mind.

He leaned back further, chair creaking, and sighed in remembrance. She had been so beautiful, and they so young. She had needed more convincing that him. Aarif knew he wasn't much to look at, never had been, but he hadn't let that deter him in the wooing of Aleena. His efforts had paid off, and they'd been married a month after high school graduation. He'd completed his undergraduate studies at Cal-Berkley, and then his masters and doctorate at Washington State. Aarif's chest tightened; those years at WSU had been the best. With no family and friends nearby, they'd grown close, their minds moving as one during the day and their bodies entwined at night.

If only we could go back there, in time as well as physicality.

Motion in the quiet hallway turned his head, but it was gone in a squeak of sneakers before he could get a good look. Finals Week at the end of the summer semester meant the Fine Arts building stayed nearly deserted.

And now here he and Aleena were, in the middle of Tennessee. Aarif sighed again. Four years ago, taking this job had seemed the right thing to do, but Aleena had been opposed; she hadn't wanted to be so far from their families. Their parents and surviving grandparents hadn't been fond of the idea either, but Aarif, as man of the house, had put his foot down.

Oh, how he regretted it now.

That first year, she had begged him to reconsider; surely he could find a position closer to where they knew the lay of the land. She didn't like this foreign country called Tennessee where people stared if she wore the hijab and the disgusting custom of preparing and eating pork was an esteemed art form.

If only I had listened!

Now their positions were reversed; Aleena had settled in, finding friends and satisfaction in her new job at that boutique. Aarif scowled. *I should've never allowed her to take that job.* That place was at the root of all their problems. She concerned herself with western fashion now and wore more makeup than he'd ever seen; when he went to visit, her coworkers whispered to each other and hid painted smiles behind their hands.

What is she telling them?

Surely nothing intimate; she was too much of a good Muslim woman to do such a thing. Women gossiped, that was all.

Things had been bad lately, true, but this morning had been an unmitigated disaster. Their fight had made him late for his lecture. How had things gone so wrong? It had been three months—three months!—since she had shared herself with him, always with the excuse of being tired or not feeling well. The frustration had built until last night when he had demanded that she do her duty to her husband. She had put him off until the morning, and then had lain under him like a board, looking up at him almost contemptuously! Aarif had pulled out of her and stood up, furious, and began yelling, thus starting the worst fight of their union.

Is she having an affair?

No. No, Aleena would not do that to him; she was a good Muslim woman, and would not violate the sanctity of their marriage before God. Still, the days of them laughing and moaning and exploring each other's bodies seemed far away.

Was she having an affair?

Knuckles rapped, and Aarif jerked upright and composed himself as Chad filled the open doorway, blond hair gleaming under the fluorescents. His green eyes immediately went to the phone sitting flat on Aarif's desk.

"Reef, are you screening my calls?"

It was a good act, but Aarif wasn't fooled. "I was busy." He would not mention the email and photos. *I won't be taken* this *time.*

His friend looked at the empty desk meaningfully. "Yeah, I can see that." Chad then considered him for all of two seconds and said, "Aleena again?"

Am I that transparent? Aarif grimaced, nodded. "Aleena again."

Chad, unfortunately, knew the whole situation. Aarif had allowed himself to consume alcohol—him, a Muslim, drinking alcohol!—and the incident had turned into a drunken, crying confession; those frozen raspberry margaritas had been sinfully good. He was a poor Muslim, no question. When had been the last time they'd gone to the mosque? Months, he knew, but they had some excuse there—neither he nor Aleena liked the new Imam. But when had been the last time he'd performed his ablutions and rak'as and offered Salat to the Prophet?

Days upon days—almost a week!

Aarif sighed yet again. He was a poor Muslim indeed.

Chad came in and sat on the edge of the desk. "Cheer up, Reefer Man; we are going to totally *hit it* tomorrow morning." Then he frowned. "We *are* still on for tomorrow, right? Tee-time is for nine sharp." He hiked his thumb at the phone. "That's what I was calling about, to make sure you're not going to wuss out on me again."

"We're still on," Aarif reassured him. Golf. Who would've thought Aarif would ever play golf? His ancestors were surely laughing (or perhaps crying), but chasing the little white ball had become a passion as well as a release; everything fell away when he was on the course: Aleena, bills, apathetic students, dead-end careers; everything but that little white ball.

Aarif eyed Chad and then waved a hand at the desk phone on the other side of the monitor. "Why didn't you call my office, moron? You didn't have to walk." The mathematics building was all the way across campus.

His friend grinned. "I wanted to walk. The view's good today."

Aarif looked a question at him though he suspected the answer.

"A bunch of fall pledges are out wandering around early." That grin deepened.

Professor Hot would never change. "How's Melissa?" Aarif asked pointedly.

The grin vanished. "Bloated and bitchy, thanks for asking."

It was Aarif's turn to grin. Chad's wife Melissa, a beautiful and patient woman (she had to be both for Chad) was seven months pregnant with their first child, a boy. The pregnancy had not been an easy one, for either of the Hottson's.

Chad said, "Hey, *most* of them are legal. Besides, if a man can't at least look, he might as well hang it up and start bowling."

Aarif stilled his tongue with an effort. Professor Hot had done more than look; after his drunken confession, Chad had admitted in reciprocal confidence that he'd cheated on Melissa with a "smoking hot" graduate student and one or two or three striking undergrads. Aarif didn't want to judge, but it had disappointed him that the rumors concerning his friend's extracurricular activities had turned out to be more than rumor.

Aarif also didn't understand; he looked, yes, but when it came right down to it, he wanted no woman but Aleena.

Aleena. What was he to do about Aleena?

Aarif noticed Chad watching him, and he attempted to gather himself again, but his friend wasn't fooled. "She's got you bad this morning, huh?" He patted Aarif on the shoulder before slipping off the desk and heading for the hall. "Don't let her in your head, man. Women are good at that: take them too seriously, and the game's over before it starts." Chad's voice echoed as he disappeared into the hallway. "See you at nine, Reef. Don't be late!"

Aarif narrowed his eyes; if he spoke, he might play right into the man's hands. Before he could get the words back, however, he had shouted out the door:

"You're not fooling me!"

Silence, and then his friend was filling the doorway once more, golden hair gleaming; his handsome face was cautious.

"What?"

"The email and the photographs; I don't know where you got them, but I'm not fooled, not this time."

Chad's face was a study; a bemused smile quickly replaced a flash of relief. He said, "I told you not to hit that crack pipe before work, Reef. Bad for the ol' career. What the hell are you talking about?"

Relieved? Why relieved? "The email and pics—original, I must admit, but I'm not buying."

"No comprende, Reef. You'll need to translate."

Aarif gave in, snatching the mouse and opening the mail and pictures again. He turned the monitor. "This, you dick. I'm onto the game, but where'd you get them? They're very…interesting." Fascinating was more like it, but he wasn't about to admit it.

"What are you…?" Chad read and then reached out to grab the mouse. "Scoot over, man. What *is* this?" Aarif obliged, and Chad moved behind the desk. Aarif rolled his chair a little further away; the man's cologne was all-consuming. Chad studied the pics and said, "You think *I* sent these?" He stood up with a dismissive wave at the monitor. "That's impossible. Someone's having fun with you, but it isn't me. What language is that, Arabic?"

"No," Aarif answered slowly. "I don't know what it is." Only a small lie, but he would not share his suspicions until he'd done some research. "You had nothing to do with this?"

A grin popped up like the rising sun. "Got you good with that last one, didn't I? You're all jumpy now." Chad laughed and then shrugged. "It wasn't me, but someone is messing with you, because that's impossible."

"You said that already, but what do you mean? It's right there."

Chad's expression said Aarif was a particularly slow student. He pointed at the monitor. "What does that look like to you? Study it closely, then tell me."

Aarif considered the photos; two were open, the close-up with the woman or teenager kneeling in the background and one from a distance. He said, "It appears to be a particularly unsightly megalith comprising some indeterminate stone covered with intricate, sunken-relief carvings standing in an overrun rose garden somewhere. So what's impossible about it?"

Chad grabbed the mouse and opened all four close-up photos and rowed them up sequentially. "There. What do you see now?"

"A big, rune-covered rock in an overgrown flower garden; again, not impossible." Chad's attitude was grating on his already thin nerves.

"Don't look at the *symbols*—look at the pattern the symbols *form*." Chad traced a tan index finger near the screen. "See this major sequence? See how it replicates itself here? Here also? Then wrapping around the upper part of the stone here?" Professor Hot straightened and spread his hands wide as if revealing the finale to a magic trick. "It's a fractal."

That word tickled something, but when he only stared, Chad snatched up Aarif's iPhone and presented it. "Remember our talk about the antenna in these? You're the one who asked *me* about them, genius."

It dawned, then. Last year Aleena and Aarif had watched a PBS special on fractals—well, Aarif had suffered through a few minutes worth, long enough to learn that engineers had used computer fractal generation to develop the antennae in cell phones to improve signal reception so they could all walk around with little computers capable of transmitting and receiving huge amounts of data; without those enhanced antenna, they'd still be stuck with only voice transmission. He'd also learned that fractals were represented all over the place in nature: veins in leaves, snowflakes, sea shells, who knew (or cared) where else. Aarif had made the mistake of asking Chad about it two days later at the driving range.

"So it's a fractal," he said. "So what?" He pointed at his phone. "You said they're everywhere."

"All right, you asked for it."

Aarif groaned. "Keep it short."

"Short. The man wants fractals short." Chad scratched his jaw, and then suddenly jabbed his scratching finger at the monitor. "How old do you think that thing is?"

"The lith?" Aarif stared at the photos. "It will take radiocarbon dating to tell for sure, but…old. *Very* old."

"The term 'Fractal' wasn't even coined until the mid-seventies," Chad said. Aarif got a glimmer of where this was going, but let his friend lecture: "In fact, it's been about three hundred years since fractals were even discovered, and lots of equations and theories later, here we are in the twenty-first century. And because of CGI we can *see* these babies now, not just theoretically calculate them." Chad's features had taken on a cast of excitement; Aarif watched him with a tiny smile, reminded that behind that handsome mug was a facile mind, even if only for something as tedious as math. "I've worked some of these and believe me they're a bitch without a computer. See what I'm saying? We couldn't do something like that *thirty years ago*. How do you think they managed it *thousands* of years ago? Some guy sat down with his bronze hammer and chisel and chipped out something that mathematically precise? I don't think so."

"It's a hoax."

"Has to be. Somebody's messing with you, man."

Reminded of his earlier suspicions, Aarif shot Chad a dark look. Professor Hot raised his bronzed hands palm-out. "Wasn't me, Reef. Not my style. You know that."

Aarif nodded, conceding the point. But who? Why? What was to gain by sending him this twaddle?

"Call the guy."

"What?"

"He put his number in the email. Call him. By the way, do you recognize that thing?"

"What, the stone?" Aarif's mind was busy spinning around an elusive yet astounding idea; it flashed and dimmed, as if lit by lightning from a distant storm, but it was definitely there.

"No, the rose bush, dip-shit. Yes, the monolith. Do you recognize it? Something like that would make a splash if it was just discovered, right?"

"No, I don't recognize it, and yes, if it were suddenly found, I think I'd hear about it."

"I thought so. *I* haven't heard of it, and I think I would." Aarif's minuscule office went silent for a minute as they both thought, and then Chad snapped his fingers. "This guy said he took these while he was on vacation with his family, right? Where were they?"

Aarif scrolled through the short email. "Doesn't say."

"Call him."

Aarif gave in, and as he dialed he realized it was a local area code and prefix. What this pertained he didn't know. He watched Chad as ringing filled his ear; he was half expecting a matching ring to come from his friend's pocket, but the call went to a generic voice mail. Aarif hung up without leaving a message.

"No answer."

His cell buzzed. He looked at the number, and then up at Chad.

"It's him."

"Well, answer it."

Aarif jabbed the button. "Hello?"

A man's suspicious voice said, "Yeah, I just got a call from this number?"

"Is this Dan Sims?"

"Who's asking? Who is this?"

Aarif exchanged another look with Chad, who was leaning over the desk to hear. "This is Professor Aarif Hameed at Middle Tennessee State University, Mr. Sims. You sent me an email with—"

"Hey, yeah, Professor, thanks for calling me. Can you translate that? Is it Arabic? What's it say?"

Another look at Chad, and then Aarif cleared his throat: "Mr. Sims, I have questions—"

The shrill klaxon of an alarm blared, and Aarif held the phone away from his ear; he thought he heard the man curse, and then the noise stopped.

"Hello?"

"Hello? Sorry about that. I've got guys here doing some work…hold on a sec." Aarif heard a muffled conversation; a dog was also barking furiously in the background. Chad waved to get Aarif's attention.

"Put it on speaker."

Aarif did and put the phone on the desk. Chad leaned away, thankfully taking his cologne with him. Dan Sims came back, voice filling Aarif's office with an electronic rasp.

"Let me step outside." The noise of a barking dog swelled; it sounded like a small breed. "Can you translate that writing, Professor?"

"I—"

"*Shut up, Mr. Yoda!*" The dog went silent. "Sorry, what were you saying?"

Aarif and Chad exchanged yet another look. "Mr. Sims, in the email you stated that you took those photos while on vacation. May I ask where that was?"

"Look, Professor, where I took them isn't important. Can you translate that mumbo-jumbo or not?"

Aarif frowned. "Mr. Sims, may I remind you that *you* contacted *me* for help?" Silence. "Now, before I help you, we have a few reasonable questions." Silence. "May we ask our questions, Mr. Sims?"

"We?"

"Yes, ah, there's a colleague here with me who's interested in the photos as well. We were wondering—"

"Who is he? Another Arabic professor?"

Chad shot Aarif a look that said he was an idiot. "Mr. Sims? My name is Dr. Chadwick Hottson. I'm a professor of mathematics here at the university. Dr. Hameed brought this to my attention because, well, what is shown in those photographs is, for lack of a better word, extraordinary."

"A *math teacher?* Why would a math teacher care about this?"

"Do you know what a fractal is, Mr. Sims?"

"A fractal? No. Should I?"

Chad launched into his lecture, and Dan Sims lasted about as long as Aarif would have—in other words, not very.

"Yeah, yeah, okay: snowflakes, lightning bolts, fern leaves, great, whatever." A deep line appeared between Chad's golden eyebrows, and Aarif smiled. "Look, guys, does anybody besides you two know about this? Shit, I should've thought of this."

Chad and Aarif exchanged another look. "What does—?"

"Just answer the question, doc. It's important that this stays between us three, and *why* it's important, I'm not really up to explaining." There was a pause. "Look, if you can't agree to keep this between us, then I'm hanging up. Maybe I should send the photos to someone else."

"No! We agree! We agree, Mr. Sims. It stays between us."

"I don't hear the math teacher saying anything."

Aarif rolled his hand, urging Chad; the lightning was flashing closer, illuminating his idea. He could *not* lose this opportunity! Chad shot Aarif a grimace, but then acquiesced.

"All right." Dan Sims' own reluctance was clear. "I didn't find it on vacation; I lied about that. I found it on a bike ride last Saturday morning. It's sitting in the middle of a cemetery that's about five miles from my house."

The silence in Aarif's office was deafening. Chad, who'd been leaning over the phone with his fists planted on the desk, abruptly stood up and moved away.

"And where do you live, Mr. Sims?"

"I live just inside the city limits of a little shit hole called Centerville. Are you at the MTSU campus, Professor?"

"Yes."

"Centerville is a little over twenty-one miles southeast of Murfreesboro—which means, doc, that right now you're sitting about twenty-five miles from that ugly rock in the photos."

Aarif glanced up to find Chad standing on the far side of the tiny office with his arms crossed and a disgusted look on his face; his friend cut his eyes to the phone and freed one hand long enough to make a slashing motion across his throat.

A volatile mix of hope and disappointment swirled through Aarif. What Dan Sims suggested was plainly impossible; something like this would've been well-documented long ago.

But if it *was* true?

He had to proceed with the utmost caution. "Mr. Sims, if this is a joke, we—"

"It's not a joke, Professor. The thing is right where I say it is."

Hope surged. "Then we need to—"

"Let me guess. You want to look at it. Am I right?"

"Well, yes. Verification is—"

"That's not a good idea, doc."

It was said softly, all traces of amusement gone. Professor Hot rolled his eyes; Dan Sims' reluctance to provide proof had only cemented his suspicions.

"Why isn't it a good idea, Mr. Sims?"

"Okay, doc, put-up-or-shut-up time: can you translate that language or not?"

"Yes," Aarif answered quickly, not sure of that at all. "I just need to do some research and then I'll—"

"Is it Arabic?"

Aarif hesitated. "No, but I believe it's an ancient precursor to the family of languages that Arabic evolved from." He wasn't completely sure of that either, but he wanted Dan Sims to believe that Aarif could provide what he was seeking; his beautiful idea was glowing now, glowing from the lightning striking all around it. "It's difficult to tell in the photos," he continued glibly. "If I could get a closer look, perhaps I could decipher it." He waited, trying to think of other arguments for a physical examination.

Dan Sims sighed. "Fine. But I still think this is a bad idea. It's on private property, and…and other reasons."

Chad jumped on that. "If it's on private property, how did you discover it? Trespassing is illegal, Mr. Sims. And a *cemetery?* This is preposterous. And who is that woman in one of the photos?"

Aarif considered standing up and hitting Chad with his chair.

He'll ruin everything!

Dan Sims said, "Are you still there, Math Boy? Don't you have snot-nosed teenagers to teach algebra equations to? That woman is my wife; as to the rest, I'm speaking to Professor Hameed."

"That's *Doctor* Math Boy to you, and I think this whole thing is—!"

"Professor Hameed?"

Aarif glared at Chad and motioned him to be quiet. "Yes, Mr. Sims. Sorry about that." Chad threw up his hands and stalked back across the office.

There was silence. Aarif held his breath. Finally the man spoke:

"All right, doc, I'll give you my address. Like I said, the cemetery is only about five miles from here. Got a pen?"

The lightning struck home. Hope glowed. "Yes, just a second…go ahead."

Dan Sims gave his address and directions to this Barron Cemetery. Aarif stared at the notepad. So close. *This just has to be true.*

"It's on a hill in a valley, smack dab in the middle of some woods; Barron Woods, as a matter of fact. I found that out yesterday while doing a little research of my own. You'll be able to drive right up to it." A man spoke in the background. "Hold on." Bits and pieces of a conversation about high-security deadbolt locks drifted over the line. Aarif's hope shined so brightly it hurt to even consider, let alone look at.

This has to work.

He glanced at Chad, expecting more anger or derision, but his friend stood gaping at the phone.

Aarif's smile slid away.

"What?"

Chad jabbed his whole arm at the phone. "That's the guy!"

"What guy?"

"Centerville! The people who got attacked! The home invasion! That's the guy!" At Aarif's blank look, Chad shook his head. "It was on the news. That's *him!*"

"You know I don't watch the news."

"Hello? Professor Hameed?"

"I'm here, Mr. Sims."

"When are you planning to head this way?"

"Well, I have a two o'clock class, but then I thought—"

"After two o'clock is fine. I have to go, doc, the locksmith's here, but first I want your word on something. Two something, actually."

His word? "I'm listening."

"Promise me that as soon as you know what that rock says, you'll let me know. You think you'll know something by tonight? I need to know what it says. It's important."

Aarif hesitated. "Probably not tonight, Mr. Sims…um, say late tomorrow afternoon?" Aarif wasn't even sure he could deliver by then, but he had to give the man something.

Important? Why was it so important?

"That's fine, I guess. And I want your cell number, just in case. That way I can call if I don't hear from you."

"All right." Aarif reluctantly recited it.

"Okay, good. Now, there's something else I want you to promise me, Professor."

"And what is that?"

"That you'll get in and get out. Look at that thing and get what you need, whatever that is, and then get the fuck *out.* For God's sake, don't hang around out there. It's not a good place."

Aarif's eyebrows drew together. *Not a good place?* Was Dan Sims trying the scare him? Doubt began the dim the hope.

What was this man's game?

He seemed to sense the confusion in Aarif's silence. "Look, doc, I know it sounds crazy, but humor me. Help me feel better about this. Just promise, okay?"

"I promise I won't, um, linger, Mr. Sims. I'll authenticate the find and leave."

"All right, I gotta go. Remember, tomorrow afternoon, you promised."

"Yes, Mr. Sims. I keep my word."

"Good. Oh, and don't go by yourself. Take Math Boy if you have to. Even he would be better than nothing. I think." The line went dead.

Aarif stared at the silent phone. Not a good place? What in Allah's name was *that* supposed to mean? He looked at Chad, expecting to see anger at the parting "math boy" shot and all the rest, but his friend stood staring through Aarif's wall.

"That *was* him. What does it mean?"

"Him *who?* Do you know this guy?"

Chad blinked and came back. "No, I don't know him. It's the guy from the… you *have* to start watching the news, Reef." He jumped behind the desk and grabbed the mouse, and Aarif rolled away before the cologne funk could envelop him. Chad opened the web browser and clicked and clicked. Then: "Here. Read."

"You could just tell me."

"Read. It'll be faster."

Two minutes later Aarif looked up, eyes wide.

"Holy shit."

"Yeah, holy shit."

"You think this has anything to do with what he sent me?"

"It *has* to be connected." Chad spread his hands at Aarif's expression. "Think about it logically, Reef; this guy and his wife were attacked by a psychopath and they barely escaped. Now he contacts you with this—whatever *this* is. They're connected, have to be, we're just missing part of the equation." Aarif nodded, conceding the logic. "But it doesn't matter," Chad continued, and Aarif glanced at him, hearing the excitement.

"So you're going with me?"

"Hell yeah, I'm going with you. Try to stop me."

They grinned at each other like boys, and for the first time Aarif considered what a find like this would do for Professor Hot's career. It had to be similar to what it would do for Aarif's.

If this was legit.

If.

As if reading his thoughts, Chad held up his hands in a hold-it gesture. "But first—"

"We need to go look."

"Right. We need to look at it."

They stared at each other.

"Shit!" Chad paced Aarif's office, covering the tiny space in two abbreviated strides.

"What?"

"Melissa and I are supposed to go to dinner with Jenifer and Thomas; we're meeting them at Russo's."

"Can't you get out of it?" Aarif had his two o'clock and then he was free; he'd planned to be at this Barron Cemetery by three-thirty, four at the latest.

"No." Chad resumed pacing. "I, uh, I had to work late last night, and I missed dinner with Missy and her parents. If I skate tonight, I'll never get out of the doghouse. Jenifer's throwing Melissa's shower next week, and we're finalizing the plans tonight. I *have* to be there."

Aarif nodded but said nothing; he'd missed dinner with his wife also, but not by his choice. She'd texted that she was going out with friends from work, and she hadn't gotten home until very late; that insult had led to his demand she fulfill her duty, which had led to the disaster of this morning.

Chad stopped pacing and snapped his fingers. "I know! I'll go to dinner and then beg off early; I'll come up with some excuse. Then I'll meet you back here. We'll probably get out there about seven-thirty or so. That all right with you?"

Aarif reluctantly agreed. He could make inquiries while he waited; and missing dinner with Aleena again would be no problem. He would text he was going out with friends. *It'll serve her right.* Aarif tried to feel satisfaction at turning the tables, but he knew she would have no problem with missing *him.*

Chad must've read his face; he slapped Aarif on the back before heading toward the door. "Hang in there, Reef. I'm late to meet Smithson." He paused in the doorway and looked back. "Call me if you find anything."

"I will."

Aarif understood. If he found something about this strange megalith, they might as well save their gas; in truth, he expected to be disappointed in the next ten minutes. Surely a thing like this had been documented log ago. Nevertheless, Aarif clung to his glowing hope.

If this is real, and we're the ones that discover it...

"See ya, Reef."

"See ya."

Aarif listened to Chad recede down the hall and hit the stairwell; his fingers hovered over the keyboard. He closed his eyes and reviewed his plan.

It was simple: he needed to get Aleena back to their mothers.

Both matriarchs had never given up trying to get them to move back, but quitting this job to hunt for another was no plan, times in academia being what they were. But with his name attached to this discovery, he could pick and choose where he taught, even if—when, not if—others more qualified took over the project...yes, he could see it. Aleena would be back in the traditional fold of their families. There would be no need for her to work. She would be away from that awful boutique. Aarif should have never let her take that job. Perhaps he could convince her to open her own boutique in San Francisco.

Perhaps they would even talk about children again.

Hope burned in Aarif's heart, but he did not fully embrace it. Not yet. There was work to do first—and, of course, he needed to see the stone; more, he needed to *touch* it, to make sure it was real.

After all, it was the rock on which his hope was based.

Aarif took his glasses off and wiped a tear from the corner of his eye; for all its brightness, it was a slim hope, but for Aleena he would grasp at any hope at all.

For Aleena, he would do anything.

The world came back into focus as Aarif slid his glasses onto his nose. He seized the mouse and started clicking.

A Change in Plans

Beth finally escaped Miss Mary's Little Lamb Childcare and forced herself to walk-not-run to her car. She paused and searched up and down the busy street, then scanned the surrounding businesses and their parking lots; no sign of the bearded man in the dark-green Accord.

She climbed behind the wheel and slammed the door.

This is stupid.

Why would someone follow her? She was becoming as paranoid as Daniel.

Beth took a few seconds to compose herself; that had been worse than she expected. As soon as they'd stepped through Miss Mary's front door, every adult face in the building had turned, making Beth feel like the only fish in the tank. It got worse after she gave Lizzie a hug and watched her run to her friends, because then the adults had swooped in, faces and voices sympathetic, eyes alive with curiosity; even the daycare's normally reticent Mexican cook had waddled out of her kitchenette to stare.

Beth had dodged all the delicate-yet-probing questions and had bobbed her head in agreement when presented with such inane banalities as They-Were-Lucky-To-Be-Alive; she didn't need strangers telling her that, but this morning they seemed compelled to do so anyway. That's about when she had mumbled some excuse and fled, leaving a stony Miss Mary at the head of a gaggle of equally offended women.

Beth sucked in a deep, deep breath, then blew it out; she needed to clear her head. She started the car and pointed it toward the USA Drug down the street; her next stop would be the dojo. A dose of honest sweat would do her a world of good.

After the drugstore, it took fifteen minutes to make her way across Murfreesboro in midmorning traffic; Beth kept a sharp eye out for the green Accord but didn't spot it. When they'd pulled into Slo Eddie's earlier that morning, Beth had seen the green car behind them turn into the Starbucks next door and hadn't thought a thing about it—but when they'd left, she'd watched the same Honda pull out and get behind her again, this time two cars back. The man driving it had curly reddish-brown hair and a cropped beard of the same rusty color and wore rectangular prescription glasses. He'd made all the turns and followed them right to the daycare, but when they'd pulled in he'd driven past without looking at them.

Beth shook her head while checking her mirrors once again; still no green Accord. She couldn't *believe* she'd let her husband's paranoia infect her.

She parked at the end of the dilapidated strip mall that housed the dojo and retrieved her bag from the back seat and got out of the car and slammed the door and locked it with the fob. Beth also couldn't believe her brainless husband planned to go back to that idiotic cemetery at night. He'd even bought night-vision goggles.

Night-vision goggles!

It's just a cemetery!

No, she was done thinking about her idiot husband. Beth would not let him ruin her day off; she hadn't *planned* on a day off, granted, but killing Scott Rison had given her one, and however she'd earned it, she was going to make the most of it. She unlocked the dojo with her key and went inside.

Takamatsu Sensei was in Osaka visiting his surviving brother and two sisters; he went every summer for a month, and would be gone for another two weeks. Sensei had entrusted her with the honor of teaching while he was away, and she had been taking three hours off each Tuesday and Thursday evening to do so, getting the other managers to cover in return for closing. She'd missed Tuesday, but under the circumstances her students had understood. Beth refused to miss tomorrow.

Sensei had called her early Monday; she didn't know if one of the other students had called him, or if he'd been keeping up with local news on the Internet, but when she'd answered the international call, she'd known exactly who it was. Beth had been afraid he would take her duty away in the mistaken belief she needed to recover from the assault, so she'd been both surprised and relieved when he had listened to an abbreviated (very abbreviated) account of Sunday afternoon and then simply told her to keep up her training and make sure the others did too. Beth had hung up with a smile, grateful that at least one person wasn't treating her differently. She should've expected as much from her unflappable teacher.

Beth dressed in her white gi and black belt and bowed her way onto the tatami and began her warm-ups; she would have to be careful of her shoulder, but not too careful. That's why she'd hit the drugstore on the way. She also could have called in one or two of the advanced students who didn't work days to come train with her, but Beth wanted to be alone today.

A sweaty two hours later, she bowed toward the Shomen and re-hung her wooden practice weapons in the wall racks and then bowed off the mat and went into the unisex restroom; she was the only female student at present, and the bathroom was her dressing room. As she cleaned the crusted blood from the reopened cut on her shoulder and examined two of the torn stitches, she decided that the peace of mind the workout had brought her had been worth the trouble. The cut would heal ragged now, but what was one more scar? What bothered Beth the most was the blood on her white gi. She would just have to pre-soak it and bleach it and then hope for the best.

She slathered Neosporin on the cut and then bandaged and wrapped her shoulder carefully to preserve her range of motion, then toweled off and put on deodorant and got dressed. While she did, a long list of thoughts she'd successfully suppressed while training shoved themselves back into her brain despite her wishes.

And at the tiptop of that list was her idiot husband: Daniel and his unhealthy fixation on that bizarre cemetery, and his stubborn refusal to talk about her past—

and that stupid cop! Showing up at the hospital, filling Daniel's head with nonsense! Old Mr. McFarlane? Really? The *farmer*? Please. As if they didn't have enough crap to worry about. Still, Scott Rison had worked for McFarlane…the more Beth thought about that, the more she didn't like it. No, McFarlane was just some fat-cat cattle farmer; he couldn't control what his hired hands did on their own time.

And then there was work! Her temper heated as she remembered how everyone had acted when she and Lizzie had walked in the door this morning. Beth had put up with it for about thirty seconds, and then she'd stuck Lizzie in a Pit booth with a lemonade and a pack of crayons and a kid's coloring menu and gathered everyone in the back of the house by her office and let them all have it.

No one would look at her or speak to her when she left though Lizzie had cutely waved and told everyone bye. That was okay by Beth, though, because her employees understood the situation perfectly now.

Nothing would be different because of Scott Rison.

Unfortunately, Beth had also had the dubious pleasure of meeting Terrance, her new MIT from the Atlanta store; he'd been transferred in to fill the void left by Mark's firing and now her two-week "convalescence". Supposedly. Terrance was a tall, thin black man about her age. She'd heard he was the best stick at the Atlanta Slo Eddie's, and she looked forward to getting him on the Pit table and finding out just how good he was. Terrance didn't blink when she informed him that she would *not* take two weeks off, which meant he'd already talked to Clint. Beth and her boss had argued about that Monday, and she'd won; she didn't need two weeks off, or want them. She would be back to work Friday night—and taking even that much time didn't please her. She'd tried to argue against sending Terrance at all, but Clint had already paid for the hotel.

The other, unspoken reasons Beth suspected Terrance had been sent from Atlanta ramped her temper toward Def-Con 5.

No. No thinking on her day off. Beth had gotten her training in, and now she was going to the bookstore. Hanging out at the bookstore and perusing the shelves was one of her favorite activities, and she couldn't even remember the last time she'd had the chance to do it.

So, that was the plan for the rest of the day: go haunt her favorite indie, buy a few titles she'd wanted forever from her much-loved authors, and then pick up the Lizmonster and head home and deal with her mule-stubborn idiot of a husband.

No thinking necessary.

Killing Scott Rison had given Beth the day off, and she intended to enjoy it, damn it.

She locked the dojo and walked to her car and climbed in, and when she turned around to put her bag in the back seat, she saw him.

Beth froze for the smallest second and then turned back around and started the car and pulled her phone out of her purse and lowered her face like she was texting.

The old shopping center had two other tenants besides the dojo, a coin laundry and a Subway; the rest of the spaces were at present For Lease. The dark-green Accord sat around the corner, on the far side of the coin laundry. Curly Beard was inside the car, pretending not to watch her as she pretended not to watch him; he was positioned so he could see her car and stay mostly out of sight, and if she hadn't had her antenna up, Beth would've missed him.

Fury *boiled.*

I'm being followed!

Who was he? What did he want?

Beth forced herself to calm down, and an idea formed; she permitted herself a nasty smirk that only her phone witnessed. Yes, it would work, and she would only have to make minor adjustments to her hard-earned day-off plans. She chunked her phone back into her purse and backed out and drove out of the shopping center's lot.

Beth watched the mirror as Curly followed while staying a discrete three cars back.

Her wicked smile twitched higher.

This will be fun.

Dan was standing on the castle's front porch playing with the remote to the new alarm system and trying to decide on the new code—nothing trite, like their anniversary or Lizzie's birthday—when his phone rang again.

"Fuck."

They were answering their phones today, and Dan had already turned down four interview requests. He'd also fielded more calls on his listings than he'd had in months; fruits of his new alleged celebrity. He'd referred the people who had wanted showings today or Thursday to Steve and scheduled three showings for Friday, the day he and Beth had decided to go back to work. Two of those had sounded suspicious, and he figured some sneaky smart reporters had winkled out how to use his job to set up ambush interviews; but even if they had, Dan suspected they wouldn't broadcast or print any of those interviews because of FCC regulations.

In fact, I'll make fucking sure of it.

Those numbers he hadn't recognized, but the face now popping up on the screen hit him like a kidney punch. How long since they'd talked? Dan had called to tell them about the move and give them the castle's address early last December, and then the obligatory holiday calls and cards, but nothing since.

Shit. He almost let it go to voicemail, but steeled his nerve and answered.

"Hello?"

"Hey, little brother."

"Hey big bro, how's it hangin'?"

Heavy silence. Dan had kept his tone flip on purpose and could tell he'd already annoyed William. He'd always had a talent for that.

"Saw what happened on the news," Will said. "Donna and I hadn't heard from you, so I called to make sure you guys were all right. Happy belated birthday, by the by."

There were so many undertones in all of that Dan couldn't even begin to sort them out. "Thanks. Yeah, it's been hectic around here. I was going to call you guys when things settled down." Dan hit himself in the forehead with the heel of his free hand, forgetting he held the remote, clunking the plastic off his thick skull. He rubbed the new sore spot absently. He hadn't even thought *once* about calling Will. What did that say about their bond as brothers? William was Lizzie's godfather, for Christ's sake! "Sorry, man."

"Yeah, no problem."

More silence, and then they both tried to talk at once. They cut off and Dan said, "Go ahead, bro."

"I was just sayin'...*Jesus*, little brother! What a fucked-up deal. Beth actually *killed* that guy? Is Lizzie okay? Did she...?"

"She's good. She wasn't here when...when it happened; she doesn't know anything. And yeah, Beth killed the bastard." Dan banished the image of his wife's naked body bathed in crimson, her face a mask of rage, knife flashing...well, pushed it aside. *I'll probably be sitting in a fucking wheelchair when I'm ninety thinking about it.*

Dead space filled the line. Dan could hear his brother breathing.

Will, like everyone else, wanted details.

He would not get them.

"All right, little brother, I guess you're busy. Just wanted to make sure you guys were okay. I'll let you—"

"Hey, Will, sorry man. It's been crazy around here, you know? I should've called and let you guys know we were okay. I'm glad you called to check on us. I appreciate it."

"Yeah, no problem, Danny." Dan flinched; it'd been a long time since someone called him Danny; last time he'd talked to Will, in fact. At least his brother sounded mollified now.

Dan said, "How's Donna and...and..." Shit! His only niece and nephew! "How's Tiff and Casey?" He wanted to smack himself in the head with the remote again.

"They're great. I'll tell them their uncle Danny says hi."

"Look, man, I'm sorry. I—"

"Forget it, little brother. I've got a bunch of work to do. You take care of those girls, okay?"

Dan sighed; he really was an idiot—just like Beth had called him this morning. "I will. And thanks for checking on us. I mean it, man. We should've called."

"No problem. You, uh, you ring us if you guys need anything."

"We will."

"See ya, little brother."

"See ya, bro."

Dan stood on the front porch for a long time, grimacing at the fancy gizmo in his hand. It could do about a zillion things, but it sure hadn't made *that* call any fucking easier, had it?

The sound of a car made him look up, and he beheld a beige Crown Victoria with a light bar and CENTERVILLE POLICE DEPARTMENT stenciled in green and gold on the door. It was cruising slowly by on Daisy; a buzz-cut cop with Aviator shades perched on his square, unsmiling face sat behind the wheel. He stared over, so Dan raised a hand in greeting.

The cop looked away.

Dan lowered his hand. "Asshole."

When he passed the mailbox, the officer gunned the big-block interceptor and zoomed off. Dan watched him go. It was the fourth time he'd seen the fuzz drive by today, and he hadn't really been paying attention. They were sure being diligent about patrolling the area now; at least some good had come from this mess.

Dan scowled at his phone; everyone in the multi-verse had called him today except Beth. She'd flat-out refused to say where she was going or what she planned to do after dropping Lizzie at daycare. He shoved the phone back in his pocket. *I don't fucking care what she's doing.* He wasn't about to call her and ask, either.

What the hell *was* she doing?

Dan's head came up again when he recognized the low rumble of a different engine approaching down Daisy. He groaned. Sure enough, a few seconds later Helen's black-and-silver '83 Silverado appeared over the rise. He willed it to keep going, but no such luck. Helen hit the brakes and whipped into the castle's driveway without bothering with a turn signal.

"Fuck me."

This day just kept getting better and better. Helen stopped in front of him and killed the engine. The door opened, and then she stepped out, cane emerging first. Helen was clad today in a tasteful combination of blue pumps, yellow dress, red headscarf, and enough cheap jewelry to choke a Gypsy.

"Good morning, Helen." She gave him a sharp look, not bothering to return his salutation, and then set to adjusting her headscarf. Dan saw her glance at the overgrown yard and sneer. *Bitch.* "They aren't here."

"I know that, Daniel. I saw 'em drive by this mornin'." She put both hands on her cane and squared her shoulder pads. "I stopped by to talk to you."

"Great."

She scowled. "I didn't drop in for a social; I came to deliver a message. John McFarlane wants to talk to you."

Dan was caught flat-footed as that name jangled in his brain; he put the grin on though. *Never let 'em see ya sweat.* "Does the man always use crippled old women as his messengers, or were you just handy this morning?"

Helen's eyes glittered. "I've said my piece." She opened the truck's door while gathering her skirts. "If you were a *smart* man," she shot him a look, letting him know where her opinion lay on that matter, "you'd go see him." She climbed in and slammed the door. The Silverado's engine rumbled to life.

I've been summoned.

Outstanding. What did McFarlane want? Was he going to apologize for his rapist asshole employee? Helen pulled away, and Dan hopped down the steps, waving for her to stop; as much as it hurt to ask, he needed more information. Helen hit the brakes and rolled down the window.

"Yes?"

"So I'm just supposed to drop everything and scuttle over to the farm? I'm busy, Helen. You could've given him my number. He does believe in phones, right? What does he want?"

She hung her elbow out the window and looked him full in the face. "I'm gonna give you a free piece of advice, boy, and not because I like you, but because Beth likes you, and because you make pretty babies." She cackled. "I suppose you're good at making them, too! Lord knows a woman has to pay for that when it comes to men. My Henry wasn't good for much else, God's truth, and God rest his soul. Now listen up because I'm only gonna say this once." She leaned out and fixed him with her clear gray eyes. "There are men in this world, and then there are *men*, and when a *man* like John McFarlane says he wants to talk, why, a man like you should hop."

Anger surged through Dan, hot and quick, but his grin only widened. "So I'm just supposed to show up? He didn't say when? What if *the man's* out getting a pedicure? Or what if *the man's* out getting his knob slobbed? What am I supposed to do then? A good little messenger gal would've given me a time. Maybe you aren't qualified for this gig, Helen."

Her snarl was yellow. "Why, if he's not there, you wait for him to come back, boy, and be grateful. But don't you worry, he'll be there. Now, can I tell John you'll be dropping by for a visit?"

"Oh, I suppose I might swing by later in the week, when I have the time."

"You do that." She punched it and shot around the driveway and squealed out onto Daisy, and then the small-block 327 really kicked in and she fishtailed and roared away.

Dan coughed and waved tire smoke from his face and looked down at the new black marks on his driveway and then up and down the road.

Where's that asshole cop when you need him?

"Crazy old cunt."

Dan went inside and slammed the front door. He made something up and jabbed the new master code into the alarm keypad, repeated it when prompted, then slammed the cover and stomped into the kitchen, jerking open the fridge door to stare inside even though he knew what he would see.

Or, more correctly, what he *wouldn't* see.

He was still out of beer.

"Fuck."

He shut the fridge and stood thinking. *Fuck it*, he decided. *Let's get this over with.* Dan would go see The Man, and if showing up this fast caught him off guard, so much the better.

And if The Man *doesn't like it, then too fucking bad.*

Dan would stop and get more gas for the mower (his pal Scotty had used up what was in the can) and also grab a twelve pack after he'd found out what the old fart wanted; it's not like he was in a hurry to mow, anyway. He fetched his wallet from the computer desk, hesitated, then pulled out Scandlin's card. He stared at it for a minute, then put it back; he would see what *The Man* had to say first.

Mr. Yoda barked, tongue protruding and eyes bulging as he stared in through the French door's lowest pane. Dan had planned on leaving the little fucker outside until he got back, but the thought of explaining to Lizzie how her new puppy had died of heat stroke made him walk over and open the door. Mr. Yoda trotted inside and straight to his water bowl.

"Shit on the tile, not on the carpet, okay?" The dog ignored him, lapping. "Glad that's settled."

Dan retrieved the Smith; he also slipped the little five-shot Eagle into his front pocket. *Never leave home without 'em, baby.* He got his keys and hat and shades, then checked his mug out in the downstairs bathroom mirror; the swelling had gone down, but he still looked like a beat-up, hung-over raccoon—thus the Chi Sox cap and shades.

The dog followed him to the door. Dan punched the code and went out after it beeped. "Remember what I said about the carpet. And if any rapist scumbags try to get in, you eat 'em up, 'kay?" Mr. Yoda wagged his tail. "Good boy."

Dan waited for the alarm to beep again and then shut the door and used his shiny new key to lock the two shiny new Schlage deadbolts and then went to his truck; he needed to clear space in the garage so he could park in it, but he'd been kinda busy and hadn't gotten around to it yet. He shoved the Smith under the front seat before he started the engine, backed up, then followed the driveway around to Daisy, stopping and checking for traffic. Nada. He pulled out and got the Toyota up to the speed limit and held it there; nothing like carrying two illegal, unregistered firearms to make you a better driver. Everyone should try it.

What the hell could the old sonofabitch want?

Whatever it was, this shouldn't take long.

Pink in the Middle

Dan rolled to a stop at the three-way intersection of Daisy Road and McFarlane Farm's Road, hit the blinker, checked for traffic, and then, for the first time since they'd moved into the castle nearly eight months ago, turned left.

The unlined asphalt petered out after an eighth of a mile, morphing into smooth-graded dirt. There was little dust because of the recent rain, and his tires popped on rocks through several twists and turns as he zigzagged up the long slope of the ridge.

An army of cows was watching when he stopped at an open gate; the gleaming steel lines of a cattle grate stretched between the gate's thick posts. On the cow side was a sign. Dan vibrated over the grate and then stopped and rolled his window down.

Sign, hell—it was a goddamn billboard. The thing was the size of his Tundra; flat white, it rose on three stout posts, the lettering such a dark blue it took Dan a minute to realize it wasn't black. He hung his arm out the window and craned his neck to read:

McFARLANE FARMS

Proudly serving Rutherford County since 1871

Angus and American Wagyu Beef

www.McFarlaneBeefUSA.com

God Bless America

Welcome

1871. A hundred and thirty-nine years. He rolled up the window and kept going. A hundred and thirty-nine years was a long damn time to stay in one spot. You just didn't see that much anymore; matter of fact, Dan made his living because people didn't do that much anymore. He went around a broad curve and over a small, steep rise, and then slammed on the brakes.

"Shit!"

Dan had suddenly come radiator-to-radiator with a spanking-new black Chevy Tahoe XL. The driver, dressed in a charcoal suit, white shirt, and navy tie, slammed on his own brakes and slid to a stop. The passenger, a guy dressed exactly like the driver down to the solid blue tie, put his hands on the dash to catch himself. They both had dark shades and the dark buzz-cuts to match.

It's the fucking Men In Black.

Dan saw the flash of a lighter suit and a more inspired tie as someone in the back seat leaned to look out between the front seats. They all sat there and looked at each other; something would have to give. The dirt road was narrow here, and the ditches were deep and steep; there was no way the two big automobiles would fit by each other. Maybe they could pull in the driver-side mirrors and inch by with two wheels barely hanging. That should work.

He was reaching for his window control to roll it down and suggest they do just that when the driver flicked the back of his hand toward Dan, two fingers extended, as if shooing a bug.

Dan stared.

The suit did it again.

Dan stared some more and then returned the gesture exactly; back of the hand, two fingers extended. Then he did it again, just to make things even.

He put his hands back on the wheel and waited.

They all stared at each other some more. Then the driver and his twin sphincter-buddy turned as the colorful tie in back said something, and then they looked at each other, and then they looked at Dan, heads moving in sync. The driver said something, and the passenger smiled, took his seatbelt off, adjusted his tie knot, and then flung open the door and hopped out.

"Ah, shit."

Suits, skull-gripping haircuts, black SUV: these guys were government, and from their build and bearing, ex-military to boot—or maybe even current military. The passenger suit shut the door and started toward him, and Dan sized him up; about three inches over six feet, his unbuttoned jacket was pulled snug over thick arms and shoulders; worse, he wasn't smiling anymore.

Dan would've also had to been blind to miss the black semiautomatic in the snug combat holster peeking out from underneath the unbuttoned jacket.

"God DAMN it!"

Dan slammed the Toyota into reverse and backed over the little steep rise, still cursing. That curve he'd just passed had a flat shoulder big enough for them to squeeze bye; he would not put his truck in the ditch, not for these pricks; not for anybody. He saw the passenger suit jump back in and the SUV follow.

He also saw them laughing.

Face burning and jaw clenched, Dan backed to the curve, pulled over on the muddy soft shoulder, put the Toyota in drive, and waited.

Those smug smiles vanished when Dan raised one middle finger and pressed it against the side-window glass. The SUV stopped with their mirrors almost touching, the driver's face expressionless behind the dark glasses. Dan pressed the other middle finger next to the first and wiggled both, just in case those shades weren't prescription, then jammed the accelerator to the floor.

The truck fishtailed, and Dan could hear rocks hitting the wheel wells and undercarriage; he could also see a fantail of mud cover the back of the Chevy, turning that shiny black brown. The tires finally caught, and Dan raced to the top of the small hill where all this fun in the sun had started.

He slammed on the brakes and watched his mirror.

The Chevy's reverse lights came on, glowing dimly through the mud.

"Uh oh."

It sat there for an endless minute, and then the reverse lights went out and the SUV slowly drove away.

Whew.

Seeing mud-spattered government plates on the Tahoe didn't surprise him. The G-ride vanished around the curve, but he watched his mirror for over five minutes, hoping they weren't just finding a better place to turn around. While he waited, Dan looked on either side of the road at the fields full of cows. *Suits and guns and G-ride;* those guys stuck out here worse than a goat in a grocery aisle. Who the hell were they? Had their GPS gone on the fritz and shucked them out to the boonies? Maybe the suits had been grab-assing and hadn't noticed until they'd hit the ridge. That must've been it. They'd sure looked like playful types.

Dan let off the brake and cruised on, the dirt road mounting up and up, heading for the buildings crowding the ridge above; one more curve, two more zags, another steep zig, a second battalion of cows, and then he finally drove through another wide-open gate and vibrated across another shiny steel cattle grate and stopped.

A tall red barn to his left had a bale escalator leading to a square hole near the roof peak. Two men were using wicked-looking hooks to pick up rectangular bales from a flat-bed trailer and set them on the belt which chugged the hay up and dropped it through the square hole. They paused when they saw him, looked at each other, smirked, then went back to work, hooks punching and shoulders heaving.

Considering how they were sweating—and the fact both sported heavy ink and were in their late thirties or early forties—Dan doubted either was McFarlane. He let off the brake…and then cursed and stamped it again as a dark-green tractor with back tires taller than the roof of his truck came around the corner of a metal building on his right and crossed the road three feet in front of him. The man in the enclosed cab looked down, hard, tan face below a camouflage baseball cap swiveling to mark Dan, but the tractor didn't slow as it moved around another building and disappeared.

Friendly bunch.

He drove on. Carefully. On his right, several large red-and-white metal buildings of indeterminate use became a long field filled with straight rows of apple trees bursting with fruit, and then the apple trees turned into the biggest damn garden he'd ever seen; it was easily an acre square, maybe more, with rows of corn, beans, tomatoes, and every other vegetable known to man.

On the other side of the apples and the mega-garden rose rank upon rank upon rank of giant trees.

Dan stopped the truck; he recognized those trees. Huge and old and impressive, their thick limbs were heavy with summer leaves and their wide trunks marched away and dropped off the backside of the ridge; he could see past the first row into open air. He oriented himself, charting the turns, and knew he'd been right; he was among the cluster of buildings he'd seen glimmering on the far rim of the valley last Saturday morning.

Were the professor and Math Boy down there right now?

No, he remembered. *Hameed said he had a two o'clock class, and then he was—*

Dan twitched in surprise as a familiar figure stepped around the end of a row of tall chicken-wire cucumber baskets. She wore a blue-plaid man-shirt instead of red plaid today, but she was sporting the same floppy straw hat and white ribbons and faded jeans and boots and startling green eyes. Despite that hat, she shaded those eyes with her hand as she stared his way; her other hand was occupied by a five-gallon plastic bucket filled with what looked like green beans.

At least those big damn clippers are missing today.

Dan waved somewhat lukewarmly. She didn't wave back, but walked to a familiar Polaris four-wheeler, set her beans on the little trailer, and then motivated his way.

Shit. Dan rolled down the passenger window when she got near and attempted to put a smile on his face.

"Hello, Dan Sims."

"Hello, ma'am." He still didn't know what to call her; there were no roses in sight. "The Keeper of Cucumbers", perhaps?

She rested her impressive forearms on the door—she had to raise them up to chins-ribbon level to do it—and peered in at him. "You've come to visit with John, I expect."

Dan paused before answering; the words were neutral enough, but from her tone and her frosty expression, it was clear she wasn't pleased with the prospect of his "visit with John".

Or maybe that's just her natural face. Yikes. "Uh, yes ma'am. He sent a message he wanted to talk."

"I see." Her eyes narrowed.

Behind her, birds twittered and swooped over the garden and through the apple trees; off in the distance Dan heard the rattle of an air ratchet—some sort of machine shop, obviously. A cow mooed somewhere.

He swallowed, unable to look away from that treacherous, bright-green gaze. "I, uh, I better be, um, you know, going now, ma'am."

She didn't answer. Instead, she took her arms off the door and turned and looked at the top of the ridge, as if she were examining something in the distance—

and not something she was very pleased with, either. Dan followed her dangerous green squint, but saw only the ass-end of some long, low-slung metal building.

Oookaay…

Suddenly she spoke, and despite that deadly face, she sounded amused. "I believe John is in for quite the surprise with you, Dan Sims." Before he could ask her what the hell she was talking about, she stepped back and waved him on. "Check up at the house first. If he's not there, one of the girls will know where he is." She took another step back and looked at his Toyota. "Nice truck."

"Um, thank you." Dan peered up the gravel track. *House? Girls? Surprise?* There was no house in sight, or girls for that matter—and if Dan had anything to say about it, no surprises, either.

Her cold voice brought his head back around to meet those eyes again; they glowed fiercely at him from underneath the hat while somehow leaving the rest of her face in shadow.

"You'll want to park it out of the way somewhere," she told him. "The boys like to race those tractors around and they might not see it until it's too late." And with that sanguine piece of advice, she turned and walked back toward the garden, gray-streaked strawberry ponytail swaying between her shoulder blades as her thick body cut through the sunlight.

"Thank you, ma'am!"

She lifted a hand in acknowledgment, but didn't turn around. Dan blew out a long sigh of relief, then frowned after her. *McFarlane summoned me, so how could there be a surprise?* Dan shook his head. Weird bitch. Conversations with the Keeper, he decided, were not exactly his favorite pastime.

And then Dan scowled and looked around. *If some blind farm-boy runs over my truck, there's going to be a fucking problem break out around here.* He let off the brake and rolled his window back up; the reek of cow manure was a physical thing.

A minute later he came upon a low-slung corrugated metal building gleaming hotly in the sun. It had the back end of a flat-bed truck sticking out of an open bay door; the concrete slab underneath it was stained with oil. Where the edge of the sunlight met darkness, he could see the truck's hood standing open. Dan pulled the Toyota in next to it and nosed up to the building on the down-slope side, thus making sure he was out of the way of even the most ignorant tractor-jockey. He killed the engine and got out and shut the door, and then almost got back in again. Fuck it was hot out.

An Eagles' track played three times daily on a thousand classic-rock stations across America oozed past the open hood, blending with the roar of a floor fan; then the music cut off and two faces appeared, one looking over the shoulder of the other. The chap in front had dark hair and wide Latino features; denim-overall straps bulged over his bare, massive chest and shoulders. Big boy had a big wrench in one big hand and a long grease smear under his clenched jaw. Tattoos covered his chest, arms, and neck like a nest of blue wire. His taller, thinner, paler, and dirtier buddy had almost as many tattoos, but at least he had a shirt on.

"Hi, fellas." Dan gave them a little wave. "All right if I park here?"

They exchanged glances, smirks bloomed, and then they turned those smirks on him. Then without a word they vanished back into the greasy darkness. The radio came back on, louder than before, Aerosmith replacing Eagles; the burnt smell of used motor oil wafted out like an invisible fog.

Well. "I'll take that as a yes."

Dan locked the truck with the fob and started walking. He could feel them watching from that oily darkness as he moved around the flat-bed and crunched up the dirt track through more buildings and then past a cluster of turkey houses occupying a long, flat plateau to his left; the houses sweltered side by side, the huge fans on the end throbbing. Dan could see the future Thanksgiving guests massing past the blur. They looked hot.

I know how ya feel, friends.

He was beginning to think he'd abandoned the truck (and its air conditioner) way too soon, but then he spied a house at the crest of the ridge; set back among the tall trees at the lip of the valley, it was big and white, with thick, fluted columns marching across a deep front porch. Dan stopped and took his Chi Sox cap off and wiped sweat from his face; he scratched around his staples before putting the cap back on.

That old beauty looks like it fell out of Gone With the Wind.

Motion to his right turned his head.

There was one last building below the house. It sat on the steep slope long-ways, the far end cut into the earth, the end nearest to Dan eight or nine feet off the ground, supported by a cinder-block foundation; long, low, and barn-red, it had six bay doors opening onto a wide expanse of concrete. The second to the last bay door was open, and a car had been pulled out; a girl was washing that car, green hose trailing from her hand, a bucket of sudsy water at her feet.

A girl was washing a car—but not just any car, and not just any girl.

The car was a Mach 1 Fastback Mustang, glossy black, with twin pearl racing stripes from nose to spoiler. If Dan was any judge—and he was—it looked like a '71. It also appeared someone had lovingly restored it to original; if so, there was a 351 Windsor lurking under the hood, or maybe even the 390 FE.

Nice.

The girl continued to hose the Mustang off, oblivious to his presence, the sweep of spray moving with her hand. Her hair was the color of a new penny and trailed down her back in a thick braid; tall but not too tall, her long, barefoot legs glistened in the back spray. Those legs climbed to a stunning bottom that was almost covered by tight blue-jean cutoffs; a pair of neon-green flip flops were stacked over to the side. A plain white tee-shirt covered her, but it was obvious she didn't have a bra on; evidently it was cold over where she was standing as well.

Dan didn't know her exact year model, but if he was any judge—and he was— he'd say she was in her mid-twenties. She had on little oval mirrored sunglasses, and Dan could see a smattering of freckles on her nose and cheeks.

Mm, freckles.

She was just as much a classic as the car—and, also like the Mustang, she looked built for speed and handling.

"Beautiful, idn't she?"

Dan whipped around to find a man scowling behind him; a few inches shorter than Dan, but with a bull's chest and shoulders, his full head of short, iron-gray hair reflected the sun. He was clean-shaven, and somehow he wore a long-sleeved green plaid shirt buttoned to the wrists and neck under dark-blue denim overalls—in this heat! He had mud-crusted work boots on his feet. He was sixty, maybe sixty-five, and his lined, tan face was strong-nosed and strong-jawed. His eyes were sharp and hard, gray mixed with shards of green; storm clouds laced with summer leaves.

Dan had no fucking doubt who he was.

And then the question and the scowl registered, and he turned a shade to match the girl's hair.

"Uh…"

That scowl cracked, and then the man bent over in a guffawing laughing fit, grasping his knees. Dan stood there nonplussed until the man finally pushed back up and wiped his face with a bright-red handkerchief he produced from a back pocket.

"Ah, me. That was just too good to resist. Your face…" He smiled, tight and toothless. "The car, son, the *car*…but my daughter ain't so bad neither, eh?"

Daughter? Christ. "No sir, she's not bad at all."

The man chuckled, then thrust out a thick mitt. "John McFarlane."

"Dan Sims." McFarlane's hand was sandpaper over rocky crags, and his grip was as strong as advertised. "Helen said you wanted to talk?"

"That's right." The last of the grin vanished as the old farmer looked at Dan somberly. "I wanted to say I'm sorry for what happened at your place the other day. Scotty was family—worthless and lazy, but family." He shrugged. "I gave him a job and tried to teach him something, but you can only do so much with bad stock, family or not."

Dan didn't know how to respond; so Rison had been related to McFarlane as well as the Sheriff *and* everybody else? *Jesus, what manner of hick nest have we landed in?* And the man was *sorry?* Well, good for him. Dan was sorry, too. He just nodded, not trusting himself to say anything.

That seemed enough. McFarlane nodded back slowly and then squinted up at the sun. "The boys've already fed, but the girls and I are 'bout to sit down ta dinner. Care ta join us?"

Dinner? Oh, he meant lunch; regional colloquialisms. Dan opened his mouth to turn McFarlane down and then hesitated; the tone had been casual enough, but there had also been a weight behind the question. He didn't need Helen's warning to see that John McFarlane was not a man to cross, and Dan hadn't bothered to eat breakfast, so lunch, er, dinner, sounded like a fine idea—just not here.

McFarlane's eyes narrowed.

"Dinner would be good," Dan said quickly. "Thank you, sir."

The old man's brow smoothed. "Fine, then." He checked the sun again. *Jeez, doesn't he own a watch?* "We've got a bit," he said, then moved past Dan, waving for him to follow. "Since you were starin' so, I'll introduce ya." McFarlane laughed at his expression, then winked. "To the car, a'course."

Dan followed, face hot. The redhead was now bent over cleaning the front-passenger wheel, so he stared desperately at the glistening car. As they approached she straightened, picking up the hose to rinse the wheel. She looked Dan up and down, and then quirked her full, pink lips.

"Rebecca, this is Dan Sims, our neighbor come to visit. Dan, my daughter Becca."

"Nice to meet you, ma'am."

The redhead didn't respond, but she kept those tiny sunglasses pointed toward him; the little quirk stayed, too.

McFarlane glowered at her and then faced Dan. "Sorry about that, son. Becca's yet to learn good manners. I keep meanin' to teach her, but I'm afraid I spoil my girls somewhat."

Becca lifted the nozzle and sprayed them. McFarlane laughed and danced back, nimble for an old guy. Dan wasn't as quick.

The old man gave him a long-suffering look. "Ornery! See what I mean?"

"Yeah," Dan said. The redhead continued to stare at him as he bent over and wiped water from his legs; his right sock and shoe were soaked.

Dan stood back up. Ornery? He had another word, but doubted her father would appreciate it. He pointed at the Mustang's hood.

"That have the 351 under there?"

McFarlane gave him a speculative squint. "You know Mustangs, son?"

He shrugged. "Always wanted one."

McFarlane grinned like a big kid. "You'll 'preciate this, then. Come with me." The farmer strode off toward one of the closed bay doors to their left. Dan followed, squishing every other step; he could sense the redhead quirking at his back.

Ornery.

The old man heaved up a door and vanished into the dark.

Dan stepped inside, and after his eyes adjusted, he saw a line of vehicles arrayed behind the bay doors. Two new Chevy pickups were on the far end, one a big dually diesel and the other a four-wheel-drive Z71. Down at the other end was a whole herd of Polaris four-wheelers, dried mud crusting their knobby tires. He barely noticed all that crap though; a red Cobra Mustang with tinted windows sat right in front of him. It was fifth generation, a 2008 or 2009; the hooded snake in the center of the grill seemed to stare at him.

"Nice."

"Bah." McFarlane waved a thick arm at the Cobra, dismissing it. "That's the girls'. It's a hell of a lot of fun to drive, I'll grant ya, but it's got no heart. Dee-troit don't make 'em like they used too." He walked to the next spot where a car sat hidden under a soft gray cover. He reached out and grasped it and then smiled at Dan. "Not like this."

He pulled the cover off with a flourish.

Dan's breath caught.

"She's a '67 Shelby Cobra GT 500, fully restored. Took me four years and I don't even want to think about how much money, but there she sits."

Dan nodded, but he didn't need the exposition; he had stood and drooled on a convertible blue one at a car show way back when he'd been nineteen, and he'd fantasized about owning one ever since. This beauty was solid black, a hardtop, no racing stripes, with chrome wheels and black side pipes.

"Original motor?"

Dan had tried to keep the envy from his voice and knew he'd failed when McFarlane smiled.

"Original everything, son. She's mine." The old man sighed, then tugged the cover back over the Shelby. Dan was sorry to see her go. "Bought a used '67 when I got shipped back from Nam and been in love with 'em ever since. My one vice." He winked. "The one my goddamn doctor let me keep, anyhow."

"She's beautiful, sir."

"Thank you." He finished covering the Shelby and patted the hood. "C'mon. You look hungry. My youngest will just about have everything ready, so we'll go slap the steaks on."

Dan followed McFarlane outside and watched him roll the overhead door back down.

Steak for lunch?

Why the fuck not?

McFarlane looked over at the redhead; she was drying the Fastback with a mitt. "We'll eat in about twenty. I expect you there, girl."

"Maybe I'm not hungry."

She said it while staring straight at Dan, and he shifted, sock squishing; he wasn't exactly hard on the eyes (at least not normally), but he was no Brad Pitt, and girls usually didn't stare like this—especially girls that looked like *that*.

That full-lipped quirk was giving him the heebie-jeebies.

"Twenty minutes," McFarlane said, hard, and then turned and trudged up toward the house. He was muttering as Dan hurried to catch up: "Shoulda started beatin' her a long time ago, just on principal." He shot Dan a dark look. "You *do* eat steak, don't ya, boy? You ain't one of those fools that won't eat meat, are ya?"

"I love steak, sir."

McFarlane grunted and kept trudging. The old man had served in Vietnam? Dan considered inquiring after the suits in the G-ride…but, even though he would never admit it to Helen, she'd been right about John McFarlane.

So, for once in his life, Dan kept his mouth shut.

He trailed McFarlane, so he risked a glance over his shoulder; when Rebecca saw him looking she picked up the hose again and grasped the nozzle and pointed it at herself and squeezed. Water blasted out and plastered the white tee-shirt to her chest.

Yeppers, no bra.

Dan turned back around hastily. Jesus Christ.

The house was drawing closer, the trees in the yard casting wide pools of shade that looked wonderful to a sweating Dan. He told himself it was the sun. Then three low, dark forms appeared from the tree-shadows; a deep bark sounded, then more, and then the dark shapes raced toward them with astonishing speed.

Dan stopped. McFarlane kept trudging. Two of the dogs were German Shepherds—*big* fucking German Shepherds—with tan bodies and black faces and huge, black, pointy ears, but the one in front had gray fur and black ears and wasn't as heavy; a mix of some sort. They barreled past McFarlane and stopped in front of Dan, snarling.

He held perfectly still; the sweat streaming down his face had turned cold.

McFarlane was standing there watching with a smile playing across his face. *The fucker's enjoying this!* The mutt in front snarled closer, pale-blue eyes full of hate, and then crouched, ready to spring.

"Ah, sir?"

"You afraid of dogs, Dan?"

"A little," he admitted. "Could you, um...?"

"They can sense that, ya know." Now that smile was proud. Proud! Dan was about to get eaten, and the old man was just going to stand there and watch and smile.

This is what I get for listening to Helen. He had a wild idea about the .22 in his pocket, but kept his hands at his sides.

Then McFarlane said, "Down!", and all three mutts shut up and lay on their bellies. "Heel!" They popped up and trotted over to sit at McFarlane's feet; the two giant Germans stared up at their master adoringly, but the smaller—smaller hell; it had to weigh eighty-five pounds—gray one kept its pale gaze locked on Dan. He met its hate-filled stare, and a black upper lip peeled silently away from amazing yellow teeth.

McFarlane walked back to Dan and pointed: "Reagan! Mark!" The blue-eyed dog came over and sniffed at Dan's legs; the hair on the back of his neck stood up as its nose snuffled his crotch.

After forever, the dog raised its head. "Good girl. Sit." She sat, eyes locked on Dan.

"There. You don't have to be frightened anymore, son. Reagan knows you're a guest, now." He glanced up at the sun again. "I don't know about you, but we work hard on a farm, and I got a hole in my belly." With that he turned and started toward the house again.

Dan followed, almost stepping on the old man's boots as Reagan and her two furry associates trotted at his heels. He could feel their hot breath on his legs.

Asshole.

McFarlane had done that shit on purpose—and the implication that Dan didn't work hard, that only *farmers* knew what hard work was…bullshit. Fucking *bullshit*. Dan had worked his whole life, but just because he didn't get up at four in the morning to milk *chickens* or whatever…he'd already had enough of McFarlane and his prick-tease daughter and his fucking hairballs and his goddamn superior attitude, and Dan had the sudden and strong urge to turn on his heel and walk back to his truck and leave, "dinner" be damned.

He didn't, though, and he knew why he didn't: curiosity. Despite McFarlane's claim he just wanted to say sorry—sorry!—for his rapist dirt-bag relative, it was obvious to Dan that the old man wanted something.

But what?

So Dan swallowed his anger and most of his pride and kept squishing; eventually they stepped beneath the shade of magnificent trees, the emerald grass mowed short underneath, and when he could see the entire house, he stopped involuntarily. The hairballs almost ran into him.

It was white, and it had four huge, fluted white columns in front that rose all the way to the roof, with a balcony looking out on the front yard between the middle columns; the balcony's wrought-iron railing was intricate and low. Dan could envision ladies in wide dresses and hats, their busts squeezed by whale-bone corsets, mint juleps and parasols in their hands, sitting on that balcony and having a slave review or some shit.

Dan smiled up at that grand lady of a house, a thing from another era.

What a place.

McFarlane had stopped and was looking back at him. Dan caught up. "Nice house."

"Thank you, son. My great, great…" The old man scratched behind his ear with a calloused finger, "great, great Granddaddy started it, and my great, great Granddaddy finished it about forty years after the War of Northern Aggression was in the books." They trudged and squished past the front porch and its giant columns and around the west side to a red-brick patio where an enormous stain-less-steel wood-fired grill sat smoking. Their smelly, panting escort peeled away and sat, finding something else to stare at besides Dan.

McFarlane laughed; three sets of triangle ears twitched and then went back to the grill. "They know, don't they?" He picked up a colossal homemade wire brush and began scraping slotted grill slats; he motioned with his chin. "Go on in there and introduce yourself and grab the steaks. Mindy'll fetch 'em out of the icebox for ya. Run 'em back out here and we'll get this party started."

Dan looked where the chin had indicated; three brick steps led up to a screen door, the solid door behind it open into darkness. He walked to the steps and up, shaking his head in admiration. It was a detached kitchen—a *huge* detached kitchen. Dan had sold houses that were smaller. He shouldn't have been surprised, really; back in the day, they often set the kitchen apart because of fire concerns. Over to his right, he glimpsed a covered walkway that connected it to the main house. He shook his head again, then knocked on the screen door.

"Come on in!"

The voice was sweet and young. Dan saw a flash of blonde hair through the screen as he opened it and stepped inside. He stopped and looked around, and two things were immediately apparent to him:

The first was that, despite the anachronism of a detached kitchen, there was nothing old-fashioned about it. It was as modern and as well-appointed as any he'd ever seen, with granite counter-tops and stainless-steel appliances; the tile was almost a match for the kitchen in the castle, a shade of green that Beth loved and Dan tolerated because she did. An oval, solid-oak dining table and six matching chairs sat beside sliding-glass doors that let onto the patio and a stunning view across the sun-dappled westward slope.

The second thing he noted was that McFarlane was a blessed man; the owner of the sweet voice stood bent over with her head in the open door of the side-by-side refrigerator, a mass of honey-blonde curls falling across her face. She was barefoot and had on black polyester shorts that rode high on the backs of her legs—*way* high. Dan whipped his eyes up as she straightened and gifted him with a smile as sweet as her voice.

"Hi! I'm Mindy."

"Uh, hi, I'm Dan. Your dad sent me for the steaks."

"Sure!" Mindy reached in the fridge and pulled out a tray piled with two-inch thick rib-eyes and shut the door with her hip, and then a third thing became obvious to Dan: like her older sister, Mindy didn't approve of bras; her large breasts bobbled beneath a gray sleeveless wife-beater, and boy, was it cold in here, too.

What's wrong with bras, anyway? Maybe he'd missed another billboard coming in: MCFARLANE FARMS—NO BRAS ALLOWED! Not that he was complaining, really.

She put the steaks on the counter and hooked a strand of honey hair behind her ear and beamed at him. "I hope you like potato salad, Dan. I just made some fresh."

"I like potato salad." He didn't, but he knew he was going to eat it.

Suddenly her smile turned upside down. "Oh!" She moved toward him, hands outstretched. Nonplussed, Dan held his ground as she crossed the green tiles on shapely feet. "Your poor face!"

With no trace of self-consciousness, Mindy pulled his ball cap off and then the sunglasses and put them on the counter next to the steaks without looking. Then she spider-walked her fingers over his forehead, nose, and cheeks; her hands were soft and warm and smelled like pickles. She was shorter than her sister, and her shirt pulled tight over her chest as she reached. Dan forced his eyes back to her face, which was about a foot away now; her irises were dark blue, the color of an autumn twilight just before the stars appear.

"Um..."

"Shh."

She ran her hands through his hair slowly, front to back, stopping to finger the shaved spot with the staples behind his ear, and then back to front; she placed the pads of her fingers underneath his eyes and held them there. Dan's scalp tingled, and warmth spread across his face and down his neck and through his whole body. He stared down into her eyes, having wild thoughts about her father walking in right then. She quirked her lips just like her sister and slowly lowered her hands and gripped his forearms; her chest was lightly touching his stomach, now.

Yep, bra-free farms, gotta love 'em.

"Did Scotty…?" Mindy lifted one hand and tapped his nose; there was some smell—her smell—underneath the pickle. Intoxicating. "Did he do this?"

That brought him back to reality—somewhat. "Yeah."

"You poor thing, I'm so sorry." She hesitated. "And your wife and your little girl? Are they…?"

"They're fine." That brought him all the way back. Christ, he was married, so married, with a family, a beautiful family.

"I'm glad." She pressed her breasts against his stomach. He realized then that he'd gripped her arms back at some point.

Dan felt himself stirring. *If this goes on much longer, she's going to get a surprise.*

Suddenly she released him and spun away, mass of curls flailing, and walked back to the fridge. "Scotty, Scotty, Scotty." She clucked her tongue like Scotty had just forgotten to put the toilet seat down or something. She opened the fridge and brought out a big blue bowl with Saran Wrap covering the top and shut the door with a hip again and set the bowl on the counter. "How old is your daughter? Five, right? And her name is…?"

"Lizzie." Dan swallowed. "She's four. She'll be five in September."

"Lizzie. What a beautiful name." She laughed. "*Almost* five, then. That's a fun age. Does she like chickens?" Mindy slid out a drawer and dug, coming up with a big spoon. When he didn't answer she cocked one dark-blue eye at him and hooked that long, curly hair behind an ear again.

What? Oh, chickens. "She likes chickens." Dan didn't have the first fucking clue if Lizzie liked chickens or not. "She also likes cows." How old was this girl? Nineteen? Eighteen? "She really loves horses." *I am an old man, a dirty old married man.*

Then Dan frowned and rubbed his nose; it felt better—much better. And his headache wasn't completely gone, but his brain felt better than it had since he'd woken up in the hospital Monday morning.

What the hell?

"Oh, good," Mindy was saying. "We have horses. You must bring her by for a visit so we can go riding. Say you'll bring her by, Dan. She'll have *so* much fun."

That sweet smile again, and those incredible eyes on his, waiting.

"Sure," he heard himself say. "I'll bring her by."

"Great!"

Mindy removed the wrap from the bowl and fetched a smaller bowl out of the cabinet by her head and transferred heaps of potato salad; she had turned sideways to him, and Dan could see one big nipple outlined. After a minute she put the spoon down and faced him and reached one hand up and slowly hooked honey hair behind her ear and smiled, but naughty had shoved most of the sweet onto the tiles; her eyes were as smoky and as knowing as any woman's he'd ever met.

"You can take those steaks out to my daddy now, Dan. Tell him I'll be ready when they are."

"Uh, sure."

Face on fire, he picked up the platter and hustled to the screen door, then stopped and went back and set the platter down and grabbed his cap and sunglasses and stuck them back on. Dan snatched the steaks up and fled outside.

Her soft laugh followed him out, and there was nothing sweet about it at all.

Dan let the screen door bang shut and paused to collect; he was sweating like he'd ridden the 'Goose twenty miles. He raised his free hand to touch just below his eyes where Mindy had pressed her fingers; his face was barely even sore anymore.

What in the fuck?

He looked toward the grill and saw that Rebecca had joined them and was talking to her father; there was a Polaris parked nearby, its motor ticking. He'd missed the sound of her arriving while he'd been…occupied inside.

Seventeen? *Jesus fucking Christ.*

Their conversation cut off as Dan walked up. "Steaks, sir. Mindy said she'll be ready when they are."

"Fine, then." McFarlane looked at Dan…and was that a knowing glint in the old man's eye? *Of course not, I'm just paranoid. Beth even said so.* "How do you like your steak?"

"A touch past medium-rare, sir, if that's all right."

"That's fine with me, son." The old man chuckled. "Pink in the middle; a man after my own heart."

McFarlane slapped the steaks on the grill; the sizzle and the smell were mouth-watering, but Dan didn't notice. He looked at Rebecca; her tee-shirt was still wet, and her nipples were little hard rubies poking through the fabric at him. She looked back, then raised her shades to rest in that copper hair, and Dan saw deep-green eyes the exact tint of the August leaves fluttering over her head.

Then she quirked those lips and spoke, and her voice was as soft and as hot as the breeze that moved the leaves:

"Pink in the middle," she breathed.

He smiled weakly and looked away. *Well, at least this one is in her twenties.* McFarlane gave with the deep chuckle again, and Dan decided he would punch the next idiot who tried to tell him a farmer's daughters' joke. The three mutts stared at him, triangle ears erect and yellow-gray tongues lolling over giant teeth as they panted; the steaks might as well have been on the moon.

This is going to be a long damn lunch.

THE ENEMY

ETH DROVE the speed limit back across Murfreesboro because she didn't want to lose her new friend, and curly beard didn't disappoint, staying with her but avoiding detection (or so he thought) by keeping three or four cars back at all times. *Good boy.*

She noticed a license plate on the front of his car. Tennessee only required plates on the back, but Ohio mandated them on the front and back. She'd gotten used to seeing them only on the back for the past six years, so this guy stood out; a mistake on his part. He stayed too far away for Beth to see which state (it wasn't the right color for Ohio), but the fact that he was from out of state was telling—but telling exactly what she didn't know.

Who is he? What does he want? Beth concentrated on not losing him; she would find out who he was and what he wanted soon enough.

A few minutes later she pulled into the parking lot of the mega-chain bookstore, and guilt stung her; normally she went out of her way to support the independents, but she needed the open space and the crowd for her plan. Beth consoled her conscious: from what she'd heard, all bookstores needed her support these days.

She pretended to dig in her purse and watched the mirror from the corner of her eye as the dark-green Honda drifted through the crowded lot and found a spot two rows behind her. She saw the plate; he was from Illinois—or at least his car was.

Beth got out and walked across the sweltering lot; she could *feel* curly beard's eyes on her. It made her skin crawl. She wanted to turn and give him the finger, but kept her cool as she opened the heavy door and stepped into an air-conditioned foyer.

There were mounds of sale books lining the walls of the small space; everything from regional nature-photo collections to cook books to astrology charts to the latest celebrity tell-all memoir (extra-steep discount for that one). She held the glass-paned inside door for three small boys who rushed out yelling, followed by a harried young mother. Beth shared a smile with her and then walked through the electronic theft-deterrent towers and into the cavernous store.

The enticing smell of coffee laced with the crisp scent of thousands of new books made Beth grin as she hurried over to one of the floor-to-ceiling front windows and peeked outside. Curly beard was sitting in his car with his head down, tapping on his phone with both thumbs.

Beth made her way deeper into the store and found the restroom and used it; if her plan went awry, she might have to hold it for some time. After washing her hands she walked to a different front window and checked on him again; he was now talking animatedly on the phone while keeping one eye on the front doors and the other on her car. He seemed upset, waving his free hand around for emphasis. *Good.*

She walked to the fiction section; on the way, she passed a smiling young woman who tried to interest her in an e-reader—the mega-chain's house brand, of course—but she turned her down politely. Beth preferred the smell and feel of a real book.

She picked up what she wanted with little hesitation; the latest F. Paul Wilson Repairman Jack adventure. Well, latest to her; she was several installments behind. Beth pictured her husband's new truck and then pulled three more from other authors she loved. She'd cut back her book habit since moving into the castle, trying to stick to their budget, and it turned out Daniel had been sitting on all that money!

Beth unclenched her jaw and vowed not to let thoughts of her idiot husband ruin her day off.

She went back to check on her bearded buddy (he was still sitting not-so-pretty) and then paid for her books, turning down the offer to sign up for the mega-chain's "rewards" card. Then she lurked in the busy coffee shop and waited for the right table to open; it didn't take long. A mother/teenage daughter tandem with bags of clothes and books at their feet and phones in hand and purses on the table began arguing, and, still arguing, gathered everything and left. Beth swooped in and moved a chair around so she could see the parking lot and checked her friend; no phone, now. He was swiveling his big, bearded head from the back of her car to the front of the mega-chain, impatience almost oozing from him.

Beth smiled, then settled in to out-wait her enemy.

She was about to lift her sunglasses off her nose and onto her hair—she'd kept them on the whole time walking about the store and while peeing, just in case—but then hesitated, glancing around; she'd seen the picture of her they were showing on television. It'd been posted on the Slo Eddie's website, from a store manager's meeting in Philadelphia two years ago, and her hair had been longer then; with no makeup and a shorter ponytail plus the glasses, no one appeared to recognize her today, though.

Satisfied, Beth lifted the shades onto her hair and got all four paperbacks out of her bag and lined them up on the little round table. She picked up first one and then another of her treasures, riffling the edges of the pages with her thumb, breathing in the new ink and paper. *Which one to start?* She'd meant to open the latest Jack, but she hadn't read Michael Connelly in far too long. She put that down and picked up the Robert Crais, then put that down and sadly fingered the James Crumley mystery. She put that back down reluctantly; Beth would savor it. Relishing her dilemma, she smiled as she picked up F. Paul Wilson again.

After a few pages she marked her place with a finger and glanced at the line; she was thirsty, but the prices on the board above the barista's head made her shudder. She could sprint to the water fountain in back, the one the big chain did its best to hide by the bathrooms; it was doubtless a code violation if they didn't put one in, or Beth knew they wouldn't have bothered.

No, she had to keep tabs on her enemy. Putting thirst out of her mind, she checked on him again; still there, but he was slumped in the seat now, and he looked bored out of his bearded skull.

Anytime now.

She was walking down the teeming sidewalks of New York City with Jack when motion in the lot brought her head up. Curly beard was ambling toward the front doors.

Beth sized him up: mid-forties, he was older and also taller than she'd thought, easily Scott Rison's height, five inches over six feet, but unlike Rison this man was non-athletic, with a pot belly and man boobs jiggling beneath his nondescript tee-shirt. Still, he was a full-grown boy; two-seventy or two-eighty, with long, hairy arms and strong-looking hands; the wire-rimmed glasses looked dinky perched in the middle of his wide face.

Beth snatched her purse and dumped her books in the bag and vacated the table, moving fast toward the back of the store, losing herself among the shelves. She glanced at her watch; he'd lasted almost forty minutes. She picked a corner where she had multiple sight-lines, pulled out her Wilson, and continued reading while standing. Five minutes later he spotted her and slowed, and then he actually turned into her aisle and pulled a book off the shelf and stopped a few feet away.

They stood that way for several minutes, both pretending to read as they watched each other. Back here they were nearly alone, only the occasional worker or browser strolling by, so Beth was patient; she needed witnesses for her trap, the more the better. It would sting her pride to play the frightened stalking victim, but her pride had taken so many dents of late that one more wouldn't kill her. She took the opportunity to study her enemy; he had a strange-looking notepad sticking out of the back pocket of his knee-length denim shorts; it was over a foot long, but narrow, with large red spirals. There was a fancy gold pen attached to it.

Her patience paid off when he suddenly shelved his book and meandered toward the front of the store on those long legs. Was he going back out to his car? If so, Beth would have to hurry; in front of that nice young lady selling e-readers would work. She would make a perfect witness, and the registers weren't far away; if he was going to the bathroom, she could wait and then ambush him by the front doors.

Beth marked her place, closed her book, and began stalking her enemy.

He noticed her following and stopped two rows down and she walked another three over and pulled a book off a shelf at random; he waited, studying her openly now, then strolled past the end of her aisle. Beth followed. This went on for about five minutes as they leapfrogged each other, working their way to the front. Curly beard finally walked into the coffee bar and got in line, turned slightly to keep an eye on her. He wore an uncertain frown now, but that was all right—he'd made his last mistake.

The café is perfect.

Beth shelved the "best-seller" she'd feigned reading and moved in for the kill, rushing up behind him in line. He stiffened and faced forward. She let him sweat for a minute, enough time for one customer to be served and move off and two more to join the line behind her. Three people were still in line in front of curly beard when she triggered the jaws.

"Why are you following me?"

Beth hadn't bothered to lower her voice; in fact, she'd raised it while putting in a terrified tremor. Several heads turned. His shoulders stiffened, but he didn't turn around. She reached up and tapped one.

"Why are you following me?" Louder: "You've been following me since before I dropped my daughter at her daycare. Why were you following us? Who are you? What do you want?" Beth's voice rose with each question.

That got everyone; even the harried barista had stopped and was peering around the line of staring customers. *So far so good.* None of them, if questioned by the police later, would forget her words.

But then he surprised her. Instead of stammering an explanation or slinking away, he turned smoothly to face her and pulled out that long, narrow notebook and flipped back the embossed-leather cover and clicked the gold pen ready and said, rapid-fire, "Mrs. Sims, I'm sorry for upsetting you, but I've left several messages indicating my wish to talk to you. I've also left several with your husband, but have received no response. My name is Brian Brennan, and I'm a freelance reporter. I'm writing a story on the home-invasion assault you suffered at the hands of Scott Duane Rison Sunday afternoon. Is it true you stabbed Scott Rison forty-seven times?"

He waited, but Beth didn't answer. She'd recognized his name and voice—as well she should; she'd deleted at least five messages from him.

A reporter! She should have known.

"I heard you were bound with duct tape," he continued, still rapid-fire, as if he thought he had to get his questions in before she walked away. "Is that true? And if so, how did you get free?" He looked at her, pen poised. Beth still didn't respond, but her silence didn't faze him. He flipped to a page deeper inside that notebook and consulted it: "You earned your third-degree black belt in Kuk Sool Won at the age of twenty, then your fourth-degree black belt in Goju-Ryu Karate at twenty-six. And now you take Aikijutsu, in which you hold a second-degree black belt rank. As a master of the martial arts, did you use your martial training to thwart your attacker and save yourself and your husband?"

Whispers burst to life around them, and Beth felt the attention she'd so carefully placed on him land feet-first on her. *They sure recognize me now!* Beth's face flamed; her trap had been neatly turned. A reporter.

She stared up at him and he stared back, gold pen hanging, notebook hovering; he looked satisfied with himself, mud-brown eyes beady behind the little glasses.

An idea took root, then; she liked it, so it quickened and then bloomed, but Beth only said, "I'm just a student."

"Sorry?"

"I'm not a master. There's no such thing. I'm only a student."

"I see." The pen plunged; he scribbled something.

"Green tea."

He lowered the pen and notebook. "What?"

"Buy me an iced Green tea and I'll talk to you. I'm thirsty." She motioned toward an open four-top table. "I'll wait right there."

"How do I know you'll be there when I turn around?"

Beth ground her teeth in a smile; she wasn't used to people questioning her word. "Because I said I would be." She walked over and put her purse and book bag on the table, then scraped a chair back and sat and crossed her legs and folded her hands across her knee, the picture of a woman at ease. She even kicked her foot a little. He watched and then nodded eagerly; he would finally get his interview.

Life in the coffee bar lurched back into motion, and Brennan kept one eye on her as the line crawled forward. That heated her temper, but she stayed outwardly calm as her mind worked furiously: *How to play this?* The whispers intensified, multiple stares pressing her face like hot spotlights, but Beth ignored them as best she could. She had underestimated her enemy, true, but she saw a way to turn this to her advantage; she and Daniel had been fools, Beth finally understood: instead of wishing the media attention away, like children, they would use the powerful tool they'd been handed—starting right now.

It wouldn't have been necessary had things truly been over, like she'd insisted to her husband, but more and more Beth had been thinking about that phone call to Rison from a mystery man—a mystery man who had seemed to both know and approve of the terrible things that Rison was about to do to her; the phone call and mystery man that the police also seemed to be ignoring. In addition, there was that girl's handwriting on those bizarre pages full of knowledge that *no one* could have known.

Beth grimaced. She hated to admit it, but Daniel had been right; there was something strange going on—although she wasn't fool enough to believe it had anything to do with a stupid cemetery in the woods! Regardless, getting their version—a carefully edited version—of events out there via Brennan might be just the way to find out what it was; and more importantly, get out ahead of it before it could harm her family again.

Warning?

I'll send them *a warning they'll never forget!*

A cell phone camera, the electronic shutter loud among the whispers, interrupted her thoughts. Beth turned in time for two more people, as if freed by the audacious action of the first, to snap her picture. She snatched her phone from her purse and took some pictures of her own. *Let's see how they like it.* The sitting area went dead quiet; the people who'd taken her picture appeared sheepish.

Then a man's laugh broke the silence; a guy three tables away deliberately snapped her picture with his phone. Mid-twenties, dark-haired, and handsome, he laughed again when Beth took his picture in turn; half a dozen photos each later, he winked at her.

Was he *flirting?*

Beth lowered her phone and stared at him, letting some of what she was feeling radiate.

His confident smile fell onto the little round table. "Jesus, lady, it's just a picture."

He gathered up his keys and book bag, leaving his latté, and exited the sitting area; he glanced back uneasily as if to make sure she wasn't following. He had on sparkly new running shoes and white ankle socks and a blue Nike tee-shirt with white athletic shorts emblazoned with a green Nike swoosh. His legs were especially nice: *great legs, bad attitude.* There were zillions like him, and Beth had stopped paying attention to them long ago. When legs scuttled out of sight, she glanced around; no one would look at her. It seemed the impromptu photo session was over. She put her phone back in her purse.

Brennan eventually returned carrying what looked like a small cup of plain coffee and her iced tea and more napkins than ten people needed; he had already shoved a red straw through her lid.

How thoughtful.

Suddenly Beth could stand it no longer. She got up, grabbing her book bag and purse. "I don't want it," she told him. "Throw it away. I want to go somewhere else." She stalked out of the tables, ignoring the stares, using the same exit as legs. When Brennan didn't follow, she turned.

"Well?"

"You're not going to drink this? It cost nine bucks! *Before taxes!*"

Beth didn't feel sorry for him at all; following her, scaring her. "I said I want to go somewhere else." She moved off, and then turned around again and arched an eyebrow when he just stood there like a big, bearded lump. "Do you want this interview or not?"

He scowled, then shoved everything into the nearest trash can and clumped toward her and angrily opened his mouth—and then shut it again, beady eyes focusing on something behind her.

Beth turned.

A tall, attractive blonde stood there wringing her hands, leather clutch hanging from a wrist. Well-dressed, she was maybe forty-five, and Beth recognized her as one of the people who'd joined the line before she'd confronted Brennan. Hesitant blue-gray eyes shifted between her and the reporter.

"Mrs. Sims? I'm sorry to bother you, I…I wanted to tell you how much I admire you." Her gaze lingered warily on Brennan, flinched away: "Could we talk somewhere private?"

Beth's stomach did a slow roil; she had a bad feeling she knew where this was going. At least she was fairly sure this woman wasn't another reporter. Nodding, she shot a warning look at Brennan and led the taller woman off the main aisle to a deserted spot between some stands of funny greeting cards and a long shelf heaped with board games; the reporter's eyes followed them, alive with curiosity, but he stayed put.

"How can I help you, Ms.—?"

The woman stared at her. "Oh!" She stuck out a hand, and Beth shook it. "My name is Gail Dempsey. I…" Her face crumpled; tears the size of breakfast eggs rolled down her cheeks. "Two men raped me my sophomore year of college. They…I knew them, they were friends. I *knew* them, and they still…" She sobbed, trembling. Beth stared up at her and waited, powerless. Finally Gail composed herself. "I've never told anyone that, not even my husband or my children. Like I said, I wanted to tell you how much I admire you, Mrs. Sims, and—"

"Call me Beth."

The tall and lovely woman smiled through her tears; she wiped her face, smearing makeup. "I respect what you did, Beth. If I could, I'd go back and do the same." Her bony fists clenched, the little purse swaying as she bared perfect white teeth. "I would kill them over and over! God help me, I would," she whispered.

Beth shifted her feet. *What does she want from me?* At last, she passed her book bag to the hand that held her purse and reached out and gripped Gail's forearm and held on to the trembling, warm flesh. Gail wiped her face again and looked at her.

Beth said, "No you don't."

She let go and walked away.

When she got back to the main aisle she glanced around; Brennan stood scribbling furiously in his notebook. He stopped when he saw her, face full of questions as he craned his neck around, looking for Gail. Beth stamped toward the front doors. She didn't care if he followed or not. No one was in the foyer so she slammed through, and would've done the same with the thick doors to the parking lot but remembered the three little boys; she opened that door carefully and then stepped into the swelter.

Beth moved to the side, closed her eyes, and took a long, long breath. She clutched her purse to her chest like a shield and dropped the book bag on the concrete. What did the woman expect? Beth couldn't help her, no matter that they shared even more than Gail suspected.

I can barely help myself!

The door opened and Brennan came out and she picked up her book bag and wiped her cheeks, once more glad she'd skipped the makeup. The reporter stopped when he saw her, then sidled over.

"What'd you say to her? She's standing in there bawling." Beth looked at him. He backed away and raised his hands. "Just asking."

She stalked towards her car. "Come on." Guilt laced with golden veins of fury kept her moving; she could do nothing for Gail. *NOTHING!* Beth felt like she'd left a slice of her soul back by those board games.

He called after her: "Where are we going?"

"Does it matter? You either want this interview or you don't." She used the fob to unlock the car. Behind her, she heard rapid footsteps.

"All right, all right, I'm coming."

He waited as she cleaned out the passenger seat; he had to move it all the way back to squeeze in, and then sat hunched and filling the front of her Nissan, studying her and then Lizzie's car seat in the back while trying to pretend he wasn't. She pulled onto the busy street, turning right. Beth had no idea where she was going. She just knew she couldn't stay at the bookstore.

Reminded that Brennan had ruined the small amount of joy she was trying to wring out of her day, she tossed him a look. He felt it and glanced at her uneasily. Beth stilled her anger; she needed him—for now. She would have to walk a tightrope; give him what she wanted and not what he wanted, but still somehow leave him satisfied enough to write the story.

To write what *she* wanted.

"Um, where *are* we going, anyway?"

"Somewhere less crowded."

Beth saw it up ahead. *Perfect.* She whipped over two lanes and hit the turn signal and pulled in. Someone honked. They hadn't even been in the car for a minute. She cruised through the jam-packed lot, stopping to let a line of children cross to the doors with the golden arches emblazoned on them. She found an open spot in the back near the Dumpsters and parked.

Brennan wrinkled his nose. "*This* is less crowded?"

She ignored him and got out. The McDonald's was packed, granted, but she didn't care as long as there were no Gail's inside. To make sure of that, Beth popped the trunk and found one of Daniel's golf visors. It was bright white and said PING on the bill, whatever that meant. She adjusted it way down to fit her head, pulled her ponytail over the back, and settled her sunglasses firmly on her face. She bent down to study herself in the side mirror; short of a false nose and a clown wig, she was as disguised as she was going to get.

Beth noticed Brennan watching and straightened. Was she *amusing* him? He blanked his face and looked away; smart man. She strode across the lot, threading her way through the long line of cars waiting in the drive-thru. Brennan stuck to her heels like he was afraid she would make a break for it.

Once inside, the smell of French fries assaulted her and her stomach growled, but today she was too wound up to eat; what she could, wouldn't, and had to say filled her brain as she looked for an open table. A couple with two small kids began to gather up trays and booster seats and Beth moved through the crowd to stake a claim. They watched the couple wrangle the kids out of the booth, the little tow-headed boy smiling shyly. Beth managed to smile back. Then it was theirs.

She made Brennan wait as she wiped the table with a handful of napkins, trying not to shoot the young couple dirty looks and almost succeeding. *People should clean up after themselves!* Once she was satisfied, Beth slid into the hard plastic booth, the reporter squeezing in across from her. He already had that notebook and pen out.

When he opened his mouth, Beth held up a hand.

"I'm still thirsty."

He stared at her, mouth open, for about three seconds, then snapped it closed and eyed her narrowly. "And what can I get you to drink, Mrs. Sims?" Teeth flashed in his beard. She thought it was supposed to be a smile.

"Unsweetened tea." She pointed at the multiple lines snaking from the cash registers. "Better hurry. I only have so much time for this." She had all afternoon, but he didn't need to know that.

Muttering, he squeezed back out and stomped over and got in line, but Beth ignored him; she heard those words every day from Daniel. The important thing was she'd gotten what she wanted—*both* things she'd wanted; she really was thirsty, and now she had a few minutes to order her thoughts. How was she going to play this? Glancing around, she could see that no one was paying any attention to her so she took her sunglasses off and hung them from the front of her shirt.

Beth had made some hard decisions by the time he set the tea and straw in front of her and shoehorned himself back into the booth; now she just had to get Brennan to play along.

Of course that was easier thought of than done; before she could utter a word he had that notepad out, gold pen poised, and hit her with the question that Beth had *known* he would ask!

"Were you sexually assaulted by Scott Duane Rison, Mrs. Sims?" Then he leaned back away from her. "I have to ask these questions," he assured her hastily, "but you don't have to answer."

Beth *so* wanted to drive folded knuckles into his larynx and snap it like a pencil, but unfortunately that wasn't an option; she slowly tore the paper sheath off the straw and inserted the straw into her tea and took a sip. Once she had control again, Beth spoke:

"No questions. I will tell you about Sunday. You will listen without interrupting and then go write a story."

His face worked. "'No questions'? I'm a reporter, Mrs. Sims, asking questions is pretty much my job description. How do you expect me—"

"Fine." Beth gathered her tea and keys and purse and slid out. "I will only do this once. I'm offering you a—what do you call it in your profession, an exclusive?" She shrugged. "But if you don't want it," she stuck her hand in her purse, then held up her phone and wiggled it at him, "I'm sure one of your many colleagues who left messages would be happy to have this interview on my terms. Have a nice day, Mr. Brennan."

"*All right!*" Heads turned. "All right. We'll do it your way. Please sit back down." Beth did. "You'll give me the exclusive?"

"You have my word." Did he really think she wanted to do this more than once? His greedy smile slipped a little when she stuck a finger in his face: "*If* you don't interrupt—and no questions!"

"Agreed," he said smoothly—too smoothly—and Beth knew it wouldn't be that easy.

THE THIRD SISTER

WHEN THE steaks were done, the humans went inside while the hairballs ran around and sat in front of the sliding doors, panting and staring in at Dan through the glass with their black ears at full mast and their long tongues hanging and dripping. *Yum.*

He tried to ignore them as he took the chair Mindy indicated was his; he tried to ignore her saucy smile, too. McFarlane sat across from him, and at a meaningful look, Dan snatched off his Chi Sox cap and shades and set them to the side of his plate; the girls bookended them at the narrow ends of the oval. Mindy had set places for five, but no one said anything about the empty plate to McFarlane's immediate right. Dan also had the old man pegged as a grace man, but they just dug in; after a second, he joined them.

McFarlane read him. "We're pretty informal 'round here, Dan." He lifted a hip off the chair, then flicked out a worn but razor-sharp four-inch Buck and started carving, disregarding the wooden-handled steak knife Mindy had set out; she rolled her eyes but kept her peace. "And during the summertime, farm folks get up early and work when it's cool, so breakfast's usually kinda skimpy. That's why we're puttin' on this feed, in case you were wonderin'." He pointed at Dan's plate with the Buck. "Try that beef and tell me what ya think. That's some of my own."

Dan obliged, cutting off a chunk. He chewed and swallowed with relish, then washed it down with a mouthful of iced sweet tea. "That's the best damn rib-eye I've ever had, sir. Sorry about my language, but that's a good steak."

McFarlane laughed. "Don't worry about it, son. Nobody here's got virgin ears. Glad you like it."

The clank of utensils and the tinkle of ice cubes were the only sounds as everyone set to; Dan tried to concentrate on his free grub, but it was hard with five sets of eyes fixed on him, and sometimes six when the old man looked up from his plate. When a bare foot rubbed against his calf, he dropped the steak knife; it landed on his plate with a clatter.

McFarlane glanced up, and to cover Dan retrieved the knife from a pile of potato salad and pointed it at the empty plate. "Will, uh, will the Keeper be joining us?"

Knives and forks froze in mid-air, hanging all around the table.

McFarlane's gray-green eyes had turned as cold and as calculating as an IRS examiner's soul. "The *Keeper*," he said. He seemed to be trying on the word and not much liking it; then the old man snorted. "No, Dan, the 'Keeper' has other concerns to be about." That's all he said, but those winter eyes stayed pinned to Dan. The foot, which had paused, resumed rubbing below the table.

Dan cut a piece of steak and chewed and tried to swallow; as buttery as it was, it didn't seem to want to go down, for some reason. When he was fairly sure he wouldn't choke, he said, "Oh."

Silence descended; no one was eating except for him. Dan focused on his plate and vowed not to ask any more fucking questions. He also decided to ignore the foot because he couldn't tell whose it was; he just prayed to Holy God and Baby Jesus that he hadn't missed the old man kicking off his boots.

McFarlane squinted across the table at Dan for an entire minute before saying, "I'd forgotten that you'd already met her down at our cemetery."

"Yes, sir," Dan said, but he had a feeling that the farmer had done no such thing as "forget". He thought about apologizing for trespassing, but then decided he would only if McFarlane made a huff about it. Dan also thought about asking the old man about his wacky graveyard, now that the subject had been not-so-safely broached, but, considering how the touchy bastard was looking at him, his vow of no more questions was emerging as smarter and smarter. So instead, he lied. "She, uh, she was real nice."

The old farmer's face didn't change, but his voice was suddenly dry. "She is that. And her name is Melissa, not that other foolishness. She's an old friend of the family. She helped me raise the girls after my wife passed."

"I see," Dan said.

So this "old family friend" Melissa wanted to be the Keeper of the cemetery, but McFarlane didn't *want* Melissa to be the Keeper? Or did he object to her *calling* herself the Keeper? And there sure seemed to be a big ol' dose of hostility in the man's tone for someone who was a "family friend"—one that had helped raise his daughters, no less. What the fuck was that all about?

No. No more fucking questions, Dan-o. Ever.

McFarlane continued to watch him without eating; finally he cut a big chunk of rib-eye with the Buck and stuffed it into his mouth and spoke around it: "That plate is for my oldest, Dan. She should be down any minute." He looked at Rebecca. "You told your sister we were about to eat?"

The redhead shrugged as she too resumed eating. "She knows. I don't think she's hungry." At McFarlane's look, she gave a low chuckle. "Don't worry, she's not going to miss this."

Mindy laughed. McFarlane frowned at Rebecca, and then at Mindy, and then shifted that frown to Dan, who clicked his teeth shut and bent back to his plate. *There's a third one?* Dear God. The foot under the table moved higher, and he shot Mindy a glare—Dan was sure it was her—who gave him innocent. She almost pulled it off.

Wait. Miss what? He shifted his chair to get away from the foot, trying to be unobtrusive, and stared when Rebecca shifted her own chair to follow, toes now reaching for his crotch. Dan frowned at her, and she smiled. He should've known; those legs were long enough to reach anywhere he tried to run.

Dan ate faster. His only goal was getting out of there without being shot. *Holy Mother of God, there's a third one.* Outside, one mutt whined, then barked.

Mindy scolded, "No, Ike. You can wait. Poor babies, they want their treat now." This with a look at him that turned it into something dirty.

Dan crossed his legs to fend off Rebecca and shoveled steak.

And then, despite his vow of no questions, his mouth betrayed him—as usual. "Ike? And Reagan? What's the other one's name, Carter?"

Nobody laughed. McFarlane said, "Not Carter. It's Nixon." He beamed. "Eisenhower, Nixon, and Reagan, the three finest Presidents this great country has ever been blessed with. Don't you agree, son?"

"Uh, sure." Dan went back to his plate. Nixon? *You've got to be fucking kidding me.* At least none of the toothy fuzz balls were named Bush; Dan might've gotten up and walked out.

More clinking knives and tinkling ice, and then he jumped when another foot came snaking in from the opposite side to join the party. Dan shot a glare at Mindy and she gave him more innocent.

These horny bitches are going to get me killed.

He fended them off as best he could while trying not to squirm too much; maybe the old man thought everyone had ants in their pants or britches or whatever because he seemed to take everyone twitching around as a matter of course. Dan grew tired of the game and picked up his tea and took a drink and reached his free hand under the table and found a smooth, taut calf and grabbed skin and twisted. Mindy squeaked, and a foot vanished from Dan's lap.

The old man gave her a long look, and she managed to blush and lower her head and shoot Dan a pouty glare all at the same time. Dan reached for the other smooth calf but Rebecca yanked it away and favored him with a tight smile.

The meal continued. Dan was almost through with his steak and feeling a little smug when he felt a foot return, but way down by his ankle, where he couldn't reach it. He stifled a curse; these sluts were out to get him shot, he just knew it. Then the sound of a door opening turned his head, and Dan forgot about the steak, and the foot, and the hairballs staring at him like he was a giant treat, and the prickly old man and his horny daughters.

He forgot about everything.

A woman stepped into the kitchen from the covered walkway and shut the door. She was about his age or a little younger, thirtyish maybe. Her hair was a glossy blue-black and flowed across her shoulders. Dressed in a simple gray tee-shirt and frayed cut-offs, she went barefoot like her sisters. She undulated across the kitchen to stand behind McFarlane, resting a slim hand on his shoulder. He reached up and patted it. The woman ignored her sisters and put her consideration on Dan and kept it there like she had no intention of looking at anything else ever again. Her skin was flawless alabaster, and her big, big eyes had long, dark lashes and irises that were the depth-less black of a starless sky. They were so dark he couldn't differentiate a pupil.

Dan stared into them and felt himself drowning.

McFarlane chuckled. Dan blushed, but he still couldn't look away. "Alexandria, this is Dan, our neighbor finally come for a visit. Dan, this is Alexandria, my oldest."

Dan worked spit into his mouth. "Hi," he whispered.

"Hello, Dan. You can call me Alex, everyone does."

He stiffened and swayed in his chair. Her voice had sent a wave of…something…crashing down his spine; it was low for a woman's voice, and melodic, and he'd never heard one quite like it.

Or had he?

Dan frowned and shook his head and then put his knife and fork down and raised his fingers to his temples and rubbed; for some reason, a sharp pain throbbed just behind his right eye. He could *swear* he'd heard that voice before, but that was impossible; he'd never met this woman before this moment.

He dropped his hands and looked up, and then Dan realized four things: one, the foot had vanished; two, Alex seemed to watch him cautiously now; three, the kitchen had gone utterly silent; and four, the old man was giving him the death-stare again.

McFarlane leaned and looked back and up at his eldest daughter's face, and then he leaned back just as slowly and looked across the table at Dan. "You two know each other?"

His soft question crackled in the hushed kitchen.

Alex cut her black eyes at her father. "Of course not."

The old man stared at Dan, waiting.

"No, sir, we've never met before." He tried to smile. "I think I'd remember if we had."

McFarlane's mouth smiled back, but he kept those suspicious lasers trained on Dan. "Somethin' else, idn't she?"

"Yes, sir, she is."

Mindy was attempting to pout a hole through her plate, but Rebecca stared a challenge at her older sister; it didn't last long. The redhead dropped her head and played with her food, and Alexandria turned those midnight eyes back to Dan with a cool smile of triumph.

He looked down hastily and cut up the last of his steak and stuffed it in his mouth and chewed as fast as he could. A charged, dangerous silence still roamed about the room; moron that he was, he decided it needed company.

"They're all beautiful, sir. You're a blessed man."

"Thank you, Dan. Kind of you to say."

Blessed? Cursed was more like it, with three spectacular daughters. Dan shot a look at all their hands; no engagement or wedding rings. Suitors should've been lined up outside the door and down the road and past the cow army and all the way to fucking Nashville.

Why are none of these women married?

He dared a look at Alex again and found those eyes still on him; she wasn't smiling, not this one, and it went without saying she wouldn't be playing footsies under the table with him, but there was something…considering…in her stare that made Dan suspect she was a lot like her sisters, despite her current demureness.

He jerked his eyes away from those inviting dark depths and tried to chew faster. Alex was near his age, so why wasn't *she* at least married? And then a thought struck Dan like a thrown brick; he furtively took in each woman.

Sisters?

Their coloring and features couldn't have been more different. And something else was bothering Dan—the fact that these beauties had come from *this* guy; not only did they not look like each other, they didn't look a thing like McFarlane, lucky them.

And then his stupid mouth opened again: "Their mother must have been exquisite."

Outside, three growls started, deep and throbbing.

Dan took a drink of tea to wet a suddenly dry throat. "Did I say something wrong?"

"Don't dissemble, Dan. There's nothing in this world I hate more than a dissembler. You know these girls aren't sisters."

Mindy surged to her feet, glaring at Dan, breasts swaying under the wife-beater. "We are *so* sisters!"

"Hey, I didn't—"

"We *are* sisters." He looked at Rebecca; the summer green's held hard on his: "Our bond is as strong as blood."

Alex said, "Stronger than blood could ever be."

Her velvet voice sent tremors through Dan again. *Why does it sound so familiar?* "Look, I didn't mean you weren't…" *Shit, I didn't even SAY it!* "I—"

McFarlane raised his hand. "I know you meant no harm, son, but take what I said to heart: I don't tolerate liars at my table. And it's true, these girls aren't sisters in the normal sense. My Muriel, rest her soul, was barren. They're adopted." He glanced over his shoulder. "Sit down," he told Alex. "You're givin' me the grips standin' behind me like that."

"Yes, Father."

McFarlane turned his attention back to Dan, who was busy shoveling the last of his potato salad. Alex sat across from him, and as she did, Dan glanced up just long enough to confirm that yes, yes indeed, it was a bra-free farm. That fun fact notwithstanding, as soon as he finished, he was fucking *out* of there; he'd had enough of these loonies.

"Where was I?" McFarlane had a faraway look. He'd cleaned his plate and pushed it aside.

"Uh, adopted, sir?" Two more bites and Dan was history. All three sisters were zeroed on him, unblinking, unsmiling. One more bite. Outside, the mutts were still staring at him through the glass; they had their ears laid back as they growled, low and throbbing.

"That's right. Yes, son, they're adopted, but loved no less for it." The old farmer picked up his knife and cleaned it on a napkin and folded it and lifted a hip off the chair and slid it back into his pocket. "I used to regret that Murial and I couldn't have children, but then I realized it was a blessing. When you have kids you gotta take whatever pops out, fair or foul, but when you're lucky enough to adopt, you can pick and choose." He reached and took his daughter's hands to either side; Mindy stretched to join in. They sat like that, holding hands and staring at Dan.

"I like to think we chose the cream, son."

Dan wiped his mouth with the green cloth napkin and pushed his plate away and took a drink of tea. "That's great, sir." He pulled his phone out. "Would you look at the time? Thanks for lunch, and it was nice to meet you and your daughters, but I'm afraid I have to go." He scraped his chair back, but the old man let go of Rebecca's hand and waved him down.

"What's yer hurry? We haven't had our dessert yet."

Dan hesitated. "Okay, but then I really do have to go."

McFarlane nodded. "Girls, clean this up and bring the goodies." Mindy and Rebecca got up to clear the table. Alex sat where she was and stared at Dan. "They're gonna have watermelon later, but right now you can join me in my kind of dessert, if you'd like."

"What kind's that, sir?" Dan did his best to ignore Alex—and also Mindy when she pressed full and unfettered breasts into his shoulder as she reached for his plate. Dan got his answer when Rebecca appeared on his other side, a half-full bottle of Maker's Mark in her hand and two heavy glass tumblers in the other. She plunked one down in front of him and raised a ginger eyebrow.

"Whiskey," the old farmer supplied.

"Why not?" It was dark somewhere, and it was quicker than watermelon. Rebecca poured generous dollops from the bottle with that distinctive runny red-wax seal, her father's first. McFarlane lifted his glass, and Dan reached across the oval to clink them together.

"To new friends."

"To new friends." The smooth whiskey delighted Dan's tongue and burned his throat going down. He coughed.

"Use another, son?"

"No thanks," he croaked. Dan could've used seven more, but he wasn't sure seven would be enough.

"Smart man." McFarlane waved a hand, and Rebecca cleared off the glasses and took the bottle away. She seemed disappointed. "Fools kill themselves with that stuff. They don't understand that it's medicine." He thumped a fist against his thick chest. "One a day keeps the goddamn money-grubbin' doctor away, that's what my daddy used to say." He laughed, and then added, "A'course, Daddy never took his own advice. But I'm smarter." He studied Dan, cold and hard and probing. "It's a shame it took that bad business Sunday for you to have a reason to visit. Neighbors used to know each other, look out for each other." He grimaced. "Just one thing that's wrong with this country nowadays." Storm eyes glinted. "I tried not to take offense."

It had never even occurred to Dan he was insulting McFarlane by not swinging by to introduce himself. "I'm sorry, sir, we didn't think—"

"No need to apologize, son. I know the younger generations play by different rules—not better rules, mind you, just different."

Mindy spoke from the sink where she was rinsing plates before filling the dishwasher. "Speaking of that, Daddy, Dan promised he would bring his little girl by for a visit. Lizzie. Wasn't that her name?"

They were all looking at him. "Uh, sure." *Promised?* "I mean, yeah, that's her name."

"Yes, you must bring her by. We'd love to meet her." That was Rebecca; the sun shot golden highlights through her copper braid as she opened the sliding-glass door and tossed the hairballs their scraps. Dan noted that Reagan got first choice even though she was smallest.

"Yes, you must bring her." Alexandria's voice, vibrating honey, pulled him back. He looked at her, and it was hard to look away.

Behind him at the sink, Mindy began to sing, sweet voice filling the kitchen.

"Yes, you must bring her," McFarlane added softly. Rebecca slid the glass door closed and then turned and raised her voice and melded it to her sister's; Dan listened and watched, bemused. Apparently it was post-lunch-sing-along time on the farm.

Alexandria got up and walked around behind him; as she did, she threaded her voice into the song…and suddenly it took on a new quality as it surged around and somehow *through* him; not a comfortable feeling. There were words, but they somehow slipped past his perception; they weren't English, he could tell that much. His eyelids drooped, and he forced them back open. He tried to turn and look at Alex (Dan didn't like her standing behind him any more than McFarlane had), but his head felt like it was trapped in molasses.

McFarlane stood up and leaned toward him across the table, hands splayed. "Don't worry about not dropping by before, Dan. You're here now, and everything is friendly between us. You bring little Elizabeth on by for a visit and let her meet my girls. Say you will, Dan. I want to hear your promise. Promise you'll bring Elizabeth by to meet my girls, Dan. Promise you will…"

Dan's eyelids had cinder-blocks attached to them, so he shut them. The song was more than a song; it was a physical force, a solid thing. He was surrounded and infused by it, buoyed as it carried him away. He felt his forehead thump on the table.

Dan looked around in amazement; he was still on the farm, but not in the kitchen anymore. They were standing in the big house's front yard. Wait, kitchen? Of course he wasn't in the kitchen, but he and John would probably end up hanging out there after dinner to shoot the shit and have a snort or three of Makers while enjoying the sunset on the westward patio. His best friend was loyal to all things Tennessee, except when it came to Maker's. Said if someone in Tennessee could make a whiskey as silky as what they cooked up in Loretto, Kentucky, well then by God he'd drink it, but as it hadn't happened yet, Maker's it was.

Lizzie let go of his hand and ran to Mindy, who had just appeared from the giant trees looming behind the house. She scooped her up with a big hug, and then Rebecca and Alex appeared and joined them, getting their own hugs, laughing and chatting. They all turned to wave, and Dan waved back, watching them disappear beneath those trees.

Lizzie was learning so much from her sisters…

Sisters? No, that wasn't right, they weren't sisters—even though they acted like it…Dan heard singing. He tried to look around for the singers but he couldn't move his head, for some reason. Lizzie had her own horse now, stabled here to ride when she visited; John had bought it for her. She was so happy here. John appeared, inviting him in for a chat, the girls would be awhile; they were walking in the woods today. There was something they wanted to show Lizzie…

Something is wrong.

It was a thought that seemed to echo in Dan's head, a thought that stubbornly refused to be subsumed by the song, buzzing around like an annoying fly. There was something missing from all this…or some*one* missing? The song grew louder, pulsing in his head, his heart, his fingers and toes, his penis:

Beth.

Beth wouldn't like this.

Where *was* Beth? Where was Lizzie's mother?

John took his elbow and guided him toward the house. The girls would be back for supper, and they needed to get the makings together for them to cook or the men would never hear the end of it.

Lizzie was so excited to have finally found her sisters…

No.

Something wasn't right.

Dan's head was on a table, his cheek pressed against the wood, and his eyes were closed. A wind was blowing his short hair around, and there was a song throbbing in his ears and head and body, a song with voices but no words he could understand. He could also hear howling. Dan fought, tried to sit up, but his arms were rubber, his hands numb.

With a grunt, Dan pulled his cheek off the wood and pushed against the table and sat up.

The song died raggedly, one voice falling away after the other. The wind stopped. Dan forced his eyes open. The howling ceased.

They were standing around him, all four, their hands outstretched over his head, palms down, fingers almost touching. As he sat up, they lowered their arms uncertainly.

"What…?" His mouth felt like someone had stuffed it with fiberglass insulation. He wobbled, and would've fallen out of his chair if he hadn't already gripped the table. He was trembling so hard he was twitching. They were all staring at him with a blend of fury and astonishment; when he met her eyes, Mindy backed away from the table with a look that was easy to read: fear.

"Why…?" Memory returned, and comprehension. The whiskey! Dan staggered to his feet, knocking his chair over backwards with a clatter. "You drugged me!"

McFarlane didn't answer, just stood there looking at him as if he'd never seen anything like Dan before. Alex moved out from behind Dan and around to his right and stopped, and there was no considering look now; she glared like she wanted to skin him alive, then crossed her arms under her breasts and looked an angry question at her father. Dan held on to the table as they stared at each other; time stretched. He glanced at the other two and found them watching McFarlane and Alex as well, waiting. The mutts were on their feet now. They watched Dan through the glass. Waiting.

Why had they drugged him? Wait, they'd drunk from the same bottle. Then why did he feel this way? Singing…why the *fuck* was he thinking about singing? And Lizzie's sisters…

Lizzie didn't have any sisters.

What the hell is wrong with me!?

Finally Alex grimaced and nodded as if she was conceding some point even though no one had spoken a damn word. McFarlane nodded back, his face resigned as he slowly sat back down.

Resigned? Resigned about what?

No, I don't fucking care. I've had enough of these screwy people.

Dan oh-so-casually stuck his hand in his front pocket and gripped the butt of the little .22. Reassured, he opened his mouth to tell McFarlane he was leaving, neighborly bullshit be damned, when Alex fixed him with a look of such black-eyed fury that his tongue shriveled. Then she turned, blue-black hair swirling, and flounced out, slamming the door behind her with a crash.

McFarlane said, "Pick that chair up and have a seat, son. We need to talk."

"What did you do to me?"

"Me?" He smiled. "Didn't do a thing. You musta been tired, is all. You nodded off right there on the table."

"Bullshit." Dan almost pulled the pistol then, but hesitated. Doing that would open a whole new can of worms—worms like the police, and he'd seen enough cops lately to last him the next three lifetimes.

"I said *sit down*, son."

"*Fuck you*, old man, and I'm not your goddamn son, so can it with the 'son' shit."

"You know," McFarlane's tone was friendly, "I meant what I said earlier, about being sorry for what happened at your place." Rebecca sat down and sipped her tea. Mindy was back by the sink, from the sound of it doing dishes again.

"Goody for you."

"I truly am sorry," McFarlane insisted. "Sorry Scotty couldn't follow simple instructions; sorry he got so caught up by that little whore of yours he thought with the wrong head. If he'd a done what I told 'im, it would've saved us a whole heap 'o trouble. It's my fault, though. Scotty always was a screw-up, and I shoulda known what would happen, sendin' a boy to do a man's job."

There was a space shuttle blasting off in Dan's head, but he managed to choke out a whisper: "You motherfucker." He started to jerk the revolver out but suddenly a firm body pressed against his back. Mindy! Dan went still as her slender arm snaked under his from behind, holding up a shining, foot-long butcher's knife; showing it to him. She held up the other hand and showed him a slightly smaller knife.

"Sit down, son. We need to talk."

"I'd do as my daddy says if I were you, Dan." Her breathy whisper tickled his ear. "He has a gun in his pocket, Daddy. I felt it earlier." She giggled, heavy breasts jiggling against Dan's back. "It's not a very *big* one, but it'd do the trick, I think." She pressed the edge of that enormous fucking knife against his belly, and Dan knew it wouldn't take much pressure to send his guts spilling onto the table.

"Does he now?" McFarlane glanced at Rebecca. "Get it. And fetch me his phone and keys while yer at it."

The redhead stood up and swayed around the table. He slowly removed his hand, and she reached in and dug around in both pockets until she had everything. Then she pressed herself against him.

"It could've been so good, Dan." Her whisper came a second before she bit his earlobe. Hard. He flinched, and she laughed. So did Mindy. Rebecca let go with her teeth and then grabbed Dan's dick and squeezed, cupping his balls in the bargain. She released him and stepped away with a smoking smile.

"Ooh, maybe *not* so little. Too bad."

McFarlane held out his hand, and she passed everything to him and sat back down; the old man didn't seem to give two mangy shits about his daughters' antics. He looked at Dan's phone and the little pistol contemplatively before setting them on the table, and then he tucked Dan's keys into his breast pocket.

"Sit down, boy."

Mindy picked his chair up and he sat. She positioned herself behind and leaned against him, one breast against the back of his neck and one in his ear. Incredibly, she began to massage his shoulders. Dan could see one big, silvery blade flash out of the corner of his eye.

"You people are fucking nuts, you know that?"

No one said anything.

Finally, McFarlane leaned back in his chair and heaved a deep sigh. "Well, son, looks like we're gonna have to do this the hard way."

Discoveries

I T WAS almost three-thirty when Beth parked next to Brennan's Honda.

Instead of getting out, though, the reporter looked over/down at her and said, "I know I told you I was packaging this for Sunday's run, but…" He took off his dinky glasses and cleaned them with the hem of his tee-shirt.

"'But'?"

"But it's just too juicy." He smiled, then hooked his glasses back on and jabbed them up the bridge of his nose with a big thumb. "My editor will want to let the world know you're talking—you know, build anticipation. Let's say…" His muddy eyes went far away, but he was still smiling. "We run it out on the wire as soon as Friday, a teaser for the website on Saturday, and *then* do the big Sunday write-up." That smile told Beth that whatever his editor wanted, this was what Brennan wanted. "Just giving you a heads-up. The weekend will be a little nuts for you guys now, especially you, but Sunday will still be the real circus. Is, uh, is that okay?"

Beth stopped glaring at him with an effort. *I knew what I was signing up for. Doesn't mean I have to like it, though.* "We'll deal with it."

"Good," he said, relieved. "Is there any chance Mr. Sims would talk to me exclusively as well?"

This again. The man was nothing if not dogged. "Like I said—several times—I'll ask him."

"Have him call me tonight."

Beth sighed. "I'll see what he says, no promises." And then she added (even though it was none of the reporter's business), "Daniel and I aren't exactly seeing eye to eye at the moment."

"Try to convince him if you can. It would be better for the piece to have both of your perspectives. And even if he doesn't agree, remember that *you* already promised me the exclusive."

"I keep my word, Mr. Brennan."

"I know that's what you say, Mrs. Sims, but I've been burned before, and when it gets out you're talking…well, let's just say there'll be mucho greedy little ink-stained fingers dialing your number and knocking on your door, hoping you'll talk to them too, but you tell them you've already promised it to me."

Beth stared across the console at him. "I know what I promised."

He shied back into the door. "Okay, okay, just making sure." He fumbled for the handle and climbed out, then leaned down and offered his hand. Beth shook, her hand engulfed in his hairy mitt. "Thank you again, Mrs. Sims." His grin reminded her of an eager boy's. "I've *got* to go see this for myself!"

"Be careful."

It had just popped out. She'd considered this man an enemy, and maybe she still did; he wanted to exploit her family tragedy for his own gain, and anybody who harbored that agenda Beth would always consider an enemy. But over the past two-plus hours, something had happened; she'd softened toward him somehow. Whatever her feelings, she'd meant it. She even repeated it, holding his eyes with hers.

"*Be careful* out there."

He stared in at her, looking like he understood the message behind her words even if Beth didn't, not really.

"I will," he said, then thrust his glasses up his nose with his thumb again. "But don't worry about me. I told you, no wannabe-thug rednecks will scare Brian Brennan off. You should read about the lowlifes I've exposed in Chicago." His sudden chuckle was sour. "Besides, I have an ex-wife living in Wisconsin with her new husband and three of *my* kids who call *him* Dad—in other words, Mrs. Sims, I've already given everything for this job." He shrugged. "What can a bunch of hicks do?" He waved with his notepad, which was much fuller than it'd been two-plus hours ago. "I'll be in touch." He stood up and shut her door, and she watched him jump into the Honda and speed off.

Beth squeezed her eyelids shut and gripped the steering wheel with both hands.

I should be happy. Ultimately, she'd gotten what she'd wanted: "The enemy of my enemy is my friend," she whispered. Beth had turned her enemy to her cause, and she had then set that enemy on the trail of a greater enemy.

That was all well and good, except Brennan had already been hot on that trail; he'd come down here because something had "smelled funny" about how the investigation into Scott Rison's death had been handled, and that had set his reporter's nose to twitching; and what's more, after listening to all he had to say about John McFarlane, Beth realized that she'd never truly believed she'd *had* a greater enemy.

She shook her head. The man had only been in town for two days, and he certainly hadn't been idle! Beth now had to face the fact that if even half—a quarter!—of what Brennan had hinted at was true about John McFarlane, then perhaps her husband and this Special Agent Scandlin weren't so paranoid after all.

Beth let go of the wheel and sat up determinedly and pulled her phone from her purse. The First Rule of War was "Know Your Enemy". She didn't care about all that crap people spouted about terrain; learn your enemy first, *then* worry about the ground you were fighting him on.

She hesitated, glancing around; if Brennan and Gail could find her, so could others. She drove back to the McDonald's and parked in the back by the Dumpsters again, this time facing out, all while watching to see if someone had followed her from the bookstore. After five minutes and one incurious McDonald's employee swinging bags of trash up and over the lip of the giant bin, Beth decided she was safe enough and turned the air up full blast and used her phone to get on one of the big search engines.

Who are you, John McFarlane?

Twenty minutes later she lowered her phone and absently watched a family with six kids pile out of a dirty white Suburban and troop through the doors emblazoned with the golden arches. There was little about McFarlane to find out there—and only one picture, amazingly. Still, even with the paucity of information, she had gleaned tidbits. A few of those bits synced with what Brennan had said: i.e. the meteoric and mostly unexplained rise to fortune back in the mid-eighties; a certain shadowy clout in Rutherford County (and beyond, if she credited some of Brennan's darker and more outrageous claims) that didn't necessarily run along established authority lines, although that last was hard to prove with a web search. She'd just have to take the journalist's word about that part—for now.

However, most of the things she'd found out about McFarlane seemed to contradict Brennan's doom-and-gloom suspicions: voted Rutherford County Farm Family of the Year three times? Farm Family of the *Year!* Three times! *This* was the big, bad man? McFarlane was also a Vietnam veteran, a hero with two Purple Hearts and the Silver Star, no less. He and his corporation, something called The McFarlane Group, also gave generously to more charities than Beth had fingers and toes.

So why would a man like that give two licks about my little family, good or bad?

Beth had no earthly idea, so she put that question aside and mulled over what was really bothering her: the photograph.

The *one* photograph she'd found.

She raised her phone and looked at the photo again; it was from a newspaper article that had ran in 1991, announcing that the McFarlane clan had won Rutherford County Farm Family of the Year for the third time in five years. The faded color print showed a stocky man wearing denim overalls and a straw cowboy hat tilted so that the frayed brim hid most of his suntanned face except for a straight nose, a hard, unsmiling mouth, and a strong jaw-line.

Beth frowned. In other words, he could have been just about any of the farmers she passed on the road going to and from work every stupid day.

The girls, however, were a different story.

The youngest had a fluff of blonde hair and was still in diapers—and, like her father, she wasn't smiling. The next youngest, the one with a cap of red hair and a healthy crop of freckles, was standing in front of McFarlane while holding her little unsmiling sister in her arms. She wasn't smiling either. The oldest, a girl of about ten or eleven, stood a little apart, and she most *definitely* wasn't smiling. Beth had never seen such a dour family, especially considering they were winning an award and getting written up in the local rag for it.

Maybe Farm Family of the Year soured after the second time or so.

Her attention kept getting pulled back to the oldest girl. At first Beth told herself it was that wave of blue-black hair, and those features; if this girl had grown into the woman those stunning looks promised, then she would be a world-class head-turner now, no question. But eventually Beth realized it wasn't the hair, or that face. It was those imperious black eyes; those eyes stared an arrogant challenge out of the photograph, so much so they made Beth almost edgy after a while.

She lowered the phone back into her lap. It was strange enough that there was only one picture of John McFarlane, but the girls in that photo from '91 would now be in their twenties, or close enough, and Beth could find nothing else about them— not even their names! The caption below the photo only read, "The McFarlane Family: Winners of the 1991 Rutherford County Farm Family of the Year". Beth had searched and searched and searched but had found not a thing else about those girls; no Myspace pages or Facebook pages, *nothing*. And if that wasn't weird, Beth didn't understand the meaning of the word; she worked with dozens of women in their twenties, and to a girl they lived and or posted most of their lives online.

Beth raised her phone and looked at the photograph again. Not these three, though. In fact, if she hadn't stumbled across this image, she wouldn't have known they even existed.

And there it was, what was truly troubling Beth.

Helen.

Helen had never once mentioned that her late sister Muriel had been married to John McFarlane—of course they had never even *talked* about McFarlane, and why would they? To Beth he had just been their neighbor up on the ridge, just some old farmer who owned all the land and the cows around her new house; so she could maybe understand Helen leaving that out, *maybe*, but the fact that Helen had never mentioned her three beautiful nieces…?

Beth tapped her lips. Muriel wasn't in the photo; she'd died before they took it, obviously…maybe that was it, the pain of losing her sister…Beth shook her head. No. Her friend had gobs of pictures of Jacob and Jacob's dad Paul and her late husband Henry and the rest of her family hanging all over her house, and even a couple of Muriel, now that she thought about it. Helen kept the one of Ryan on the end table, beneath the lamp right next to her spot on the couch, and except for her youngest son, Helen had no trouble talking about *any* of them, dead or alive.

So why had there been no mention of her nieces? No photographs on the walls proudly showing them off? Beth didn't know, but she vowed then and there that she and Helen were going to sit down and have a long talk, and soon.

She raised her phone again and looked at the thick-necked man in the frayed straw cowboy hat and the dark denim overalls. This *is the monster?* The man that, according to Brennan, made everyone in Rutherford County hop, whether they knew he pulled their strings or not? This man, who was a war hero and gave generously to every charity on the books and who had also raised three daughters by himself after his wife had passed?

Beth snorted, staring out the windshield but not seeing anything.

Ridiculous. Absolutely ridiculous!

Except…

…except Scott Rison had worked for him. And, if what Brennan hinted at was even partly true, and if Daniel and this Special Agent Scandlin aren't completely paranoid…

Then he's not just some goody-goody widower farmer, now is he, Beth?

She sighed. Beth didn't know what to think anymore—about anything, let alone John McFarlane—but she decided that *who* she needed to talk to at that moment was her husband.

He hasn't called me all day…

Beth told herself that was a good thing as she put the phone to her ear. He would not be happy about the deal with Brennan, that's for sure.

Six calls later and no answer, Beth sent him a text asking him—politely!—to call her, then lowered the phone and watched kids swarm over the multicolored slides and tunnels in the McDonald's play area. Lizzie loved those tunnels. It was hard to get her out sometimes. Luckily, Beth was small enough to go in after her when needed.

What is Daniel doing? Why hadn't he texted or called her back by now? She was going to *strangle* him; they were supposed to be answering each other's calls today! And then there was his brainless idea to go look around the cemetery at night. What was the stupid *point?*

That reminded Beth: she needed to do a little scouting. If they were actually going to do this idiot thing, someone might as well be smart enough to check the lay of the land first.

Google Earth was popping up on her phone when Beth squeezed her eyes shut. *Am I really going to participate in this foolishness?*

She sighed deeply, then opened her eyes and typed in her address and got the grainy satellite view of the castle centered on the screen. Beth couldn't let him go by himself; he'd just get into trouble without her.

But she wasn't happy about it.

From the castle she found the ridge to the northeast and then McFarlane's sprawling farm, then scrolled the view quickly across the valley behind it and found the cemetery on its hill. Her lips twisted. *That stone is ugly even from space.* She followed the ruts that cut through the trees, curious to see what was in the circular clearing. She couldn't *believe* she was actually considering this! Her brains must be turning as soft as—

Beth's eyes widened.

The circular clearing wasn't a clearing.

It was a giant sinkhole.

A *sinkhole?* Wait, what did they call those things? *A cenote, that's it.* Beth knew this area of Tennessee was riddled with them because of all the groundwater eating through the limestone (although not nearly as bad as Florida), but not only was this cenote almost half-a-mile wide, it was deep enough to have giant trees growing inside! She'd never even *heard* of one that big, let alone seen one. She tried to roll the view down closer but she was at max magnification.

Beth squinted at the screen. There was something in the center of the hole; a clearing devoid of trees, round like the hole; a circle within a circle.

What in the world?

Frustrated by the poor resolution, Beth punched off the net. She would have to do all that again on the computer at home, but no matter how clear the image, the questions remained:

Why was there a big hole in the woods? Was it really a giant cenote, like it seemed to be? And if it was, how come she had never heard of it before? And why did that rutted track lead straight to it from the cemetery?

She thought about the gate with the lock and the chains and the forbidding KEEP OUT and NO TRESPASSING signs and realized there was another question:

What are they hiding?

Beth shook off the uneasy feeling that even a second-hand sight of the giant cenote had given her and tried to call her husband again. No answer. She sent a text again.

No answer.

"Where *are* you, Daniel?"

THE HARD WAY

THE HARD way? What the hell did that mean?

It was everything Dan could do not to launch across the table and grab the little hold-out pistol and empty all five shots into the old bastard. *He sent Rison! He fucking ADMITTED it!* Common sense kept him in the chair, however; common sense and the knife hovering near his carotid artery. Mindy continued massaging his shoulders, fresh-honey curls cascading around his head. The redhead watched it all with a contented smile, long legs crossed, bare foot kicking. She thought him nicely caught. She was probably right. *Bitch.*

McFarlane popped the Eagle's cylinder and removed the .22 Magnums and set their hollow lead points upright on the table one by one; he then reassembled it, thick hands moving expertly. When he was done, he pointed it at Dan and put the bead straight between his eyes, then lowered the little revolver and stuck the bullets in the breast pocket of his overalls—Dan heard them clink, one after the other, on his keys—patted it, then set the empty pistol down.

Mindy giggled in Dan's ear.

I am so fucked. "What do you want, old man?"

McFarlane chuckled. "I want a lot of things, *boy.* You'll hafta be more specific."

"We've never done a damn thing to you. We don't even *know* you. Why would you do that to us?"

McFarlane said, "Truth be told, boy, I didn't send 'im, I just gave 'im permission. Scotty had his faults, but he woulda never made a move like that without gettin' the nod first. He wasn't dumb, just green foolish. He had his eye on that little whore of yours months before—"

"She's not like that anymore, goddamn you, and don't you *ever* call her that again! I'll fucking *kill* you if you—!"

McFarlane's hand was a blur. Pain exploded in Dan's skull as his broken nose bent to the side; his world swam around a bit, and he would've fallen out of the chair if Mindy hadn't held him.

Quick. He's old, but he's quick. Jesus, *he's quick.*

"Watch your filthy mouth at my table, boy. Truth hurt? Once a whore always a whore, I say."

Dan held himself back. Barely. "Call her that again. I dare you."

McFarlane grinned. "Got sand, don't ya? I like that. Not enough like you around. But listen here, boy, I want to know somethin'." The old man leaned forward. "Why did you go to that cemetery?"

The question caught Dan off guard. "Well, I…" McFarlane was staring at him like he wanted to eat him. Rebecca was watching just as intently, although from that little smile, eating was far from her mind. Mindy's rubbing hand had gone still on his shoulder as she waited for the answer. Even the mutts had quit growling; they were now staring through the glass with their ears perked…as if waiting for his answer.

Why did *I go, anyway? Something about a song…*Dan shook his head. Why was he thinking about music again? *What the hell is wrong with me?* "I, uh, I went exploring, and then I just found it, that's all."

Silence, and then McFarlane leaned back and picked up his tea and took a drink, shaking the glass and making the ice tinkle. His eyes were narrowed in unalloyed suspicion as they watched Dan over the rim. "Explorin', huh?" Then he looked at Rebecca, for some reason. She shrugged freckled shoulders. McFarlane looked past Dan at Mindy, and Dan felt her curls sway against his neck as she shook her head. McFarlane put the glass back on the table and turned his suspicious squint on the door from which Alexandria had departed. He held it there for a long time before picking up his tea again and taking another sip, measuring Dan over the rim once more.

Tinkle-tinkle.

"So. You met Melissa down there. Y'all have a nice chat?"

"I guess."

"What did you two gab about?"

Outside, the hairballs started up again, this time with a low, snarling rasp that held a promise of pain. "I told her I liked her roses, and, uh, and then I asked her if I could bring Beth to see them. She said that would be fine with her."

Dan had decided not to mention the "strong enough" crap, partly because he didn't understand it, but mostly because some intuition was warning him to say as little as possible on the subject. It didn't take a whiz-kid to suss out that McFarlane and The Keeper or Melissa or whatever she was called weren't exactly best buds, "old family friend" or not. "She also said it was a private cemetery, and then she pretty much showed me the gate before riding off on her four-wheeler."

"Did she now?" McFarlane seemed to relax a fraction. He took another drink of tea, watching Dan over the rim. Tinkle-tinkle. Then he set the tea back and smiled, although the eyes didn't soften. "Thank you for answering, Dan. Now, you asked what I want. What I want is you and that little whore and your brat gone. And I'm tired of lookin' at that eyesore you call a house. I want y'all out of there, and I want it burned or bulldozed to the ground. I want cows walkin' 'round and eatin' good green grass and pissin' and making cow flops on that ground, they way they shoulda been all along. *That's* what I want."

Dan stared at him in outrage bordering on awe: "Who the hell do you think you are? You can't tell people where they can and can't live!"

Mindy put her lips next to his ear. "You'd be surprised what my daddy can do, Dan."

"*Very* surprised," Rebecca said.

"I'll call the police and tell them you're threatening us, and that you sent Rison to attack us!"

The old man threw back his head and laughed. "You will? Well, good fer you, boy. Which police are ya gonna call? We're out in the county here, so the Sheriff? Go right on ahead." His grin was vicious. "Tell Cousin Willy I said howdy, ask him if he likes that handmade walnut gun-rack I gave 'im for his birthday." He let that sink in. "Or the State Police? I know folks there too, boy, lotsa folks. The TBI?" That grin was sly, now. "Lotsa folks there, too." McFarlane shook his head in disgust. "You're dumber than I thought if you think the law will do anything for ya. No, the only choice you got is to pack up and git. Go back to livin' in an apartment in Murfreesboro. Better yet, skedaddle on back to Ohio. It's where you belong. You pickin' up what I'm puttin' down, boy?"

Lightning crackled through Dan's brain.

Crazy, he's crazy, but it sounds like he'll let you go, so just SHUT UP!

As usual, his mouth didn't listen.

"Fuck. You. Beth and I bought that house, and that's where we will stay, and for as long as we damn well please. You think you'll scare us off? If you think that, old man, you don't understand a goddamn thing."

McFarlane's nostrils flared. "*Understand?*" It was a hiss. "*I* don't understand? Let me tell you somethin', boy, and if you have a single ounce of smarts between yer ears, you'll listen up and listen up hard. There's so much about me, about this here situation, about this *world* you don't *understand* that I almost feel sorry for ya. I could explain it, but you're too goddamn dumb to comprehend. What I will do is tell ya—in simple language even *you* can *understand, boy*—the consequences of not haulin' yerself and that whore and yer brat on down the road." The old man brought out Dan's keys and tossed them to Rebecca. "Drive that pretty nip truck up here." He sniffed. "Goddamn Japanese pickup truck. What, good old-fashioned Dee-troit rollin' iron ain't good enough for ya?" McFarlane waved a meaty hand. "Don't get me started. We'll be here all afternoon, and I got a farm to run." Rebecca was still in her chair. McFarlane scowled at her. "Well? Git on with it."

She stood up with a glower pulling down the freckles. "I don't like this," she announced. "Push him outside and let Reagan and the boys play with him. It'll be interesting to see how long he lasts." Dan went cold all over. *Is she fucking joking?* "We'll…deal…with the rest, after. It'll be better that way, Father. Don't go through with this."

The fucking bitch was serious! Wait. Deal with the rest of what?

Go through with what?

There was silence as Mindy shifted her boobs against his back. McFarlane was still scowling, but his eyes stared past his middle daughter.

Dan's breath caught.

Holy Mother of God, he's considering it!

"No," McFarlane finally said, slowly, as if he were unsure and could still change his mind: "Your sister and I agreed that this is the best way." His voice firmed. "Go on now, girl, do as I say."

The redhead stood there staring at her father, and then she slammed her chair into the table so hard it rebounded and fell over sideways. She turned, fixed him with a murderous stare, and then flounced toward the door. Dan was suddenly glad that Mindy was the one with the knife to his throat. The screen door slammed open and then crashed shut. The Polaris cranked over, and then it roared down the hill and out of earshot.

Dan sagged against Mindy's breasts. Sweat ran out of his hair and trickled down his forehead. He could hear the mutts snarling and feel them staring at him through the glass; he refused to look at them.

Sweet Christ.

"When Becca brings your nip truck back, Dan, yer gonna climb in and drive to that blemish you call a house, and then if yer smart, you'll start packin' right away. What is today, the fifth?" The old man scratched his cheek. "Well, no matter. I'll give y'all till September first ta get gone. That's three weeks or so; plenty of time."

Dan was speechless for one of the few times in his life.

This fucker is serious!

"Don't believe me, do ya, boy? Tell ya what, if you don't think I mean what I say, just go talk to James Fulbright." It took Dan a second for the name to register; when it did, he stiffened. Mindy patted his shoulder. "That's right, James Fulbright. Man thought he was a wheeler and a dealer, comin' out here and pesterin' me to sell him some of my land so he could throw up houses." McFarlane snorted. "Last thing I want is this land spoiled by a goddamn suburb; told him so, but he wouldn't listen. Then he went and built that house. He did it just to spite me, too, buildin' it close like that. I warned him not to, Dan. We sat here at this very table and I warned him not to build it, so what did he do? He left and built the damn thing anyway." The old farmer's thin lips pulled up at the corners. "Well, he learned not to cross me. Don't ya think so, Dan?"

He forced the words out of his dry throat; they passed his lips as harsh croaks, denying: "It was an accident. Fulbright's wife was in an *accident.*"

"Was she?" McFarlane took a drink of tea and wiggled the glass. Tinkle-tinkle. "That's what everyone says, so I guess it must be true." That horrid death-smile vanished, only to be replaced by the death-stare. "Accidents happen, boy, 'specially when I don't get what I want. You remember that."

Dan ignored the blade at his throat and leaned forward and gripped the edge of the table. "If anything happens to her, I'll kill you."

McFarlane chuckled. "If I call her what she is, you'll kill me. If anything happens to the little slut, you'll kill me." He grunted. "Like you know a goddamn thing about killin' a man."

"Let me tell you a story. Might be maybe you'll learn somethin'. We got ambushed 'round sunset in, oh, June of 67', I b'lieve it was, in the Song Ve River Valley, right up against that stinkin' hole of a river. I took one in the leg, went down, hid in that big grass as the firefight moved on up the riverbank. I staunched the wound, was about to get up and follow when the gookers came back, twenty strong, and made camp not sixty feet away. Seems we were in their favorite campin' spot. My guys thought I was dead, but I wasn't dead yet." The old man leaned across the table; three feet now separated their faces.

"So I laid there with the bugs and the leeches in the mud, stewin' in my own blood and piss and sweat. I knew they would spot me in the dawn light, so in the darkest part of the night I started crawlin'. And where did I crawl, boy? Not away, that's fer goddamn sure. I crawled right into their camp and killed seven slopes with my bayonet. The eighth made a noise and woke the others, so I opened up with my Thompson. Two sentries popped up and joined the party; one of 'em got me in the shoulder, but I killed those slants, too. My click heard the shots and came back for me, but so did another company of Charlie down-river; it was a race that the good guys won, but barely. I took another in the gut, and they killed two of my buddies." McFarlane thrust his face even closer. "Long story short, boy, if you think I'll have any trouble with a piss-ant *salesman* like you, think again."

Dan ground his teeth together.

Where's that psycho cunt with my truck?

Mindy shifted; her breath was hot on his clenched jaw. "I'd listen to my daddy if I were you, Dan." She nibbled his earlobe.

McFarlane didn't even glance at his youngest daughter as she molested Dan. He just leaned back and picked up his tea once more. Tinkle-tinkle. "But you don't have to worry 'bout me. No, it's my boys I'd be frettin' over if I wuz you. They're not happy 'bout Scotty. He was the young'n of the bunch, and all the boys looked out for him, kinda like big brothers." The old man pointed a thick finger across the table at Dan's face. "Scotty did some fine work all by his lonesome, fine work indeed, so what do you think's gonna happen if I send half a dozen over to play?"

"Don't get me wrong now, Dan, they're good boys—not that they always were, but I make sure they straighten up and fly right when they come stay with me. Most of 'em are on the Centerville volunteer fire crew, like I used to be." McFarlane sneered. "Those city council fools up 'n told me I'm too *old* now, but that don't stop me from rollin' out when a neighbor needs me. But that's neither here nor there. Point is, my boys are all hard workers, and good to have 'round the farm, and handy when yer house is busy burnin' down, but *nice* boys? No, not nice boys, Dan. Not nice boys at all. And when they come, it'll be rough on that whore of yours. And your little girl? Well, let's just say some of my boys might not care that she's four. Get my meanin' there, son? So take my advice: pack up those two pretty little girls and git on down the road."

Dan twitched. It took every ounce of willpower he had to stay in the chair. And for once in his life, he kept his mouth shut; he'd said what needed to be said. He thought about the .38 under his truck seat, and he didn't smile, but it was a near thing. The problem was numbers; he only had six bullets. McFarlane and his nutty slut daughters made four, plus at least six farm hands, and can't forget the three hairballs.

I'm carrying extra ammo from now fucking on.

But would the old man really let him go? After admitting to killing Fulbright's wife? It'd been a semi versus car wreck on I-29 south of Nashville. How the hell had he arranged that? Unless McFarlane was bragging about something he had no part in, which meant he really was crazy.

A cold hand gripped Dan's spine.

Or unless he was telling the truth, and he truly wasn't afraid of the authorities. Where was that bitch with his truck?

He heard a vehicle pull into the yard; the dog's ears perked higher, but they stayed focused on him through the glass. They looked hungry.

Dan was visited by a cruel vision, then: they led him to the screen door, his truck and his .38 sitting only feet away…but the dogs were waiting.

He wouldn't make it three steps.

Would McFarlane do that? Give him hope, and then…?

Oh God, please let me see Beth and Lizzie again, please oh please oh please.

The screen door creaked open and then banged shut. The redhead appeared and his keys hit the table and slid to McFarlane. Dan glanced at those long, long legs and those yummy freckles and that blazing copper hair and that gorgeous face that wanted to feed him to her puppies.

Then he saw what she held.

She hefted his Smith, showing it to him, making sure he saw it, and then handed it to her father butt-first across the table. "I found this under the seat."

McFarlane took it with a knowing smile. "What do we have here?" He inspected it. "You should clean yer weapons proper, Dan. Could save yer life some day." He took the bullets out and set them on the table one by one and then laid the Smith down next to the smaller revolver. "Came loaded for bear, didn't ya, boy? Much good as it did ya." McFarlane spoke past Dan's shoulder. "Let him go." Mindy stepped away, and the blades disappeared. He rubbed his throat and felt a sting, then looked at his fingers; blood. He glanced around at her: dark-honey blonde, blue eyes, two gleaming knives in her small hands, big nipples erect. She saw him looking and smiled, sweet as pie.

Dan turned away.

McFarlane had his Buck open and in his right hand by then; he chunked Dan's keys across the table with his left and then waved the Buck at the pistols. "Hand him his pea-shooters, Becca. He'll need 'em later, I think."

Dan picked up his keys. Such fucking arrogance…no, whatever the reason, he was letting Dan go…*just get the fuck out, Danny boy; keep your goddamn smart mouth shut and git while the gittin's good*…Rebecca passed Dan the pistols. He stood up and put everything except his keys in his pockets, and then he looked out at the dogs.

They were on their furry feet now. They trembled, eager, watching. Waiting.

Dan pulled his gaze away from them with difficulty. "What about my phone?"

McFarlane cheerfully replied, "Oh, yeah," but Dan had a feeling that the fucker hadn't forgotten about it at all. The farmer picked the iPhone up and contemplated the darkened screen. "So. I figure those pictures you so foolishly took are still on this thing. Am I right, Dan?"

Dan said nothing, just stuck his hand out and waited.

McFarlane looked up at him, eyes glinting. "Not a smart move, taking photographs of that stone like that; not a smart move at all, Dan. Dangerous, in fact. *Very* dangerous," he finished softly. He tilted the phone back and forth. "I suppose these are the only copies?" Dan said nothing. "Haven't dropped 'em inta yer computer, or inta that little whore's phone?" Dan said more nothing, still with his hand out, but McFarlane should have turned into a pile of steaming glop on his chair. "Maybe even sent 'em somewhere to see if someone can tell ya that weird writin' means, huh?"

Dan tried not to let his shock show; he just stood there with his hand out, glaring.

McFarlane watched him shrewdly, tilting the phone back and forth, back and forth as the silence stretched. Then he said, "Bah!" and slid the device across the table, almost contemptuously. "Keep 'em. I done decided they don't matter."

Behind Dan, a strangled sound of protest came from Mindy, and Rebecca stared at her father with mixed anger and disbelief. "*They don't matter,*" he told his daughters, sharing a hard look between them. "That place had its uses once, I'll admit, but I've moved beyond it. You both know that." Mindy said nothing, but Rebecca nodded reluctantly. "And besides," he told them, "things is hapinin' fast now. We ain't got time to worry 'bout pictures."

Uses? Moved beyond it? A fucking *cemetery?*

And things happening fast?

What things?

Dan stared at the old farmer.

You are one insane son of a bitch.

McFarlane focused on Dan again, and then his face twisted. "Git," he snarled. "Before I change my mind. Remember, boy, September 1st. Go on. *Git!*"

Dan picked up his phone and put it in his pocket and turned away without a word. It was the hardest thing he'd ever done in his life. Out of the corner of his eye he saw the mutts run around the building.

Aw, shit.

Mindy said, "Bye, Dan." She giggled. "I'll be thinking about you."

Dan stepped up to the screen door as the fuzzballs appeared at the bottom of the steps; he looked out through the flimsy screen and met Reagan's eyes and her ears laid flat and her black lips peeled up to reveal long yellow teeth set in red, red gums. Dan put his hand on the door handle, prepared to open it and step out, then hesitated, looking at the other dogs; they snarled from behind Reagan, black-and-tan juggernauts of muscle and teeth.

Oh, this is going to suck.

McFarlane suddenly yelled, "Go lay down, Reagan! Down Ike! Down Nixon!"

The dogs quit snarling and perked their triangle ears. Reagan whined. Then they trotted to a grassy spot a few feet from the steps, laid down, and put their heads on their paws.

Dan started breathing again and went down the steps and stopped when he saw his truck fifty or sixty feet away, parked in the grass just past the smoking grill. There were men standing around it, waiting. The waiting men wore dirty ball caps and ripped tee-shirts and faded jeans over scuffed work boots, and all had crude blue-ink tattoos covering their arms and shoulders. There were even a few stylish neck tattoos. Outstanding.

Dan walked toward them, ignoring the mutts' snarls as he went past. One waiting man held a rusty crowbar, another a dented aluminum softball bat; the rest held various other party favors. Dan recognized the two that had been chucking hay up by the front gate; they still had those wicked-looking hooks with the T handles. *Shit.*

Dan walked closer, and then stopped beside the grill and waited for McFarlane to yell for them to go lay down, but no such luck. The men spread out, and one sauntered out to meet him, the big Latino grease-monkey from the machine shop; he seemed to be the leader, probably by dint of sheer size. Dan doubted it was for intelligence. Muscles and tattoos rippled as he tossed a dirty claw hammer from hand to hand.

"Where's your bitch, homes? She not here to fight for you? I think you're in trouble, meng." The men laughed, adding their own comments. The big man swished the hammer. "Scotty was my little brother. You're gonna pay. Right now." The other men began to circle.

Dan pulled the Smith from his pocket and cocked the hammer and held it down by his leg; he didn't want them to see the empty cylinder.

They stopped. Confident grins were wiped away, and they cast several questioning glances behind Dan. That's when he knew for sure that McFarlane was standing back there, watching. He waited for the old man to implode his bluff, for the circle to tighten and the beating to commence. He eyed his truck; twenty feet, and only one man in the way now that they'd spread out.

Can I make it?

He'd have to try.

Then came the shout and he tensed, ready to make the dash, but the words surprised him; him, and everybody else.

"Let 'im go, boys! He's got packin' to do!"

The men eyed him, anger twisting their faces, but they obeyed, opening a path to the Toyota. The big one's lips pulled back in a snarl remarkably like Reagan's, yellow teeth and all.

"This ain't over, homes."

Dan nodded, holding the man's dark eyes with his own, not trusting himself to speak. The others added their own two cents, promising payment for Scotty. Dan strolled through them, memorizing faces; none were as big as the Mexican with the hammer, but all were lean and tough; hard men. He got to the truck, opened the door, and climbed in. Rebecca-scent lingered in the cab. It smelled like an invasion. He put the useless pistol on the passenger seat, fumbled the key in, and started the engine.

Dan had never heard such a sweet sound in his life.

He backed around in front of the main house, then put it in drive and rolled the window down. McFarlane and Rebecca stood back by the kitchen, just outside the screen door; Mindy was squatting in the grass, scratching Ike behind the ears. His long tail thumped in pleasure.

Something made Dan glance at the big house, at the balcony between the two center columns; up there, a slim hand held a white curtain back, and behind the glass he saw that perfect face staring down at him. He met Alexandria's black eyes, and instead of the fury she'd shown him earlier, a gleeful, almost naughty smile spread across that face. Then she pressed her upright finger to her lips, like he was supposed to keep some big secret or something.

Dan scowled up at her.

Crazy bitch. Just like her father.

They were all watching, mutts, sluts, thugs, and farmer, so let them all hear: "If you come anywhere near my family," Dan yelled, "I'll fucking kill *every last one of you!*"

McFarlane stepped forward. "So be it, boy! You reap what you sow in this life! Remember that! You reap what you sow!"

"So be it," Dan whispered.

He let off the brake and rolled the window up and drove out of the yard and down the hill past the buildings and out the gate and down the road, not looking back and barely seeing anything. Five minutes and two cattle grates and a billboard and a cow army later he was back on pavement. Two minutes after that he pulled around the castle's driveway. He parked in front of the closed garage and shut the engine off.

His breath was ragged. Dan looked at his trembling hands and then clenched them around the steering wheel. He turned his head to the northeast and looked up at the not-so-distant ridge and saw metal buildings set among the trees; they glittered cheerfully in the afternoon sun.

So close. So fucking close. A nest of insane vipers.

And he'd moved his family in right next door.

Right next door!

They'd been *ordered* out of their own house. *Our own fucking house!* Unbelievable. Those men…hard men, all of them; when they came, it would be bad. Dan pictured Beth and Lizzie…no. He really would kill them all before he let that happen.

We need help, he realized. Can't go to the police. *That fucker McFarlane knows them all, or so he said…*

Or can *we?*

Dan raised his hip and pulled his wallet out. He retrieved Special Agent Scandlin's card and stared at it for a long stretch, then got his phone out and started dialing.

CHAD POINTED. "That's it, Barron Road, turn here."

"I see it, I'm not blind."

Aarif was fuming. They were supposed to have been to Barron Cemetery and gone by now, but Chad hadn't arrived at Aarif's office until seven-thirty and now it was after eight and the sun was setting. Aarif had even been stopped for speeding in Centerville! He had no particular reason to be in such a hurry other than a vague, childish fear of visiting a cemetery at night, but he wasn't about to voice that weakness to Chad.

And then there was Aleena. She had been all too happy when he'd informed her he would be out late; she hadn't even bothered to ask him where he would be. *Where is* she *tonight? What in Allah's Holy Name is she doing?* Out with friends again, he supposed—not that she'd bothered to say.

Damn the woman. At least Chad had offered to pay for the ticket. Aarif would make sure Professor Hot did just that.

He slowed as Barron Road crested the steep, rocky ridge, and then squinted as the red ball of the setting sun swelled above the horizon in all three of his mirrors, bathing his face and arms in a ruddy reflection; a few seconds later the red glow vanished as they dropped over the far rim into a vale already filled with deep dusk. He turned on his headlights.

They stopped at the bottom next to a rusted and canted sign. Chad rolled the window down and clicked his flashlight on and shined the beam on it.

BARRON CEMETERY

Their heads swiveled in unison as they followed the arrow to the other side of the road, where a leafy tunnel swallowed unlined blacktop; in there, it was already deepest night.

The only sound inside the car was the air conditioner.

Finally, Chad said, "You found nothing? No mention at all?"

"Nothing. What about you? Did you ever talk to that historical mathematician at Purdue?"

"I did, and he's never heard of anything even remotely like it. Asking raised his flag way up high, too; the guy's sent me seven emails and left four messages at my office last count, and that was three hours ago."

"So we'll be the first."

"Yes."

More silence as they sat and stared down the lane—a lane that vanished into solid darkness.

And then Chad said, "Are we going to do this or not?" Aarif looked at him. "It's just an old cemetery. Let's go in there and confirm it, take some pictures, drive our asses back to civilization, grab a brew and a raspberry margarita, and bitch about women. Simple."

Aleena. Aarif would do anything for Aleena. Besides, Chad was right; despite Dan Sims' enigmatic warning, it was only a cemetery.

He cranked the wheel hard left and drove into the tunnel and flicked on the high beams; they lit up enormous trees sliding by as the unlined blacktop took them deeper and deeper within their ranks. Chad stuck his head out the open window like a dog, craning his neck around.

"You ever seen trees like this, Reef?"

"No."

"Me either. Maybe this is a state park, or some sort of preserve. Did you find anything like that when you were doing research?"

Aarif leaned forward to look out the windshield; through scattered holes in the towering canopy, he could see the sky was darkening, but still streaked by red, orange, and pink clouds. It was light, of a sort, and no matter how weak, that cheered Aarif; down here on the ground, his headlights pushed through an inky black that seemed to give way reluctantly and then close in behind his Camry eagerly, making his tail and brake lights dim. It was all just his imagination, of course.

The road dipped and became a gradual slope, and soon a one-lane wooden bridge appeared in his beams; about forty feet long, it sported low rails on each side as it arched over a busy stream; drooping willow trees lined the banks on either side. Chad pulled his head in and looked at him.

"Aarif?"

"I wasn't worried about trees," he said. "I concentrated on the symbols. Besides, Mr. Sims said this was private property, remember?"

Chad made a face but didn't reply as they rattled across the span. The blacktop climbed on the other side, and high above them, about a quarter-mile away, he saw an opening; its pink-and-orange striated purple brightness contrasted sharply with the surrounding gloom. Aarif had never seen anything quite so inviting.

Chad was staring up at that glowing opening, too. "Speaking of that, did you ever find out what language that was? You mentioned something about it earlier, but then you started bitching about me being late."

"I need more information before I can state any definite conclusions."

It was only a small lie. Aarif was certain he knew the language the symbols had been derived from—or at least mostly certain—but he needed to verify it with his own eyes because if he was right, the ripples of this discovery would spread far and wide, and not only through the linguistic and mathematics and archaeological communities, but the religious scholars as well.

Aarif kept telling himself he should be happy about that.

Chad stared at the side of his face and then relented. "Okay, Reef, be mysterious. The language doesn't matter anyway, as long as the pattern it forms is an honest-to-God, measurable fractal. We're going to be famous!"

"Yes." Though if what Aarif suspected were true, infamous may be more accurate.

They finally drove out of the murky tunnel and into a glorious red-tinged sunset. A dark-green oval hedge just like Dan Sims had described enclosed the crown of the hill above them, stark against the fading sky; at the crown of the tor, the top few feet of the twisted black megalith poked above the hedge, and relief that it was really real warred with sudden foreboding.

At least there's still plenty of light up here, Aarif told himself. Then his eyes widened, and he hit the brakes, jerking them to a stop.

Chad leaned forward. "Whose car is that?"

"How should I know?" A green Honda Accord sat in the small parking lot; its headlights were on, illuminating a hillside of red roses.

"Illinois plates."

"I can see that."

Then Chad whistled, glancing around. "Sims was right. Somebody sure likes roses."

Professor Hot had a firm grasp on the obvious. Aarif was about to inform him so when Chad pointed past his shoulder. "We've got company."

Aarif turned to see a man holding a flashlight. He was standing on a path that cut through the flowers. The man saw them looking and waved and headed their way.

Aarif said, "Who is that?"

"The owner, maybe?"

Aarif pointed at the Accord. "From Illinois?"

Chad motioned impatiently to an empty spot. "Park and let's find out."

"What if he asks us to leave?" Aarif pulled his Camry into a space two away from the Honda, watching his own headlights fill with crimson roses.

"Then we'll sneak back in when he's not here." Chad got out.

Aarif shut the engine off and followed suit and immediately began to sweat in the thick August air; unlike Chad, who'd taken his sweet time and had changed into shorts and tennis shoes and his ridiculous MATH IS SEXY tee-shirt, Aarif still wore his lecture attire. The Accord had been left running, he discovered, but the soft thrum of its engine was no competition for the hordes of insects screeching from the surrounding wall of trees. Aarif sniffed and then grimaced; normally he enjoyed roses, but this was too much. The stranger slowed and then stopped at the edge of the lot. He seemed nervous.

"Hi, fellas. Um, I was just leaving. I got turned around, and, uh, ended up here; you know how these damn GPS' are…" He frowned, then used his flashlight to look them over. The stranger was taller than Chad, which meant he had six inches on Aarif at least, and big with it. His curly hair and beard needed trimming, and rectangular wire-framed glasses sat on his nose; Aarif used to have a pair just like them. "You're not McFarlane's people," the big man said, almost accusingly. "Who are you guys?"

Chad stretched to his full height. "Who are *you?*"

The bearded man ignored Chad and walked to Aarif's car, where he leaned down and looked at something on the windshield. Who *was* this man? And who on earth was McFarlane?

Professor Hot intoned, "I inquired who you are, sir."

The stranger stood up and came back; a long, thin spiral notebook with a gold pen attached to the leather cover jutted from the back pocket of his knee-length denim shorts. The man stopped in front of Chad and shined the light on his shirt.

"Math is sexy. Cute." He waved the beam toward Aarif's car. "That's a Middle Tennessee State faculty parking sticker, which makes you…a math professor?"

Chad flexed his jaw, but remained silent.

The big man turned to Aarif. "Are you a math professor as well?"

"I teach Arabic." Him, teach math? Allah forbid.

The man's brow furrowed, but before he could say anything Chad stalked by him and opened the back door of Aarif's Camry. "Don't talk to this guy, Aarif." He reached in and pulled out his camera bag and hooked the strap over his shoulder, slamming the door back. "If he's not the owner, then screw him. Come on." Chad started across the lot toward the pathway, and Aarif hurried over and opened his trunk to retrieve his own camera; it wasn't as nice as Chad's, but it would serve. When he turned back around the bearded man had his hand out. Aarif shook it warily.

"Brian Brennan. I'm a freelance reporter…" His broad features twisted in alarm, and he released Aarif's hand and jabbed a finger in his face. Aarif backed up, bumping into his trunk lid. "*She* sent you, didn't she?" Brennan turned and jabbed that accusing finger at Chad, who had stopped at the edge of the roses to watch. "Didn't she?" He cursed and smacked a fist into his palm, rattling the flashlight. "Exclusive my hairy ass. She's a mean little bitch, but I didn't think she was a liar."

Aarif and Chad looked at each other.

A reporter.

This is not good. She? She, who?

Brennan noted their exchange, and relief swept beneath the short, rusty beard. "She didn't send you. Then how…?" He snapped his fingers. "The husband!" Once again Aarif and Chad exchanged a glance, and once again Brennan read it. "Damn, I'm good." He clenched the flashlight in his armpit and pulled the notebook from his back pocket and freed the gold pen and wrote feverishly. "This is great! It corroborates what she told me, crazy as that shit is…" The big man shook his head, still writing. "I almost didn't believe her. Hell, I *didn't* believe her, but…" The pen paused as he stared up at the oval hedge, or perhaps at the top few feet of the crooked megalith outlined against the bellies of the orange and scarlet clouds. "But why would Rison care? Why would *anybody* care?" Then he laughed, and Aarif blinked as the big reporter danced a jig right there in the middle of the parking lot. *"Who fucking cares?* I'll find out! Perfect!" Brennan went back to his notebook; he appeared to have forgotten Aarif and Chad existed.

Aarif watched him uneasily. A reporter. This could ruin everything, but what to do about it? He looked at Chad again, who jerked his head toward the top of the hill, pausing to glare at Brennan before starting up the path. Aarif followed, stepping wide around the large, excitable man.

"Wait!" Aarif froze. Chad halted as well. "You thought I was…you don't know who owns this place?"

"Why should we care?" Chad mocked. "We won't be here that long. Come *on,* Aarif."

Brennan laughed. "Oh, that's rich. For a couple of smart guys, you two don't know shit, do ya?" He eyed the camera in Aarif's hand, then ran to his car and pulled out a camera bag bigger than Chad's, extracting an instrument with a heavy strap and a long lens. He jogged back, the spot from his flashlight bobbing. "What are we taking pictures of, gentleman?"

"Don't talk to him, Reef! And *come on!"* Chad was following the walk around the hill through the roses. Aarif trudged after him, mind whirling.

A reporter!

"Yeah, don't talk to me, Reef, I'll do the talking. So what did Mr. Sims say that got you two out here?"

Aarif eyed the big man sideways, and then, since he seemed so fond of questions, stopped at the edge of the parking lot and fired off one of his own. "Who's this McFarlane? Is he the land owner?"

Brennan halted with him and gave Aarif a toothy smile through the beard. "And why should I answer your question if you won't answer mine?" Then he waved his hand breezily. "Just kidding, Professor, I'll tell you. Maybe you'll even loosen up and reciprocate. John McFarlane is indeed the owner of the hill you are standing on—and all of *that,* too." The reporter turned and swept his arm in a wide arc. "And *that,* my friend, is Barron Woods, or The Barron's Woods; depends on how old the map is. Whatever its name, this valley is a spooky place—or so local legend would have you believe." Brennan's expression was one of wry disgust as he stared out over the shadow and mist-shrouded vale. "Not that I can find a shred of real evidence to back that up, of course."

Aarif swallowed. "'Spooky place'?"

"That's what the old-timers around here say—the bare handful that would even talk to me, anyway, and all off the record: ghosts, goblins, strange lights in the woods leading hunters astray; standard boogeyman stuff, in other words, and none of it provable, but it'll make a hell of a good background for my story. There were even two people killed out here, which is even better." Aarif stared at him. The writer made a calming gesture. "It happened a long time ago, back during the second Eisenhower administration."

"How…how were they killed?" A thought struck him, and he glanced up at the hedge looming over them. "Were they killed here?" He swallowed again. "In *there?*" For some reason, Aarif had whispered the last.

"No, they died when they fell into a sinkhole." Brennan hiked his thumb past the bulk of Barron Cemetery's hill. "There's one down there, at the center of the valley. Sinkholes form when groundwater erodes the underlying stone beneath the soil, usually limestone—"

"I'm familiar with the concept of sinkholes."

"Okay, well, there's a big one in here; one of the largest in the world, as a matter of fact. John McFarlane lets no one get near it though, because it's not done sinking; there's some sort of underlying strata of rock that's tougher than limestone, and that means most of the bottom hasn't collapsed all the way to the water table yet, although it's just a matter of time." He chuckled. "*Geological* time, at any rate; give it a few million years. And when you throw in that lovely little stream we all crossed to get up here dumping into it, that means whatever ground is left down there is marshy and treacherous." Brennan shrugged. "Supposedly, anyway. I guess McFarlane would know; the two people killed were his first and second cousins. He was just a kid when it happened, and he was with them, goofing around near the mean ol' crumbly edge when the two boys fell in. It took them three days to recover the bodies. I've seen it on satellite view, Professor, and that thing is almost half a mile wide, and so deep it has trees growing right down in it, so I believe that last part."

Aarif said, "Half a *mile?* You'd think something like that would be famous, or at least talked about, but I've never even heard of it."

"You would have if you were a Geology professor, Professor; all of *them* know about it. McFarlane fields about five-dozen requests a year from rock hounds and spelunkers from all over the world who want to explore it, not to mention those insane freshwater cave divers, but he turns them all down, says it's too dangerous." Brennan's grin suddenly peeked through his beard. "That didn't stop some tenured big-shot UMass dirt-grubber from driving all the way down here with a handful of grad students about, oh, fifteen years ago, though. Thought he could charm the old man into changing his mind. When McFarlane sent them packing, they tried to slink into the woods to get—"

Chad came stomping back down the path. "Aarif, come on! *And don't talk to this guy!*" He stomped away again, LED beam highlighting the scarlet roses on either side of the footpath as he swept it side to side.

Aarif hurried to follow, and Brennan kept pace just behind. "What, uh, what happened to them? The geologists that tried to sneak in?"

"They met McFarlane's dogs, that's what."

Aarif stopped dead, but the reporter kept going, taking his flashlight with him, so he hurried to catch up. Why oh why hadn't he thought to bring his own flashlight?

Because I wasn't supposed to need one, that's why!

Damn Chad and his tardiness! "Dogs?"

The big reporter wasn't grinning anymore. "Yeah," he said. "Dogs. Big ones. German Shepherds. McFarlane keeps them to scare off trespassers."

Aarif swallowed, hard. "Trespassers like *us*."

Brennan slapped him on the back, causing Aarif to stagger and almost fall into a rose bush. "Don't worry, Professor. Like I said, he uses them to scare people away from that sinkhole, but I've heard he mostly keeps them close, up on that farm on the northwestern rim. I don't think we'll see them down here at the cemetery." Brennan's uneasy gaze roamed out over the roses toward the closest shadow-filled tree line. "Or at least I hope not."

"You *hope* not?"

"Hey, no guarantees, Professor. Why do you think I left my car running? The first bark, I'm history."

Aarif swallowed yet again as they made a ninety-degree turn and trudged up the incline. Brennan went on in a cheery tone. "And it's not just McFarlane's physical property you've trespassed on. I'm assuming that, like me, you and the math prof there aren't big hunters, and so, also like me, you're standing without official permission inside the most exclusive hunting club in the state of Tennessee: The Barron's Hunting Club." He shook his big, shaggy head. "You wouldn't catch me out here during the first weekend of modern gun season, that's for damn sure."

They were nearing the lichgate. Chad waited for them under its wrought-iron arch, roses entwined over his head, his flashlight pointed at their faces. Aarif raised a hand to block the light, squinting past him; there were white roses inside the hedge, and only white roses, just as there were only red outside—exactly as Dan Sims had described. *WELCOME TO BARRON CEMETERY* vaulted overhead.

Brennan was still speaking; he seemed to enjoy the sound of his own voice: "And boy oh boy, if I told you the *names* of the members of The Barron's Hunting Club you'd fill your little pink panties, Professor; they're the names of businessmen, politicians, prosecutors, cops, and judges—hell, anybody who's anybody in Rutherford County." His voice dropped, almost to a whisper. "And they're not just from Rutherford County. That reminds me." The reporter halted and shifted his camera and flashlight around to dig a cell phone out of his pocket. Aarif stopped with him, watching curiously. Brennan cursed. "Still no signal." He lifted the phone toward the purpling sky. "There's a bar…it's gone. Shit." He stuffed the phone back. "There's a guy I use sometimes, a private investigator. I flew him down here to do some digging, and…well, let's just say that if this thing has the legs I think it does, then I will blow the lid off this whole goddamn backwards-ass shit hole!"

Aarif shook his head. Legs? They continued to the entrance, where Chad was still waiting for them; his friend's face was a tan stone.

Uh oh. Aarif had seen that look before.

Professor Hot squared on Brennan and held up his hand, palm out. "That is far enough, sir. I appreciate your professional curiosity, but Dr. Hameed and I have business here—*private* business. When we're finished, we may answer some of your questions, but we go alone from here."

Aarif almost cursed. Did Chad have to use his last name? Though he supposed it didn't matter; a reporter would have no trouble finding out about him.

The silence made him glance up at Brennan, and what he saw caused Aarif take a step away; the quiet stretched, filled only by the pulsing screech of millions of insects. Then Brennan spoke, voice soft the way concrete is soft.

"First, it doesn't take a genius to figure why you're here: that weird megalith, right?" He looked at Aarif. "Arabic. That's what that language is." Aarif said nothing. "Right, Professor?" Aarif still didn't answer, and the reporter looked at Chad again and shrugged. "Can't figure what a math teacher is doing out here, but it doesn't matter, I'll find out. Second, I served six years in the Marine Corps. I was in Desert Storm. I would've re-upped, but they had to cut that thing out of my leg, so…" He eyed Chad up and down. "You look like you workout. Gym muscles might impress the coeds—and I'm sure they do—but not me. Bottom line, *Professor*, is that you can try to stop me from going where I want to go, but I don't think you can."

Another insect-filled silence stretched as the two men faced each other, and then without another word Chad turned and walked into the cemetery.

Brennan snapped his heels together and saluted. "Semper Fi, asshole." Professor Hot hunched his shoulders, but kept walking.

The big stringer winked at Aarif and then followed Chad in. Aarif hurried to keep up, passing under the arch with its entwined red and white roses; what he wouldn't give for his own flashlight! He caught up and eyed Brennan sideways; all in all, he thought Chad had chosen wisely.

Aarif looked toward the top of the hill then and beheld the entire length of the tall, twisted stone outlined against the fading sky.

His hope.

Finally.

The sight made his heart clench and breath quicken. Aarif became aware of Brennan watching him as they made their way between black gravestones and white rose bushes. "What's so special about that thing, Dr. Hameed?"

Then, Chad's voice from above: "Oh my God, Aarif, it's real!" He stood by the lith with his flashlight trained on it.

Aarif ran the rest of the way up and stopped next to Chad. Behind him, Brennan said something else, but he neither caught it nor cared; the lith, and the symbols carved into it, revealed magnificently in the white LED beam, filled his mind. *Praise be to Allah, it's not a hoax!* He reached over a bush full of white blooms and brushed the tiny sunken-relief carvings with his fingertips.

Aarif jerked his hand back, grimacing and wiping his fingers on his shirt; the thing was…greasy. And *cold*, even in this muggy heat. This close, he could also see the stone that comprised the megalith wasn't black, as it appeared even from only a few feet away; instead, it was an unsightly swirl of dirty white, gray, brown, charcoal, and ebon.

How strange.

Aarif was about to lean in for a closer look—without touching—when Chad moved the beam up and down the lith.

"What are you doing? Shine it here!"

Chad ignored him. "It's a…!" He scowled at Brennan, who stood behind them, watching. "It's what we talked about. It's impossible, but it is. It *is!*"

"I can't *see!* Shine—!" Chad raised his camera, and Aarif squeezed his eyelids shut just in time as a white flash lit the hilltop like silent lightning.

"I've got you, Dr. Hameed." Brennan held his light at Aarif's shoulder, shining it on the swirling symbols. "What's got Goldilocks so worked up, anyway?" There was another flash from the other side. Aarif blinked the spots out of his vision, then leaned close.

After a few seconds, he had no doubt…but why here? And *how* here? He stepped back and took in the lith from its twisted, bulbous top to where it vanished into the pale roses; Brennan moved the beam to accommodate him.

How in Allah's name has this come to be here?

"This *is* what they call a megalith, right Dr. Hameed? Like one of those stones from Stonehenge? Although I've never seen one like this. Or even heard of one."

"Actually, considering the location and the etchings, this would be termed a stele." Aarif stooped and moved thorny branches aside, and Brennan stepped close and put his beam where he peered.

Dan Sims had told the truth again; the stone—and its etchings—disappeared into the soil.

Brennan said, "Damn, she was right; the symbols go into the dirt." Aarif released the thorns and stood back up. "Is that normal for these, uh, steles, Dr. Hameed?" The reporter had pulled his thin notebook out and was scribbling again, all while somehow holding the light steady.

"The plural is stelae," Aarif answered slowly, staring at the stone. "And I don't know if it's normal. Such knowledge is beyond my expertise."

"Well, I can tell you there's something funny about this cemetery, and it isn't just this big ugly rock. I tried to find a little background info on it before I drove out here, and you know what I dug up?"

"What?"

"Stop talking to him, Aarif!" Flash.

"Nothing, that's what; as far as I can tell, this place doesn't exist."

Aarif stared at the journalist, and Chad moved back around the stone and looked at him as well. "Of course it exists," he said, breaking his own prohibition. "We're standing in the middle of it, Brennan."

"Normally I'd concur, but everything's in a database now, boys, and I couldn't find Barron Cemetery on Rutherford County's official cemetery registry—nor, for that matter, could I find it on the state of Tennessee's. I couldn't find it *anywhere.* I even called the Rutherford County Historical Society, but the lady I talked to didn't know thing one about this place—or so she said—despite the fact there are graves on this hill over two hundred years old." Brennan made a disgusted noise. "As soon as 'Barron Cemetery' popped out of my mouth, she clammed up on me, then put me on hold and shuffled me off to some flunky who knew even less than her, if that's possible."

Chad made his own disgusted sound before turning and raising his camera to the stone again. Flash. "That's absurd. It has to be listed somewhere. You must have made a mistake. Maybe you should consider another profession, Brennan."

"Yeah, maybe," the reporter said softly while watching Chad. Then he turned to Aarif with that grin shining through his beard. "But it doesn't matter; I'll just come at it from the other direction." He tap-tapped his notebook with the gold pen. "Before you ladies turned up, I was busy copying names. I'll contact the decedents' families and find out all I want to know about this place, and then some."

Aarif considered the stone and the swirling text again, his mind seething: *What did it all MEAN?* Add in what he suspected concerning the language, and he liked nothing about this situation; he most certainly didn't like that he had based all his hope on it.

Brennan sidled over, pen poised. "So is that Arabic?"

Aarif answered before he thought, distracted by the possibilities—and the fear—churning through his brain. "No."

"Then what is it?"

"Don't talk to him, Aarif!" Another flash.

"What is it, Dr. Hameed?" The reporter's question was as hushed as the surrounding graves.

"It's an ancient form of Aramaic." Aarif frowned. "Or perhaps a *precursor* to Aramaic would be more accurate. Again, not my area of expertise."

There was total silence then, but it didn't last long; Brennan got there first.

"Aramaic! Holy fucking shit! You're kidding, right?"

Chad came around the stone again. "Aramaic? Why does that sound familiar?"

Brennan answered. "I didn't say *holy* fucking shit without a reason, numb nuts. Don't remember your Vacation Bible School, huh? *I* do. Aramaic was the language spoken by Jesus Christ."

Chad whispered, "Holy fucking shit."

The reporter shined his light around the cemetery. "What's this thing doing *here?*" He turned back to Aarif. "Well? Can you read it, Professor?"

Aarif scowled at them. Christians. So ready to assume that everything revolved around *their* beliefs; however, he didn't feel up to giving them a language history lesson—not that they would appreciate it if he did, or care. He glanced at the stele, hesitated, and then held out his hand. Chad passed his flashlight over without a word.

Aarif put his finger out, careful not to touch the stone, tracing the symbols. "I...may have misspoken when I said the language was Aramaic; the *symbols* are those utilized in ancient written Aramaic, or at least closely related, but many of them are...inverted, twisted. Corrupted." They were staring at him. Aarif backed away from the looming stone. "Whichever language that is, I cannot read it—and frankly, I don't think I want to."

There was a heavy silence. Aarif could hear all three of them breathing as they stared up at the crooked lith blotting out the stars; there seemed not to be another sound in the universe.

And then Chad said, "All right," and glanced at Aarif's camera. "I've got what I need. Are you going to take any pictures? Do it and let's get the hell out of here, I'm ready for that beer."

Brennan wrote furiously in his notebook. Aarif watched him, thinking they would need to announce their discovery as soon as possible—like tomorrow.

"Reef?"

"Um, yes." Aarif snapped a picture and then checked it in the display; good. Behind him, another bright flash lit the cemetery.

Brennan.

The big reporter moved around the stone and took another picture. Flash. "So," he said. "I still haven't figured out why a math professor is interested in this thing." He moved behind a scowling Chad. Flash. "Why are *you* here, sexy?"

"I'm not speaking to you."

"That's fine." Flash. "As soon as I get out of here and catch a signal, I'm going to the MTSU website. I'm sure I'll be able to find your smiling face in the faculty bios, with a name underneath." Flash. "Maybe even the name of your boss. I'm sure he or she will be very intrigued that you're running around out here tonight."

Chad's teeth grinding together was audible from ten feet away. "What I do on my time is my business, so talk to whomever you like."

He left Brennan standing there and cut through the flowers and thorns toward another path; suddenly he stumbled and cursed and caught his balance by grabbing the top of a black headstone. Chad freed his tee-shirt hem from the thorns before continuing on; he sounded like an angry gorilla crashing through the jungle.

Aarif had been using the digital zoom to study the clarity of the symbols in the pic he'd just taken when he suddenly looked up, and something fluttered in his chest as he strained his ears; the cemetery and the surrounding trees were utterly silent.

Where are the insects?

Their cacophony had been so prevalent they'd faded into the background of his awareness, but now they were gone. He looked toward the west and beheld a dull orange line above the trees crowding the ridge; overhead, vast multitudes of stars twinkled.

"…could just tell me, sexy. If you cooperate, you'll get a mention, and believe me when I say this story will go national. Having your name inside would do wonders for your career."

"Screw you, Brennan."

"Gentlemen, please." The fluttering in Aarif's chest had spread, making him tremble. Where were the insects? It wasn't just the cemetery and the surrounding forest; the whole valley had gone silent. "I think we should leave."

"Screw *you*, Goldilocks."

"*Shut up!*" Aarif's voice crashed across the tor. "Listen!"

They stared at him in shock.

"What?" Chad said.

"Shh!"

In the stillness that followed, their ragged breathing sounded like three chugging locomotives.

"Where'd the bugs go?" Chad whispered.

Brennan's voice was unsteady as he shined his flashlight around. "I don't know, but I think Dr. Hameed is right. It's time to leave."

Panic was crawling up Aarif's spine, rising from somewhere deep inside, where the old instincts lived—instincts not dulled by time or modern living.

Yes, it was time to leave. Past time.

Aarif and Brennan took two steps down the path toward the lichgate, and then a crash spun them around. They both trained their flashlights on Chad thrashing in a rose bush. He rolled out, then to his hands and knees, head hanging; a grunting, hacking sound came from his throat as he swayed on all fours.

"Chad?"

"What the hell's wrong with him?"

Aarif stepped forward. "Chad?" Closer. "Chad, are you all right?"

His friend gathered his feet under him and stood, unrolling in a strange, boneless way, hands hanging at his sides; Aarif could see his fingers twitching. When Chad's face appeared in the flashlight's beam, he gasped and stumbled backward into Brennan.

Chad's eyes had rolled so far back only the whites were visible, and the mouth… his mouth stretched in a maniac grin that went from ear to ear, like the Joker from the Batman movies; his lips had cracked from the strain, and beads of blood ran down his chin as Chad's heavy breath rasped, the sound filling the cemetery.

Brennan seized Aarif's arm in a crushing grip. "What the fuck?"

A detached part of Aarif's mind, the part that wasn't gibbering in terror, noted he was clutching the taller man back; their beams wavered, making Chad's horrible new face jump from the light to the dark and back.

"Chad?"

Chad's head turned toward them like a balloon floating on a string; the whites of his eyes glowed above that huge, bloody grin.

Brennan whispered, "Jesus Christ!"

Chad fixed those horrible white orbs on the reporter. "No."

That wasn't Chad's voice; deep and harsh, it had to be the most awful voice Aarif had ever heard. The part of his mind clinging to sanity howled in terror, telling him to run, to flee, but Aarif's feet stayed rooted. He couldn't just leave his friend.

"Chad, are you…?"

That ponderous head swiveled to regard him, and Aarif got another shock; Chad was…swelling. He was now as large as Brennan, and his outline undulated, like a bed sheet drying on a clothes line.

"Chad," the voice boomed. "Yes, this mite Names itself that. So important it thought itself." A resonant laugh peeled forth. Aarif was shaking so hard he could barely hold the flashlight, let alone keep the beam steady, but he could see that the torn lips and the terrible face that had been Chad's had never moved during that speech, or that awful mirth.

Brennan was clutching him so hard Aarif found it hard to breathe.

"Oh my God oh my God oh my God—!"

The laugh cut off. "It is still here, mortal. Do you wish to hear what it thinks of itself now?"

A scream filled the cemetery, a howl on the edge of madness, perhaps beyond. It was Chad.

"*Ahhhhhhhhhhhhhh God help me! Ahhhhhhhh! Help me please God help me pleeeeeaaaase! Ahhh—*"

The scream chopped off, and silence filled the cemetery once more except for three sets of breathing; two rapid and panicky-loud, one sonorous and even louder; the things mad, impossible smile had never altered through all of that.

"Do you hear, mortal? It knows its place, now." Chad took a long step towards them; he was over eight feet tall. Aarif and Brennan staggered back, still clutching each other. "Soon *all* will know."

Chad. Chad was still in there somewhere; the part of Aarif's mind that was still sane rebelled, repulsed, but he knew:

His friend was *still in there.*

Aarif then did the bravest thing he'd ever done in his life. He took a step forward, dragging the reporter with him, brandishing Chad's flashlight at the thing that used to be Chad.

"Let…let him go!"

Brennan hauled Aarif back again. "OhmyGodohmyGodohmy*God*—"

"I said let him go!"

The thing's smile abruptly shrank to almost normal as it stared at Aarif, and then it returned, stretching wider than ever. And then both he and Brennan screamed, their screams chasing each other around the cemetery and echoing across the hushed valley as a red tongue that was two feet long and forked, but hollow, like a tube, snaked out of the thing's mouth and slurped at the blood pouring down Chad's chin. It talked while the tongue worked, lips never moving, impossible smile never wavering.

"Ah, Loyalty. One of the so-called Virtues. Misplaced and misguided, as ever. Tell me, mortal, would you feel Loyalty to this flesh if you knew it had been keeping time with your mate? With your precious she?"

Aarif stopped breathing.

"No."

"Yes." More deep, rasping laughter issued, mocking and cruel. "This is the thing you give your Loyalty. Would you like to understand your folly with your own pitiful senses, mortal?"

The cemetery filled with two voices: his Aleena's beautiful laugh sounded, followed by a moan; Chad's voice. Chad's moan. The thing's lips never moved; its tongue still flailed like a stepped-on snake, those glowing white eyes fixed on Aarif; it was over ten-feet tall now and still growing.

Chad and Aleena's voices. They were…they were…

"*No!*" Aarif ripped free of Brennan and covered his ears with his hands, dropping his camera and almost knocking his glasses off with the flashlight. He was trying to block out the sound of his wife's moans and gasps. His wife and his friend's.

"No! Stop it! *That's not true!*"

Then Brennan shoved him. Aarif caught his balance and turned to look at the reporter; the bearded man's complexion was as white as the roses surrounding them.

"You guys are playing some kind of trick on me, but I'm not falling for it! You people are sick! Well, I'm *done!* I'm fucking *out* of here!" With that he turned and jogged down the path toward the lichgate, his flashlight bobbing a circle of brightness in front of him; by the time he crossed under, he was running.

Aarif turned back to Chad—or what had been Chad. Aleena. Aleena and Chad…no. It could not be.

"Chad?"

The thing ignored him, balloon head turning, terrible glowing white eyes tracking something Aarif couldn't see.

"Chad?"

It continued to ignore him while looking down the hill toward the parking lot; it was now enormous, towering in the night next to the twisted stele like a grotesque Professor Hot parade float. The animal part of Aarif's mind pleaded with the remaining part to run and keep running, to run and not look back, but he had to know. He had to hear Chad say it.

Aleena, my beautiful Aleena…with Chad…no. No, it could *not* be.

Could it?

"Chad, did you sleep with my wife?"

Aleena.

Then there was a shout; the shout contained words that were indistinct, but he recognized that voice. Brennan. Another shout, louder, and then one word, "No!", and then a scream, followed by more screams, horrible screams, like an animal caught in a trap. Aarif turned toward them involuntarily. Brennan. Aarif could hear the reporter pleading for mercy between ragged howls, for God to save him, and then the screaming got even louder, spiraling up beyond human hearing before cutting off as if chopped with an ax.

Silence.

Then that voice throbbed behind him, full of anger—and hunger. "They feed without me!"

Aarif spun back around just in time to see a normal-sized Chad collapse like a marionette whose strings had been cut. He immediately stirred and mumbled something, tried to sit up and fell back.

Aarif stepped closer. "Chad?"

Chad got to his hands and knees, shaking his head, swaying, and then he climbed to his feet. When Aarif shined the flashlight on his friend's face, he gasped.

The coeds wouldn't smile at Professor Hot now; his normally tan, firm face was sagging and twitching and bloodless-pale; red, red blood still dripped from his torn lips and ran down his chin. Chad raised shaking hands to cover that ruin of a face, and then a keening wail came from behind those fish-belly white hands.

"Did you sleep with Aleena?"

Chad either didn't hear him or ignored him; that soft wail turned to a shriek, ripping from Chad's open mouth; fingers turned to claws, drawing more blood as Chad howled at the stars.

Aarif stepped up and slammed a fist into that twisted face, dropping Chad to the path, and then winced and shook his hand; he'd never hit anyone before in his life. Chad scrambled back to his feet. At least that horrible caterwauling had stopped.

"*Answer me!* Did you sleep with my wife?"

Aleena.

Chad blinked and then focused, and Aarif knew Chad was seeing him when those sagging features crumpled further. "Reef…I'm sorry. She came on to me, and…and it just happened. I'm so sorry." He took a step forward, and Aarif stepped back as the cemetery tilted and spun.

No.

"I wanted to tell you, man, because I'm not the only one. She's been…" Chad stared wide-eyed over Aarif's shoulder, bloody mouth gaping, and then he shrieked louder than before and tore off through the cemetery.

"Chad!" *Not the only one?* Aarif whirled and shined the light where Chad had stared, but saw only black headstones and white roses. He ran after him, beam bobbing wildly. "Chad, wait! What does that mean, 'not the only one'? *Wait!*"

Professor Not-So-Hot ran full-tilt out from under the lichgate and down the path. Aarif stopped under the arch, panting, and watched as Chad got to the turn in the walk and didn't, instead crashing into the mass of red roses. He was still screaming as he plowed a straight trail all the way through to the trees and disappeared; his shrieks echoed from the forest.

Aarif took a few stunned steps down the walk and stopped, shining his flashlight on the path Chad had carved. The beam shook as he turned it toward the cars. He could see both of them down there, and Brennan's lights were still on.

Where was the reporter?

He called out, but with little hope. "Brennan?"

Aarif had tried for a shout, but a shaky croak was all that emerged. No answer. The silence pressed in on Aarif, and cold numbed his feet, creeping up his legs toward his heart.

Cold?

How can it be so chilly in August?

Aarif stumbled down the path, shaking so bad it took three tries to shove his hand in his pocket. *Yes, away, that's where I need to be, far away, somewhere else.* As he made the turn, he realized he was praying; in English or Arabic, he couldn't tell which. He finally got his keys out, dropping them and scooping them up, and when he straightened she was in front of him.

"Don't leave."

Aarif froze as terror blazed through him, and then terror faded to relieved confusion; a little girl stood on the walk. *I'm not alone, praise be to Allah!* But where had she come from? Aarif stepped closer, shining the light full on her. She didn't flinch from it, didn't raise her small white hand to shield her eyes, just stood and looked at him; she had big dark eyes, and she wore an antique ivory dress, a thing from another century, with lace and a long train. Her pale feet were bare, and she had brown hair in two long braids down her back; she was nine, maybe ten.

"Don't leave," she said again. Then: "I need you."

Where in Allah's name had *she* come from? Aarif shined the flashlight around but saw no one else; the cars in the parking lot were just a few dozen feet away, now.

"We have to leave," he told her. "It's not safe here." Aarif stepped forward, holding out his hand. He would find her parents once they were—

He stopped.

Everything about her was normal except for her eyes: dark eyes, he'd thought, and he'd been right; eyes as black as the lith looked up at him—eyes without a sclera, iris, or pupils; eyes like holes bored into a starless sky.

The little girl that wasn't a little girl smiled and reached for his hand; her sweet voice filled the cold, empty air.

"I need you," she said.

The part of Aarif's mind that had somehow held it together until then snapped, and he shrieked and turned and plowed a path through the roses parallel to Chad's, thorns ripping into his stomach and thighs and hands, but he didn't care. When he reached the trees he stopped, and then hesitantly turned back and shined the flashlight up at the cemetery.

He immediately wished he hadn't.

A silent throng had joined the little girl; they were maybe a hundred all told, men and women and a handful of other children. A double handful of the men wore antiquated military uniforms from several eras. Some people stood on the walk, others in the roses, and more stood under the lichgate and in the cemetery beyond; at least a dozen surrounded the twisted lith, their motionless outlines joining the stone's against the star-filled sky.

They were all watching him.

Aarif fled into the darkness beneath the trees.

Trunks flashed by on either side. He was flying downhill, down and down and down, and had just skirted a massive trunk when he tripped over something and went sprawling; he slammed belly-first into the loam, his left elbow striking something hard, and he cried out as the flashlight went flipping away.

Aarif held his elbow, thrashing with the pain; when he could feel his fingers again, he climbed to his feet and spotted the flashlight glowing a few feet away. Allah be praised, it hadn't broken and gone out.

That's when he realized everything was blurry.

He'd lost his glasses.

Raw panic engulfed him. *I can't see!* The tree trunk to his right—he'd tripped over one of its roots—was a dark blur against the black; only the flashlight was clear to him. He squinted desperately near his feet, but it was no use. His vision was bad even in the light; in the dark, without his glasses, there was no hope. He needed to get to the flashlight and then find them with its beam.

Aarif felt the loam ahead with his hands, walking like a chimpanzee, making sure he didn't crush his glasses inadvertently, and made it to the flashlight, sending another prayer of thanks to Allah. He stood up, shining the beam around, and spotted a gleam in front of the big knob of root he'd tripped over. He went over and picked his glasses up and put them on; they now sat crooked on his nose, but the lenses were still intact, praise be to Allah.

Aarif's panic was gone, blasted away by the pain in his mashed elbow. He gave the root a swift kick and kept going downhill, but walking now, and with a purpose: that stream should be down here somewhere, it had to be, gravity said so, the stream with the bridge and the willows, and if he followed it back to the bridge and the willows, he'd find the road, and once on the road he could—

A scream shattered the hushed forest. Aarif turned toward it, heart hammering. Another cry, pure terror and pain that echoed through the trunks; it was close, and coming from further down the hill, and from Aarif's right.

Worse, he recognized that voice.

Chad.

Another pain-and-terror-filled shriek, another, spiraling up and up and up, another, and then they stopped.

Shaking, Aarif angled away from where the screams had come, from where the screams had stopped, jogging now, not running, no, but not walking anymore, that's for sure. There was no sound except for crunching leaves and his whistling breath. *Chad, oh merciful Allah, that had been Chad.* What had happened to him? Chad and Aleena. No time for thinking, keep moving. The stream appeared, and he followed it to his left. He'd found the willows! The bridge should be up ahead, and the road, the blessed road out…the bridge! There it was!

Aarif scrambled up the embankment and stood on the blacktop. He looked to his right, at the wooden bridge, and then to his left, up the hill; far above he could see the tunnel opening filled with stars. The parking lot was up there, and his car.

He patted his pockets and realized he'd lost his keys somewhere. No matter, Brennan's car was still running. He would run up there, jump in the reporter's car, and be away from this horrible place in a cloud of rubber smoke…

But that meant he would have to go back, *up there*. He glanced at the road past the bridge. Perhaps it would be best to walk out. Once he escaped this abhorrent valley, he'd have a cell signal, and he could call for help for Brennan and Chad.

Chad and Aleena. No. Yes. That was best. No *way* was he going back up there; he would walk out—no, *run* out; no *sprint* out—and then call for help.

Decision made, Aarif turned, took one step, and stopped.

She was standing in the middle of the bridge.

"No," Aarif moaned, backing up. "No, please." He trembled so hard that her pale, sweet face and infinite eyes jumped in and out of the flashlight's beam.

"Why did you leave?" She moved toward him, fast, off the bridge and onto the road. "I *need* you."

Aarif opened his mouth to scream, and nothing came out but a hiss of air. He turned and lunged off the road back toward the trees and had taken two long strides when something caught his foot. He went down hard, glasses flying, but he somehow retained his grip on the flashlight. He tried to yank his foot free, but it was held tight so he sat up and shined the light on it.

A pale hand had thrust out of the crumbling leaves of untold past seasons and grabbed him, a hand with curved, black claws instead of fingernails; a hand covered with lesions and boils. A sunken, narrow face pushed out below the hand, all gaping mouth and needle teeth and bottomless black eyes, and bit a chunk out of his calf.

Aarif howled.

He smacked the hand with the flashlight and jerked his foot away, but more clawed hands thrust out of the detritus to grip his arms and legs; a dozen mouths opened below, hundreds of teeth. The flashlight rolled away. They held him on all fours as he thrashed, and his screams bounced from the uncaring trees.

Aarif shrieked for Allah to save him, please save him. Motion drew his head up, made him cease his struggles even as parts of him disappeared down bloody, grinning mouths. The little girl came to stand before him and leaned her face down, close enough for him to see, and for the first and last time in his life, Aarif wished he were blind.

It wasn't pretending to be a little girl anymore.

"Your God cannot hear you," it rasped. "This is our place." Its jaws gaped impossibly wide and then snapped forward, ripping his nose and left cheek off.

Aarif thrashed, screaming until what he could scream with was gone, and then with a final horror he realized what was left of him was being pulled beneath the loam.

No! Anything but that! Allah the Merciful, ANYTHING BUT THAT!

Aarif's consciousness fled, and he found himself falling down a long, black tunnel just as they dragged his body beneath the ground; a small mercy.

His last thought was of Aleena.

Book III

Things
That Should Not
Be

A ROBOT HAND

ANIEL JUMPED up and scurried over and peeked out the front window, the one nearest the foyer this time; the hand that didn't have a beer in it hovered near his pocket. Beth knew the big revolver was in there because she could see its weight pulling down that side of his khaki shorts; it was the tenth time he'd gotten up to peer out one living-room window or another since they'd started this idiotic movie.

And evidently there was still a bunch of nothing out there because he came back and plopped back down on the far side of the couch. Lizzie sat between them; her eyes were wide, and her mouth was ajar. They were watching her "New *Star Wars* Movie", known to the rest of the galaxy as *The Empire Strikes Back*, and to Beth as *Not This Stupid Movie Again*.

And Daniel wasn't even watching! He stared at something on the wall beyond the flat screen while his hand stroked his pocket, the one with the gun; he seemed unaware he was doing it, or of her study.

What in the world has gotten into him?

He glanced over at her; his blue eyes were startling in those caverns of yellow-and-green contusions, although Beth had noted his face was looking remarkably better. Suddenly he popped up again without a word and vanished into the kitchen; her husband was also moving easier, as if his back and shoulder weren't bothering him at all, now. Beth was glad he was feeling better, she supposed, but it was… strange…how fast he was recovering; this morning, there had still been swelling, especially around his eyes and nose, and those eyes had been ringed by eggplant. He'd also been hobbling like an old man, but now…strange.

Beth scowled.

And strange didn't even *begin* to describe how he was acting, forget how he looked or how he felt! She hadn't felt like cooking following her battle with Brennan, so after picking Lizzie up she'd snagged carryout from their favorite pizza joint, Gussano's: a large deep-dish Chicago-style pepperoni and sausage pie for Daniel, a small mushroom and pineapple for her, and a small cheese for Lizzie. When they got home, Lizzie and Mr. Yoda greeted each other with laughs and licks and then went tearing outside to play in the backyard; as for Beth, she had cornered her husband, determined to tell him they needed to talk, or else. But before she could say a word, he had caught her flat-footed by looking at her intently and saying, "After pizza, we need to talk."

Beth had just stared up at him, her thunder stolen, and then said, "All right."

So then they'd called Lizzie and Mr. Yoda back in and eaten dinner, Daniel hardly touching his food while drinking beer nonstop and glancing out the window every five seconds like he thought something was going to crash through and get them, Lizzie full of energy, kicking her legs over the edge of her new chair and talking nonstop; she'd picked up a word at daycare today: now everything was "cool". Pizza was cool. Mr. Yoda, who was extremely cool, sat on the tiles below her chair, ears lifted as high as they would go. Lizzie had been the only one with any appetite—well, Lizzie and Mr. Yoda.

Afterwards, Lizzie demanded to watch her cool new *Star Wars* movie, about which Beth had mercifully forgotten. Daniel whispered, "After the movie, when she goes to bed," and she'd had to be content with that, even though she'd thought it was totally uncool.

Now not only was he not watching the stupid space movie with them, he had vamoosed out of the living room!

Beth had had enough.

"I'm going to talk to your daddy."

Absorbed, Lizzie didn't respond.

Beth sighed, kissed the top of her daughter's oblivious head, squared her shoulders, grabbed her determination in both fists, and strode off to find her annoying idiot of a husband.

She didn't have to look far. He was standing in the empty formal dining room, staring through its triple windows; out there the sun was setting, indigo sky streaked with orange and pink wisps of cloud, darkness creeping over the fresh-mowed grass and engulfing their old patio furniture, her bag gallows, and Lizzie's swing set; lightning bugs winked and blinked in the gloom out by the fence.

Daniel glanced at her, then slipped the revolver into his pocket. Why on *earth* had it been out? She didn't want Lizzie seeing it—she didn't want her daughter anywhere *near* it! Beth fought for calm; blowing up would serve no purpose, other than making her feel better.

He cocked his head, ostentatiously listening to the laser blasts interspersed with Chewbacca's warbling roar, then took a sip of beer and pointed his idiot face back outside. "So the movie's over?"

"Yes." She could be sarcastic, too. "It's time to talk."

"I think we should wait 'till she goes to bed, at least."

"I think *now* is a good time." Beth followed his twitching gaze outside, but there was nothing to see except their backyard and the stuff that lived there; the tension in his manner and posture had her on edge. "I found some things out today."

"Oh yeah?" he said, dry as dust. "I found some things out today, too." He tipped the beer up and drained it, then set the empty on the bay ledge. She waited, but her husband offered nothing else, just stared out at the fading sky.

Deep. Calm. Breaths! "Fine," Beth growled. "*I'll* start."

She left nothing out except the woman at the bookstore, Gail. Beth was about to tell him what she'd found during her scouting when he spoke without looking at her:

"I thought we agreed we wouldn't talk to any fucking reporters."

"Yes we did, just like we agreed to answer each other's calls today!"

"I *told* you I couldn't hear the phone because I was mowing the yard." He slapped up the switch next to the window, bathing the patio and yard in white light. "See, Beth? See the cut grass?"

She crossed her arms, trapping her hands in her armpits. Beth was *not* going to strike her husband; if it ever came to that between them…of course, she wouldn't have to hit him; with that nose, she could just grab and twist and he would be on his knees so fast…she stalked two paces away and turned back. It was safer over here. For him.

"So this reporter we weren't supposed to talk to wants me to call him tonight?"

"Yes."

He shrugged. "I *guess* I could…but help me out here: wasn't it *you* that insisted that everything was 'over', and that I was 'compensating'?"

"I decided you were right," Beth said oh-so-calmly, "about *some* of it, anyway." She wasn't about to bring that stupid cemetery up again. "The phone call Rison took in our bedroom should have been followed up on, but they just closed the case. I want to know why. And this business of a 'warning'…" She shook her head. "I'm not sure I buy it, but wishing the media attention away is foolish, Daniel. We should tell our side of the story while we can—while anybody still cares. And if there truly is a 'they', then putting what really happened out there will let them know we're not just going to sit here and take what they throw at us. At the very least we'll get some sort of reaction, and that will help us pinpoint who's against us."

He faced her for the first time, an unreadable expression on his bruised face, and then he suddenly started laughing. "*Reaction?* Oh, it's gonna get one of those, I can fucking guarantee it." Beth frowned, but before she could ask what was so darn funny he said, "So this Brennan cat told you some things about John McFarlane, huh? Well, I went straight to the source. Helen came by, said McFarlane wanted to talk, so I drove over to his farm and ate lunch with the man—excuse me, 'dinner'."

Beth gaped, and then spluttered, "Well? What did he say?"

"Oh, he had lots to say." His ragged amusement was gone.

"Daniel, what did he *want?*"

He told her.

Beth paced the kitchen like a caged panther. She thought she might explode. McFarlane had sent Rison to attack her! "*Who does he think he is?*" She spun and stalked the other way, flicking out the blade of her Carson, folding it and flicking it out; fold, flick, fold, flick. She was going to break something, or someone; this was unbelievable. "Does he really think he can *threaten* us like that? That we'll just *move* because he doesn't like our *house!?* At least he gave us until the first!" *McFarlane sent Rison!* "We have to call the police!"

"And which police would those be?" He was back to staring out the window even though he'd turned off the flood lights, and it was now full dark. "It's his word against mine. And you heard me: the fucking Sheriff is his cousin—*cousin Willy*, he called him. Smug bastard bragged about knowing people in the State Police, too." He eyed her significantly. "*And* the TBI."

"So we're not going to do anything?" The TBI? Who did he know there? Wait. Beth squeezed her eyes shut, the connections forming. Her stomach twisted.

"Weren't you listening? I'm meeting Scandlin tomorrow at three o'clock at some Cajun restaurant in Nashville. The guy seems to know a lot about McFarlane; maybe he'll know who can help us. Until then we'll—"

"I know who McFarlane knows in the TBI," she said, snapping her eyes open. "Or at least I *think* I do."

"Who?"

"Scarborough."

"*Special Agent* Scarborough?" Beth nodded. "As in the guy-in-charge-of-the-fucking-investigation Special Agent Scarborough?" She nodded again.

He looked pole-axed. "Shit."

"Yeah."

"How can you be sure?"

"I did some digging today and found an obituary for McFarlane's late wife."

"So?"

"So she was Helen's sister."

"*Helen* is McFarlane's sister-in-law?"

"She never told me, Daniel."

He grunted. "I wouldn't claim the son of a bitch either. But what's that got to do with Scarborough?"

"Don't you…?" Beth did a mental double-take; she'd been so worried about his sanity last night she'd forgotten to tell him about Rison being related to Helen and Scarborough. She filled him in, and he walked over and stood in front of her, looking down into her eyes. Beth held her breath at his closeness.

"Okay," he said, "so Scott Rison was apparently related to the entire state of Tennessee: the Sheriff of Rutherford County, some bigwig District Attorney, Mc-Farlane, Helen, and Special Agents galore. That doesn't mean—"

"Rison was related to McFarlane too?" Then she got it. "Cousin Willy!"

"Right, Cousin Willy. That's why the old man gave *Scotty* a job—"

"That's not funny, Daniel. Don't call him that. Don't you *ever* call him that, not where I can hear."

He looked uncomfortable. "Sorry. Anyway, I'm not surprised Helen's related to him—to both of them. I remember her saying she was connected to everybody within a twenty-mile radius, in one form or another." His laugh was sour. "Sometimes I think we're the only ones in this damn county *not* related to everybody else.

Beth, McFarlane might have the in with Scarborough, but you can't tell me you think Helen would…look, I'll be the first to admit she doesn't like me—and you know the feeling's mutual—but she's your friend, and she loves Lizzie. She loves *both* of you. You know that."

Beth hesitated and then nodded; he was right, but she didn't trust herself to speak. He was so close, now, and he smelled like gasoline and grass clippings and cigarettes and beer and him, and despite the cigarettes, she wanted nothing more in the world than his arms wrapped around her.

Their eyes stayed locked; his hand lifted toward her cheek slowly.

"Beth, I—"

"Mommy, Daddy, Mommy, Daddy!" Lizzie ran through the kitchen, bare feet slapping on the tiles. Mr. Yoda was hot on her heels, toenails clicking.

Daniel said, "What is it, baby? What's wrong?" Beth saw his hand go into his pocket as he looked over Lizzie's shoulder, as if he expected someone to be chasing her. An hour ago Beth would've been exasperated, and maybe still worried about his sanity.

Not anymore.

She turned away and tried to compose herself. *So close.*

Lizzie skidded to a stop. Daniel squatted in front of her. "What happened?"

"Darth Vader is Luke's *daddy!* And he cut his *hand* off! And now Luke's got a robot hand! Daddy, if you cut my hand off, can I get a robot hand?"

Beth watched Daniel's mouth work with some satisfaction; she'd *told* him that Lizzie was too young for *Star Wars*.

"You know I would never cut your hand off, sweet pea." He shot Beth an annoyed look; he knew what she'd told him as well. "And Luke didn't *really* get his hand chopped off, that was just movie magic. You know that, right? That movies and stuff on TV, they aren't real?"

Lizzie nodded uncertainly. Then she grinned. "Can I get a robot hand anyway? It was *so cool!*"

Daniel laughed, and Beth managed a smile as he scooped their daughter up and kissed her and tickled her. Lizzie giggled.

"I'll see what I can do," he said.

"Can I watch my new *Star Wars* movie again?"

"Once is enough for tonight. It's time for a bath and then bed."

The sweet giggles evaporated. "I don't *want* to go to bed!"

"Lizzie, it's late—"

"No!" She squirmed, fighting him, and he put her down. She ran off. "I don't *want* to go to bed! I want to watch my new *Star Wars* movie again!" She retreated into the living room. "*I DON'T WANT TO GO TO BED!*"

Beth made slow circles on her temples with the tips of her index fingers; she felt like a balloon animal that had been over-inflated.

Daniel was watching her warily. "I'll run a bath and get her into her rabbit jammers," he said. "She's tired."

"You think?"

His face hardened. "Yeah," he said. "I think."

Mr. Yoda whined, and they looked at him; he was staring toward the living room. He whined again, then looked up at them, and it was obvious to everyone whose fault this was. Then he gave a little doggy sigh and trotted after his mistress, ears drooping. Beth watched him slink into the living room, where from the sound of it Lizzie was in full-tantrum mode:

"I DON'T WANT TO GO TO BED!"

Welcome to the family, dog.

Her husband strode off toward the commotion.

"Daniel, I..." Beth couldn't bring herself to apologize. He looked at her, still walking, and she motioned toward the bottle he'd left on the deep ledge. "Do you have any of those to spare?" She needed something to take the edge off or she really would pop.

Her husband stopped dead, staring, and then he shrugged and nodded in the general direction of the fridge. "There's plenty, help yourself." He disappeared around the corner.

Beth had never been a beer drinker, but any port...she fled outside as Lizzie's yells got louder, then shut the French door and turned to peer through the glass in time to see her daughter go wailing up the stairs. Daniel stopped at the bottom, shoulders slumped. Beth saw him look down at Mr. Yoda and say something; the tiny dog wagged his tail. Daniel picked him up, and they climbed after Lizzie.

Beth pressed her forehead against the cool glass for a minute and then twisted the top off her beer and took a sip. She made a face. How did he drink this crap? She walked over and stood next to their patio table, looking over the fence to the northeast, toward the lights crowning the darkened ridge:

John McFarlane's farm.

Did the man really think he could just order them to move? And that they would do it? And he'd sent Rison! Or gave the psycho the 'green light', as Daniel had said, which amounted to the same thing; fury washed through Beth, making her shake. *Who does he think he is?* She chugged the beer, belched, set the bottle on the table with a clink, and went back in to get another. Beth stood in the open fridge and listened as she twisted the new cap off and took a swig: bath water running, and normal voices drifting down the staircase; the storm had calmed.

She was anything but calm.

Beth stalked back outside, slamming both the refrigerator and the French door, and sat her beer on the table. She picked up a patio chair and carried it across the yard to the fence, then went back for her beer—the things weren't *that* bad—and climbed on the chair; when she stretched tip-toe, she could just see over the fence. A handful of lights glowed in the distance, shining among the trees on the ridge.

She took a big drink, then raised her middle finger to those lights.

John McFarlane thought he was such a *big deal* he could just *order* them off, and all because he didn't like their *house?*

Outraged anew, Beth pulled her phone out and thought seriously about dialing 911 right then and there, but Daniel was right; it was McFarlane's word against his. She put her phone up and emptied the bottle down her throat, swayed, caught the top of the fence, and then graced the distant lights with her middle finger again before hopping down. She needed another beer.

Brennan had been right. John McFarlane really did have connections every-where; and judging by Beth's own discoveries, everyone believed he was some sort of pillar of the community. *What are we going to do?* Standing in the open fridge, she raised her new beer to her lips and took a long, long pull; these things were pretty good. No wonder he liked them. Beth heard the sounds of splashing bath water and Lizzie's piping voice, and then her laugh.

Good for Daniel.

Beth slammed the fridge and went back outside.

Suddenly she had an idea. *That's it!* She plunked her beer on the patio table and got her phone back out and then dug in her shorts until she came up with the McDonald's napkin she'd made Brennan write his cell number on.

If they couldn't go to the police, she'd have Brennan put everything into his story! *That* would light a fire under the old man's balls!

Her call went straight to voicemail.

She tried again; same result. Again. Same. Again. Same. Again. Same. Beth scowled, then snatched her beer from the table, tipping it back. Men. Beth didn't understand why they were even allowed to *have* cell phones. She stood, swaying, and went inside.

The patio was waving in and out, in and out, but she made it back and dropped into her chair and tilted her fresh beer up; she lowered it, but kept her head back and her gaze pointed up at the swimming stars. Brennan. Where *was* he? A tinge of worry hit the new warmth in her belly and melted. He'd just had to go see that stupid cemetery for himself. It was just a cemetery! Stupid men. Bane of her ex-istence. September first. What would McFarlane do if they didn't move? Send the goons Daniel had told her about? She needed bigger knives. Helen.

Beth sighed, then settled deeper into her chair. Helen. She was going to have a loooong talk with Helen tomorrow. So many stars. If she only had the eyes to *see!* She wanted a telescope. She'd wanted one since they'd moved in, but didn't think they could afford it, not even a cheap one. Beth rolled her head around and looked inside. That stupid bag full of money still sat on the kitchen island. No, she wouldn't spend *football* money. Daniel had a gambling problem, but he wouldn't admit it—oh no, not him! Brennan. Where *was* he? Beth tipped the beer up, then shook the empty bottle.

Never trust men. Oh, you could trust them to do what they *wanted* to do, but nothing else. Daniel was no exception. So many stars. Brennan wasn't the only reporter in the universe; they were like stars that way. An idea began to form and then dissolved. Her beer was empty. She set it the on the table next to the others. How many was that? She focused. That was four. Onetwothreefour. Time for numero five; she stood up, then made her way inside and grabbed a beer and twisted the cap and saw the Gussano's. Pizza! She fumbled out two of her mushie and pineapple slices and had finished the first when a noise made her peer around the edge of the open refrigerator door.

Daniel was standing there watching her with a weird look on his face. Beth chewed and swallowed, then shut the fridge with her elbow. It *whumped* closed with a tinkling crash, and he winced.

"What?"

"Uh, Lizzie's clean and in her rabbit jammers. I told her she could stay up 'till ten if she played in her room."

"Fine by me."

"Are there any of those left?" He pointed at her beer.

"Of course there are! This is only my second one." She tried to go back outside, but she either needed to finish the pizza slice first or grow a third arm. Daniel opened the door for her, and Beth made it to her chair as he got his own beer and came outside and sat down across from her. She could see his face in the weak glow from the kitchen window.

"What are *you* smiling about?"

"Not a thing."

Beth finished her pizza and settled back with a sigh; her stomach felt *much* better. She looked up at the stars again; they were swimming slower now, but they were still breathtaking; thousands upon thousands, and trillions upon trillions beyond them she would never, ever see.

What's really out there?

"Beth, listen to me." She rolled her head around so she could see him. Why was he talking like that? "I want you to take Lizzie tomorrow and get a hotel room and stay there for a few days."

She sat up, then gripped the edge of the table to make everything stop swaying around. "What? Why would I do that?"

"You know why."

"No."

"Beth—"

"No!" She stood up, then grabbed the edge of the table again. "I'm not running from that…that…" She couldn't think of any words bad enough, so she settled for some of his favorites: "Fucker. That *asshole*." She turned toward the distant lights glowing on the ridge. "Fucking asshole!" She tucked her half-empty beer under her armpit and raised both middle fingers, then fell back in her chair and took a drink. "This is good beer."

"It is."

Beth glared across the table. "What's so funny?"

"Nothing. Look, it would just be until we—"

"I am *not* running." Beth had run once before, but she'd been just a teenager, a baby, and in a bad situation. She'd had no choice. But she was a fighter now, a warrior, and she would never run again. "*You* take Lizzie and go hide in a hotel room, and I'll stay here and do what needs to be done."

"Fine. But if I do, I want you to carry that pistol I bought you."

"Not going to happen."

He sighed. "Beth, I'll teach you how to use it. I found a range to join; I'm going there tomorrow, before I meet Scandlin. Guns aren't dangerous if you know what you're doing."

"No."

"God damn it—"

"No!" Beth lurched up and slammed her half-full bottle on the table; the empties fell over, two rolling off the edge before Daniel could grab them. One landed in the grass, but the other shattered on the patio's flagstones with a pop, scattering brown glass everywhere. "Guns are for punks." She jabbed a finger toward his shorts. "Does carrying that make you feel *safe?* Make you feel like a *big man?*" She staggered around the table to stand over him; he didn't move, just looked up at her. "I knew a bunch of guys who carried guns once—four guys, to be exact. They used their big, bad guns to scare people, to hurt people." Her stomach gave a lurch. Maybe she shouldn't have stood up so fast. "They used them to keep me quiet when they raped me, Daniel. All four. They took turns."

They stared at each other. Crickets peeped and creaked on the other side of the fence; up in Lizzie's room, Mr. Yoda barked.

Beth turned away from the look in his eyes. Her stomach gave another lurch and a gurgle. "But you *don't want to talk about it*, so fine, we won't *talk about it*, but I'm not carrying a gun. I'm no coward." Her gut twisted, and she held onto the back of the chair.

"Beth—"

"Shut up." She made it to the edge of the patio and dropped to her hands and knees; his chair scraped, and she felt his warm hand on her back as he knelt beside her.

"Let me get—"

"*Don't touch me!*"

The warm hand vanished.

Why had she said that? She wanted nothing more than for her Daniel to touch her, to hold her again…

Beth heard the French door open and shut softly as he went inside, and then she threw up on the grass.

Outside the downstairs bathroom, Dan sat cross-legged in the hallway with his back against the plaster. Lizzie stood in front of him, facing the closed door. Mr. Yoda sat on the hardwood next to Dan, watching Lizzie.

"Mommy, are you done getting sick?" It was the third time she'd asked that in the last two minutes.

"Almost, baby." The toilet flushed. "I'll be out in a sec." Water ran in the sink.

Lizzie turned to him, all big-eyed and earnest and cute as can be. "Daddy, will we get sick too?"

"No, sweetie, only Mommy's pizza was bad. Ours was fine. We'll be okay, I promise." Four of them. Jesus. He held his arms open. "C'mere."

She shuffled over, and he gathered her onto his lap with her head tucked under his chin; her hair smelled like cherries tonight. She'd wanted the Dora shampoo instead of the Elmo. Mr. Yoda whined, and Lizzie reached out a small hand and patted him on the head; that got a wag.

Four of them. Holy Christ. No, *not* going to picture that; there was nothing he could do about it, anyhow. It had happened long before he'd met her.

Not a goddamn thing he could do.

Four of them.

"Daddy, you're hurting me."

"Sorry, babe." He eased up and kissed the top of her head.

The water shut off, and a moment later the door opened to reveal Dan's wife toweling her face off, hair wet and stringy. Lizzie scrambled off his lap, and Beth scooped her up.

"Are you done getting sick now, Mommy?"

"Yeah, sweetie, I'm done."

"Daddy said only your pizza was bad, so we won't get sick, too."

"That's right, you guys will be fine."

"Did it taste funny?"

"What, the pizza?"

"Yes. Mrs. Lincolmb told us not to eat stuff if it smelled bad or tasted funny. You're s'posed to throw it out."

Beth gave a ghost of a smile that didn't touch her bloodshot eyes. "I'll remember that next time."

"Okay."

Beth glanced at her watch. "It is *way* past your bedtime, little girl."

"Daddy said I could stay up and make sure you were okay 'cause you were sick."

"Did he?" Her eyes slid over him like he wasn't even fucking sitting there, and then she walked toward the stairs, still carrying Lizzie. Dan unclenched his jaw as he used the wall to push himself to his feet and followed, trailing Mr. Yoda. "I'm fine now, so you go on up to your room and get your dog tucked in. I'll be up to kiss you goodnight after I talk to your daddy." She set Lizzie down on the bottom step.

Dan stood behind them and watched; his wife couldn't be bothered to look at him, and she didn't want him to touch her, but at least she would talk to him.

I suppose I should feel gratitude.

"Is your room still dirty? Are you gonna sleep with me again tonight?"

Beth squeezed her eyes shut; Dan knew she'd forgotten all about cleaning their room. He'd thought of it earlier, but the last thing he wanted to do was walk into that room again, let alone scrub rapist blood from the walls and floor and ceiling, so he hadn't minded when the subject wasn't broached.

"It's still dirty. Do you mind if I sleep with you again?"

"It's cool, Mommy."

Beth smiled, a real one this time. "Thank you. Now go—"

"Is Daddy gonna sleep in the spare room again?"

"Yes. Now go do as I—"

"No he's not," Dan cut in firmly, and they both looked at him, Beth with that dangerous crease between her eyebrows. He focused on Lizzie. "I'll sleep in your room with you guys tonight."

"Yay!"

Beth's lips compressed into a line (quite a feat for her), but all she said was, "Time for bed, kiddo."

"C'mon, Mr. Yoda!" Lizzie shot up the stairs.

Beth walked into the kitchen without so much as a glance at him. Dan watched Mr. Yoda scale the risers—he was slow, but he was getting the hang of it—and then followed her and found her by the island making a phone call. "Who are you calling at *this* hour?"

She gave him one of those looks, but didn't answer. Dan forced his jaw to unclench and waited on her pleasure; whoever it was, they didn't pick up. She scowled at the screen, then muttered "Zen" or "Hen" for some reason before she jammed the phone back in her pocket, but he couldn't be sure which.

"I tried to call Brennan."

She was back to not looking at him, staring somewhere past his shoulder.

"The reporter?"

"Yes, the reporter."

"Why?"

"Since we can't call the police, I thought we could get McFarlane's threats into his story."

"I don't know if that's such a good idea. Let me talk to Scandlin first, see what he—" She dug a wadded-up something out of her pocket and bounced it off his chest. Dan caught it before it hit the tiles. "What's this?"

"Brennan's cell number. The reporter. Call him if you want. As a matter of fact, *tell* him what you want, I don't care." She brushed by him, heading toward the foyer. "I'm going to bed. I shouldn't have drank that much. I don't feel very well."

"Hold on, there's something I want to say."

"It can wait until morning."

"Just listen for a minute, and then we'll all go to bed. Please."

She stopped next to the refrigerator, keeping her back to him. Dan watched her for a few seconds, then cleared his throat. "First, I, uh, I'm sorry about…about what happened to you, about what those men did." He struggled for something to say besides "I'm sorry", but for the life of him couldn't think of a single goddamn thing. "I'm sorry."

Beth turned around and crossed her arms beneath her breasts.

"Thanks," she said.

Dan hurried on. "I've got that appointment with the nose doctor at eleven, and then I'm supposed to swing by the hospital so Doc Williams can take my staples out and put stitches in, and then I'm going to the range, and then I'm supposed to meet Scandlin in Nashville at three, so long story short I'll take Lizzie to daycare if you can pick her up. I know you said you want to talk to Helen, but I don't know what else you have planned for tomorrow."

She considered him before saying, "That's fine, but I'm teaching tomorrow night, so be home by seven at the latest or I'll have to take her to the dojo with—"

"I put your blanket and pillow in my room, Daddy!"

"Thank you, baby!" He could see Lizzie's legs and feet as she stood looking down at them. He started to reach for Beth's arm to move them deeper into the kitchen and then let his hand fall; his beloved wife didn't want him to touch her. *Man. That hurts.* Instead, he waved her over, and she followed without expression, those arms still crossed, those hard, bloodshot eyes still looking up at him. "I'll be home by then," he continued, voice lowered, "but my point is, you'll be here by yourself tomorrow, and I know you won't carry the gun—"

"Never."

"—I know that, but what I'm trying to say is, well, don't do anything stupid, okay?"

Dan winced.

Maybe I should have put that a better way…

Beth smiled, and he had to force himself not to step back. "Why, whatever do you mean, dear?"

"You know what I mean. There are six of them, for Christ's sake, and that's not counting McFarlane. I know you've got knives, but knives won't do much good against six plus. I want you to promise me you won't go anywhere near that farm tomorrow."

"Six? What about the daughters? He has three grown daughters, right?"

Dan thought fast; he'd deliberately left the sluts out earlier. "Yeah, McFarlane's got three daughters, but trust me, they're as crazy as he is." Crazier. "My point is we need to talk to Scandlin first, and I suppose Helen, before we—"

Her eyes dropped to dangerous slits, and now her foot was tapping; not good. "What are their names? What do they look like?"

"Their names? Uh, Mindy, Rebecca, and Alexandria. And, you know, they look like farm girls. I want you to promise me—"

"I noticed you didn't mention *them* earlier, and Helen never told me she had three nieces. What is it about these girls that nobody wants to talk about them?"

"Uh, well, it's not that I didn't want to talk about them, I just sorta, you know, forgot about them. They're nothing special, really." *Keep a straight face, Dan-o, for the love of God.* "But you're changing the subject. I want you to promise me you're not going anywhere near that farm."

"I'm not promising anything."

"Beth—"

"I'm going to bed, Daniel."

Shit! "Wait. One more thing." She kept walking. "Please."

She stopped. "What?"

"Saturday night, before I go check out the cemetery…" Dan forced it out. "We'll talk. About anything you want. Everything."

If Dan had expected her to be happy, he had another think coming; his wife turned back around and looked at him for a long time, but her face was uncertain, almost frightened.

"All right," she finally responded. "We'll talk Saturday." She still didn't seem happy about it. She turned to walk up the stairs.

"Wait."

"*What!?*"

"I need to show you the alarm." He went over to the new control pad by the front door, Beth following silently. He explained how to work it and punched in the code, repeating it to her. "There. We're locked in for the night. Oh, and I'll give you your new key in the morning; it'll work both of the new deadbolts."

Beth wasn't paying attention to him or the alarm; instead, she was staring at the foyer closet. Suddenly she reached out and opened it and pulled two bulging suitcases out and hip-checked the door closed. She rolled them to the steps, lifted, and carried them up.

Dan's wife spoke while ascending, and without looking at him. "I didn't get a chance to tell you about the sinkhole, but I'm too tired, it can wait until morning. And I'm going with you Saturday night, even though it's the dumbest idea I've ever heard in my life. You'll just get into trouble by yourself. Maybe we can get Janet and Bill to babysit. And I guess Lizzie and I won't need these now that you've decided to talk to me."

She and the suitcases vanished upstairs.

Dan stood perfectly still for a long, long while, and then he moved through the castle's downstairs, making sure every window was locked.

Sinkhole?

What goddamn sinkhole?

Four of them.

No, not going there. So not going there.

There was something else he'd left out besides the crazy, bloodthirsty sluts; McFarlane's mad claim about Fulbright's wife. He wasn't sure he believed it—and he was damn sure he didn't *want* to believe it—so Dan had decided he needed to talk to Scandlin first before he told Beth. He also wanted to talk to Fulbright; he had heard through the realtor grapevine that Fulbright had stage-four pancreatic cancer now, on top of the stroke he'd suffered after his wife's accident, so *if* the man was still alive, and *if* he could talk, Dan had a plan to find him and have a little chat. Then he'd tell Beth. Maybe.

He stopped at the bottom of the staircase; he could hear them up there, his girls; they were brushing their teeth. Beth said something foamy, and Lizzie laughed; she responded, equally foamy, and they both laughed.

What would it be like?

What would it be like to be alone in this house and not hear that laughter? To not see those faces looking back at him across the table at breakfast, only empty chairs?

Dan fetched the Mossberg down from its hidey-hole on top of the kitchen cabinets, double-checked the garage to make sure the door was down, went upstairs to check the windows, and did his best to stop thinking about what it would be like.

MEETING

DAN GOT to Roscoe's twelve minutes late. He had tried to call Scandlin to let the man know he was running behind, but had the TBI Agent bothered to answer?

Of course fucking not.

That seemed to be the theme of the day: no one wanted to answer their god-damn phone, at least when Dan called. Well, Steve had answered—not that he'd had much choice; and he hadn't exactly been *glad* to hear from Dan, but at least he fucking answered. Steve was more than ready for him to come back to work tomorrow so he could stop "being Dan's bitch". He had even known what Dan wanted to find out: James Fulbright was in Rolling Heights, an exclusive hospice on the east side of Murfreesboro—or as Steve had put it, where the rich went to rot.

Dan slid the Tundra into an empty spot in Roscoe's almost empty lot, then checked his phone again. Beth still hadn't called or texted him back, and he'd be damned if he'd call or text *her* again! What was she doing? Surely she wouldn't go over to McFarlane's, she wasn't stupid, but during breakfast he hadn't been able to wheedle a promise out of her to stay away from that farm (and boy, was his wife grouchy when she was hung-over), but she had grudgingly said she would wait to talk to Helen—and also see what Scandlin had to say—before she did anything. So that had made him feel somewhat better, but why didn't she answer, or at least call or text him back?

He touched his throbbing nose. Gently. Dr. Gertsteiner had re-straightened it, and "Gert" hadn't bought Dan's story about running in to a door frame. Christ, Mc-Farlane had quick hands, especially for a sixty-something old man. Dr. Gertsteiner had then cheerily informed Dan that if he didn't refrain from future confrontations with rogue "door frames", he'd soon end up in the surgery suite to correct breathing problems. "Gert" had seemed happy with that proposition. Dan had thanked the smiling, affable doctor, paid the gorgeous receptionist—who was also, Dan noted, Mrs. Gert—and got the fuck out.

At the hospital, after Dan had gotten a big hug from Nurse Stefanie, Doc Williams had taken his staples out, and then after commenting several times on how fast Dan was healing, Doc decided the gash where Rison had hit him with the knife handle would be okay without stitches. So that was good, but Doc hadn't believed him about the headaches, so now Dan had to haul his ass back up there next week for more tests.

Fuck.

And he didn't even want to *think* about the fancy indoor range; after a solid hour of expensive practice with the Smith, Dan could now confidently hit a Greyhound bus broadside from forty feet; if the bus was shooting back, however, he was screwed. So except for Stefanie's well-padded hug and finding out where Fulbright was shelved, his whole day had been a fucking waste.

Where the hell is Beth?

Dan got out and slammed the door, locking it with the fob.

God his head was *killing* him!

He stopped and looked around, then snorted and kept walking; he had no damn clue what Scandlin drove; either the man would show, or he wouldn't. Dan jerked open the front door and walked into Roscoe's. He'd heard about the chain—and the smell that greeted him boded well—but he'd never had the pleasure.

If they didn't have beer, he was fucking leaving.

Dan found a deserted host stand, so he wandered deeper and seated himself in a giant booth. It was three o'clock, shift-change and prep-time in Restaurant Universe—so he'd learned from his lovely, non-phone-answering wife—and there were only three occupied tables in the whole place. Soon a cute brunette waitress appeared. Her name tag said Sara.

"Sir, these booths are reserved for three or more people," she said, pointing at the big sign that said **Booths Reserved for Three or More People**. "We have seating at the bar if—"

"I'm meeting some people, Sara. Bring me a beer." One people, but Sara didn't need to know that. He took his ball cap and sunglasses off, then scratched gently around the gash over his ear; the damn thing itched constantly. "And a menu." Dan wanted to see if the taste matched the smell.

The brunette paused, taking in his bruises; he was getting used to that reaction. "What kind of beer would you like, sir?"

"Shiner Bock, on tap if you've got it."

"We don't stock Shiner, sir."

"Of course you don't."

He ended up settling for a Sam Adams in the bottle. Sara walked away, and Dan decided with her coloring and features, she could pass for Beth's little sister; a little sister that was seven-inches taller. No freckles, though. Shame, that.

Speaking of Beth…

She still didn't answer; Dan waited, and she still didn't text or call him back. He gripped the edge of the heavy wooden table until his knuckles cracked. *God, if anything's happened to her…if those crazy fucks…*no, he couldn't let himself think like that or he'd call 911 and send in the cavalry. She was fine and dandy; she was just punishing him for not answering her calls yesterday. And McFarlane wouldn't do anything yet; he'd given them until the 1st.

Dan laughed, eliciting a look from an older couple eating with two small kids; they had 'till the first of the fucking month to get out of their own, motherfucking, *house!*

He laughed again. It was better than screaming.

Dan checked the time: 3:19. Where was Scandlin? Sara brought his beer along with a frosty mug, and then slapped a menu down, ignoring his thank you. Dan watched her stalk away, back stiff, cute ass twitching. *Yeah, a whole lot like Beth.* He poured the beer and took a drink; *much* better. Then he tried to call Professor Hameed's cell phone again; still no answer. Where the hell *was* the man? Hameed had promised to call *him* by now, so where the fuck was he? He wanted to know what that writing said, goddamnit!

Sara came back, but he'd forgotten to open the menu so he ordered a bowl of house gumbo; the place was Cajun, so they had to have gumbo, it was like a fucking law or something. He was right. He also ordered another Sam before she snatched the menu and flounced off. Dan took another pull from his now not-so-frosty mug.

Should've asked Sara to dip her pinky in it.

He was sitting and brooding and drinking and thinking about wives who wouldn't answer their phones and language professors who didn't answer their phones and reporters that supposedly wanted to talk to him and wouldn't answer their phones and cops who not only didn't show up when and where they said they would but *also* didn't answer their fucking phones, when the hum and crackle of clashing light-sabers issued from his iPhone.

It was a text from Scandlin.

You're late.

Dan spluttered, spitting beer on the table. *He* was late? He wiped his chin and looked around, but glimpsed no sign of L'il Howie or his graying flattop. His fingers twitched, but he managed to control himself: **I'm here. Where are you?**

Had 2 make sure u wrnt followed. Meet me @ Carmody's on Briscoe. 10 minutes.

"God damn son of a *bitch!*"

Heads turned, and Sara popped up at the end of his booth as if by sorcery.

"Is there a problem, sir?" The frost was gone; she now had the cautious look of someone trying to decide if she was dealing with a crazy man. Dan sucked air through his nose and relaxed his jaw; it wasn't her fault Scandlin was playing games. It also wasn't her fault she looked like his wife—a wife who had better be goddamn motherfucking okay!

He jammed his cap and glasses back on and downed his beer and slid out of the booth and stood up. She stepped away. "That was who I'm supposed to meet, but it looks like I'm at the wrong place." Dan handed her a credit card and tried not to notice the obvious relief on her pretty face. "I'll take that gumbo to go."

"Um, it won't be ready for about ten minutes, sir."

And the smells were so nice… "Tab me out, I can't wait. Give it to them." He hiked his thumb toward the grandparents, who were still staring; maybe those brats liked gumbo.

Dan stood there and fumed and didn't look at the now-whispering family and signed the receipt when she came back, leaving her a twenty-dollar tip. He stamped out into the heat and ignored Sara's startled and grateful "Thank you, sir!" as the door swung shut behind him.

This talk with Scandlin had better be fucking worth it.

Beth had to be okay. She just had to be.

Carmody's turned out to be a rundown neighborhood pub—which meant it fit into its neighborhood quite well. Roscoe's had been near a shopping mall roughly the size of a beached aircraft carrier, but there sure as shit wasn't any mall on Briscoe Street. Instead, there was some sort of abandoned industrial facility behind Carmody's. It came complete with a rusted chain-link fence with concertina wire swirling along the top and multitudes of faded NO TRESPASSING signs. There were long, jagged cracks in the immense and empty lot beyond the fence, with green and brown and clear beer-bottle glass glinting among the weeds growing out of the cracks. Dan looked up and down Briscoe and saw nothing but bars, cheap motels, third-hand used car lots, check-cashing businesses, and pawn shops. Nice.

He crunched into the gravel lot and killed the truck, joining two other pickups and a pod of tricked-out Harley Davidson's. There was a neon Pabst Blue Ribbon sign hanging in the barred window. Dan got out and made double-sure the truck was locked; there were no good aromas wafting from Carmody's.

Then he opened the front door and found some: sour beer, fried food, and stale cigarettes. *Hey, at least I can smoke.* Dan took his shades off, and when his eyes adjusted, he saw several people staring at him, most notably Scandlin. The Special Agent sat all the way in the back facing the door, his bulk squeezed into one of the three booths. His flattop and suit and tie made him look as out of place as, well, Dan.

Four bikers hunched in the middle of the room, leaning over a pitcher of golden beer that rested on a small, round table. Dan nodded and got no response as he squeezed by and walked toward Scandlin. The biker's heads swiveled to follow. There was no sound except for a Chicago song playing on an honest-to-God Wurlitzer hulking in the corner.

There's got *to be something on that old beauty besides Chicago.*

He slid onto a cracked red-vinyl booth seat patched with red duct tape. Classy. The Special Agent had a tall, dark concoction with lots of ice by his hand. Before Dan could say anything a waitress appeared; forty-fiveish, deep, freckled cleavage, and earrings that would give Helen pause.

"What can I get ya, sugar?" Her voice was a testament to the miracles of whiskey and cigarettes.

"I'll have what he's having."

Her smile—a tremulous thing to begin with—went missing as she turned back toward the bar. "One Coke with ice coming right up." She patted a plus-sized biker on his bare, tattooed deltoid as she went past; the tattoo was of a grinning skull smoking a joint. "Big spenders today, boys." The bikers laughed.

"Uh, wait." She stopped and turned. "What do you have on tap?" He knew better than to ask for Shiner.

She gave him a wry look and pointed a long green fingernail toward the bar where Dan glimpsed a whole three tap handles poking toward the stained ceiling.

"I'll have a Michelob, please." The lesser evil.

"Comin' right up, hon." She swayed away. "You hear that, boys? 'Please'. That's called *manners*." The bikers didn't laugh this time.

Dan faced forward as several connections sparked in his slow brain: he'd assumed that his entry had caused the silence, but as he eyed Scandlin, Dan reassessed; the man looked like a cop, only a cop, and nothing but a cop. He glanced over his shoulder and found the bikers still watching and turned around again. These guys had rode into their favorite watering hole after a hard day of doing…whatever it was they did, only to find the five-o sitting here, and now here was Dan, meeting with him. They probably thought he was a narc.

I'll be lucky to make it out of here without getting my ass kicked up between my ears.

Dan lit a cigarette to calm his nerves, dragging over a beat-up red-plastic ashtray from against the wall. Scandlin still hadn't said a word, but his cop-eyes flickered over Dan's shoulder; at the bikers or at the door, he couldn't tell which. Dan would bet the man didn't give a shit about bikers, so that left the door. What was he watching for? Did he think Dan hadn't come alone? And what was all this shit about being followed? Beth had been followed by that reporter, Brennan; maybe the Special Agent was right to be paranoid. The woman brought his beer then, not bothering with a coaster, and from the condition of the table, Dan wasn't surprised; he also saw the look she gave Scandlin.

Yep, everybody knows. Out fucking standing.

"Start you a tab, honey?"

"Please." Why not? He handed her a credit card, and she swayed away, shaking her head.

When the silence went on and on and even the bikers had started communicating in low rumbles and snarls, Dan decided he wasn't getting any fucking younger.

"So how's the world treatin' ya, Scandlin?"

The big man grunted, studying Dan's face. "*You* look a hell of a lot better. You called this meeting, Sims, what do you want?"

Dan kept his expression smooth and resisted touching under his eyes, where Mindy's pickle-scented fingers had rested. Doc Williams had said the same thing; in fact, Doc Williams couldn't shut up about how fast Dan was healing.

Then the rest of what Scandlin had said registered, and he grimaced wryly. *I should've known.* When the Special Agent had come to Dan in the hospital, he'd been the one wanting something. Now their negotiating positions were reversed, and the veneer of friendliness had been washed away. Dan had no problem with that.

He took a sip of beer—at least it was cold—and a deep drag on his cigarette and then blew smoke past Scandlin's ear; no change in the cop-eyes, but that jaw flexed.

"I had lunch with John McFarlane yesterday."

"Yeah?"

"Oh, yeah. Real nice guy. He informed me we had until September first to get out of our house or he would send his thugs-disguised-as-farmhands over to evict us—or worse." Dan took another drag and drink, watching Scandlin's face. Nothing. "He also admitted he sent Rison to attack us—excuse me, gave the dirt-bag *permission*, but he knew about it and approved. Man doesn't like my house, apparently."

Scandlin's eyes narrowed; after a long pause, he took a drink of his Coke, and Dan noted that he wore a plain gold wedding ring.

Then the Special Agent gave him a sardonic smile. "That sounds like him," he said.

Dan drank and smoked and waited, but no further wisdom seemed forthcoming. The Wurlitzer began cranking out Van Morrison—now *that* was more like it. He downed his Mick and waved the mug at the waitress who was evidently the bartender as well because she was back there wiping ineffectually at the stained wood with an even darker cloth. She smiled at him and nodded and Dan turned back to Scandlin.

"He didn't come right out and say it, but he also pretty much admitted that he had James Fulbright's wife killed."

That got a reaction; Scandlin's jaw clenched so hard that Dan thought it was going to dislocate and ping across the room and crack the Wurlitzer. The big man controlled himself with a visible effort, then folded his hands on the table.

"Can you prove any of this? Were you smart enough to wear a wire?"

Dan opened his mouth and then shut it. Wear a wire? He didn't even know *how* to wear a wire. "No, but—"

"Then why are you wasting my time?"

"Because I need help, goddamn it! That fucker threatened my family!"

The only sound in the bar was Van singing about brown-eyed girls, a subject upon which Dan and Van agreed wholeheartedly; he could feel everyone staring, but he didn't give a shit. "I told him I'd go to the cops and do you know what the old man did? He *laughed* at me and said go right ahead! Said say howdy to his cousin, who happens to be the Sheriff of Rutherford County! Said it would be my word against his and nothing would come of it. He also claimed to know people in every fucking law-enforcement outfit on the planet, including the TBI. Is that true?"

Scandlin nodded, square face sour. "It's true."

Dan felt ice spike his gut. "Shit." He took a trembling drag and then stabbed the butt out in the ashtray. "So can you help us? I mean, there has to be someone you can put me in touch with that will do *something*. The crazy fuck *ordered* us out of our own goddamn house, for Christ's sake!"

Scandlin considered him for a long moment, then said, "What did you burn in the fireplace?"

Dan hesitated. "You won't believe it."

"Let me be the judge of that."

The waitress slash bartender dropped his beer off and Dan thanked her and waited for her to smile at him and go away, and then he told him.

It turned out he was right; halfway through Scandlin got this disgusted look and slid out of the booth. "I don't know what game you're playing, but—"

"It's the truth."

"C'mon, Sims, a cemetery? If you're going to waste my time, I—"

"Why would I lie?" Everyone was staring again. Softer. "Why would I lie, Scandlin? I came to *you* for help, remember? Why would I lie about this?"

Scandlin slid back into the booth and tried to scowl a hole through Dan. "Rison claimed he attacked you because you went to that old cemetery out there?"

"I know what it sounds like, but I swear…wait, you know about it? The cemetery, I mean? Barron Cemetery?"

"Sure I know about it. Seen it once when I went deer hunting out there with my daddy, a long time ago. Musta been twelve or thirteen. And a lot of people know about it; there's been a cemetery on that hill since before the Civil War, or maybe the Revolutionary War, or something like that. I don't think anyone uses it anymore, not even McFarlane, and that's my point—why would Rison care if you camped out in the middle of it? Doesn't make sense, Sims." The jaw flexed. "If you're lying to me…"

"I'm not."

"And you said he knew things, things about your past, you and your wife's?"

"Yeah he did, stuff nobody knows; stuff we've never even told each other. He wrote it down…" Dan hesitated, remembering the loopy girl handwriting. "…or somebody wrote it for him, but he stood there and read from our pasts like it was some kind of sick book report. He rubbed it in our faces that he knew so much about us, and then he…" Dan shuddered and took a drink.

"The Internet," Scandlin said. "Smart killers research their victims, and in today's world it's even easier."

"You're not listening. Do you know what an EM meter is?" Scandlin nodded. "Well, I bought one thinking someone bugged that house while it sat empty, before we bought it, you know? I mean, how else could he have known all that? The whole time, though, I was thinking it didn't make any sense, because Beth and I didn't tell each other most of that." God, if it was only possible to *un*learn something…he drained his beer and waved the mug again. "Point is, I crawled all over that house yesterday morning and found nothing: no bugs, no listening devices, no microphones, no whatever, and I'm not surprised, because what was on those sheets of paper was stuff that *nobody knew*, stuff that Beth and I never discussed…" *God help me.* "…stuff that sure as *fuck* wasn't on the Internet."

The big Special Agent stared at him as the woman brought Dan's beer, and then she raised her eyebrows when Scandlin ordered two shots of Jack Black. They watched each other in silence until she returned. The cop paid with cash. Dan had thought maybe one of those shots was for him—he wouldn't have turned it down—but Scandlin threw one back like an old pro and dumped the other in his Coke, stirring with a thick finger.

"All right, finish your story."

Dan did. It didn't take long. "…and so that was what we burned, that envelope and papers. Then we called 911 and the shit storm started."

"What was on the papers?"

"It's private. That's why we burned them."

"Fair enough. A goddamn *cemetery?*"

"Yeah."

Scandlin scowled, and Dan thought he muttered something about "be that stupid", but couldn't be sure. They were quiet for a stretch, nursing their drinks and listening to more Van Morrison, Scandlin still somewhere else as he worked it over. Dan pulled his phone out; it was past four and Beth *still* hadn't called him back.

Shit shit shit!

"So can you help us or not?"

Those cop-eyes weighed and measured him from across the chipped table. Finally he said, "If I do, it won't be easy. McFarlane, that son of a bitch, really does know a lot of people, but I'll tell you something, Sims." Scandlin gave him a feral smile. "Not everyone's a John McFarlane fan, including yours truly."

Cautious relief flooded through him; maybe they *weren't* all alone with this. That had also been raw hate in Scandlin's voice when he spoke of McFarlane, or Dan had never heard it.

"What'd he do to you?"

That ghoulish, dead-eyed grin didn't alter. "It's private."

Dan slowly leaned away. "Fair enough." Beth. Where was Beth? "I gotta make a phone call. If you decide to help us, let me know."

He slid out of the cracked booth, intending to settle up and vamoose out of this shit hole, but Scandlin grabbed his forearm; feeling that grip, Dan wasn't sure he could break it if he tried.

"Sit down, Sims. You need to listen for a second."

He did, and Scandlin let go. "What?"

"Even if we talk to some people I know, people that might be able and willing to do something, you need to get your wife and little girl out of there."

Dan felt the ice in his gut spread. "I already came to that conclusion." Goddamn Beth! Where was she? *Shit!* "My wife's not having it, though. Said she wouldn't run from anybody."

"Stubborn, huh?"

"You could say that." Where on God's Green Earth was she? What the *fuck* was she doing? "Look, I appreciate you at least considering helping, but I've got to—"

"You want to know what McFarlane did to me?"

The tone was casual; the look on Scandlin's face was anything but. Dan nodded.

"I believe what you said about Fulbright's wife, Sims. Know why I believe it?"

"Why?"

"Because McFarlane had my wife killed, too."

Oh. God. Beth. "What…how do you know? And why the fuck isn't the sick son of a bitch rotting in a jail cell somewhere?" *Oh God.* "What happened to her?"

"She was found in the ditch on the eastbound side of I-40, about fifteen miles west of Nashville. She'd been raped, multiple times, and then beaten to death." Scandlin took a drink of his Jack and Coke, a long one; his big, square face was still, but his eyes were the scariest thing that Dan had ever seen. "As for why McFarlane isn't in jail, I can't prove he ordered it done, but as for how I know, that's easy. He called me and told me."

Dan just stared at him.

Beth. Oh God, Beth.

"I was investigating him on my time, and somehow he found out. He told me to back off and mind my business, and that what he'd had done to Jess was only a taste of what he could 'make happen'. His words." Scandlin took another long drink. "If it's the last thing I do in this world, Sims, I'll see John McFarlane in jail. That, or dead."

Dan surged out of the booth. "I have to call…she's alone at the house today, and she hasn't answered since…I need to call her."

Scandlin nodded. "Go call. But come back. We still have things to talk about, Sims."

Dan stumbled toward the door. Had that been *sympathy* on the Special Agent's face? Dan didn't want his fucking sympathy; he wanted to know that Beth was all right. Jesus God, Scandlin's wife *and* Fulbright's?

The bartender called, "What about that tab, sweetheart?"

"I'm just going outside to—"

One biker scraped his chair back and stood up and barred Dan's way. "The lady wants you to pay your tab, sweetheart." His deep voice was smug, and his grin was confident above the braided goatee. "Please." His buddies laughed. They liked that.

Dan looked up at him; six-three, maybe six-four, maybe two-fifty without the chains and leather, maybe two-seventy with.

He didn't give a fuck.

"I'm going outside to call my wife."

Dan waited.

The biker's grin slipped, and he looked at Dan for about three seconds before he turned to the bartender and yelled, "He's going outside to call his wife!"

He moved out of the way, and Dan pushed through the door and into the sun, already dialing. No answer. *Fuck!* He called Helen and found out Beth had been by to visit earlier in the afternoon, but Helen hadn't heard from her since. Then Dan called Lizzie's daycare and asked if Beth had been in to pick her up but found out Lizzie was still there. He called Slo Eddie's, but she hadn't been there all day.

Terror squeezed Dan until he couldn't breathe.

He called Beth. No answer.

Oh God.

Dan dialed 911.

Not Enough

Beth pulled into Helen's; the dash clock read 1:36. Helen's Silverado was in the carport, but no other cars besides Beth's were in the driveway.

The old lady didn't have company.

Beth told herself that was a good thing.

How in the world *am I going to do this?* Helen was one of the few people she called friend…

Beth steeled her resolve and stepped out into the swelter; she had spent the morning scrubbing a dead rapist's blood from her bedroom's floors, walls, and ceiling, and all while suffering through the nightmare memory of how it had gotten there *and* the worst hangover of her life.

She could gently pry some information from a stubborn old woman, no sweat.

The multitudes of statues, birdbaths, windmills, signs quoting scripture, and other less-categorizable junk that crowded Helen's front yard shimmered in the heat as Beth wound her way through to the porch; the half-dozen permutations of Jesus in various benevolent poses seemed to stare at her with their creepy blank statue-eyes as she walked up the steps; a white flag with a red border was displayed in the front window. It held two stars: one was a solid blue, for Paul; the second star was gold edged in blue, for Ryan.

Pickle barked from the backyard when Beth rang the doorbell. She ignored the three-foot-high stained-wood cross that hung beside the bell, recalling her first visit and the way she'd struggled to keep from staring, and maybe even giggling.

It's amazing what you can get used to.

No one answered. Perhaps Helen had ridden into town with one of her church/gossip-monger friends to get their hair done or go marketing. Beth rang the doorbell again; if Helen didn't answer this time…no answer. She turned around and dug in her purse and pulled out her silenced phone; Brennan still hadn't called her back, but she had six missed calls and four texts from her husband.

Beth smiled grimly and put her phone back. *Let's see how* he *enjoys being ignored.*

The door opened behind her, and she spun around. Helen peered out at her through a six-inch gap.

"Helen! I didn't think you were home…are you all right?"

"Yes, dear, I'm fine, but this isn't a good time. Maybe you could come back later, after you call first."

Beth flushed. Every time before when she'd come to this house, even unexpectedly, she'd never been greeted with anything but hugs and smiles. She didn't know what to say. Beth took in Helen's slumped shoulders and lost expression and concern overrode embarrassment.

"What's wrong?"

The old lady looked down. "Nothin's wrong, dear. I'm just not feelin' well today, that's all."

"Is there anything I can do? Maybe make you some tea, or some soup?" Beth knew Helen was pushing seventy—or had blown right past; she didn't discuss her age—but besides her hip, Beth had always admired her vitality. Maybe there was some other health issue affecting her. She stepped closer and peered up through the narrow gap. "Helen, let me help you."

Her friend's eyes slowly lifted to hers, and then she squeezed her lids shut, as if in sudden pain.

Truly alarmed now, Beth said, "What's wrong? Are you—?"

The old woman snapped her eyes open. "*I* should be feedin' *you*, not the other way 'round; a woman should have some meat on her." Helen threw the door wide and turned away, cane thumping. "Git your skinny butt in here." Beth smiled, then stepped in and closed the door behind her; it was reassuring to see the hot spark that burned in her friend flare to life.

"And you just park that narrow bee-hind somewhere; nobody's gonna serve tea in my own damn house but me." She thumped out of sight, muttering; the sound of rattling pots wafted from the kitchen.

Beth put her purse on the coffee table and sat in the old recliner; an even older couch covered with a handmade coverlet was to her left. She knew from experience that both were comfortable, despite appearances. More dire mutters and metallic clanks came from the kitchen as Beth took in Helen's living room, as usual feeling like she'd landed in the aftermath of a church rummage sale that had been hit by a tornado.

There were three more statues of the savior in here, one a bobble-head resting on the cluttered coffee table in front of her. Beth smiled at it; she'd always wanted to ask where Helen had found it but knew better than to start down *that* road. The journey would lead to Helen's church, where, according to the Gospel of Helen, Beth and Lizzie and especially Daniel should be attending regularly.

There were three more crucifixes as well, one each above the entryways to the kitchen, the hallway that led to the bedrooms, and the small mudroom slash laundry room that contained the door to the backyard. Pictures of Jacob were everywhere, of course, and Jacob's father, Paul, a tall, handsome man with red-gold hair. In most he was dressed in desert fatigues; two were full-dress uniform. Beth saw two black-and-whites of Muriel, the sister, and one black-and-white of a much-younger Helen and her late husband, Henry. Helen had a slew of those in her bedroom, she knew.

Beth carefully surveyed all four walls, confirming there were no photographs of nieces. Maybe they were also displayed somewhere in Helen's bedroom, but for some reason, she doubted it.

She glanced at the nearest end table, where the only photo of Ryan usually sat, ensconced in its ornate, easel-back frame. It wasn't there. It was face-down on the handmade coverlet, as if Helen had been sitting on the couch and holding it and had put it down when the doorbell rang.

Beth grimaced.

She just might know what was bothering her friend.

She heard the *fwump* of a gas burner, and then Helen came back, using her cane to maneuver around the coffee table to the couch. Beth's suspicions were all but confirmed when she saw that her friend was wearing her Gold Star lapel pin; she'd only seen her wear it once before, on Memorial Day. Helen picked up the picture of her dead son and put it back in its spot beneath the lamp, then sat with a heavy sigh, leaning her cane against her knee.

"I'm sorry, Helen, you're right, I should've called first. I'll come back when—"

"Oh, hush." She gave Beth a wan smile. "You're always welcome here, you know that, I'm just a she-bear today." She looked at the photo of Ryan, and then picked it up and held it in her lap, staring down at it. "If he'd a survived Bush and Cheney's Oil War, he'd be turnin' thirty-seven Sunday. Sometimes it all comes back, you know. He was such a beautiful little boy. A handful, true, but aren't they all?"

Beth leaned and took her hand and squeezed; her friend squeezed back.

"I'm so sorry, Helen."

Helen squeezed again and then let go to put the photo back on the end table. "God only lets us stay on this earth for a short time before He snatches us back," she said, gaze lingering on Ryan. "I don't know why that's so, but I know for damn certain it is. And it's no use arguing with Him about it." Beth saw the steel glint in Helen's eye, and despite the caveat, she had a feeling the arguments had been long and hot. She faced Beth. "But you didn't come over to listen to all that mess. There's somethin' on your mind, unless I miss my mark by a mile."

"There is," Beth confirmed. "Uh, you delivered a message to Daniel yesterday, from John McFarlane?"

Helen's lips twisted; pure distaste. "I did."

Beth watched that expression, not knowing if it was for Daniel or McFarlane. When Helen offered nothing else, Beth plowed ahead. "Well, he went over there, and they talked."

"Oh?"

Beth hesitated; Helen wasn't looking at her now. She seemed to be staring at Bobble-Head Jesus. "Yes, they did. Helen…did you know *why* McFarlane wanted to talk to him?"

It was Helen's turn to hesitate; she still wouldn't look at Beth. Then she gave a laugh devoid of any mirth. "No, dear, I didn't. John don't confide in the likes of me, he just told me to carry the message." The kettle whistled, and Helen grabbed her cane and heaved up from the couch and thumped into the kitchen. "You take honey in yours, right dear?"

"Yes." Despite her age and hip, the old lady could still move when she wanted.

Beth swallowed a lead lump in her throat. Helen didn't want to tell her something, that was obvious; she seemed reluctant to talk about McFarlane at all. Worse, before now Beth would have said that Helen wasn't afraid of anyone, but it was plain she was afraid of John McFarlane.

Helen reappeared carrying the tea tray, her cane absent because she needed both hands; her limp made progress slow. Beth stood up. "Let me help with—"

"Sit down, girl. You're the guest in my house, so I'll serve the blasted tea. I'm not that crippled."

Beth cleared a spot on the coffee table, displacing Bobble-Head Jesus and setting her purse on the floor. Helen poured and steeped the bags; the house was silent except for the ticking of the coo-coo clock, and that hush drove home just how upset her friend was; Helen always had gospel music playing on the radio, or one of her soaps on the bulky old Zenith in the corner. Not today.

Helen handed Beth her tea and moved to the couch. Beth reached out and lent her a hand, and Helen accepted it; when she'd settled, the old lady gave her a pat and a "Thank you, dear." Helen picked up her own tea, and they drank; after a minute of tea-slurping, tick-tocking silence, Beth decided that there was just no easy way to do this, so she dove in head-first.

"McFarlane told Daniel that he gave Scott Rison permission to attack us. And he threatened to hurt us again if we don't move out of our house by September first. Apparently, he doesn't like it much."

The old lady heaved a forlorn sigh. "I figured as much, dear, knowin' John." Her cup rattled on its saucer. "Tell me."

She did; halfway through the bird shot out of the clock, startling her, letting them know it was two o'clock. Beth *hated* that thing. Helen never interrupted, but she set her barely touched tea down and picked up Ryan's picture again and held it against her stomach, stroking it. She didn't look at Beth, but she did mutter and scowl in places; Beth had never heard the old woman use such language. She was giving Daniel a run for his money.

Beth wound down with, "…and I, um, I know that he was married to your sister." She paused to let Helen answer the implicit question, but when the old lady just sat there stroking Ryan's picture, Beth continued: "Is he serious? Does he truly think he can just *order* people out of their homes? And what if we don't go? Will he really try to run us out or hurt us again?"

And if you knew John McFarlane was behind Rison's attack, why didn't you say anything to Scarborough, Helen? Or me, for that matter? Are you that terrified of him?

Sadly, Beth now believed that last was true.

Instead of answering any questions, though, spoken or unspoken, Helen suddenly thrust a finger at her, and Beth shied back; the old lady's eyes were almost throwing sparks.

"You listen here, missy, we need to set the record straight! That woman is no 'old friend of the family'!" She shook the picture of her dead son at Beth.

"I—"

"Friend of the family? Ha! Keeper? Ha! That woman's no more the 'Keeper' of anything than…than…" Helen clutched Ryan's picture with white knuckles.

"You don't have to—"

"Let me finish, girl. I'm sorry for snapping at you, but that woman brings out the worst in me. Keeper? That's a good one."

"If this Melissa's not a friend of the family, then why would John McFarlane say she was if she wasn't? And why would she tell Daniel that she was the Keeper of Barron Cemetery if she wasn't?"

The anger visibly drained out of the old woman, and Beth watched as something replaced it—something like fear. The evil coo-coo clock ticked and tocked. Then Helen licked her lips and answered Beth's questions—sort of.

"Not everyone's as blessed as my Henry and I were, dear. Oh, we had our fights over the years, and I could never teach the man to take his boots off before trampin' across my clean floors, but it was a loving marriage. You seem to have the same with that husband of yours." She snorted, like she always did when she mentioned Daniel. "But Muriel wasn't so lucky."

Beth digested that. Was she saying…?

Helen rolled her eyes. "You're a grown woman, honey. Do I have to spell it?"

"Okay…but they *did* have three daughters—your nieces," she added. Pointedly.

Helen's face turned to rock. "They're not my nieces."

"How could they not be—"

"*Those girls…!*" Helen's nostrils flared, and she took a deep breath before continuing in a quieter voice, if not softer. "Those girls are *not* Muriel's daughters. My sister was barren. They were adopted."

Daniel sure hadn't mentioned that part, which made her wonder what else he'd left out about them; as she had noted, he didn't seem to want to talk about those young women at all—not unlike Helen. Beth stared at the cup in her lap while trying to regain her bearings; her picture of McFarlane didn't jibe with a man willing to raise three girls not his own. Helen had fallen into stony silence, and Beth studied her in snatches, trying to come up with more questions, but the fear and hate hadn't left her friend's face.

What kind of family swamp have I waded into?

Beth sipped her tea, and then suddenly realized that Helen had never answered the only question that mattered: Would McFarlane follow through on his threat?

"Do you think…?"

She frowned. Helen was staring toward the hallway that led to the bedrooms; her eyes were wide open and horror stricken, and her breath was rapid and shallow. Beth shifted fast and looked, spilling warm tea on her shorts, but there was nothing there. She looked back at the old woman, alarm giving way to confusion.

"Helen, what is it?"

Instead of answering, she grabbed Beth's hand in a crushing grip, clutching the picture of Ryan with the other. "Pray with me, girl! Quick now, pray!"

"What—"

Beth went silent as Helen bowed her head and began to recite the Lord's Prayer: "Oh Heavenly Father who art in Heaven, hallowed be Thy Name. Thy Kingdom come, Thy Will be done, on Earth as it is in Heaven…"

She didn't join in, though that prayer had been etched onto her heart long ago. Beth refused to pray to a God that would allow…that would let the things that had been done to her happen to little girls.

Helen finished, and then began the Lord's Prayer all over again, voice strident. Beth wanted to pull her hand away, and as if sensing this, Helen gripped harder. She frowned at the top of her friend's head, beginning to fear for her sanity. Beth eyed the picture of Ryan clutched against Helen's chest; perhaps with good reason.

Beth craned her neck to peer down the hallway again. Helen's bedroom was at the end, with two more rooms, one to the left and one to the right as you went; one was her sewing room, and the other was the spare bedroom that Jacob and Lizzie slept in when they stayed over, and where she and Lizzie had slept Sunday and Monday. There was nothing in the hall except sunlight slanting in from the sewing room on the left, making the polished hardwood floor glow a deep mahogany.

What had made Helen act so—?

A shadow shifted, blocking the sun, and then the slanting light came back as strong as ever; dust motes floated in the glow, dazzling bright in the darkened hallway.

Beth frowned; that must've been a high, fast-moving cloud crossing the sun, or an airplane, but the sky had been blue and hot and cloudless all day, and she couldn't hear any plane.

Her gaze lingered in the hall, but she saw nothing else so she shook her head and turned around and waited as Helen said the Lord's Prayer a third time, and then watched as the old woman raised hesitant, fearful eyes to the hallway. Whatever she saw this time, she seemed relieved, sagging into the couch, releasing Beth's hand and double-clutching the picture of Ryan. Her full bust rose and fell with each panicked breath.

"Helen, what—?"

The old woman sat up. "Oh dear, I'm afraid I'm not much for company today." Her gaze shifted to the hallway and away, to Beth and away. "If you want to come back tomorrow that would be fine, but I'm just not myself right now. You understand, don't you, dear?" Helen's eyes darted around the living room.

"I understand." Beth stood and enveloped her friend in a hug. Helen reached around one hand to hug her back, murmuring "Oh, oh." She let Beth go, started to speak, and then burst into tears.

Beth stared; this was uncharted territory. She spied some Kleenex on the other end table and brought them to Helen, who hiccoughed a thank you. Beth sat back down and took her hand, feeling useless.

"Oh honey, you're such a good friend, and I'm…" Helen gave Beth's hand a hard squeeze before letting go. "I'm just not fit for company today. Would you be a dear and take the tea back to the kitchen? I'm just not myself."

"Of course." She gathered everything and left Helen to compose herself.

What would it be like?

Beth never, *ever* wanted to know.

Helen's kitchen was yellow: yellow cabinets, yellow counters, yellow tile, yellow splash guard, even yellow cabinet knobs and yellow drawer handles. Beth was drowning in yellow as she carried the tray and tea set to the sink—thankfully *not* yellow—washed everything, and placed them aside without putting them away; she didn't know where Helen kept them. Somewhere yellow. Something caught her eye then, and she pushed a yellow-gauze curtain aside and went on tip-toe to peer out the window over the sink.

Helen's small backyard was its usual riot of flowers and vegetable garden and Jacob's toys and Pickle's doghouse. Beth could see his white paws sticking out the front as he napped in the shade under Helen's mulberry tree, but Pickle wasn't what had grabbed her attention.

The dummies slouched at attention against the back fence; the photos tacked to their stuffed heads were ragged and sagging, wet from the recent rain. Beth couldn't tell which was Dick and which was George and supposed it didn't matter. The dummies themselves weren't what had caught her eye, though; she was used to seeing them out there. No, what had her staring was what was sticking *out* of the dummies.

Arrows.

No, not arrows, she realized, too short; they were crossbow bolts. They had brown-and-black-striped fletchings, and their red-plastic nocks glowed like brake lights in the strong afternoon sun.

Beth let the yellow curtain fall. Her heels thumped on the yellow tile.

Those sure aren't BB's, she thought uneasily.

A noise made her turn. Helen stood in the entryway to the kitchen, her face blank. Beth said nothing. What was there to say? She was just glad those Secret Service goons hadn't seen this; Beth doubted they'd have found it amusing. Helen retrieved her cane from where it leaned near the refrigerator and then moved up next to Beth and stared out at the bolt-riddled dummies.

"When Ryan's battalion rolled into Baghdad," Helen began softly, "the children ran next to his tank, shouting and laughing and waving. He saw them pull that statue of Sadam down; he was there that day." A tear tracked down Helen's cheek, and Beth reached out and squeezed her arm. "He was so *proud*, honey, so proud. He joined up after 9/11, you know, like a lot of those boys, I reckon." She turned to Beth. "Did I ever tell you how he passed?"

"No." She'd wondered, but Helen had never brought it up, and Beth had never worked up the courage to ask.

"My youngest son died in a traffic accident." Beth blinked. "Yes, a traffic accident. Ryan went through all that trainin' to go half a world away and git run over by an out-of-control delivery truck." Helen shook her head. "Can you imagine? They had him directin' traffic in all that chaos after the invasion, and he was run down in the dusty street like a cur. Sometimes, and I'm ashamed to admit this, and may He forgive me for sayin' it, but sometimes I think God must have a cruel sense of humor."

"I'm so sorry, Helen."

"But that's not the worst." Beth stared as Helen's red lips peeled back in a snarl that put Mr. Yoda to shame. "Do you know what those children were shouting at Ryan, the ones runnin' next to his tank? He told me, but he didn't know what it meant—it was in their jibber-jabber, a'course—but later I found out; looked it up in some big-city newspaper article on the Internets." Helen waved a multi-ringed hand toward the window, as if the Internet was in her backyard. "They were shouting 'Ulooj', 'Ulooj'. Do you know what that means, dear?"

Beth shook her head.

"It means 'Little Donkey', or sometimes 'Rat of the Desert'." Something more than hate moved across Helen's face. "Those are the people my son died for. They called him filthy names and didn't care a lick about him or that he died for them. *Didn't care a lick.* I hope they all rot in Hell." Helen pulled in a deep, shuddering breath, and then blew it out. "That's why I shoot Henry's old crossbow at the dummies sometimes, 'cause sometimes, the BB's just ain't enough. Can you understand that, dear?"

"I can, Helen."

"Good." She patted Beth's hand and turned back to the window. "You go on home and take care of that precious little one and that husband of yours. I'm sorry I'm not much company today, but this time of the year, 'round his birthday…it's hard."

Beth felt the tears come, and she wiped them away and hugged Helen from the side. "I'll let myself out. You call me if you need anything, and I mean *anything*. To talk, or…or whatever."

Helen patted her hand again, her stare pointed out the window and far away. "You're a good girl, thank you. Go on, now, I'll call you if I need you. Go on."

Beth hugged her one more time, and then left her staring out the window and leaning on her cane, lavender pantsuit clashing horribly with the yellow kitchen. Beth retrieved her purse from the floor next to the coffee table and eased the front door closed.

Poor Helen. Poor, poor Helen. Beth wiped tears from her cheeks; she would have to think of something to cheer her friend up, but she had no idea what that something could possibly be. *Poor Helen.*

She dug in her purse and found her phone; still no Brennan, and Daniel had called three more times and sent four more texts, but the anger she'd felt at them was gone. Helen had reminded Beth that there were worse things in this world than idiotic men and their phones.

Besides, her idea from last night had resurfaced from the beer fumes: Brennan wasn't the only reporter in the world. Beth had been thinking on it all morning while scrubbing Scott Rison's blood from her bedroom; she'd promised to give

Brennan the exclusive about the attack, but she hadn't promised him anything else, and once his story came out Sunday, she would be free to talk to anyone she chose. Bottom line, she had shackled them by using only one reporter.

Why not utilize all of them?

Yes. She was liking this idea more and more, but she needed to discuss it with her stubborn idiot of a husband first, get him on board. Beth glanced at her phone, and then resolutely stuffed it back into her purse. That conversation could wait until tonight.

Let him stew for today, see how he likes it.

Beth slipped her shades on and weaved her way out to her car and stopped and stood in the blazing heat, looking up and down a shimmering Daisy Road. Helen hadn't answered a single one of her questions, at least not directly. Beth had also intended to quiz her about McFarlane's connection to Scarborough, but maybe she'd feel more like talking after Ryan's birthday had passed. *Poor Helen.*

Beth stared down the road to the east, toward the castle and beyond, where, according to Daniel, it eventually wound up to the crest of the ridge, to McFarlane's farm. She looked for a long time at the top of that ridge, at the buildings glinting among the trees.

Who was this man that thought he was so far above the law he could flat-out *order* them to move—and that they would do it? A man that had given *permission* to a rapist to attack her! A man that Helen obviously feared and hated, but would still deliver messages for?

A man who also had enough kindness in his heart to adopt three girls and raise them?

Beth patted her hip, where her Carson was hooked and concealed under her shorts. *Six of them.* She would have to stop by the castle for more knives. She hopped in and fired the engine, cranking the AC up full blast, then backed out and drove toward home.

It was time for Beth to meet this conundrum named John McFarlane and judge him for herself.

Poof, Gone

S EVENTEEN MINUTES after he dialed 911, Dan trudged back inside Carmody's and sat down again. Scandlin pushed a heavy shot-glass full of amber liquid in front of him.

"Everything all right?"

"Yeah." *No.* "What's this? Jack?"

"Does it matter?"

"Nope." Dan tossed it back; it burned all the way down. He clunked the sorta-clean glass on the table. "Thanks," he croaked. Scandlin nodded.

Dan coughed and looked around. The bartender slash waitress, she of the enormous and freckled cleavage, was busy chatting up customers that had their bellybuttons pressed against the stained rail; happy hour had blossomed while he'd been outside sweating and wasting his time. Two more motorcycles had thundered into the lot as well, swelling the pod, along with several older-model cars and pickups. Their scruffy owners had given him looks as he'd stood in the sweltering gravel and argued first with the 911 dispatcher and then Beth, but they could've been three-eyed tattooed space aliens for all Dan had cared. He got the woman's attention, motioning to his empty beer mug, and saw Scandlin do the same with the shot glass.

"Comin' right up, boys!"

The two new bikers had joined the others, making the count six; alternates for the Mensa debate team. The little round Formica table in their midst resembled something helpless about to be eaten. They eyed Dan and Scandlin, but the overall mood in the place was relaxed. Maybe it was because the TBI Agent was drinking, but Dan was still surprised; the odds of a warrant or perhaps even a parole violation or three floating about in the glorious happy-hour ambiance of Carmody's were pretty darn good. He turned back to find Scandlin watching him.

"Did you talk to her?"

"Yeah. I, uh, I panicked a little, I guess. I sent your buddies in blue out to the house, said she might be in danger." Dan swallowed. "They got her out of the bathtub."

Scandlin winced. "Ouch."

"Tell me about it."

Scandlin's gaze went far away, and Dan figured it wasn't Beth's interrupted bath he was thinking about. The bartender brought their conversation oil then, leaning over the table, earrings scraping the chipped wood as Dan enjoyed a spectacular view, the freckles more numerous than the stars in the firmament; a green-and-blue tattoo peeked at him from the inner slope of the right one before she stood back up.

"Thank you," he said. "And this round's on me."

She pinched his cheek with strong, cool fingers. "Ooh, polite, cute, generous, *and* married. All my favorites." She winked and swayed off.

Scandlin came back from wherever or whenever and said, "Your wife's mad, and you'll pay for that, but you were right to be worried, Sims, because Fulbright's wife and my Jessica aren't the only people McFarlane's murdered."

"You know this for sure?" The big Agent nodded. "Then why the hell isn't this asshole rotting in jail?"

"Several reasons." Scandlin dumped the shot into his glass and stirred it with a finger; there couldn't be much soda left in there. "The main one being I have no hard evidence; a lesser is that no one wants to listen."

"McFarlane's cronies. But you said not everyone's a fan, so surely there's someone who—"

Scandlin waved that away. "It's not just them; the guy's a *hero*, Sims—or at least some fools see him that way. He talk about his 'Nam days?"

"He mentioned them."

Scandlin nodded. "John McFarlane was awarded two Silver Stars by the United States Army for gallantry in action during two separate combat operations in the Song Ve river valley in 1968."

Dan whistled. "*Two?* He never mentioned that."

"He wouldn't. He also takes care of his fellow vets; McFarlane's heavily involved in the Wounded Warrior Project, stateside military family assistance, and about five other vet charities. And not only them; he gives millions to cancer research, children's hospitals, you name it, every year."

"Millions every *year?*"

"Yeah, he's loaded. Why, couldn't tell?"

"Well, I've heard rumors, and I know he has all that land, and I saw the Shelby and the other toys, but I just figured he had a good financial adviser or that farm was doing well or whatever."

"The man likes his Mustangs, don't he? It's his one vice—besides killing people, that is. And believe me, Sims, he could drive anything he wants; a while back I called in a favor and got a peek at his tax returns from six years ago. McFarlane's worth two hundred and ninety million dollars."

"Two hundred and ninety million."

"And that was six years ago. Probably north of three hundred by now, even with the turmoil in the markets and all he gives away—*well* north."

"Fuck."

"Yeah."

"Maybe I should start farming. But that farm can't be doing *that* well."

"It's not. Let me start at the beginning. Back in '85, the TBI was part of a multi-agency gangbang that was investigating McFarlane's money. It came too quick, you see; short of winning the lottery, people just don't get that rich that fast without something fishy going on. Before '79, the guy was just a farmer; his family's had that land forever, true, but he was no different from every other farmer: land-rich and cash-poor."

"What did you find? Drugs? Guns?"

Scandlin shook his big, square head. "Drugs? McFarlane hates drug pushers, especially meth dealers. I know of at least four times he's passed on information that got some major methamphetamine operation busted, or some pipeline for Mexican meth shut down; *how* he knows I don't have a clue, but Rutherford County is the cleanest county in five states, at least as far as meth goes. The local tweakers sure aren't fans of his. It's another reason some see him as a hero."

"Why does he hate drugs so much? I mean, they're bad, I get it, but—"

"You know about his daddy?"

"No."

"A drunk and a pill-head and a wastrel from the jump—at least that's what the old-timers say, including my dad, who used to chum around with him before Daddy sobered up and headed off down the right track. Momma saw to that, believe me. Any who, Papa McFarlane 'bout ran that farm into the ground when he had the reins. There were also rumors of abuse, if you can call McFarlane's momma and him sporting shiners like yours there and bruises most of the time 'rumors'." Ice clattered as Scandlin tipped back his drink, cop-eyes scanning past Dan's shoulder. "Papa McFarlane died when his red Farmall tractor rolled over him in January 1969, 'bout three months after junior got shipped home from the jungle. It managed to roll over him three times."

"And nobody thought that strange?"

"The incident was 'investigated' and then written off as an 'accident' by the then Rutherford County Sheriff, a lazy, corrupt tub of guts who's since died, a tub of guts by the name of Bill Burgess—but yes, there were folks who thought it queer, my mom and dad among them. But nobody cracked their teeth because the consensus was no matter how it happened, the world was a better place without Papa McFarlane stinkin' it up."

"Oookaay…so how'd McFarlane make his money?"

"Investments."

"*Investments?*"

"Yes. Stocks and commodities, at least to start."

"So what the hell's illegal about that?"

"Not a thing. But listen to me, Sims—he made all the right moves." Scandlin's graying flattop was so short Dan could see pink scalp beneath the bristles as he leaned forward, his deep voice dropping to a whisper; his tie made a red pool on the chipped table. "*All* the right moves; he'd made his money by '85, nearly eighty million in less than six years. That would raise eyebrows anytime, anywhere, but high school's the highest level of education the man has, and he was finding companies nobody knew about and getting in—and more importantly, getting out—at

just the right times. There're pros, hedge-fund managers and whatnot, fat cats livin'
up there in New York City who're in charge of billions of dollars who *wish* they
had a track record a tenth as good as this uneducated farmer living in the middle
of Tennessee."

"How'd he do it?"

"He said he subscribed to the Wall Street Journal and the Financial Times and
then he applied his 'farmer's smarts' of commodity markets to companies. Made
some no-name broker from Nashville nearly as rich as him, and that's where everyone thought he was getting his advice until it came out in the investigation it had
been McFarlane calling the shots all along. He's settled down now, diversifies like
all rich people do, but when he makes a move, it's always a good one." Scandlin
snorted. "Man even owns his own bank, and he treats the local farmers well. Yet
another reason some call him 'hero'."

"Which bank?"

"River Valley Bank and Trust; they deal in farm and commercial loans, but I
hear they've expanded into residential, what with the…what's wrong?"

River Valley Bank and Trust. "Nothing, I…he owns *that* bank? Are you sure?"

"Does that mean something to you?"

"No."

What *did* it mean? Then Dan saw the way Scandlin was looking at him; the
Special Agent wasn't pointing across the table and shouting "liar", but his stony
expression told the tale.

"I've done business with them," he admitted. "You're right, they've expanded
into residential. I deal with one of their loan officers, guy name of Rickson Aldridge." God, what did it *mean*? "It just surprised me to find out I'd been making
that asshole richer." Scandlin nodded slowly, watching him, and Dan kept his face
smooth. The Wurlitzer was booming AC/DC "You Shook Me All Night Long."
Something to distract the man; Dan knew just the topic. "Was that what made
McFarlane, um, do what he did, you know, with your wife?" The look on Scandlin's
face made him want to lean away again. "Was that what you were investigating on
your own? His money?"

"No." That shovel jaw unclenched, and Scandlin seemed to consider Dan before continuing. "In March of '04 I was in D.C. for three weeks of feeb training
when I got word that Sammy Glick had come to TBI headquarters in Nashville
and said that he wanted to talk about McFarlane. Sammy also informed the agents
on duty he would only talk to me." Scandlin waved at the bartender again, holding
up two fingers.

Dan let out a silent breath. *Keep asking questions, Dan-o, think about the damn bank
later.* Ho-lee-shit, what did it *mean*?

And what was he going to do about it?

"Who is Sammy Glick?"

"Who *was* Sammy Glick; he was a farmhand, not to mention a paroled rapist and suspected murderer from Illinois who worked for McFarlane from August of '99 until the day he walked into HQ. Sammy was dead by the next morning."

"From Illinois? What the hell was he doing down here?"

The bartender came then, depositing their drinks, leaning over and offering that view again, but neither man paid attention. She left in a huff.

"Let me ask you something, Sims. You went out there, right?"

"Right…"

"Did you meet his 'boys'?"

"What's this got to do with—"

"What was your impression of them?"

"I don't know, jeez, they looked like farmhands. I mean, they seemed like hard cases, but—"

"Hard cases," Scandlin interrupted. "That's a good observation. Notice a lot of tattoos? Blue-ink tattoos? Jail 'tats?"

"You can't mean…"

"All of McFarlane's 'boys' are on parole or were released after maxing out for rape, murder, assault, or all of the above. Did you see a big Mexican? Bigger than me, with a neck tattoo? A spider web with a number in the center?"

"I had the pleasure."

"That's Jesus Menendez. That number's his prison I.D. He went down in Arizona for murder two; should've been murder one, and he only did six years on the two because one witness disappeared and the other recanted. Jesus used to be an enforcer on the north side of the line for the Los Zetas Cartel. Ever heard of them?"

"Yes," Dan managed. He took a drink of his warming Michelob, but his mouth stayed dry.

"They suspected Menendez of at least eight murders, but they could only try him for the one. In June of '89, during his second joke of a parole hearing, McFarlane shows up out of the blue to speak for him, and the next thing you know it's not funny anymore because good ol' Jesus is living smack dab in the middle of Tennessee and working on the farm, even though supposedly no one just up and quits Los Zetas." Scandlin shook his head. "It's like that with all of them. McFarlane hears about them somehow and goes to collect them; some he speaks for and helps get paroled, others he waits, but the result is the same: they come work for him on that farm." Scandlin grunted. "The parole boards and the PO's love it, too, because there's no recidivism: zero percent. Once those boys are here, they're clean; not so much as a goddamn speeding ticket. Yet another reason some fools see him as a 'hero'."

Rapists. Murderers. Dan had moved his family in right next door to these people. There was a buzzing between his ears; he barely heard himself say, "Well, that explains Rison."

"Yeah, but Scott Rison was just a baby compared to most of these guys, especially Menendez. You'd be wise to stay away from him, Sims. From all of them."

"I plan on it." Right next door. "So, uh, what happened with this, um…" *Holy fuck*. "What's his name, Sammy? What did he have to say about the old man?"

"I don't know. He was dead before I could talk to him."

Dan swallowed more beer; it still wasn't helping. "McFarlane?"

"We're not sure; the circumstances of Sammy's death were…odd." Scandlin leaned closer, voice dipping again. "And I didn't drop everything and rush back from D.C. just to gab with some ex-con who wanted to have a chat with me; before Glick clammed up, he made two statements, and then named two names. The first thing Sammy said was that he 'didn't sign up for this crazy shit', those exact words, and then he stated he wanted immunity for his cooperation."

"'Didn't sign up for this crazy shit'? What the hell does that mean?"

Something flickered in Scandlin's eyes, but then they cleared. "Not a clue, Sims. But what got me back on the first flight available were the two names he tossed off—two names Sammy Glick should've never heard of or known anything about." Scandlin weighed and measured Dan again, and he seemed to reach some decision before continuing. "They were the names of people who'd vanished without a trace; one in '01, from Tampa, Florida, and the other from Spokane, Washington in '03."

"That's on both ends of the country. How could—"

"Just shut up and listen." Scandlin took a cautious scan around the smoky bar, then continued, voice a low rasp. "I told you about McFarlane's money. Most people like that travel all over the world, winter on some island, have vacation houses, so forth and so on. Not John McFarlane. Except for collecting his new 'boys', the man never leaves that farm, not even for groceries or supplies; he sends his daughters or his boys to fetch them, or has them delivered. Says he doesn't *need* to go anywhere else, that nowhere on earth is as beautiful as his farm." Scandlin snorted. "He might be right; that's some prime Tennessee dirt he's sitting on, but the point is, he's not your typical rich guy." He flagged the well-endowed bartender down, holding up one finger. Dan decided he'd have one more beer and did the same; she brought their libations without saying a word, her sulk now a thing of silent, freckled beauty.

When she left, Dan said, "What's this got to do with people vanishing?"

"I'm getting to that, Sims. Christ, zip your lip and open your ears for once in your life."

Dan clamped his jaw shut. See if *he* asked any more fucking questions!

"Charles Duperies, age thirty-six, husband and father of two, a boy and a girl; owned three upscale restaurants in the Tampa area and was in the middle of opening a fourth. He vanished on his way to hit a bucket at the range five minutes from his house. Poof, gone."

Scandlin took a drink, eying him over the rim, and Dan ground his teeth and kept it zipped; the Special Agent nodded in approval, which made Dan's jaw ache.

"Vivian Rawlins, twenty-nine, newly married, an up-and-coming riparian-rights lawyer; she vanished on her way home from the office. Poof, gone. That was in Spokane two years later."

Scandlin sipped and waited, and Dan could have punched him; the man had about eighty pounds on him though, and they weren't potato-chip pounds. He contented himself with taking a pull of his beer and fantasizing about smashing the mug in the cop's face.

"I know what you're thinking, Sims." *Oh no you don't.* "Two people with no link to John McFarlane or Sammy Glick or Tennessee, period. That's what I thought too, but then Jessica and I had some vacation time saved up back in January of '05, time we had to use or lose, so I talked her into checking out Tampa for a few days. Figured it was a long shot, but if I didn't find anything we could still lay on the beach and get a sunburn and a Piña Colada buzz."

"I began by showing around photos of McFarlane and Sammy and Menendez; Jesus is the old man's crew leader, the one who's been around the longest, so I figured if they were snatching people for whatever sick reason, he'd use Menendez, but no one in Duperies' circle of family or friends or business acquaintances recognized any of them. I'd about given up and was sitting on that beach with Jess when I had an idea." He swirled the ice in the glass, watching Dan, then said, "You met those girls, right?"

Dan's eyes narrowed. "I met them."

"Lookers, aren't they?"

"Oh yeah."

"Think you'd remember them, even four or five years later?"

Dan nodded.

"You're not alone. I didn't have pictures, but women that look like that, well, men notice them; women, too. Five employees and one business partner of Charles Duperies saw those girls talking to him two days before he vanished from the face of the earth."

"So you're saying three *girls* abducted this guy by themselves? In 2001, the youngest, Mindy, would've been about seven, and the oldest, Alex, would've barely been twenty! You've got to be fucking kidding me, Scandlin! *A seven-year-old?* What did they do, take these people home and play Barbie with them?"

The agent just nodded. "Farfetched, I know. And the youngest was nine; she's pushing nineteen, now. As for doing it themselves, I think they had a chaperone, a woman by the name of Melissa Bane. She's supposedly an old friend of the McFarlane family."

"The Keeper," Dan whispered, thunderstruck.

Scandlin frowned. "The what?"

"Melissa…*Bane*, you said her name was? She's the Keeper of the cemetery. I met her."

Scandlin stared at him from across the table, and even though the wide, hard face didn't change, Dan could feel the intensity. "You didn't mention this before."

"Why should I have? I didn't know you knew her. She was lurking in the cemetery the Saturday I found it, popped up from behind a rose bush when I was checking out that weird megalith and scared the shit right outta me. Why? What does it matter?" Dan studied the Special Agent; the man was sitting as still as a statue. "You said she was 'chaperoning' those sluts when they snatched this guy from Tampa? What does *that* mean, exactly? Who is she, Scandlin?"

Something moved in the big man's eyes again and then was masked; it had been so quick that Dan wasn't even positive he'd seen it this time…but if he had seen it, he was sure he knew what to call it.

Fear.

Fear? Dan couldn't imagine Special Agent Scandlin afraid of much, and certainly not some middle-aged lady who liked roses and hanging out in cemeteries, no matter how creepy she was.

So what is he afraid of?

Scandlin didn't give him a chance to wonder further. "'Weird megalith'? There's no megalith of any kind in that cemetery, Sims, just a bunch of weed-choked, falling-down gravestones. I saw it when I was younger, remember?" Somehow that face hardened even further. "If you're making up stories, you can forget about me helping—"

Dan clicked his teeth shut. *No megalith?* "There *is* a megalith! I swear! It's big and black and ugly and sticking out of the ground right at the top of that fucking hill! I can prove it, I took pictures." Dan brought the pics to the screen of his iPhone and handed it across the table. Scandlin took it, but he had his cop-eyes pinned to Dan's face.

"The pictures Rison wanted."

"That's right. Look at them and tell me that's not a big fucking rock in the middle of the cemetery, Scandlin. Tell me it's not, I dare you."

The Special Agent stared for another few seconds, and then he lowered his gaze to the iPhone. Suddenly he frowned, swiped twice with a sausage finger, and then chunked the phone back at Dan. It clattered on the tabletop before he could catch it.

"Hey, that's expensive!"

"I don't know what game you're playing, but I've had enough. I offer to help your family, and this is how you treat me? Lying and playing tricks? That's not even the right cemetery!"

"*Not the—!*" Heads turned. "That's Barron Cemetery. I swear it is. Call my wife if you don't believe me. Beth's been out there. I took her to see the roses that Sunday afternoon, before Rison ambushed us. That's when I took those pics." Scandlin stared at him. Dan wiggled the phone. "Call her. She'll back me up. That's Barron Cemetery."

Scandlin reached for the phone again and sulkily swiped through the photos. "There was no megalith when *I* saw it," he said, still sulking and swiping, "and no roses either, just a buncha overgrown graves on a hilltop in the woods. By God, I see the hilltop and the woods are still there! But that green hedge wasn't around back then either, and the gravestones were all falling-down fieldstone—all shapes and sizes, too, not this uniform black. Half were so weathered you couldn't read them." Scandlin looked up sharply. "Are you *sure* this is Barron Cemetery?"

"Call my wife."

He passed the phone back. "No, I believe you." He settled back into the cracked red booth and stared somewhere past Dan's shoulder, but Dan didn't think he was taking in the atmosphere of Carmody's now.

"And Melissa Bane is this new Barron Cemetery's…Keeper."

Scandlin said it so soft and so low that Dan had almost missed it because of the Crosby, Stills & Nash (sans Young) now oozing from the Wurlitzer; he watched the Special Agent's face and didn't like what he saw.

The news that Barron Cemetery had evolved, and that Melissa Bane was its caretaker, had shaken the big man, but why? What did it matter what she did? And so they'd upgraded the cemetery, big deal. Dan could've done without all the flowers, and he would've chosen a more attractive rock to stick in the ground, and he certainly would have inscribed it with some good old-fashioned English, but each to his own.

"Scandlin. Scandlin!"

The man blinked and then scowled at him. "What?"

"Why do you think this Bane woman would snatch grown men? What do you know about her?" Scandlin just stared at him with those cop-eyes. "C'mon, man, you know *something*. McFarlane said the same as you, that she was an old family friend. He also said she helped him raise those girls after his wife died. What else do you know? Who is she?"

Scandlin seemed guarded as he said, "Who is she? She's Melissa Bane—at least that's the name she goes by. Whatever her real name is, she showed up about thirty years ago, around the time McFarlane's wife took sick and died from a mysterious illness. She helped raise those girls, there's no doubt about that. There were rumors she filled other roles the dead wife left behind."

"You mean…?"

Scandlin shrugged the lineman's shoulders. "You do the math." He glanced at his watch. "But we're getting off track, and I've got an appointment. Let me show you something." He picked up a scuffed brown-leather briefcase from the seat beside him and set it on the table. Dan hadn't noticed it, likely because of the poor lighting; Carmody's wasn't exactly the kind of place where people wanted to see or be seen clearly. Scandlin popped the latches and pulled out a photograph, glancing at it before sliding it in front of Dan. "That's Charles Duperies."

Dan didn't look at the photo; instead, he watched Special Agent Scandlin.

Why doesn't he want to talk about Melissa Bane?

The man's reluctance to do so was as plain as the bruises on Dan's face. He wanted to push the subject, but some instinct warned him off, so he let it go for now and picked up the 8 x 11 color print; a well-built, handsome guy with dark hair standing with his arm around a statuesque blonde stared back at him; blue sky and a palm tree hovered behind them.

"Okay, that's Chuck. So how did two women, a teenager, and a nine-year-old girl abduct this guy? What, did the little one tackle Chuck around the knees and then the others sat on him and tied him up?" Dan shoved the picture back. "This is fucking ridiculous. I mean, sure, I met them, and yeah, they're bat-shit crazy—they held me at knife point, remember?—but going around abducting grown men? *Why?* What would be the fucking point? What could be worth getting caught and going to prison? This makes no damn sense."

Scandlin stowed Chuck in the briefcase, then presented Dan with another picture. "That's Vivian Rawlins."

Vivian was a slim, well-dressed woman with short blonde hair. "Okay, that's Vivian Rawlins."

"I took a trip out to Spokane about three months after…after Jessica died. Lied and expensed it as TBI business, but the point is, I talked to Vivian's family and friends; three of them remember seeing McFarlane's girls speaking to her in the days before she vanished."

Dan just stared.

Scandlin put Vivian away and pulled another photo out of that damn briefcase, and Dan took it with numb fingers. "That's Jim Briscoe. He was a landscaping contractor, a successful one. Employed three crews, about three-dozen people. Had enough work lined up to last two years. Had a wife and three young kids, two girls and a boy. Jim vanished from Lexington, Kentucky, in August of '05; on his way to Starbucks, according to his wife. I talked to his next-door neighbor; three days before Jim vanished, the neighbor came home from Kroger and looked across the driveway and saw Jim standing on his front porch talking to a brunette in her twenties. The neighbor remembered her because you don't see a face like that or hair that blue-black shade every day."

Dan handed Jim back. Scandlin passed him yet another photo, and he took it reluctantly. "That's Roger Cartwright, a well-respected Entomologist from Georgia State University, in Atlanta. Disappeared while working out at the gym late; left his car in the parking lot and his wallet and keys and cell phone in the locker, not to mention his wife and a brand-new baby girl at home. I found half-a-dozen people who saw him speaking to a stunning green-eyed redhead in the campus cafeteria the day before. This was last year; September 17th, to be exact. That's the latest one—that I know of. Let's go for a change of pace." Scandlin took Roger back and shuffled photographs, holding the ones he didn't want out to the side in one big hand.

Dan stared in horror.

Dear God.

"Here we go." He handed Dan a warped and sepia-toned Polaroid; it showed a brunette in her thirties with big 80s hair and the clothes to go with it. Two dark-headed children clutched her hands; they looked about seven or eight, a boy and a girl. "That's Sue Ann Wilson. Dallas, Texas. She vanished on her way home from work in July 1985. Poof, gone. When I talked to her sister, she recalled a beautiful little five or six-year-old girl with blue-black hair. A woman was with her.

Sue Ann's sister described Melissa Bane perfectly. She saw them standing in Sue Ann's driveway, talking. That was four days before Sue Ann vanished."

"*Jesus Christ!*" Heads turned and conversations stopped. Holy Mother of God, rapists and murderers and egomaniac farmers with knife-wielding slut daughters he could handle, but *this?* Dan pointed at the briefcase; his voice dropped to an involuntary whisper. "How many are in there?"

"I've found seventeen so far."

Dan tried to take a pull on his beer but spilled most of it down his shirt; the mug rattled when he sat it down. Seventeen. So far. Beth and Lizzie. Were they home yet? He didn't want them to be home yet, he wanted to call Beth and tell her to come to Nashville and they'd get a hotel room, any hotel room. Holy fuck.

"Who else have you told about this? And what do they do with the bodies?"

"How would I know what they do with the bodies? Get a grip, Sims. And I've told no one but you, and for several good reasons, the primary one being motive; in law enforcement, we like to establish a motive. It makes things simpler. You asked the right question earlier: why. *Why* would Bane and these girls take people? I don't know, and until I do, I don't have a case. What I have is unofficial eyewitness accounts—and in some of those, there's a twenty-year gap between what they think they saw and when I took their unofficial statement, as with Sue Ann Wilson's sister—that these girls and Melissa Bane were seen in the company of people who disappeared, sometimes as much as a week before. That's it. No one heard any threats from Bane or the girls, no one saw the people being coerced or abducted, and without any of that to back it up, the dumbest DA in the world wouldn't bring charges on this evidence."

"But…but…"

"There's another reason I haven't told anyone." He gathered the photos and placed them in the briefcase and closed and latched it, then left it there with his hand resting on it, almost protectively. "After…after McFarlane called and told me… told me to back off, and *bragged* about Jess…" Scandlin wiped his face, and Dan studied his beer mug until the man regained his composure. "Long story short, I went a little ape-shit over John McFarlane. I couldn't prove anything, though, just that he'd called me, and when they asked him, he said he'd reached out to offer his condolences because his daddy and my daddy used to know each other." Dan watched pure murder move across Scandlin's face. "My point is, I can't go to anyone with this, not about McFarlane. You understand? It's like the boy who cried wolf, now."

"I get that, but there's too much here. We have to tell somebody."

"Look at it from someone else's perspective, not yours or mine, someone whose family hasn't been attacked and threatened, or wife…someone who still thinks this guy's the hero he pretends to be. If you didn't know what you know, and you just knew about the good works McFarlane does, would you believe any of this?"

Dan felt sick. No one would believe it, not without more proof.

Proof…

And then it hit Dan like a concrete block from the sky.

"The cemetery," he whispered.

Scandlin leaned toward him. "What?"

"Barron Cemetery. That's where they're putting the bodies. That goddamn cemetery." Scandlin was shaking his head. "What? It explains why Rison was so worked up about us poking around out there."

"No," Scandlin said, still shaking his head. "It doesn't make sense." When Dan opened his mouth, he held out a hand. "Hear me out."

"All right."

"I'll admit that when you first mentioned Rison's fixation on that place, I was, well, interested. But McFarlane wouldn't be that stupid. That old man is a lot of things, but stupid he's not."

"I don't know what you're talking about, and I don't care. Rison said—"

"This is a guy who makes *all the right moves,* Sims. He has an entire county fooled; hell, he has the whole *world* by the shorthairs. Do you think he'd risk that? Because if they found a bunch of missing people's remains on his property, that'd be the ballgame, and as much as that thought gives me a warm fuzzy feeling, I don't believe it for a second. No way would McFarlane be that dumb. No way."

Dan nodded, conceding the point. Still, he'd come here for answers and he was just piling up more goddamn questions. And no one else but Dan seemed to think there was something wrong with that fucking cemetery and it was royally pissing him off.

"Fine," he said, "let's forget all about the cemetery that the psycho who broke into my house and tied me up and raped my wife wouldn't shut up about." That jaw clenched, but Dan couldn't give a shit less. "You never told me what happened to this Sammy guy. Why *you,* by the way? Why did he want to talk only to you?" By God, Dan would get an answer about something!

"Let's just say that when the investigation into the old man's money ended, I didn't go quietly." His sudden grin was fierce. "I raised a bit of hell, truth be told. We couldn't find anything illegal, true, but there were still unanswered questions, questions like how McFarlane was privy to information that the biggest investment gurus in the country didn't have; this was the 80s, mind you, before the Internet. But what really got me was how it ended; it stank to high heaven, Sims. Word came down from on high—and I mean *way* on high; out past the top ranks of the TBI— to end the investigation. Nothing official, you understand, just a back-channel warning we'd be smart to drop it. That didn't sit plumb with me, and I wasn't shy about saying so, not that it did any good. McFarlane got to enjoy his money, and because of my mouth, his friends made sure my career was over." Seeing Dan's expression, Scandlin said, "Oh, I've put a lot of scumbags behind bars since then, and I'll continue to do so until I retire next year, but I guarantee you I'll retire the same rank I was then, as I am now: Special Agent. The old man's friends have seen to that."

"Scarborough," Dan said, not a question.

"He's one, and there are a lot more where he came from, but the point is, Glick must've heard about my opinions and thought I would listen." He shrugged. "Who knows? They stuck him in a lock-down cell—Sammy's request, that—to wait for me, but by the time I arrived at HQ, he was meat."

"How did they get to him if he was locked down?"

"That might be the strangest thing of—"

The bartender appeared, freckled gorge leading the way. "You boys ready for another round?"

Scandlin drawled, "I'm good, darlin', I gotta skedaddle, but I believe I've taken a shine to this place. I might just make Carmody's my regular stop."

She stared, then painted a smile on. "You come back and see us, sugar." She turned to Dan, and Scandlin winked at him. "And what about you, handsome? You leavin' me, too?"

"Yeah, uh, I've got to go. Tab me out, please." Scandlin had a sense of humor. Who knew?

She sighed. "Please. I'm gonna miss that, and those pretty eyes. You come back and see Miss Sheri, now—after you're all healed up, a'course." Sheri's smile downshifted to something with a promise before she swayed away.

Dan turned back to Scandlin, but there was no playfulness in the big man now. "I told her the truth, Sims, I have to go, but before I do, you listen and you listen good. Sammy died, and no one saw anything, no one heard anything, but when I got there at four in the morning and had them open the door, we found this." He popped the latches on his horrible briefcase again and took out another damn photo.

It was an 8 x 11 black-and-white that showed a cramped and furniture-less room; the walls were two-tone, darker on top and a dirty white or beige on bottom. A lidless steel toilet and a steel sink stuck out of the left-hand wall like cheerless modern art. Something was crumpled in the corner opposite the toilet; it resembled a big doll with the stuffing ripped out. Blood covered the walls above the doll's head, as if splashed by a mad painter. The blood had streaked toward the floor; to Dan, it looked like the wall was weeping black tears.

"What...who did this?" He'd almost said *what* did this because it appeared as if Glick had been ripped apart by a bear or a lion or something; something big, with claws. *Big* claws. "You said no one heard anything, or saw anything? How the hell could that be? This was in the middle of a police station! What about his guards? What about security cameras?"

Scandlin looked tired. "We interviewed everyone who had access to Glick, and then they took a polygraph; they all passed. Every CCTV recording was reviewed. There was only one thing—"

The bartender appeared with Dan's card and tab; he signed the receipt and handed it back to her. "So what—?" A squeal, and then he was dealing with a face-full of soft freckles.

"Thank you, sweetie! You remember what I said: Sherri's always here at Carmody's." She winked again and sashayed off. Dan watched her go.

"Sims. Married man, remember?"

"I wasn't—"

"Keep it in your pants and focus. I've got five minutes, so listen sharp. Are you listening?"

"I'm listening," Dan gritted.

"Everyone with access to that room checked out, and there was nothing on any of the recordings that wasn't supposed to be there, except…"

"Except?"

"The ceiling camera in the hall outside that lock-down cell worked perfectly until 3:07 A.M. Then it went dark for thirty-four seconds and change, and then it showed an empty hallway again."

"Could someone have gotten inside that cell in thirty-four seconds without a key? It *was* locked, right? And *dark?* Do you mean someone disabled the camera, or it glitched?"

"It worked fine when we tested it. No outages, either, not even a flicker or a surge; we checked. As for someone to disable it, they would have shown up on the cameras in the adjacent hallways and had to pass a guard station besides. And when I say dark, I mean like a shadow moved across the lens. I've watched the video a hundred times, and I've seen the same thing a hundred times, although I still don't understand it; a shadow, as black as anything you've ever imagined, moves from left to right, and by the timer you can see that the camera is recording the whole thirty-four seconds plus. And then the shadow moves off, and just like that, the hallway's as bright as it's supposed to be."

A black shadow…

Scandlin was watching him, so Dan kept his face still. It had to be a coincidence. It had to be; things were getting screwy enough without…

He tried to focus. "So who killed him?"

Scandlin smiled; Dan had never seen an expression so bitter.

"Sammy killed himself."

"Suicide?"

"Yes."

Dan looked at the photo. He looked at Scandlin. "Bullshit."

"That's what the Davidson County Coroner officially ruled, Sims. Why, don't you believe it?"

"You don't believe it either."

"Oh, I believe that's what the coroner ruled. I believe that completely." He looked at his watch and then tapped the photo in Dan's hands. "See how his wrists are torn open? Human teeth did that; inconclusive they were Sammy's, but who else was in there with him?"

Dan stared at what was left of Sammy Glick; there was no way someone could do that to themselves. He was still looking when Scandlin spoke again:

"Ol' Sammy there also ripped his own scrotum off. They found it, and his partially masticated testicles, in his stomach."

Dan swallowed, hard; the Michelob was trying to come back up. "He chewed his own…?"

"That's what the ME said."

"This coroner, the one that ruled it a suicide? Let me guess, he's a friend of McFarlane's."

"You bet your ass he is, along with almost every elected official, judge, and half the cops in both Davidson and Rutherford Counties."

"Jesus," Dan whispered.

"Have you ever heard of The Barron's Hunting Club?"

Dan's brain rocked, trying to keep up. "A *hunting* club? What the hell's a hunting club got to do with…did you say *Barron's* hunting club? As in Barron Cemetery, or Barron Woods?"

"Yes." Scandlin's cop-eyes were blazing. "It all comes back to that hunting club, Sims. Everyone who's anyone in both Rutherford and Davidson Counties is a member, along with several people from the Nashville entertainment scene; people you would recognize. Others, too. Does the name Thomas Rattling ring a bell?"

It took Dan a second, and then he quit breathing.

"Tom Rattling."

Scandlin nodded.

"As in *Senator* Tom Rattling?"

"The same. Thomas Rattling, senior Senator from the great state of Tennessee, a shoe-in to win a fifth term next election, sitting member of the Senate Armed Forces Committee, and unless the man gets caught diddling his secretary or the Democrats lose their majority in the Senate, destined to become Senate Majority Leader after Jim Altenburg decides he's had enough, or dies. John McFarlane's been a major contributor to Tom Rattling's war-chest for over twenty years."

They stared at each other. Scandlin checked his watch again, then slid out of the booth and stood up, carrying his horror-filled briefcase in his right hand.

"Listen, Sims. You want my help, and I'll give it to you, starting with a little advice; get your family out of there. If McFarlane's fixated on you because of that house…" Scandlin frowned. "Or whatever reason, the man won't quit until he gets what he wants—and believe me, John McFarlane is used to getting what he wants."

Beth. There was no way she would run. Dan said as much, then added, "I thought there were people we could talk to, people that could maybe get something done."

"There might be, but three weeks isn't enough time." He stuck out a thick paw. Dan shook in a daze. "I'll do whatever I can, you have my word, but you need to talk to her, help her see the wisdom of a tactical retreat." The big man smiled wistfully. "The best ones are stubborn, but sometimes stubborn isn't the best course. You being out there, right next to him…" Something moved in Special Agent Scandlin's eyes then, and this time Dan recognized it easily: terror. "McFarlane's evil, Sims.

Not just bad—I know bad men—but evil like I've never seen. Get them far away." He glanced at his watch. "Call me tomorrow night, after eight. We'll talk more." He walked out.

Dan sat for a time and then got up and zombied toward the door. Sheri called, "Bye, hon! Remember to come back and see me!" He managed a wave for her.

One biker growled, "Bye, hon, come back and see us!" His pals laughed, but Dan didn't bother to look at them as he stumbled out and through the sweltering gravel and to his truck; he cranked up the AC, then sat there staring out the windshield at Carmody's but not seeing it.

Evil.

This from a man who'd dealt with the dregs of the earth for thirty years; not just bad, but evil. Rapists and murders and crazy sluts that make people go poof, gone.

And Dan had moved his family in right next door.

Now that Scandlin wasn't staring at him, Dan let himself think about the rest: River Valley Bank and Trust. He knew that bank, and not just from work. River Valley Bank and Trust was where Dan had his safe deposit box, the one with all the football money. He'd gone there Tuesday and removed the money; he still had the box, but he didn't just have a box at that bank.

River Valley Bank and Trust held the mortgage on the castle.

McFarlane owned his house.

Beth and Lizzie. Dan fished his phone out and called his wife. She answered on the third ring.

"Hi." Radio*active* pissed.

"Hi." Dan couldn't care less. "Are you guys home?"

"Yes." Lizzie piped something in the background, and Mr. Yoda barked. Dan gripped the phone so hard its case popped. He eased up and wiped his eyes.

Thank you, God. Thank you. "I'm heading that way. We need to talk."

"Yes," she said, "we need to talk."

She didn't mean it the way he meant it, but Dan didn't care about that either. "I'm still in Nashville. I should be home in about forty-five minutes to an hour." Traffic heading south out of the city would suck this time of day, but shitty traffic didn't seem like much of a problem anymore, for some reason.

"Make it faster. I want to get to the dojo with time to stretch before I teach class." She hung up on him.

Dan put the phone up and drove home, fast, but it was still the longest drive of his life.

The Sharing of Oxygen

ANIEL APPEARED in the laundry room doorway. He watched her for a time, and then he stuck his hands in his pockets and observed for a longer time. Beth folded laundry.

"I read her *Yertle*," he finally said. "Now she's playing with Mr. Yoda in her room." He chuckled. It sounded forced. "Well, she read it to me. I can't believe how smart she's getting."

Lizzie had been reading for over a year, and Beth knew how intelligent her daughter was.

She folded laundry.

He sighed. "I'm sorry, okay? I was worried sick that—"

"We made the news again," she informed the washcloth in her hand. "Those idiots were parked in the driveway when Lizzie and I got home." Beth slammed the folded washcloth on top of a stack of folded washcloths, but it wasn't satisfying; washcloths didn't slam well. "I had to make them move to get in my own stupid garage."

Beth took a load out of the washer and threw it into the dryer, picked up her basket, and left the laundry room; Daniel had to scramble out of her way or she would've run him over. She went down the hall and crossed underneath the chandelier to the stairs; he didn't speak until she was five risers up.

"Steve called to see if we were okay, and Irene, and about ten other people. I guess the media picked it up on the police band."

"You think?"

Beth stomped the rest of the way up and into their bedroom and past the ruined mattress and box spring and into their walk-in closet. She almost threw Daniel's clothes on the floor, but decided that would be petty. Beth would not be petty; furious, yes, petty, no.

When she was done hanging his stupid shirts, she stepped out to find him standing next to their bed; he was looking down at the bare and bloodstained mattress, and the memory of what she'd had to do there was etched across his face.

Beth turned away before he saw her watching and went into the bathroom to put away towels and washcloths.

He followed her in. "The bedroom looks great, but I wish you would've let me help."

Beth wiped at her suddenly leaky eyes. "No," she said, "it does *not* look great. We need to fix the bullet holes in the drywall and the ceiling—not to mention *repaint* the walls and the ceiling!—and I don't have the first clue what we'll do about the bloodstains on the hardwood. And I don't think we'll *ever* get that smell out!" Beth whammed the linen closet door shut and turned to look at him; he flinched, then offered a weak smile that wavered and died when she finished with, "*Help?* Oh, you're going to *help.*" She stalked past him to their ruined mattress and box spring and jabbed her finger at them. "See those? Get rid of them."

"Beth—"

"You can haul them off in that new truck you're so proud of, the one you bought with your *football* money. You can carry them down by yourself, too, because *I'm* not going to help."

A line appeared between her husband's eyebrows, but he kept his voice smooth—just. "I'll take care of it, but right now we need to talk about other—"

"Surely you can manage *that* much."

"Yeah, I think I can manage it."

"Wonderful."

"Beth, c'mon, I was scared to death something—"

She tramped out of the bedroom and down the stairs; she had more stupid laundry to deal with.

Beth had just dumped the detergent in the washer when Daniel popped up in the doorway again. "We need to talk."

"About *what!?*"

"What do you think? You were supposed to talk to Helen today, and I had that meeting with Scandlin, remember?"

Beth started the new load and then stood straight, not looking at him, fighting for calm; it wasn't his fault he was a stubborn idiot, he was just made that way. She stared at their old dryer; the thing was as ancient as the chugging washer—they weren't a matched set—and it took three times as long to dry a full load as it should, but it kept on trucking.

Beth suspected those were the two ultimate secrets to life: stay calm, and just keep trucking. She forced herself to look at her husband.

Calm. Trucking.

"So tell me what this *Special Agent* had to say."

They sat across from each other in the breakfast nook, drinking iced green tea, and she banked her fury and sipped her tea and listened until the end without interrupting, although keeping her lip zipped was about the hardest thing Beth had ever done in her life. *What utter nonsense.* He kept glancing out the window as he blathered, fingering that idiotic gun in his pocket, even getting up and going outside to scan the backyard twice. His paranoia was giving her a headache—well, okay, making the headache worse; she'd never quite lost the one from this morning, another reason her temper had claws.

When the baloney ran down Beth said, "So not only are we neighbors with a man who thinks he can order us out of our own house, but he employs paroled rapists and murderers?"

"Yes."

"And his three daughters and this Keeper woman Melissa have abducted dozens of random people and have been doing it for years?"

"Yes."

"Why would they do such a thing, Daniel?"

"I know it sounds—"

"And what do they do with them? Oh, that's right, you think they're killing them and burying them in that cemetery."

"Yeah, I do. How else do you explain what Rison said?"

"Rison said a lot of things, Daniel."

There was a stretch where neither looked at the other. Lizzie's sweet laughter drifted down the stairs.

Beth felt numb, although she should have been furious and terrified; her husband, with this moronic Special Agent's help, had finally dove head-first into the deep end with this cemetery craziness. But the drivel he was spouting was so out there, and she was so tired after a long day that had started hung-over and cleaning her rapist's blood from her bedroom and then had ended with a two-hour session at the dojo teaching class—not to mention the fruitless talk with Helen and all the crap she'd dealt with in between!—that Beth just changed the subject before she strangled him.

"You haven't asked me about Helen."

"So tell me."

She tried, but it didn't take long for him to interrupt. "Scandlin hinted that Muriel died rather conveniently not long after Bane showed up, but it was some sickness, so I don't know how she could've been involved."

Of all the foolishness this Scandlin had filled her husband's head with, the story of the so-called Keeper, this Melissa Bane, intrigued Beth the most—if it was true, and not just some grieving widower's paranoid fantasy, although Helen's obvious loathing for the woman was real enough. She was also curious as to how, and more importantly why, the cemetery had been completely remodeled—if remodel was the right term for bone yards.

Beth said, "And she appeared out of the blue thirty years ago? Where did she come from?"

"Who cares where she came from? My point is these people are *dangerous*, Beth. We should get a hotel room, at least until we decide what to do."

"The answer is still no. I will not run."

"God damn it, these people are DANGEROUS! Don't you get that? Rapists and murderers! Guys who make Rison look like a fucking Cub Scout! That's enough reason right there, forget all the wacky shit about farm girls making people vanish! Rapists and *murderers*, Beth! They could be out there past the fence right now, or hiding in that corn field on the west side of the house! We'd never know until it was too late!"

"Don't yell at me."

He gripped the edge of the table; she could feel it tremble. "I'm just thinking about you and Lizzie," he said through clenched teeth. "If anything happened to you two…look, it would just be until we could—"

"I will not flee from my home."

"McFarlane is dangerous. He murdered Mrs. Fulbright and made it look like a traffic accident somehow. He had Scandlin's wife raped and beaten to death and dumped in a ditch. He threatened to do something similar to you if we don't move out by the *fucking first of the goddamn month!*"

"Don't you *dare* speak to me like I'm stupid!"

"You don't believe me. You don't believe *any* of this!"

"Did you really expect me to?"

"Call Scandlin." He tried to hand her his phone; when she didn't take it, he set it on the table in front of her. "Call. He'll tell you what he told me." His face soured. "Maybe you'll believe him. Call him. Talk to him."

"John McFarlane supposedly admitted to a police officer he'd had that officer's wife raped and murdered?"

"Yeah, that's what the arrogant fuck did."

"And why is he not in prison?"

"The old man has a lot of friends, not to mention the lack of evidence and motive…" He pointed at the phone. "Scandlin can explain all that shit better than me." He grunted. "The guy's pissed, though, and I've got a real good feeling that if he doesn't manage to put McFarlane in jail…well, let's just say the old man won't have to worry about throwing a retirement party."

Beth felt something slow, cold, and hard move through her.

"Perhaps that isn't such a bad idea."

Daniel put his palms flat on the table and stared at her. "C'mon, Beth, we can't just kill the guy. Last time I checked, they put people in prison for that."

"Except for John McFarlane, apparently."

He stared some more. "You're serious."

Beth massaged the back of her neck; had she ever felt this drained? "I'm just talking, forget it. I'm also tired, I don't feel well, and now you want us to run away from our own home." She smiled. "You haven't asked me what I did after I talked to Helen."

He squinted, suspicious. "What did you do?"

Beth took a sip of tea. "Nothing much, I just drove over to the farm to have a little chat with this man who thinks he can order people out of their own homes."

Daniel sat up straight. "You—! What if they—? God *damn* it, don't you realize these people are dangerous?"

"No big, *baaad* farmers attacked me, dear. See me sitting here, alive and un-harmed?"

Beth thought steam might come shooting out of his ears, like a Saturday morning cartoon. He practiced his curses—her Daniel possessed quite the eclectic collection—and ground his teeth for a bit. Eventually he grated, "Well? What the hell *did* happen?"

Beth lost her satisfied smile. "Nothing. They had the front gate shut and locked. I honked, even got out and yelled that I wanted to talk to McFarlane, but no one let me in."

"So they just…what, ignored you? How did they even know you were—Helen. She must have told them you were coming."

Beth nodded wearily. "I didn't tell her, but she must've figured it out somehow. It's the only explanation I can think of." That Helen would do such a thing still twisted Beth's heart. "But the real question is why would McFarlane invite you to lunch but lock the gate on me?" She left out the tiny fact she'd taken three of her biggest kitchen knives in addition to her Carson, and that McFarlane wouldn't have had nearly as much fun threatening her as he had Daniel, but there was no way Helen could have known that either, so it still didn't explain why.

He said, "The gate was locked? Huh, they must've been gone."

"Oh, they were there. You didn't let me finish."

"So finish."

"When I first pulled up, two guys came around some red metal building about a hundred feet away, looked at me, and then walked off." She didn't tell him they'd spoken to each other and then *laughed* before disappearing; Beth didn't enjoy being laughed at. "Another guy driving a green tractor saw me, leered, and kept going."

"Maybe the old man took off for some reason, although Scandlin said he never leaves unless he's collecting new assholes from prison. I bet the—"

"Daniel."

He showed her both palms. "Please continue to enlighten me, dear."

Beth's nostrils flared. Lizzie's laughter drifted down the stairs; she took a deep breath into her *itten* before continuing.

"Those jerks weren't the only ones who made an appearance. I was standing there like an idiot, shouting that I wanted to talk to McFarlane, when a redhead rode a four-wheeler around the corner of the closest building and shut it off. I asked to speak to her father, but she didn't say a word. She just sat there and looked at me." Beth left out the challenging, arrogant smirk the young woman had directed at her, and the way contempt had *oozed* from her; Beth still felt like she would pop. "She was very beautiful."

"Yeah, that was Rebecca."

"Oh? You're on a first name basis?"

"I told you McFarlane introduced me to them. Just count yourself lucky you didn't meet the other two."

"Are they as beautiful as Rebecca?"

"I suppose," he said without looking at her, taking a careful sip of his tea. "The youngest, Mindy, is a blonde, and the oldest, Alex, has black hair."

"Last night you told me her name was Alexandria. Now it's *Alex?*"

"She said I could call her Alex, everybody does…" Her obtuse husband finally took note of her face: he leaned as far away from her as the ladder-back of his chair would allow. "Who fucking cares what they call themselves or what they look like? They're as crazy as their father." He sat forward again; more fool him. "That's my point—these people are *nuts*, Beth. We can't stay here. Let's get a hotel room until we figure out what—"

"*No.* Get it through your head: I will *never* run, not from them, and not from—"

Lizzie suddenly yelled, and Daniel stood up fast and put his hand in his pocket. Beth rolled her eyes as she heard her daughter pound out of her room: "Yuck! No, Mr. Yoda! Bad dog!" Mr. Yoda barked. "Mommy, Daddy, Mr. Yoda pooped in my room again! It's gross!"

"Okay baby, hold on." Beth stood, but Daniel said, "I'll help her," and hustled out of the kitchen.

She plopped back down with a scowl; Rebecca and Mindy and *Alex*. What she hadn't told her husband was that she had met them all—or at least seen them.

After the redheaded skank had given Beth her green-eyed smirk for a minute, she had started the four-wheeler again and puttered away up the dirt track. She hadn't gone far when she was joined by her sisters; the blonde rode a four-wheeler around a building on the right, and the other stepped out from behind a building on the opposite side. All three were barefoot, and wore tee-shirts and frayed blue-jean cutoffs, like they were ready to serve at Slo Eddie's. They were certainly attractive enough to pull it off. The one on foot was the oldest, and her raven hair cascaded to mid-back; even from a distance, Beth could see that the promise of the girl in the newspaper photo had been fulfilled, and then some.

The dark-haired woman's appearance didn't bother her (although she wanted to drag *Alex* to Slo Eddie's so Tracy could see her), so much as how the three had acted: they hadn't said a word, or made any gestures; they'd only…watched her… while keeping their distance.

It's almost as if they were afraid of me, or at least leery.

Beth snorted, dismissing the thought once again; it was ludicrous. Oh, she'd had her Carson ready and waiting in its spot, of course, and her biggest kitchen knife shoved blade-first into the back of her shorts so that the wooden handle had stuck up along her spine under her shirt; and her second biggest reversed in her hand with the blade hidden along her forearm; and her third biggest waiting in the passenger seat of her Nissan—but the women couldn't have known any of that.

So what had they been afraid of?

After two or three minutes of silently staring while she yelled that she wanted to talk to their father, they'd simply left, the blonde and redhead riding off, and the raven-haired beauty vanishing around a corner; there'd never been any sign of McFarlane, the man she'd gone to confront.

Daniel was right.

They had *ignored* her.

Beth had been so furious that she'd thought about ramming the Nissan through the gate. Let's see them ignore her then! But she hadn't wanted to damage her car, so she'd just fumed for a minute, flew the bird at the farm in general and everyone hiding from her inside it in particular, and then spun dirt and rocks as she drove away.

And then to top it all off when she'd arrived home after being ignored she'd found the not-so-lovely Ms. Jenifer Hayden of the Rutherford County Child Services waiting for her—and most definitely *not* ignoring her! This time Ms. Hayden was by herself, and when Beth had finally gotten rid of the snooty, judgmental bitch and tried to unwind in a much-deserved bath the cops had come pounding on the castle's front door saying her husband had called 911 and said she could be in danger so she'd had to stand in the stupid foyer wrapped in a towel with ten cops ogling her until she'd convinced them she was fine and that it was a false alarm!

Beth heard a toilet flush and then Lizzie chattering as they came down the stairs; she stopped rubbing her neck and took a deep breath and turned her chair to face the kitchen and fixed a smile upon her face. She heard Daniel say, "It's late, ask your mom if it's okay," and then her daughter bounced into the kitchen.

"Hi Mommy!" Mr. Yoda followed, tongue lolling and toenails clicking. Daniel came last, and he froze when he caught the look she threw him.

Passing the buck! "Hi, baby. Did you guys get the yuck cleaned up?" Mr. Yoda trotted straight for his water and food bowls; reloading for his blitzkrieg on Beth's floors.

Lizzie made a face. "Daddy made me pick it up 'cause Mr. Yoda is my doggie and I have to take sponsability. I used *lots* of toilet paper. It was so gross!"

"I'm proud of you, baby."

"Can I watch my new *Star Wars* movie?"

"It's after nine-thirty, you and your daddy can watch it tomorrow night." Beth would be at work, thank goodness.

"Please, Mommy? *Pleasepleasepleasepleasepleaseplease?*"

Beth was too worn-out to argue. "All right."

"Yay!"

"But only until ten-thirty. You can finish the rest tomorrow."

"Okay!" Lizzie threw her arms around Beth's neck and gave her smooches; she smelled like little girl and green-apple shampoo and dog. Then she shot toward the living room. "I'll start it!"

Beth glared at her husband. "Thanks for making *me* the bad guy."

"Hey, I'm going back to work in the morning, remember? You guys can sleep in." He got a worried look, and Beth's temper grew spikes; she knew what he was thinking: they would be here alone, without *him* to protect them! Any second now he would start that crap about getting a hotel room again; Beth didn't know whether she'd scream or kick him in the jaw or both.

"I wish you'd reconsider about the hotel room. I know you think it's running, but think of it as doing the smart thing. There are six of them, Beth—six I know of—and if that asshole sends them all, I don't think the cops can get here in time. What about Lizzie? What if they hurt her?"

"Then I'd kill them. *And* John McFarlane."

He stared at her. "Yeah, well, I guess so, but I still think we should—"

Beth was *so* tired of this subject; it was time to go on the attack. "Do you still intend to go traipsing through the woods in the middle of the night to stare at graves?"

"Yeah, Saturday night, like we planned. Why? Did you change your mind about going? It's okay if you don't want—"

"I'm going. In fact, after hearing about how the cemetery has changed, I'm looking forward to it. Have you ever heard of a maker's mark?"

"The whiskey? Sure, it's good stuff, but I don't see what—"

"Not the whiskey, the marks on gravestones that monument masons put on them to identify their work."

"No…although I suppose it makes sense; those things are expensive, so there's probably some trade group—"

Beth kept attacking; give him a toehold, and she'd have to listen to more of his drivel. "I don't buy this stuff about vanishing people, but don't you think it odd they would revamp the cemetery? I've heard of restoring old headstones, or even replacing them when they wear out or break, but if what your paranoid cop buddy said is right, that place underwent a complete transformation. Why bother, especially if no one is using it anymore?"

"That is strange, but—"

"Yes it is, Daniel, *very* strange, and if I discover maker's marks, we could find the mason and ask him—or her—some questions. I also want to take down names, see what I can find out about them, maybe even talk to the families. *That's* why I'm going. And to keep you out of trouble."

He gave her a wry look, then sat across from her. "Whatever the reason, I'm glad."

"The movie's starting!"

"We'll be there in a minute, baby! Mommy and Daddy are talking!"

"Okay!"

Beth said, "She won't even realize we're not there once it starts."

"Yeah, I know. Look, doing the smart thing isn't running, and it would just be for—"

Keep attacking. "And since we'll already be out there, I want to get a look at that sinkhole."

"Are you ever going to let me finish a goddamn sentence? You said something about a sinkhole last night, but what's a fucking sinkhole got to do with—where are you going?"

Beth sat down in the computer chair and clicked onto the net. "Remember that foggy, circular clearing in the center of the valley?"

"Yeah."

"It's not a clearing. It's a cenote."

"A say-what-tay?"

"Say-*no*-tay. It's Spanish for 'big hole', I think. That stream we crossed to get to the cemetery drains into the cenote and makes a waterfall, which explains the mist that won't burn off."

He came over to the computer desk. "How'd you find this out?"

"I figured if we're really going to do this idiot thing, somebody should be smart and scout a little first."

Daniel moved close and stood by her shoulder; Beth scooted further into the desk. He stepped back. She found Tennessee and then Centerville and then the castle and then McFarlane's farm and then the valley. She centered it over the cemetery and rolled the view down to max magnification; the megalith was an ugly dark lump at the top of the hill.

"Barron Cemetery."

"I see it."

She dragged the overhead satellite view along the ruts that led from the north side of the cemetery's knoll and stopped when she got to the circular clearing; blaster bolts and the dramatic music blaring from the living room were nearly drowned out by an angry warble from Chewbacca.

"Lizzie, that's too loud! Turn it down!"

"Yes, ma'am!" The volume decreased. Beth wasn't going to *listen* to the stupid movie, either.

Daniel put his face close to the screen. "Son of a bitch, that thing's *huge!* There's fucking trees growing right down in it!" His finger traced the stream to where it dumped into the cenote; his eyes narrowed, and he leaned closer. "There's something at the center." He reached for the mouse, and his hand enveloped hers, so warm; he jerked back like her touch burned.

She wouldn't cry. "Here." Beth pushed the mouse toward him.

She would *not* cry!

He didn't look at her as he manipulated the satellite view; after a few seconds he said, "There *is* something down there. It's hard to make out because of all the trees, but I think it's a perfect circle, just like the sinkhole. This is so fucking *weird*. What the hell *is* that thing?"

Beth couldn't stand it anymore; she rolled the chair away and stood up. "Maybe we can find out Saturday night." She wiped at her cheeks.

He looked at her uncomfortably and then straightened and took a step toward her. "Beth…"

She raised a hand, and he stopped. "I have three things to say, Daniel, and then I will finish my bath—the one the police interrupted."

His voice was soft. "Okay."

"When I got back from being *ignored*, that lady from child services, Jenifer Hayden, was waiting in the driveway."

"Shit."

Beth told him how she'd let Ms. Hayden paw through their house again, and how the esteemed Ms. Hayden was obviously disappointed by not finding it dirty, or perhaps a new meth lab in the downstairs bathroom; she didn't mention it was everything she could do not to put the sanctimonious woman face-down on the floor in a nasty wrist lock.

"She was alone this time, but when I picked Lizzie up from daycare I found out from Miss Mary that the nosy bitch had been by this morning asking if Lizzie had ever showed bruises, or if she was ever dirty or hungry."

"Motherfuckers. Well, you said they'd have to check everything. Mary told her we don't abuse Lizzie, right?"

"Of course, but Ms. Hayden and I didn't exactly get off on the right foot the other day, Daniel, and I don't think she's going away no matter what anyone tells her. She doesn't like me."

"That's hard to imagine."

Beth glared, but she let that slide—for now. "Where I'm going with this is, we may have to hire one of those smart and nasty lawyers after all."

"If we do, we do. We'll cross that bridge when."

"Fine. Second, we made a mistake by only using one reporter. I want to use *all* of them to back McFarlane off." She took a deep breath; this would put Beth's family under the hot spotlight again, but it had to be done. "We'll call a press conference next week and tell the world about Rison, and about how McFarlane's threatening us. Brennan's story will be out by then and it'll give credence to what we say."

He gaped, and then spluttered, "Didn't you listen? This guy is *loaded!* If we go accusing him with no proof, the asshole will drown us in lawyers!" His laugh was wild. "Forget running us out, he can just sue us right off the fucking planet!"

"Stop yelling at me!"

"Talk to Scandlin. If he thinks it's a good idea, I'll go along. Hell, he may even help us."

"We have to do it soon, while the press still wants to hear what we have to say—and I *will* do this, Daniel, I don't care what some *Special Agent* says." Beth knew he was right, though; she wasn't about to admit it, however.

He retrieved his phone from the table and tried to hand it to her. "Call him. He's a good guy—for a cop, anyway—and he hates McFarlane more than we ever could, trust me." He shook the phone. "*Call* him."

Beth sighed, then pulled her own phone out. "All right, but not tonight; I'll talk to him tomorrow. Give me his number." Daniel seemed happy with that as he rattled it off.

Then he said, "There's something else we need to talk about. I wasn't going to say anything until I did some calling around tomorrow, but—"

Beth slowly held up three fingers.

His scowl was impressive. "I'm waiting with bated breath for number three, dear."

She crossed her arms under her breasts and stalked over to the French doors and looked into the backyard; that nasty wrist lock would work on him, too. The hum of a light saber and a trill from R2D2 wafted from the living room.

How to make him understand? "Do you remember growing up with your mom and dad and brother, safe and warm in your very own house?"

He sighed. "I know you didn't—"

Beth spun on him. "Shut up, I want to say this. I *need* to say this."

"All right."

"I didn't grow up like that. I've lived in someone else's home my whole life, Daniel, moving from place to place, family to family; just visiting. Even when I was grown and on my own, I rented. Oh, I thought about buying a little house and fixing it up, just to say it was mine." Beth had done more than think about it; she'd planned it out twice, but it had never made enough financial sense to pull the trigger. "But now I have a home." The wonder of it filled her anew, and she brushed her fingertips across the door jamb. "My very own home; not my host family's; not my landlord's. Mine. And I know the castle is too much for us, and that this was an investment, and that someday we'll sell it and move on…" Beth took a step toward him, jabbing a finger, "but I *will not* let some jumped-up farmer *order* me out of my own home! I won't run, Daniel, not from him, not from anybody! Do you understand?" That smile was infuriating! "*What?*"

"You just reminded me of something, that's all." His blue eyes were soft on her. "I get it, we won't run. We'll back him off. Somehow." Then his grin popped out, the one Beth had always liked. "I'm digging this press-conference idea, too. Maybe we'll give the old fart an ulcer."

Perhaps he *did* understand…her Daniel was watching her. Beth watched him back. He stepped closer and reached a hand toward her face, slow, and she wanted him to touch her, to kiss her, to hold her, so much that it hurt.

His hand floated there between them…and then fell to his side.

Beth walked away.

"Have you heard from Brennan today?"

She stopped at the bottom of the stairs, but didn't turn around. "He hasn't returned my calls."

"I tried to call him, like you said he wanted, but he never answered."

She waited, but Daniel said nothing else so she went on up. Beth had decided that the reporter didn't matter because she'd gotten what she'd wanted from him; Brennan's story would reveal McFarlane for the trash he was, and her press conference would drive the final nail; the world's eyes would focus on the old farmer, and he wouldn't be able to follow through on his threats against her family. Mission accomplished. Oh, it stung that Brennan had used her and was now avoiding her, but she could live with it.

He just better hope he never crossed her path again.

She passed the blood-splotched mattress and box spring, locked the door, ran the water, dropped in her favorite lavender beads and lit all her candles, put her biggest, fluffiest towel out, stripped, turned on the jets, and settled into the scalding, bubbling water with a sigh.

Then the tears came. Beth sat forward and hugged her breasts to her thighs, rocking and sobbing.

How can we stay married if we can't even touch each other?

She wanted so much for him to hold her, but he wouldn't, or couldn't, and for some reason she couldn't reach out to him.

Scott Rison had caused this…

Her tears dried in a sudden and sudsy fury.

No. Rison hadn't caused this. It was the man he worked for, McFarlane.

He was the cause.

Beth leaned back and let the hot water embrace her body. John McFarlane thought he could get anything he wanted, push people any *way* he wanted; and if what this Special Agent had told Daniel was true, the man was also a murderer. McFarlane's daughters, and this Melissa Bane, and the people who had disappeared… ·could this supposed Keeper and those girls truly be responsible?

Beth dismissed the thought with a wet snort. It was crazy. In fact, this whole business with the cemetery was utterly insane—and now, thanks to this crackpot TBI agent, her stubborn idiot of a husband was now even *more* fixated on it!

It's just a stupid cemetery!

She had to make him see reason somehow…Beth tried to relax, sinking deeper into the swirling water…maybe after they had tramped around out there and he saw the place wasn't anything special, they could move on…yes…stay calm, keep trucking…tomorrow night she went back to work, and Terrance would be there, so she could let him handle everything while she barricaded herself in her office and called this oh-so-Special Agent Scandlin…she would express condolences about his wife, but then she would tell the man to quit filling her husband's head with garbage, there was enough crap up there already…and on Saturday, Janet would pick Lizzie up to watch her so they could talk before they went for their idiotic hike…

Dread filled Beth, and water sloshed as she sat up again.

She'd wanted this talk, *fought* for this talk, but what if he couldn't handle what she'd been? What she'd done?

What if he leaves me?

Beth relaxed into the water once more; she was too exhausted to think about all that; besides, it was too late to turn back now. Calm. Trucking. She would deal with his reaction Saturday night, whatever it was, and then they would go look at the stupid cemetery in the dark, and then they would hold the press conference next week and back McFarlane off, and then their lives would finally return to normal.

Normal? How will we ever sleep in that bedroom again, let alone make love there? Even when we get a new bed, how?

Beth grimaced. McFarlane. *He* was who she needed to focus on, not future beds or haunted bedrooms or even making love to Daniel. McFarlane was the one threatening her family. McFarlane was the one ordering her out of her own home.

John McFarlane, this man who wouldn't face her today; John McFarlane, this *coward* she'd never seen in person, but whose arrogance was spinning her world like a top.

John McFarlane, the man who had decided to set himself against them because he didn't like their *house!*

Well, other people could decide things, too. Everyone had to decide to share their oxygen with each other every single day, for instance; friends, family, or complete strangers, it didn't matter: they all had to decide to share. But if McFarlane didn't heed the warning of her press conference, if he continued to threaten her family…

Beth closed her eyes as lassitude crept over her. She would have to make a decision concerning her oxygen, and whether she was still willing to share it with John McFarlane.

She would have to make that decision soon.

HEART

D AN PULLED the receiver away from his ear, looked at it, and then threw it back into the cradle.

People are crazy. It's not just McFarlane and his sluts; the whole damn planet is bug-fuck.

Steve stopped typing and peeked around his monitor. "What's up?"

Their desks were pushed together facing each other at the back of the communal agent's room, up against the wall by the emergency exit; they had both agreed it was a good location in case of fire, or if a client incensed over forking out eight percent strolled through the front door and opened up with an AR-15, or for the day Irene inevitably exploded, sending Irene-juice splattering everywhere.

Steve was waving a meaty hand. "Earth to Dan."

"What?"

"You look like somebody just shit in your Cheerios."

"That was the Jacksonville whale."

"Yeah?" Steve's cynical eyes sparked with interest as he dug around in a drawer before pulling out a King-Sized Snickers. He peeled it like a banana. "Think he's for real?"

Dan shrugged. "He talks big, but you know." Many acted like they had the juice, but when they got to the table, most didn't even have the down payment; talk was just that, talk.

Steve chewed and swallowed before responding—thankfully. "They always do."

"He's supposedly coming up in two weeks and bringing the wifey to look at houses; their son and daughter go to MTSU, and they want to be closer. Separation anxiety. Guy's talking five-bed four-hole min so little miss and little junior can stay over. He also wants to tour lots. He's looking to expand his tractor and farm-supply business into Tennessee, says he's already got seven locations spread across northern and central Florida and lower Georgia. Supposedly."

"Little miss and little junior are gonna love that."

"Yep." Nothing like getting that taste of freedom and then having Mom and Dad crawl back up your butt.

Steve polished off the candy bar and wadded the wrapper and chunked it toward the trashcan; he missed by two feet. "I tried to tell the guy I could take care of him, but he wanted you." Steve shook his wide head, unapologetic at his attempt to steal Dan's business. "Being famous is hell."

"I suppose. He also wants to take us out to dinner so the wifey can meet—and this is a direct quote—'the little lady who did for that sicko Rison'. Says we're good, solid Americans, the kind he likes to do business with. And he wants to see the house." Dan lowered his voice. "He'll probably ask for a tour of my fucking bedroom."

"One of those, huh?"

"One of those."

"You gonna show it to him?"

"If he has the green, you bet your ass."

Their laughter cut short when Victoria clacked up in her two-inch heels. "Welcome back, Dan. I was so sorry to hear what happened. Are, um, are your wife and daughter doing all right?"

Steve said, "Their names are Beth and Lizzie, Vicks."

She shot him a glare. "I know their names, and I told you I prefer Vicky or Victoria."

Steve grinned and eyed her up and down. "Sorry about that, Vicks."

Victoria sniffed, then pinned her megawatt smile on Dan; her blonde hair fell past her shoulders in the latest carefully untidy fashion, and her makeup and clothes were faultless; two years older than Dan, Beth's age, Victoria Damon was a knockout. She wasn't just a showpiece, however; Victoria wielded her beauty and intelligence like twin machetes to carve what she wanted out of the world. The "Vickster"—her sobriquet around the office (never to her face)—was the top agent at Dalton-Reed Realty and had been since she'd jumped from Century 21 three years ago. Dan idly wondered what she was doing back here; Victoria rated her own office just down the hall from Irene's. He supposed she was out slumming, granting the little people their viewing.

Steve continued to eye her brazenly, and Dan was fighting his own grin—it was obvious the Vickster had forgotten Beth and Lizzie's names—when she reached out a perfect nail and traced the yellowing bruises around his eyes.

"Ooh, poor baby." She gave him a kiss on the cheek, her light, flowery perfume enveloping him as he got a glimpse of the most spectacular tan cleavage that money could buy; no freckles, though, point against her. She cupped his chin. "You let me know if there's anything I can do. Promise you will, Dan." Her smile got even warmer, and her big blue eyes widened; they made her seem innocent if you didn't know her.

"I will, Vicky. Promise."

She winked and clacked away, and despite knowing her game, Dan found his eyes lingering; in a slew of great features, Vicky's ass was the tops. Steve leaned into the aisle and watched until she vanished down the hall; the audience with the commons was over.

Steve straightened and gave a low whistle. "I'm tellin' ya, Danny boy, you need to cut that."

"Just one problem."

They looked at each other and spoke at the same time:

"Not enough money!"

They laughed; as much as Victoria liked to flirt, she preferred a certain type of gent, one that was both rich and married—and in that order. Dan was definitely not the first and most assuredly the second.

"Besides," he said, "If I did, Beth would sew us both up into the same sack and drop us in the river." Beth had met Victoria once. Dan shivered. Once had been enough; the Vickster had made a special point of flirting with him ever since.

Steve's laugh boomed. "She would, wouldn't she."

Dan sobered. Beth. He glanced at the clock on his monitor; it was almost eleven. She'd been home all morning by herself; he'd taken Lizzie to daycare, even though Beth had planned to keep her until she went to work this afternoon, and when Dan had explained *why* he'd wanted to do it that way, it had nearly started WW3. And his argument that there was no telling what McFarlane would do when the reports she was talking to Brennan hit the news wires had just made her even madder. But she had agreed, eventually; with no grace and a tight jaw, but eventually.

He pulled his iPhone out; no calls from Beth, or from Brennan, even though the man had told Beth he wanted Dan's part of the story. The reporter also wasn't responding to the message Dan had left him this morning—*two* messages! Well, if Brennan still wanted to talk, he could call and ask nicely. Dan might even answer his phone when he did. *Might.*

And it wasn't just Brennan: they had figured the media would descend on Dan again when it became known that Beth was talking, hoping he'd changed his mind as well, but nada; even the four showings this morning had all been actual, honest-to-God, credit-worthy buyers.

Where are all the goddamn reporters?

"Hey."

"What?"

"Have you, uh, heard anything this morning?"

Steve poked one eye around his monitor. "Heard anything about what?"

"Never mind." If he had, Dan wouldn't have had to ask. Steve gave him a strange look, but then his desk phone rang and he grabbed it up. "Dalton-Reed Realty, you've been blessed with talkin' to Steve, how may I help you?"

Dan went online, and it took about ten seconds to figure out it hadn't leaked that Beth was talking to Brennan; there were only old stories about the assault, and one posted yesterday on the so-far fruitless search of Center Hill Lake up in Decalb County for the still-missing young woman, Lisa Rene Stalls. Dan double-clicked on Scott Rison's teenage mug shot, maxed it until it filled the screen, stared into those unforgiving blue eyes, and then clicked it away.

Fucker. Rot in hell.

Maybe Beth had misunderstood about when and what would leak; maybe Brennan had experienced a change of heart and had done a story on little-old ladies baking cookies to benefit orphans instead. Sure. Dan glanced at his iPhone again;

he itched to check on Beth, but his wife had pulled him out of their daughter's earshot this morning and made it clear what would happen if he did. So yeah, he could call her, but then he'd have to be satisfied with humping his right hand for the foreseeable forever.

Dan decided not to call.

And then there were all the other people Dan had expected to hear from by now: he'd left a message first thing this morning at River Valley Bank and Trust for Rickson Aldridge to call Dan back a.s.a.p., but the receptionist had said Mr. Aldridge would be in meetings most of the morning…and now most of the morning was toast, but still no Rick. Dan had also finally remembered the math prick's name: Hottson, Chadwick Hottson. *Sounds like some kinda wannabe Ivy League douche bag.* After he'd dialed the MTSU main number and got connected to Math Boy's office, some woman had answered, and when Dan asked to speak to Professor Hottson, she'd sounded hesitant, saying Professor Hottson wasn't in, but she could take a message. Dan had obliged her, but Math Boy hadn't called him back yet. Dan had also called Professor Hameed's office six times, but just got voicemail, and Hameed's cell had gone straight to messages, like it was turned off or out of charge.

Still. Just like Brennan's.

Dan grimaced. He would give Hameed 'till Monday to make contact, and then he was sending the pics to some bighead at the Field Museum of Natural History in Chicago; with the circus that would spring up after their press conference added to the stir Brennan's eventual story would cause, Dan figured he'd have no problem getting a brain to tell him what that writing said. That's all he wanted, damn it.

Wait. Cell phones. Dan dug in his card file for five minutes; he had every business card on the planet except the one he was looking for. He searched the drawers, but came up empty; he must've taken it home. "Yo."

"What?" Another wrapper sat peeled and empty on Steve's desk, dark bits of chocolate clinging to the pearly inside like grateful refugees.

"You got Call-Me-Rick's card? I need his cell."

"Hold on." Steve rummaged and then held out a crisp cream card scissored between two fingers. "Here."

Dan stood up and took it. "Thanks."

"No problem. Whaddaya wanna talk to that asshole for?"

"The usual," Dan lied. He sat back down and snatched the desk phone from its cradle and punched numbers.

"Ah. Well, tell Rick I said hi and to go fuck himself."

"I will."

"Thanks."

Dan listened to it ring, and then Rick's smooth voice informed Dan that Rick was unable to grace Dan's call with an actual presence, but nevertheless it was important to him, so please leave a message. He repeated his call-me-a.s.a.p. from this morning and then hung up and checked the time; eleven-twenty. Dan had only been in the office an hour, but it felt like a month. Besides, he wanted to talk to

James Fulbright today; he wasn't sure the guy would breathe much longer, so time was of the essence.

Dan collected his phone and keys and stood. "You wanna grab some lunch and check out the new truck?"

The candy bar wrapper was still on the desk, and its mate was still crumpled on the floor two feet from the trashcan, but Steve looked up with interest. "Where ya goin'?"

"I was just gonna grab drive-thru somewhere on the way to, uh, to Rolling Heights…" Dan realized too late he'd stepped in it.

Steve leaned back, chair squeaking in protest. "You never told me why you wanted to talk to that mean old fart."

"It's, uh, about the pool." *Shit.*

"You don't have a pool."

"It's, um, it's about where they were going to put it in the backyard, you know, when they first built the place. We were thinking of dropping one in, and I can't find the original plans…"

"Uh huh."

Dan sighed. "It's not about the pool."

"I picked up on that."

"It's…well, it's complicated. There's a lot going on between Beth and me, you know, after what happened."

Steve suddenly wouldn't meet Dan's eyes; he cleared his throat. "I bet, man, I bet. Hey, you go talk to Fulbright and count me out for lunch." He made a face. "Amy's got me on this new goddamn diet, anyway. You believe that shit? Woman's six-months pregnant and hooverin' up everything in sight, and she wants *me* on a fuckin' diet."

Dan raised both eyebrows and made a point of staring at the wrapper. "What?" Steve looked down at it and then back up at Dan. "It's true!" He reached into his desk and pulled out a Tupperware container with a dark-green lid and opened it and showed Dan a scattering of lettuce leaves with some tomato wedges and slivers of hard-boiled egg and three croutons on the side. There was no dressing. "See?"

"Yum."

Steve rolled over and dumped it in the trashcan. "Mmmm, that was tasty. Can't wait to see what she packs tomorrow." He put the Tupperware back in the desk and dug out another King-Size Snickers before slamming the drawer closed; he must have a box of the things in there.

Dan laughed, then walked out to his truck thinking about what he wanted to eat and how bad the traffic would be during the lunch rush and how long it would take him to drive across town because of it.

He just hoped Fulbright didn't croak before he got there.

Beth spent her Friday morning cleaning the kitchen and bathrooms—and, of course, doing laundry.

She'd never thought much about laundry when she was single, even when she'd had that crappy little apartment and she'd had to haul everything down to the coin mat and back. But now, with a family, their laundry somehow multiplied by a factor that was greater than the number of people in said family; Beth wouldn't be surprised if she looked right now and saw clothes magically piled in the basket she'd just emptied! If she ever got rich, she was going to hire someone to do her laundry; she would clean the rest of her house, they'd just have to do her laundry.

Every. Stinking. Day.

When Beth finally got their clothes put away, it was after nine o'clock; she pulled her phone out of her pocket and frowned at it. She'd been expecting it to blow up by now, and to have to chase at least one camera crew out of her driveway, but nothing. Beth glanced out the front windows; perhaps there was other news happening out in the wide world. She wouldn't know; she didn't have the TV or the radio on and hadn't been online. The castle was peaceful this morning; she'd only had the chirping of birds and the mooing of cows and the occasional passing car for company—and Mr. Yoda, who looked lost without Lizzie.

Where is everybody?

Beth decided to enjoy the peace while it lasted; the media would get around to her little family all too soon.

She changed into her work-out clothes and retrieved her bokken, and then Mr. Yoda followed her out into the backyard and watched as she worked both sword kata she needed to demonstrate for her upcoming test, flowing across the grass, smooth in her footwork, fierce in her cuts, imagining real opponents; it was easy enough to come up with faces for those. A distant part of her mind noted the dog now over by the fence, moving in a tight circle, butt tucked under as he strained; he was doing his business somewhere besides her carpet.

Amazing.

Beth finished with the weapon and then flowed into her empty-hand forms, spinning and striking back and forth across the grass; she'd been at it for over twenty minutes with no break, but she didn't pause before she launched into push-ups, crunches, squats, lunges, mountain climbers, and jumping jacks, straining her muscles and breathing deep into her *itten* for energy; an enemy wouldn't let her stop to rest, so she didn't either. The dog eyed her while panting in the shade under Lizzie's slide, most likely thinking humans were insane.

When she finished she bowed, hands pressed together between her breasts, and then toweled off while staring at the silent cell phone on the patio table; no calls all morning, not even from Daniel. While that was gratifying—her husband had heeded her warning, as she'd thought he might—the silence bothered her; even so, Beth decided to put it out of her mind until she'd finished her workout.

Here and Now.

"C'mon, Mr. Yoda." The little dog followed her in with a grateful wag and trotted straight for his water bowl as she went into the living room to stretch; standing routine first, a series of movements to loosen her from neck to ankles, and then floor-work.

Mr. Yoda finished rearming and came in to watch, plopping himself in the corner by the fireplace, chin on paws. After stretching, Beth sat Zazen with feet tucked under her in seiza, counting her breaths in the still house until her mind was a calm pool; she even forgot about the dog staring at her. When she'd showered, changed, and was standing in the kitchen eating a nonfat-blueberry yogurt, Beth thought about the phone and its silence again; she picked it up to make sure it was on and had a signal. Check, check.

Where the heck *was* everyone?

Beth gave in and sat down at the computer and soon discovered no one knew she was talking to Brennan. She swiveled back and forth and thought about that; the reporter's wish to build suspense before Sunday's big story hadn't happened, obviously—not yet, anyway. He'd said Friday, but he hadn't specified a *time* Friday, so maybe it would be later this afternoon or this evening. Ultimately, she knew, it didn't matter: as long as the truth about Rison and McFarlane came out before their press conference next week, her plan would still work.

So now what?

Beth tapped her lips with a finger; she didn't have to be at work until five…

She retrieved her books from the car with a grin, made tea, and was strolling down the teeming sidewalks of New York City with Repairman Jack again when she heard a powerful motor rev out on Daisy. She folded a corner to mark her place, hopped off the couch, went to the window, and beheld a red Mustang sitting in the road in front of her house. The passenger window was toward the castle, and Beth couldn't see through the dark tint, but a glimpse of copper hair through the windshield made her smile.

"Well, well, well."

She opened the front door and walked out onto the porch. Beth could see shadows moving behind the tint, so she knew there were others besides the redhead in there—her sisters, maybe? Beth could only hope. The motor screamed, and the Mustang squalled forward before braking to a stop, tire smoke billowing.

"I'm impressed!" she yelled. "Why don't you come over here and we'll discuss how impressed I am!" Beth had her Carson on her, as always, but she wouldn't need it for these bitches.

The Mustang abruptly roared off down the road towards Helen's, and smoke wafted into Beth's yard, bringing the smell of burnt rubber. She gave the retreating red car her middle finger and went back in; if they came back, maybe they'd be dumb enough to get out if she hid in the house.

Beth soooooooo wanted those girls to get out and play with her.

Then Mr. Yoda began barking furiously, so she threw both new deadbolts before dashing across the castle. She found him in the dining room trying to eat through the French door.

"What's wrong, boy?"

The sound of heavy machinery brought her head up; a large truck with a square cab and a round tank, like a gasoline tanker except shorter and much dirtier, was trundling along on the other side of her fence; a nozzle poked out of the back of the tank, and liquid sprayed from that nozzle in a wide fan.

Beth opened the door, and the raw reek of ammonia slapped her in the face; the rumble and squeak of the truck almost masked mens' coarse laughter as Mr. Yoda darted past her ankles to the fence, keeping pace with the tanker, snarling and barking; brown liquid seeped between the cracks and ran down the inside, streaking the wood.

"Oh, I don't think so!"

The tanker finished with the back and turned towards the far corner of the house as Beth darted to the side gate, yanked it open with a squeal, ran through, slammed it with a clang, and then sprinted along the wide alley between her property and the tall, green corn next field over. She was barefoot, and she had to keep a careful distance from her beautiful fence because the stinking brown liquid coated the grass along with the outside of the boards.

They were spraying *shit* on her *fence!*

She came around the corner at full speed and saw the tanker just making the wide turn out into the field, done with its nasty task. Two men were in the cab; the one driving wore a dirty white-and-green John Deere ball cap. They saw her coming and stopped, idling and rattling, saying something to each other and laughing. Beth ran up and planted herself in front of the bumper; the smell coming off the tanker was like a physical blow, but she ignored it while glaring up at the men with her fists planted on her hips.

She raised her voice over the clattering motor. "I think you got something on my fence!"

The driver leaned out his open window. "Yeah, oops, sorry 'bout that! We was just fertalizen' 'n got a little close! My apologies, ma'am!" They both laughed uproariously at that, and John Deere leaned back in the cab and high-fived his buddy.

"No harm done! I'll just hook up my hose and you boys can clean it off! Won't take but a few minutes!"

The laughter cut off. They looked at each other. They looked at her. They looked at each other again, and then the passenger leaned forward, as if to see her better through the grimy windshield; he wore five-dollar sunglasses above a week's growth of golden scruff, and the shag of blonde hair on his head looked like it'd been washed the day before the tanker.

He spit out his window. "We ain't cleanin' nothin', bitch!"

"Now that's not nice! Tell you what! If you clean it off, I'll let bygones be bygones! If not, then I'll have to do something about it!"

Mr. Yoda continued to yap hell on the other side of the fence, sounding bigger than he was as the two men exchanged another look, and then the scruffy blond cursed and violently threw open his door. Green hat grabbed his arm, gesturing toward Beth, arguing, but goldie shook him off and hopped out, leaving his door open. The driver yelled, "Goddamnit, Tommy, you heard what John said! Git back in here! We'll just drive around 'er!"

"Shut it, Zack! I ain't takin' no shit from no bitch, and that includes you!" Tommy came around the front and stopped, then grinned and gave her the slow-eye up and down; he was shorter than Daniel, but not by much, and he wore scuffed work boots topped by faded and ripped jeans and a stained white tee-shirt with the sleeves cut off; hard, tan muscles etched with crude tattoos flexed as he hooked his thumbs in his front pockets and leaned back on one heel. "Well, ain't you the feisty bit. I think you ain't gonna do a damn thing, little girl. I think you'd best skedaddle back inside your fence there before I put you over it."

Beth didn't bother to answer; she only stood still and waited.

His cocky grin wilted. "Don't listen so good, huh? You got 'bout five seconds before I teach you a lesson."

"You're gonna git us in fuckin' trouble! Git back in here!"

"Shut up!" Tommy raised a calloused finger. "One."

Beth held up two fingers. "Two."

He blinked and dropped his hand.

She added another one. "Three."

"Why you little…!"

"God damn it, Tommy!"

"Four and five," Beth said, completing the hand.

Tommy's face contorted, and then he lunged, trying to grab and dominate. Beth waited until the last instant and then slapped his hands to the inside, pivoting and driving the point of her left elbow into his temple. Tommy's cheap shades flew off as he staggered and cursed, and then he turned and lunged for her again, this time seizing a handful of tee-shirt with his left as his right balled up to hit. She trapped the left against her shoulder and dropped her center forward, letting the right flash past her ear.

There was a crunch, and Tommy screamed and fell to his knees, cradling his ruined wrist against his chest. He opened his mouth to scream again, and Beth drove her knee into his face; there was a louder crunch, and blood splattered her legs and feet as Tommy slumped to the grass, out cold.

So much for muscle.

"The fuckin' hell?" Zack scrambled out of the cab and stared at Tommy. "I'll be goddamned!" He took off his dirty John Deere cap, scratched his head, and then yanked it back on; he was bigger that his unconscious friend.

Beth stood still and waited.

Zack took an angry step towards her, glanced at Tommy again, and then stopped with an uncertain expression.

"I'll go get that hose for you."

"Fuck you, lady, I ain't cleanin' any goddamn—" Beth moved toward him, and he backed away. "John told us to freshen the fence, and nothin' else." He circled wide around her, wary, and toed Tommy, who groaned and stirred. "Damn, you fucked him up good." Zack laughed. "Tough guy, huh? Got yer lunch handed to ya by a *woman*. He ain't never gonna live this shit down."

Tommy suddenly sat up, and then stood, quick to his feet. He winced and cradled his wrist, then reached up and touched his swelling nose with his good hand, fingers coming away red. He stared at them and then shifted that stare to Beth; his eyes were like a mad bull's. He reached into his back pocket and flicked out a lock-blade; it looked like a Buck knockoff.

"I'm gonna carve you a new asshole, bitch, and then I'm gonna fuck it."

Beth didn't show Tommy her Carson, not yet; when she did, it would be too late for poor Tommy. She only stood still and waited.

Zack raised his hands high and backed away. "You're a dumb shit, man, you heard what John said. Fuck abuncha this." He climbed into the tall cab and slammed the door; the engine clattered, and the stinky tanker reversed across the field.

Tommy watched it go and then cursed and put those bull eyes back on her. He pointed the knife at her heart. "This ain't over, slut. You'll be seein' me again." Zack ground into gear, and Tommy took off, snatching up his cheap shades and closing his cheaper knife before he climbed in the cab one-handed and banged the door shut. They rumbled away across the field, scattering cows; Beth could see the men watching her in the big wing-mirrors, and when the tanker stopped, she wasn't surprised.

Zack stuck his grimy green-and-white hat out the window, forty yards of courage in his voice: "If yer smart, you'll do as the man says and clear out by the first!"

Beth showed him her middle finger.

"Bitch!" He ducked back, the engine gave a roaring clatter, and then they bounced across the field and over the rise; suddenly she found herself alone with the herd of red-on-white cows that had stood in a clump and watched the whole thing with cud-chewing aplomb.

"Well," she told them. "That was fun."

For some reason, Beth felt better than she had in days. She rubbed the sore spot on her right knee; it was a good reminder: faces were *so* much harder than a heavy bag. She turned to survey her fence; she hadn't gotten them to clean it, but she wasn't *too* disappointed, considering. Mr. Yoda whined from the other side.

"It's okay, boy, you did fine. Good dog." He barked. Mr. Yoda fit right in with their little family, Beth decided then; he was as big as a sneeze and crapped on her carpet, but he had heart, and heart was what counted.

Then she peered down at the blood dotting her shirt hem and shorts and sighed; more stupid laundry. Beth went back inside, cleaned Tommy's blood from her legs and feet, stripped, put her clothes in the sink with some presoak, changed into new clothes, added some socks and shoes, then opened the garage and went to the road to view the new black marks. She looked up and down Daisy, but no red mustang. Disappointed, Beth went around back and hooked her hoses together and washed her fence inside and out; it took almost an hour, and the ammonia reek lingered, but the smell didn't bother her.

She lived in farm country now.

Beth was curled on the couch with Jack and a fresh tea and still with two hours to kill before she had to get ready for work when she threw back her head and laughed.

If burning rubber and spraying crap on her fence was the best McFarlane had, then he was in a *lot* of trouble.

THE WAR TO END ALL WARS

INSPIRATION STRUCK as Dan was driving across Murfreesboro.

He'd been worried about whether they'd just let him walk in and talk to Fulbright; did you have to be family? He hoped not. Dan could claim to be a friend, or a coworker; that should work. Either case, he needed a prop that would ease his way in; hospice lube, so to speak. After hitting the Wendy's drive-thru, he stopped at the first florist he saw.

Fulbright was sick, and people brought flowers to sick people.

Simple.

Not so, it turned out.

The door chimed as he stepped in, and a woman with a Spanish accent called from the back, saying she'd be right with him. Dan waited in the center of a mass of flowers he couldn't name, breathing through his mouth because the combined weight of their scent was about to make him pass out, and realized he was at a complete loss. *What kind of flowers do you get for a guy, for Christ's sake?* And not only a guy, but somebody he'd met once, somebody he didn't particularly like, and somebody dying of stage-whatever pancreatic cancer; maybe this hadn't been much of an inspiration.

There was a rustle, and a bone-thin Latino woman appeared from the jungle, dark hair wound into a wispy ball on the back of her head. "May I help you?"

Dan told her he needed something for a friend who was sick, and with an eager smile she produced a wicker basket overflowing with unfamiliar red-and-orange flowers and little sprigs of green stuff sticking up all around and half a dozen shiny foil balloons floating on colored strings tied to the handle and it cost a hundred and fifteen dollars. He said his friend wasn't that sick. Her lips pressed together, but five minutes later Dan escaped the cloying shop only $14.99 plus tax poorer with a small brown plastic-weave basket containing exactly five yellow mystery flowers and one sprig of green stuff and one foil balloon on a stick that shouted GET WELL SOON.

When he got to Rolling Heights and parked, he looked at the balloon on its little stick, then pulled it out of the basket and threw it in the floorboard with the crumpled Wendy's sack. Dan wasn't sure, but telling someone who had stage-whatever cancer to "get well soon" maybe wasn't so cool. He took a last drag and stubbed his cigarette out in the portable ashtray he'd bought because the Tundra hadn't come with one for some fucking reason and grabbed the basket by the handle and locked the truck and walked toward the entrance.

He was almost there when R2D2 bleeped and whistled from his hip carrier. The doors slid open and two twenty-something brunettes wearing light-green scrubs passed him on their way to the parking lot, one unlimbering a pack of Camels and a red Bic lighter. The brunettes smiled; Dan smiled back and then pulled his phone out and checked the screen.

Call-Me-Rick had called him back. *Whaddaya know.* Dan moved to the side, staying just beneath the burgundy awning to escape the sun. "Rick, good to hear from ya."

"Dan, sorry it took so long to hit you back, been one of those mornings. Know what I mean, buddy?" Rick's easy laugh sounded then, but Dan didn't feel special; Rick was everyone's buddy. The bogus laugh wound down and Rick said, "What can I do for you? So sorry about that bad business out at the house, by the way. I left you a message on Monday but never heard back. How are Beth and Lizzie doing?"

"Good, they're good." Shit. He'd erased Rick's message without listening to the whole thing or thinking about it twice. "Thanks for calling, and, uh, sorry I didn't call you back, it's been hectic."

"I bet, buddy, I bet, and it's no sweat, glad everyone's okay. So, you back on the job?"

"As of today. Listen, I wanted to talk to you about our mortgage."

"Is there a problem?"

"Not exactly, I just had a question about—"

"Because if there is, I'm not the one you should speak to. We have a dedicated staff that can work with you to see if you're qualified to have your payments adjusted—"

"It's not—"

"—to something you can afford, although I must say you got quite the deal on that place—"

"We're fine with the payments." *For now.* "My question is about something else."

"Good to hear it. So what can I do for you, buddy?"

"Why did you offer the house to us? I mean before anyone else, before it came on the market. Why us?"

An office phone did a double-burr in the background, a woman's voice answering and saying the bank's name before Rick spoke: "What's this about, Dan? Are you guys unhappy out there? Let me state for the record that the deal you got was very sweet—very, *very* sweet—so sweet I had to pull more than a few strings to get you in at that price, so I don't understand what the problem is; if you're having trouble with the payments, we have a team who—"

"Rickson. Focus. Listen to my words. We're not having problems with the payment. What I want to know is, *why us?* There were any number of better-qualified people you could've gotten into that house; you said yourself we only did it with some generous math. So why us?"

"Dan, please, call me Rick. I don't know where this is coming from, and I don't appreciate the ingratitude I'm hearing here, buddy, but as to *why*, you said yourself last year—I remember it was on more than one occasion—that you were tired of renting and that you and Beth were looking for just the right place, one with profit potential. I'll be frank with you, buddy; we make each other money, and I was trying to do you a favor. If I may say so, I *did* do you a favor; you wouldn't have gotten it without my intervention. So if there's no problem with the payments, I don't understand or appreciate this line of questioning."

Dan grimaced. He'd handled this badly; time to smooth Call-Me-Rick back down. "You're right, I apologize. I'm just…it's been hard, these past few days. Beth and I…well, it's been hard."

"All right, buddy, I understand." Rick didn't *sound* like he understood, or mollified for that matter, but there you go. "I have another meeting starting in fifteen and I need to prepare my—"

"Hey, uh, almost forgot, I might have some people to send you; I'm waiting to hear from my seller, but I prequed the buyers and they look doable: two good jays, steady history, high sea-score. You'll like 'em, Rick."

It was a big fat lie; the buyers he'd taken offers from this morning already had financing—a nice change, that—but Dan needed an olive branch; he had another question, the most important one, and a good feeling Call-Me-Rick wouldn't like it much, either; he wanted Rick with his guard down when it landed.

Rick hesitated, but he sounded almost normal when he said, "Okay, buddy, that's good, let me know when—"

"How's John McFarlane doing these days?"

A solid quiet settled onto the line; when Rick finally answered, Dan almost checked the iPhone's speaker to see if little icicles were growing out of the tiny holes.

"I suppose he's doing fine, buddy, but I don't know for sure. I've only met the man twice."

He's lying. Dan would've bet the farm on it if he had one.

Rick said, still icy, "If I've answered your questions, I need to—"

"Did McFarlane have anything to do with us getting the house? Did he sign off on it?"

"Dan, buddy…where is this coming from? It's true River Valley Bank and Trust is owned by Barron Equity, and yes, it's also true John McFarlane is the CEO of The McFarlane Group, the principal partner in Barron Equity, but the man doesn't involve himself with our day-to-day operations—and as a general rule, the upper tiers of management do not concern themselves with transactions as *small* as yours."

"We're neighbors. Are you telling me McFarlane doesn't know his bank holds the paper on the house next door?"

"I…was aware of that, but it's hardly of note; John McFarlane is a pillar in the business community of Rutherford County, and through his holdings with Barron Equity, as well as various other entities, he has a financial stake in many properties."

"Has anyone ever told you you're full of shit, Rick?"

"Hey, buddy, I'll tell *you* what—since you're neighbors, why don't you do the neighborly thing and drop by and ask him? I look forward to hearing from your buyers. Good day, Dan." Call-Me-Rick hung up.

Dan pulled the phone away from his ear and looked at it. "Steve says hi and to go fuck yourself, *Rick*."

A well-dressed man and woman in their thirties frowned at him; the woman was tugging on the hand of a five or six-year-old little boy wearing a suit as the man pushed a dried-up old lady in a wheelchair under the burgundy awning and through the sliding doors and inside. Dan mumbled "sorry" as he put his phone away and followed them in.

Fuck Rick. He hadn't answered any of Dan's questions—or rather he'd *not* answered them and therefore answered them in a way—but maybe Fulbright would give him some straight answers. It would be a nice fucking change. If he knew anything. If he could still talk. If he was still alive; the way Dan's luck was running, the old bastard had keeled over while he was standing outside wasting breath and daylight with Rick. The little boy fighting the tug of his mom's hand looked utterly miserable.

I feel ya, kid.

Dan carried his basket to a circular reception counter parked Starfleet-style in the middle of the lobby; a vast woman with skin the color of pricey chocolate was sitting behind a command console and speaking into a telephone. When he stepped up, she lifted one cherry-red nail into the air without bothering to look at him, finished her conversation, and then hung up; a badge pinned to her light-green scrubs on the upslope of her colossal bust said C. WELLS. She eyed him and his basket and didn't appear impressed with either.

"Can I help you?"

"I'm here to visit James Fulbright."

She blinked eyelashes the size of mainsails. "James Fulbright?"

"Yeah, James Fulbright. Is there a problem?"

She considered the five yellow flowers again, still not much impressed. "Are you family?"

"No, ma'am, just a coworker. I heard about his diagnosis and thought I'd stop by, you know, give him my best." Dan tried to keep his face open and honest. *Maybe I should've practiced in the mirror.*

She rolled her chair over and picked up a clipboard holding a lined sheet and a red pen attached by a blue string. "Sign in, please." He did, feeling her watching him. "You say you're a coworker?"

"Yes, ma'am."

"Is anyone else gonna come see that poor man?"

"I'm the only one that's visited him?"

"Oh, you not the *only* one, honey. His son been here twice to bring his grand-kids by," she held up two red-nailed fingers, as if he couldn't figure out what two was without help, "but not one of his coworkers. It's heartbreakin', what it is." She waved a tree-trunk arm to Dan's right. "You go on down that hall and take the first left. He's the third door on the right…" She tilted her head to read, "Mr. Sims. Room 410." Suddenly she sighted down her finger like a rifle. "But don't you disturb that man if he's asleep! Mr. Fulbright needs his rest, and Miss Cherry's people're taken care of good roun' here! If he's asleep, you just put that somewhere and tip-toe on out, come back and visit some other time, or I'll give you somethin' all over to match those decorations you sportin'. Hear me?"

"Yes, ma'am." Jesus.

She lowered that finger and shook her head. "Um, um, um, heartbreakin'. Go on, now."

"Yes, ma'am."

He picked up the basket as she rolled over to another woman in light-green scrubs seated at an adjacent command console and said something; they looked at him, and then their laughter pealed forth, following him across the lobby. Heart-breaking. Miss Cherry was all busted up inside. He carried his basket of flowers down the hallway and left her to her misery.

Dan was mouth-breathing by the time he found 410. *Piss and cleanser mélange, nummy.* The door was open, but he knocked anyway and then stepped inside. James Fulbright lay propped in a hospital bed, shiny rails hemming him, tubes and wires trailing out of him, hooked to three expensive-looking machines that went ping; he also appeared to be asleep. *Shit.* A half-full colostomy bag hung from the side of the bed. Ick. Dan slunk past and sat the basket on an empty round wooden table that had two square chairs pushed under it and stared at what was left of James Fulbright.

The only other time he'd been this close was back in '06 at the Nashville Con-vention Center. James Fulbright had been the toast of the GNAR Awards that year, though Dan couldn't remember the award he'd received; probably Douche Bag of the Year. Fulbright had worked the giant room like a silver lion, glad-handing his way through his fellow real-estate assholes in his three-thousand-dollar suit, and Dan had shaken his hand when offered, introducing himself, but Fulbright's dark eyes had slid past him, and Dan had known the man had forgotten his name already.

He hadn't held it against him—well, not much—and Dan had continued to track Fulbright around the room; so had everyone else, not a few with glittering stares, but love or hate the guy, he'd made himself into what everyone in that room aspired to be: rich as snot. James Fulbright had been living the American dream by *building* the American dream, tract after tract. Of course that was back in the golden years, before the bubble had burst, dropping everyone into the yawning void beneath, Fulbright included. Dan included.

That silver lion was gone; the widow's peak was still there, but the slicked-back hair was now dull and sticking up in clumps, and the deep tan hard-earned on exclusive golf courses had turned into the yellowed, splotchy hide of an ailing old man. He was snoring with his mouth open, and Dan could see it'd been a long stretch since James' last tooth bleach. *How the mighty have fallen.* He looked around the room, but his pathetic basket was alone; being an asshole didn't pay long-term dividends, apparently.

Oh well, it didn't matter; the man was asleep, and after his encounter with the force-of-nature otherwise known as Miss Cherry, Dan wasn't about to wake him up, either; she had to outweigh him by a hundred and fifty pounds. He would do as she'd "suggested" and come back later.

He was moving back around the foot of the bed when Fulbright's eyes fluttered and opened.

Dan stopped, watching him blink and focus. He could see the effects of the stroke; the right eye didn't want to open, and Fulbright's mouth drooped on that side; his scleras were a sick ochre, and bloodshot.

"Who are you?" Fulbright asked with the darkest suspicion; the resonant, self-assured voice that Dan remembered was now a raspy croak.

"Dan Sims. We met several years ago, at the 2006 GNAR Awards."

Fulbright relaxed visibly and closed his eyes again, but Dan didn't think the man remembered him, or cared if he did. "What do you want?"

"I need to talk to you about John McFarlane."

Fulbright's eyes flared back open, and one gnarled hand reached out to grip the bed rail. "Get out! Get out of here! I told him I wanted nothing to do with him or his sick friends! *Get out!*" He was panting now, and one machine had started pinging faster. Dan glanced toward the doorway, half-expecting Miss Cherry to come through it like an avenging WWF wrestler in scrubs.

"Mr. Fulbright, McFarlane didn't send me. I came because he's threatening my family and I wanted to see if you could provide information I could use against him." Fulbright didn't respond, but at least the machine pinged slower. "We bought your house, and he sent a man to rape my wife and kill us both. We fought back and got away, but now…" Fulbright had lost his droopy snarl; he watched Dan without blinking. "Sir, if you can tell me anything that will help us, I'd be grateful. I…I know he murdered your wife. He told me." *Sort of.*

The hand on the rail tightened until the knuckles cracked. Fulbright's face cramped, and he shuddered; a tear formed and rolled past his ear to vanish on the pillow. "Yes," he rasped, staring mournfully at something Dan couldn't see. "Yes, he did. Son of a bitch killed my Alice, my beautiful old girl. We were high-school sweethearts, you know. Would've been together forty-six years last June." There were more tears and another ping-filled silence, and then Fulbright focused on Dan. "You said you bought our house? You're talking about the one we built out there but never lived in?"

"Yes, sir. McFarlane doesn't like it much. He wants my family out, wants the house bulldozed and gone. He said that's why he had your wife killed, because you built it right next door. To spite him, he said."

Fulbright stared up at Dan with shiny black-and-orange crow-eyes in a wasted body. "Is that what he told you?"

"Yes. Why? Is there some other reason?"

Fulbright shook his head, even that small gesture weak, and released the bed rail and folded his hands on his stomach. "You want to know about John McFarlane, son?"

"Yes, sir."

"Well then, the first thing to know is that he lies. Lying isn't even second nature to the man; it's his only nature. Nothing about him is what it seems." Fear had replaced rage in that hoarse voice. "Nothing."

Dan wondered how much pain medication they were giving him. "Uh, that's great, sir, but what I had in mind was—"

"Shut up and listen, son, and I'll tell you what you need to know, not necessarily what you want to hear."

"Yes, sir." Maybe that silver lion wasn't completely gone.

A few-dozen pings went by before Fulbright spoke again; shapes moved across the doorway, shoes squeaked in the hall, but Dan watched the dying man in the bed.

"First off, McFarlane knew all about us building that house. His bank funded its construction. Hell, it was his land we built it on. All that land out there is his, except for patches here and there." Fulbright's droopy mouth twisted. "He fooled me, suckered me in. I made a deal with the devil, in more ways than one, and I paid for it."

Why had McFarlane lied? "I don't understand, sir. What deal?"

"When everything fell apart in 2007…you said we met in '06. You in real estate, son?"

"Yes, sir. I'm with Dalton-Reed."

Fulbright nodded. "Then you know. When it all went south, McFarlane came to me, said he and I together had an opportunity. Said when it turned around—as it eventually has to—with my genius and his money, we'd make a fortune; plucked my ego like a banjo string. Such a goddamn greedy *fool* I was."

More slow pings; Dan waited, and when Fulbright continued, it was in a near-whisper; he had to move to the side of the bed to hear. "We consolidated everything in River Valley Bank and Trust. He paid off all my creditors." The old man rasped out a bitter laugh. "After that, he owned it all. He owned *me*. And for doing all that, all he wanted was for me to join his hunting club." Fulbright's dying crow-eyes jerked from side to side. "Hunting club, what a joke." He trembled, and more tears slid onto the pillow; two of the machines pinged faster.

Hunting club…

Scandlin had mentioned something about a hunting club, and that it was tied to everything about McFarlane and his friends, but Dan had been reeling about River Valley and the violent ex-cons living next door to his family and the horny sluts that not only held people at knife point but made them go poof gone, and the TBI agent had left before he could think to ask about it.

Dan stepped closer, grasping the rail. "Why is that a joke?" The eyes continued to twitch. "James, tell me about the hunting club."

Fulbright focused on him again, and suddenly the old man seized his wrist in a grip that was still strong. "It's not a hunting club, boy, not even close."

"Then what is it?"

"I'm not sure, but it's no hunting club. I drove out there…" The eyes went unfocused; Fulbright was seeing something besides Dan and the hospice room again, but that grip tightened to the point of pain. "I was told to come to McFarlane's farm on a certain night. I was told to be there by eleven-thirty at the latest. This was late May 2008, several months after we made the deal; the house was three-quarters built by then. When I asked him what the hell were we going to hunt in the middle of the night, not to mention out of any season, he told me this was just a meet-and-greet with some far-flung affiliates, so don't bother bringing my rifle." That raspy, bitter laugh: "That was a lie too, but like the fool I am, I showed up." The crow-eyes stopped roaming and pierced Dan. "There were cars and trucks parked all over that farm, wherever they could fit them, dozens and dozens, and damn few from Tennessee."

"Why were they there? What happened?"

"We all went for a midnight walk in those woods, that's what happened." His strained whisper was barely audible above the pinging machines. "There's a trail behind that big house. It leads down into the valley. And I knew right away it wasn't a 'meet-and-greet' because no one bothered to introduce themselves. Nobody said a damn word until that black-haired girl ordered us to turn our cell phones off, and instead of kicking up a fuss they all pulled them out and did it, so I had to. That was another thing that told me it was more than just a social gathering, those girls; they were wearing white formal dresses, like they were heading off to their Cotillion, not for a hike through the damn woods. No one had brought any flashlights, either; we just stumbled along in the pitch black behind those white dresses floating ahead of us like ghosts. McFarlane and his daughters seemed to have no problem seeing without flashlights, but maybe they were just familiar with the trail. Those big dogs went with us too, one trailing each daughter like a puppy after its momma."

"I wanted to ask why we had to turn our phones off and why we couldn't have flashlights and just where the hell were we going, but some instinct told me to keep on keepin' my mouth shut." Fulbright shook his head, lost in memory. "Those girls were dressed to the nines, but McFarlane wore those denim overalls he never seems to take off, with a long-sleeved plaid shirt underneath, buttoned to the neck and wrists as usual, even though I remember it being a warm spring night, almost summer-like. I know *I* was sweating. After a couple of miles, we came to a clearing in the trees, and a…a hole, in the ground, and we stopped."

Sonofabitch, he's talking about the cen—the say-no-whatever, the sinkhole Beth found.

Dan was almost disappointed; he'd been positive they were all trooping to the cemetery. That thought made him realize who was conspicuously absent from Fulbright's account of this midnight hike.

Where was Melissa Bane?

Fulbright was droning, "…millions of stars. The moon had set, so they were bright and clear overhead. The hole was so deep there were full-sized trees growing in it, but it was hard to see how wide it was because of the fog hovering out over it—but it was big, I could tell that. That fog glowed like a silver blanket in the starlight. It was eerily beautiful." Fulbright focused on Dan again. "There's a creek that dumps into the hole. It makes a waterfall. I couldn't see it, but I could hear it. That's where the mist comes from, that waterfall."

"Okay," Dan said. *I don't give two green shits about fog or waterfalls, old man.* "I have a quick question."

"What?" Petulant.

"You said McFarlane and his daughters led everybody down into the valley, right?"

"Right."

"Was there anybody else with them?"

The old man stared up at him, and that droopy expression said Dan was a complete idiot. "I just told you, boy, there were dozens and dozens of—"

"Not them, I meant somebody else. She would've been leading, too." Dan couldn't see the Keeper hanging out at the back of the pack like a shrinking violet. "Her name is Melissa Bane, and she's supposed to be an old family friend of the McFarlanes'. She's in her late forties, early fifties maybe, short and stocky, long strawberry hair with a few gray streaks, and she's got these startling green eyes." *She also has this creepy habit of looking at you like she wants to eat you.* Fulbright was just lying there, staring up at him. "Doesn't ring a bell?"

"There was nobody like that out there that night, leading or otherwise. Melissa… *Bane*, you said? And she's an old family friend? Well, if she is, I've never heard of her before this."

"Yeah," Dan said. "Melissa Bane." He was a little crestfallen, but he supposed he shouldn't have been surprised; there seemed to be some kind of rift between McFarlane and the Keeper, "old family friend" who'd helped raise those crazy sluts or not. Dan just didn't know what, or why. "Never mind, it's not important. What happened after you got to the sinkhole?"

Fulbright licked his lips; he seemed reluctant to go on. "We…we stood around for a few minutes, like we were waiting for something, still quiet, still not speaking; even so, I was working up the courage to say something, maybe something about what the hell we thought we were doing, and then McFarlane walked up to the edge of that hole and looked down into it with this strange smile and announced, 'It's time.' And that's when I realized we were going down in there."

"Well, I didn't want to go, as you can imagine, and I didn't think it was possible, anyway; it sure looked like there was no way to get down short of jumping, but I was wrong. There's a way, but it's hidden. The youngest daughter, the blonde, pulled a coiled rope ladder out of a thicket and she and the redhead secured it to a tree and then unrolled it out over the edge. Shimmy down that twenty feet or so and you can step out on switchback steps concealed under the lip, steps carved out of sheer bedrock. They're narrow and there's no handrail and they're treacherous slick, because of the vapor, but they'll take you down and down and down to the bottom."

"The dogs had to stay up top, though they didn't like that much, snarling and growling and yipping and all, but those girls soothed them down. It took a long time to get all of us over the edge and down that ladder, especially us older ones, but everyone kept silent while we waited for our turn. When it came mine, I almost bolted, dogs or no dogs, but I went in. God help me, I did."

"What's down there? What did you see?"

"I saw…there were trees, terrible, perverted trees, and the ground was one big swamp, but there was a raised, dry path that wound between the warped boles and the twisted roots…and shadows, shadows under the diseased leaves, shadows that moved; shadows that were *alive*. They whispered to me, and they knew my name. *They knew my name!*"

Dan felt a bone-deep chill.

Shadows.

He was going to ask more about these "living" shadows, but then he got a good gander at Fulbright; the old man looked like he and sane had never gotten up and brushed their teeth together. Dan wanted to back away from the bed, but Fulbright still had his wrist trapped in a death-grip.

The old man kept talking while staring wild-eyed at something Dan couldn't see. "McFarlane and his oldest daughter led us down the raised path through the trees and the shadows to the center of the hole. There was a blue light shining down there, and a huge, round, flat stone at the lowest point, thrusting up out of the ground. It had…symbols…carved all over it. It was some kind of language I've never seen. They had…they had two people, a man and a woman, tied up… they were on the slab, in front of the blue light, and they were naked. The oldest daughter cut them free, and then she made them do things, awful, unspeakable things, with each other, *to* each other, while we stood there and watched, *but that wasn't the worst, not even close!*"

"What, James? What was worse?"

"There were *things* in the blue light! I could sense them in there. I thought I was going insane, but when those two pitiable people were about used up, McFarlane commanded the things to come, and they obeyed, stepping out of that blue light… they were *horrible*…things that should not be…and the things snatched up the screaming man and the shrieking woman and they…they started to…NO!" He thrashed, but kept his grip on Dan's wrist. "And the *song!* God, that dreadful SONG! When the things appeared, everybody started singing in some strange, harsh language, and when I saw what the things were doing to the man and the woman, I ran, and the people closed in around me, tried to stop me—the *song itself* tried to keep me! It was like I was running through cold molasses, not air, but McFarlane shouted for them to let me go and suddenly I was free so I ran all the way back through the swamp and the shadows and up the switchback and climbed the rope ladder. I thought those dogs would rip me apart. They acted like they wanted to, but then they just snarled and backed away, so I ran out of the woods and to my car and I left. I called McFarlane early the next morning and said I was going to the cops and he warned me not to. I didn't listen, and the next day my beautiful Alice was dead." Fulbright bared his yellowing teeth. "They said it was an accident, but it was no accident. McFarlane called an hour after the wreck and said that if I kept talking, my son and my daughter-in-law and my two little grandchildren would be next, except that he'd make sure they ended up down in that hole, lying on that slab in front of that awful blue light. I couldn't let that happen, so I had to recant what I'd already told the police. They thought I was a crank even before I recanted, but I had to."

Singing…Dan raised his free hand and wiped cold sweat from his forehead and then watched his fingers tremble.

Singing…a song…

Why did that sound so familiar?

"And you want to know the absolute worst part?" Fulbright now wore this incredulous expression on his ravaged face; it almost drowned out the terror and the hate and the madness. "McFarlane still wants to be my friend." At Dan's look, he nodded jerkily. "That's right. Even after Alice, even after threatening my son and my dear grandchildren, even after those…those…" Fulbright shuddered. "He says that's why he let me go, because there's a war coming, and that he needs people like me on his side. Says I have to choose of my own free will, though, or it won't count. He keeps calling me or sending those hoodlums every few months to renew his offer of friendship, and to remind me that time is running out, that it's time to pick a side, that the war is coming. 'The war to end all wars', he calls it. That's who I thought you were when I woke up and saw you standing there, one of McFarlane's thugs."

"'The war to end all wars'? What does that mean?"

Fulbright didn't hear him. "He still wants to be my friend," the wasted man said again, slowly, as if tasting the words. Then he sort of laughed, but mostly it was a sob. "He even claims he can heal me, cure my cancer and reverse the effects of the stroke both, if I say yes and be his friend." He looked Dan square in the eyes. "The man is stark-raving mad."

"Yeah," Dan said, once more speculating on just how much pain medication they were giving James Fulbright. "I'm picking up on that."

Suddenly Dan's wrist was jerked forward, his hand coming off the rail and onto the bed, and he grabbed the rail with his other hand to keep from falling across Fulbright's lap.

Furious, dying eyes stared into his from a foot away. "You said you live in my house, the one I built for my Alice, out there by McFarlane's farm?"

"Yes."

"You said you live there with your family?"

"Yes, sir, I—"

"Get them out. You hear me, boy? Get them out! *Take them far away, as fast as you—*"

Fulbright's attention flicked over Dan's shoulder, and then his mouth opened as wide as it would go, eyes bulging, tongue protruding like Jabba's when Leia was choking him with her chain; and then the old man shrieked in his face, crow-eyes still fixed on something over Dan's shoulder. He let go of Dan's wrist to raise clawed hands, like he was warding something off, and shrieked again.

Ears ringing, gagging from Fulbright's halitosis, Dan staggered away and turned to look.

A bathroom with a wide, wheelchair-accessible door sat in the corner where Fulbright was staring, a sunlit window opposite, the beige wall between holding a wispy floral Cezanne print. There was the round table with Dan's pathetic basket, and the chairs tucked underneath; besides a blank flat-screen television hanging in the far upper corner, there was nothing else.

Dan glanced back at Fulbright; the old man still had his bulging eyes fixed on the open bathroom door. He screamed again; the pinging machines were rocking and rolling, now.

"What the hell?" Dan rubbed his wrist and looked again, and the breath froze in his lungs.

Something…a shadow…moved, flowed, in the darkest recesses of the lavatory where the sunlight from the window didn't reach.

He was aware of someone running into the room to Fulbright's bedside then, and he heard urgent questions being asked of him, but he kept his focus on the darkness swirling in the depths of the restroom.

If I walk over there and look in, what will I see?

Dan wasn't sure he wanted to find out.

Fulbright stopped screaming and someone shouted at him and Dan looked around, awareness dropping back into chaos; there were a handful of scrub-clad people crowding the doorway, and one of the twenty-something brunettes he'd met walking in was holding Fulbright's clawed hands and trying to soothe him, but instead of smiling she alternated glares at Dan with puzzled frowns toward the restroom; the machines hooked to the old man were about to blast into orbit. And then Miss Cherry shouldered her way through the people in the doorway like a linebacker on her way to the quarterback, and Dan was the quarterback.

She fixed him with that finger, brown eyes blazing. "You—!"

"Miss Cherry?" The brunette at the bedside was staring at the readouts on the pinging machines. "I think we need Dr. Solomon."

Miss Cherry took in the situation with a glance, and then snapped toward the doorway, "Page Dr. Solomon, and git him back here if he's already left!" Someone disappeared at a run as Miss Cherry whirled back to Dan, that finger coming up again. "I *told* you not to wake him up!"

"I didn't! He was awake when I walked in." *Kind of.* "We were just talking, and then he had, uh, some sort of fit."

Dan's eyes were pulled back to the restroom; it had only been seconds, but he could now see the stainless-steel handrails attached to the wall on either side of the toilet. *Could I see those before?* He didn't think so.

When he looked back at Miss Cherry, she was frowning at the bathroom and looking from Fulbright—who hadn't taken his bugged-out crow-eyes from it the entire time—and then back to Dan. Then she cracked wide hands together, and everyone jumped.

"It don't matter, I told you not to disturb one of my people, and now look at 'im!" She advanced on Dan, and it took an effort of will not to back up; not only did she have him by a hundred and fifty pounds, she was two inches taller. "Git on outta here! I'm tempted to call the po-leese! You'd be goddamn lucky if I *do* call 'em cuz you don't want me to do it m'self! Go on! *Git!*"

Dan got.

He made it back down the pissy hallway and across the Starfleet lobby and out the front doors and to his truck and then sat there, trembling. Two scrub-clad people came outside and stood talking under the burgundy awning, and then one pointed at him so Dan started the Toyota and drove some direction and found a strip mall and pulled in and parked; there was a light pole at the front of his spot; its wide concrete base was covered in chipped yellow paint. Dan had graduated from trembling to shaking, so he shut the air off and rolled all four windows down, letting the hot midsummer wind blow across him, but it didn't help; he only shook harder.

A man and a woman, bound and naked, forced to do awful things to each other, and then unspeakable things done to them by…things. Things that should not be.

Who had the man and woman been? Were they two of Scandlin's missing?

The world tilted, and Dan gripped the steering wheel and looked desperately toward the shopping center and saw a State Farm office; two doors down was a salon by the name of Naughty and Nice Nails, and next to that was a Firehouse Subs doing a brisk lunch business; normal things and normal people in a normal, sunlit world, God bless 'em. What Fulbright had said just couldn't be true. Maybe the stroke had zapped more than the muscles in his face, or the meds had scrambled his brain, or something. Anything.

A man left the sub shop and walked by whistling and twirling his key fob, and then he saw Dan's face and grabbed the fob out of the air and stared, brows furrowed over sunglasses.

Dan looked straight ahead until the guy got into a black F-150 and drove off. He let the hot asphalt-stinking wind blow through him and got his shaking under control before he picked off points on twitching fingers; Dan was trying to "reason this out", although he had a bad feeling reason had been left in the dust some time back:

Fulbright was sick and on gobs of medication, so he couldn't be trusted; a group of people, strangers, getting together and trooping into the woods in the middle of the night and then down into a big hole to do…whatever had been done to those unfortunate people? Right. And can't forget the "things that should not be", things that supposedly came out of a blue light. Sure.

And a *war?* "The war to end all wars", no less—whatever the hell that meant. And healing…

He touched just under his eyes, where Mindy's pickle-scented fingers had rested. *Everybody keeps telling me how fast I'm healing…* No. No, it just wasn't possible…but why had the mention of singing made Dan's brain clench?

And shadows…

He thought about the CCTV recording at TBI headquarters, the one from the night Sammy Glick had been ripped apart. Dan thought about what he'd seen Saturday night outside his own dining-room window; he'd assumed he'd had a panic attack, but had he? Had he really?

And what the FUCK was that back there in the goddamn bathroom?

Dan began to shake again, despite the sweat trickling down his ribs. He looked over at Naughty and Nice, at the State Farm, at the people eating lunch in Firehouse; normal things and normal people in a normal, sunlit world.

Fulbright *had* to be zonked on meds. Had to be.

Dan sat for a long time, cold and shaking in the sweltering truck, and thought about things that should not be.

Good People

THE SUN was a carroty glow on the northwest horizon by the time Special Agent Jeff Scandlin turned onto his street; he flicked his headlights on as the small homes and duplexes sank into shadow. He was looking forward to working out and going to bed; after that talk with Dan Sims yesterday, Jeff had hardly slept a wink. His duplex came into sight as he considered saving the workout for tomorrow; the good Lord knew he didn't have any Saturday night plans.

Jeff saw them as he neared the wide driveway he shared with the other side of the duplex, their garage doors separated by a low brick partition with faux Parisian gas lanterns mounted on each side. Duplexes just like his stretched for blocks, most deteriorating. He'd sold their house over in Ranchero Place; he hadn't been able to stand living where everything was still alive with Jessica. Her smells had been the worst: lotion, perfume, potpourri, bath beads, you name it; his wife had been in charge of a heap of smells that don't pop on a man's radar until it's too late, and like her presence, he'd taken them for granted; they had floated through the house like scented ghosts, tormenting him, reminding him of what he'd lost.

His jaw clenched.

Not lost; what they had taken from him.

So he'd bought the duplex, renting out the other side and living on his side free, if there was such a thing. The plan had been to move on after a couple of years and rent both sides, but a couple of years had come and gone three years ago. Jeff hit his turn signal and stopped in the street and waited for them to notice him; he wanted to smile, but kept a stern expression.

Austin, the oldest, spotted him first and shouted; small faces looked toward his truck, and then they scrambled to clear the driveway; the youngest, Marigold, was snatched up by her brother Dallas and carried to the lawn. Austin directed Tyler to drag their toys and bikes out of the way, and then all four lined up at the edge of the grass like little soldiers.

Jeff parked on his side of the partition and grabbed his suit coat and briefcase and climbed out, loosening his tie as he walked around the tailgate. None-too-clean faces beamed as they started bouncing, although Austin, now ten, didn't bounce, or wave or beam; he only gave Jeff a nod, as if to an equal. Jeff felt a swell of pride; it was hard growing up without a father, but Austin was coming along just fine.

He noted the door open on their side of the duplex, letting cool and expensive air spill into the humid evening, but only growled, "I thought I told you kids to keep your toys out of the driveway."

Tyler shouted, "We moved 'em for ya, Mr. Scandlin!" The boy was always running or shouting or both. He made Jeff plain tired.

"We picked them up, sir, just like you told us," Dallas said, and then he grinned, both shy and proud. It surprised Jeff he'd spoken; normally the kid stuck to Austin's heels like a blond shadow.

Jeff allowed the smile to split his face then and held out a palm for a high-five. Dallas obliged. "Good job, son." He held the palm out to Tyler, who jumped when he high-fived, laughing. Jeff then turned to Austin and stuck out his hand, offering to shake, man to man. The boy puffed up and put his small hand in his and shook. "Thanks for getting everybody lined out," Jeff told him. "That was good work."

Somehow Austin puffed further without splitting at the seams. "Thank you, sir."

Sir. It hadn't started out "sir"; the children and their mother had moved in five months ago, and Jeff had put up with them running around like wild Apaches for about a week until one memorable Saturday afternoon. It'd been "Yes, sir" ever since.

Now if I could only use that same belt on their mother...

Jeff bent low, putting his hands on his knees. "Thank you, too, Mari."

She stuck a finger in her mouth and then pressed her face into her brother's leg. Jeff poked at her smooth little belly where it hung out over the Big Bird pull-up; she giggled, watching him out of the corner of her eye. He smoothed her soft blonde hair and stood; the back of the pull-up almost drug the grass, and he could smell urine.

Jeff didn't want to ask, but he had to know, so he looked Austin dead in the eye.

"Is your mother home?"

"Yes sir, she's—"

"Mamma's home, Mr. Scandlin!" Tyler ran into the yard, circling the bikes like an excited dog. "Mamma's home, mamma's home!"

Austin watched his little brother with a scowl that promised retribution, then looked up at Jeff. "She's home, sir."

Motion at the open door drew all eyes. Tiffany stood there holding the youngest girl on her hip; the baby, clad only in a diaper and all of seven months, swayed and watched her brothers and sister with a gummy grin, and then locked eyes on Jeff like he was the most interesting thing in the world, but it was her mother's eyes that made him uncomfortable.

"I'm home, Jeff." She managed to sound angry and hurt and defensive and tired all at once. "It's gettin' dark," she told her children. "Y'all get inside and stop botherin' Agent Scandlin."

"They're not a bother. They're some good kids."

"They are for *you.*"

As if it was his fault they rode roughshod over her. Jeff noticed she didn't tell the children to bring any of their toys or bikes in, but that didn't surprise him; after five months of living next to Tiffany Bach and her brood, nothing much surprised him anymore.

"Night Mr. Scandlin!"

"Goodnight Mr. Scandlin!"

"Goodnight guys. Be good for your mama, now."

"Yes, sir."

"Yes, sir!"

Tyler hopped up and down, blue eyes fastened on Jeff's Colt 9mm where it hung under his left armpit in the tactical holster. "Mr. Scandlin, did you shoot any bad guys today?"

"Tyler!"

"It's okay, Tiffany. No, son, but I just might tomorrow." *Ya never know.*

"Cool!"

"Git inside, Tyler."

"Yes, mama! Night Mr. Scandlin!" Tyler scampered in, a blond monkey with a grin.

Tiffany gave Jeff a flat stare and then shifted the baby to the other hip; her wavy gold hair was in a loose ponytail today, and she wore bright-green shorts and a tight white tee-shirt that bared her stomach, with a dark-colored sports bra underneath. A gold-nugget stud pierced her belly button, and a barbed-wire tattoo encircled her left ankle. She still bore some pregnancy weight, but she was a fine-lookin', curvy woman, and knew it; she also looked tired, but Jeff figured squeezing out five kids before you were thirty would do that.

"You don't have to ask them if I'm home every time."

He shifted, embarrassed. "I know. I'm sorry. It's none of my business what—"

"That's right, it ain't your business." Despite her words, she sounded more resigned than anything. "I just don't want you telling my parents stuff about me again. You know I just got the kids back, and I don't want nuthin' to screw that up."

"I know." There were about six hundred other things he wanted to say to her besides "I know", but Jeff kept his mouth shut; it really *wasn't* his business. He tried to change the subject. "I see little Abby's feelin' better." He made a funny face and wiggled his fingers, but the baby just stared, rapt, like Jeff was about to give away all the world's secrets.

"She is," Tiffany said, then stalked inside. Jeff watched the flaming sun tattooed above her tail bone twitch; it was peeking over the lip of her shorts, and he couldn't decide if it was rising or setting. When he realized what he was doing, he jerked his eyes away just before the door slammed. Tiffany was young enough to be his daughter, for God's sake.

"Old fool."

Five years without a woman, that was the problem; he turned the ring on his finger, watching the plain gold gleam in the lamplight. Jess was gone, but in his heart Jeff was still married, and that part of his life had died with her, never to be again. He accepted that, but sometimes…

He eyed the bikes where they lay in the grass; this was a quiet neighborhood, but leaving them out was tempting fate, and he'd bought them for the boys a scant three months ago. Jeff glanced at the closed door; he could hear shouting behind it, and then a child crying, but he'd learned those were normal noises. He thought about knocking and telling the boys to put their bikes in the garage, then set his briefcase and suit coat on the pavement and picked up two bikes by the crossbars and carried them down the side of the duplex to the fenced backyard; best not to antagonize Tiffany further. Jeff let himself through the unsecured gate and deposited them and turned around for the third; when he carried the last one back, the crying had changed to laughter, and Jeff smiled as he walked around front; it was often like that here now, a circus of life that, for good or bad, was rarely quiet.

Jeff considered the pile of toys and decided if some numbskull wanted to steal a plastic toy, that was his lookout. He retrieved his coat and briefcase and locked his truck, then stood listening to the chaos as the woman next door rode herd on five children.

Pure East Texas trailer-trash…but who the hell was he to judge? Jeff just hooked 'em and booked 'em; it was someone else's job to pass sentence, thank God. Still, the evidence was cut-and-dried: Dallas and Austin and Tyler and Marigold and Abilene, and the rent paid by cashier's check mailed by her parents from a zip near Beaumont. He'd met the parents once, and talked to the mother twice on the phone, but he didn't know them; they paid the rent on time, that's what Jeff knew—that, and they seemed resigned to their daughter's choices. Tiffany was a singer (and a darn good one, judging by the snatches he'd caught through the wall), and had come to Nashville to chase her dreams in addition to making a new start with her kids; she was also trying to get away from the girls' father, an abusive piece of garbage that Jeff almost hoped would show up some day.

He sighed, then trudged down the short walk to his porch and used his key on the deadbolt and went inside.

None of my damn business.

He put the briefcase on the kitchen counter. The boys had a different father; by the look of them, maybe a different for each. Jeff grunted. Still none of his business. He listened to the racket coming through the thin wall as he went upstairs and changed, then stowed his badge and service nine and tactical rig in the nightstand and re-strapped his .32 Beretta Tomcat to his right ankle; he knew it looked ridiculous riding above his sock, but with scum like Jesus Menendez loose in the world, Jeff never went unarmed, even at home.

He did a light stretch in the hall and then opened the spare bedroom door and poked his head in; two years ago he'd converted it to an office he rarely used, and the computer and file drawer and bookshelves were dusty. He shut the door and finished stretching and then went down to the garage. Jeff didn't have much of a social life—hell, he had no social life—but tonight he had a date with some weight.

He tuned the old clock radio perched on his workbench until it scratched out classic rock and then started pumping iron. Jeff had a bench and stacks of plates and a rack of dumbbells and a Nautilus machine and a treadmill crowding his garage, which was why he had to park his truck outside. No one messed with it, though; everyone in the neighborhood knew he was a cop.

Jeff hummed along to Aerosmith's "Walk This Way" as he threw the weight around, fatigue forgotten. He relished being in shape and enjoyed taking down punks who thought gray hair meant he was soft; there'd been more than one scumbag learn a hard lesson that way.

He finished his benches, sliding the 45lb plates off the ends of the bar and re-stacking them with soul-soothing clanks. Jeff toweled off, and then eyed the treadmill before he turned it on and climbed aboard, pulling his Velcro ankle holster off and setting the Tomcat on the workbench within easy reach; for a second there, he'd thought about only doing five miles instead of the usual ten, so he set it to twelve; he would not be soft. As extra punishment, he dialed it to random hilly.

Jeff had passed the warm-up portion when a crash came through the wall, loud enough to be heard over music and treadmill. He paused the program and stepped off, then turned the radio down, listening, thinking about going next door and seeing if everything was all right; there were no other noises, though, so after a minute he scowled and turned the music up louder and climbed back on.

None of his business.

Those boys needed a real father; the treadmill inclined, and he bore down, running faster. Jeff had become their de facto father over the past five months; sad but true. He and Jess had tried for years—both had been checked out and found healthy—but no luck. They'd eventually accepted it wasn't meant to be and had decided to enjoy their freedom, although sadness had crept into Jessica's eyes whenever she'd watched children play; the treadmill leveled off, and he eased up. Now here he was, a surrogate father in his fifties…and Tiffany had supposedly moved to start fresh with her kids, but as far as Jeff could tell, she was living the same life in a fresh zip code. Take six weeks ago:

He'd gotten home from work that Sunday evening to find the door to her place wide open and the four oldest kids out wandering like feral chickens and Tiffany and the baby gone. Austin said his mother told him to watch his brothers and sister, took the baby, and left in her little blue Dodge Neon. The boy was sketchy on when that was, but Jeff got the feeling she'd been gone most of the day, so he'd gathered them up and fed them, stuck them in front of a cartoon, and watched the clock and worried. He'd tried her cell when she hadn't shown by nine, but no answer. If the baby had been there, he would've dialed 911, certain that something had happened to her, but by ten and at wits' end, he called her parents in Texas. Tiffany's mother's voice had grown tears, but she hadn't sounded the least bit surprised as she'd promised she would call her daughter, thanked Jeff for his concern, and hung up.

Twenty minutes later Tiffany had shown up with baby Abby on a hip, reeking of marijuana, glassy eyed and sullen, with a tall, good-looking, twenty-something kid in tow. The kid had spiked blond hair and diamonds in each ear like a nigger and he'd sneered at Jeff until Jeff gave him the stare, the one he saved for the hardest cases; the punk turned pale and wouldn't look at him as Tiffany gathered her clutch without a word and took them across the driveway and home. He'd been angry enough to give the woman the lecture she needed, but Austin had watched him as they'd left, and the boy's eyes were hard to take.

He glanced down at the display; two miles to go. Jeff wondered when she would turn up pregnant again. One mile; would she name it after a town in Tennessee? A half-mile; what would happen to those kids when she left? He knew Tiffany would eventually move, and sooner rather than later; it was as certain as sunrise.

What will happen to me when those kids are gone?

Jeff's cell phone rang with a quarter-mile to go, and he hopped off and listened; he'd left it in on the kitchen counter, and it was sounding the default tone. He glanced at his watch: 9:46. What stranger would call this late? The ringing stopped, and he turned the treadmill and radio and lights off and went inside after grabbing the Beretta from the workbench.

Jeff toweled off while he checked the number; he didn't recognize it, but it had a Rutherford County prefix. Had it been Sims? He'd told the man to call him after eight if he wanted to talk more, but Jeff hadn't been sure he would.

He was attempting to access the call menus, big, clumsy thumbs preventing any grace or speed with the task as usual, when the phone rang again, startling him; same number. He answered with a cautious hello; it was Rutherford County, after all.

A woman said, "Are you Special Agent Scandlin with the Tennessee Bureau of Investigation?"

"Who's this?"

"Beth Sims. I believe you spoke to my husband yesterday."

"Yes," he said, surprised; Sims' wife. Like her husband, she didn't have a southern accent. He remembered her picture from the news; a beautiful woman with full lips, dark-brown hair, and intense mahogany eyes. This little lady had done for Scott Rison, and he hadn't gone easy; Jeff could hear some of that iron in her clear, high voice. "What can I do for you, ma'am?"

"You can stop filling my husband's head with nonsense, that's what you can do for me."

Nonsense? "Ma'am, I—"

"This week has been hard enough without you pushing your agenda on us, Special Agent."

"I don't have—"

"Daniel has been jumping out of his skin since yesterday, thinking the big, bad farmer next door will send his goons to kill us all."

"He just might."

There was a silence, and when her voice came back, it had dropped ten degrees. "So you say. I don't know what your grudge against John McFarlane truly is, and I don't care. Daniel said something about the man murdering your wife, but I don't believe that for a second."

"It's true!"

"You're a police officer of some sort, and you can't tell me you'd let a man walk away after he'd admitted to killing your wife. No, there's some other reason you're interfering, and I don't know what it is, but I want you to stop. You ought to be ashamed, using your wife's death to—"

"Don't you DARE suggest I'd use Jessica's death for some kind of gain, goddamn you!" He placed a hand on the briefcase. "It's true, Mrs. Sims, every word, whether or not you want to believe it."

When she spoke again, her tone was gentle. "I'm sorry, Special Agent. I'm truly sorry for your loss, but I had to know if you were working an angle."

She'd played him like a fiddle. He was starting to like this woman. "Thank you, Mrs. Sims, but you need to understand that McFarlane is a monster. And I'm not sure why he's set his mind against you—maybe it's like he told your husband, that he just doesn't like your house…" Jeff frowned and shook his head, because he wasn't sure he believed it; McFarlane wasn't a man who gave fair warning, for one thing. "Whatever the reason, I know he's arrogant enough to think he can get his way."

"I will not be driven out of my home, Special Agent Scandlin; not by some farmer who thinks he's Caesar, not by anyone for *any* reason. Do I make myself clear?"

Jeff grinned. Sims had his hands full, that was plain, and that bastard Rison hadn't stood a chance.

"Yes, ma'am."

"I know it's late, but I would like you to tell me what you told my husband about these missing people. Perhaps I can believe, or at least understand better, if I hear it from you."

"I can do that, ma'am, but please, call me Jeff."

"Only if you call me Beth."

"All right, Beth."

"Thank you, Jeff." Then: "I hope this doesn't sound ungrateful, but would you first tell me *why* you're helping us?"

He thought of how to respond as he snagged a bottle of water out of the fridge and grabbed the briefcase and sat down at his dusty kitchen table; the round wooden slab seated four, but he always ate standing at the counter or on a TV tray in his recliner.

Beth Sims misread his silence: "Again, I don't mean to seem ungrateful, but it's been my experience that people rarely help other people without an ulterior motive."

He cracked the water and took a big glug; despite the sweet voice, she was a woman with hard edges. Jeff liked her even more. "You're right," he said. "I was hoping Rison would've maybe said something more about other women, something you'd forgotten to tell the officers. Maybe even…"

"Said something about your wife."

"Yes. When Jess died, Rison was still a teenager, and not even working for McFarlane yet, but I thought if the others had bragged—"

"These 'others' being the paroled rapists and murderers John McFarlane uses as farmhands?"

"Yes." Jeff clenched his fist around the water bottle, and then carefully set it on the table before it ruptured; when they'd pulled Jessica's nude body out of that ditch, the ditch where she'd been dumped like some piece of litter, her face had been crushed, her teeth broken, her privates torn; the officers on scene hadn't wanted him to see her, but they hadn't been able to stop him from looking.

Shuddering, Jeff brought a picture of Jessica into his mind as she was in life: beautiful, vibrant, loving, laughing. That was how he remembered her, not the other way.

Never the other way.

"I'm so sorry," Beth said; he'd let the silence stretch too long. "We can talk tomorrow if that would—"

"No." Jeff wiped at his eyes and smoothed his voice. "Now's as good a time as any. And the reason I'm helping you is that people brave enough to take on John McFarlane are worth helping."

There was a pause, then: "Thank you, Jeff."

So he repeated what he'd told her husband about the missing, and she interrupted only once, when he heard a woman say something in the background and she excused herself; when Beth came back she apologized, saying she was at work and hiding in her office. When Jeff asked if she needed to go, she got that irritated tone again and told him her staff could handle it, and that she was just there to prove a point, whatever that meant.

He finished and then waited; he didn't have to wait long.

"So you've had this information about these poor missing people for over six years, but Daniel and I are the only ones you've told?"

The way she'd said it made him sound negligent, so he explained how an adult missing-person investigation proceeded once it was determined that foul play was involved and not just some greener-pasture urge, and also when you were lucky enough or diligent enough to pinpoint a suspect: you searched for connections between the victim and the suspect, and if you had multiple missing persons, between victims. Jeff told her how he'd struck out trying to connect McFarlane or his "boys" to any of the missing, and then his inspiration about the daughters and how he'd found several semi-reliable eyewitness accounts they—and unexpectedly sometimes Melissa Bane—had had contact with the missing in the days before they vanished, although some of those IDs were more than twenty years old.

Jeff also told her that, unfortunately, he could find no other link between the vanished themselves.

Guilt twisted him; it was a lie, plain and simple. It was the same lie he'd told Beth's husband, however, and Jeff still believed it was a necessary deception; they weren't ready to hear everything.

They might never be ready.

The reason he hadn't come forward, Jeff continued, was that prosecutors had scant desire to appear foolish; they wanted hard, prosecutable evidence before they filed charges, and there just wasn't any here. Lack of motive was another factor, along with McFarlane's status in the community and swarms of hidden friends; bottom line, most wouldn't believe it, and those that did would keep their mouths shut. That was all pure truth, and it soothed Jeff's conscious about lying to this courageous woman—somewhat.

Beth Sims was quiet when he finished. Jeff was so tired he swayed in the chair. At last she spoke: "So it looks like there's no connection between these people from every corner of the country, but we know there is?"

"Yes." *Oh, yes.*

More quiet, then: "I'd like to hear your opinion on something, Jeff."

"Shoot."

"We've been avoiding the media, but now we're thinking of calling a press conference and announcing that Scott Rison was sent by McFarlane, that our own neighbor had me raped and tried to have both of us killed, and that he's threatening to try again unless we move away from our home. My question is this: do you think that would make John McFarlane back off and leave my family in peace?"

"Possibly." Jeff could see several large problems looming, but found himself liking it; it would piss the old man off no end, for one thing, but…

Beth said, "I realize you don't owe us anything," and Jeff knew what she would say next; he cringed inside, hating himself for it, "but if you will stand with us at the press conference and give your evidence, perhaps some authority would have no choice but to investigate. It would also lend credence to what we say, having an officer of the law at our side."

"It'd sure stir the anthill." *Boy, would it.* "But there's a problem."

"Oh?" That chill was back. "What problem is that?"

Jeff explained how rabid he'd been for McFarlane in the year after Jessica's death, and how he was now like the boy who'd cried wolf; what he didn't say was that his career had died with her, and that only in the past two years had his superiors trusted him again with cases that mattered; all that would end when he appeared at their press conference. He might as well retire early; in fact, Jeff might *be* retired early, whatever he wanted. He didn't say any of that, but he had a feeling he didn't have to; this woman was no fool.

When he finished, Beth said, "I see." Jeff had expected her to be upset, but she only sounded thoughtful. "And my original question? Would McFarlane back off?"

"Again, possibly, but if he did, it would only be for a time; the media's a fickle bitch, pardon my French, and all he'd have to do is wait, and when time went on and nothing happened, you and your husband may end up in the same pasture as me, crying wolf. And then there you'd still be, right next door to him." Jeff could see the old man biding his time, like a big, denim-overalls-wearing spider in a web. "There's also the legal issue; if you accuse him with no proof…well, slander and defamation of character just to start, is what I'm thinking."

"Let me ask you another question, Special Agent."

He sighed. "Call me Jeff, please."

"Why did you gather this evidence if you won't use it against the man who murdered your wife?"

"I—"

"Don't you have any compassion for these poor families? Are you such a coward you would let McFarlane and all the rest run free because you're afraid of what your cop buddies think? The man who had your wife *raped* and *murdered*, Special Agent! Will you let him get away—"

"I WILL NOT!" Jeff glanced toward the slim wall that separated his kitchen from Tiffany's. "I will not let him get away with what he did to Jessica! I've arranged for this to go to the right people, people who aren't McFarlane's, and they'll do what they can with it. They'll get it when…" He tried to recover. "What I mean is—"

"You're going to kill him."

"I'm a sworn officer of the law."

"But not for long. You told Daniel you're retiring next year. So that's the plan? Wait until your actions won't reflect so badly on the TBI and then get your revenge?"

Jeff didn't believe someone had his line tapped—what reason would they have?—but he kept caution. "Ma'am, what you're implying is—"

"My husband and I have agreed to hold a press conference next week, and we would like for you to join us, but I understand if it's an *inconvenience* for you to help catch the man who had your wife raped and killed, Special Agent Scandlin, so I—"

"I didn't say no, Mrs. Sims."

There was a long silence, and then she said, "Thank you, Jeff."

"Don't thank me yet; my participation may hurt your cause. Oh, the media will get stirred up, but in law-enforcement circles, where it matters…well, you may be better off without me." It hurt to say, but he knew it was true.

"Nonsense. We'd be much better off with you by our side."

The warmth in her voice stirred him. "Thank you, ma'am." Jeff wiped at his eyes. What the hell was wrong with him? He was like a goddamn sprinkler all the sudden.

"As for the other matter, my family doesn't have a year to wait." Her laugh was clear, and biting. "We have until the first of September! And I also happen to agree with you; the world would be a much happier place without John McFarlane in it."

Jeff sat silent. "Yes," he finally said. "Much."

He heard a voice in the background, a man's this time, and Beth excused herself and then came back. "I have a few more quick questions, if you don't mind."

Jeff shifted on the chair; Lord, he was tired. "Go ahead."

"Those girls, the daughters…I know they were adopted, but if I hadn't seen them for myself, I might think they didn't exist. I've been trying to learn more about them, but I can't find any Facebook or Myspace pages or yearbook photos or anything else."

Scandlin grunted. "They were home-schooled. They got their GEDs by the time they were sixteen. And I doubt they're the social-media types; they stay out there on that farm and pretty much keep to themselves."

"Except when they're traipsing across the country abducting people."

"Yeah, except then."

"And then there's Melissa Bane, this supposed 'Keeper' my husband met. You say she may be helping those girls take people? And you told Daniel that she showed up thirty years ago, about the time Muriel McFarlane fell ill and passed away?"

Jeff sat up straight, suddenly not tired anymore; he had to be careful here. "Yes and yes."

Something in his tone must have given him away. "I see," she said slowly. "Daniel also implied she may have had some role in Muriel's death. Is that true, Agent Scandlin?"

He'd avoided this line of questioning with her husband, but Jeff had a bad feeling Beth Sims wouldn't be sidetracked so easily; she was like a wolf with a bone. "All I know is that the timing was handy. I guess you've heard Bane replaced the wife in…certain ways?"

"Yes."

"Well, stir that in with McFarlane and Bane going halfway across the country to adopt the oldest daughter—while the wife was teetering on the far edge of her deathbed, no less—and you can see how some might get that idea. But Muriel McFarlane's death certificate lists 'Unknown Illness' as the COD, so it's beyond me how Melissa Bane could be responsible. I found the sawbones who treated her, Dr. Aldus Murphy, but unfortunately for Aldus and me, by the time I found him his practice was closed and he was dead. The storage facility that housed his records burned to the ground over twenty years ago, so I could find nothing on this 'unknown illness'. I did track down an RN who worked for Murphy back then, and she told me that no one had ever seen such a terrible wasting sickness that wasn't viral or bacterial or fungal, and that they did what they could to make her comfortable, but in the end there was little that could be done to save Muriel McFarlane."

Jeff clamped his teeth together and hoped that satisfied Beth Sims.

He should have known better.

"So tell me what you *do* know about Melissa Bane."

"She's an old friend of McFarlane's family—"

"Don't insult my intelligence, I know you tried to backtrack her. Who is she? Where did she come from?"

Not a bone; a starving wolf with a whole deer carcass. Dan Sims must be tougher than he looked. "Who is she? Why, she's Melissa Bane—or at least that's what she tells everyone. Where did she come from? I heard a whisper she was from 'up north', but up north covers a lot of territory. I searched online and found some Banes and called around, but none had heard of a Melissa relation of her age and description, 'up north' or anywhere else. She doesn't have a driver's license or a Social Security number, she's not registered to vote in Rutherford County or the great state of Tennessee, and she doesn't file tax returns or collect benefits."

Jeff drank water and waited, convinced those dribbles wouldn't pacify this woman.

He was right.

She said, "And now you know through my husband that Bane claims to be the 'Keeper' of Barron Cemetery."

"Yes," he said. "Now I know that, too."

There was at least five seconds of silence before she spoke again.

"Do you believe these young women and this Melissa Bane have been making people vanish for almost three decades? Do you *truly* believe that, Special Agent Scandlin?"

"My belief or disbelief doesn't matter; what matters is what I can prove to a prosecutor, and what I can prove is that during an unsanctioned investigation I discovered sketchy eyewitness accounts and took statements—statements that wouldn't be admissible to any grand jury or during any trial in a single courtroom in a single courthouse in America—that John McFarlane's three adopted daughters, sometimes singly and sometimes in a group and sometimes with Melissa Bane, were seen conversing amicably—not attacking, or threatening, or even arguing—conversing *amicably* with the victims in the days before their disappearance, but that's all I can prove."

"As for explaining *why* they would take these people, I don't have a clue how to start, ma'am. I believe…I *know* that John McFarlane is evil. As to the rest, I don't know what to think. And if *I* don't, you can be damn sure no one else will."

"One more question."

Jeff suppressed a groan. "Go ahead."

"My husband is convinced these missing people are being interred in Barron Cemetery. What do you think?"

"I think that would be stupid of John McFarlane, ma'am, and he's a lot of things, but stupid isn't one. And now we're back to the why. *Why* would he bother to do that?"

"I've had similar thoughts." Beth Sims sounded satisfied. "That leads me to another question. You told Daniel that you saw Barron Cemetery years ago, when you were a boy. I believe he said while hunting with your father?"

Alarms went off in his head, but Jeff answered smoothly. "Teenager, actually, but yes, I saw it."

"He also said you viewed the pictures on his phone, and that you were surprised by the transformation the cemetery has undergone. Is that correct?"

"I'd say that's accurate."

"I see. And since you were on McFarlane's property, am I to assume that you used to be good friends? This would be before he supposedly murdered your wife, of course."

Jeff pulled the phone away and looked at it before putting it back to his ear; Dan Sims must have three-inch thick skin. "Ma'am, as I told your husband, my dad and his dad were good-time buddies. We could hunt in that valley back then, but Daddy went on the straight-and-narrow and they lost contact. We moved to Nashville a few years later."

"And this move…did it occur around the time Melissa Bane showed up?"

"Thereabouts," Jeff said, carefully nonchalant; her arrows were hitting close to the bull's eye. "As for McFarlane, he and I were never friends. He's about fifteen years older than me, and we only crossed paths two or three times. And there's no goddamn *supposedly* about it! John McFarlane had my beautiful Jessica raped and murdered!"

"So you grew up in Rutherford County?" Her question was cool and calm; she had ignored his outburst like a passing summer shower.

"Yes," he grated.

"And why did your family move?"

"I don't know," Jeff said, and it was the second lie he'd had to tell this gutsy, annoying woman. "You'd have to ask my momma and daddy, but they're dead." He didn't feel guilty—much—because they were heading down a path she wasn't ready to walk.

"I see. So, you are familiar with Barron Woods and its valley. Tell me, Agent Scandlin, have you seen that cenote out there?"

It took a second to remember what a cenote was. "That big hole?" *Why would she ask about that old sinkhole?* "I glimpsed it while Daddy and I were hunting, but we steered clear. Some kids were screwing around by the edge and fell in back in '58— it was McFarlane and his cousins, as a matter of fact. Anyway, it's deep, and they couldn't get out, and two of them died before they could be rescued." A thought struck, making his blood quicken. "Why? Did Rison say something about it?"

Jeff had long ago considered and then discarded the idea that the missing's bodies could have been dumped in that sinkhole, and for the same reason he now doubted they were buried in Barron Cemetery; it was still McFarlane's property.

But if Rison…

She uprooted his slim hope before it could bud. "No, no, he didn't mention it." And then Beth Sims hesitated, and when she spoke again, she sounded uncertain for the first time. "As for why I'm asking, let's just say I have my reasons."

Jeff's ears perked; it seemed he wasn't the only one with secrets. Before he could press her, though, a man's baritone spoke in the background, she replied, and then she said, "I have to get back to work. Thank you for answering my questions, Special Agent Scandlin—"

"Jeff, please."

"Jeff, then. And I'm sorry to put you on the spot, but I need a definitive answer. Will you stand with us at our press conference next week?"

"I'd be honored." Early retirement wouldn't be so bad, as long as they left his pension and benefits intact.

"Thank you, Jeff."

"You're welcome, ma'am."

"We need to compare notes. Would you like to come to the house for dinner, say six o'clock Sunday? You can meet our daughter, Elizabeth."

"That would be fine, ma'am."

"Beth."

"That would be more than fine, Beth."

"Good. I look forward to meeting you. Perhaps then you'll be kind enough to tell me all you suspect about Melissa Bane. Goodnight."

She hung up, and Jeff looked at the screen before setting his phone on the table; his rueful grin faded as he thought about the lies he'd told, and also about what he hadn't dared reveal:

His daddy *had* said why they'd moved away from Rutherford County, but he hadn't said it to Jeff; he'd eavesdropped on his momma and daddy through the wall in the new house while they'd fought about the sudden move, and his daddy had declared something strange that he never forgot, something that had rang clear and strong through old plasterboard and faded wallpaper:

"I'll have no truck with their blasphemy!"

Years later, after he'd grown into a man and worked up the courage to ask his still-imposing father, the old man wouldn't talk about it; the only thing he'd said was, "Don't you go a messin' with those folks down there in Rutherford County, son, they're bad news." And then he'd refused to speak of the move or "those folks" again until his dying day.

Jeff squeezed his eyes shut.

But I didn't listen, did I? And Jess had paid for it.

And then there were the missing.

Dan and Beth Sims couldn't see the pattern because they didn't know all the details and weren't trained investigators, but Jeff had eventually seen it, and when it all came out at this presser, so would others of his kind; what they would make of it was another matter:

There were no connections as far as the lost knowing or communicating with each other, but the *type* stayed spot-on across the board; it was a statistical fact that most American adults who up and vanish exist on the fringes of society: prostitutes, gang members, drug dealers and the like; not so with those connected to McFarlane's daughters and Melissa Bane. Instead of hanging on the fringe, they had been solid citizens, and for the most part devoutly religious, though that wasn't the case for all.

But all had been hardworking family people; people who gave to charity; people who volunteered in their churches and the community…

Good people.

And now there were these new puzzle pieces: Bane telling Sims that she was the "Keeper" of Barron Cemetery, and how that cemetery had been transformed…the new pieces connected with the others he already had, and the puzzle congealed on its own, but Jeff scattered it, refusing to view the picture it tried to form.

There has to be some other explanation.

But the pieces weren't so easily discarded, standing out clear in his reluctant mind; those puzzle pieces and the picture they were determined to make were the reasons sleep had eluded him last night no matter how many prescription sleeping pills he'd popped:

What his dad had said about "those folks", and his obvious fear when he spoke of them; the three daughters; the good people vanishing; and now this about Bane and that old cemetery, a cemetery that had been inexplicably redone and revitalized; and then there was the growing power, wealth, and influence of John McFarlane and his cabal of friends. Jeff had stood on the sidelines and watched the farmer's meteoric rise, and always with his daddy's words whispering in his ear…

And, most of all, what he'd seen on the CCTV recording of the night Sammy Glick had died; that oozing black shadow…Jeff had never mentioned to Dan Sims how that shadow had seemed to be looking back at him through the camera; and not only through the camera, but through time and space, as if it were watching him and marking him out even as he watched it.

He shivered. Impossible, of course. Nuts, even—but impossible and nuts or not, judging by how everyone reacted after viewing that recording, Jeff didn't think he was the only one who'd felt it.

The pieces gravitated toward each other again, forming a nightmare picture, but Jeff scattered them once more.

It was insanity; absolute, utter, insanity.

And that was the *real* reason he'd brought none of this forward, forget McFarlane's friends in the TBI, or his reputation of hating the old man. If Jeff voiced these suspicions, being marginalized and ridiculed by the law-enforcement community would be the least of his problems; having his badge and gun yanked while being put through a psych-eval before being forced into retirement would be the least of his problems:

Jeff might end up doped to the gills and locked in a soft-walled room somewhere for the rest of his life.

But I'll tell the Sims' over dinner Sunday night, won't I.

He sagged in the chair as a vast release of tension blew through him. *Yes.* He would do it. Jeff would lay all the pieces on the board and see if another rational person could see the same terrifying picture form; if anyone could believe, it would be these courageous people who were already willing to buck McFarlane.

Jeff rubbed his face with both hands; he needed a shower and his bed. Whether or not they saw the same picture, it would be one hell of an interesting conversation. Beth Sims might regret asking him to tell her everything he suspected of Melissa Bane, and she'd probably change her mind about him speaking at her press conference, but it wouldn't be his burden to bear alone anymore, this mad idea that—

A hard breeze gusted through the kitchen, and Jeff started up from his thoughts and watched in astonishment as the paper towel at the end of the roll flapped. He caught a whiff of spoiled eggs as his eardrums popped and whined; he reamed a finger in his ear and cracked his jaw. Was there a storm brewing? Had he left a window open? And where had that damn awful *smell* come from?

Jeff stood, and then froze and glanced up at the ceiling as a *thud* came from overhead, but then he snatched the Velcro holster off the counter and pulled the Beretta. The smelly wind from nowhere died as suddenly as it came, and he strained his ears in the silence that replaced it; that had sounded like something falling upstairs, something heavy. Had it come from Tiffany's side? It was after ten, so those kids should be in—

Another heavy thump overhead; adrenaline blazed through Jeff's body, flushing away the weariness. Someone was in his house. If they'd searched his bedroom, they might have his service pistol. They must've gotten in somehow while he was in the garage.

He held his breath and tried to listen over the hammering of his heart.

Silence.

Whoever they are, they broke into the wrong place.

"Who's there?" Jeff called, and then displaced to the entryway to the living room and put his back to the thick jamb, pistol up and ready. He listened. Nothing.

"Who's there?" Silence. "I'm a policeman and I'm armed!"

Nothing. Well, Jeff had given fair warning. He listened more: still nothing, and no sound from Tiffany's side. He glanced over at the wall they shared. Those kids…if there was going to be shooting, Jeff wanted them out of the line of fire; he couldn't live with himself if he let those children be harmed.

He peeked into the living room; empty except for his television and his recliner and the table with the lamp he always left on and the Larry McMurtry oat opera he was reading beneath it. The sofa that never got used was pushed up against the far wall; the steep, narrow stairway to the second floor was on the other side of the television.

"Who's up there?"

Jeff sprinted across the room and crouched behind the far arm of the sofa, the end of the Tomcat's barrel never leaving those stairs. He was now on the far side of the duplex; those kids should be out of harm's way. He listened again and heard more nothing, but his nose crinkled as the stench strengthened; it was like a cross between spoiled eggs and rotting meat. He put his free arm over his face.

Lord, what *was* that?

"Hello? Is someone up there?"

Silence.

"Come down with your hands over your head and I won't shoot!" No answer; maybe something had fallen off a closet shelf…

Twice?

"Hello?" No answer. Maybe—

"Jeff?"

Everything inside him went hot and loose.

"Jeff, is that you?" The stairs creaked as a pair of bare feet descended, the light from the lamp revealing a dark-green dress swirling around shapely calves.

He tried to stand on mile-long legs and staggered into the wall. The Beretta fell from his numb fingers and hit the carpet.

"Jeff? Baby?"

She stood at the bottom, half in the lamplight and half in shadow. She brushed reddish-blonde hair from her face in an achingly familiar gesture and peered into the living room, squinting as if the light hurt. Her eyes found him, and she smiled.

"Jeff."

"Jessica," he whispered. The room lurched, and he kept one hand on the wall or he would've crumpled to the carpet.

His dead wife held her arms out. "Baby, I've missed you." Those arms, slender and beautiful in the green dress, stretched into the soft yellow light while the rest of her stayed in shadow. He could see her two-carat diamond ring glinting on her left ring finger; the last time Jeff had seen that ring, he'd handed it to the funeral director so she could be buried with it.

Understanding came then, and hot disappointment: *I'm dreaming.* He had dreamed so many times that Jess was still alive, that there'd been some terrible mistake, that they'd found some other man's wife broken and violated in that ditch. He always woke from those dreams with a rip in his soul that had him clutching himself and crying like a baby, but for those few, wonderful moments, his Jessica wasn't gone, and he wasn't alone.

Jeff was asleep and dreaming of his dead wife. She still had her arms out. He pushed off the wall and walked toward her, intending to enjoy every second of this while he could.

"God, baby, I've missed you too."

One red-gold strand of hair shined on her shoulder, caught by the edge of the light. He took another step and kicked something hard, sending it sliding across the carpet. He looked down; the Beretta. Jeff held a hand to his head, swaying; it felt real, that hand, and so had the pistol. He could feel his aching muscles, still swollen from his workout, and that rotten smell filled his nostrils, so strong it almost made him gag.

This is the strangest dream I've ever had.

Something made him look up. Jessica hadn't left the stairwell, but she had lowered her arms, and her expression tore his heart. "What's wrong, baby? I've missed you so much. I love you." Her face, half in shadow, was even more beautiful than he remembered.

His eyes filled. "I love you, too." Jeff took another step, and then stopped again; her hands were at her sides, the left hand with the diamond gleaming in the lamplight, but he stared at her right hand, the hand that hung in shadow.

Needle-sharp ebony claws clicked as a massive scaled fist clenched; the fist was on the end of an arm that dangled to the floor, an arm that was longer than Jess was tall; it rippled with black scales and bulging muscles that were nowhere near human.

Jeff's heart was trying to hammer up out of his throat, terror like he'd never known choking him. His eyes found hers.

"Jess?"

She stepped forward and…shimmered, causing him to blink, but then she stood before him fully in the light and all Jessica.

His breath hitched. "Oh, baby…"

It was Jess as she'd been long ago at the Buster Bowl one lane over, laughing with her friends, a plastic cup of foamy amber beer in her hand, and he'd hardly been able to take his eyes off her, bowling so poorly that his squad had made fun of him, but she was looking back so he got the courage to turn around and talk to her over the hard plastic backs of their chairs and she was so sweet and genuine and beautiful he felt like a teenager again, sweaty palms and all, and he'd asked her out and she'd said yes and they'd married eight months later and he didn't care if this was a dream or how strange it was he missed her so much, God he missed her, his beautiful Jess with her flashing eyes and bad temper sometimes and sweet nature the rest, so mercurial but he loved it, and oh God oh God, Jessica.

She lifted her slender arms toward him once more. "I love you."

Jeff took that last step and wrapped his dead wife in his arms.

Not Fair

Tiffany blew smoke toward the rattling vent fan, then grabbed the air freshener from the sink counter and sprayed. She closed the toilet lid and sat and rested her forehead in her free hand; the other held the hemostat out, thin smoke-trail rising.

Life was so not fair.

She'd just gotten Abby down in her crib, Mari was zonked in Tiffany's bed, and the boys had finally settled after she'd yelled at them for the tenth time to lie down and be quiet. Tiffany didn't care if they went to sleep; she just wanted them to keep it down so the girls could. She didn't care because it didn't matter what time they got up; school didn't start for almost three weeks.

"C'mon school," she told the empty toilet-paper roll. When the boys started school, Tiffany would talk her mom into paying for daycare for the girls, and then she could concentrate on her singing career.

Summer couldn't end fast enough for Tiffany.

She drew on the shrinking roach and set the hemostat by the sink while she reached for a fresh roll and threw the cardboard tube in the trash; she blew smoke toward the fan, automatically spraying after.

"*C'mooooon school*," Tiffany sang, her voice low for a woman's and sexy as hell, made for county-rock or rockabilly; everybody said so. She thought about the three Xanax she'd stashed, but Abby had been sleeping fitfully since coming down sick, and Tiff wanted to hear her crying. She picked up the hemos and took a last hit, then stood long enough to flush the ash.

"*C'mooooon school!*"

Her voice would make her a star, she just knew it; throw in her looks, and it was only a matter of time. That producer she'd met two weeks ago agreed. He'd said he worked for Columbia, and she'd even blown him, but he hadn't called in over a week, now. She'd left messages every day, but nothing.

"Asshole." He was just like all those other assholes at the Purple Palace outside Houston; finish them in the back room with her hand or her mouth, and still no extra tip.

Tiffany took the baggie off the counter and fitted another roach into the clip, locked it, grabbed her lighter, and fired up. She held the hit and did the vent and the spray and then eyed the baggie; a few bowls of shake and three roaches left. She'd have to call Mike. Mike could score the chronic, not that Mexican dirt-weed she used to get in Beaumont, and if she did him, he wouldn't charge her. He was cute and good in the sack and all, but *God* he was dumb, and Tiffany would have to go over to his apartment. Mike wouldn't come over to her place anymore because he was scared of Jeff. Why did she have to have a cop for a landlord?

Tiff giggled. It wasn't *all* bad; five weeks ago, Dominique had called out of the blue—she still didn't know how he'd gotten her new number—and threatened to come take the girls even though she'd gotten a court order saying he couldn't have contact with her or them and he hadn't even *seen* them in months and months, but when she'd told him about Agent Scandlin (making a point to mention how big he was), Dom hung up.

She giggled again. Guess he didn't like hitting people who were big enough to hit back.

Dom was King of the Assholes.

All men were assholes, even her dad, who would barely speak to her anymore, and especially Jeff, ratting her out like that! She wouldn't have stayed out all night! Austin, her little man, had just been watching his brothers and sister for a few hours, that's all. It's not like he hadn't watched them before, but Big Bad Special Agent Asshole Jeff Scandlin freaked out and called her mom and dad, and now her mom was all calling all the time and up in her business.

Life was *so* not fair.

Okay, yeah, she'd fucked up before, but she was off the meth, and yeah, she smoked a little because her kids, God, they stressed her out, but she was a good mom. Tiff smiled. Her little man, Austin, and her quiet one, Dallas, and, God, Tyler, there was something wrong with Tyler, she would have to put him on medication, she just knew it. And her girls; shy Mari and precious little Abby. How could such sweet girls come from an asshole like Dom? She still couldn't believe she'd gotten pregnant again; she was so fertile it wasn't even funny, because she'd totally made him wear a condom, even if it didn't feel as good, but she *still* got pregnant!

Life wasn't fair.

"C'mooooon school!"

Tiffany hid the weed and the hemostats in their spot under the sink and sprayed a cloud of air freshener. Austin, her little man, was so smart, and she didn't like the way he looked at her sometimes since she'd gotten him back from her parents; it'd gotten worse since they'd moved. She frowned. It was because of Mr. Up-In-Tiff's-Business Scandlin. She appreciated the bikes he'd bought the boys, and she could tell Austin worshiped him, but she wished Jeff would stay out of her life.

Why hadn't that producer called back? Maybe he'd lied. Maybe he wasn't a producer for Columbia; maybe he wasn't even a *producer*. But his card had looked so official, with gold lettering and everything…Tiff sighed, then plopped down on the toilet lid again; she needed to get some sleep because Abby would be up soon. She'd been sure the other kids would get sick, but so far luck was with her; she couldn't handle all of them sick at once.

"C'mooooon school!"

Why hadn't she heard back from *anyone?* She'd submitted demos covering so many good songs, giving them her own twist with her smoky voice: Elvis, Buddy Holly, Reba, even a Roy Orbison "Only the Lonely" that she'd nailed better than Roy ever had, in her opinion; add her head shots, and they should've been knocking her door down.

Tiffany was destined to be a star, she just knew—

The shriek shattered the quiet, and she was up off the toilet with her back pressed to the door before she'd realized she'd moved. There was shouting in a man's deep voice, and then a crash, and then another scream. Tiffany covered her ears as this one trailed up past where a man's voice couldn't and shouldn't go, sounding like a woman or maybe a tortured dog, and then cut off.

Quiet again.

Tiff dropped her shaking hands. That had come from Jeff's place; it was too loud and too close to have come from anywhere else, but that couldn't have been him, it—

Abby's wail brought her back, and she heard Mari's crying mixed in.

"Mom!"

"Mama?"

The boys were up. She snatched up the towel and opened the door and stepped into the hall, glancing into her bedroom. Abby was standing in her crib, and Mari was out of bed; she ran to Tiffany and hugged her leg. Austin and Dallas and Tyler boiled out of their room, sleepy and scared.

"Did you hear that?"

"What was it, Momma?"

"I don't know." It had to have come from a passing car; people were always blasting their music, day or night. Tyler ran to the leg not taken by Mari. Abby watched them from her crib and stamped her feet and held out her arms and wailed.

Austin said, "It was Mr. Scandlin! I heard him shouting!"

"No it wasn't." It couldn't have been.

"Yes it was!"

"No it wasn't." Abby was in a full-tilt fit. "Go get your sister."

Austin looked at the rolled towel in her hand; he went to the bathroom and leaned in and sniff-sniffed, then gave her one of those looks she didn't like before doing as he was told. She dropped the towel on the hallway carpet when he brought a hiccuping Abby to her. Dallas joined his brother and sister at her hip as Abby stretched out, and Tiffany took her; the baby clung, shaking.

Austin glared up at her, defiant. "It *was* Mr. Scandlin! I think he's hurt!"

"Hush! Listen!"

"We need to see if he's okay!"

"*I said be quiet!*"

He crossed his arms in that stubborn way, but he shut up; they stood in a little trembling group, only Austin apart, being the big boy, and listened.

Silence.

"It *was* Mr. Scandlin, Mom! I heard him!"

"Go get my phone, it's on the dresser. We'll call and make sure he's okay."

Austin dashed into her room and came out with the phone. She handed Abby to him and scrolled through her contacts and then froze as she had a thought.

Tiffany swallowed.

"What's wrong?" Austin shifted Abby to the other side and bobbed her up and down. "Mom, what's the matter?"

"Nothing." She avoided his eyes as she found the number and hit the button. Jeff should've been pounding on their door; he was so protective of the children, and that scream had been so loud…*He should've been here by now.*

Austin turned and looked down the stairwell. "I hear something."

The call went to voicemail; Jeff's baritone told her she knew what to do, and then the beep. Tiffany hung up and tried again.

Austin said, "I hear music." He was still looking down the stairs.

"I hear it too, Momma." Tyler peered up at her from beside her leg with scared blue eyes.

Dallas said, "I do too, Mom." He let go of her reluctantly, then moved to hover behind Austin. Mari held her arms up, whimpering, and Tiff picked her up; she pressed her face into Tiffany's neck.

"Y'all listen while I try again." Tiffany worked the phone one-handed, and this time they all heard it; music, so faint she could barely make it out; she hit the call-end button, and the music stopped.

Austin turned and looked at her; Abby's eyes had never left her, one little fist in her mouth; she was teething. That had been Jeff's phone. They could hear it ringing through the wall.

Why isn't he answering?

"Let's go downstairs." They couldn't just stand there in the hallway all night. She grabbed Tyler's hand, and Dallas stuck to his brother's back as they trooped down in a knot. Abby's eyes were glued to her over Austin's shoulder. They stopped at the bottom, and Tiffany caught a whiff of something rotten. Hadn't Austin taken the trash out to the garage like she'd told him?

"Here," she said to Dallas, handing him his sister. Mari whimpered, but that's all. Abby still watched Tiffany; they all did except for Austin, who stared at the wall separating her kitchen from Jeff's. "Go sit on the couch." Tyler obeyed, subdued for once; Dallas followed, carrying Mari.

Austin ignored her. "I think Mr. Scandlin's hurt. We need to call 911."

"Go sit with your brothers and sisters."

"Call 911, Mom, he's hurt!"

Unease churned through Tiffany, but she said, "He's old, Austin." Over fifty; that was *way* old. "He's probably asleep." She pointed. "I said take Abby and sit with your brothers and sisters!"

He glared, then slowly walked over and sat on the couch, where the rest of her children huddled like puppies; Abby had drool running down her fist.

"Y'all stay quiet."

She stood near the refrigerator and hit the button; it rang on her end, followed a heartbeat later by music through the wall, and now she could make it out: George Strait's "All My Exes Live In Texas." Tiff frowned. Why did he have *that* ring-tone? Jeff was from here in Nashville, or at least that's what she thought he'd said. The ringing stopped, and then the song from beyond the wall.

Silence.

"Call 911, Mom."

She looked at her son, and his quiet certainty sent a chill through her. Tiffany raised the phone again, then hesitated; the pot. Would the cops find it? She didn't know why they'd have a reason to come inside her place, let alone search under her bathroom sink, but maybe they would smell it; she didn't need that hassle on top of everything else.

"No," she said, "I'll just hop over and check on him."

Austin didn't argue, only watched her; they all did. She'd never seen them so cowed. She'd never heard screaming like that either. Tiff went to the front door and put her hand on the knob and turned to look back at them. "Stay there." She opened the door, and the humid night air flowed in; she looked at them one more time, then went out, leaving the door open.

Tiffany padded down the short sidewalk to the driveway and across, her toe ring clicking on the warm concrete every other step. She squeezed between the front of Jeff's truck and his garage door, then went down the walk to the porch. His light was off, and the blue metal door looked gray in the dark; the doorbell beside the knob glowed like an orange eye.

She glanced up and down the street, but didn't see a wreck; a car zoomed through an intersection two blocks away, but there were no lights on in any of the duplexes surrounding theirs and no one standing out in the street. There was an empty lot on Jeff's side where the boys liked to play; it'd been overgrown when they moved in, but Jeff had mowed it for them.

Tiffany looked up and down the street again; all quiet except for a dog barking somewhere and the faint hiss of the expressway; she couldn't find the moon, and the stars were bright in a black sky.

She pushed the doorbell.

There was a loud buzz, and then a *DING-DONG!* made her jump; she'd forgotten that the bell was right next to the door, just like on her side. She listened; surely he'd heard that, but there was no deep voice yelling he was coming or asking who it was. Maybe he *was* hurt. Maybe he'd fallen in the shower or down the steps; he was old, and that kind of stuff happened to old people all the time. Tiffany pushed the glowing eye again.

Buzz, *DING-DONG!*

Still no answer, but a smell like spoiled ass made Tiffany's nose crinkle. She leaned and sniffed the door; it was coming from Jeff's place. She chewed her bottom lip; something was wrong. Jeff's truck was here, so he hadn't left. Something had happened. She would have to call the cops, and since Jeff was a cop, they would swarm this place like angry hornets.

"Shit!"

Tiff would have to flush the baggie and spray, then pray no one smelled it; hopefully they would be so occupied with Jeff they wouldn't worry too much about her place, but you never knew. She raised her fist and knocked, hard.

"Jeff?" Nothing. She pounded. "Jeff! It's Tiffany!" She listened; more nothing, but that smell was making her eyes water. God, what *was* that? Tiffany turned and stepped to the edge of the porch, facing the street with toes dangling. She looked at the phone in her hand and sighed.

What a shit-the-bed hassle this is.

Life was so not fair.

Tap. Tap. Tap.

Tiffany spun, then staggered backward onto the short grass. "Jeff?"

No answer, and no more taps. Needle pricks started on her scalp and flowed down her back to the soles of her feet; the blue-gray door grew huge in her vision, big enough to take up the world.

"Jeff?"

Was he playing a *joke* on her? She'd never known him to be a prankster, but people could surprise you; if he was, it wasn't funny.

"Jeff?"

"Mom?" Austin poked his head out, then saw her in the yard and came across the driveway. "Is Mr. Scandlin okay?" His nose wrinkled. "What's that smell?"

"Go back inside."

The peephole was a gleaming black dot in the middle of the upper door, and somebody watched her through it. Tiffany didn't know how she knew that, but she did. She backed further; the grass was prickly, but cool between her toes.

"Mom?"

"I said go back inside!" Out of the corner of her eye she saw Austin start to do it, but then he stopped on their walk and watched her. "Jeff? This isn't funny. I'm going to call—"

Her throat seized as a loud *skreeeeeeel!* came, like metal dragging across metal; in the orange light, she saw the door shudder violently.

Austin darted back across the driveway. "What was *that?*"

Tiffany ran. Austin's eyes bulged. "What—"

She grabbed him as she flew past. "Inside!" Tiffany dragged him, their bare feet slapping on the concrete.

"What about Mr. Scandlin?" Austin fought her as Dallas and Tyler appeared, and then they scrambled back as she pulled him inside and slammed the door.

"What about Mr. Scandlin?"

"Shut up!" Mari took one look at her and burst into tears. Abby, propped in the corner of the couch, did the same. Dallas and Tyler were crying, too.

"Did you see Mr. Scandlin? Was he—"

She slapped him. The crying ceased as they all stared in shock. Tears welled in Austin's eyes as he placed a hand on his cheek, and a distant part of Tiffany's heart broke, but instincts long buried, instincts from the cave-and-tree days, were telling her it was time to run.

Take her kids and *run!*

"Get Abby," she whispered. She jerked her gaze to Dallas. "Get Mari. Go!" The crying started up again, but they minded. Tiffany snatched Tyler's hand; they had to get out and find help.

We have to get out!

Tap. Tap. Tap.

They stared at the kitchen wall, even Abby; the cheap old refrigerator, the only kind Tiff could afford, chose that moment to click to life; its hum was loud in the utter silence.

Austin looked up at her, his cheek scarlet from her hand. "Is that Mr. Scandlin? Why is he tapping on the—"

Tap. Tap. Tap.

Tiffany took the baby from him. "Open the front door!" She was shaking so hard she almost dropped her daughter. Austin's hopeful face had turned uneasy as he watched the wall. She took a whimpering Mari from Dallas, who didn't notice as he stared with a slack jaw. She pushed Tyler towards Austin. "Follow your brother!" She clutched her daughters and shoved Austin with her foot. "Take your brothers and run! *RUN!*"

He staggered, and then Tiffany heard a noise from the other side of her kitchen, and her oldest son's eyes popped and his mouth opened and he screamed.

Tiffany turned in slow motion.

The wall bulged as an enormous hand pushed through, the wallboard and paint stretching like a balloon; needle claws longer than her fingers flexed, and somehow they didn't pop the balloon as a face from a Halloween mask appeared beside it, pushing out its own balloon, nightmare features outlined tight. The claws moved back and forth, back and forth, and teeth as long and as pointed as the claws appeared in that horrendous face.

It was…smiling and waving at them.

A buzzing, clicking noise filled her head, and it took a second for Tiffany to comprehend she was screaming. They were all screaming. Abby was trying to crawl over her shoulder, and her shy little Mari, who could talk but rarely did, was shrieking "*Moner! Moner!*" in Tiffany's ear. Austin was at the front door yanking at the doorknob, his brothers glommed onto him and each other while they screamed.

"It won't open! *It won't open!*"

"Unlock it!"

"It *is* unlocked, but it won't open!"

The balloons and the hand and that dreadful, angular face suddenly vanished, leaving the wall next to the refrigerator looking like any other wall.

Tiffany took a shaky breath. They could—

It stepped through, then, like her wall was mist, or air; it shimmered and then solidified, and then it was standing in her kitchen.

Her children shrieked anew, wretched sounds, but Tiffany was silent as a strange lassitude stole over her. Black scales covered it from hairless head to clawed toe, overlapping like a dark fish; impossibly long arms dangled from massive shoulders; jet-black claws scraped and clicked on her linoleum, leaving smears of blood. It had brought its smell with it, a musky wild-animal scent with a big dose of rotten eggs.

Tiffany met its merciless yellow eyes, and it smiled again, thick lips pulling back from a fence-row of pointed, bloodstained teeth. Those eyes glowed in that hellish, dark face; they had narrow vertical pupils, like a viper's, and its small, pointed ears swiveled toward her independently, like the kitten Daddy had given her when she'd been Austin's age, the one that had gotten run over in the dirt road a week later. Muffin, that's what she'd named it; it'd been such a tiny little thing.

This thing's wide head bumped her ceiling eight feet up.

"Moner, Mommy!"

Book IV

Back to the Cemetery

Be Kind

ANIEL SHOWED the officers to the door, and Beth yanked her phone out and cycled through her contacts and found Jeff's number and hit the button; it didn't even ring, only went straight to his deep voice telling her she knew what to do. She hung up without leaving a message and tried again: same.

Her husband slammed the front door and came back and looked a question at her; Beth shook her head. His face was grim as he went to the window.

She tried again: same. Beth sank onto the couch.

It must be true. Jeff was gone.

"They're standing out there talking," Daniel grated. "Look at 'em! They don't like the son of a bitch, either."

Beth didn't bother to respond; the tension between Special Agent Robert Scarborough of the TBI and the Murfreesboro detectives had been palpable, and her heart was still trying to wrap itself around the terrible news all three had brought.

Daniel said, "I think you and Scandlin might be right."

"About what?"

"About Scarborough being one of McFarlane's bunch."

"I'm one hundred percent positive we're right."

"How can you be so sure?"

"Do you really think he drove all the way out here just to tell us Jeff and this Tiffany Bach woman and her five kids ran away together?"

"I guess not." He shook his head, still staring out the window. "How did he even know we were talking to him?"

"Maybe you were followed that day you met Jeff in Nashville, but however he knows, I know he just gave us another 'warning'." The tall TBI Agent had been as smug as a cat sitting in a bowl of cream when he'd delivered it, too. "The *real* question is, what would he have said to us if Jackson and Frisbee hadn't been here?"

"Good point. I wish they hadn't been, now."

Beth wiped tears from her cheeks. Jeff was gone…and that poor woman and her children…and the professors from Middle Tennessee State…had they done something to Brennan as well? Is that why she hadn't heard from him?

If Brennan had been kidnapped or killed or whatever McFarlane was doing to all these people, then there would be no story to lead into her press conference; and with Jeff gone, there would be no evidence connecting McFarlane's daughters and Melissa Bane to the missing, and no officer of the law standing by their side when they stepped in front of the cameras. It would be just them and their word against McFarlane and all his money and hidden friends.

The icy hand of fear gripped Beth's heart, and squeezed.

Her husband had turned and was watching her. "Scandlin's wife *has* been dead for a long time," he said gently. "Maybe he fell in love, just like his resignation email said."

She looked at him, incredulous. "You know how dedicated to his profession *and* his wife's memory he was—*is*. Do you really believe he would just up and quit his job and run off with some woman more than twenty-years younger, not to mention her five children?"

"Well, sure. I mean, I would've ditched the kids, but…"

"This isn't funny, Daniel, and you don't believe it any more than I do. He wouldn't give up his revenge against McFarlane. And I told you he agreed to come to dinner tomorrow night to compare notes, so he also wouldn't leave without contacting me." A tear ran down her nose, and Beth swatted it away. "That evil old man did something to them. I don't know what, but he did, and now Scarborough and McFarlane's other butt buddies in law enforcement are helping him cover it up!"

"Are you okay?"

"Do I *look* okay?"

Daniel turned back to the window; after a second he said, "Well, the good news is Jackson didn't arrest me." His laugh was sour. "Not yet, anyway."

Beth clutched the phone in her lap; the handsome MPD detective with the build and the dark hair, Jackson, had sat on the love seat while the slender one, Detective Frisbee, had stood by the fireplace with his suit coat unbuttoned and his hands stuffed in his pockets, watching while his partner informed them that two people that Daniel was perhaps acquainted with, Middle Tennessee State University professors Aarif Hameed and Chadwick Hottson, had been missing since Wednesday evening. She and Daniel had expressed their concern and shock, although Beth wasn't sure how well they'd pulled off that last considering how Frisbee had zeroed on them.

Then the interrogation began, and Beth had to admit Jackson was good; he'd kept it circumspect, prying out information while keeping them from invoking their rights. They'd had no desire to be hauled in for formal questioning, however, so Daniel had freely told, and Beth had corroborated, of their Sunday trip to Barron Cemetery; they'd made no mention of the attack later that afternoon, and neither did Jackson nor Frisbee, but the poison presence of Scott Rison had hovered in the investigators' eyes as they'd listened.

Jackson had been scrolling through the pics on her husband's iPhone and Frisbee was busy staring at Beth unblinkingly when into the middle of it all had strode Senior Special Agent Robert Scarborough of the Tennessee Bureau of Investigation.

When Daniel answered the door, the man pushed his way into the castle uninvited and ignored his Murfreesboro colleagues to inform them about Jeff and his supposed resignation email and his supposed decision to run off with his twenty-something-years-younger tenant and her children. Scarborough had delivered this improbable news with a smirk that had made Beth want to pull her Carson and slice his lying lips off—cop or no cop, cop witnesses or no cop witnesses.

She'd also thought Daniel might throw the man out bodily; like her, however, he saw the effect Scarborough's arrival and attitude were having on the MPD detectives. Frisbee had even lifted his stone stare from her and pinned it on the TBI agent. Jackson had quickly wrapped up the interview, and Beth had no doubt that was also because of Scarborough's sudden and slimy presence.

But Jackson hadn't gone away happy. He'd handed Daniel his card and said if they remembered anything else, please call him; his tone and face had more than suggested he knew they were holding something back, and that he doubted they would call.

Daniel is right. They hadn't seen the last of Jackson and Frisbee.

The only question for Beth was why on *earth* had her husband sent a mathematics professor to the cemetery? Not that she'd been about to inquire in front of Jackson or Frisbee, particularly Frisbee…

She opened her mouth to ask, and Daniel announced, "Janet's here."

"She's early." Beth joined him at the window. The two Murfreesboro detectives were by their squad car with the tall form of Scarborough; their crisp navy suits and bright ties were a stark contrast to the Special Agent's unshaven jowls, disheveled charcoal suit, and crumpled paisley tie.

The jerk must've had a long night.

The men watched Janet climb out of her white Tahoe; she'd parked behind Scarborough's dark-blue Crown Victoria, which was parked behind the MPD slick. All three exchanged polite greetings as she carried her purse past them on the way to the front steps, and Beth wanted to groan; Janet's face was composed, but her eyes were alive with curiosity. She'd hoped the cops would be gone before her friend arrived to pick Lizzie up, and now there would be questions—not that Janet was rude enough to ask them, but they'd be in the woman's mind, and she'd certainly talk to Bill.

Janet disappeared from view as she mounted the porch, and Beth focused on the cops loitering in her driveway; whatever their interrupted conversation had been about, it seemed to be over. Detective Jackson said something to Scarborough before slipping his wraparound shades back on; the Senior Agent said something sharp back, but Jackson only gave him a tight smile and hopped in the slick and slammed the door. Detective Frisbee had already climbed behind the wheel, and she heard the engine race before it sped around to the road; they paused there, then turned left.

Daniel grunted. "They're heading toward the cemetery."

Beth studied Special Agent Scarborough's scowl as he watched the Murfreesboro detectives drive east on Daisy.

"*He's* not happy."

"Shame, ain't it?"

Scarborough turned that dire expression toward the front porch for a moment, and then he whirled and stalked toward his Crown Vic; his angry dark eyes flickered to the window, and he froze. Daniel stiffened, and Beth knew some sort of idiot macho staring contest had begun; the doorbell bonged as her husband raised his middle finger and pressed it against the glass.

"Like that, motherfucker?"

"Daniel!" Beth put her hand on the knob; the bell bonged again. "*Daniel!*"

"Yeah? *Yeah?* Well, fuck you, too!"

Beth heard a car door slam, and then an engine rumble to life. She opened the front door in time to see Scarborough hurtle around her driveway and screech to a stop at the road; she was sure he would follow the Murfreesboro cops, but he zoomed off toward Centerville; apparently the speed limit didn't apply to Special Agents.

When he was gone, an uncertain Janet faced her, purse dangling from a forearm. "Is everything all right?"

"Yes," Beth lied.

"Was that…was that a police officer, like the other two?"

"Yes." *Not really.*

Janet made a face. "You know he was giving your house the finger, don't you?"

"I figured as much. Come in, Lizzie's so excited. And thank you for this."

She could see questions piling up at the back of the woman's eyes like floodwater behind a levee, but, like the nervous townsfolk downstream, Beth was grateful the dike somehow held because for the life of her she didn't know how to answer any of those questions in under an hour—or without Janet thinking she should be carted off to the booby hatch.

Janet stepped inside, and Beth closed the door.

"Hello, Daniel."

"Hey, Janet, thanks for watching her, we appreciate it." Despite his words, her husband's face and voice were tight and furious; he seemed to realize it and took a deep breath, then actually shook himself before offering Janet his lopsided grin. "We needed a night out. It's been a helluva week." That was the story, that they were going out to dinner to enjoy some them-time.

"I'm sure it has." Janet grasped Beth's arm and gave it a squeeze, then pulled her into a hug. "I'm sure it has."

They held each other, and then Beth stepped back and wiped her face with the neck of her tee-shirt. Janet dug in her purse and handed Beth a tissue.

"Where's that pretty little girl?"

Beth blew her nose before answering. "Up in her room."

Daniel walked to the bottom of the staircase. "Lizzie? Janet's here."

Beth watched with what felt like the first smile of this awful Saturday as her daughter appeared. She was carrying Mr. Yoda.

"Hi Ms. Janet!"

"Hey you! Well! Who do we have here?"

"This is Mr. Yoda! He's my doggie! Daddy got him for me! His name is Mr. Yoda cuz he's got ears like Master Yoda in my New *Star Wars* Movie." Lizzie came down, and when she reached the last step, she held her dog up for inspection. "See?"

Janet laughed. "Why so he does! Aren't you the sweetest thing!" She reached out an elegant hand to pet Mr. Yoda, who trembled and licked her fingers, unsure of this new giant.

"Wanna hold him?"

"Of course, sweetheart, just let me set my purse down…" Mr. Yoda got passed up to her. "Oh!"

"Sorry about that," Beth said on the way to the kitchen. "Let me get you a paper towel."

"Shoot, it's only a little piddle!" She held Mr. Yoda up to her face. "He just doesn't know me yet, does he? Aren't you precious! Yes you are!" Mr. Yoda began a full-out tongue-assault on Janet's cheek; by the time Beth returned, both Janet and Lizzie were giggling, sounding remarkably alike. Janet put him down on the hardwood as Beth handed her the towels; the older woman wiped absently, not even looking to see if she'd gotten it all off her cream silk blouse.

"I'll get her bag." Beth ascended the curving staircase.

"Ms. Janet, can Mr. Yoda come with us to your house?"

Beth stopped and glanced back at her husband; he stepped forward. "You'll only be gone for one night. He'll be fine until you get back."

"Please?"

"We don't want to impose—"

"*Pleeeease?* Please please please, Daddy, *puuleeease?*"

"I said no, young lady."

Janet said, "Oh, phooey, he can come!"

"Are you sure?" Beth asked her. "He's not housebroken yet."

Janet laughed, then bent to scratch Mr. Yoda, who was sniffing her beige pump. "Mr. Bill's twice as messy on his best day as this little guy on his worst, I can guarantee it." She stood back up. "He'll be no bother."

Beth and her husband exchanged another look, and then she shrugged.

Daniel said, "All right, but he's your responsibility, Lizzie, so you'll have to clean up after him, just like we talked about."

"Yay!" She did the happy dance on the bottom step. "I will, Daddy!"

Despite everything, Beth smiled as she went up to Lizzie's room and retrieved the overnight backpack; thoughts of the professors and Brennan and Jeff and some poor woman and her five kids resurfaced, and her smile was a quivering thing when she came back down. "Okay," Beth announced, wiping her leaking eyes yet again. "She's all set."

But of course she wasn't. Daniel had the idea to pack a small container of dog food, and then Lizzie clamored to take her New *Star Wars* Movie. Janet said that would be fine, and Beth's daughter and husband went into the living room to fetch it.

"Sorry. Daniel's got her hooked on *Star Wars* now."

Janet patted Beth's arm. "There are worse things to be hooked on, dear."

They came back, and Lizzie suddenly yelled, "I forgot Mr. Fred!" and shot up the steps.

"That's her giraffe, right?"

"Yes. I thought the dog would replace him, but she loves them both."

"She's got enough love to go around."

"Yes," Beth said. "Yes she does."

Lizzie appeared again. "Now I'm ready!" Holding Mr. Fred against her lavender Powerpuff Girls tee-shirt, she made a stately procession down the steps, nose in the air, conscious of all the watching adults. Beth wanted to roll her eyes.

Lizzie made her eventual and elegant way to the bottom, and then they got smooches and hugs, and then extra smooches and hugs on the front porch, and then she was down the red-brick steps and running toward Janet's Tahoe, her orange and red Dora LED light-up sneakers flashing at the heels, Mr. Yoda gamboling at her feet and Mr. Fred flopping in her grip. Her dark hair fanned across the top of the green and red Elmo backpack as it jounced; she hadn't wanted to put it up after her bath this morning.

"Love you Mommy love you Daddy, bye!"

Beth had to swallow a giant lump in her throat. "Bye, baby! Be good for Ms. Janet and Mr. Bill!"

"I will!"

"Love you, sweet pea!"

Lizzie stood on her toes and pulled open the Tahoe's back door, picked Mr. Yoda up and put him in, chunked Mr. Fred inside, and then climbed up and in, giving them a gap-toothed grin and a wave before slamming the door.

Janet was standing at the bottom of the steps. "Don't worry, she'll have a great time."

Beth wiped her face and did her best to compose herself; Lizzie would be safe, at least for one night. That was the important thing. "I know she will, Janet, it's just been a long week. Thank you so much for doing this."

Daniel said, "Yes, thank you."

"She's welcome at our house any time." Janet snapped long fingers. "I *knew* I was forgetting something. I need to borrow a car seat; Bill took Trevor's out of his truck for me, but I forgot it this morning."

Beth pulled her keys out. "I'll get it out of my—"

"No need," Daniel said, hopping down the steps while reaching into his pocket. He pointed his fob at his truck where it sat in front of the open garage door; it chirped and unlocked. "I bought one. Janet can use it."

Beth frowned. She was still pissed off about that stupid truck. Daniel carried the bulky seat over to Janet and said, "I'll put it in for you."

Janet's bony fists went to her hips. "What, don't think I can do it, Mr. Big, Strong Man?"

He blinked. "Uh, well, I just…"

She snatched it from him. "I'll have you know I'm a mother *and* a grandmother, and an old hand at car seats, thank you very much."

"Sorry." Daniel retreated up the steps, and Beth smiled when Janet winked at her; her friend started to walk away, and then she hesitated and looked up at them.

"It's not my place…" she began, and Beth felt herself tightening. Janet studied them before continuing: "But I'm gonna say something anyway. Bill isn't my first rodeo. Marriage is hard, damn hard some days, the hardest thing in the world, seems like." They stared at her, and Janet suddenly looked uncomfortable. "Be kind to each other, I guess is what I'm trying to say. Be as kind as you can bring yourselves to be. Forgive me if I've overstepped."

She nodded briskly and walked off, head held high. They watched her secure the seat and get Lizzie buckled in, and then she started the Tahoe and pulled around. The smoked back window rolled down, and Lizzie's gapped grin appeared; she was waving, little arm going back and forth. Mr. Yoda barked.

"Bye Mommy, bye Daddy!"

"Bye, baby!"

"Bye, kiddo! Be good!"

"I will!"

Then the window rolled up and Janet pulled onto Daisy and drove past Helen's house and vanished over the hill.

A huge tension drained out of Beth; she felt like sitting on the steps and putting her head in her hands: her daughter was safe.

For tonight at least, Lizzie would be safe.

She felt Daniel looking at her, so Beth looked back; they stood like that as the late evening sunlight slanted in on them.

He broke the silence. "We need to talk."

"Yes."

Her husband went inside and she followed, shutting the front door. Beth stood in the foyer and listened; the castle felt empty without the energy of a little girl and a puppy filling it. Daniel seemed to feel the lack as well. He looked around the living room and then blew out a breath and flopped on the couch. "She's safe for tonight."

"Yes." Beth went to the fireplace and considered those impossible, unexplained ashes that still sprinkled her fake logs. Then she turned, and they spoke as one:

"I think we should—"

"There's something I didn't tell—"

"Let me say it, Daniel."

He sat up and rested his elbows on his knees. "Go ahead."

"You were right, and I was wrong. We should stay at a hotel, at least until after the press conference."

He gaped. "Ooookay, well, I'm glad you came to your—" He cleared his throat. "I mean, yeah, if they're going to make *cops* disappear, and those little kids…" He looked sick. "God, what did they *do* to them?"

Beth had been trying hard not to think about that. "I can't even imagine. So what didn't you tell me?"

"What?"

"You said there was something you didn't tell me."

"Um, there are a couple things, actually."

"Of course there are."

"Hey, you said you wouldn't leave this place no matter what, so I didn't—"

"Just tell me, Daniel."

Beth stood in front of her kitchen sink; outside the little square window, shadows were creeping across her grass and growing on her fence; the sky to the east and overhead was a deep violet and sprinkled with early stars; to the west it glowed pink and orange and lavender, streaked with crisscrossing contrails that were bright white on top and a fiery red-orange below.

The beauty, however, was lost on her for the moment.

John McFarlane owned her house.

John McFarlane owns my HOUSE!

A thought pierced her, and Beth turned to find her husband leaning against the island with his arms crossed. "Didn't McFarlane say he had Mrs. Fulbright killed because Mr. Fulbright built this place against his wishes?"

Something guarded entered his face; he shifted his weight before answering. "Yeah."

Beth's eyes narrowed. "Didn't he also tell you he doesn't like the castle, and that not only does he want us out, he wants it bulldozed and cows walking around and pissing and crapping on the ground it's built on again, or something idiotic like that?" She crossed her arms, matching his negative body language. "Isn't that why he gave Rison *permission* to attack us? To get us out of here?"

More cautious look; the shift came again. "He said that, too."

"Why would he say all that if he owns it? What aren't you telling me? You said there were *two*. What's the other?"

"Those same things occurred to me, so I talked to Rickson Aldridge yesterday."

He recounted his conversation with their loan officer, and Beth listened with growing anger and confusion. "So you think Aldridge lied about knowing McFarlane, and also about McFarlane signing off on the deal we got on the castle?"

"Yes and yes."

"So if everybody's lying, then McFarlane *wanted* us in this house, or at least approved, but now he wants us out and the castle razed to the ground?"

"I've been thinking about it for a day and a half, and there are only two answers I can see. Number one is simple: John McFarlane is a crazy man."

"All right." *That would explain a lot.* "What's the second?"

Instead of answering, he stared at her directly, and although he still seemed guarded, there was…judgment…in that look; worse, that judgment found her lacking.

Beth spoke through gritted teeth. "What *is* it?"

"Well, if McFarlane's not crazy, then that means there's more going on here than we thought."

"More going on than we thought."

He sighed. "Just listen—"

"More going on than, say, a farmer who thinks he's Emperor of Tennessee sending some punk to rape me and kill you because he doesn't like our *house?* The one it turns out he built in the first place, and that his bank still holds the paper on?"

"Beth—"

"And when that didn't work, he just *ordered* us to move by the first of the month? And if we don't *obey*, he'll send more rapists and murderers to finish the job?"

"Would you—"

"And we can't tell the cops because he knows and or owns them all?"

"I get your—"

"And let us not forget, his daughters and their 'family friend' have a habit of making dozens of random people disappear! Is *that* what you mean? *There's more going on than THAT, Daniel?*"

He sighed again and looked away from her. "Yes, Beth, more going on than that." He gathered himself before facing her once more. "I know this will be hard to believe, but I learned something from Fulbright—"

"There's something else you haven't told me? Why am I not surprised?"

"Please just listen—"

"You're going to say something about that cemetery, aren't you."

"*Would you let me finish a fucking sentence, for Christ's sake?* I'm sorry for yelling, but—"

"Don't you think we have enough to deal with without starting that foolishness again?"

"God *damn* it!" He glared, then just shook his head. "Never mind. This is why I didn't…never mind." He squinted at her. "Foolishness? If it's so dumb, then why are you going with me?" Beth opened her mouth, but he bulled right over her. "And don't give me that horseshit about maker's marks or keeping me out of trouble."

It was her turn to sigh. "I *was* going along for those reasons—and you do need looking after—but since I heard about Jeff and the others, I'm hoping to find fresh graves."

"*Hoping?*"

"You know what I mean." Then all her fears came out in a rush: "Without Brennan's story or Jeff's backing, we'll sound like crackpots, Daniel. Nobody will believe us. We need *evidence*, and if Bane and McFarlane's daughters are going to make people vanish, why not put them in that cemetery? Fresh graves for the authorities to exhume would solve a lot of our problems."

Her stomach twisted, and she turned and braced both hands on the counter and hung her head over the sink, but Beth was only sick in her heart. *What a thing to hope for!* And she couldn't believe she was buying into his idiot theory, but at the moment she had nothing better.

But she kept thinking about what Jeff had said, how he didn't think McFarlane would be dumb enough to bury missing people on his property. She had to go out there and check, though, because if they found Brennan or Jeff or those two professors or that poor woman and her children under that tangle of white roses, they could put McFarlane and his daughters and Bane and the rest of those thugs away forever.

A tear rolled down her cheek; she swiped it away.

I'll never meet you now, Jeff. Beth would also never hear what he'd truly thought about Melissa Bane. *What were you hiding? Why were you so frightened of her?*

After a time when her husband said nothing, she looked over her shoulder; he was watching her with a bleak expression.

"Yeah, about that." He eyed her warily and then said: "I think you should check us into a hotel while I go to the cemetery."

She spun to face him. He held up his hands. "Just hear me out. We both don't need—"

"I'm going, end of discussion." How could he think she wouldn't know what he was doing? How could she be so *mad* at him and want his arms around her at the same time? They hadn't held each other or kissed in almost a week, let alone made love; it felt like ten years.

"Fine," he growled. "*God*, you're fucking stubborn! But if you're going, I want you to carry the shotgun."

"No."

"It's not like a pistol. You don't need any training to use it, just some minimal instruction and a few safety pointers, and I can give you those. You don't even have to aim, just point it in a rapist's general direction and pull the trigger—boom, Insta-Rapist-Goo."

"*No.*"

"God damn it, these people are *dangerous*, don't you get that?"

"I know they're dangerous! Jeff and Brennan and those professors you sent out there know they're dangerous, too! Besides, I'll have my knife, and you'll have all your big, baaaad guns to protect me."

"Beth—"

"I won't touch a gun, Daniel. *I will not.*"

Her husband threw up his hands, then glanced out at the deepening twilight. "*Fuck!* All right, just stick close to me." He squinted at her again. "What if we don't find anything? Maybe we should put off calling the press conference until—"

"It goes on next week. I don't know *when* next week, we still need to decide, but it *will* happen."

"Beth—"

"Don't you see? That's what they want, for us to run away and keep our mouths shut! Just because I agreed to take my daughter to a hotel for a few days doesn't mean I'm running, Daniel. I will *not* run from these people! I will make them pay for Jeff, and for Brennan, and for that poor woman and her children, and for the professors, and for who knows how many others. If we can find fresh graves in that cemetery tonight, so much the better, but even if we don't, we'll *still* tell everyone what they're doing. It'll be harder to convince people, but McFarlane won't dare touch us then, not with the eyes of the world glued to him! And you said it yourself: not everyone is a John McFarlane fan, so there has to be another cop who suspects that old farmer isn't what he seems. Maybe our conference will shake that person loose."

He scrubbed his hands over his face. "I guess you're right. Jesus, we'll have lawyers setting up shop inside every orifice we've got."

"They have to be stopped. No matter what it takes."

He nodded tiredly, then glanced outside again before walking away. "Let's get this show on the road." He disappeared into the foyer, voice trailing. "We need to get dressed and go or we'll be out there all night. I've got work tomorrow, and you've got to pick Lizzie up after Janet's church lets out. We'll pack first thing in the morning, enough stuff for a week I think, and then we'll—"

"You promised."

Silence.

"You *promised*, Daniel."

He reappeared by their fridge. "I know I promised, but we have more important—"

"You promised."

He grimaced. "All right, but I still think we should get ready first. Then you can tell me…whatever you need to tell me, and we can leave right after."

"That's fine."

Despite her words, terror fluttered in Beth's core. *What if he can't handle what I was, what I've done? What if he leaves us?* Some of her dread must have shown, because he walked over and looked down into her eyes.

"I know this means a lot to you—"

"Everything."

"But I want you to know I was serious about what I said the other night, about the past not mattering. I'm no angel, trust me, and I don't care what you did, so you don't have to tell me anything if you—"

"It's not about what I want or what you want anymore. I *have* to tell you. What Rison said…that was just a twisted half-truth, and I won't have it festering between us. I should've had the courage to tell you a long time ago, I understand that now, and I'm sorry, but here we are, and you need to know what happened to me. What I did. What I was. Then if you can't stand to be with me anymore—"

"Beth—"

"—we'll deal with it."

They looked at each other for a long time before he turned away. "We should eat something. This will be a long night."

"I'm not hungry."

"Yeah," he said softly, "me either."

Her husband went upstairs.

Beth stood with her arms wrapped around her middle, hugging herself hard and trembling.

I can still get out of this.

He didn't want to know; she could just tell him they'd talk later in the week, or maybe next month; he'd be good with that.

No.

Beth straightened her spine.

No! She would not be a coward. And he was right; they needed to get their gear together and get dressed, and then…

And then Daniel would learn what kind of woman he'd married.

Beth followed him up on shaky legs.

Falling Through Darkness

ETH LOOKED up at their picture on the mantle.

Lizzie was in the middle, with Beth's arms around her and Daniel's arms around them both. It'd been taken over a year and a half ago at one of those studios in the mall and had turned out well despite that horrid plum backdrop. She stood on tip-toe and retrieved it; her daughter had still been a toddler, barely three, and Beth marveled at the changes such a short time had wrought. Lizzie was a little lady, now.

Beth heard him shift on the couch, so she stretched and put the frame back and stared at the ashes behind the mesh-iron curtain, ashes from pages of unexplained and impossible notes in a woman's loopy hand, notes that contained information on events in her life she'd never told a soul about—until tonight.

For now, Beth didn't wonder how that could be.

Now she just had to tell him.

She was frozen at the edge of the cliff; the darkness that shrouded her past waited below, but she couldn't bring herself to jump. Beth had left that darkness behind so long ago, fought tooth and nail with every fiber of her being to mold herself into a different person, a *better* person; a warrior.

But now she had to go back.

She took a deep breath, opened her mouth, and jumped.

She was five when the Morrisseys adopted her. Before them she played and slept with large groups of children, the adults in her world passing billboards telling her how pretty she was, how smart, how sweet, looming and then gone. She knew she had no parents, but that was all right because none of her friends had any either.

He interrupted to ask if she recalled those two names from the ashes, and Beth suppressed a flash of anger; she'd jumped, and now all she wanted was the bottom, the quicker the better, but she supposed she should be grateful he was participating and not just sitting there like a lump. So she told him the truth: she didn't remember, and considering the source, she didn't know if the names were even accurate, and wasn't sure she cared either way. She hadn't decided what to do about it, regardless.

He had nothing to say to that, so Beth kept falling; it was easy up here because it was still mostly light. The true darkness waited below.

Then the Morrisseys took her in. Beth told him about being the daughter of a Methodist lay-minister and a home maker, an older couple who'd raised two college-age boys and then decided they'd wanted the light and laughter of a little girl in their lives. She told him about her dog, Spankey, a medium-sized brown-and-white mutt with a long, shaggy tail who she'd loved more than life itself, and the chickens and the goats and the cows on the tiny farm they'd all lived on in Summervale, Ohio, about thirty miles northeast of Cincinnati.

He said, "Spankey?"

Beth ignored him and told about dressing up for church and how she'd sit and listen to her Daddy preach about God and his son Jesus and she was happy as she kicked her feet out over the edge of the pew; bored, but happy, waiting for the singing. Beth rarely sang now, but back then she'd loved it when everyone would stand up with a rustle of good clothes and belt out a hymn. After church they would go to the Sizzler buffet, or even better have a potluck, with the ladies bringing their finest dishes; there were casseroles and pies and fried chicken and things she couldn't name, but everything had been tasty. And since it was Sunday afternoon, her father would let her out of most of her chores, but not all; they had a dozen chickens and four cows and several goats, and they all had to be fed and the cows and goats had to be milked, but on Sunday he would let her go play with Spankey by the pond, or wander through the small woods behind their house when her few chores were done.

Sundays were her favorite day…

Beth choked off, the ashes blurring. *Good memories shouldn't be so painful.* She could feel him watching, so she gathered her courage and kept falling.

She was seven the first time it happened. It was a Sunday afternoon. Mommy had left with Mrs. Draper and Mrs. Broomfield to go shopping in town. Daddy had been in a strange mood, which was okay because sometimes he did that, got in a mood, but he always got in a good mood again, and then he would tickle her and read with her and play ball with her and Spankey. But that afternoon, after Mommy left, he called her into the barn…

She didn't want to, but he said it was part of being a family so she let him, even though she didn't like it and it hurt, but he seemed to enjoy it. After, they knelt in the hay and prayed to Jesus for forgiveness. Then he told her not to tell Mommy because even though what they had done was part of being a family, a good and righteous part, Mommy wouldn't understand, and would get mad at her, so she had to keep it their secret. Then he let her go outside to play with Spankey.

It happened four more times over the next three years; every time, after, they'd pray to Jesus to forgive them and he'd tell her not to say anything to Mommy, that it was their secret. She didn't like it, didn't like the things he made her do, but she did them because it was part of being a family and he was her Daddy, but in her heart Beth knew it was wrong.

Then one day a boy from her home room, Bobby Hews, didn't come to class. She sat at her small desk surrounded by the other children and watched her teacher, Mrs. Haverchamp, whisper with the counselor, Mr. Mark, who had come into their classroom just after first bell. Mr. Mark was a bearded bear of a man who had a rumbly voice and a kind smile, but he wasn't smiling that morning. Then

Mr. Mark left and Mrs. Haverchamp stood behind her big desk at the front of the room looking all upset and told them that Bobby wouldn't be there for a few days and that it wasn't right for anyone to touch them in their privates, and to tell a grownup they trusted if someone did that, and if they couldn't tell a grownup, tell a police officer. Mrs. Haverchamp then asked them if they understood her, and they'd answered in chorus:

"Yes, Mrs. Haverchamp!"

So she'd ridden the bus home armed with this new information and waited.

Her tenth birthday passed, and then one Saturday afternoon he came to her room; he'd been in a mood all week, and her mother was visiting and wouldn't be back until dinner, and Beth was ready for him—or so she'd thought. She told him she didn't want to and that Mrs. Haverchamp said it was bad, but he got angry and made her, and the more she fought, the more he seemed to enjoy it; after, she refused to pray with him and ran out to the woods to hide and wait for her mother to get home.

It'd been different that time, rough, and she was hurting and even bleeding down there a little, but when her mommy got home, Beth would tell and Mommy would make him stop and everything would be better. He came to the edge of the pond and called, sometimes mad and sometimes sweet, but she didn't answer. Spankey got bored and went sniffing around the base of the trees, trailing squirrels, but she hugged her knees until Mommy got home, and then she jumped up and ran to the house, but Daddy beat her there, slamming the door and locking her out.

He came out a short time later and didn't look at her as he walked toward the barn. She found her mother looking sad and tried to tell, but Mommy got mad and told her not to tell fibs, but Beth told her anyway, and then her mother got screaming mad for the first time ever and told her to go to her room until she stopped fibbing, so she ran and curled up on her bed and cried.

Beth wiped her eyes; the pain of their betrayal was still somehow fresh after twenty-five years. Daniel was silent, so she risked a glance over her shoulder; he sat on the edge of the couch, head hanging, looking at the carpet between his feet without blinking.

She turned back to the ashes and kept falling.

Her Daddy came in for dinner, and Mommy knocked on her door and said she could come eat if she promised to stop fibbing, but she kept quiet, and Mommy went away. She heard them talking in low voices, and Beth knew *he* was telling more fibs; after a time she heard him get up and go back outside.

She got mad then, furious, and stomped around her room and threw a few things, trying to work the amazing anger off, but it didn't help, so she stormed out of her room and up to her mother, who was at the sink doing the dishes, and told her she was telling the truth and that he was fibbing and that baby Jesus didn't like it, and then she blasted through the screen door and outside. Beth didn't know what she would do, but a cold, clear-eyed fury burned through her.

She found him working beneath their pickup truck under the bright lights, just inside the shop he had for his tools, the one right next to the barn; a front wheel was off, and the big jack with the long orange handle he let her pump sometimes held the front end off the ground.

He heard her coming and slid out with a gleaming wrench in his hand and raised his head, and Beth would never forget that moment; gone was the kind expression he'd showed old Mrs. Ferguson when Mr. Ferguson passed, or the wise look he got when standing at the pulpit telling them what God and Jesus thought and how they should all live; his eyes *danced*, and he had a little boy's naughty grin that said, "Ha, ha, I got away with it!"—an *evil* grin—and…and then it vanished as if it'd never been. She'd wondered if she'd really seen it as he donned the wise face and used the Daddy voice to tell her to go back to her room, that they would talk about it later, but his eyes still danced, and that's when Beth knew she hadn't imagined it, that that grin was real, and that now he was just hiding it, and that maybe he hid it every day.

Then he slid back under the truck, and something inside her snapped.

Beth walked over to the jack…no, she hadn't walked over to the jack…well, she didn't *remember* walking, but she must've because she remembered pushing it with everything she had, trying to make the truck fall on him and squish that terrible grin, and she *had* pushed it, she knew that, but she couldn't remember walking…

Beth gathered her wits; she'd been so young, and it'd been so long since she'd let herself think of that day, and she'd been so mad at him, that she just couldn't recall all the details now. That must be it.

So she walked over to the big orange-handled jack and she pushed as hard as she could and he shouted as the truck rocked and the jack slipped and he tried to roll out and then it all came down with a crash, and he screamed and screamed and screamed and screamed…

 From behind her, she heard one word:

"Good."

Beth tried to smile, but couldn't; she was plummeting through the darkness now, and nothing would stop her but the bottom.

The police came, and she told them like Mrs. Haverchamp said, and they took them both to the hospital where a nice lady doctor examined her down there, and then the nice lady doctor got this look like she was going to throw up and left the room, and then her Daddy went to jail and Beth never saw him or her Mommy or Mrs. Haverchamp or her homeroom or her friends at school or her congregation or her house or the pond or the cows or the chickens or the goats or Spankey ever again.

Then she was back in the system, and she was still pretty and smart, but she was no longer sweet; two families wanted to adopt her that first year, nice people who would give her what she wanted most of the time, but Beth hated how they'd whisper to each other when they were in another room, like she was stupid and didn't know what they were talking about, so she'd do something to upset them and then they'd take her back to the place with all the other kids. That place became her *true* home, although the building itself changed over time, as well as the children; after a while, Beth always went home.

She was fifteen when she met Chris.

Mary Dorn had been her guardian then. Mary was a young widower, and although she'd been a stickler about homework and chores, she'd let Beth have her space while providing stability and guidance. The memory brought a sweet ache; Mary had been one of the good ones. She'd tried her best with a difficult teenage girl, and in a way had been a friend. Beth remembered how she'd treated Mary, and shame seared her; she hoped Mary was well and still taking in fosters. If she was, those kids were lucky.

Beth first saw Chris when she walked off campus to eat lunch; she still hadn't known many people and always ate lunch alone. He was standing in the parking lot talking with some guys she recognized as seniors, but she'd never seen him before, and Beth would've remembered if she had; he had curly light-brown hair and big blue eyes, and she walked into a parked car when he smiled at her. The other guys laughed, but he came over and asked if she was all right. She stammered something and escaped, but his smile lingered, so she forgot about lunch and hid behind a tree at the edge of the lot and spied on this beautiful boy. Beth thought maybe he was new, like her, and that she just hadn't seen him before, but he slapped hands with the seniors and climbed into a black Corvette and roared away.

The rest of her day was a blur.

Beth spent the next three weeks asking questions and walking through the parking lot every lunch hoping to see him again; she learned his name was Christopher Olsen, and that he wasn't in school because his family had money, loads of money, and that he'd dropped out and gotten his GED, and now he was free to do as he pleased at seventeen. *All* the girls knew who he was, and stared and whispered when he drove his Corvette to Friday night football games, but it was Beth he asked to the movies the third time she smiled at him in the parking lot.

She snuck out of her room the next Friday night—Mary wouldn't have approved—and they went and he kissed her, and Beth found to her wonder the memory of that night was still magical, even knowing what would happen later.

It wasn't long before she quit school and ran away to live with Chris. Beth left a note for Mary…her face burned, but she told him how she wrote that she and Chris were in love, and that she would marry him. She didn't inform Mary about his big house in Willow Brook, a gated community on the north side of Cincinnati, because she would tell the police. Beth did promise to call and let her know she was okay, but she never called, worried they would somehow find her.

So then Beth moved in with Chris. They call their house the castle as a joke, but Chris's house really was a castle; it had six bedrooms and five bathrooms, and a pool and a hot tub, and a game room with a beautiful pool table covered in red felt. He lived there by himself because his dad had divorced them and moved to London and his mother traveled all the time; his dad sent Chris money every month, a *lot* of money, and they had parties every weekend and people coming over all the time. Chris got her to smoke heroin by saying it would make her feel wonderful, and that he loved her and wanted to share it with her, so the next six months were a blur of getting high and having sex and playing pool, with no cares or worries in the world.

She'd been so young and stupid she'd thought it would last forever...

Beth turned around. Daniel still sat on the edge of the couch, but his head was up, and he was staring at the wall next to the flat-screen with a pinched expression. Maybe she shouldn't have mentioned the sex, but it'd been incredible, with them being so young and thinking they were in love. Beth sure didn't mention *that* part. Instead she said, "I'm sorry I lied to you a few years ago. I told you my adopted father taught me how to play pool, but I learned in Chris's game room. I taught myself, at least initially."

"I forgive you. Are you done? It's late and we've got shit to do."

Beth turned back to the ashes, trying not to be angry with him and failing; she wasn't anywhere *near* done, and he knew it.

About three weeks after her sixteenth birthday, Chris's mom showed up on a Friday night in the middle of a big party. Chris talked to her all the time on the phone, but that was the first time Beth had met her, and it turned out to be memorable; Mrs. Olsen took one look and called the cops.

They hid the drugs, and his mom knew they did—she didn't want her son to go to jail—but the police made them pour out all the alcohol. Then Chris and his mom got into a huge fight, and part of what they fought about was Beth; the woman wanted her gone as of yesterday, but Chris said he loved her and that he was going to marry her.

The most awkward two days of Beth's life followed; Mrs. Olsen ignored her like a stray cur, refusing to speak to her but not *about* her while she urged Chris to do something with his life; she'd been addicted to several kinds of pills and had gotten clean at one of those rich-people places where she'd received holistic foot massages and volcanic mud facials to reinforce her Twelve Steps; she now carried the mantle of righteousness only the newly sober could boast. Mrs. Olsen had also decided that acting like a mother suited her again, but Chris was having none of it, so she zoomed away in her black Mercedes, bound for Aspen, she said; she also threatened call Chris's father.

What Beth remembered most about the day his mother left, though, was how bad she was hurting. The woman wasn't even out of the driveway before they were scrambling to get the stash and the spoon and the rig and the lighter; they'd graduated from smoking to skin-popping by that point.

She was hooked, they both were, and it was about to get far worse.

Chris's father called; then the money stopped. The big parties stopped too, but strange people started coming around, mostly at night; she knew what he was doing, and they would fight about it, and he would scream that it was her fault because his mom and dad wanted her gone, but then he would tell her he loved her and that he didn't care what they thought or wanted because he would turn eighteen in two months and he was going to marry her and be with her forever; they'd get high and make love and everything would be okay for a while, and then the whole scene would repeat itself. She was in a bad situation, but Beth was so far gone she couldn't see the truth, let alone figure how to get out.

"I *admired* Chris. I thought the fact that he could do what he wanted was special, but now I find it sad, maybe the saddest thing of all. His parents abetted their son's downfall. If they had cared, they would've set rules and been there to guide him. Even with what he did to me, I still feel sorry for Chris."

"What did he do to you?"

Chris turned eighteen, but there was no more talk of marriage. His mom put the house on the market, and Chris threw the For Sale sign into the street; there followed a chain of events she didn't clearly recall, but it started with Chris getting a lawyer and ended with the house in his name.

They were on their own.

One night about a month later, almost Christmastime, four guys showed up late; Chris seemed nervous, but they went upstairs to talk business and Beth went back to playing pool. She'd hardly paid attention anyway, being used to his late-night meetings.

That turned out to be a mistake.

A little later they all came back down, and Chris had a busted lip and was keeping a bloody towel filled with ice pressed to his face. She ran to him and asked what happened, and he told her he'd fallen, it was nothing, but he seemed scared.

Beth looked at the four men and noted they were all staring at her; they were older, in their late twenties or early thirties, and two were huge, one black and one white. The big guys stood in the background while the other two did the talking; a dark-haired, wiry guy did some, but the bookish one with the wire-framed glasses and long blond ponytail did the most, speaking to Chris in a soft voice while watching her. Chris introduced them: the hulking black guy was Mike, and his bigger white friend was Tuck; the wiry, intent guy was Johnny, and the leader, the handsome one with the soft voice and the glasses and ponytail, was Simon.

Beth said hello, but she didn't like the way they were looking at her so she pulled Chris around the Brunswick and through the sliding-glass doors to stand beside the scummy, iced-over pool. She remembered snow crusting the scum and their breath pluming the air as she asked him what was going on, and he held her and kissed her and told her he loved her and that he needed her to go with these guys to pick something up; Chris would give her the money, and then they would bring her back. He had to stay because he was waiting on some other guys to deliver a lot of stuff.

Beth told him to jump in the frozen pool.

They were still standing out in the cold arguing when the glass door slid open and two of the men grabbed Chris by the arms; the giant white one, Tuck, grabbed her. Chris yelled, "Don't hurt her! Don't hurt her! I'll get your money!" Then Simon backhanded Beth across the face, and she would've fallen to the icy cobblestones if the big guy hadn't held her up. Simon told Chris he'd already agreed: "The girl for what you owe." At those words, Beth's world fell through a black hole that opened beneath her wobbly feet.

Chris had *traded* her.

He went wild then, fighting, but they beat him to the ground. Simon kicked him one last time, and they dragged Beth out to their car, a black four-door Caprice, and took her away.

She remembered rough hands pawing at her breasts, between her legs, the coarse laughter as they drove across the city and down to an industrial area by the river. They stopped at a chain-link fence with a gate, and Mike got out and unlocked it and let them through and they drove to a long metal warehouse and pulled her out of the car.

"Stop."

There was another woman inside, a blonde, but the blonde fled when she saw what was going on. The front of the warehouse had been converted to living space, with two bedrooms and a living room and a kitchen—

"Stop!"

—and one bedroom was a loft with a spiral stairway, and they took her up and she tried to fight them but they had guns and they were so big and strong and they hurt her, so she pretended she liked it to make them stop hurting her, and they laughed and called her a little freak and took turns, but sometimes she had to do two or three at a time, and once even all four while they were high-fiving each other and laughing and laughing—

"Stop! *Please* stop!"

Beth was on her hands and knees in front of the ashes; she didn't remember falling. Her tears dripped onto the carpet. Then he was there saying her name, and at his touch she struck out, and he grunted as she connected, but he wrapped his strong arms around her and wouldn't let go. She stopped fighting him and clung, and he picked her up and carried her to the couch and held her on his lap and whispered that she was here with him and not there anymore, that it was all right. He was shaking and crying, too, and he kissed her hair as she let out twenty years worth of pain and terror.

The tears and shaking finally stopped. "Do you want a glass of water?"

"Yes, please."

He eased her off his lap and went into the kitchen, and she wiped her face and blew her nose, using a tissue from the box on the coffee table. He came back and handed her a tall glass of ice water and sat down. Beth drank and set the glass on a coaster, and he took her hand.

"I'm proud of you. It took guts to tell me all of that. It's getting late, we need to go."

He thought she was done…no, he just *hoped* she was done…Beth pulled her hand from his. "I still need to tell you how I got away, and…and some other things." Those "other things" made her heart quail, but Beth had fallen this far; she wasn't about to stop now.

"Did the blonde help you? Who was she? Did you go to the cops? Tell me those fuckers are in prison."

Beth licked her lips. *This is so hard.* How would he react?

"I didn't escape that night. They held me captive for over five months."

Outrage filled his face, and he jumped up and cursed and paced around the living room. Beth thought he would punch a hole in their wall, but he stopped dead and looked at her, taut as a live wire: "Tell me those rapist pukes are dead or locked up, or so help me God I'll find them and kill them myself."

"They're dead. Please sit down so I can finish."

He stared at her, breathing hard, and then slumped onto the couch and lowered his face into his hands.

Beth took a sip of cold water and continued falling.

The blonde was Sadie. Sadie was Johnny's. Simon claimed *her*, although he didn't mind sharing. Simon was the leader; he owned the warehouse and the computer wholesale and repair business that occupied it, but that was just a front. Drugs were his business, and business was good. Simon and Johnny lived there; they were the brains, although it was Simon who ran things. Mike and Tuck were just muscle, but they hung around a lot because they liked house pussy. That's what they called her and Sadie, house pussy.

The old shame and humiliation flooded through her, and Beth fought the urge to get up and break something, or stab someone. Out of the corner of her eye she saw him raise his face and look at her, but she didn't meet his eyes. She couldn't.

Somehow Beth dredged up the strength to keep falling.

"You're wondering why it took me five months to get away."

He nodded, still watching her.

"It wasn't from lack of desire."

There was no phone, and only one way in or out of the converted living space, and Simon kept it locked; the greater part of the warehouse was filled with broken computers and monitors and copiers, and there were two big roll-up doors to load or unload trucks back there, but those were chained and padlocked inside and out. And Simon really was a computer expert, despite his diversion into drug supply; he'd designed state-of-the-art surveillance and alarm systems, with cameras she and Sadie could see—and, as they found out the hard way, hidden cameras they couldn't.

But Simon didn't need cameras or locks to manage them; Beth was a full-blown heroin addict by that time, Sadie too, and he controlled their supply; if they did what he wanted, they got what they wanted.

If not, not.

Beth had been there a month when she'd lost it, demanding they take her back to Chris, screaming that he loved her and that he wouldn't have traded her, that he wouldn't have done that to her. But they just laughed and got rough and were going to rape her again, and she fought, biting and scratching, until Simon told Johnny to hold her down; it took all of them. Then Simon came out of his office and plugged something into the outlet next to where she was pinned, and he…he…

Beth raised her shirt and ran her fingers over the silvery ridges: "A soldering gun. Simon was always building motherboards or other computer stuff..." She let her shirt fall and pulled another tissue and blew her nose. "So now you know how I got my scars."

She almost died; not from the pain or the burns, but from Simon's other punishment. He wouldn't let her have anything for five days, and the withdrawal on top of her wounds, combined with her heartbreak over Chris...

"I *would* have died if it hadn't been for Sadie. She was older, twenty-three or four, and she'd also been hooked far longer and knew the tricks. She had pills, some that they let her have, and some that she stole from Johnny somehow; without those pills, I wouldn't have made it. Sadie did that for me even though the guys used her hard while I was healing. I could hear the slaps and the grunts and the screams from the other room. It was about three months after that when she was killed."

"Jesus," he said. "What happened?"

"Johnny happened."

They were all mean, and Simon could be cruel when it suited, but Johnny was the scary one; the others would hurt you if you didn't do what they wanted, but Johnny would hurt you just because. He had a temper, too, rage on a hair trigger, and because he'd brought Sadie back from a run to Denver, Johnny thought in some sick way that he owned her. He would get jealous when the other guys used her, but not always; stability wasn't exactly Johnny's modus operandi.

"Johnny beat Sadie to death one night while I listened in helpless horror from the next room."

"*Shit.*"

It started a big fight between the guys; Sadie had been alive when they'd finally intervened, but by the time they'd finished arguing about what to do, she had stopped breathing. Then they all looked at *her*, and Beth knew she was in trouble; she was a witness. They discussed it out of earshot, and she thought they would kill her; she was even looking forward to it because it would be an end to the hell she was living, but for some reason they didn't; probably couldn't stand to be without house pussy.

Then Simon and Johnny and Mike carried Sadie's limp, smashed, and bloody corpse out the door. Beth never knew what they did with her. While they were gone, Tuck forced her to clean up the blood and then give him a blowjob.

"Jesus Christ. Can we skip to the part where these pieces of shit die? Please?"

"Sadie," Beth said quietly. "Her name was Sadie, and she saved my life. I never knew her last name. I don't even know if Sadie was her real name. Sadie was from Denver. She had a little boy, Tristan. When we'd get high, she'd talk about him; he was seven or eight by that point, but Sadie would gush about how he'd looked when he was two, the last time she'd seen him; about how he'd laugh when he played with his toy cars, and how he'd run to her and say 'Momma'. Sadie from Denver. I want you to remember, because Sadie deserves to be remembered, and we might be the only two people on the planet who care. Sadie had been a street walker and a drug addict, and she had a little boy named Tristan, and she saved my life. Sadie from Denver."

"Sadie from Denver," he said, soft.

They sat in silence; a car went by out on Daisy, headlights splashing through the darkened living room. Beth swallowed. There was more. He would think it the worst; it wasn't, not to her, not by far, but he needed to know:

"They made movies."

He twisted to face her. "What?"

"They took pictures, too, of Sadie and me. The guys made us…you know… together…and then one or two or all four would join in. I recall a tripod set up next to the bed at least twice; it might have been more. I was so messed up back then, it was probably more."

Beth couldn't look at him; it felt like there was a hydrogen bomb about to go off in the living room. He staggered to his feet, then leaned against the wall behind the television, both palms flat like it was the only thing holding him up.

"I thought you should know."

"I didn't fucking need to know *that*."

"Yes you did. It's been almost twenty years, and it would be a drop in the ocean of smut that's out there now, but Simon may have posted the videos or the pictures. I've never found them, but then again, I've never really looked."

He pushed off the wall and put his back to her; another set of headlights flashed across them. When he spoke, his voice sent a spasm of fear through Beth's heart.

"Are you done? Can we go now?"

"No, I'm not done. Will you please sit down?"

"No thanks, I'll stay standing."

Somehow, *somehow*, Beth kept falling.

"After Sadie was gone, I lived with them for over a month."

She let that float there, but said no more because even though she loved him and he deserved to know who he'd married, Beth had no desire to relive what little she recalled of that time.

What she did remember was enough.

He got it, though.

"Jesus," he breathed.

Then the guys made a mistake.

Beth was asleep when a man dragged her out of Johnny's bed by the hair. She didn't know him, a blocky, bald gentleman in a suit with no tie. The hand not tangled in her hair held the biggest gun she'd ever laid eyes on, and when he dropped her onto the carpet in the living area, she found that everyone had preceded her; Beth also saw something she'd thought she'd never see.

Simon was scared.

So were Mike and Tuck; only Johnny looked the same, pissed off. Facing them were more men like the one who'd dragged her: blocky, shaved heads, suits sans ties, their gleaming white dress shirts unbuttoned to reveal tufts of graying chest hair. Big guns. The guys had their guns out too, though nobody was pointing them at anybody yet. But the two groups were shouting at each other, and one newcomer was doing most of the shouting; the chest hairs spoke English with a heavy accent, Russian or Yugoslavian or something; to this day Beth didn't know and didn't really care. She knew they weren't from Cincinnati.

The first chest hair had dropped Beth dead center between the men, and she was so scared she could hardly understand what was going on, but the gist was the Russians or whoever wanted to be paid; they thought the guys had cheated them, or maybe cut in on their territory. The guys thought different, but there were six of the scary chest hairs and only four of them. One extra-wide chest hair hung by the door, blocking the exit; the leader stood almost on top of her, jabbing a thick finger at Simon as he made his demands while his men stood fanned out behind him, watching everyone, including her.

Simon told the boss chest hair he didn't have any money or drugs.

Then he pointed at Beth and offered her instead.

The leader looked down at her for the first time; his eyes were heavy-lidded and as glittery as brown gems, and he could've been examining a rock or a bug for all the life in them. But evidently Beth passed muster because he snapped something incomprehensible and one of the lesser chest hairs grabbed her and hauled her across the room and passed her to the super-sized chest hair guarding the door; his giant hand encircled her arm like a shackle. She gave an experimental tug, and he snarled something and shook her like a doll; the flunky chest hair went back and stood behind his boss again.

There followed more negotiations, if you can call them that. Beth didn't bother to listen because despair almost overwhelmed her; she'd been *traded* again. As bad as her situation was, at least the guys were a known quantity.

Beth did *not* want to go with those strange, hairy men.

She stopped talking.

Daniel turned to scowl at her, waiting, his arms crossed, waiting…but should she tell him? All these years later, and she still didn't understand; but in for a penny…

"Then something happened, and it's the strangest thing that's ever happened to me in my life; time seemed to…to slow, and…and I raised my head and I looked at Johnny, and I knew he would shoot the lead chest hair in the face." *How* she'd known, Beth still didn't get, but she'd been sure, so she'd shifted to stand behind the big man guarding the door. He didn't acknowledge her move beyond tightening his fist, so she poked one eye past his huge arm and waited for what she knew would happen.

And then Johnny shot the leader in the face.

"You *knew?* You mean you saw it, like a vision?"

"Not like a vision," Beth said carefully. "I just knew." She shared the conclusion she'd come to after thinking about it over the years: unfortunately, she'd known Johnny, and her subconscious must have seen the signs and warned her.

He grunted. "What happened then?"

Relieved he was dropping it, Beth kept falling:

"Blood and brains and bullets everywhere, that's what happened." The man who held her went down right away and fell on top of her, almost crushing her; she lay under him with her hands covering her ears and saw Simon go down without firing a shot. Johnny got the one behind the leader before dying. Big Mike killed a chest hair before falling, and Tuck, who was bigger than Big Mike and so tough he liked to beat sixteen-year-old girls when they didn't suck him off good enough, screamed and dropped his gun before they cut him down.

Beth knew if she just laid there, they would kill her; a burst of fear adrenaline gave her the strength to push the heavy man off, and she opened the door and ran.

Incomprehensible shouting, and then three shots blasted, pinging the closing door. She saw two idling cars sitting inside the gate, so she ran the other way. It was night, and misting rain, and pitch black away from the security light by the door, and her bare feet slapped the wet asphalt; all she had on were soiled panties and one of Johnny's Nirvana tee-shirts.

The door slammed open behind her as a tall and rusted chain-link fence loomed out of the dark, and she thought she was done, but the warehouse abruptly ended on her right and there was a dark alley between the fence and the back of the building. It was her only choice, so she ran down it.

Beth heard shoes pound to the corner behind her, and then two more blasts, and two bullets whined past her ear…but only two; she didn't know why at first, but then she heard the sirens. A Dumpster appeared out of the dark, pushed up against the fence; she crouched behind it. There was more shouting, curses from their tone, and then retreating footsteps and engines revving and tires spinning on wet pavement.

She found where the bottom of the rusted fence links were bent back and slithered under. There was a wooded slope on the other side, with thorn bushes on the lower part and cans and bottles and fast-food wrappers scattered everywhere. She crawled through the thorns and the trash and up the slope to the scraggly trees and buried herself in moldy leaves just as blue-and-red lights strobed the hillside.

"You hid from the cops? Why did you do that? You could've told them what those pieces of shit did to you! They would've *helped* you! Why did you hide?" He sat on the couch next to her again. "Why?"

It mortified Beth to admit it, but…*in for a pound.* "I was one messed-up little girl, and I was hurting and confused and afraid and ashamed. Would they charge me as an accomplice to what the guys had done? It sounds stupid now, but back then I just wanted to hide. And…" Deep breath. "I knew the police wouldn't let me go back to Chris."

He stared at her, then snorted and looked away.

Face hot, Beth kept falling. Somehow.

There had to be some mistake, she'd thought; Chris had fought the guys when they'd taken her, so he really did love her. She would go back to his house, his big, warm, comfortable house, and then he would fold her in his arms and say he loved and missed her and everything would be all right again.

So she hid in the leaves all that night and the next day, watching from the slope as swarms of cops tore the warehouse apart; then the drug dogs and their handlers came, and she thought they'd sniff her out, but they stayed focused on the building. Beth figured they'd removed the bodies at some point, but she didn't see it because she was on the back side, which didn't bother her; but she cared about what else they might have taken:

Simon's stash.

Surely the police couldn't have found *everything*, right? So Beth told herself as she lay there, thirsty and hungry and hurting; besides, she needed clothes and shoes.

She snuck back under the fence when they were all gone; out of her bed of leaves, it was one of those spring nights in Ohio when the wind blows down off the lakes; it might as well have still been winter. Shaking, her feet turning numb, she crept back to the corner of the warehouse and peeked around; crime-scene tape was pasted across the door, and there was a new chain and a big gleaming padlock securing the gate. That's when she saw the flaw in her plan: what if the door was locked? She had no way to get in if it was…she'd never been so cold in her life… if it didn't open…but it did, and she hurried inside, yellow tape ripping and falling; Beth couldn't do anything about that, so she'd just have to be quick.

Then she discovered why they hadn't bothered to lock the door; there was nothing left to steal. Desperate, Beth ignored the splotches of dried blood and went to where Simon had kept his personal stash, a baggie and kit taped to the bottom of his dresser; you had to tip it back and reach under…she stopped and stared when she got to the top of the spiral steps.

The dresser was already tipped over, the clothes scattered. She ran to it and looked; the stash was gone. Beth realized at that moment she was in bad, bad shape: she was freezing to death, and so thirsty she couldn't swallow, not to mention she couldn't remember when or even *what* she'd last eaten…and all she could think about was the drug.

She needed help.

But first she needed to drink something and clean herself and scrounge some warm clothes and get out of there; if the cops caught her, they wouldn't let her stay with Chris. So she drank a gallon of water at least and washed up and put on her shoes and three layers of Johnny's clothes; they were the closest fit, but she still looked like a tiny bag lady. Beth thought of something else she would need, money, and did a quick search without much hope, but she had more luck there, finding forty dollars in a pair of Simon's jeans and another hundred folded into a sock. Beth felt better about her situation then; she could afford a cab. She'd been dreading a trek across the city, and hitchhiking, trusting a stranger, was out of the question.

Beth walked out without a backward glance.

She went back under the fence and up through the trees; there was a thruway on top of the hill, eight lanes of roaring traffic. She'd been listening to it for hours, but Beth knew she couldn't get a cab there, so she walked in the bushes and grass and trash well out of the glare of the headlights while looking for a way under. She could see the buildings of downtown Cincinnati soaring on the other side; if she could get downtown, she could hail a cab.

The sun was filling a low strip of sky in the east by the time she made it to the feet of those glass-and-concrete giants; a strange hope had also filled her, because she had worked out a plan. Beth needed help to get off the heroin, and so did Chris. She would convince him to stop dealing and get clean with her, and they would get jobs and live in his house, and eventually they would get married. Her vision kept her walking through the terrible withdrawal sickness; all she had to do was reach Chris and talk to him, and then everything would be okay.

It was full dawn when she finally flagged a cab; *five times* she had tried, but when they slowed and got a look at her, they'd sped away. Beth knew how she looked; the people in nice clothes coming and going from the buildings behind her knew how she looked too; some regarded her with pity, but most turned away in disgust. So she combed out her hair with her fingers and put a smile on her lips and held a fist-full of money out to the sixth cab. He stopped.

She couldn't remember Chris's address, but she remembered Willow Brook. The cabbie had many questions in his eyes as he watched her in the mirror, but he never said a word. The ride cost thirty-seven dollars; she gave him fifty and told him to keep it. A rent-a-cop guarded the gate, so she had to climb over a ten-foot stone wall to get in, but after what she'd been through, walls were nothing.

Beth trudged through the beautiful homes glowing in the spring dawn and up to Chris's door and rang the bell; he had mowed the yard at some point that spring, but it needed it again, bad. No one answered. She rang again, heard footsteps, and then the door opened and a face peered out at her from under the security chain.

It wasn't Chris.

She had blonde hair and pouty lips, and she was all of maybe fifteen; the girl was also wearing one of *her* shirts, and not much else. Beth felt her heart break right there on the front steps, but she only asked for Chris. The girl wanted to know who she was. Beth said that if she didn't go get Chris and bring him to the door, she would call the police and tell them about the drugs; two minutes later, a bleary Chris opened the door all the way, and his eyes widened in shock.

But he was no more shocked than Beth, because the Chris she'd known was gone; he'd lost more weight, and he had scabs on his skinny arms, and his face was ten-years older. He stammered something, but she only said she needed her things, and enough stuff to last two days, and then she would leave. Five minutes later she walked back down the steps with a suitcase full of her clothes and enough junk for two days plus a rig, spoon, and lighter. They stood in the door watching her go, and she couldn't help herself:

"I looked at the girl and said, 'Chris lied. He doesn't love you.'"

Then she turned away for the last time, and as she walked down the street, Beth heard the fight start behind her.

Silence. Silence. Then: "I'm sorry that happened to you."

"Thank you."

"We need to go if we want any sleep tonight."

"I'm almost done." The bottom was close, but she hadn't hit yet.

He sighed. "Tell me the rest, then."

Beth walked to the bus station; she could only think of getting away from the city where *he* lived. She'd gotten worse since *he* knew her, though, and the two days of stuff he'd given her only lasted one, so she used some of her money to score more; when she made it to the terminal, Beth didn't have enough for a ticket to Cleveland.

"*Cleveland?*"

"Cleveland. I'd gotten it into my head that I would head up to Cleveland. To this day I don't know why."

"Okay," he said. "Cleveland."

Her Daniel watched her, waiting for the rest; Beth swallowed, twice, then dove and hit bottom:

"I was holding my suitcase and smelling diesel fumes and watching the buses arrive and depart and wondering what I should do when a man approached. I knew what he wanted, and I figured it was the only thing I was good for anyway, so I followed him into the alley behind the terminal and I…we…he gave me fifty dollars, but I still didn't have enough for a ticket to Cleveland, so I bought one to Columbus, and you know the rest: I stayed at a shelter and went to NA meetings and got clean and got my GED and trained in the martial arts and worked as a hostess at Slo Eddie's and got my own place and kept clean and kept training and worked my way up to kitchen manager, and…and that's when I met you…"

Beth couldn't look at him; the quiet was thunderous. She risked a glance; his face was a wooden mask.

"Are you done?"

"Yes."

He stood and picked up his stupid guns and his bag full of toys and walked out.

Beth stared at the impossible ashes.

When she heard his truck start, she got up, checked that her Carson was secure, and followed him out.

Within the Cemetery

BY THE time they found the road Beth was so angry she thought the willows would catch fire.

She swatted her way through their feathery branches and kicked up through seasons upon seasons of moldering leaves and reached the blacktop and marched across the bridge; the wooden slats clacked beneath her hiking boots.

From below and behind her came a hissed, *"Wait!"*

Screw waiting—and especially screw waiting for him!

She paused on the far bank to savor the cool, loam-scented air, then shined her heavy MagLite around and discovered that over here was a lot like back there; no matter where she pointed it, rank after rank of giant, night-shrouded trunks swallowed the bright beam. At that moment Beth could also count no less than five owls *who-who-who*ing at each other; on their way in she'd seen several sitting on branches, feathery heads swiveling to track her and Daniel; a few had taken startled flight, ghosting off on dark or sometimes speckled wings.

Owls weren't the only creatures she'd seen tonight: deer, opossum, red fox; even a pair of glowing-eyed coyotes had made an appearance before slinking away. And she'd almost forgotten the valley's strange, energized air; all that oxygen had Beth feeling like a girl again; her step was light and quick, and she'd barely noticed the miles or the hour.

In fact, there were only three things ruining this gorgeous midnight hike: where she was going, the circumstances under which she was going there, and…

She heard him scramble up the embankment and then clack across the bridge after her.

Beth took off walking again.

"Wait!"

She kept going.

"God damn it, *wait!* We need to talk about this first!"

Beth stopped dead and turned; he jerked to a halt when he saw her expression, then approached warily.

Now he wanted to talk? They'd hid his stupid football-money truck behind a dilapidated barn in an overgrown field at the edge of the valley and then hiked up and over the ridge and meandered more than two miles while following the creek downstream to the bridge and he'd uttered five words the entire time and those had been "I did some scouting, too" when she'd asked him how he'd found the abandoned barn. They could've driven. Beth could've been home and asleep in Lizzie's bed by now, where for the first time in six days she could have slept without a little girl's cold feet pressed into the small of her back! But nooooooo, he had a stupid plan!

Beth spoke through gritted teeth: "What do you want?"

"We need to look around before we go up there."

"Why? It's after midnight, and like you said, we need to get *some* sleep."

He peered from side to side, as if he expected something to leap out of the woods at them; those goggles looked ridiculous. "Just think for a second," he said, then pointed toward the top of the hill with the big pistol; he'd been carrying it since they'd left the truck. "There might be cameras up there."

"*Cameras?*"

Beth walked away.

He wouldn't *talk* to her, oh no, but she'd caught him *staring* at her with those stupid goggles several times. She'd finally snapped and told him to quit looking at her, but now Beth didn't care. *Let him look.* She'd take Lizzie and find another man, a man that would talk to her, and this time she'd tell the lucky guy her shame up front, not wait seven years.

Apparently that doesn't work.

Staring at her.

Judging her.

Beth had bared her soul and threw it at his *feet!* Why wouldn't he say anything?

Daniel ran up behind her and grabbed her arm. She looked at his hand, and he hastily let go; smart man.

"Rison knew we'd been here, damn it!" He lowered his voice. "*They* knew, re-member? And did you see anyone that day? I sure as fuck didn't. There had to be someone watching from back in the trees, or some kind of surveillance system, maybe even motion detectors."

Her eyebrows shot up. Motion detectors? Beth almost walked away again, but she remembered Scott Rison, and what he'd said, all too well; maybe Daniel had a point.

"You wait here while I sneak a peek at the back of the lot," he blathered. "If there are cameras or motion detectors, that's where they'll be."

Him and his stupid toy. Had he offered to share it, even once? And him? Sneak? Please. She held out her hand. "Give me the goggles, I'll do it."

"I don't think—"

"I want a turn. You can hold the flashlight for a change."

He hesitated and then pulled them off, and they made the exchange. Beth ad-justed the strap—why did he need such a big head? It's not like there was anything in it—and then dropped the bulky things over her eyes.

The black world lit up in shades of green. She looked around, impressed; *much* better than a flashlight. He wouldn't be getting these back soon…she frowned and tugged at the sides of the goggles; her peripheral vision was severely restricted, and there didn't seem to be much she could do about it. Beth didn't like that.

"*You* wait here," she told him, then left the greentop and slipped through the green trunks; she would make her way around the hill and then head up to the back of the lot and look for Daniel's cameras and *motion detectors*, as preposterous as—

She stumbled over a low bush, then sprang to her feet and furiously brushed leaves from her clothes and hair.

He shouted in a whisper: "See? They're hard to get used to! And fuck waiting!" He crunched after her.

Okay, so maybe she shouldn't have laughed when he'd brained himself on that branch earlier; the goggles *were* hard to get used to. And transitioning from looking at an object far away to looking at something near was jarring. And she didn't enjoy having no peripheral vision; someone could sneak up on her from the side. Maybe the goggles weren't so hot. Beth decided to keep them anyway.

It'll serve him right.

She let him blunder up to her. "You might try to be a little quieter."

His scowl was green. "I *am* trying, but I'm heavier than you, and my feet are bigger. That's why you sneak better, those tiny feet."

She moved off again, watching for bushes and low-hanging branches. Daniel followed. He was making less noise, Beth admitted; he sounded like a single buffalo instead of the whole herd. When she thought they were far enough around she went straight upslope, looking for the edge of the trees. After several minutes she crept up behind the last wide trunk and peeked around. Daniel crunched and crouched beside her; at least he'd had the presence of mind to turn the flashlight off.

"Do you see anything?"

"Be quiet and let me look."

Beth had hit about where she'd aimed; the lot was on her left, empty of cars. The hedge loomed, glowing green. She glanced at the sky above it, but the angle was wrong to see the crooked lith, and the goggles washed out all but the brightest stars; the new moon was due tomorrow night, and the shaving of silver she'd enjoyed earlier had already disappeared behind a tree-lined ridge. On the other side of the lot, the green walkway parted the green roses and disappeared around the green hill; she saw no cameras, and no stupid motion detectors.

Beth stepped into the lot.

"What are you doing?!"

"There's nothing here, Daniel."

"There could be cameras flanking the path, or someone spying from the tree line on the other side. We need to make sure before we go up there."

"You're insane if you think I'll crawl all the way around this hill. I'm going up; stay if you want. Here." She pulled off the goggles and held them out. Beth wanted her peripheral vision back. "Give me the light."

He traded with her again and she clicked the Mag-Lite on; the mass of scarlet roses jumped into the beam as she craned her neck; overhead, the Milky Way blobbed and sparkled.

Hello, home galaxy.

She walked across the lot, bright beam leading.

"Beth!" She kept going. He cussed a blue streak, then ran to her side and whispered, "Would you at least turn that off? We don't know if—"

"Use your little toy. See any cameras? Or *motion detectors?* Or anyone else dumb enough to be out here at—" Beth shined the light on her watch, "one oh four in the stupid morning? Well?"

He got the strap readjusted and slipped the goggles on and looked around while she waited, tapping her foot.

"All right, I don't see anything." He sounded disappointed! "But that doesn't mean there's not hidden cameras in the roses, or someone on the other—"

Beth stalked away before she kicked him. He cussed some more and followed. They wound around the hill and were about to make the turn up when she saw a glint of red on the walkway; she stopped and picked up an emaciated petal. There were dozens scattered on the concrete, and the bush they'd come from canted back, as if someone had tried to stomp it flat. Beth shined the beam into the mass, and her eyes widened; someone or something had plowed through the red blooms, cutting an unbroken line downslope all the way to the trees.

"Daniel, look at this."

"There's another over here." Beth shined her light where he indicated and saw a second line churned down to the forest. "That's not all." He pointed to the other side, to the slope below the hedge; dead bushes and wilted blooms were scattered on the surrounding plants, as if they'd been ripped up and thrown about; the destroyed area was about seven feet square.

"Why would someone tear them up?"

"I don't know. Why would someone run through them?"

"We don't know it was a *someone*; it was probably just a deer." But wouldn't a deer jump? The lines had no breaks, as if whoever or whatever had plowed straight through. She winced; those thorns had to have hurt.

"Beth." Below the goggles, his cheeks were drawn, mouth tense.

"What?"

He reversed the big revolver and held it out. "Now would be a good time to change your mind about guns."

They stood on the walkway and stared at each other as the night insects thrummed and the vivid constellations wheeled overhead.

At last she said, "I won't ever touch a gun, Daniel. Get it through your brain."

He simply nodded, then removed the smaller revolver from that idiotic ankle holster he'd insisted on wearing. "All right," her husband said when he stood back up. "Let's go.

Beth let the withered petal fall, and side by side they walked up the hill. She shined her light on the lichgate; tonight the mingled crimson and white climbing blooms were stark and somehow unlovely in the beam:

WELCOME TO BARRON CEMETERY

They passed under.

Pale blooms blanketed the hilltop, broken only by the walkways and the occasional ebon headstone that managed to poke through; the megalith loomed and jutted, a twisted void among the stars. Daniel's hoarse breathing was the only sound. Beth could hear numberless insects making a racket from the trees and in the reds behind her, but between the hedges, all was silent.

The bugs are just startled to see us, that's all; they'll do their thing once they get used to human intruders.

"Let's split up," she whispered. "The search will go faster." Why was she whispering? There was no one to hear; even so, whispering felt right.

"I go where you go," he said in a tone that didn't invite argument. "And don't forget to look for crosses. Bet a dollar you won't find any."

She glared, but the effect was spoiled because he was frowning up at the megalith. Not the "no crosses" idiocy again; she'd thankfully forgotten about *that* bit of paranoia.

Beth pulled her leather gardening gloves out of her back pocket and yanked them on and started searching just above the lowest path, the one that circled inside the tall hedge. The plan was to shift a few feet up as she got back to the entrance and spiral her way to the top; there could easily be fresh graves hidden beneath all this, and she didn't intend to miss one.

She tugged the gloves off after the tenth headstone and got her phone out and stuck it in the thorns and snapped pics of each monument, the iPhone's flash flickering beneath the pallid blooms; ten should be plenty. Tomorrow she would search for descendants and see if they could tell her anything about McFarlane, or why Barron Cemetery had been overhauled, or even about this mysterious Melissa Bane, the supposed Keeper.

Somebody has to know something about that woman. Beth thought sadly of Jeff. *And be willing to tell me...*

She put her phone up and slipped her gloves back on and got to work; when she discovered a headstone, Beth made sure not to touch it, even with the gloves, although she had a hard time articulating why; it just seemed...wrong...to disturb them, somehow.

Daniel followed and said not a word as she worked all the way back to the lichgate and didn't find a single fresh grave. She also didn't find any crosses; she hadn't seen religious symbols or pictograms of any sort, just the cold impersonality of names and birth-and-death dates. Beth made note of those death-dates; she'd searched about a quarter of the cemetery, and the newest grave was 1979. She suspected that if she explored the entire hill, '79 would hold...

...which meant no one had been interred in Barron Cemetery since its revamp thirty years ago.

Beth shined her light around. Why go through the trouble and expense of replacing the crumbling old tombstones, not to mention planting the roses and the hedge and sticking that ugly rock up there, if you weren't going to bury more people? She could understand a for-profit cemetery doing a remodel—a much more *tasteful* remodel—but why bother in a private cemetery, especially if you didn't plan to utilize it again?

This makes no sense.

Daniel stood almost on top of her, goggles pointed up at the tall, twisted stone; the insects were still screeching and buzzing out in the valley, but the cemetery's mount remained an island of stillness.

Beth tried to quash the creeped-out feeling stealing over her as she shifted up and began another circuit, but all she found were more sharp thorns, more white blooms, more dark and heartless headstones, and no fresh graves; a terrible certainty was also growing in her heart: whatever McFarlane had done to poor Jeff and Brennan and the others, they weren't here. Jeff had been right. The old man wasn't dumb enough to put them on his property, and she wouldn't find anything to use against her enemy at the press—

Then she remembered the maker's marks.

I'm as big an idiot as my husband.

Beth got down on hands and knees and pushed aside fragrant white blooms and parted the thorns and examined the nearest headstone with her Mag-Lite; the marker belonged to one **Abigail Arlene Whit/December 10th, 1908/November 13th, 1918**. Little Abby had nearly made it to ten, poor thing. Careful not to touch it, although she still couldn't express why, Beth squirmed close and shined her beam on the front and back and even all around the edges, but found no symbols or initials or company logos.

She extricated herself from the thorns and considered checking other tombstones, but instinct told her it would be fruitless; whoever had crafted these hadn't wanted to be associated with this place.

Beth shined her light around Barron Cemetery again.

Not that I can blame them.

Daniel jerked, then cursed and pointed his guns back toward where she'd already checked. Beth shined her light that way and was greeted by pasty blooms and dark stones. Was he trying to scare her?

It would be just like him. "Would you stop that?"

He slowly lowered the revolvers. "I thought I saw…"

The hairs on the back of Beth's neck stood up, and she whirled and put her light on the memorial at her feet while backing away at the same time. She bumped her husband's hip, and he spun and thrust both guns over her shoulder.

"What is it? Did you see something too?"

She didn't answer, just kept bumping him back until they stood on a path; she still had her light pinned on Abigail's black-granite marker where it glittered half-seen in the thorns; a few seconds ago, Beth could've *sworn* there was someone standing on top of the little girl's grave—right in the middle of a rose bush.

"Damn it, did you see something or not?"

"I…I thought…" Beth shook her head at her own foolishness. "I've never been in a cemetery after midnight, and now I know why. I think I'm a little freaked out."

"Yeah, me too. I don't like this place. We won't find them here, Beth. We need to go. We need to go *now*."

Her eyes dropped to dangerous slits. "We won't find them *here?* There's something else you're not telling me, isn't there." Despite the heat of her anger, Beth shivered; the August night air, while still damp-rag humid, had abruptly turned freezing.

Must be some weird valley temperature inversion.

"I—" He whipped toward the lith, pistols coming up fast. She shined her light up there but only saw a big, crooked rock.

"Stop trying to scare me. It's not funny."

"I'm not…look, I'll tell you where I think they are, but first I have to get the fuck out of this place." Daniel took several fast steps down the path until he was on the one circling just inside the hedge. He looked up at her. "Come with me, Beth. Please. I'm serious. We need to go."

Beth considered all the overgrowth she hadn't searched; she did *not* enjoy failing. "Fine," she groused.

Without another word he turned and strode beside the hedge and out under the lichgate and kept going, and with his long legs, Beth had to run to keep him in sight.

She wasn't running because she didn't want to be alone in Barron Cemetery.

That was silly. It was just a cemetery.

Smart Squirrels

Daniel didn't let up with those long, quick strides until he made the parking lot, and then he squared around on the cemetery with both guns raised like he thought it would leap down after them and he would have to shoot it.

When Beth caught up he said, without looking at her, "You owe me a dollar."

"I didn't agree to that bet."

"But you didn't find any crosses."

"You insisted on scuttling away before I could check all the markers. I'm sure I'd have found one eventually."

The goggles lowered, found her. "You don't believe that."

"There's no law that says people have to put crosses in their cemeteries!"

"There's no law, but don't you think it's kinda strange? We're living in the fucking buckle of the Bible Belt here, Beth. Finding a cemetery with no crosses is like… like discovering a cemetery outside a kibbutz in Israel with no Stars of David or menorahs or whatever."

"It *is* strange," she conceded, "but—"

"It's not just strange." Daniel looked up at Barron Cemetery again. "It's not right," he whispered.

"Ooookay, I've had enough, it's time to go back to the truck. We'll give the press what Rison said and tell them how McFarlane threatened—"

"What about this hole you wanted to see so bad, the whatchamacallit, the cenote?"

Beth squinted at her husband; there had been a not-so-subtle weight to the question. She shined the light on her watch. "It's almost two." She sighed. "I'm really not going to get any sleep tonight, am I?"

"Let's go," Daniel said, and then he scurried out of the lot while watching the cemetery over his shoulder. He vanished down the tunnel.

Beth followed slowly—unlike him, she was *not* going to flee from a stupid bone yard—but the moonless dark squeezed in around her beam, and she was very aware of the burial ground looming at her back.

She also felt watched.

Beth tugged her gardening gloves off and tucked them into her back pocket and kept walking. Slowly. She'd just gotten a little freaked out, that's all, but she would not give in to this preposterous fear. It was just a cemetery.

Despite her resolve, by the time she reached the leafy tunnel the certainty that someone was behind her had grown so strong she pulled her Carson and spun around.

Nothing.

Beth shined her light in the lot, down the path, into the flowers on both sides, and then up at the hedge crowning the prominence; nobody, but her breath began to plume; that peculiar temperature inversion was spreading downhill, it seemed.

And, even though she couldn't see anyone, she still felt…observed.

Daniel whisper-shouted, "Beth! Come on!" She risked a glance over her shoulder, but he was lost in the black.

Something pallid flashed, and Beth jerked around with her heart in her throat, but her beam only revealed waves of crimson roses. She tried to swallow and had to work spit up to do it. What in the world had *that* been? An owl, she decided. Beth had glimpsed an owl swooping over the flowers, hunting dinner…

A white owl?

She backed into the tunnel, eyes wide. There were white owls, sure, but none in Tennessee—at least that she knew of. But evidently there were, since an owl was what she'd seen. *Only a stupid owl.* She was almost running backwards now, light fixed on the star-punched oval above her.

Something blurred across that opening, in and out of the beam so fast Beth didn't register what it was.

Something pale.

She turned and sprinted down the hill, beam bobbing wildly. *Owl!* She steadied her light and saw her husband; the small revolver glinted as he rolled it at her to hurry, hurry. He was off to the side near the trunk of a giant elm in a drift of leaves up to his calves, and he had the big revolver pointed up the road behind her. Beth reached him and stopped, panting, and realized her breath had stopped pluming; the air down here held no more chill than the relative cool of a humid nighttime forest.

"What happened? Did you see something?"

"No, I…" Beth shined her light up at the tunnel's mouth, but it was too far away now; only a black oval greeted her.

Why is it warmer down here? And what the heck was *that?*

He tilted the goggles to consider the blade in her hand.

"Yes you did."

Beth grimaced, then folded the Carson and put it away. "An owl startled me, that's all."

He stared at her for a moment, then glanced up the road again before slipping between massive trunks. "This way," he whispered.

She followed, kicking an irritated spray of leaves with every step. He didn't go far before he crouched in a dell behind a towering white oak and splayed one gloved hand on the bark and peered around the trunk. Beth squatted behind him and wiped sweat from her face with the hem of her tee-shirt. When her husband was apparently reassured that the cemetery wasn't coming after them, he faced her and sagged against the trunk and lifted the goggles off and wiped his face on his sleeve; he was sweating buckets, too. Beth held the flashlight low, and the beam bounced off the loam and cast fractured shadows across his bruised face.

"Coming back here was a mistake," he said.

Beth's mouth worked, but no sound emerged. He held up a hand. "I know it was my idea, but that place is *not* just a cemetery. You just don't want to admit it. I saw how you reacted."

"I *said* I'd never been inside a cemetery this late, and that I got a little freaked out, but that doesn't mean—"

"I saw how you reacted in the daylight too, and you can't tell me with a straight face that there's anything about Barron Cemetery you find wholesome or agreeable whatsoever."

"I'll admit—again!—that I don't like Barron Cemetery, but that doesn't—"

"You saw something. That's why you ran."

"I saw an owl hunting mice in the roses. It startled me, that's all."

"Sure," he said. "An owl." Before she could do more than bristle he added, "*I* saw something, and it wasn't a fucking owl."

Beth licked her lips. "I thought you were trying to scare me."

"I wouldn't do that…well, not tonight, anyway. And I'd planned to snap better pics of that writing, but I couldn't even make myself walk up there. Part of it was I didn't want to leave you alone, but mostly it just seemed like a bad idea to go near that thing tonight. *Very* bad."

"Daniel…"

"I know, I know, it's just a cemetery, whatever. Point is, I'm done with that place. Third time's the fucking charm for Dan-o. I don't even care what that whacked-out writing says anymore." At her look, he amended, "Okay, I do, but if I send those pics again, sure as God made poor people and little fishes the egghead who sees them will want to 'authenticate the find' just like Professor Hameed, and then I'll have another missing know-it-all on my conscious. No thanks."

"Are you suggesting you saw a ghost? A *ghost*, Daniel? Ghosts only live in Hollywood. They put them in movies to sell tickets to teenagers."

He scowled, then yanked the goggles back on. "Make fun of me all you want, or call it whatever the hell you want, but I saw what I saw. And it doesn't matter because I meant what I said: I'm *done* with that place." He pointed the big revolver at her pocket, the one with her phone, and she shifted away and glared. "I saw you get the names, and I hope you find out what you want, because if you come back out here to get more, you're on your own."

"It's—!"

"—just a cemetery. Right. I've heard. So why are you fixated on this big sinkhole? Tell me that."

That's when Beth put it together.

"You think McFarlane's dumping the bodies in the cenote, don't you."

He regarded her, blank-faced behind the goggles, for what seemed a long time, then shrugged. "I'm no killer, but it makes more sense to chuck murdered people into a big hole in the middle of the woods where nobody goes than to bury them in a cemetery accessible from the road—if 'sense' is the right word for any of this. So yeah, maybe I do think that."

Beth raised the flashlight, and he turned away. "Quit."

She lowered it, but Beth didn't need to see his face to know. She knew him. "There's something you're not telling me. *Again.* What did you find out?"

"Tell me why you're so obsessed with it."

"I'm not obsessed—"

"Yes you are."

"Oh, like you aren't obsessed with that stupid cemetery up there?"

"Maybe I was, but I'm over it now. And at least I've *been* there. You've never even laid eyes on this hole, but ever since you found it on Google Earth you've been yammering about getting a look at it. Tell me why."

Yammering? Jeff had asked her essentially the same question—albeit much more politely—but Beth still had no good answer. Truth was, ever since she'd seen the overhead view of the half-mile-wide cenote, something about it had called to her— although "call" wasn't right. Whatever it was, she would not inform her husband; no telling what his paranoia would make of it. Still, something was pulling her toward the giant sinkhole; maybe it was simple curiosity.

That's it, I'm curious.

Beth said as much, and he just shook his head and stood up. "Let's go satisfy your 'curiosity', then." He slid between two trunks and was gone.

And *she* was stubborn? Beth clicked her Mag-Lite off and followed, stepping lightly until she was right behind him and matching his footfalls.

"Tell me."

She got the satisfaction of seeing him jump. When he landed, he spun around. "Fuck! It's a good thing Dad taught me to keep my finger off the trigger!"

"*Tell me.*"

"You won't believe it."

"Why wouldn't I?"

"Because you're you. Besides, we're going there now, and if what I was told is true…well, let's just say we'll both know it."

Away to the north, deeper in the valley, coyotes yipped as they closed on prey. Beth watched her husband for the entire minute it took for the pack's death-song to trail off, then clicked her flashlight on and walked past him up the hill.

"*Where are you going?*"

"The roses. We'll follow them around to the gate."

"Oh." He ran to catch up, then settled a tree behind. "As long as we're not heading back to that cemetery. You can count me outta that shit."

"You've made that abundantly clear."

He muttered something she didn't catch, which was probably good for him.

Beth found the flowers and clicked her light off once more and led by starlight while staying just inside the first rank of trunks; the cemetery's tor humped on her right. Beth glanced at the top; the lith was a crooked black tooth biting the stars. She didn't have to look to know that Daniel was staring up at it.

They drew near the warned and chained gate, and Beth glimpsed the "road" it guarded; two narrow ruts with a mound of grass between. From here, the cenote was a little over a mile and a half away, at the exact center of the valley—at least according to Google Earth it was. She flanked the gate, edging between packed trunks; deprived of the stars again, Beth was nearly blind, but caution kept her flashlight turned off.

The runnels appeared, and she stepped out guardedly; the forest was alive with that strange energy she'd noted before, as well as a disharmony of insect noise, but Beth couldn't see ten feet. She looked a question at her husband; he peered around with the goggles and shook his head. Beth chose a rut and walked deeper into this odd basin. He chose the other and followed.

They hadn't taken twenty steps when light sparkled through the limbs overhead. They froze like startled deer. Then Beth was blinded as three small vehicles popped over a rise about a quarter-mile ahead and sped down the ruts toward them, their engines changing tone as the riders shifted gears.

"Shit! Those are four-wheelers!"

"Over here!" She sprinted into the trees.

Daniel cursed as they wove their way deeper, then pressed their backs to a wide trunk and listened; the ATVs were motoring closer, but hadn't left the ruts, and didn't seem to be in a hurry. Beth leaned and peeked, but saw only headlights.

Daniel peered around his side. Then he gasped.

"The Presidents!"

"Presidents? What are you—" He seized her arm. "Let go of me!"

"Big fucking dogs, Beth! We have to climb! *Now!* They'll smell us and—shit! No branches low enough!" The goggles swiveled. "There!" He pulled her stumbling to the next tree. It was a little smaller, and there was a thick limb sticking out more or less parallel to the ground about eight feet up.

Beth considered breaking his hold—there were several ways, although he wouldn't enjoy any of them—but then she heard deep barks. Her hair tried to stand up. *He's right, those are big dogs.* She looked behind; the four-wheelers had stopped where they'd entered the forest, headlights angled their way.

Then Beth squawked as he seized her under the armpits and threw her toward the branch. She grabbed it and lost her Mag-Lite; it tumbled into darkness.

"My flashlight!"

"Climb! Climb!"

She pulled herself up. "Look out!"

A huge dog raced toward her husband's back. It leapt just as Daniel jumped and chinned, swinging his legs high. The animal passed beneath and crashed down, sliding behind the next tree over.

Two even bigger dogs appeared as his legs swung back down.

"Daniel!"

"Grab my hand!" Together they managed to get him up as all three dogs leapt and barked and snarled; their jaws snapped inches below.

Two four-wheelers left the track and headed their way.

"Climb higher! Go!"

It was an easy ascent—for her. This southern red oak was small compared to some Beth had seen out here, but it was still almost seventy feet tall, and its branches were thick and sturdy. Daniel cursed and struggled as they scrambled higher and then higher still while the four-wheelers stopped at the base. Beth could see the third one still out on the furrows, single headlight slanted toward them. She pressed into the trunk, hiding as best she could.

They were forty feet up, and they were trapped.

Daniel peered toward the ground and whispered, "They have rifles. We're sitting ducks." The goggles swiveled to her. "Sure could use that shotgun right about now."

Beth's face went hot. He'd tried to get her to carry it for him, but she'd refused to touch it, even with the case, so it had stayed in his truck. "You've got those," she whispered, indicating the pistol he was clutching to his stomach with one hand; the other hand held a branch above his head as he tried to keep from falling and hide at the same time. "What happened to the little one?"

"I dropped it. And they have *rifles*. It wouldn't make a—"

Daniel hushed as the riders shut the engines off. Two dogs continued to leap and snarl and bark, but the smallest now sat off to the side, muzzle raised as it peered into the tangle of branches. Beth could see its pale-blue eyes glowing in the headlamps, and she had the strangest feeling it was looking straight at her.

And then she forgot about the stupid dog as a deep cracker voice she recognized said, "You reckon them's some squirrels, Tommy?"

Beth peeked; sure enough, her pal Tommy had just climbed off an ATV. He was holding a lever-action rifle in one hand; the other hand dangled in a cast.

This is not good.

"If they are, they're the biggest damn squirrels in creation!"

They laughed uproariously at that. The first speaker was the bearded camo-loving muscle man who'd dined and dashed at Slo Eddie's with Scott Rison; he was still sporting head-to-toe camo.

Then Tommy slung his rifle butt to his shoulder and pointed the barrel up into their tree. Rison's friend from the restaurant did the same without dismounting.

Beth and Daniel jerked behind the trunk.

Her husband's whisper was almost inaudible. "Shit!"

Then Tommy shouted, "Shut yer yaps! A man cain't hear hisself think with all that racket! Nixon, Ike, shut the hell up! They ain't goin' nowhere!"

Nixon and Ike; now Beth got the "Presidents" thing. Cute. The dogs continued to leap and snarl and bark.

"Goddamnit!" They peeked again in time to see Tommy step forward and swing his rifle stock in wide, threatening arcs. "I told you mutts to *shut up!*"

Camo boy rumbled, "That ain't a good idea."

"I don't give a rat's ass! These fuckin' mutts gotta learn their place! I said *shut—*"

A gray flash, and the third dog was no longer sitting off to the side. Ike and Nixon dropped their paws from the trunk and turned to face Tommy as well; all three crouched, snarling and snapping. Tommy stood frozen with a look of almost comic surprise on his pocked face and the rifle held across his chest; the cast Beth had gifted him glowed a dingy white in the headlamps.

Camo lover said, "I *told* you, dumb-ass."

Tommy backed up. The dogs followed, snarling and snapping. "I didn't mean nothin', Reagan. Good girl. Good boy, Ike, good boy, Nixon. Good doggies."

The three massive animals inched closer to Tommy, lips skinned from impressive yellow teeth, hackles bristling. They were German Shepherds—or at least Ike and Nixon were. The President out front, Reagan, the one who'd seemed to watch Beth, wasn't as heavy or as thick across the shoulders, and had a longer snout and gray-silver fur; Husky hybrid, or perhaps wolf mix.

Tommy's narrow butt hit the four-wheeler's headlamp, and Beth wouldn't have been surprised to see a dark stain spreading on the crotch of her old pal's dirty jeans. And then a sound wafted through the darkened forest; it was so out of place it took Beth a second to recognize what she was hearing.

A woman was singing.

Low and lovely, her voice somehow came from every direction; her song contained words, but they were in a language Beth didn't recognize. The three dogs stood from their deadly crouch, ears pricked. Then they bounded away toward the third ATV, which still sat back on the ruts, engine idling, headlamp spearing the dark.

The song faded.

Beth let go of the branch over her head and reamed a finger in her ear. She looked at Daniel, and even in the dark and with the goggles covering half his face, the shock of recognition was plain; no need to ask if he'd heard that or not.

Down below, camo boy said, "You're a fuckin' idiot, Tommy."

"Screw you, Nelson! They weren't gonna do nothin'! They was just riled, is all." Despite his boast, Tommy sounded shaken.

"Shut yer trap. We ain't got time for yer bullshit."

Nelson, the formerly nameless camouflage-loving friend of Scott Rison, slid his bulk off the ATV and raised his rifle and sighted in their general direction. Beth grabbed her dazed and oblivious husband and yanked him behind the trunk.

"Hey! You *squirrels* listen up good! This here's private property, and if you're *smart* squirrels, you'll scamper back out the way you came in, and as fast as you can git! You hear me up there?"

Beth and Daniel exchanged a look and then peeked around both sides of the trunk again as Tommy erupted:

"*WHAT?*"

"Shut up!" Nelson addressed them again. "Smart squirrels only get one warning." He lowered the rifle and hooked its strap over his shoulder.

Tommy jabbed his rifle up their tree one-handed. "You know who that is? I ain't leavin' 'till—"

Nelson seized Tommy and whispered in his ear. Tommy jerked free and hissed back.

Daniel murmured, "What are they saying?"

"I don't know."

The argument ended with Nelson climbing back on his four-wheeler and starting it. Tommy hopped back on his as Nelson motored away. Tommy cranked his ride, and then looked up, straight at Beth.

"This ain't over, cunt. You and I still got it to settle. I'll see ya soon." His laugh grated. "*Real* soon."

He clunked it into gear and circled the trunk, gunning the motor and slinging leaves, then rode back to the ruts, where Nelson had already joined the third mystery rider. Then they all puttered away; Beth glimpsed low, shaggy forms loping out ahead.

They clung to the branches and stared at each other as the night settled around them again.

He spoke first. "They knew we were here."

"Yes."

"They know *who* we are."

"Yes." Beth shifted to peer in the direction the riders and the dogs had gone; back they way they'd came, deeper into the valley…towards the sinkhole…

Then she saw light stab through limb and leaf, and a jag of excitement burned through her.

"You were right!"

"I was? About what?"

"They're keeping us away from the cenote! Remember what Camo Boy said? 'Scamper back out the way you came in.' You were right, it *has* to be where they put Jeff and the others!"

"'Camo Boy'?"

"Nelson. He was the cracker with Rison at Slo Eddie's last Saturday, the one Scarborough never bothered to question."

"Oh yeah. *Scarborough*. Goddamn crooked bastard. I think I want to nail him worse than I want to bring McFarlane down. But how do you know they're guarding it?"

"I saw their headlights swing this way before they turned them off. You've got the toy, look for yourself. They're on that rise they first popped over. I think."

He dropped to a limb below her and wrapped the oak's trunk with one arm and leaned out and stared into the black for a long, long time. "I see them," he finally said. "Shit, they're just sitting there waiting for us."

"We can go around them. This is a big valley."

"Are you nuts? Didn't you hear me? They're just *sitting* there and *waiting* for us to do something stupid! Something *else* stupid! And I think their scopes were NV, which means they can see us as well as I can see them, probably better."

"There's something down there, Daniel, something important. Maybe it will be the key to putting them all away."

He stared up at her.

"*What?*"

He looked off toward the center of the valley.

"Maybe your right," he said, voice soft.

"I am." *Keep your secrets.* It didn't matter what he'd "heard" about the cenote, because now she knew there was something down there, something significant.

Beth didn't know how she could be so certain, but she was.

He said, "But we won't find it tonight."

"We could—"

"We'll come back, I promise, but right now they have us outgunned, and that's not counting whoever was on that other four-wheeler." He turned the goggles away from her. "I don't know why they're letting us go, but I'm not inclined to spit in the gift horse's mouth. Come on, let's be smart squirrels and get the fuck out of this tree." He climbed down, cursing and feeling for branches with his feet.

Beth swung past him and skittered to the ground and retrieved her flashlight; she thought about Nelson and her buddy Tommy while she waited, along with the Presidents, and...

Someone else.

Who had been singing? And why would someone *sing* in the middle of the woods at night? And what language had that been? And why had the dogs reacted that way?

Daniel dropped beside her. Finally. "So," he said while brushing twigs and cobwebs from his hair. "Want to catch me up on you and Tommy?"

Beth did so while he searched for the small revolver. His glaring pout was a thing of beauty, even in the dark; she could tell he wanted to say something about how she could have been hurt, but his only comment was a muttered, "I thought it smelled worse than usual back there."

She led them out after he found the tiny pistol, not bothering to sneak anymore. Beth wanted to bite someone; the purpose of this excursion had been to provide answers, but she'd only found more questions:

How had they known she and Daniel were out here?

Why were they letting them go?

Who was that woman singing? *Why* was she singing? And how did Beth's husband know her?

Why didn't he want Beth to know that he did?

Was he just going to pretend she hadn't laid out the darkest secrets of her heart for his viewing pleasure?

Would he say *anything* about what she'd shared?

Ever?

So many questions, but Beth knew one thing for absolute sure; if it was the last thing she did, she would discover what McFarlane was hiding and use it to bury him in his own stupid cemetery.

Impossible

DANIEL PARKED in front of the garage and pushed the button and the door chugged up, revealing her Altima and his bicycle and her bags of Rose Feed and his riding mower and the rest of their crud; the pickup's dash clock read 3:49. He held his keys in his lap, but he made no move to get out.

Beth stared straight ahead.

The light over her car finally clicked off, plunging the garage into darkness.

She opened her door.

"Wait."

"What?"

"We need to talk." She just looked at him. "Please."

Beth shut the door and folded her hands in her lap, but her heart was pounding. What if he wanted a trial separation, to think about things? A separation would be its own little sadistic Purgatory; she might as well go ahead and file for—

"Are you absolutely, positively, one-hundred percent sure you want to have this press conference?"

I should have known!

Beth controlled her voice with supreme effort: "It's the only way to back McFarlane off until we can get more evidence or find more people in authority like Jeff. You know this."

"It'll be messy; lawyers, lawyers, everywhere." He paused, and then added, low and ominous: "And that's just to start."

"I'm willing to risk it. He has to pay for Jeff and Brennan, and that poor woman and her children."

"Don't forget Professor Hameed. And Hottson, I suppose, although the guy was a total prick."

"Detective Jackson said his wife is seven months pregnant," Beth remembered sadly. "That reminds me, why send a math professor? I understand the Arabic."

"It wasn't my idea. Hameed showed Hottson the pics and Math Boy got a big hard-on."

"Why would a mathematics professor care about bizarre symbols?"

"It wasn't the symbols; it was the pattern they formed. Hottson said it was a… oh, what the hell was it…he was nattering about lightning bolts and leaves, and the antenna in our smart phones…" Daniel snapped his fingers. "Fractals! That's what he called 'em."

"Fractals." Beth pictured the miniscule carvings, following them in her mind's eye as they twisted and swirled up and down and around the oily rock.

But what does it MEAN?

"Yeah, fractals. They're these patterns that occur in nature all over the damn place: lightning bolts, veins in leaves, even the way streams and rivers flow toward the ocean. God knows or cares where else. And apparently some smarty-pants figured out how to use them to reconfigure the antenna in our phones so they can transmit and receive data. Good thing, too, or we'd all be walking around with expensive walkie-talkies. Anyway, that's what Hottson was—"

"I know what fractals are." He couldn't be bothered to mention what she'd revealed about her past, but he could wax poetic over an obscure math equation!

"You do?"

"I read an article in Popular Science."

"Ah."

Beth waited, grinding her teeth.

"Did Hottson say *why* it was significant, Daniel?"

"Oh. Well, no, actually. We never got that far."

Beth dropped her face into her hands.

"Hey, don't blame me. Hottson was prattling on and I had the alarm guys here and Mr. Yoda was raising hell and then the locksmith showed up…" He shrugged. "I just wanted to know what that weird writing said. Besides, they were all fired up to go look at the thing, and I figured I'd learn what they knew, you know…when they got back."

"I wish you would have mentioned this earlier. I would've went up there and looked for myself." He didn't respond, and when she glanced at him, his face had turned to rock.

"I said—"

"I heard you, and now I'm glad I never mentioned it. Messing with that stone tonight would have been a bad idea, Beth. A really *bad* fucking idea. Trust me."

She shook her head, exasperated. "It's—"

"—just a cemetery. So I've been informed. But if it's 'just a cemetery', what's so damn important about the pattern that writing forms? If it's 'just a cemetery', why do you give a rat's ass?"

"Well…"

His laugh was unforgiving. "Just a cemetery, right. It doesn't matter anyway because Dan-o meant what Dan-o fucking said. You want to stare at the swirly symbols, be my guest, but you're going alone—or at least without me." He shuddered. "Never again, that's a *promise*. And I'm not sitting out here at four o'clock in the morning to talk about math, or that goddamn cemetery. You want the good news first, or the bad?" Before Beth could choose he said, "Vivian Rawlins."

"Who's Vivian Rawlins? And is she good news or bad news?"

"Good, at least for us. Sure as hell not for Vivian; she's one of the missing. Scandlin told me about her, showed me a picture. Charles Duperies. He's another. We can give their names to the press. There was also some landscaper from Lexington, Kentucky, and an entomologist from Georgia State in Atlanta. There were more, but I can't remember their names. I remember Chuck and Vivian, though, and we can look the landscaper and the bug doc up on the net."

"Daniel, that's wonderful!" Beth grimaced; it was anything but wonderful. "You know what I mean."

"Yeah."

"Still, the reporters will run with the names, and then it'll all hit the fan and McFarlane will be too busy to worry about us! Wait. You learned this when you talked to Jeff in Nashville?" He nodded. "Why didn't you say anything? I've been worried *sick* about what we could give to the press!"

"I wanted to see what we found tonight. For all I knew, we wouldn't need them."

Beth pulled her phone out and opened the Notepad app. "Vivian Rawlins?"

"Vivian Rawlins."

Beth typed it in. "And Charles…?"

"Duperies."

Beth sat looking at the names, crisp and black against the luminescent background; the names made it all real. She would look them up tomorrow, find out what she could before she gave them to the press, along with the landscaper from Kentucky and the entomologist from Georgia State. *And these four are just the tip of the iceberg.* According to Jeff, there were thirteen more—and those were just the ones he'd known about.

Why were they taking these people from their families? What sort of monstrous thing were they doing with them?

Beth touched Vivian with the tip of her index finger.

"Who were they? Where did they come from?"

"She was some sort of lawyer from Spokane. He owned restaurants in Tampa Bay. She disappeared in '01, and he in '03." Daniel frowned. "Or maybe it was the other way around." He shrugged. "Doesn't matter for our purposes, I guess; as soon as that pack of reporters figures out who they were, they're gonna go bananas."

Beth touched Vivian again. "Did she have children?"

"I don't know. Scandlin said she'd just gotten married. Chuck had kids, though, a boy and a girl. Had a hot blonde wife, too."

She gave him a look.

"What?"

Beth shook her head and went back to staring at the two names; those poor children's pain, and Vivian's bereft newlywed husband's, were additional marks on the tally sheet that she would make John McFarlane pay.

In full.

"Beth, look at me." She did. "It's time for the bad news. There are a few things I haven't told you, but I think you need to hear them before we go through with this press conference."

She sat up ramrod straight. "A *few?*"

"Just listen to the end without interrupting." He barked a laugh. "Then you can call in the guys with the butterfly nets. Hell, I might go with them willingly; a padded room with all the happy-drugs I want sounds tempting right about now."

Butterfly nets? Padded rooms? "This better not be more nonsense about that cemetery."

"It's not. It's something else. Do you promise to listen without interrupting?"

"I'm not promising anything, and it's too late for all the dramatics. Tell me."

As she listened, Beth fought the urge to laugh hysterically.

And I thought his obsession with the cemetery *was bad!*

She cut him off mid-blather. "You don't really believe this, do you?"

"I know it sounds farfetched, but—"

"*Farfetched?* I'd say that's an understatement."

"Would you let me fin—"

"Shadows? And *things?* What *kind* of things? And why a blue light? Why not red, or green, or even purple?"

"Fulbright said they were 'things that should not be', and I wish you'd let me finish before—"

"'Things that should not be?' What in the world does that mean?"

"God damn it, would you just *listen*—"

"And McFarlane and his daughters leading a bunch of people down into the cenote where these two people were tied up naked? And *things* coming out of a blue light while everyone chanted?" Beth's eyes flew all the way open. "You don't think they're dumping bodies, you think they're…what, *sacrificing* the missing to these 'things' that McFarlane supposedly called out of the light?"

"Yes."

Beth licked her lips and studied his mottled face where it hovered in the darkness on the other side of the cab; her husband stared back at her calmly, looking not at all like a raving lunatic.

"I saw them, Beth. The shadows, I mean. I've seen them three times. Fulbright saw the third one, too, in the bathroom at the hospice. He saw it before I did. And I already told you about the second time. Remember when Lizzie and I surprised you on my birthday, and you asked what was wrong and I said I thought I had a panic attack? It wasn't a fucking panic attack, it was…well, just listen." And then Beth sat there with cold dismay constricting her heart as he talked about shadows that stood around in backyards, and shadows that oozed across window panes and looked in at him, and shadows that moved in bathrooms and then disappeared like smoke on the wind.

He believes this.

Beth's husband actually believed he'd seen living shadows.

His mind must have snapped last Sunday afternoon, up in their bedroom. She'd feared as much after he'd fixated on that cemetery, but she hadn't *wanted* to believe it, and now…now here Beth was, battling their megalomaniac and possibly psychotic neighbor for their home and perhaps their very lives, and she was doing it with a husband whose frontal lobe had melted.

She had to get him help, and before they called the press conference. Beth could just see him ranting to the world about shadows and blue lights and things that could not be or should not be or whatever; not only would they be dismissed out of hand as crackpots and not receive any help against McFarlane, they'd be laughed right off the edge of the planet…

He'd asked her a question.

"What?"

"I said, you don't believe me?"

She searched for words that wouldn't set him off. "Maybe you did see something, but—"

"I knew it." Instead of angry, though, like she'd expected, he sounded smug, as if he knew something she didn't.

"We'll just agree that you saw *something*, okay? I don't know what—"

"Scandlin saw the shadows, too."

Beth stared at him.

"Did he tell you about Sammy Glick?"

"No. Who's Sammy Glick?"

"I didn't think so." Smug wasn't even in it, now. "Listen." He told her about this rapist and ex-con and apparently disgruntled McFarlane farmhand Sammy Glick, and how Sammy had mentioned two of the missing people's names when he'd run to Jeff—the very two she'd saved in her phone. When Daniel told her how Glick had died, she watched him carefully again, but he still showed no signs of lunacy.

"…so Scandlin saw it, along with every other TBI Agent who's watched that recording." He went silent then, watching her watch him. Then he grimaced. "You *still* don't believe me!"

"Maybe if I could view the footage…"

"If your precious *Jeff* had told you about the shadows, you would have swallowed it whole. You guys got to be buddy-buddy on the goddamn phone, didn't you?" He snorted. "You'd believe *him*, but you think I've slipped a cog."

"I don't—"

"It's all over your face. Well, here's another wacky tidbit for you to choke on, sweetheart. It wasn't 'chanting'."

"I don't know what you're—"

"What Fulbright heard all those people doing when McFarlane called the things out of the blue light. A minute ago you said it was chanting. That's not what *he* said. It was singing."

"Singing, chanting, what's the—" He was watching her, that self-satisfied look now cemented. "*Singing?*" He nodded. "Like…like we heard tonight in the woods?"

"Yes."

Beth squinted. "You *knew* her. I could see it on your face."

"Yeah, I knew her. I knew her the second I heard her voice."

"Who was she?"

"That was the oldest daughter, Alex." He saw her expression and cleared his throat. "Uh, Alexandria, I mean."

Alex. "How can you be sure? You've only met her the once, right? It had *better* be just once, Daniel!"

"It was, I swear."

"Then how could you know that was her? And why would *Alex* sing in the woods at night? Why would anyone?"

"I don't know why, but as to *how* I know…" Beth's husband seemed to brace himself. "I know because that's the third time I've heard her singing."

"You said you'd only met her once!"

"It *was* only once! Christ, calm down."

"You better not be lying."

"I'm not! Jeez! The first time I heard her was…"

As Beth listened, her jealousy was swamped by crushing fear for his sanity again; first shadows and blue lights and things, and now…this!

"So the first time you heard her, she, what, *lured* you to the cemetery? Like one of those Sirens in the Odyssey? That's the most absurd—"

"I know what it sounds like! But I'm not crazy! I heard her singing, and then I rode the 'Goose to the cemetery, and I don't think I would have done that on my own! So yeah, maybe it *was* like that boring fucking story they made us read in high school!"

"Stop shouting at me!"

"I'm not shouting!" He shouted. "And I really did wake up with my forehead planted on McFarlane's kitchen table! And Alex and those other two sluts were standing over me, singing! *Even the old man was singing!* And those fucking mutts were sitting there on their furry butts just outside the sliding-glass doors with their heads thrown back, howling! And I didn't fucking *imagine* any of it!"

"This is—"

"And while I was down there, I was having the weirdest dream of my life! Lizzie and I were on the farm, and I was chumming around with McFarlane while Lizzie was hanging out with those three and calling them her sisters, but you were nowhere to be found! That's what made me realize it was a dream, and when I opened my eyes and sat up, they were all standing around me and *they were fucking singing!"*

Something slow, hot, and terrible moved through Beth.

"Sisters?"

"Stupid, right? But that's what I was dreaming, and when I woke up, they were all standing around me, singing in some strange language. I'm not making it up, and I'm not crazy. It happened."

Sisters?

Beth tossed the thought away like the garbage it was. Lizzie had no sisters. Besides, it was just some ridiculous dream. That brought up a good question:

"Why would you go to sleep on the table in the middle of lunch?"

"I don't know. At first I thought they'd poisoned me."

"*Poisoned* you? Why would they do that?"

"I don't know! But I was conked out and dreaming on the goddamn table, and when I woke up, they were standing around me, singing. That's a motherfucking *fact*, by the by, but *why?* Don't have a goddamn clue. And here are more *facts* for ya, babe: I *saw* something in the backyard, and outside those bay windows. It looked like a shadow come to life, but what it really was, I don't fucking know. I saw something in that hospice bathroom, too; so did Fulbright. That's a *fact*. Tonight was the third time I've heard Alexandria singing, and that's also a *fact*."

"Daniel…"

"Want to know the worst part? I didn't remember until I heard her in the woods tonight! The other two times came crashing back, then. You saw me! I almost fell out of that damn tree! But *why* I forgot…?" He shook his head. "The answer to 'why' is in short fucking supply right now, Beth. For a lot of things."

He believed it. Her husband believed this nonsense about a voice calling him to the cemetery and shadows and sacrifices and all the rest.

He actually believes it!

Daniel started to say something else, but she couldn't stand it anymore. Beth felt like she was treading water far out in the ocean and he was with her, her life raft, her lone hope of salvation, only now the current of his madness was causing him to drift away.

So like the drowning woman she was, Beth reached for him.

He'd leaned toward her while ranting about "facts" and "why", draping his left arm over the steering wheel, so she lifted her hand and gently cupped his cheek. He started, and for one agonizing moment she thought he would pull away from her touch, but then he nuzzled her hand and wound his long, strong fingers into hers.

His skin was so warm…

Beth sobbed, "You can't be…" *Crazy? Insane?* She would not utter those words; she wouldn't even *think* them! "You have to stay…focused…so you can help me with what we need to do, Daniel."

"Shh." He wiped her tears away, then raised the back of her hand over the console and kissed it.

"Don't shush me! You want 'facts'? McFarlane is threatening to throw us out of our own home if we don't move by the first of the month!" She deepened her voice: "That's a fucking *fact!*"

He chuckled, then brushed his lips over her right eyebrow, making her shiver.

She pushed him back. "I'm serious."

"I know you are." He tried to kiss her again.

She fended him off. "Do you? Then you should know you're really scaring me with all this…this talk about shadows and things and blue lights and *Alex* luring you to the cemetery with her stupid voice! And I mean *really* scaring me. I *need* you, Daniel. I need you…whole and paying attention to what we have to do to back

McFarlane down, not talking about all these things that are…well, they're just *impossible*, that's what they are! Absolutely, utterly, IMPOSSIBLE!"

He pulled back and studied her face, then sighed. "Okay, I'm sorry I scared you—"

"You should be."

"But you heard her singing, too."

Beth frowned.

"You can't deny it. I was there."

"I'm not denying it, but—"

"You *heard* her, so you know I'm not making it up or that I imagined it because I'm crazy. You heard her singing. Admit it."

"I said I'm not denying—"

"Admit it."

"Fine! I heard *Alex* singing! Does that make you happy?"

"Actually, yes. It means I'm not nuts." At her raised eyebrow, he said, "I've wondered myself the last few days. But if you heard the singing, that means it's real. I don't know if I trust anything Fulbright said, but we both saw the shadows, and that means *they're* real. And if you had seen them, you'd know they're real, too. Damn it! I wish Scandlin…well, maybe the TBI will let us take a gander at that security recording, although I doubt it. Wouldn't hurt to ask, I suppose, but…Beth? Beth!"

But Beth was no longer face to face with her husband while holding his hand and sitting in his stupid football-money truck in front of their open garage at four-something in the morning. She was a half-mile down Daisy on the left at Helen's house and it was a steamy Thursday afternoon, but it was cool and dark in Helen's living room. The loathed coo-coo clock had just shot out of its wall-mounted prison twice, making her jump—

…the shadows…

"Beth?"

—as usual, and then Beth had looked at her friend and found Helen staring down the hall toward her bedroom and the spare that Lizzie and Jacob used when they stayed over and her sewing room on the other side, but Helen wasn't just staring. She was bug-eyed and terrified. Then she'd snatched Beth's hand and fervently recited the Lord's Prayer over and over and over, and Beth, alarmed, had glanced over her shoulder and down the hall and—

…if you had seen them…

—a black shadow had moved in and out of a bright beam of sun slanting from the sewing room. She'd chalked it up to a passing cloud or an airplane, but—

"Beth!" Fingers snapped in her face.

…you'd know they were real…

—if it was just a cloud or a plane, why had Helen reacted that way? And Daniel sounded so sure of himself and not crazy at all when insisting he saw these oozing, vanishing shadows; and now that she thought about it, the one in Helen's hallway had been oozing away from the living room—

She felt him take her by the shoulders and gently shake her. "What's wrong?"
—and so if it wasn't a plane or a cloud, what had she seen in the hallway? *What did I really see?*
"That's impossible," she whispered.

He stopped shaking her. "What? Are you okay? You look like you're about to get sick. Do me a favor and open the door first. I happen to like that new-truck smell, and I want to keep it around as long as—"

Beth slammed her palms into his chest, knocking him back.

"Ow! Hey, that hurt! Why'd you—"

"IT'S IMPOSSIBLE!"

He leaned further away from her in shock.

"It is *impossible*, Daniel! It's all impossible, so I don't want to hear another word about shadows, or things, or sacrifices, or ghosts in the cemetery, or stupid blue lights, or that twat singing! *Especially* her! We have enough real things to deal with without all this…this…" What did you *see*, Beth? *What did you really SEE?* "It's flat-out impossible, and I don't want to talk about it anymore!"

"Okay, okay, Jesus!" He rubbed his chest. "I'll have bruises for a fucking week! Like I need more!" He faced the steering wheel. "Let's go inside. I want to wash the bug spray and the sweat off before I go to sleep." He was still sulking and rubbing his chest as he reached for the door handle.

Beth caught his arm before he could; here they were, finally touching after an agonizing week of *not* touching—and for Beth, wondering if they would ever touch again—and now she'd let her idiot temper ruin the moment.

"I'm sorry, I shouldn't have hit you." She drew him back, and after a second he faced her again. He was still glowering; he was so cute when he pouted. Beth pulled his other hand away from where it was rubbing and kissed both sets of big knuckles. How did his hands stay so warm? "You know that I'm right, though. This stuff—shadows and things and blue lights and all that—it's just impossible."

His scowl turned into an uncertain grimace; then he glanced at the dash clock. "It's almost four-thirty. I'm too tired to argue. You can crash at the hotel before you have to pick Lizzie up from Janet's, but I've got a long day ahead."

He tried to pull away, but she held on. "There's another reason I'm mad at you." She'd *sworn* that she wouldn't be the first one to say anything, but here she was, about to say it.

"What'd I do now?"

"When you said you wanted to talk, I thought…Daniel, I bared my *soul* to you. I told you things I've never told anyone, and you haven't said a word. It's like you're trying to pretend I never opened my mouth!"

She could feel him drawing away in every aspect but physically, and then he did that as well, freeing his fingers from hers almost roughly. He looked into the blackened garage, face empty.

Beth rested her hands in her lap; she felt nothing but frozen inside.

"That wasn't part of the deal," he said at last. "After Rison, you had to tell me about your past. I get that. And I had to listen. I get that, too. But I never said we'd hold a forum about it, after." He looked over at her then, and she almost wished he hadn't; those eyes were cold. "I won't leave, if that's what you're worried about. I love you and Lizzie too much." He looked away again. "But that was a lot to take in. I need time to process. We'll talk about it someday, if you want, but right now—as you're so fond of pointing out—we have real shit to deal with."

Daniel slid out and retrieved the shotgun and his other toys from the back seat, then walked into the garage. She watched, numb, as he flipped on the light and punched the code into the new glowing keypad. There was a faint beep. He opened the door and went inside. He didn't look back.

Beth stared up at the castle, and then out at the remote and uncaring stars, and then she sighed and wiped the tears from her cheeks and got out and locked the truck before slowly following her husband.

Everything Changes

Beth tossed her gardening gloves onto the workbench, then watched the garage door churn down before locking the interior door. Daniel was in the foyer, standing in front of the master keypad, cradling the shotgun in one elbow and reading the instructions on the inside cover while muttering curses. He didn't look around as she walked behind him and into the living room. She sat on the couch without collapsing into the cushions, but only just; without the valley's strange, hyper-oxygenated atmosphere, the hour had definitely caught up to her.

The alarm pad gave three quick beeps; they were now locked in and safe from the big, bad world. Daniel shut the cover and trudged upstairs; their bedroom door opened and shut, and a minute later the shower started.

Someday.

That's when he would talk about her past…if, that is, she really wanted to discuss it. Beth laughed, but it came out more like a sob. He would never mention it if she didn't bring it up first, that was obvious to her now, but he was also right; talking about it hadn't been part of the deal.

She listened to the shower and decided he'd had a good idea for once; there was no way she was climbing in with him, though, so Beth went to the downstairs bathroom and stripped and stepped beneath the spray, letting the heat pound into her neck and shoulders and the top of her head.

Someday.

She pawed for the shampoo in the little alcove, and its unfamiliar shape made her open her eyes. It was Daniel's brand. He'd put a spare bottle here for the times he didn't want to wake her up, like when he had to work early and she was scheduled to close and she and Lizzie were sleeping in…

Beth leaned her shoulder against the slick stall, and soon more than water was running down her cheeks; she was avoiding him, yet now she would smell like him all day.

Someday.

She straightened and dumped out a handful of the man-shampoo and washed her hair, then rinsed it and her tears away and climbed out and grabbed two fluffy towels from the linen closet; Beth wrapped one around her hair and another around her middle, knotting it between her breasts. Her clothes were filthy, so she retrieved her phone and keys and knife and carried her soiled garments to the laundry room.

Back in the kitchen, she stood barefoot on the tiles between the sink and the island and cocked an ear toward the ceiling; the shower upstairs had stopped, but she could hear him thumping around. What was he doing now? Why hadn't he gone to bed yet? Beth was more than ready for bed herself, but wherever he was sleeping, that's where she wouldn't be sleeping. She'd thought it might be different, what with the way he'd kissed her out in the truck—and considering this was the first night they'd spent alone, without Lizzie, in a week—but…

Beth sighed, then slipped over to the computer desk on the far side of the breakfast nook and put her phone and keys and Carson down, then fell into the chair.

She swiveled back and forth, back and forth, waiting to see where her husband would choose to sleep; if he crashed in Lizzie's bed, she couldn't hold it against him. She'd been there all week while he'd been stuck on that uncomfortable air mattress. Beth might as well seize the initiative and grab some spare blankets and hit the couch; they would get up in a couple of hours to pack anyway, and she was tired enough it wouldn't matter.

Decision made, Beth stood up to go to the linen closet, and then their bedroom door opened. She froze. When she heard him come downstairs, she dropped back into the chair and spun to face the blank monitor, heart thrumming. Why was he coming down? Had *he* decided to sleep on the couch?

He walked into the kitchen; by the sound, he was barefoot, too. He stopped. Beth waited for him to say something, anything, but he just stood behind her and stared at the back of her towel-wrapped head.

Someday.

Then, soft and strong and clear:

"I'm proud of you."

Beth's brow furrowed; maybe she had water in her ears.

"What?"

"I said I'm proud of you." Daniel came closer and used the back of the chair to swing her around. He cupped her chin and leaned down and kissed her, then stood her up and pulled her against his chest, and she wrapped her arms around him and held on tight, as hard as she could; as hard as she'd ever held anything.

"I'm so proud of you," he whispered. He freed one arm to take the towel off her hair and let it drop, then kissed the top of her head. "I've never been so proud of anyone in my entire life."

Relief and joy bloomed in Beth's heart, so hot they shamed the sun. She put a hand on his chest and pushed him back so she could see him through her tears.

"How can you be proud of me? Rison was right, I was a prostitute."

He held her eyes with his bright-blue stare and gravely considered her question. "Let me ask you something," he said at last.

"What?"

"You just did it that one time, right? For the bus money?"

"Right."

"And you don't plan to do it again?"

"Of course I don't plan to do it again!" Beth was tempted to hit him. "How can you ask me that?"

"Well, because if you *do* decide to do guys for money, then I guess we'll have a serious problem—unless you cut me in. As the husband, I'm entitled to sixty percent." His lips twitched.

Beth gaped, and then she *did* punch him. He grunted, but didn't lose that smile. Then they were laughing, and they held onto each other until it wound down. She had her cheek pressed to his chest. She could hear his heart beat. He was so warm.

He used her chin to lift her face to his. "How could I *not* be proud of you? I mean, God, after what you went through, most people would still be curled in a dark corner somewhere with their thumb stuck in their mouth." He ran his fingers over her cheeks, her eyebrows, her lips. "I'm proud you're the mother of my child," her Daniel said. "I'm proud to be your husband."

Beth seized his ears and pulled him into a kiss; it was late, but she wasn't tired anymore. He grabbed the back of her head and pressed the kiss deeper. She let go with one hand and undid the knot in her towel and it slid to the tiles, making a moist white puddle at her feet. She reached down and gripped him through his boxers as they kissed again, melting into each other.

He scooped her up and carried her upstairs, trying to kiss her the entire way and stumbling and nearly falling twice. Panting with need, they dragged some blankets out of the linen closet and fetched her pillow from Lizzie's room and then they went into a spare bedroom and shut the door.

Beth dropped to her knees, slid his boxers to his ankles, and took him into her mouth, all the way. He gasped. She had one instance of worry that he would think of Rison, but when she rolled her eyes up, he had his head thrown back. She took him out and licked up and down the length of him and then took him in again and he moaned; she stroked up and down, up and down, faster, faster, and then stood up and nearly ripped his shirt off and lay back on the tangle of blankets. He spread her legs and then he was inside her, deep inside, all the way to the back as he pounded, harder, harder, harder, and her cries echoed through the room. He turned her over and put her face in the pillow and grabbed a fistful of her hair and drove into her and she felt pain but it was the good pain, and she shuddered as she came, her screams reverberating from the wall near her head. She came again, and then again; she couldn't come any more, he couldn't go any deeper, there wasn't room, she didn't have anything left, again, her shrieks filling the castle now, and then he moaned as he released inside her, the wonderful warmth spreading.

They lay shoulder to shoulder, trembling and gasping and looking up at the ceiling, and then she took his hand into both of hers and held it between her breasts.

"I love you."

"I love you, too." He groaned.

"What's wrong?"

"My knees have carpet burn. We need another goddamn bed."

Beth laughed and kissed him. Somehow the blankets had ended up across the room, so to spare his poor, hardworking knees, she crawled over and dragged them back and covered them up.

And then they talked and laughed and argued about how to best handle the upcoming press conference as the smell of sex and new carpet permeated the spare bedroom. He went downstairs for their phones and Beth's knife and his pistols and a much-needed glass of ice water, then lay back down on the floor with her; along about the time the new sun was driving away the stars and filling the world with a rosy glow, they made love again, slow, their need not so great this time, with her on top like they both liked.

They fell asleep not long after, limbs and hearts entwined, and as Beth was drifting off, she realized she'd been wrong: he hadn't left her, and it wasn't over; he'd accepted her past, accepted *her*.

But she had also been right: after Scott Rison, nothing could ever be the same between them.

It could be better.

The tinny sounds of AC/DCs "You Shook Me All Night Long" rocked the sun-drenched spare bedroom, and Beth clawed awake; her brain felt stuffed and mounted. What time was it? Daniel didn't stir, even when she lifted his arm away and crawled to the phone.

She blinked crusted lids: 7:34. She focused, and the first tingles of alarm ran through her. Why would Janet call so early? Maybe Lizzie wanted to say good morning. She'd done that before when staying over at Helen's.

Beth fumbled the phone to her ear.

"Hello?"

Book V

The Binding

THREE DAYS

Dan was dreaming of a storm.

It was a big sucker, too, one that would've made Katrina resemble a polite sneeze. He was caught in the middle of it, and—

—he was actually *feeling* the storm pulse around him, so he wasn't—

He sat up in alarm, but instead of a raging cyclone, Dan saw his wife standing with her back to him, rigid in the middle of the empty spare bedroom; her right hand held her iPhone crammed to her ear. She was as naked as him, but instead of all the fun things he could have looked at, Dan stared uneasily at her left hand, which she held down by her leg; that hand was knotted into a fist. Even as he looked, that bony knot unraveled to make a deadly claw; the claw sprang shut and became the knot again as she trembled from head to heel; the fine blond hairs on the back of Dan's forearms were standing stiff and waving like wheat swaying in the breeze.

The hell?

"No," Beth whispered. Then: "No. *No!*"

A surge of adrenaline brought him staggering to his feet in the spitting air; holy crap, he was sore. "What the fuck is going on?"

Beth spun. Her lips were skinned back from her teeth, and her eyes darted like a trapped animal's.

"They took her!"

"What?"

That awful face crumpled, and she stumbled. He caught her.

"They took her, Daniel!"

Dan stood perfectly still with his arms around his wife as Janet's panicked voice called Beth's name from the phone's tiny speaker.

"Here! I have to get pen and paper!" She shoved her phone against his chest, but he didn't react; it thumped onto the thick blue carpet, Janet's frantic voice rising from between his bare feet now. Beth rushed naked to the door and jerked it open and ran through; from far away Dan heard her bounding down the stairs.

He bent over in glacial motion and picked up Beth's phone and put it to his ear.

"Beth! *Beth!* Where did you go? Oh my God, we have to call the police, I don't care what the note says!"

Dan spoke, his voice leaking down from the stars:

"It's me. Where's Lizzie?"

"Daniel! Oh thank God, Beth's not—"

"Where's Lizzie, Janet? Where is my daughter?"

The only answer was the sound of Janet weeping.

"*Where is she!?*"

"She's gone! Someone took her!"

"Who? *Who* took her?"

"I don't know! Bill got up at four to get some work done in the paint bay so I got up with him, and we had coffee and took a peek at her before he left and she was sound asleep, Mr. Yoda too, and then when I went to wake her at seven-twenty to have some waffles and get her dressed for church, she was gone! Mr. Yoda's gone too, and her backpack with the clothes you sent for her; even her toothbrush and that *Star Wars* movie are gone! The only thing left was a note!"

Gone. A note. Gone.

"What does the note say?"

Janet crying.

"Janet! What does the note say?"

"It says…it says not to call the police or they'll know, and you'll never see Lizzie again." Janet sobbed, "Ohmygod!"

Dan knew there was more. There had to be more. *Please God, let there be more.* "What else does it say? *Janet!* What else does it say?"

"There's a number. It says to call you and give you the number, and not the police. You're supposed to call the number by eight-thirty this morning. If you haven't called by then, she'll be…Oh my God, who *are* these people?"

"What's the number?"

Beth blasted into the room carrying a pen and the spiral notepad they kept on the computer desk. "There's a number to call!" She thrust the pad and pen at him and tried to snatch the phone. "Let me talk to Janet again!"

She was quick, but he moved faster, holding it up and out of her reach; her face contorted, and for one long second Dan was sure they would have another naked throw-down right there and then, and not the good kind; then Beth shuddered and turned away.

Dan put the phone back to his ear. "Repeat that, Janet."

She did, and he read it out while Beth carved it into the pad. "Hang up, we have to—"

"Read the note to me, Janet."

"Why would they take the dog? Who kidnaps a child and takes the *dog?*"

"Janet! Read the note!"

"You have to call the police. They can trace that number and get her back, I saw it on CSI."

"We don't have time for this! We have to call! We have to make sure she's all right!" Beth looked around wildly until she spotted his iPhone poking from under a fold of blanket, then darted and snatched it up.

"*Wait!*" Dan held his free hand out. His wife snarled, and he figured it was even odds whether she would stab that pen through his palm or not. "We've got 'till eight-thirty, and it's not even seven-forty-five. Let's hear the whole note first."

Beth closed her eyes, then nodded; glistening tears the size of robin's eggs squeezed from under those long lashes and leaked down her cheeks.

"Plea—" He cleared his throat, tried again: "Please read the note, Janet. And describe it to us. Hold on, let me put this thing on speaker. Okay, go ahead."

Lizzie.

Oh God, Lizzie.

Janet said, "Can you hear me?"

"Yes," Beth said. She clutched his phone and the pen and pad between her breasts.

"The note's in blue ink, on lined yellow paper. It's written in cursive. It's…it's a woman's hand. It says, 'We will not hurt her. No cops. If you involve the authorities, we will know, and you will never see her again in this life.' Oh my God, what kind of woman kidnaps someone's child?"

"*READ THE REST OF THE FUCKING NOTE!*" Dan fought for a scrap of control, any scrap, any scrap at all, found it: "Please, Janet."

"It just says to call you and give you the number, and that you're supposed to call it by eight-thirty, and then it repeats not to call the police." Janet hesitated. "You know who took her, don't you."

They looked at each other.

"We know. Or at least we think we do."

"You…! Well, then you've got to call the police! *Now!* I don't care what the note says, the police can—"

"No police. They'll know, just like the note says, and then…" Dan couldn't finish that thought; wouldn't *allow* himself to finish it.

"Well, for God's sake! What're you going to do?"

"We'll call the number."

"And *then* what? Tell the police! They can—"

Beth said, "Daniel's right, no cops. Not yet, anyway."

Her voice seemed to break something loose in Janet. She sobbed, "Oh, I'm so sorry, dear, *so* sorry, she was fine when we checked on her! I swear! And we had such a good time last night! We watched her *Star Wars* movie, even Bill watched, and he doesn't take to science fiction stuff, and we had strawberry ice cream and she wanted to wear those Bugs Bunny pajamas she loves so much and we put her in the back bedroom, the one Terry and Allie always sleep in when they visit, and she insisted Mr. Yoda sleep in there with her. Bill didn't like it, but we let them, and she went right to sleep!" Janet wailed, "We didn't think to watch her all night! I'm so sorry!"

The pad and pen and his phone slipped from Beth's fingers and tumbled to the carpet as she put her face in her hands; a keening howl filled the spare bedroom.

Dan heard himself say, "It's not your fault, Janet, I need to let you go, we have to call this number."

"You…you have to let me know what…if there's anything I can…Oh my God, I need to call Bill and—"

"No!" Dan yelled at the same time as Beth let her hands drop and said, "You can't tell Bill."

"Why not?" Now she was angry. "Someone broke into our house and we didn't hear a thing, and I can't even call the law! *He* at least needs to know—"

Beth said, "You can't tell him. He may call the cops no matter what we want, or he may say something to someone—"

"He wouldn't do that."

"I'm sure he wouldn't, but we can't take the chance. If the authorities somehow get involved, and the people who took her hear about it—"

"And they will," Dan said. "I know of at least one TBI Special Agent on their payroll, and I suspect there are a lot more. And not just with the TBI."

There was a stunned silence before Janet whispered, "Who in the Lord Jesus' name are these people? And what do they want with poor little Lizzie?"

"We don't know." What *did* they want? Dan wiped his eyes roughly and decided it didn't matter; they had his daughter, yes, but he would get her back, end of fucking discussion. "Let us call this number and then I promise we'll let you know what's going on. In the meantime, you can't tell Bill, or anyone. This has to stay between us three for now. Please."

"Please, Janet," Beth said.

"All right." Janet blew her nose with a big honk, sniffled, then: "God! This is…I guess I'm not attending services this morning." She gave a broken laugh. "In fact, I know where Bill hides the single malt, even though he thinks I don't. I haven't had a serious drink in seventeen years, but this morning calls for one. Dial that number and then call me right back. I might be four sheets to the wind by then, but call me anyway."

"We will," Beth said while bending down to retrieve the pad. She left his phone and the pen on the carpet. "Thank you, Janet."

There was a final sob, what sounded like ice clinking into a glass, and then she was gone.

Dan and Beth looked at each other; clear snot ran from his wife's nose and dripped on her full lips. Her eyes were red and puffy and frightened and furious. She was still naked and so was he, and Dan suddenly wanted to put clothes on before they called; it was ludicrous, but they seemed more vulnerable this way. He also wanted to scream and punch a hole in the drywall, but none of that would do Lizzie any good. The warm sunlight slanted in on their bodies as birds fluttered and swooped and chirped outside; it was a gorgeous Sunday morning.

Then out of the blue Beth announced, "She's all right." She sounded relieved, and her leaking eyes were focused elsewhere. "Lizzie's okay," she whispered, as if to herself.

Dan frowned at her; she seemed so certain, but he didn't know how that could possibly be. He nodded anyway; at this point he would take any comfort he could get.

"She's okay," he agreed. The urge to put clothes on was still strong. "Read the number."

She did. He dialed. It rang. They listened.

He answered on the third ring.

"Hello?"

Dan forced himself to say the name; it came out like an animal's snarl.

"*McFarlane.*"

"Why hello there, boy."

"Where's Lizzie? Where is our—"

Beth snatched the phone out of his palm so fast Dan barely saw her move. "Give her back!" She held the iPhone in front of her face with both hands and screeched: "*Give Lizzie back to us! Who do you think you are? You have no right!*"

"Ah, The Mother! It's nice to finally meet you, my dear. I've been looking forward to it with great anticipation."

"*Fuck you! Give us our daughter back!*"

"All in good time, all in good time; we have business to conduct first. And right off, let me offer my congratulations. You've created an extraordinary little girl."

"Give her back, you goddamn piece of runny shit! I'll fucking *kill* you if you don't! I *promise* I'll kill you!"

McFarlane chuckled again; he sounded like he was having a fine Sunday morning. "Fierce little filly, ain't she, boy? Such strength. Such *spirit.* I suspect you didn't have a damn clue what you was marryin', and in more ways than one. You could've been somethin' special, girl; a candle to the sun compared to this astonishing little lady of yours, true, but special in your own right, no doubt about it. But it's too late, now—or mostly, anyway, and for that to happen, you would have to have a change of heart and mind the likes of which you couldn't begin to believe or accept. Yes," McFarlane finished sadly, "it's too late."

Dan exchanged glances with his wife and then snapped his mouth closed and looked back at the phone.

He was insane; McFarlane was insane.

A crazy man had kidnapped their daughter.

God help us.

"Let her go, John." It seared his soul to beg this man. Dan did it anyway. "Please. If you bring her back now, we won't tell the police. We'll move away, sell the house, anything you want, just please give Lizzie back to us."

"We're way beyond that now, boy. Things have been set in motion, and I won't have them interrupted. I cain't allow it."

Things in motion? "Let her go, John. *Please.*"

"Don't hurt her!" Beth wailed.

"Hurt? Don't even think it, my dear. You have my word, as a man and as a father, that nothin' I do will bring her harm." That easy chuckle again: "Just the opposite of harm's what she'll get from me."

Beth and Dan exchanged another wondering glance; McFarlane sounded sincere.

Then the breath whooshed out of his lungs at a piping voice in the background, a voice as familiar and as precious to him as anything in the world. "Lizzie!" Dan grabbed the phone and held it along with his wife:

"*Lizzie!*"

"Lizzie!"

"Just hold on! Jumpin' Jupiter, you people got some *lungs* on ya! Man cain't hear himself think with all that caterwaulin'! Simmer down and I'll let you speak to 'er. Poor mite's been askin' to talk to her Mommy and Daddy all mornin', anyhow."

"You'll let us talk to her?"

"Of course, dear, I wouldn't be so cruel as to deny you that. Besides, she's young; she needs her Mommy and Daddy." He paused. Then he said something that made Dan's spine turn to polar ice. "For now."

And then thoughts of just what the hell that had meant were driven out of his mind as Dan heard Lizzie's sweet voice come closer, and then a familiar bark. Mr. Yoda! Wherever that bastard was holding her, Mr. Yoda was there, too! For some reason that broke loose a flood of his own tears.

Lizzie asked Mr. John if she could talk to her Mommy. Beth looked like she would jump through the phone if she could. McFarlane answered yes, calling her sweetheart, but said he needed to talk to them for just a minute more.

Dan's tears dried in a sudden furnace.

The sonofabitch called her sweetheart.

Kidnaps her and then calls her *sweetheart!*

Lizzie said okay. Dan's daughter sounded happy, not upset or scared: happy. Mr. Yoda barked again.

McFarlane came back; his voice was lowered, as if he didn't want Lizzie to hear.

"Three days. That's the deal."

"Three days? What the fuck does that mean?"

"It means three days, boy. We keep her three days, do what needs to be done, and then I'll bring her back to ya myself on Wednesday mornin', 'round this time. She'll be right as rain—better, in fact. You have my word."

They both stared at the phone like it had sprouted an ear. They looked at each other. They looked at the phone. Dan said the only thing he could.

"You're crazy, old man."

McFarlane gave the deep chuckle. "Am I? Guess we'll find out soon enough." A rustle, then:

"Hi Mommy!"

"H—hi, baby."

"Mommy, why are you crying?" Dan wiped his face; somehow, Beth had been right. Lizzie was okay. In fact, she sounded like she was doing a helluva lot better than they were.

"I'm—" Beth took a deep breath, blinked, and smoothed her voice. "I'm okay, sweetie, I'm just so happy to hear you, that's all."

"She's okay, baby. We love you." Dan didn't know what else to say. "We love you."

"Hi Daddy! Love you!" A small bark sounded. "Mr. Yoda says he loves you, too!" She giggled.

"Are you okay, sweetheart? Where are you?"

Dan darted a look at his wife and found her looking back intently.

He shook his head and whispered, "Don't—"

"I'm okay. We're at Mr. John's farm, Mommy. They have horsies and chickens and turkeys and whole bunches of moo cows and piggies and I got to ride on a tractor, it was *so cool*, its tires were way up taller even than Daddy's truck, and…"

They ran to the window in lockstep and he yanked the cord and almost ripped the blinds off the wall as they pressed their faces to the glass, craning their necks to the right; only part of the ridge was visible, with its gleaming buildings scattered along the crest, but it was enough.

Lizzie was still telling them about the tractor ride as Beth raised her free hand and pressed her fingertips against the glass.

"She's right there, Daniel. *Right over there!*"

That goddamn egotistical son of a bitch! Not only does he kidnap Dan's daughter, he takes her next door! And judging by how he was letting Lizzie talk, he didn't care if they knew! It wasn't a child abduction, it was a forced sleepover! Dan fought the urge to grab his guns, crash through the window, drop to the grass, jump the fence, run the four or five miles, kill everyone in sight, then bring his daughter home, all while still naked; Beth could fix them a late brunch when they got back.

"…please, please, please, please, please, *puhleeeaaase*, Mommy? Daddy said I was too little to ride a horsie, but I'm big now, almost five! Ms. Mindy said she'd teach me, and I promise I'll clean my room and pick up Mr. Yoda's poop forever and ever and ever even though it's so gross I wanna ride a horsie so bad please say I can please?"

Beth had a lost expression on her snotty face.

"I…"

"You can ride a horse," Dan said. *This can't be happening.* "Just promise me to be careful, okay? Listen to Ms. Mindy and do as she says."

"Yay!" The unmistakable sounds of his daughter jumping around in glee came over the line. "Thank you, Daddy, thank you! I promise I'll be careful!" Mr. Yoda barked.

Three days. Why three days? She would ride the horsies and feed the chickens and see the moo cows and pet the piggies; not a forced sleepover, more like an involuntary mini-camp, one sponsored by the local Nazi branch of the FFA. They would roast marshmallows over a campfire and she'd come home toting a cross-section of pine with Popsicle sticks glued to it. It would read, "I was kidnapped and survived McFarlane Farms' Summer Camp 2010."

Madness.

Lizzie, who had been going on about the horsie she would ride—a pretty red girl one with a white diamond on her forehead and one white foot—suddenly giggled. "Stop it, Ike!"

Dan heard panting, and then a deep bark; the heavy panting was right in the phone. Dan and Beth looked at each other, eyes wide: the Presidents. More panting; Lizzie giggled harder. "Stop it, Reagan!" She laughed. "They're so silly." Mr. Yoda barked. "Stop it, Mr. Yoda, don't be mad." She giggled again. "He's jealous."

Dan was going to throw up, he just knew it. He didn't have a chance, though, because he heard Lizzie speak to someone, then: "Some baby piggies were born yesterday and Ms. Alex and Ms. Rebecca are going to show them to me! And I get to hold one! Love you Mommy love you Daddy bye!"

Beth yelled, "Wait! Lizzie, wait! Come back!"

"Lizzie!"

It was no use; she was gone.

McFarlane drawled, "Alrighty then. You've talked to her, and as you can hear, she's havin' the time of her little life. Farm livin's good for young'uns, I've said it afore and I'll say it again. Now, I need to know if you agree to the deal."

"You *steal* her," Dan raged, "and then you act like it's a fucking—!"

"Agree or not. I need to know. Right now."

"You sonofabitch, I'll—!"

"Callin' me names ain't gonna get the job done, boy." The old man's voice hardened. "You know what I can do, what I can make happen. Don't believe me, just ask yer pal Special Agent Scandlin." He let that sink in. "I know you been lookin' inta me and my business. You think I wouldn't find out? I know a helluva lot more about this world than just farmin', boy. Even a numb shit like you shoulda figured that out. I'll warn ya one last time: say no, and she'll be gone. You know I have the resources to take her anywhere. It'll be a pain, I won't kid ya there; this is a special place, and I'd prefer to do what needs to be done here, but it's not unique. We can do it any number of special places scattered about this world. It would just be…bothersome…to arrange at this late date." McFarlane cleared his sinuses, spit. "Decision time. What's it gonna be?"

They looked at each other.

"Time's a tickin', yes or no."

Special places? What needed to be done? Pure insanity, but they didn't have a choice. Dan nodded, and after a slight hesitation, Beth nodded back.

"All right, you fucking bastard, three days, but not a second more! You hear, McFarlane? Not a single second more!"

McFarlane sighed, and in it Dan heard a clear note of relief. "A deal, then. We have a deal."

Dan spluttered. Asshole made it sound like they'd just bought a car! "You listen to me, you sick fuck! Three days, and she better come back without a scratch on her!"

"Can we talk to her again?" Beth said. "Please?"

"I don't think—"

"*Please?*"

Dan let go of the phone and stalked away, fists clenched; Beth begging was as alien as trees talking.

I will kill you for this, old man. I swear to God I will.

"Tell ya what," McFarlane said, magnanimous. "I'll let ya talk to her twice more, once tomorrow and once Wednesday at this time of the mornin', right before I bring her back and put her in yer lovin' arms. That sound good?"

"That sounds fine," Beth whispered.

Dan turned around, then took an involuntary step back. Scotty Rison had seen that face, there at the end; the fingers resting on the pane had morphed into the claw. She raked it slowly down the glass.

"That's it then, a deal! Good, good, good!" Then the jolly-old-farmer routine vanished. "I'm aware that yer of the opinion that yer smart folks, and that smart folks do stupid things 'cause they think they're smart but they really ain't. What I'm a-sayin' is, don't call the police. I told ya I had friends everywhere, didn't I, boy? And now you know it's true. Oh, I'd have to abandon everythin' I've built here, and that'd be a pain *and* a shame, no doubt, but I'd do it at the drop of a hat for yer little girl. She's that important. Call 'em, and she'll be long gone before the first law dog turns down my road. Forever. Hear me?" That last had been harder than steel.

"Yes," Dan whispered, swallowing his rage. "We hear you."

"Good. And don't try none o' that foolishness you tried last night, either. Sneakin' onta my property. Like I wouldn't know." His voice turned sly. "Didn't find what you were lookin' for, did ya?" He laughed. "All my boys are on the lookout sharp, so you just stay there in that eyesore you call a house and wait three days. I gave you my word, as a man and as a father, and I'll give it again: after three days, I'll bring her right to ya myself, and no harm will come to her." McFarlane laughed again, a rich belly buster this time. "Harm? Hurt's the last thing that special little girl will get here."

Beth said, "What will you do to her?"

"If I told ya, you wouldn't understand, and even if you understood, you wouldn't believe. You wouldn't let yerself." He grunted. "No, it's best to just let us do what we gotta do." Then he laughed yet again, and this time it was as wild and insane as advertised. "You'll see the results! Believe me, you'll see!" That mad mirth cut off as if chopped with an ax. "Still there, boy?"

"I'm here, you cocksucker."

"Remember what I told ya, when you was over to my place?" Dan didn't respond, and the old man prompted him: "Remember what I told ya?"

"That you like it in the ass? Yeah, I remember."

"I told ya that ya reap what ya sow in this life. We coulda done this the easy way, been friends, but because of you and that smart mouth, we gotta do it the hard way. *Reap it*, boy. Tomorrow mornin', this time, a different number. She'll call you."

The line went dead.

They stood naked in the window, looking at the farm gleaming on the ridge; numbers churned through Dan's brain, but they weren't encouraging. Two against six farmhands plus the old man and the singing sluts made ten; eleven, counting the Keeper or the family friend or whoever the fuck she really was. Fourteen counting the hairballs.

Can't forget them, oh no, can't forget them!

Three days.

Lizzie was right over there, but with those numbers, she might as well have been on Pluto.

Beth shifted to face him, and he looked down into her wounded eyes.

Two. Fourteen against two. Three days.

"What will they do to her?"

"I don't know. He's crazy. They all are."

"Yes."

"Let me ask you something. Do you trust him to keep her for three days and not harm her, not take her anywhere, and just bring her back to us like nothing ever fucking happened?"

Beth looked up at him for the longest time, then squeezed those eyes shut and whispered, "No."

"That's pretty much how I feel about the goddamn situation." Fourteen against two; they had to whittle that ratio down, and Dan thought he saw a way.

"But what can we do about it? We can't call the cops, and we can't go back over there; he'll know and take her somewhere far away and we'll never see her again! Maybe we should just wait, like he said."

"So you *want* to leave her over there for three days with him doing God knows what to her?" She didn't answer. "Well? Do you?"

Beth looked out the window again. "No," she admitted.

"Good, because I have a plan to get her back, and get her back tonight. Fuck three days."

"How?"

He told her. She listened. They argued. Then they got dressed and went downstairs and argued some more; Dan reluctantly admitted that she had a few ideas that improved his plan. They both called in sick. Beth had no problems there, what with her new MIT Terrance up from Atlanta, but Irene wasn't happy with Dan, not happy at all. He couldn't have cared less if he tried. Then Beth called Janet.

Dan listened to the women talk, thinking feverishly: *"Things" had been "set in motion"? A "special place"? Lizzie was "too important"? What the fuck was that supposed to mean? Complete insanity. It doesn't matter, she won't be there long.*

After Beth had smoothed Janet down again, they hashed the plan out, putting in the final touches, and when they were done his wife stood at the dining-room bay window, looking toward the distant farm. By then it was past ten in the morning, and the August sun shot warm rays through the kitchen as Dan walked over to the island and put his hand on the Nike bag; the money inside was hers, even though she didn't think of it that way.

"We'll spend most of this, you know."

"You think I give a flying fuck?"

"I guess not."

"You guessed right."

Dan divided the cash into two piles; his pile was bigger because he had more stuff to get, but they both had a list. Beth was crying again, a soft, helpless sound that made him blink and lose count and start over twice. He couldn't stop now. If Dan stopped, he would curl into a ball and shrivel up and die; he would never stop, not until he had Lizzie safe in his arms again.

Never, ever stop.

"Daniel?"

"Yeah?"

"Tell me this will work. Tell me we'll get her back tonight."

Dan put the bills down and walked over and turned her around. She pressed her face into his chest, and he rested his chin on her hair and gazed at the distant buildings nestled among the lush trees on the ridge, at the ripe fields sprinkled with cows, all of it shining in the sun like something out of an evil fucking Rockwell.

"This will work. We will get our daughter back tonight."

"Promise?"

"I promise."

She pulled back and peered up at him.

"You could go to prison."

"So could you, but it doesn't matter as long as we get her back."

She nodded. "It doesn't matter, as long as we get her back."

They left the other truth unspoken; one or both of them could die tonight. They'd made contingency plans for that as well.

They divvied the cash up, each with their list, and then they packed overnight bags. Without hesitation, but also without looking or saying anything to him, Beth packed a bag for Lizzie. Tears dripped from her chin as she did. Dan said nothing, just kept going; they were splitting up and taking both vehicles to save time, and for other reasons.

Beth started her car and backed out of the garage; she shut the garage door, and he opened his truck with the fob. They both looked up at the castle, and then at each other. He went to her, and she lowered the window and they kissed, and then she drove off and Dan got in and pulled around the driveway and stopped facing Daisy. He looked left, toward McFarlane's farm. Then he hit the blinker to turn right, towards town.

Away from Lizzie.

"We'll be back. We're coming to get you." He wiped his streaming eyes with the neck of his tee-shirt. "We'll be back, baby, I promise. I love you."

Dan turned right, heart ripping. Then a fierce grin split his face, pulling his lips away from his teeth.

"We'll be back."

He wasn't talking to Lizzie, now.

"We'll be back, motherfucker."

The Longest Day

I T WAS the longest day of Beth's life.

She kept checking her watch to make sure she wasn't losing it, but it was true; a minute took an hour, and a normal hour took a week. It was a good plan her husband had thought up, and it was even better after she'd plugged the gaping holes; they had a chance to get their daughter back and get her back tonight. Daniel was right, fuck three days. There was no way she would leave Lizzie in McFarlane's clutches that long.

It was killing Beth to leave her until tonight.

What are they doing to her?

"Mommy's coming, baby."

"Um, may I help you, ma'am?"

The clerk at Cabela's frowned uncertainly as Beth scrubbed away tears and moved up to the register; the man who'd been checking out in front of her was gone. She ignored the watchful checker and paid for her purchases and wheeled the cart to the car and loaded the trunk and drove away.

Two weeks later Beth stood in line at Wal-Mart and looked around at the thronging moms and dads and kids, just another Sunday out shopping with the fam, and it struck her how much apart from these people she felt, like she'd beamed down and taken human form to stroll among them; the Earthlings didn't understand how it really was. *They took my daughter!* Beth wanted to rave at them, but they wouldn't believe, or they'd grab their kids and shy away. Some would even run screaming if she told them the truth:

It could be your child next!

She waited in the queue and shuffled forward with the clueless humans; to keep from shrieking, Beth bit the inside of her cheek until she tasted blood and swallowed it and stayed quiet and paid. The cashier, a young woman with a diamond stud in her nose, watched her leave, but Beth didn't care; two more stops to go.

Her first had been Slo Eddie's. Everyone had looked at her funny—she'd called in sick, after all—especially Terrance, but Beth had simply walked to her office and shut the door. It took her a week to type everything up and print out two copies, and then each copy had gone into its own manila envelope.

Everything, no matter how embarrassing or outlandish: What Rison had said during the assault, along with the details of the assault and what was written on those impossible pages she'd burned; what Jeff had told them about his wife and the missing and the daughters and Melissa Bane and McFarlane; what Brennan alleged about McFarlane; what they suspected had happened to those poor children and their mother and Jeff and Brennan and the MTSU professors; and finally, how McFarlane had threatened them and who took their daughter and what they planned to do about it.

Everything.

In case they didn't come back.

One envelope Beth addressed to Tennessee's Attorney General; she'd had to look his name up, but he was getting the first copy. On the good chance he was McFarlane's butt buddy (like everyone else seemed to be in this stinking, backwoods state), the second copy was going to the offices of the Associated Press in New York City.

One way or another, Beth would take McFarlane down; even if she was already dead, she would reach out from her grave and snatch him down with her.

She gave the sealed and stamped envelopes to Terrance and told him if she didn't show up to open Monday, he was to put them in the outgoing mail. Then, ignoring the questions flickering in his eyes, Beth left without another word.

One way or another.

"Mommy's coming, baby."

It took three eons to drive from Wal-Mart to the Army Surplus store. Beth was going knife shopping. Hooray. *What are they doing to her?* She was still an eon away when Daniel called with the name of their hotel and their room number and said they were holding a key card for her at the desk. He asked how she was doing. She asked how did he think? He only replied yeah, me too, and then said he had to go—she could hear voices in the background, and some sort of machinery—and that he loved her and would see her at the hotel and hung up. Beth kept driving, tasting copper. She grabbed the tissues from the glove box and spit a glob of red into one and folded it up and put it in the trash. She told herself to quit chewing on the inside of her cheek, it wasn't helping anything, but she'd used most of the tissues by the time she parked in the surplus store's lot.

The only thing keeping Beth sane was the feel of her daughter, although "feel" wasn't right; whatever it was, somehow she knew that Lizzie was safe and unharmed and still on the farm. Beth didn't know *how* she knew, she just did, and at this point she didn't much care how. It was enough that she knew.

Why did they take her? What do they want? What are they doing to her?

Tears dripped onto her tee-shirt; it took an hour to walk across the lot and through the glass doors.

"Mommy's coming, baby. I love you."

Moths to a Flame

THEY ROLLED into downtown Centerville at ten o'clock on the dot; right on schedule. The temperature had dropped thirty degrees since mid-afternoon, and billowing clouds obscured the stars. The only illumination was from their headlights and the occasional streetlight and front porch; the rest of the world was gusty darkness.

They went past the minuscule Centerville City Hall and the volunteer fire station and the post office with its three empty flagpoles, tied-down ropes pinging in the wind, and then the obligatory barber shop complete with patriotic helix lit up and traveling forever up its own little pole, even at this hour. Just down from the hair hack, two churches glared across E. Main Street at each other, one Baptist and one Methodist. Helen was a fervent frequenter of the Baptist side and didn't have a good word to say about those attending the building across the street; not very Christian, if you asked Dan, but nobody was.

There was another building downtown, two blocks from Main: an abandoned and dilapidated elementary school. Spanking new in the early sixties, it had been made obsolete by the consolidated elementary in '97, and then bought and renovated in '02 by some enterprising fellows who had secured a government contract to crank out berets for Army Rangers to wear jauntily while they fought for freedom and country and oil. At its height it employed over fifty people, but in 2005 some genius at the GAO or the Pentagon had decided that America's interests would be better served by yanking the contract away from American workers and awarding it to a company in China that used twelve-year-olds. Go USA.

The old school had changed hands twice since then, but both plans to renovate it and turn it into a whatever had fallen through; it had gone back to the county two years ago, and now it sat empty and decaying, the taxpayer's burden. The L-shaped red-brick building was surrounded by a rusted chain-link fence, happy memories of laughing children and snazzy berets now dust. It was visible from nearly everywhere in the small municipality, hulking and ignored like Centerville's sad red elephant.

To Dan and Beth, it was also key to getting their daughter back.

Beth was driving her car, and he was driving the new Dodge truck. Well, new to him; it was an '84 Ram with faded coffee paint and a wheezy V-8 with over three hundred thousand miles that got about six miles to the gallon. Downhill. As a bonus, the interior smelled like a cigar, the headliner a sick amber from the accumulated smoke of a thousand thousand stogies. Good thing Dan liked cigars; however, he did prefer to breathe his own. Beth had taken one sniff and refused to even poke her head back in, but she would only have to ride in it for a minute and she wouldn't have to drive it. That was Dan's job.

Odor aside, the Dodge was a tank: four-wheel drive, with a steel brush guard over the steel front bumper and thick, knobby tires you could go anywhere and back with, and when Dan put the wide gas pedal to the floor, the wheezy engine turned into an animal.

In other words, it was exactly what he needed tonight.

The geezer he'd bought it from—eighty-five if he was a day—had it listed in the local rag for a grand. Dan called ahead to make sure it was still there and then took a cab from the hotel and found the Dodge sitting in a front yard on the outskirts of Murfreesboro next to a carport covering a dusty Lincoln. The truck had grass growing around the tires and a sun-bleached For Sale sign stuck under the cracked wiper and Dan was sure he could've talked the bastard down to five Benjamins, but after eyeing the idling cab over the clear tubes snaking over his ears and into his nose, the old man rolled his unlit cigar into the corner of his mouth and shifted his little oxygen-tank cart handle to the other hand and stuck firm to nine hundred.

Dan paid cash, got back an archaic carbon-copy receipt (not in his real name) and the title and the key and the spare, tipped the cab driver, and rumbled away.

Beth hit her blinker and turned onto the street fronting the school and Dan did the same, barely feeling the empty nineteen foot dual-axle trailer; wheezy or not, the old Dodge had more than enough power. Even when Beth's new toy had been back there, Dan had hardly felt it. They'd dropped the toy and the rest of her gear at the designated spot, but even though its brief hauling days were done, the trailer still had a part to play tonight.

Beth reached the end of the school's lot and came to a full and complete stop at the four-way and used her blinker before turning left. Dan followed, like her obeying all traffic laws to the letter; it wouldn't do to be pulled over at this stage of the game. Finding a match for Beth's Altima had been a breeze, the trailer as well, but Dan had given up trying to find a counterpart for this old gal. Stealing three sets of plates had been even simpler; just park close with his cordless and then zip-zip, ten seconds tops, and he was driving away. Simple, yes, but if the tags on the Dodge were run through the system, even the dumbest cop in the world would think it funny when they came up registered to a burgundy 2009 Cadillac CTS.

And trouble over the tags was zilch compared to the mess they'd find themselves in once said inquisitive officer shined his light under the tarp over the bed; worse, he might search the black backpack Beth was carrying. Dan didn't even want to *think* about that possibility. This was the delicate time in the plan when one slip, one piece of bad luck, or one fucking bored hick cop could derail everything before they even did anything.

Dan glanced at his watch: 10:07.

Lizzie had been at McFarlane's farm for at least fifteen hours.

God, please let Beth be right. Please, please let Lizzie still be there.

Earlier, at the hotel, after they'd accumulated and ordered the supplies and went over the plan for the umpteenth time, they had tried to discuss that prospect: the risk that Beth was wrong, and that Lizzie had already been spirited somewhere far away. But they had barely been able to talk about it, only agreeing that they'd go to the cops and the media.

That, and never give up looking for her.

Dan wiped cold sweat from his forehead with the back of a black-suede driving glove. Beth wore an identical yet much smaller pair, and neither would take them off until this business was finished, one way or another. Lizzie. Oh God, Lizzie. Dan's daughter was healthy, and she was still here; Beth said so. He didn't know how his wife knew, but he believed her. Dan had to believe her. Lizzie wasn't on a plane to Timbuktu. She was asleep in that big white house on the ridge with Mr. Yoda curled up beside her. She'd dropped off to dreamland after having a big day on the farm saying hi to the moo cows and holding the baby piggies and riding horsies.

Please, God, oh please, let it be so.

Beth wound through the quiet neighborhood and parked at the curb midway between two houses where there was no streetlight, all as planned. She hopped out and carried her backpack over to the passenger side of the Dodge and climbed in; the dome light didn't come on. Dan had taken the bulb out. He drove two blocks west; they were now one block north of the school, facing its rear; it humped dark and angular against the racing clouds, fifty-five thousand plus square feet of memories and graffiti and rats. The hole at the bottom of the fence where the local kids crawled under to explore and skateboard and practice their general vandalism skills was just ahead. They could see it if it were still daylight; after leaving the castle this morning, he'd spotted it while looking for security cameras or alarms. There were none.

He parked in front of a small white house for sale, a property on which Dan had done some discreet checking; the listing had been active for over a year, and judging by the state of the yard and what he could see of the three-bed, two-bath Craftsman, neither the realtor nor the absentee owner cared if it sold in the up-coming year, either. He shut the engine off.

Wind rocked the heavy truck, whistling through the old, dried seals; plump drops dotted the wide windshield and then stopped as fast as they'd started. They didn't speak. They watched the surrounding houses because this was another critical time, and not only a bored cop could ruin everything. Dan could just see it: some nosy biddy climbing out of bed to down some Ex-Lax or make sleepy tea and squinting out her window at a strange pickup and trailer parked down the street with two dark and dangerous silhouettes lurking in the cab.

The old girl's probably reaching for the rotary phone right now…

After a never-ending minute when no lights came on and no alarm was raised, Dan turned and found big dark eyes staring at him from the other end of the bench seat.

This was it, everything into the pot; one hand to win or lose it all.

She reached, and he slid gloved fingers into hers. Dan could feel the strength of this beautiful little lady in that grip—a lady who for some incomprehensible but thankful reason had decided to spend her life with a loser like him.

They kissed, tongues swirling, and he tasted salt as her tears ran into his mouth, mixing with his own.

Beth broke it first, laughing softly as she wiped her face, then his. She held his eyes from six-inches away for an eternity that wasn't long enough, but they still didn't speak; they'd said it all back at the Best Western an hour ago. Then she let him go and retrieved her backpack from the floorboard, glanced up and down the street, and opened the door and slid out. Dan had to restrain himself from lunging and dragging her back in. He held himself rigid as she looked at him with those eyes.

And then she whispered, "See ya," and shut the door before he could respond.

Beth strolled up the lane with her arson kit slung over one shoulder; trust her to get the last word. She was dressed as casually as she walked, in jeans and a tee-shirt and sneakers; combined with the backpack and her stature and dark ponytail, it made her look like a schoolgirl.

Dan's grin faded when his wife disappeared into the void between street lamps.

He cruised east down Main. The castle was up ahead, about four miles, and beyond that McFarlane's farm. And Lizzie. Please God, let it be so. Dan kept to the speed limit, but he swiveled his head from the old school to the phone in his hand; no sign yet…oh God, something had gone sideways. Maybe she'd gotten trapped. He should turn around and—

A wailing whoop started from the fire station next to city hall, but he didn't relax. Beth had done it, and now she needed to text him. *Now* she needed to text him. Dan watched the orange glow quickly become flames shooting into the sky; shit, the fire had spread so fast…if Beth was still in there…somehow he kept going. Dan stared at the phone in his hand as he drove. *C'mon.* More sirens, now coming from everywhere as first responders rushed to the scene; an apocalyptic radiance filled the Dodge's mirrors.

Dan reached his side-road; still no message. He was shaking as he pulled a K turn at a cross street and drove back and parked in the ditch and shut the engine and lights off and rolled his window down; he was facing the main drag he'd just left, and he was supposed to be watching it, but that drag could've been on fucking Neptune for all Dan cared.

He cupped the phone in his lap, bouncing his knees up and down.

WHERE THE FUCK IS SHE?

He glanced up as a Centerville PD cruiser roared past out on Main, sirens wailing and lights strobing, and then another, and another, and another; that was the whole force, or just about, and all coming from the direction of his house. They couldn't *all* be on McFarlane's payroll…

Could they?

Chewbacca's warbling roar issued from his hand, making him jump:

Lunchtime.

Dan slumped and blew out a long breath; he didn't know what the fuck had taken so long, but Beth had lit the candle, and now they had to wait for the moths to show up. Dinner was yet to come; there would be no discussion about dessert. Either they would have it, or they would be dead. Dessert was Lizzie back in their arms. Please, God, please, let it be so. Please. But first they had to get through lunch and dinner.

Dan watched the road.

"C'mon, c'mon."

He heard the clatter of a diesel engine, and then he saw a red dashboard strobe, and then an all-too-familiar white Dodge dually sped past with four red-tinged shadows crammed inside. Right behind it thundered the Mach-1 Mustang; it didn't have a dash light, and the dark tint prevented him from seeing inside, but there was at least the driver in there. How many of McFarlane's "boys" did he say were volunteer firefighters? Beth had pressed Dan to remember, reminding him it was important to the plan, but he hadn't been able to recall exactly; he thought most of them were, but he'd been a mite distracted at the time and couldn't be sure— although no way José would tell his wife that, especially *how* he'd been distracted. Anyway, five had come for sure…maybe all six? Too much to hope, but at least they'd neutralized some of the cards in McFarlane's hand.

He texted Beth a quick **5 for lunch** and started the truck and surged out of the ditch and up to the stop sign. The glow from downtown Centerville reflected off the racing clouds as he turned east and floored the big Dodge; speed limit, schmeed limit. Dan knew where all the cops were.

McFarlane wouldn't come. They knew that. McFarlane would stay with Lizzie because she was "important", whatever that meant. McFarlane would stay because he had "set things in motion", whatever the fuck *that* meant.

Dan gripped the steering wheel so hard his knuckles popped like a machine gun.

It didn't fucking matter what it meant.

"I'm coming for you, old man."

He slalomed right at the first intersection, not bothering to stop or use a signal. So. One rapist slash murderer, three singing sluts, the insane kidnapping farmer, the creepy Keeper, and the Presidents. Dan smiled. He had plans for the Presidents. Another screeching turn, the trailer fishtailing; halfway back to the castle now, but he wasn't going home to stay. He would change and get his gear ready and wait in the driveway for Beth to text him it was dinnertime, and then Dan was going back to the farm.

He wasn't sneaking in the back way, though, like Beth. Dan was going back right through the motherfucking front gate.

"Hold on, sweet pea. Daddy's coming."

THE DOOR OPENS

ETH CUT the barbed-wire and rode her Yamaha four-wheeler through the hole; this new field was full of corn, with fifteen-foot gaps between the tall plants and the fences. That green and dusty corn-smell filled her nose as she turned right and puttered for the nearest cross-fence; she didn't dare use the headlamp, and even with the night-vision goggles she had to be wary of deep rain-ruts and stumps and other obstacles that might wreck her. The field was gigantic, and impatience gnawed, but eventually she came to the corner; when she could see the lights shining up on the ridge again, she stopped and glanced back.

A glowing bovine mass was streaming through the latest opening she'd made; most of the dumb beasts were content to spread out in the corn and snack, but a good portion were still thudding along behind her. Those cows had stopped when she stopped, and the numbered tags in their ears blazed pale-green as they stood shoulder to shoulder and waited for her to do something else; steers, rather, if you wanted to be technical. Boy-cows. No wonder they were so dumb. Beth was just glad she hadn't encountered any big, aggressive bulls; she hadn't even considered that possibility until she was halfway across the second field and completely surrounded. It had made for a nervous time when she was down off the four-wheeler cutting wire.

A small eternity later Beth found what should be the last fence; the tree-choked ridge and its scattered buildings and lights sprawled above her, now. *So close.* She grabbed her bolt cutters and jumped off. There were no cows on the other side, just plants lined out in low rows; soybeans maybe. Beth didn't care. She cut the fence and peeled the wire back and threw the cutters over her shoulder into the corn without looking before driving the Yamaha through and then gunning a fast u-turn, facing it back the way she'd came before killing the engine and pocketing the key.

She hopped off again and checked her knives first—she'd purchased several at the surplus store and had brought them all—finishing with her trusty Carson in its new black-Nylon belt sheath on her right hip. She ignored the animals milling about her and unstrapped the Mossberg from where she'd secured it to the four-wheeler's rear rack and pulled the shotgun's shortened carry strap over her head so it slashed across her chest; the sawed-off barrel now stuck up behind her right ear, and the truncated stock jutted past her left hip.

When she'd asked Daniel to show her how to use it, Beth had thought her husband would keel over from shock—that, or cry. It was too big for her, and she couldn't shoot it, not at the hotel, but after Daniel's quick run down to the hardware store, she'd practiced shrugging out of the strap and bringing the now perfectly sized shotgun to bear in a microsecond. She'd even practiced getting the strap over her head with the new pair of night-vision goggles on her face, which changed the whole deal until you learned the trick of not ripping the goggles off.

Beth had learned.

Daniel had sat on the hard hotel bed and watched with a fascinated-yet-sick expression, and then he'd pointed out she didn't have to bring it to her shoulder to fire; now Beth was ready to shoot from the hip as fast as she could pump and pull the trigger. He'd also warned her that the shells were loaded with double-aught buck (whatever that was), and to brace the stock firmly against her hip or shoulder unless she wanted a bruise, or even something dislocated or broken, but surely the thing wouldn't kick that hard; he was just worried about her.

Beth lifted her goggles off to adjust her black ski mask and to settle the covert Kevlar vest she wore under her black full-sleeved shirt and was reminded just how dark it was tonight; there was zero moon scheduled, and the racing clouds covered the stars, so the lights sprinkling the farm above her were the only game in town.

She stared up at that glow; she could feel her daughter up there. Beth thought she could point to her; the sensation had grown that powerful.

Mommy's coming, baby.

She tugged her gloves off and retrieved her phone from the deep side-pocket of her black combat fatigues, then crouched behind the Yamaha to hide the screen's glow.

Dinner time.

Beth was stuffing her phone back when a throbbing racket caught her ear; a big motor, driven hard. The noise was coming from the far side of the farm, from the direction of the castle. She stood up and stared that way, straining her ears; no, it was *two* motors, one a deeper throb.

Then the racing engines stopped, and the gunshots began, cracking and booming in the distance.

Dread gripped Beth by the throat.

Daniel.

She yanked the gloves back on and reset her goggles, then brought her shotgun forward and sprinted down a row with the weapon held across her chest, cows scattering at her sudden movement, plants whipping against her pant legs, holding her finger outside the trigger guard as he'd taught her. More echoing booms and cracks, and then a lull as a man shouted—it wasn't Daniel; the voice was too deep, and when Beth stopped for a moment and held her breath, she thought she detected a Spanish accent. She took off again, and although she was terrified for him, Beth forced herself to focus on Lizzie; even if the plan had been followed to the letter, Daniel's safety hadn't been guaranteed. Neither was hers.

Beth heard nothing more over the wind's moan and her own heart pounding. Was he still alive? *He has to be alive.* She came to the creek that meandered along the bottom of the slope and stood, panting and listening, and then three measured shots split the darkness: *Pow. Pow. Pow.*

Silence.

Which side of those three bullets had Daniel been on?

Beth forced her panic down; she couldn't help him. Lizzie was the one who mattered. Daniel could take care of himself.

He had to.

She splashed across the shallow flow and squeezed between the lowest slats of a tall board fence and sprinted up the slope to the first building and poked one lens around the edge; yearling pigs crowding a wide pen grunted and squealed and moved toward her in a green mass. Beth ignored them and the smell and scanned the surrounding buildings; except for the mobile pork chops, she was alone—as far as she could tell.

Then came a whine and a crackle, and an amplified voice blasted across the night:

"LIZZIE, CAN YOU HEAR ME? IT'S DADDY!"

Beth sagged against the corrugated metal wall. Her husband was alive. But what he shouted through the bullhorn next made her stand straight again.

"IT'S A TRAP, BETH! THEY KNEW WE WERE COMING! THEY *WANT* YOU TO GO TO HER! *IT'S A TRAP!*"

Somehow they had known she and Daniel would come for Lizzie tonight; somehow, they had known.

But how? *How* had they known?

And they *wanted* her to go to Lizzie?

Why?

It didn't matter, Beth decided; none of it mattered. She wasn't backing away now, not with her daughter so close. She'd just have to be more careful; and a trap discovered before it was sprung could be a tactical advantage.

A trap.

Beth's scalp jumped as she watched her surroundings and listened to her husband alternately call McFarlane every cuss word he knew and yell for Lizzie and her, voice growing more and more desperate. Her phone buzzed in her pocket; Daniel had texted her what he was broadcasting. Beth turned it off. She regretted the fear and pain she was causing him, but she wasn't about to give her position away by shouting back, and she'd have to take her attention from her surroundings and put the shotgun down and remove her gloves to respond. That wasn't happening.

A trap. Speed was everything. She had to move.

Beth ran up the slope in a crouch; the next building was enormous, with a towering open doorway you could drive a semi through. She peeked inside; a row of giant glowing-green farm machinery stared back at her; the metallic reek of oil and gasoline wafted out.

A trap.

She edged back and rested her left hand on the K-9 pepper spray in the holster hooked to her utility belt and scanned her surroundings once more; those dogs could be on her in seconds, and with their sensitive noses, they wouldn't need to see her to find her. Daniel was supposed to draw them to the front gate, and maybe he'd already taken care of them (her husband had been looking forward to that part of the plan with unholy relish), but Beth had heard no barks mixed with the gunshots. She didn't want to hurt those beautiful animals. She would if she had to, though. Lizzie. Beth's daughter pulled at her like a lodestone; she gazed up at the crest where the top half of a stately house with columns glowed green against the rushing clouds.

Mommy's coming, baby.

Beth stepped into the vast doorway, intending to move past it and scout the next building, when green motion made her gasp and turn as something hard knocked the goggles askew and her to the stained concrete pad. She brought her shotgun around, but it was wrenched from her hands; Beth heard it clatter as it was thrown inside the building. A hand grasped her ski mask and ripped it away along with the goggles, and then someone took a grip on her hair.

Beth surged up and slammed her elbow into a rib cage; a man grunted and then hit her with something that felt like a brick. Her knees went wobbly, and then she was yanked face-to-face with someone who was only vaguely acquainted with a toothbrush:

"Hello there, sweet thang. Remember me?"

Cold metal mashed her cheekbone as Tommy flashed a dank grin beneath his shag of blond hair; the hand holding the gun had a cast stabilizing his wrist and encasing half his forearm, but it left his thumb and fingers free; its dingy plaster was a pallid island floating in the dark.

He saw her looking at it. "Ya like that? Got me outta playin' hero, so I guess I owe ya one." He snarled: "I'm gonna pay ya back proper, too, yes *ma'am* I am!"

Tommy walked Beth into the building and around the head-high tire of some colossal farming contraption and stopped; tall tires and towering machines now hemmed them on two sides. Beth was calm; she still had her knives, and the second she had separation from the pistol, Tommy was a dead man.

Suddenly he released her hair and shoved her away and backed up, and Beth bent and yanked out her KA-BAR boot knives, but he held his aim steady on her center-mass; they were less than ten feet apart, and Beth could throw a knife and throw it well, but if she missed...

Tommy thumbed the hammer back. "Uh uh, little girl, toss 'em over here." Beth hesitated. "Go on, and the rest of 'em, too. I know ya got a damn sight more."

Frustrated, enraged, she did as he said. A pile of knives grew at Tommy's feet, but Beth kept the slender knuckle-knife hanging down her spine on a homemade break-away black Nylon lanyard; the little blade was her ultimate backup, and hopefully Tommy wouldn't discover it until it was too late, but how had he known about the rest? For that matter, how had he known she'd be coming this way, known sure enough to ambush her?

The last of her knives clanked at the toes of Tommy's crusted boots—as far as he could tell, anyhow.

"Good girl. Now strip."

Beth glared and didn't move a muscle.

He twitched the barrel. "C'mon now, off with them clothes, I want a good gander before we start. Have I got somethin' fer *you*." Daniel's frantic voice boomed across the farm again, demanding that McFarlane bring him Lizzie. "Hubby there's cracked if he thinks John's gonna trot yer little girl out on his say-so. Yer *both* dumb. You thought you could waltz out here and take 'er, just like that?" He snapped the fingers on his uninjured hand. "You think John didn't know you wuz commin'?" Tommy lowered his voice, and even in the deep dark between the machines, the fear twisting his scruffy features was plain. "You don't have a goddamn clue what yer up against, do ya?" He found his cock-sure grin again. "Yer gonna learn, though, real quick-like. Now *off*. All of it." He stepped closer when she didn't comply. "Don't make me do it, bitch. I won't be gentle. I don't give two flips about what they say yer needed for, I'm gonna git my satisfaction first. Now *strip!*" Daniel's voice crashed across the night once more. "If it'll make ya feel better, think about hubby-pooh there while we do it." He stepped closer. "Strip!"

The pistol was now three feet from her nose, but Beth's only knife was down her back; too far. She was faster than Tommy, granted, and there were at least five ways to take that weapon from him if she could get her hands on it, but if she failed, and got shot…she couldn't risk leaving Daniel alone to rescue Lizzie.

So Beth did the only thing she could; she peeled her clothes off.

She took her sweet time, though, mind scrambling like a rat in a burning ship, but there was one option at this point; she'd have to let him inside her, and as he lost control, when he was about to release, she'd make her move.

She shuddered in revulsion and rage.

Can I do that?

And then Beth realized the answer was simple; she would do anything for her daughter.

All too soon she stood naked except for black socks, carefully facing him so Tommy wouldn't see what was hanging down her spine. He might notice the lanyard circling her throat and wonder what it was, though, so to make sure he didn't, Beth dropped to the floor without being ordered and spread her legs and arched her back and put her hands behind her head, close to the knuckle-knife; the smooth concrete was chilly on her shoulders and butt.

Anything for Lizzie.

"Eager ta get started, are ya?" He sidled in for a better look; his breathing hitched. "Now that's a sight," he whispered. Tommy dropped the pistol down by his right leg, then leaned and reached for her left-handed. Beth braced herself; anything for Lizzie. He cupped her right breast with his rough hand and rolled the nipple between thumb and forefinger and *pinched*, hard, but she didn't react. He stood back up and began unbuttoning his fly one-handed.

"This'll be one for the memory banks, sweetheart, I promise ya."

Beth glared hate and fury up at him, trying to fry him with a look…and then her jaw dropped as a shadow swirled and took shape behind Tommy, but it was no shape Beth could wrap her stunned mind around. *Something* now stared at her out of that churning darkness; something with black shadows spread wide like a dark dream of giant wings; something tall and painfully yet powerfully gaunt; something with a jaw full of hooked black teeth below two sickly green sparks.

That nightmare visage was only visible for an instant, and Beth barely had time to wonder if she'd gone stark-raving mad before those swirling ebon shadows collapsed and then a woman stood behind Tommy. She held a small but wickedly curved knife in her right hand, and as Beth gawked, she twined the stubby fingers of her left hand into Tommy's shag and jerked his head back and slashed his throat. He tried to scream, but only air whistled as hot arterial blood splattered Beth's face and body.

Tommy collapsed onto her legs, but she didn't spare him a glance as she kicked him away and rolled backwards to her feet, snatching the knuckle-knife and holding it out and ready. The Nylon cord slithered between her breasts and to the floor as Tommy's gun clattered away under the machine on her left; the woman's curved knife dripped slow crimson drops as they faced each other over a thrashing and gurgling Tommy.

Beth's rescuer was in her late forties or early fifties, with gray-streaked strawberry hair and a blocky, powerful body. Her eyes were cold and fierce, and some trick of the faint light made them glow green, just like that thing she'd seen behind… no, no, she must've imagined that. Things like that didn't exist. Things like that tall, thin, hideous winged creature weren't possible; just like appearing from a churning shadow was not possible.

The woman looked down; Tommy had stopped thrashing and gurgling.

She spat on him with sudden venom. "Fool. You could have ruined everything with your uncontrolled appetites." She had a Slavic accent, but only slight, as if she'd been here for a long time. Her head snapped up again, and Beth held perfectly still, just as she would if she were all at once confronted by a lion while out on a walk; it wasn't a trick of the light.

The woman's eyes were jade fire.

But that can't be, just like the thing in the shadows couldn't…maybe Tommy hit me too hard.

"Who are you?" Beth whispered.

The woman jabbed her bloody little knife at the pile of Beth's garments: "Clothe yourself. There are animals on this farm that do not walk on four legs. As you have discovered, yes?"

That mixed note of command and contempt tightened Beth's lips, but the strange woman *had* helped her, so she dressed one-handed as fast as she could while keeping both attention and blade pointed at the woman with the glowing eyes. It had to be some trick of the light. It *had* to be, because other than that, her rescuer looked like a normal woman; although wide, she was not much taller than Beth, and was dressed in faded jeans and hiking boots and a checkered, button-down man's shirt. Her hair was pulled into a ponytail similar to Beth's, only longer and secured by a big drooping white bow, of all things.

Beth had to put her weapon down to lace her steel-toed combat boots; rescue or not, she craned her neck to keep the odd woman in view. When all her knives were back in place except the knuckle-stabber, Beth faced her over Tommy's body; blood had formed a darkly glistening pool under the machine on her right.

"Thank you," she said. The woman sneered. Beth's lips thinned further, but she attempted to keep her tone civil. "I asked who—" Then Daniel's description crashed into her frazzled brain: "I know who you are. You're the so-called Keeper of Barron Cemetery, Melissa Bane."

Those eyes became radiating slits. "*So-called?* I have spent untold power and blood to harness that garden of remembrance and constrain those within it, and it and they are now more my chattels than anything you dare call yours, child—at least in your pitiable understanding of the concept!" She sneered Beth up and down, then pronounced: "He is mistaken. You will never be one of us. Your compassion for the simpletons trapped on this doomed world makes you weak."

Child? *WEAK?* "You don't know me!"

"I know you, child. I felt it the moment you squalled into this world. For one of your power, how could I not? But I was right to leave you to your fate, no matter how strong, *for see how events have UNFOLDED!*" The woman laughed then, laughed like a girl, and the wonder and delight in her voice contrasted sharply with that hammer of a face. "Praise to my Master! Praise Him! It is not only the Old Fool Above who works His will in mysterious ways, I am thinking." She turned and lifted her gaze toward the top of the ridge then, as if she could see through metal walls with those glowing eyes; her sudden half-smile was coldly amused: "He believes me enfeebled because I missed you. He is a fool, yet he has become strong in his power. Yes, very strong. But he chooses to forget who introduced him to the source! He will remember." She turned back to Beth. "With your aid, and perhaps your husband's, I will remind him this very night!"

Suddenly Daniel's voice blasted across the farm, much closer and louder than before; he had quit the front gate, and in that Beth understood he had abandoned their plan in his desperation:

"BETH! LIZZIE! CAN YOU HEAR ME? ANSWER IF YOU CAN HEAR ME, *PLEASE!* GOD DAMN YOU, MCFARLANE! I'LL FUCKING *KILL* YOU WHEN I FIND YOU, OLD MAN, I SWEAR TO GOD! BETH, LIZZIE, *ANSWER ME!*"

"My tool has performed well, yes? Although I suppose I shouldn't be surprised given his own astonishing strength. Still, we shall measure his true mettle when the Blood of the Mother runs thick and red."

Blood of the Mother?

Beth didn't like the sound of that.

And then that thought was washed away in a surging, white-hot fury; this strange, arrogant woman had saved her from being raped, true, but she was also using Daniel (and her!) as pawns in some…some *game* or competition with the old man!

But what was the prize?

Beth flicked her Carson out in a blur and stepped forward with both knives brandished, ready to spring and slash and stab; ready to kill:

"Where is she? *What have you done with her?*"

That *sneer* again: "If you had been properly trained, one such as this," she toed Tommy's body without looking, "could never have harmed you. Such a waste, but you are flawed within." Awe stole over Bane's pitiless features: "Ah, but your daughter! She shares the same defect, but she is young enough and malleable enough to be bound, although not without danger. And for one as potent as she, the danger will be great." Those lambent and hateful eyes lingered on Beth's, piercing her: "I have prayed to my Master, child, prayed that she is truly the One, the One I have been tasked with searching for all these tedious millennia. I suspect she is, and if in His wisdom He deems it so, the rewards will be well worth the risks." Her sneer widened into something toothy and gleeful and depraved: "Especially since I will not share in those risks!"

She bent and snatched Tommy's limp arm and backed away, dragging the dead weight of a two hundred pound man like an empty sack. Tommy's head folded to his spine and a wet, dark smear followed them as they disappeared around a giant tire.

Beth dashed after them, slipping in the blood as she rounded the tire, and then skidded to a stop; the shadowy back wall of the building is what she *should* have seen, but that metal wall was obscured by darker shadows that grew out of thin air, tendrils eddying and swelling and thickening around Melissa Bane and Tommy's body.

Beth's eyeballs felt like they would fall out of their sockets: "Where's Lizzie? Tell me what you've done with her!"

Green sparks flared within that deepening dark: "You know where she is. She is calling for you. I can hear her. So can you, even in your pathetic state." The sparks dropped to Tommy's body. "I will take this. It will be of some use to me, certainly more now than before." Those jade embers rose to Beth again; they were fading into the hump of swirling darkness. "Go to her, Mother." Not a whisper, but faint, as if from far away: "It is written that you will go to her. Go!"

The black shadows swirled faster and faster and then broke apart like smoke from a doused fire. Soon the dim back wall of the building was visible; both her false rescuer and Tommy's corpse were gone.

Beth stood rock still, staring at the smooth concrete where a dark-red slick abruptly ended. Then she staggered back and caught her balance on the tire and turned and ran, slipping and sliding. She made it out from between the machines and stumbled to her shotgun and snatched it up and sprinted out of the building.

Beth kept it pointed at the tall opening as she grabbed up her ski mask and goggles and then backed quickly into the gravel road that wound through the buildings.

She kept backing up until the tall wooden pole supporting the nearest light thumped between her shoulders and the soothing pool of luminescence lay spread around her. Moths and other hardy night bugs swirled high over her head, fighting the gusting wind, casting tiny shadows at Beth's feet. Metal buildings lay on either side and above her on the slope, their purposes unfathomable, their doors run shut, but she kept her wide-eyed gaze and the shotgun pinned on that towering black opening.

No way did any of that just happen.

No way.

It was—

"Impossible," Beth whispered.

It seemed she owed her husband an apology.

The shotgun and mask and goggles slipped from numb fingers and landed in the dirt; her stomach hitched, and she dropped to hands and knees and up came the half-digested Granola bar she'd forced herself to eat earlier. Beth regarded the reeking pile, gagged, heaved again, but that one was dry; she could hear Daniel coming closer, calling for her and Lizzie, and she could feel her daughter pulling her, stronger than before, and thunder now spoke in the distance, warning her that the weather was taking a turn for the worse, but those developments concerned a woman who was far, far away, not Elizabeth Marie Sims:

If you had been properly trained, one such as this could never have harmed you…

Trained?

Ah, but your daughter! She shares the same defect, but she is still young enough and malleable enough to be bound…

Bound?

If you had been properly trained…

Bound?

And for one as potent as she, the rewards will be well worth the risks…

BOUND!?

"No," Beth muttered.

I have prayed to my Master that she is truly the One…

The One? The One *what?* And Master? *What* Master?

The One I have been tasked with searching for all these tedious millennia…

Millennia? Had Bane really said *millennia?*

"That's…" Beth would never say the word impossible again; she wouldn't even *think* it: "Unlikely," she murmured to the goop between her hands.

It is written that you will go to her…

Written? Written where?

If you had been properly trained…

Beth lurched to her feet, dabbed her lips with a sleeve, and looked around: everything felt…off, disjointed; *she* felt off, as if the world had slipped six inches to the right and nobody had bothered to tell her; disjointed or not, she was still on the farm, and the wind still gusted, and the pregnant clouds still streamed overhead, and thunder still cracked and rolled and boomed in the distance, and Daniel still shouted for her, his hoarse, agonized voice carrying faintly over the wind; he'd abandoned the megaphone, for some reason. Lizzie still pulled, but even that barely mattered right now because right now, Beth had to make sense of what that fantastic woman had claimed. She would have to be utterly *insane* to even consider—!

But how are you "feeling" Lizzie, Beth? Explain that.

"No," she moaned.

How did you "know" she was still on the farm—know sure enough to swear it to your husband? How did you "know" she was still happy and healthy? All-day-long, you KNEW!

How is that, if what that woman said isn't the truth?

"This is…it can't be possible! It just *can't!*"

They wanted her to find Lizzie.

Why?

It is written that you will go to her…

Beth raised quaking fingers and touched her face; her gloves came away tacky. Tommy's blood. Her hair was stiffening with it; the copper reek threatened to make her sick again and reminded her of Rison.

It couldn't be.

Could it?

Could it?

"*No,*" Beth whispered one last time, a feeble denial even to her ears, and then a door appeared before her astounded mind's eye; it was the door to her bedroom closet when she was a girl; just a plain, eggshell, tri-panel wooden door with an oblong, multifaceted glass doorknob; she'd pretended it was a giant diamond, Beth suddenly remembered. Only an ordinary closet door in an ordinary little girl's room, but that closet had been her secret place; her safe place. The place she had gone… after, every time. The place she put all her favorite toys and books and dolls; a place she could play with Spankey undisturbed; a place all her own, there in a little hollow way in the back behind the winter coats and her hand-me-down church dresses and her father's old worn-out work shirts that her mother would rip for cleaning rags; a place both of her parents knew about, obviously, but respected and never intruded on when she was in residence, even *him*.

It had been the door to child-Beth's secret place, and that was well and good, but why in the world was she seeing it floating there in the middle of a dirt track in the middle of a farm in the middle of Tennessee twenty-five years later?

Beth shied back as the eggshell door suddenly bulged toward her; the 100-karat knob rattled, like something monstrous wanted to get out and at her—

And then the door burst open, and *it* was upon her.

And IT…it was memory.

That last day with her father; she'd pushed the jack out, dropping their old pickup on him, yes, punishing him, yes, but Beth had still been twenty feet away at least, and she hadn't used her hands, not even close; the night she'd *known* that Johnny would shoot the boss chest hair in the face; it hadn't been reluctant familiarity that had granted her foresight. Even the day she'd met Daniel was seen in a new light; one glance, and even though he'd been at the restaurant-league softball game with that blonde bit of bartender fluff, as soon as Beth had laid eyes on him she'd known in every fiber of her being that they were meant for each other. It was a sensation she'd never had with any other man, before or since.

"No!" Beth cried, but it was no use; the truth she'd hidden from her own mind was bursting out of her secret place.

Other banshees from the past wailed out of that doorway: that big girl in eighth grade, Megan Stroudmire; popular, with many friends where Beth had none, a bully who'd delighted in tormenting the much-smaller new girl—until the day Megan had tripped and fallen into a locker in the girls changing room and gotten locked in even though there was no lock, just a latch, and Megan's friends had tried and tried to get her out but that blue metal door wouldn't budge until the P.E. coach, Mr. Jackson, had finally and at wit's end ran and brought the janitor to pry it open and let a screaming Megan out. Megan was screaming because Megan was claustrophobic, and somehow the little picked-on new girl had known that.

"No," Beth whispered again, but the hits kept coming: that time in her early twenties when she was dating the guy from BCA league…Derek, the one with the long dark hair. They'd been in his Z-28 Camaro with him driving and another car heading the opposite way had crossed the double-yellow line and Derek had been looking down at his CD collection and Beth had screamed and Derek had screamed and yanked the wheel but it was too late they were going to hit head-on so Beth had *pushed*, and then the oncoming car had *jerked* back across the lines with a squall of rubber.

She had saved them.

"No more!" There were other memories flying out, but the door was open at last and there was no stopping them so Beth closed her eyes as tears streamed down her face.

It couldn't be.

It was.

It was.

And then the flood was over. Shuddering, crying, Beth opened her eyes and stared through the gaping door and realized there was something else in the closet; something waited back there in the darkness for her; some…potential, and Beth knew she had a choice: step through and embrace that potential, or turn her back on it and keep ignoring who and what she was.

She understood something else: if she stepped across, there would be no turning back; this would change her, and maybe not for the good. Sudden, petulant fury blew through Beth; she'd fought so hard to forge herself into who and what she was—every day she fought!—and she didn't *want* to change!

Then, faint and far away, she heard her husband calling. She felt Lizzie. Her family was waiting—and not only them. Beth's enemies wanted her to go to her daughter, to spring their trap, but if she stepped through, perhaps she could use what she found to turn the tables; use it as a weapon to save her family.

Deep breath.

Anything for Lizzie. Anything and everything, forever and ever.

Beth stepped into the darkness.

Down the Rabbit Hole

AN WAS taking a much-needed leak on the side of his garage and wondering when the hell Beth would text him when he heard the motor; he squeezed off mid-stream and listened. The throaty echo was rolling down Daisy from the direction of Centerville, and fast.

He pictured the Mach.

"Shit."

He shook off and zipped up and ran to the Dodge, then paused with his hand on the door handle, looking down at himself; black combat fatigues and a long-sleeved black shirt with black steel-toed combat boots, and he had the Smith holstered on his right hip in its new black-Nylon holster. Worse, he'd already donned the Kevlar tactical vest—also black.

"Just act casual."

Right. He took his hand off the handle and rested it on the Smith and waited. The motor throbbed closer; maybe it wasn't the Fastback; maybe it was some other muscle car out for a Sunday-night drive…it could happen…

That faint hope was dashed as the glossy Mach 1 Mustang with the twin pearl racing stripes blatted past Helen's place, following its round yellow headlights down Daisy. When it got to the castle, it rumbled to a stop near his mailbox. The window came down, and the person behind the tint made the body motions of hand-cranking; that asshole McFarlane really had restored that thing to original. Insane murderer and kidnapper he might be, but he had first-rate taste in cars. That wasn't going to stop Dan from killing him, though. It wouldn't even make him hesitate.

A thick, tattooed arm was placed on the door; a broad, pockmarked face leered in the muted glow from the instrument panel.

"Dat some slick trick with the school, homes, but I ain't no hose puller!" Jesus Menendez laughed. "Those other boys cussin' you and sweatin' out they asses 'bout now, though!"

Dan didn't reply; what was there to say?

Oh God, Lizzie.

Menendez shook his head. "You don't think John knows what you doin'? Da man *knows*, okay? Shit, you people ain't got a clue what you dealin' with." That hard face softened for a moment, pure terror making it sag. "Not the *first* fuckin' clue. They out there waitin' for your ol' lady, homes. She goin' right to 'em, jus' like they want."

Dan gripped the Smith, hard, but didn't draw. Not yet. McFarlane couldn't know everything. He just couldn't. Oh God, Beth and Lizzie. "Fuck you, Menendez, you piece of shit baby-raper."

"Fuck *you*, Sims! Come over here and say dat shit!"

Dan drew the revolver and put the bead on the big man's face as he strode toward the Mach.

"Okay," he said.

Menendez cursed and ducked, then came back up with a long barrel leading out the window. Dan crouched and crabbed sideways; would the vest stop a rifle bullet from this range? Maybe he was about to find out.

"Hold up, homes! John sent me to offer a deal!"

Another deal? Great. "What does he want?"

Menendez poked his head over the door. "Quit pointin' dat cannon at me and I'll tell you."

Beth and Lizzie. Dan trembled with the urge to kill this shit pile. "You first."

"Okay, meng, okay." The rifle disappeared, and Dan stood and lowered the Smith. Menendez sat up and gunned the motor. "Shit, I knew you di'n't have the cajones to shoot, panocha motherfucker. Here's John's deal: stay here and wait, and when he's done with your ol' lady and niñita, you can have 'em back tonight. Forget all dat shit 'bout three days."

Dan twitched. "What does he want them for?"

Oh my God my girls my beautiful girls…

"I look like a dumb-ass motherfucker to you? I don' ask no questions, homes, I jus' do as I'm tol'. Dat's it, dat's the deal. Sit tight and don' interfere, and they be back tonight. John give his word."

"And what if I 'interfere'?"

The big man's smile was a razor. "I won' let dat happen. It'd be my ass—or worse. You come out dere, and I'm gonna have to stop you. And I won' kill you, neither." Menendez licked his lips, and Dan's skin tried to crawl all the way back to Centerville. "I ain't had me a pretty boy like you since John popped me out o' stir. I'll beat you down and we'll go someplace dark and comfortable and I'll show you what I taught that li'l ride booster. You might even learn to like it, Sims. He did." He drank Dan in with dark, ravenous eyes. "You'll also never see dat smokin' wife or your girl again. John give his word 'bout dat, too."

"You're a twisted piece of dog shit, Menendez."

"Dat's the deal, Sims, take it or leave it." The Mach peeled off.

Dan watched it thunder away. Just sit here with his thumb up his ass while McFarlane did God knows what to Beth and Lizzie?

"Fuck abuncha that."

He slammed into the truck and burned out of his driveway. Menendez idled at the three-way intersection, watching him approach in the mirror, then turned left, tires smoking, back end fishtailing. Dan took the turn just slow enough so that he didn't lose the trailer; their plan was shot to hell, but maybe not all of it, so he might need the damn thing. A wall of dust raised by the Mach enveloped him as he hit the dirt road, and as much as he hated it, Dan had to slow. Would Menendez close the gate on him? That fit right into the old plan, but he wasn't sure he wanted that now. He needed to text Beth and warn her it was a trap, but at this speed he also needed both hands on the wheel to keep the ungainly Dodge and trailer out of the ditch.

"Fuck!"

He passed the McFarlane Farms' billboard and rattled over the first cattle grate, then picked up speed again and blew over the little rise where he'd had his fun with the government suits and found that a cross breeze had carried the dust into the field on the right; above, he saw the Mach's brake lights flash, then watched them disappear around the last turn before the farm. Dan floored it, the big-bore 360 clacking now, and shot up the slope and skidded around the corner and there was the gate; Menendez hadn't closed it. Dan witnessed him jump out near the corner of the first red-metal building on the left and run for cover, leaving the Mustang running with the door open and lights on.

Dan cut the wheel to the right and then hard back to the left; the trailer whipped around and crashed into the fence, blocking the gate, and the Dodge lurched, rattled, and died, steam gushing from under the hood. He slammed it into park and yanked the emergency brake, then peered through the passenger-side window at the corner of the building Menendez had ducked behind.

Where'd that rapist piece of shit get to?

He got his answer with a muzzle flash and a slug that plunked into the Dodge. A ka*POW!* accompanied the plunk—that was a big fucking rifle. Dan chucked open his door and threw himself out as another ka-pow came just as the passenger window blew out.

"Shit!"

Dan pulled the Smitty and stood up and returned fire over the hood, blasting away, emptying all six chambers at that corner, then went prone and crawled fast over behind the trailer's twin axles. Ka*POW!* A bullet whined over his head. *What happened to not killing me?* And where were those fucking dogs? Dan had planned some fun for the mutts, oh yes indeed, but if they appeared while he was in the middle of this he was puppy food. He looked under his armpit at the large black-felt bag tied to his utility belt; maybe not.

He rolled to his back and holstered the empty Smith and opened the bag and grabbed handfuls of the caltrops he and Beth had clipped out of the cross-sections of stout chicken wire and threw them over the trailer, as far out over the cattle guard as he could, scattering them across the dirt track, ignoring the pain when their razor points stabbed through his glove. He threw them all while ducking another shot from Menendez, then dropped the sack; *there* was a nasty surprise for a puppy's paws. Dan just hoped the hairballs didn't get outside the fence and come up on him from behind.

Another shot—ka*POW!*—and the bullet whanged off the trailer's railing right above his head. "*Fuck!*" Forget the damn dogs; he had Menendez to deal with. Dan pulled the knife Beth had loaned him and flicked it open and flattened all four of the trailer's tires.

When he was done, there was silence. Dan cautiously scrambled back to the Dodge's open door and stretched and grabbed his NV goggles and his new toy from the passenger seat and crammed the goggles on his face and switched them on. He crawled around to the front of the truck, flattening tires as he went, and peeked past the bumper. No sign of him; Menendez was likely reloading.

What was that thing, a lever-action .3030? Probably. He'd fired five shots, but how many shells did it hold? Six? Seven? Dan wasn't positive, but if so that meant Menendez was reloading while he could, and *before* he ran dry; rapist he might be, but the man was no dummy.

Dan took careful aim at that corner with his Colt .45 1991 Series, model 01991 CCG; he'd always wanted one, and if some maniac asswipe kidnapping your daughter and then holding her captive next door wasn't an excuse to buy one, Dan didn't know what was. He'd loaded five eight-round magazines with .45 ACP Starfire Hollow Points; plenty of stopping power for the puppies, but they would work just dandy for Menendez, too.

Suddenly he saw a crouching green figure run behind the Mach and head towards a long, low building on the other side of the dirt and gravel road; Menendez was displacing. Dan was tempted to squeeze off a shot or eight, but hitting a moving target from over a hundred feet was beyond his skill. Then he decided that the shit-bag had had a good idea.

Dan leapt onto the trailer and pounded down its length and then hurdled the fence on the other side of the gate, landing and rolling and then laying still; he was now at the far end of the same long, low building that Menendez had taken shelter behind—or at least he thought so.

Had the cock-knocker seen him?

A rifle shot ka-powed, and forty feet to Dan's right the back glass of the Dodge blew out. "Hey Sims, you gonna come out an play, or you just gonna hide like a chickenshit?" Menendez laughed and shot again; a two-inch hole appeared in the Dodge's quarter panel.

Dan grinned as he hastily thumbed fresh loads into the Smith, saving his brass in a vest pocket; he'd watched too much CSI to make that mistake. Then he went to the opposite corner and poked his head around, but didn't see the big Mexican. Was he at the end of this building, or the next one up? Only one way to find out; Dan crept along the wall, pistols leading; there was a high, tubular metal fence and an empty dirt cattle pen on his right.

Where *were* those fucking mutts, anyway?

Another shot at the truck, and then calm until Dan got to the far corner and peered around, but he still didn't see Menendez. Had the roided-out asshole ran back across the road, or retreated deeper into the farm? Dan was now even with the grumbling Mach, so he snuck toward it, and then crouched at another blast, this one close enough to make his ears whine, but Menendez was still shooting at the Dodge and trailer. Dan ran to the corner, trusting the idling muscle car to cover his movements, and peeked into the road.

The wide, glowing-green form of Jesus Menendez strutted openly toward the truck and trailer, stock hard against his shoulder and barrel up, ready and steady. "Hey! Sims! Did I already kill that sweet ass?" The big Mexican laughed, and Dan twitched, eager to shoot the fucker in his broad back, but then he saw where Menendez was walking.

A little further…

"You dead back there? I bet you are! You shoulda did what the man said and stayed home, meng!" He cackled again, but despite his words, he kept that rifle up.

Just a little further…

Menendez lurched sideways and screamed, grabbing for his foot. The rifle clattered in the dirt as he fell over on his side, and then he convulsed and screamed louder. Despite everything, Dan winced as he bolted around the corner. *That has to hurt.* Menendez heard him coming and grabbed for the weapon, but just as he swung it around Dan leapt and smashed the Colt into his face and jerked the rifle from his hands and threw it to the side.

McFarlane's enforcer spit blood, then bared bloody green teeth up at him as Dan leveled the .45 between his eyes. "Fuck you, Sims! You ain't got—"

Dan pulled the trigger. Green brains and pale green bone and dark green hair splattered the dirt behind Menendez as his body went limp and voided its bowels. Dan gagged but held his gorge as he shot Menendez in the heart and then took careful aim and shot him in the groin. He stood holding his breath and looking coldly down on Menendez as he took a fresh clip out of his vest and reloaded the Colt and stuffed the partial into a deep pocket.

Dan racked a bullet into the chamber. "That last one was for Scandlin's wife, and God only knows who else. Rot in hell." He hawked a big slimy one on the corpse, then found his spent casing and secured it before hurrying over and shutting down the Mach and turning off the headlights. He banged the door closed and kept a lens peeled and the Colt ready as he holstered the Smith and got his phone out and almost sagged to his knees when he saw the text telling him it was dinner time. She had to have heard the shots and figured the plan had gone to shit, but she didn't know it was a trap.

Beth would still be going for Lizzie.

Sick with fear, Dan sprinted toward the Dodge, slowing to pick his way through the caltrops lest he end up with one through his boot like a certain dead rapist shit-stain. He was in a near panic by the time he scrambled over the gate and snatched the megaphone from the floorboard and shook the glass off and flipped the switch; it came on with a crackling whine. He turned around and raised it to his lips:

"LIZZIE, CAN YOU HEAR ME? IT'S DADDY!" Dan lowered the bullhorn and listened; no answer. No dogs. No nothing. It was like he was alone out here. Had they taken them away already? Please God, no. He jerked the megaphone back up and screamed: "IT'S A TRAP, BETH! THEY KNEW WE WERE COMING!

THEY *WANT* YOU TO GO TO HER! *IT'S A TRAP!*" No answer. Dan called McFarlane every name he could think of and yelled for Beth and Lizzie some more, then put the thing down and snatched his glove off and hammered out a text telling Beth it was a trap.

No answer. He called her.

It went to voicemail.

Rage and almost overwhelming despair came along and shuffled Dan off to a scary, scary place, but he held it together long enough to drag the ¾ inch industrial through-hardened 80 grade chain out of the bed and run it through the trailer's axles and around the thick gate post and then repeat the process on the Dodge's front and back axles and the other post. He secured its hundred-foot length with four Brinks Boron Shackle Commercial cut-resistant industrial padlocks. *Nobody* was taking his daughter out this way; not quickly, at any rate.

When he was done, he snatched the megaphone up and shouted for Beth and Lizzie and cursed McFarlane, but there was still no answer and still no sign of the dogs.

There was no sign of anyone.

They'd taken his family. They'd taken his girls. He hopped onto the trailer and jumped the gate, then stomped through the caltrops; somehow he managed not to step on one, but Dan would have welcomed pain in his foot; it would have distracted him from the pain in his heart.

His girls were gone.

He drew back a boot and kicked the stinking rapist's corpse as he went by, then strode past the Mustang and up the dirt track between the buildings. He put the bullhorn to his mouth and shouted, but got no answer. It didn't matter. Dan would find his family or someone else to kill, whether it was on this farm or wherever in the world he had to go.

Oh God oh God they took my GIRLS!

Dan walked up the dirt track through the still farm, pausing every fourth step to shout for Lizzie and Beth and cuss McFarlane.

His destination was the big white house on the crest.

Dan had never felt so alone.

Meanwhile, the weather had turned sprightly; green lightning flickered to the west, accompanied by distant rumbles; cow-shit scented wind swirled as the green sky churned overhead, spattering him with stinging drops. Gone. They were both gone. His family was gone. Everyone was gone, not even a single goddamn hairball to exterminate, but he would not quit, not until he knew what had happened to his wife and daughter.

His sudden smile was a baleful thing full of teeth; and not until he killed John McFarlane. *That I will do, guaran fuckin' teed.* Dan had tossed aside the useless megaphone, and his voice had grown hoarse, but he still stopped and threw his head back every four steps:

"Lizzie! BEEEETH!"

"Daniel."

He whirled and saw her standing at the edge of the shop where he'd parked his truck last Wednesday.

"Beth!" He ripped the goggles off and ran to hug her…and then, for some reason, he slowed and stopped ten feet away.

Her sawed-off shotgun was clutched in one small hand, strap dangling in the dirt; the goggles and ski mask hung from her other hand. She didn't come toward him; she just stood there and stared through him. "Are you all right?" Beth didn't answer. Her ponytail had come loose, and her hair was roostered-up on one side, stiff and spiky; her face was streaked with something dark, like war-paint. "Holy shit, is that blood? Are you hurt?"

"It's not mine," she said in a weird, flat tone, then turned and looked up the ridge with that disconnected stare.

Not hers? Well, whose blood was it, then? Dan opened his mouth to inquire, then closed it and frowned; in the normal course of events, his dangerous little wife was so "in the moment", "aware-of-everything", blah blah, all that Zen-warrior shit, that it was completely fucking annoying; now…now he didn't know *what* was wrong with her, but he didn't like this eerie detachment, not even a little goddamn bit.

He stepped into her line of sight and waved. "Hello? I did for Menendez at the gate, and he said they were laying a trap for you, that they wanted you to go to Lizzie, but I think that was just bullshit, just like the three-days was bullshit. Mc-Farlane only wanted a clean head-start, and now she's *gone!* They're *all* gone! Even the fucking dogs are gone! We have to go to the police!"

"She's still here. They're all still here."

Monotone again.

"You can't fucking know that, not for sure. I think we should—"

"*I can feel her.*" Beth looked at him then, really looked at him, and Dan almost wished she hadn't; her big dark eyes were blazing, and that wild hair and the pattern of blood smears had transformed her countenance into a stranger's furious fright-mask. "She's still here, Daniel! And I know it's a trap. It doesn't matter." She let her mask and goggles drop like so much trash and gripped the shotgun with both hands. "It's time to go get her," she announced, then strode off up the road as lightning streaked and thunder boomed, the closest and loudest yet.

Those goggles had cost a fucking mint! Dan cursed and crammed his own goggles back on, then watched her walk away with that determined stride, lithe green figure somehow moving fast on those short legs. "Goddamnit, *wait!*" Dan snatched up her mask and goggles and ran after her. "Just hold up a sec, would ya? Jesus!" She stopped, and Dan tried to hand her stuff back. "Here, you dropped these."

She didn't take them. "There's no reason to hide now, and I don't need the goggles. We're wasting time."

"Don't *need* them? It's dark as a politician's asshole out here! And like I said, I killed Menendez at the gate, but there's still…uh, if it's not yours, whose blood is that, anyway?"

"Tommy's." She walked up the road again. Dan scrambled after her. How could she *see* anything? Tommy. So two down, and the other four were at the fire in Centerville—he hoped. That left the old man, the sluts, the mutts, plus the Keeper mucking about somewhere. Dan was holding out hope she would be deadheading roses down in her creepy bone yard and would choose to stay aloof from this mess, but just in case he had a Starfire ACP with her name on it.

"Did you kill him?" She kept walking. "Damn it, talk to me! What the fuck is going on?"

She spun on him and he stopped, wary. "No, I didn't kill him, but I would have if given the chance! We're wasting time, Daniel! She *needs* us; she needs me! I can't explain how I know, but she does! There's something happening!" Beth seemed to gather herself, then went on in a quieter tone, but she still sounded like she was spitting rivets: "Do you trust me?"

"What does that have to do with anything?"

"Do you trust me or not?"

"Of course I trust you, but—"

"Then no more questions; I don't have the answers, and Lizzie doesn't have the time. I'm taking our daughter back, right now, so if you're coming with me, then come. If not, wait here and I'll bring her out."

She stalked away.

Dan stared after her, then followed. He slowed and walked beside her, keeping a sharp lens out and the Colt and Smith up and ready; those furballs could be anywhere. He didn't have a third hand for her stuff so he tried to get her to take it again. She refused again, and what she said made Dan stop dead.

"I can see just fine."

He said nothing else when he ran and caught back up, but he was thinking plenty. See just fine? And if Beth hadn't killed Tommy boy, then who had? And "feel" Lizzie? That was a rung up on the wacky scale from "knowing" their daughter was happy and healthy and still hanging out on the farm; Dan had bought into that craziness all day for the simple sake of staying sane.

But "feel"?

What the fuck, exactly, did "feel" mean?

Dan kept his lip zipped with great difficulty and unease as they continued to the crest…and then Beth jerked to a halt.

"What is it? What's wrong?"

She didn't answer; she only stared toward the house with something like alarm on her face; it was hard to tell for sure with it being green and covered in blood and all. Dan looked where she was looking, but all he saw was the huge Gone-With-the-Wind house sitting there with all its tall, narrow windows blank and lifeless and their white (green) curtains drawn. Two ornate wall lamps glowed on either side of the double front doors; the fluted columns that supported the roof over the porch threw long shadows almost to where he and Beth stood at the edge of the yard; the detached kitchen where he'd enjoyed such a lovely lunch with the McFarlanes also appeared deserted.

Where the hell is everyone? And where are those goddamn dogs?

Dan started grimly toward the front doors; he'd made it five steps before he realized he was alone. He stopped and glanced back; Beth stood staring up at the house, that stricken look now plain. He pulled the goggles off and went back, keeping both eyes peeled and both guns up; his furry friends could be anywhere.

"What is it?" Nothing. "Beth! What's wrong?"

"She's not here." Dan's wife turned slowly and faced the trees, which were massed on the back side of the yard; the house was built into the verge of the forest, right at the edge of the valley. Cicadas whirred and screeched from that dark wall.

"She's down there."

Dan looked at her, looked at the silent house, and then turned and looked at the trees; he *should* have been asking how she knew. He *should* have been suggesting they search the house just in case, because if she was wrong and they went traipsing down into that valley and McFarlane got past them and the blocked gate and took Lizzie somewhere…but it was only a fleeting thought. The reason he didn't say anything was simple:

Somehow, for some reason he couldn't explain, Dan knew she was right.

"Of course she is. Let's go get her." He took a step toward the trees, but Beth put a hand on his arm.

"Wait." Then she startled him by dropping the Mossberg to the lawn and wrapping her arms around him and pressing her face to his chest; she was trembling like a leaf in a tornado. Dan hugged her back one-armed while keeping his head up and the .45 out and ready; the Presidents. Lighting crackled and thunder spoke and a wave of rain pelted them and moved on.

Beth finally pulled back and looked up at him, wiping moisture from her face with one black glove; she smeared Tommy's blood across a gorgeous cheek doing so.

"I love you."

"I love you, too."

"Do you trust me?"

Not this shit again. "What does—"

"Yes or no."

"Yes, I trust you."

"Good." Then she took one of those breaths that puffed her belly like a Buddha; his wife always did that when she was about to tell him something he didn't want to hear. "There's more going on here than we thought, Daniel."

"No shit."

Beth grimaced, then spoke carefully: "I'm sorry I didn't believe you. And I'm going to do what I have to do to get Lizzie back, but *before* I do, I want you to promise me that no matter what you see down there, you'll follow my lead and…

and that you won't do anything unless I tell you." Dan checked to see if she was kidding, but his wife's face was blood-smeared, determined, and yes, completely serious. "I'll have my hands full doing…what I have to do, and I won't be able to protect you. I don't have the control to do both, not yet."

Dan blinked, then blinked again.

Huh?

"I know you don't understand, and I can't explain, not right now. Just promise me you'll do as I say. Please."

Dan stared at her.

"If you can't promise…" deep Buddha breath, "then you'll have to stay here and wait for us."

He laughed; he couldn't help it. Maybe she'd bonked her head on something and scrambled her brains; it would explain a lot. Dan pushed her away, and he had to force himself to be gentle: "If you think I'll just stand here with my dick in my hand, you're crazy." Perhaps not the best turn of phrase, considering, but he meant every word. "I'll do what *I* have to do to get Lizzie back *and* keep you both safe, and that's the only promise you'll get, babe. And don't worry about protecting me." He showed her both guns. "I got that covered."

Beth just looked at him, eyes sad and frightened. Then: "Very well."

She strode off toward the trees.

Dan considered the abandoned Mossberg—so much for all that practice—then dropped Beth's goggles and mask on top of it and ran to catch up, slowing beside her to cram his own goggles back on. Beth produced two big green knives as they turned around the side of the house; he thought about opining something about knives being poor replacements for the 'Berg, but didn't.

Dan thought about saying a lot of things but didn't.

They crossed the sloping backyard, and Dan could see a track worn into the grass; it vanished between two massive oaks that stood like tree sentinels; beyond them, the world dropped away into windy darkness.

And then he stumbled to a halt and brought the pistols up as three low, glowing-green forms trotted from the tree line, triangle ears perked.

"Beth! The Presidents!"

She stopped beside him. "I see them." He cocked one lens at her without taking attention or aim from the mutts. She could *see* them? How the fuck? She reached out a slim green hand and pushed both pistols down. "They're here for me."

And with *that* total nonsense, she walked sedately toward the huge toothy fuzzballs, which turned and loped away and then stopped between the twin towering oaks, all three looking back with their ears at full mast and their long green tongues hanging and dripping.

Their tails were wagging.

"Fuck me," he whispered.

Beth joined her new furry pals, and then all four disappeared over the lip without even a single glance back at him; not even a "piss off" or a "how do ya do!"

Dan looked around, and then, just for shits and giggles, he took the goggles off: solid black. He yanked them back on. "Wait!" He ran and passed between the trail-head trees and stopped; the path unrolled downhill, smooth and straight as a highway, branches arcing overhead like Bambi's cathedral; Beth was already far down it, the Presidents surrounding her like a smelly honor guard.

Dan hesitated for one long endless eternal nanosecond, then plunged down the rabbit hole after his wife.

SISTERS

LIGHTNING FORKED and furious cracks and booms spoke overhead, fading to angry rumbles and then discontented grumbles. Beth walked down the wide trail, boots pressing into the moldering loam; cold rain spattered, those few drops somehow running the gauntlet of leaves and interwoven branches high above. The two largest animals bookended her, with Reagan trotting ahead, yet she felt no fear; she didn't know what the Presidents would do if she turned back, but it didn't matter; they were leading her to Lizzie, and there would be no turning back.

Beth stared around at the swaying, creaking forest; she could see as if it were dusk instead of a moonless, starless night. She could smell the dogs' hot, sweet breath, and the mustiness in their coarse fur. She could also feel their savage hunger, albeit momentarily suppressed. Daniel walked two steps behind her, and she could hear his heart pound and his blood race; she could also sense his raging love and desperate fear for Lizzie.

Her husband's growing misgivings about *her* were clear as well.

Those stung, oh how they stung, but Beth understood:

She had reservations of her own.

Something had awoken deep inside her, something that had blasted her senses wide open; something that, had she the time or the inclination to think about it, would have terrified her.

Lizzie's need pulsed; Beth had no time for fear, and certainly no time for doubts. She told herself that it was just another tool she would use to get her daughter back, as she would her fighting skills if needed; it could wait to be explored and examined.

Lizzie was all that mattered.

Despite her resolve to wait, Beth couldn't help flexing her new awareness, like a muscle long atrophied.

It felt…glorious.

Over the years, there had been times when she'd pushed herself, or her teachers had pushed her, to the point of falling down or throwing up, where vision had narrowed and blood had thundered in her ears; in those raw, exhausted moments, her sense of self, of being "Beth", had fallen away, and she'd been one with the moment, one with her opponent; one with everything.

She'd known nothing.

And it wasn't only Beth's power that was awakening.

On the phone, McFarlane had talked about a "special place", and how whatever madness he had planned for Lizzie had to be conducted in such a location; at the time, Beth had barely paid attention, consumed by her crushing terror for her kidnapped child, and when she'd contemplated it off and on during this eternal day, she had marked it a symptom of his obvious psychosis.

She knew better, now.

Beth lifted a hand before her face and felt the atmosphere crackle; if she snapped her fingers, she thought it might cause a spark; she'd sensed that energy twice before and deluded herself that it was extra oxygen produced by photosynthesis, but there could be no delusions tonight. Pure, scintillating power filled the valley to its brim, and if she chose, she could reach out with…something…not her hands; her mind, maybe, although that wasn't quite right; perhaps it was her will. Regardless of what *it* was, she could use it to harness that power and squeeze sap from these towering trees as easily as she could wring water from a washcloth; even rip them out of the ground and juggle them like giant leafy bowling pins.

The part of her that still hadn't accepted rebelled: *That's…impossible.* There was no better word for it. The rest of Beth knew it was extremely probable if she put forth just a little effort…but she restrained herself; as new to this as she was—whatever *this* was—Beth sensed that such an act would weaken her, even with the basin's might augmenting her own, and she would soon need all her strength for Lizzie.

There was something else Beth was beginning to comprehend…and fear; this reservoir was not for her to play with. It existed for some dire purpose, and her dread grew exponentially when she considered that it coincided with a confluence of people, events, place, and time…

And at the heart of it all was Lizzie.

What were they planning? To bind her, as Beth's false rescuer had said? What exactly did *that* mean? And this "Master" she had spoken of so reverently; so fearfully.

Who was He?

Beth trembled at the possibilities, and then righteous rage surged from deep within; she used it to shove aside all her fears, doubts, and questions. It didn't matter who "He" was or what they planned because Beth was going to take Lizzie back from these terrible people and away from this dreadful place and nothing would stop her.

Nothing!

Behind her, Daniel stepped on a fallen branch, the dry crack seeming as loud as a gunshot; the Presidents instantly turned toward him, as if waking to his presence. Beth could read their confusion; he didn't belong here, not like them.

Not like her.

Daniel cursed and shouldered her aside and thrust his weapons at the Presidents. "Watch out!" The dogs' vicious, rasping snarls matched their awakened bloodlust; they inched toward him, preparing to spring, rend, and tear.

"No," Beth said softly.

The Presidents looked at her; so did her husband. Reagan whined, and then all three animals turned and trotted ahead, glancing back when she didn't follow.

Reagan whined again, and this time Nixon joined her. Ike sat down and scratched an ear with a hind foot, then stood up and barked plaintively; a clear invitation.

Daniel's voice was a strained whisper: "Holy fucking shit!"

Beth had tried to warn him; he truly didn't belong here. How was she going to protect him while doing what she had to do? She stood silent, head bowed, thinking how to convince him to return and wait for them, but she knew it was useless:

He won't go back, not even if I beg.

Her husband said nothing—for once—but he shifted from boot to boot; she could sense his desire to back away from her, but he didn't.

Beth had no time for this; Lizzie's need called. She walked on, the Presidents leading now, Reagan still on point. Daniel stayed two steps behind Beth, as she knew he would. What would happen, would happen; she would do her best to protect him, and if she failed, a part of her would die here tonight, never to be reborn, but she could accept that outcome.

Right now, only Lizzie mattered.

The path leveled and curved to the right, toward the heart of the vale. The storm thrashed the high canopy, pelting them with sodden gusts as they went on without speaking for more than a mile, like travelers trapped in a dark dream: the dogs in the lead, Beth in the middle, and Daniel two steps behind, breathing harshly.

Then the song found them.

They halted as one, listening, even the Presidents; the music floated through the forest, eddying around the colossal trunks and swirling through the high boughs before dropping gently upon their senses; the tripart, a cappella melody was beautiful and powerful and fearful beyond imagining.

The dogs abruptly loped forward. Beth ran to keep up. Lizzie. Daniel cursed and dashed after them. Lizzie. There were bizarre, sickening words peppering the song; it didn't matter. Only Lizzie mattered. Three distinct female voices, first one then another taking prominence, the song's power building, layer upon layer rising.

Lizzie.

They burst into a giant clearing; at the center was the sinkhole, a circle almost a half-mile across. It was so deep trees grew inside; their spreading canopies melded just below the rim, rippling in the storm's gusts like a living carpet, fostering the dangerous illusion that you could step out and walk across. A rope ladder was tied to the trunk of a hoary walnut that grew close to the edge; knotted rungs trailed across the ground and dropped over the rim into darkness.

Three young women barred the way, mouths open in song; the jet-haired beauty stood prominent, obsidian eyes fastened on Beth's. The blonde and redhead stood behind and to either side. All three wore matching dove-gray dresses with wide, dagged sleeves hanging almost to the loam; the silky garments hugged their curves, leaving little to the imagination; a darker lace the color of the churning clouds trimmed their busts and hems. They were barefoot, and their hair blew unfettered in the wind.

Beth and Daniel halted as the Presidents ran forward and sat panting at the womens' feet: Reagan at the brunette's, Ike at the blonde's, and Nixon at the redhead's. The youngest, the honey blonde with the boobs threatening to pop her lace, scratched Ike behind the ears.

And then Daniel strode forward and leveled both pistols:

"Where's Lizzie? What did you do with her?" They didn't answer, just kept singing, but the younger two pinned outraged, glittering stares on him; the eldest continued to watch Beth. He cocked both hammers. "Better start talking, and I mean *right fucking now*, or there's gonna be three new singing-slut corpses stinking up this forest!"

The first never took her eyes from Beth as she stopped singing; the two behind closed their mouths as well, but didn't stop, not entirely, humming and carrying the melody as they glared scalding death at Daniel. Beth felt the force they'd built pause, but not lessen; whatever vileness they'd put into motion hadn't run its course, not yet.

The titanic hole beyond the three beckoned.

Lizzie was down there.

The first spoke to Beth, disdaining both Daniel and the weapons he held pointed at her face from less than twenty feet away. "He does not belong here," she said. "But you knew that already. Didn't you, sister."

Beth took stock; Alexandria's voice was vibrant and sultry and held more than a hint of contempt, and she had to suppress a flash of unease; unlike Daniel or the Presidents, Beth could read no surface thoughts or emotions from her; the other two were closed to her as well. Their power must shield them in some way…which meant that hers should shield her from them—she hoped.

Beth walked up and stood beside her husband.

"I'm not your sister, bitch."

"Perhaps not before this night of nights, but…" A mocking smile twisted her bee-stung lips: "I sense things have changed. You are one of us now, *sister*."

Daniel slowly turned his head and put the goggles on her without taking his aim from the three; Beth felt the weight of his stare, but she had no time:

Lizzie waited below.

Beth seized Alexandria's haughty black eyes with her own and held them:

"I will *never* be one of you."

That insufferable smile vanished, and hot hate blazed from all three lovely faces; and then their long hair lifted around their heads in a wild cloud as a violent wind gusted, but not from the strengthening storm above; this wind blew *up* from the cenote, the trees within twisting and rocking, leafy carpet shredded and inverted by the force, a vast flock of leaves shooting skyward and then fluttering back down as the wind died as suddenly as it had come.

Nixon spun, growling and barking, and the redhead continued to hum as she patted him while turning around and looking down into the hole with a harried expression.

The first sister ignored the strange wind from below and the commotion equally while spitting words at Beth: "You are correct, *bitch!* You do not deserve what you have been given! YOU WILL NEVER BE ONE OF US!" That hateful smile blossomed once more: "But that is of no moment; time moves apace, and what is begun cannot be stopped short of the inevitable. To even pause now risks everything; nevertheless, he must be prevented from continuing further." Those merciless eyes swiveled to Daniel, and she raised her hand, but Beth stepped between them.

"No."

Her face twisted, somehow still gorgeous: "Do not test me, *sister*. You are strong, yes, but untried, and you know his kind do not belong here, not on this singular night! His interference could jeopardize our Father's triumph as well as risk all our lives, your daughter's included. *I will not allow it!* The Mother may pass, but *he* may not!"

Something rang false.

That tiny smile, even as Alexandria shouted…that gleeful glint in her black eyes as she looked at Daniel…Beth was prevented from sensing the woman's emotions and thoughts, true, but she had been interpreting facial clues and voice inflection and body language her whole life:

Alex was lying.

But about what?

Meanwhile, the snotty cunt was still running her perfect mouth: "Or do you not wish to join your daughter? She is calling you. Can you not hear her? I can. If you want to be with her, he cannot accompany you. You have a choice, sister: mate, or offspring." Her hand came up again; slowly, teasingly, threateningly. "Choose now; time grows short!"

Daniel stepped forward. "Let the bitch try it!" Beth pulled him back, but he shook her off and began ranting at the three, threatening to kill them where they stood, women or not, if they didn't get out of his goddamn way.

Beth focused on Alexandria; did she *want* Daniel to go down into the cenote? Beth glanced at the younger two, at the fiery stares that should have crisped Daniel by now; the very *idea* was anathema to them. Beth put her gaze back on the eldest:

If she was pretending, if was for the benefit of those two.

But why would she deceive her sisters?

"Choose!"

"She ain't gonna choose *shit* for me! Get the fuck out of my way or I'll…!"

Beth looked at that hovering hand, glanced at the other two again, listened to them hum, measured the tension in their postures and the strain on their faces…

"You're bluffing. You won't stop my husband from descending, not if I oppose you."

The younger sisters glared at Beth even as they hummed, but Alexandria's small, secret smile only grew more smug—satisfaction carefully hidden from the two behind her. Beth intended to repair that situation, and right now; she spoke to the blonde and redhead in turn: "You will not stop him because you dare not risk letting what you've built collapse." She shifted back to Alexandria. "But I also agree: he does not belong here. *I* will make sure he goes no further."

The younger two exchanged an uncertain glance, but Alexandria's obsidian eyes glittered as she lost her superior little smile; she didn't react other than that, though, and Beth knew her instinct was right: the eldest was hiding her true intentions from her sisters.

But why?

And then Daniel erupted:

"*What?!* Fuck that! You're as nutty as that whore!"

Wind blasted from the cenote again, stronger than before, and the blonde with the rack glanced over her shoulder, then stopped humming and raised her voice against the gale: "As long as he is contained, what matter how? We have our own business to be about! We cannot hold much longer, sister!" She hastily took up the hum again, supporting her copper-haired sister, who had staggered and looked ready to faint at the sudden burden of sustaining the melody alone.

The eldest hesitated and then dropped her hand; something beyond hate moved across that flawless face as she looked at Beth. Then she turned those eyes on Daniel and brazenly took him in from black boots to golden hair: "I would have handled him gently, sister. He is not unattractive, and he produces *wonderful* daughters." She laughed.

Jealous fury boiled; even Lizzie was forgotten for the moment. Beth took a long step forward and pointed the tip of the Carson at her. "If you touch him, I will kill you." Reagan's black lips skinned away from long yellow teeth; she growled at Beth, deep and low.

"Ladies, ladies, this is flattering and all, but now's not the—"

Beth whirled on him. "*Shut UP!*" She faced the black-haired hussy again. "He will remain here, and he will be untouched when I return, or I'll slice you open and tie your stinking guts in a knot and then feed them to you, I promise!"

A hiss: "Your love for them will be your undoing!"

"Your love for only yourself will be *yours!*"

She laughed again, softly this time, eyes pools of black fire: "There are many things you have yet to learn, sister. I look forward to teaching you!" Before Beth could respond she spun away, midnight hair whipping. "Come, sisters! The world groans at our delay! Take your places!" With looks of vast relief, the blonde and redhead lifted their voices again, and all three sang as they walked away around the rim. The blonde swayed off by herself, Ike following; the other two undulated the opposite way, trailed by their animals. Somehow Beth knew that they would take up equidistant positions around the hole, forming an equilateral triangle...

A perfect triangle overlaying a perfect circle.

The configuration sent fear rippling down her spine.

Lizzie.

Time was running out.

"Yeah, whatever, you do that! Crazy cunts." Daniel jogged to the edge and peered over. "Lizzie's down there, right? Of course she is. I bet McFarlane is, too. And here's the rope ladder, just like Fulbright said." He holstered both pistols and grabbed up the ladder and tugged, eyeing where it was secured to the old walnut; apparently satisfied, he made ready to descend, then stood back up when he saw she hadn't moved. "Well? Come on! We gotta get Lizzie and get the fuck outta here!"

Beth just looked at him.

Realization dawned, and then anger; he came back and stood in front of her. "You can't be serious."

Beth licked her lips; her confrontation with the sisters was nothing compared to this. He had his guns and his bullets and his love for Lizzie, but Beth knew those wouldn't be enough to survive what they would find in the cenote; she'd known it back up at the farm. Beth belonged here, not him, and she was the one who had a chance to save Lizzie and return.

If Daniel went down there, he would die.

Beth was determined to save her daughter *and* her husband, but for that, he had to stay here; but she knew he wouldn't, no matter what she said, stubborn, idiot, love-of-her-life that he was.

Beth couldn't watch him die, not when she had a chance to save him.

She gave it one last try with words:

"I must go down alone."

His anger turned to astonishment, and then hurt, and then the anger came back stronger than before, but the grating, wounding sense of betrayal stung more than she could've imagined; then his face turned to rock, and she felt his resolve harden with it.

"I'm going, Beth." *Way* more than a hint of challenge entered his bearing as he not-so-casually freed one pistol again and held it down by his leg. "What, do you really think you can stop me? I don't care what fancy fucking martial-arts moves you pull or whatever this new shit is you've got going on, I'm going in there to get my daughter." He slashed the semi-auto through the air perilously close to her nose. "End of fucking discussion."

Beth didn't react, just looked up at him; the song soared to new heights, and she knew the sisters were nearing their places.

No time. Lizzie.

I have to do it, and not only to save him; that SLUT…that BITCH…she wants Daniel down there. Why? Why would she mislead the other two? What game is she playing?

But she didn't have time to puzzle it out, and in the end, it didn't matter; any-thing *Alex* wanted couldn't be good for Beth's family.

He got this haughty look and nodded sharply, misled by her silence that she'd backed down: "Now stop being stupid or I'll leave you standing here arguing about who's going down in the fucking hole while I get Lizzie." He turned away. "Let's—"

Beth shot out a hand and gripped his forearm; he looked down in surprise.

This would forever change things between them; compared to this, what had happened with Rison in their bedroom would be remembered as only a blip on their relationship's radar.

No time. Lizzie.

No choice.

Beth sank her awareness into the dark earth beneath his boots; she caressed its strength, embraced its solidity, enfolded its timelessness, and then brought it all up and into Daniel's feet and legs and blended them.

She stepped away, and his face below the goggles sagged in shock; he tried to take a step, wheeled his arms for balance, and then gaped down at his boots.

"What the hell?" He struggled to lift a foot again and failed.

"I'm sorry."

"What the *fuck?!* How—?" He struggled more, then froze like a statue as he stared at her, his astonishment so strong it eclipsed the rising song and Lizzie's pulsing beacon. "What did you do to me?" he whispered. Then rage blew away astonishment like a thunderclap: "Release me, goddamnit! *Release me! DON'T DO THIS TO ME!"*

Beth walked to the rim and looked down; the rope ladder descended into solid darkness—unyielding even to her eyes. Wind gushed from the hole once more, lifting her hair and thrashing the canopy before dying away. The song had reached a crescendo, three voices spiraling, blending, pulsating; lightning streaked and thunder boomed.

And then a virulent force surged from below, rising to meet the song, nearly drowning out her daughter's call.

It was beginning.

"I'm coming, baby," she whispered.

"Beth! Let me go with you! *Please!"*

She turned and drank in the sight of him; he had dropped the pistol and ripped the goggles off and was using both hands to yank at his booted ankle, trying to pry his foot off the ground. His beautiful blue eyes were wild and scared and furious. The wind from the sinkhole howled yet again, whipping Beth's hair around her face.

"Don't do this! Let me go with you!"

"I can't. I'm sorry."

"Please!"

"I'll bring her out, I promise."

Beth sheathed the Carson and turned and quickly descended the rope ladder. Another hurricane gust from below made it sway, banging her against the rock, but she kept going. Lizzie. The air sang and the stone before her face surged with sickening power.

Lizzie.

"Beth!"

She reached narrow, switchback stairs that had been carved out of the bedrock and stepped off the ladder, letting it go to flail and twist in the wind, waiting for her eyes to adjust to the strangely thick darkness. Finally they did, although she still couldn't see very far. She pounded down the steps; they were treacherous with moisture, but Beth didn't care.

Lizzie.

From up above came a frantic scream that cut through the howling wind and the mounting storm and the pulsating song:

"BETH! DON'T LEAVE ME!"

"I love you," she whispered.

Lizzie.

Beth ran faster, back and forth and back and forth and down and down and down; the shadows soon swallowed her.

The Die Has Been Cast

*I*JUST WENT *bat-shit fucking bonkers*, Dan thought, amazed.

Crazy was the only way to explain this; he strained and yanked, trying to lift his right boot from the ground, but it stayed put. He tried to lift his left boot. Nada. How was the wind blowing *up* and *out* of a fucking hole, anyway? Screw it, it didn't matter; he was crazy. Beth and Lizzie were down there, that's what mattered. McFarlane was down there. Dan growled and pulled harder. His girls needed him, but he couldn't lift his boots! He could feel his feet in them just fine; he wiggled his toes, just to make sure; there, they wiggled. He could also feel his knees popping and calves and thighs straining, but *he couldn't lift his feet!*

Beth had superglued him to the earth somehow. But that was impossible, as his lovely wife was so fond of saying, so it must not be happening. He was crazy. Beth and Lizzie. McFarlane. Panic spider-crawled across his brain; that kidnapping, sanctimonious, asshole was in there with Dan's girls, and he was fucking *STUCK UP HERE!*

Dan stared grimly down at his right boot. *I will take a step.* He'd been putting one foot in front of the other his whole life just as he damn well pleased, and he'd be goddamned if he stopped now.

A step, that's it; just one step, Dan-o.

Trembling, Dan lifted his right foot; a dump truck was hanging off the sole of his boot, but he lurched forward. *Yes!* Sweat dripped from his nose, and he was stretched out like he'd been caught mid-sprint, right knee at a hard angle. *Okay, now another step.*

Dan focused on his left boot, but he couldn't help do the math: twenty or so feet to the rim, then the rope ladder, and then…what? Fulbright had said something about steps carved into the rock; how deep *was* that thing—and more importantly, how many steps? And when he finally reached the bottom, he'd have to track Beth and Lizzie down…and McFarlane, oh yes, McFarlane for sure, you bet, but…

At this rate, Dan would join the party sometime next spring.

Desperation made him start yanking again, but he forced the panic away and swiped sweat out of his eyes and brought his will to bear; his whole body quivered as his left foot slowly began to lift…

Fuck'n A!

"You are even stronger than I suspected."

Dan's boot sucked back to the leaves. He flailed for balance and put his hands down to keep from toppling over, then straightened and stood stock still; that voice had come out of the pitch-black woods; worse, it had spoken directly behind him.

Worse than that, he recognized it.

Lightning flashed, inverting the night and making Dan squint; thunder cracked and then rumbled through the clouds as she stepped sedately around him and put her back to the sinkhole, facing him from ten feet away; with his legs stuck spread out, they were the same height. She was dressed in a man's plaid work shirt and jeans and hiking boots, as always, but she'd foregone the floppy hat tonight, although her ponytail was still bound by that white ribbon; a few strands of red-gray hair had come loose, and the wind blew them across her pale face in wispy, undulating stripes…

Dan's breath caught.

Her eyes…her eyes were gleaming like someone had snapped one of those chemiluminescent glow sticks and dumped them into her irises; that sickly glow lit up her eye sockets and high cheekbones in a truly dreadful way.

Dan swallowed. Then what she held in a thick-fingered hand caught his attention; there wasn't much light—and most of that was from her eyes and the flickering lightning—but what there was glinted from a small but viciously curved steel blade.

"My, my, but this *is* a delectable turn of events. Hello again, Dan Sims."

"Uh, hello." Dan kept one eye on that nasty little sickle and one hand on the butt of the holstered Smith as he oh-so-casually looked around for the .45. He found the Colt lying in the dead leaves behind him, just out of easy, twisting reach. Shit.

She observed these gyrations with some amusement, then peered at his legs. "Impressive. She learns quickly." Those shining green peepers found his face again and held.

Behind her, the wind howled from the massive hole, thrashing the trees, launching leaves and even whole leafy branches into the sky; the wind died as unexpectedly as it had come, but that torrent had lasted a little longer than the others—or at least Dan thought so; it was hard to concentrate with her staring at him like he was a cupcake in a bakery window; leaves and branches fluttered and dropped around them.

"So, it—" Dan cleared his throat: "It's good to, um, you know, see you again, but I've got to get back to…" He pointed at his boot.

"I could free you, Dan Sims."

He supposed she could, at that. The problem was, Dan was fairly fucking certain he didn't *want* her help. Fairly? *Completely* certain; in fact, he just wanted her to take her weird-ass eyes and go the fuck away.

"Thanks but no thanks. I'll manage."

"As you wish. You have the strength; that is assured. However, will you succeed in time to help your wife and daughter?"

Dan considered her narrowly while keeping a tight rein on his temper; had she taken part in Lizzie's kidnapping? Was she working with McFarlane, or against? He didn't have the time to get the answers—Beth and Lizzie didn't have the time—but she obviously had some stake in all this bullshit.

What did she really want?

They stared at each other as another blast jetted from the hole; more leaves and broken branches fluttered and dropped. Lightning walked and thunder talked; the sluts' eerie jam session had taken on a new and even darker tone, if that was possible.

"The window to help them is about to crash shut, Dan Sims. Request my assistance, and you shall have it."

She wants me to ask, Dan realized with a chill. *It's important to her.*

But why? Why was it important that he ask?

Dan gave her his best grin: "Like I said, I'll manage. And it'll be in *plenty* of time to help them; you can fucking count on that, lady."

Now her green-glowing stare could be described as nothing but predatory. *Shit!* Dan fumbled the Smith out and pointed it between those eyes. "Stay away from me! I mean it!" The barrel was trembling so badly he'd likely miss, even at this range, but that was why the cylinder held six bullets.

Those eyes narrowed, and she pursed her lips. Then: "Perhaps she will accomplish what I desire without your help—she *is* exceptionally gifted. However, they are prepared for her, and she is not likely to survive their reception." One thick, sloping shoulder twitched in a tiny shrug, as if she didn't much give a hoot either way. "Her fate—and your daughter's—will be made clear soon."

"*They?* Everybody but McFarlane and Beth and Lizzie are still up here. Who the fuck is down there wi—you're talking about the trap. Right? McFarlane's trap. Beth is walking into it."

Swirling ebon shadows abruptly folded around her; the only thing that could still be seen were those eyes, and now they were laughing at him. Dan stared into that churning, crawling darkness with sick recognition, but he only had room for one gargantuan terror at the moment:

"Who else is down there? What are they going to do to her? What are they doing to Lizzie? *Answer me!*"

Those green flames diminished, receding into some vast distance.

"Wait!" Only amused sparks now…gloating green embers, floating way off in the darkness…

And then Dan came to a decision.

A voice in his head immediately spoke up in protest; it sounded uncomfortably like a blend of his dad's voice and his older brother Will's:

She wants *you to ask, numb nuts,* said Daddy/Will. *Even you can tell that, and you ain't the sharpest knife in the chandelier. No. NO, Danny. This is a bad idea. In fact, it's the NUMBER ONE BAD FUCKING IDEA OF ALL TIME. Try to break free on your own. You can do it. She even said so.*

It'll be too late, Dan told Dad/Big Bro. *Only she can free me in time to help them. I have no choice.*

Dad and Will went quiet because they had no answer to that. Dan steeled his courage.

Beth and Lizzie.

He would do anything for Beth and Lizzie.

Anything and everything for his girls.

"I…I ask that you free me!"

The black shadows, which had begun to dissipate, solidified, and then those fading sparks flared to new, blazing life…and Dan suddenly felt like the guy in all those adventure stories he and Will had devoured up in their rickety tree house on lazy Saturday afternoons; the ones where some jumped-up idiot stumbles on a magic sword and then decides to be proactive, and now this imbecile is standing in front of the cave where the local dragon is taking a nap, and said dumb-ass starts banging his sword on the rocks and yelling for the dragon to come get some, and that's when the fiery eyes flare open deep within the darkness of the cave and the dude has second thoughts, but it's too late…

Then she spoke, and her voice seemed to trickle to Dan from a great distance; the Evil-Slut Jamboree and the storm and the weird wind gushing almost constantly from the sinkhole now should have drowned it out, but he heard her perfectly:

"There will be a price, Dan Sims. There is always a price. Do you accept this debt?"

"Well, that depends on what it is; I wash a mean car…" He stared at those glowing eyes, floating there in the swirling darkness: "…er, broom, rather. Or I could prune some roses, I guess. Beth said they needed it pretty bad…"

"Wise, to set the price. Foolish to wait until this late hour. *I* will set the price. Agree or not, Dan Sims. The Time of Choice is upon you."

Beth and Lizzie. No time to run from the dragon, and no fucking alternative, anyway.

"Yes," Dan said. Nothing but his girls mattered. "Yes, I agree."

"It is agreed," she whispered. Whisper or not, the words tolled in his head as the shadows collapsed and vanished and the Keeper of Barron Cemetery stood before him again…and then she whirled to face the sinkhole and pumped both fists in the air; the little knife was a darkly gleaming crescent brandished against the racing, flickering clouds.

"*Mine!* The choice is MINE! *THE POWER IS MINE!*" She dropped her arms and turned back, and now her face was twisted, mad, eyes glowing like green pilot lights. Black shadows billowed around her like a vast cloak—or wings—as she stalked toward him.

"*Jesus Christ!*"

Dan thrust the revolver at her, but if she cared, it didn't show; she stopped with the business end dimpling her right breast and reached and gripped his shoulder, hard, and he gasped. Her fingers were hawk's talons—and her *smell*, God! Like roadkill slathered in sex. He gagged, then held his breath to keep that stink out of his lungs as she muttered something and suddenly he lurched and fell to his knees.

He was free! Dan jumped back to his feet—

The song stopped.

Both of them spun toward the sinkhole. Complete and total silence filled the world; the strange wind blowing from the hole had also stopped; even the storm's gusts had ceased. Dan glanced up, and his eyes bugged; there was a cloud-lake hanging above him; the vapors had frozen mid-churn.

What the fuck?

The Keeper slowly raised her hands before her face, as if warding something away, then stumbled back from the edge and turned and rushed to the trees. She paused at the verge of the forest and looked at him over her shoulder; her eyes were raging green bonfires.

"What is it? *What's happening?*"

"Go, Dan Sims! Go, Husband! Go, Father! The die has been cast! Bring them out, if you can! *Go!*"

Black shadows rushed into her, swirling and churning, and then she was gone.

In the absolute stillness of the world, Dan stared at where she'd been, then faced the sinkhole again.

"Well that's encouraging."

Dan snatched up the Colt and holstered it, holstered the Smith on the other side, then retrieved the goggles and hastily slipped them on.

Three glowing-green women stood around the edge of the vast hole, each facing the center; all three had their arms raised to the sky and their heads thrown back, hair hanging to their waists; backs arched, they looked like they were frozen in agony—or ecstasy. Dan hoped it was agony. The dogs lay at their feet, heads on paws; the mutts could've been asleep, but he didn't believe it.

He looked up at the motionless lake of clouds again, and vertigo nearly sent him to his knees. Dan squeezed his lids shut and decided not to look up any fucking more. He walked to the lip and went carefully down the ladder; step off onto the stairs carved out of solid rock, just like Fulbright had said, down and down and down, back and forth and back and forth, and now he was below the canopy; there was no sound except for boot soles scraping slick rock and his huffing breath and his thumping heart.

Dan didn't know what was happening, and he didn't care; he was going to find his wife and his daughter and get them the fuck out, period. And if McFarlane got in his way, he would send him straight to hell.

Dan bared his teeth.

Maybe even if the old man *didn't* get in his way.

Still grinning like a wolf, Dan vanished into the shadows.

Mother's Blood

ETH WAS about to step off the last stone tread when she wrinkled her nose and pulled her boot back; the ground—what she could see of it—was fetid swamp, although a well-worn trail on top of a raised embankment started at the steps and cut through the wide trunks toward the center of the cenote. She thought she could hear a waterfall off to her left; the unnatural gloom apparently suppressed sound as well as sight, but the mist was thicker over there, the sludge deeper and more dangerous, so she was probably right.

She eyed the raised path; at least she wouldn't have to get her boots nasty, but even the dry soil of the levee felt…wrong. Beth carefully extended her awareness, then snapped it back, shuddering; it wasn't just the soil or the smelly bog. *These trees*…the trees thrusting out of this tainted mire were contorted, their broad leaves sickly and spotted, their trunks gashed with wounds that oozed an odd red sap. The forest giants up above had been vibrant, their strength as deep as their roots; these plants were alive, that much could be said for them.

Lizzie pulsed like a star. Beth pointed the Carson toward the middle of the sinkhole and knew that its tip was centered on her daughter. She steeled her resolve, then stepped onto the corrupted loam and pulled her awareness in tight and strode down the path. High above her the song soared, and the tortured trees creaked as they swayed in a sudden roaring wind that rushed up from the center.

Beth moved quickly between the weeping trunks, senses reeled in and knives out. Shadows shifted and flitted. Several times Beth felt certain that someone was standing on the path behind her, but when she whirled, there was no one there; eyes wide, she picked it up to a cautious jog.

Motion to the side; she crouched and peered beneath the diseased boughs, but saw nothing solid, only shadows; another movement, an airy voice whispering her name. Beth's hair tried to stand up as she spun that way, but she still saw only darting shadows.

She turned a slow circle, blades out, breathing in rapid hitches, staring at the shifting shadows that flowed between the distorted trunks.

The shadows stared back.

Beth trembled as she staggered back to her feet, prized balance deserting her, but she leaned and pushed forward. Lizzie. The shades kept pace, closer now, flowing across the path before and behind her; thin voices whispered her name, over and over and over, among other horrors she tried to not hear. She could feel their dreadful hunger, and knew that her hot blood drew them, but they didn't attack.

Instead, the shadows seemed excited, almost overjoyed by her presence; they were… they were *escorting* her.

Terror both of them and what that meant kept her moving, terror and her little girl waiting somewhere ahead, needing her, but until that moment, Beth had never considered how delicate her skin was; that fragile barrier, that thin layer of cells that kept her lifeblood from spilling onto the ground: so weak, so feeble, so easily ripped and punctured, that frail wall separating life and death…

And then Beth stopped, and the whispering, ravenous shadow-hoard halted with her; a deep voice floated through the ailing forest, words pulsing like waves crashing on a faraway beach, the language the same as that shrieking from the three above, rising higher, mounting, her hair whipping as the trees swayed in another sudden gale from the heart of the cenote, diseased leaves ripping free and streaking past her face. The shadows pulled away and milled, airy murmurs frightened now, and then they melted into the deep darkness between the twisted trunks, leaving her alone among the weeping boles.

"Lizzie," Beth whispered.

She sprang forward, fighting the hurricane wind, dodging oozing branches that dangled and swayed across the path. Lizzie. Squinting into the gale, Beth glimpsed a wide clearing ahead, and now only a few misshapen trees separated her from its open space. Lizzie was in there. A sapphire glow emanated from that clearing, bathing everything in an otherworldly radiance.

Blue. Her Daniel had been right about that, too; if she somehow survived this, Beth would never hear the end of it.

Then, with a final resonating shout, the deep voice fell silent and the howling wind died as a wave of foul energy rippled from the clearing, slamming into her like a dark supernova being born. Beth tumbled boneless to the path, went out for a moment, and then came to curled in the fetal position in piles of diseased, desiccated leaves with her back to the blue radiance and her neck muscles corded in a silent scream. To her everlasting shame, Beth knew that if her daughter hadn't been in the center of that awful pulsation she would've already been bounding away through the tortured trees like a deer ahead of a forest fire.

Something had come.

There was no sound, no sound at all, only that blue light and horrifying dread pulsating from the clearing. And Lizzie, but her daughter's star was now muted in the face of…whatever…was in there with her. Lizzie. Beth pushed up to hands and knees, swaying, hair hanging in her face. Lizzie. She lurched to her feet, shaking, sweating, newfound awareness reeling. Lizzie. Beth picked up her knives; the whole world was one vast vault of silence as she pushed herself stumbling toward the clearing.

Lizzie.

Beth stepped out from the last line of trees and stopped when she saw her daughter.

Lizzie was standing at the edge of a wide, flat, circular stone shelf that dominat-ed the center of the huge glade. She was still wearing her retro lavender Powerpuff Girls tee-shirt and green shorts and her red Dora light-up sneakers. Her short legs were scratched and dirty and her hair needed brushing; she stood still with her hands at her sides, eyes closed, as if she were asleep standing up. Mr. Yoda lay curled at her feet, also appearing asleep. The Elmo backpack lay discarded several feet away.

Then Beth saw the blood.

Lizzie had a deep cut on her left forearm, just below the elbow, and crimson streaked her little arm and dripped from her fingers.

Beth's face knotted in a snarl. *Someone will pay for that!*

A man was walking away from Lizzie and toward the stone shelf, a single-edged, heavy-bladed knife gleaming darkly in one hand, a shallow wooden bowl held overhead in the other; his barefoot stride was measured and ritualized, his pace unhurried. He was also naked—or mostly, anyway. A bright-white loincloth covered his privates and wound around to split his buttocks; the cloth was knotted on his right hip. Muscles upon muscles upon muscles rippled beneath strange tattoos covering him from shoulders to feet; they glimmered in the blue light and seemed to writhe beneath his skin with a life of their own. Even his toes were inked; only his face, neck, lower arms, and hands were free of the squirming tattoos. Beth had never met him, but she knew who he was.

John McFarlane.

She also recognized many of those tattoos; they matched the symbols on the megalith in Barron Cemetery.

It seems I owe my husband another apology.

Beth was drawn past McFarlane to the light source that lit the clearing; a tower-ing, shimmering, cobalt dome of force, two hundred feet across and nearly eighty feet high. The dome rested on the shelf, and its curtain of light flowed *up* from the stone, sending ripples to the top and back.

The tattooed man mounted the shelf via three steps rough-carved into its edge and faced the iridescent dome, a tiny dark figure against its shining mass. He presented the bowl with a flourish and placed it at his feet, then prostrated himself and spoke in a language that wasn't meant for human tongue or ears or mind.

Beth gathered herself, then dashed toward Lizzie; McFarlane hadn't noticed her yet and now was her—

A vast silhouette shifted behind the blue light, and she froze like a rabbit as she gaped up and up and up; the ground trembled, and then something spoke. Beth thought the language was the same as McFarlane had uttered, but there the simi-larities ended; if a thunderstorm could talk, it would sound like that, so immense and terrible and powerful that it was more felt in the bones than heard with the eardrums.

And then the regard of something pressed into Beth's mind, something so alien and potent that to understand it would be to go insane; the blue light dimmed in four distinct spots high above her as the dome sparked and wavered. Beth's heart threatened to burst; then the cerulean glow steadied and she let herself breathe again; whatever that thing was, the blue light confined it.

The tattooed man had lifted his forehead from the stone to watch this play out, and the pulsing sapphire glow allowed Beth to catch his stark terror, and then pure relief; it seemed McFarlane didn't want that thing to escape, either. He bounded to his feet and faced her.

"Welcome, my dear! You're right on time." He stepped to the edge of the shelf, leaving the bowl resting on the stone behind him; Beth glimpsed an identical wide yet shallow wooden bowl beside it. The storm rumbled from behind the blue light again, and McFarlane grinned down at her: "My Master greets you as well."

Beth licked dry lips and kept her eyes pinned on McFarlane; if she tried hard enough, she could see the outline of…something…behind that sheeting curtain, but Beth knew if she contemplated that nightmare shape, her mind would not leave the clearing intact. Somehow she also knew that it wasn't trying to harm her; if it wanted, even confined as it was, it could break her without much effort.

Thunder suddenly crashed loud enough to make her skeleton throb, and she had to swallow hard to keep from throwing up in her terror:

It was laughing.

The tattooed man looked back and up, startled. The deafening thunder trailed off, and then the storm rumbled again at normal volume—normal for it. McFarlane faced her once more; glimmering drops of sweat were running out of his iron-gray hair and beading on his forehead.

"My Master says He could crush you without trying, but that is not His wish. We have far greater plans for you, my dear. For your very special little girl, as well."

Beth glanced at her daughter; Lizzie still stood as if asleep on her feet. She also appeared oblivious to the horror before her, and Beth was thankful for that, at least. The tattooed man walked back down the three jagged steps and over to Lizzie and stroked her hair, smiling down at her fondly.

Beth seethed, but she was still at least seventy feet away; she began closing the distance.

"I'm here for Lizzie." Closer. Closer. McFarlane turned that compassionate smile on Beth; with that…that *thing* hulking over his shoulder, a thing he'd called here, a thing contained merely by blue light, he smiled like that! Also, the Tennessee cracker accent he'd had on the phone seemed to have deserted him; tonight he was urbane as a political commentator. Daniel had been right yet again; this moron *was* congenitally insane.

She halted twenty feet away. "I will take her, and if you try to stop me, I will kill you." The dome, and the dreadful shadow beyond, towered above her, now.

That smile became condescending. "No need for threats, dear. Of course you can take her. We require something in return, however."

"What is it?"

"The smallest of favors. The tiniest of boons."

"What do you want from us?"

"Not *us*, my dear. You. We already have what we need from her: hair with intact follicle, breath, saliva, urine, fecal matter. And now…" he held up the heavy black knife; a wet redness gleamed along its razor edge: "Blood."

Rage and fear skittered, but Beth forced herself to speak calmly: "What do you want from me?"

"Isn't it obvious? The Blood of the Mother is needed to set the Binding." He smiled down at Lizzie and stroked her dark hair again: "Once she is Bound to serve my Master, she will be of immense importance to my plans, and through me, His." He suddenly looked up and grinned at her hugely, joyously. Insanely. "Indeed, my Master has confirmed the wonderful news! Rejoice, rejoice! *She is the One!* The One foretold of in our most ancient and secret prophecies! And when she grows into her full power, she will be a force unlike anything this world has ever seen!"

"She's just a little girl! She's not…not what you said."

But McFarlane didn't hear her; he swayed, eyelids fluttering, still grinning hugely as spittle leaked down his chin: "She will subjugate humankind and force them to worship my Master, and with the Balance tipped, He will at last be free to enter this Middle plane unfettered. He will then lead the Lower and Middle against the Upper and bring the Last War to His Father's Golden Gates! We will bring war and woe to Heaven itself! *HE WHO WAS CAST OUT WILL FINALLY GO HOME!*"

Beth's blood froze solid. *He Who Was Cast Out?* Her eyes jerked up to the nightmare silhouette behind the shimmering barrier and then hastily away. *That isn't…! That's not…!* Beth forced herself to breathe, and she tried to shout that what he'd said about Lizzie couldn't be true, *none* of it could be true, but all that came out was a terrified whisper:

"You're mad."

McFarlane gently stroked Lizzie's hair again. "Am I?" Seeing Beth's frightened, sidelong glances at the dome, he said, "Do not fret, my dear. We are blessed with His Holy Presence, yes, but my Master is not, in fact, in physical attendance. Though potent beyond your understanding, what I have summoned and constrained is only…a seeming, if you will, a shadow; a paltry projection of His true might and terror. When the One has triumphed, and He enters this world for true, you will know. *All* will know." He gazed at Beth with a solemn, rapturous expression, but his eyes squirmed more than his tattoos: "Before we go any further, I would like to understand something. Your husband visited our cemetery, and when I asked him why, he said he had found it while 'exploring'. Is that the same explanation he gave you?"

Beth stared, nonplussed; why was he asking about *that?* And why now? Didn't they have bigger things on their plate? She was about to point that out, then noticed how intent the madman was; those wriggling eyes probed, watching. Waiting.

"He told me he found it while riding his bike," Beth said slowly, then added: "At first. Now he remembers Yors Alexandria luring him there with her voice."

"Ah," McFarlane breathed, and Beth tensed; despite that mild response and the benevolent smile still tugging at the corners of his hard, straight-lipped mouth, his gray-green eyes now held pure murder. He raised them slowly until they burned at something on the rim of the cenote high above: "As I suspected. Their feeble attempt to thwart my rise caused me to act before I was ready, though ultimately they have done nothing but speed my inevitable ascent. How that must vex them. Still, their insurrection, pathetic though it may be, will not go unpunished." He dropped that writhing gaze to her again, insane and saintly grin once more cemented in place: "I must apologize for underestimating you, my dear. Scotty was to bring you to me so some of your precious blood could be secured and then kept fresh using the prescribed rites. After that, you were to be discarded."

Hot wrath blazed, but Beth managed a tight smile for him: "Didn't turn out like you expected, did it?"

He laughed. "It did not! And I am grateful, because you showed me my mistake: You are too strong to waste. I have consulted my Master, and He agrees; vow to serve Him freely, faithfully, and you can be part of the glory to come. You may serve at your daughter's side—under my direction, of course."

"Of *course*," Beth said.

His face hardened. "You *both* will serve at my command; for my faithful service, I am to be raised to His Right Hand, and through His will, I will direct the new order to come." He glanced over his shoulder again, and his smile was beatific: "He has promised." McFarlane turned back. "What say you? Will you pledge to serve my Master?"

"Um, I don't think so. Kindly remove your filthy hand from my daughter and step away. I'm taking her out of here, and I'm taking her *right now*."

That smile faltered, and he sighed. "I feared you would adopt this attitude. A lesser covenant, then: give me a tiny portion of your blood and you may walk away with her; only your fresh blood and my Master's blessing are required to set the Binding. Your continued presences are not. You have my word that I will not hinder your leaving." That mad, virtuous grin returned full force as he held up the malevolent black blade: "Only a tiny slice with this, a few drops on the edge, and then you both may go."

All her intuition, old and new, told Beth that McFarlane was lying—or at least not telling the whole truth; her gut also warned that being cut by *that* blade would be a very, very bad idea. She attempted to move around him to Lizzie, and he slid between them.

"None of that now, dear. Your blood, first."

Beth glanced at the knife, then at McFarlane, and then at Lizzie:

"No."

"Then I regret—"

He whirled as a popping and crackling filled the glade; streams of cobalt sparks jumped from the dome as it *bulged* in four places, the bulges once again high above her head. Beth watched this with round eyes. The bulges disappeared, and then the thunder crashed, angry. Did the sheeting blue light look…*dimmer* now? Maybe even *thinner?* Beth profoundly hoped not. McFarlane listened until the thunder faded and then faced her again, and the terror on that deranged face was plain.

"My Master is not pleased with your defiance. I also believe He grows impatient."

"You think?" Beth moved toward Lizzie, and again he shifted to block her.

"As I was saying, I regret what will happen now; you could have been so much more."

Beth dropped into a fighting crouch, but instead of attacking, McFarlane gazed at her intently…she gasped and stiffened; her eyelids fluttered. She was being ridiculous; this was her friend. He had nothing but her and Lizzie's best interests at heart. What was a little blood, anyhow? One prick, and it would be over—no, not over: it would *begin.* This man could be a father to her, a father like she'd never truly had, and a grandfather to Lizzie.

All she had to do was give a little blood.

Was blood so much to ask?

Her knives lowered, and she slumped.

McFarlane stepped forward, dark blade held ready, his smile now one of victory.

What was a little blood?

The core of Beth, her true self, her warrior's heart, stirred: "No," she muttered, shaking her head. "*No!*" She raised her blades, gathered her will, and drove him out of her mind.

McFarlane stopped just out of reach with shock on his face.

Behind him, the unspeakable thing inside the dome chuckled, light thunder booming.

Beth said, "Get out of my way. I'm taking my daughter home."

McFarlane did not move; fury made his blunt features twist and writhe as much as the tattoos. "So," he breathed. "You have embraced what you truly are. The Gift is a powerful instrument, my dear, and only a bare handful of each generation are privileged enough to be born with it. A pity it's being wasted on fools like you and that smart-alecky, foul-mouthed husband of yours, but you produced this miraculous little girl, so I presume your potentials weren't for nothing." He raised the arm that wasn't occupied with the deadly knife, turning it in the cobalt radiance; he seemed fascinated by the symbols squirming under his skin: "I was not so fortunate. There is infinite power in pain and blood, and I was forced to sacrifice much of both for *my* Gift. Some of it was even my *own!*"

On the last word he sprang at her, slashing. Beth was ready, but she still had to roll desperately; instinct told her to keep away from that knife at all cost. She managed to stab the arm that held it, but he only grunted and kept slashing. Beth dodged, giving ground; she should've been much faster than a sixty-something-year-old man, even jacked up on steroids as he apparently was, but she was just barely keeping away. Beth also should have had the advantage with two knives, but she couldn't let his knife touch her; in a normal knife fight, the one who loses the least blood wins, but this was anything but a normal knife fight.

That was underscored as she ducked a slash and stabbed him once in the thigh and once in the kidney, barely dodging a backslash as she rolled away. She came to her feet and McFarlane crouched and gave her a feral grin, eyes wild, writhing tattoos gleaming in the sapphire glow. Blood ran down his thigh and also his ribs, soaking the loincloth, but he didn't seem slowed as he circled to her right, ebon knife probing. Beth circled left, uncertain now; how could she win if her blades had no effect? He sprang forward, incredibly fast, stabbing and slashing, driving her back; she retreated, thinking furiously, desperately:

How?

Almost too late she realized what he was doing; she stopped at the edge of the stone, the flowing light only feet behind her; the ground shook, and blue sparks popped and sizzled over her head. Frantic, Beth dodged as McFarlane rushed her, knife slashing. She rolled away from the shelf and he followed, swinging. She ducked under the arm and stabbed him in the stomach with the Carson, driving it in to the hilt. He grunted, then seized her shoulder and neck with his free hand, pulling her into him. Beth fought, but he was so *strong!* She stabbed him in that arm with her other knife but he ignored it and back-handed her in the face; her head snapped back, stunned, and he slashed her on the left bicep. Blood flew in a red arc to splatter on the dead leaves, and she screamed; that cut *burned*, searing like it was filled with magma.

McFarlane punched her again and wrenched her remaining knife free and threw it to the ground, then seized her by the hair and dragged her stumbling toward the steps, only feet away. Beth pulled her boot knives and stabbed him again and again and again, but he only laughed and took those away while still pulling her stumbling by the hair. She watched the hilt of her Carson jutting and jiggling from his belly in disbelief; as with the wounds in his side and arms and thighs, it bled profusely, but it didn't slow him.

"I only need a few drops, but I think I'll slit your throat over the vessel and let your mite strengthen the Binding. It will be payment for all the trouble you've caused me." He stopped and yanked her head back, forcing her to look up at him, and leered in her face: "Oh, you won't *die*, my dear. Like I said, my Master has plans for you, but I think you will find your new state of existence…troubling."

Beth fought wildly then, punching and kicking, but to her shame he handled her as easily as she would a tantrum from Lizzie; his strength and reflexes were like nothing she'd ever encountered.

She was dragged up the three rough steps and onto the shelf, and Beth discovered with revulsion and horror that not only were there glowing symbols gashed into the stone, but collection channels and runnels as well, leading everywhere in a mind-twisting pattern. Her boots crunched on claret streaks of old crusted blood as she was pulled to the bowl; a viscous dark fluid bubbled and steamed inside. An identical but empty bowl waited beside it.

"That is yours, there. I planned ahead, but it's a shame; if you had agreed to serve Him, it wouldn't have been needed. I believe you will find the process of component collection for your own Binding extremely uncomfortable, my dear, but we all do what we have to do to best serve Him."

The stone trembled as something appalling loomed on the other side of the blue light. McFarlane thrust her head over the bowl with the burbling fluid and pressed the heavy black blade against her jugular.

"Hey asshole!"

Daniel!

McFarlane spun, the blade leaving her throat, and Beth kicked him in the knee; he stumbled sideways and let go of her hair. She scrambled away and turned. Her husband stood in the humus below the edge of the stone shelf, the revolver in his right hand blazing blue fire, little black hole at the end of the barrel pointed at McFarlane's chest. In his left arm he cradled Lizzie; her head rested on his shoulder, little arms dangling, eyes closed, still asleep.

"*YOU!*" McFarlane roared.

"Miss me? Nice diaper. Oh, by the way, fuck you."

Daniel shot him in the heart, the report booming through the clearing. Mc-Farlane staggered back one step, and then stopped, his bare heel just brushing the dome of coruscating sapphire light. A gleeful smile grew on his face, and he took a calm step forward again. Daniel cursed roundly, then shot him again. McFarlane ignored the second hole in the center of his chest and made a grasping, twisting gesture; her husband cried out and dropped the gun.

Beth stared in mute shock; two bullets to the heart. They oozed rivulets of blood down his tattooed chest and stomach, staining the loincloth anew, but he disregarded them as easily as he ignored her knife, the hilt of which still jutted obscenely out of his belly button.

McFarlane threw back his head and laughed; the stone juddered, and behind him a monstrous silhouette grew, towering on the other side of the blue light.

"You are too late, fool! *I still win!*" He flicked the black knife at the bowl with the bubbling goo, and Beth's blood flew, several drops spattering inside; it immediately roiled faster while smoking and glowing a fiery red.

"*NO!*" Beth screamed.

Lizzie convulsed in Daniel's arms.

Her husband, who had bent and snatched up his pistol, dropped it again because he had to hold Lizzie with both hands; she was thrashing as if in the throes of a terrible seizure. "What's wrong with her?"

McFarlane laughed again, the sick sound of triumph, and Beth snapped. Shrieking incoherently, she threw herself at him and punched him in the face. Still laughing, he tried to fend her off with his black blade, but she trapped his knife arm and snapped a kick into his stomach, and her boot sole drove her Carson all the way in.

McFarlane stopped laughing; his eyes widened, and his mouth made a little o of surprise. Beth spun and drove her heel into his raw, red belly, and he stepped back again…only one, long step, just like before, but he was so close to the light that this time his right leg crossed the line of sheeting blue radiance, disappearing up to his tattooed knee.

Beth dove from the edge and rolled to her feet and spun around and looked while backing hurriedly away, and what she witnessed up on that wide stone shelf would haunt her nightmares for the rest of her life.

That hulking mass of darkness loomed behind McFarlane. Horrified understanding twisted his face just as a hand the size of a Volkswagen pushed through the compromised barrier. It had a clawed thumb and three multi-jointed, clawed fingers longer than Beth was tall. Each hooked claw was easily a foot long and tapered to a needle point. The skin and claws were both the color of the deep space found between stars. Black on black blisters bubbled where the cobalt light touched the hand, and foul smoke hissed, choking Beth.

That dreadful hand closed on McFarlane almost gently.

"No! *Master, please no! You promised!*"

The hand jerked him through the light. There was complete silence for all of a heartbeat, and then the screaming began. Beth heard answering screams from high above, on the rim of the sinkhole. Women's screams. Pain-filled howls rose, accompanying the screams. And then hideous laughter boomed, drowning out the screams.

Sick from the fetid blister smoke and nearly insane with fear, Beth ran to her family. Daniel stood with his arms around Lizzie, staring up at the dome, shaking his head so hard in negation that his short hair flailed and the night-vision goggles flew from his face. Beneath them his eyes were as big as coffee mugs, and he was mouthing *no, no, no.*

Beth snatched her daughter from him.

Lizzie.

"Mommy's got you, baby. Mommy's here." Her eyes were still closed and her small body trembled and jerked, but the worst of the seizure seemed to be over.

What did they do to my daughter?

What have they DONE?

The shrieking behind the light became tortured-animal squeals, and Beth wanted to cover her ears. Above them on the rim, three voices were suddenly raised in a ragged, desperate song, not nearly as beautiful as before, and wind rushed *into* the cenote as the dome zapped and crackled and wavered and pulsed, throwing a riot of blue shadows across her husband's slack face as he gaped up at it.

Beth shoved him, and he looked at her dazedly.

"Get Mr. Yoda!"

He snatched his pistol up again and the goggles too, then stumbled over and scooped up the dog and the Elmo backpack. Beth ran into the twisted trees, fighting the gale now blasting toward the center of the sinkhole, Lizzie cradled against her shoulder. Daniel sprinted after them, almost stepping on her heels as the pitiful screams and the thundering, maniacal laughter began to fade into some unimaginable distance.

They ran faster.

Book VI

The Reaping

One Question

ONE FUCKING question; that's all I have, really.

Beth yelled from out on the hotel's walkway: "The taxi's here!"

"Yay! Mr. Yoda, you get to ride on the airplane with us!"

Mr. Yoda barked, keyed up because Lizzie was keyed up, but the little shit didn't have the first clue that he would be stowed in the plane's belly, and thus would be deprived of the dubious joys of airplane food and of being squeezed into coach between wailing babies and rejects from the Biggest Loser; Dan figured the dog had it better.

Just one question…all right, that's not true. Dan at least had to be honest in his own head. *I have a thousand questions, and nine hundred and ninety-nine are about that insane night in the sinkhole, but one or a thousand, it doesn't look like I'm getting answers any goddamn time soon.*

Lizzie skipped into the suite's bedroom, interrupting Dan's sour musings. "The taxi's here, Daddy!" Mr. Yoda trotted at her heels, new collar jingling.

"So I hear." He zipped the suitcase shut and glanced around one more time, but Dan understood that no matter how hard he looked, he was bound to forget some damn thing; it was inevitable after ten weeks plus in a hotel. He gave up and smiled down at his five-year-old daughter. "Are you excited?"

"Yeah! Flying will be *so cool!*" She stuck her arms out and zoomed around the bed, making jet noises through pursed lips.

Mr. Yoda sat down and watched her, head cocked; after nearly three months of Lizzie's dynamic acquaintance, the mutt had embraced the wisdom of personal energy conservation. He caught Dan looking and gifted him with a toothy snarl, then went back to watching Lizzie.

"Fuck you," Dan whispered, flipping him a discrete bird. The little turd only growled sideways, then gave a doggy snort that seemed to dismiss Dan utterly and went back to watching Lizzie swoop.

Dan shook his head. Mr. Yoda had woken up meaner than hell after that crazy night in the sinkhole. He now tried to bite everyone that came near Lizzie, although most people laughed it off; it was a good thing he was so tiny or Dan doubted they'd find it amusing. Mr. Yoda sure as shit didn't tolerate *him* anymore, though the little fucker still liked Beth, for some reason; tell the truth, Dan's little family's status quo had changed in a heap o' ways since that wild night, and living in a hotel and the hairball's shitty new attitude were the least of the transformations.

Dan had called Irene and quit his job that next Monday morning, giving all his listings to a very surprised Steve (those that would sign with him; most had) so Dan could stay with Lizzie while Beth was at work. Lizzie hadn't been back to daycare, either. She had also been sleeping in the same bed as them, even though this extended-stay suite had two bedrooms.

To put it another way, Dan hadn't let his daughter out of his sight for a single goddamn millisecond.

And his job situation wasn't the only one in flux. Beth had slipped into her office after lunch rush that next Tuesday and called Eddie's best boy Clint Jennings and told him she wanted to run the new store that was about to open in California; Dan didn't know if she'd come right out and told Clint that if he didn't give it to her she would quit, but he figured it was implied.

Two weeks later it was official; Beth would run the first Slo Eddie's west of the Mississippi—the largest and most expensive Slo Eddie's, as well—and Terrance would take over the Murf store. Three weeks after that, they'd packed up Beth's car and headed west on I-40 to sun-drenched Cali to look at houses, and so his wife could survey her new fiefdom.

Shockingly (to Dan, anyhow) it had been an easy trip, with no hassles beyond the expected when you crammed three stubborn people and a vicious little mutt into a car for three days. Dan had even belted out the Marty Moose song once a day to keep spirits up; well, okay, five or six times a day. Beth got the joke, but didn't think it was funny—especially by the third day. Lizzie didn't get it, too young, but she thought the song was *hil-arious*. Dan taught her the lyrics. His lovely wife hadn't been exactly thrilled with that either, but hey, ya can't please everybody.

Then they'd arrived in radiant San Bernardino, the armpit of Southern California, although the new Slo Eddie's wasn't in San Berdo, not even close. The spanking-new flagship of the Slo Eddie's chain was in Santa Monica, on the coast if not right on the beach, and also two minutes from the front gate of the University of California Santa Monica. Dan was looking forward to the catch of servers Beth would net from *that* deep pool, yes indeed, but after thirty seconds of checking out Santa Monica real-estate prices on the web, they'd determined there was no way they would be able to afford to live near the restaurant—ever—so dusty, not-so-lovely San Bernardino it was.

But hey, San Berdo was only an hour and a half from the beach with good traffic, which meant it was two and a half because there was never good traffic in L.A. Beth would have a shit commute, to say the least, but with the money she would make, it was worth it—especially since Dan didn't have to drive it.

The second day out they'd gotten pre-approved at the local branch of a multi-national mega-bank (no more fucking small, psycho-farmer-owned banks for them, thank you very much), and then made an offer on the third house they'd toured, a single-story four-bed two-hole on a cul-de-sac in a neighborhood that until five years ago had been a heavily irrigated avocado grove. Their shiny new subdivision had been thrown up during the boom times, but with the mortgage crisis and foreclosure mess still hitting hard in South Cali, every fifth house had had a For-Sale sign planted in its sandy front yard; their low-ball offer had been accepted the next day. The new Ranchero-style Casa Sims was about half the size of the castle—in other words, just what they'd always wanted. On a whim, Dan had even applied at a San Berdo GMC dealership he'd seen a help wanted posting for on Craig's List and was hired on the spot. He started next Wednesday.

Dan was content with selling cars again, for now; eventually he would go through all the bullshit to transfer his license (real estate was where the Benjamins were, after all), but he figured it would be two years at least until a man could make real money selling houses in California; he'd had enough of battling banks over short sales to last him a fucking lifetime. Meanwhile, he would put in his due diligence while peddling Chevy's and prepare to plunge back into the mix.

Watch out, Greater So Cal Real-Estate Market! Here come Dan, da Listin' n' Sellin' Man!

Beth popped in the doorway: "Earth to family! The cab is here, it's time to go! Why isn't Mr. Yoda in the carrier? Lizzie, get that dog in his cage!"

"Yes, ma'am! C'mon, Mr. Yoda, we're gonna fly to our new house!" Lizzie picked him up and scooted out, and Dan couldn't help but note Mr. Yoda's lack of enthusiasm; the little guy wasn't too fond of that pet taxi.

Good.

As Lizzie ran by, Beth reached down and brushed her fingers across the silver streak that was growing into their daughter's dark hair, just over her right temple.

That streak wasn't gray, and it wasn't white; that streak was pure silver. It had only been a few gleaming chrome strands at first, but now that shiny band was nearly four-inches long and an inch thick; at that rate, it would be all the way through her hair within half a year. Beth often touched that vein of silver anxiously, but as far as Dan could tell, Lizzie paid zero attention to it.

To her, it was as if the streak had always been there.

When Lizzie was gone, Beth let her hand fall, and then raised her eyes slowly to his. They stood there looking at each other as, out in the living area, their daughter attempted to coax her dog into his mobile prison cell.

I dreamt about that silver streak, he wanted to inform his wife but sure as fuck didn't. *I had a* dream *about something happening BEFORE it fucking happened! Why? How, for God's sake?*

Now *there* were two great questions—but, like all the others, Dan knew he wouldn't get any answers. *Not from Beth, that's for sure.* Still, Dan wanted to ask, *so* wanted to ask, but he wasn't going to, and the reason was standing there staring up at him with those big, gorgeous, frightened, furious eyes.

Beth didn't want to talk about that night in the sinkhole. Beth didn't want to talk about the chrome band growing in their daughter's hair. Beth wanted to pretend the whole thing had never happened, although after what they'd seen and gone through, Dan didn't understand how that would ever be even remotely possible.

Oh, he had *tried* to talk to her about it. Once. "The Talk", as Dan had come to refer to the event in his head, although "The Talk" was a grand label for something that had lasted less than two minutes and had comprised only four questions, two answers, one non-answer, and two outright lies.

"The Talk" occurred exactly one week after they'd snatched their daughter back, on a humid mid-August Sunday night. She'd finally given in to his pestering and they'd put Lizzie and Mr. Yoda to bed, and when those two perpetual motion machines were asleep, they'd retreated to the suite's spare bedroom. Dan had opened with this salvo:

"So how the fuck did you superglue me to the ground that night?"

"It," she replied, stone-faced.

"It." Beth nodded. Dan waited, and when he realized nothing else was forthcoming he said, "What the fuck is 'it'?"

Her face had grown even tighter, and she'd crossed her arms beneath those breasts, but she'd eventually answered; Dan hadn't been sure she would. "It doesn't matter what 'it' is, Daniel, because I will never use 'it' again. It's faded since that night, anyway—and besides, I refuse to be like *them!*"

Them.

Now *there* was something Dan understood, although knowing didn't bring comfort—he'd been standing right beside her when all that shit about "sisters" had been flying around, and he didn't like it now any more than he had then—but just when he was about to inquire further, she'd drawn a question from her own pile and smacked him upside the head with it.

"How did you get free? You shouldn't have been able to."

Well, Dan wasn't about to bring up the Keeper or their bargain, that's for ever-fucking sure, so he supposed he was the one who'd started the lying—but it was only a *little* lie when he'd said, "I just broke free, that's all." *I would have eventually;* she *even said so.* Beth had then hit him with the Super Squint, so he'd hastily thrown out another pile-dweller to distract her: "What were you and McFarlane talking about?"

"We never talked about anything."

Dan had been so astounded by the bald-faced lie he was struck speechless; eventually he'd spluttered, "Beth, I got there right before you two started trying to kill each other, and I could *hear* you talking. I couldn't make out what you were saying, you were too far away, but I know I—"

"You must have been imagining it, Daniel. We never talked about a thing." Beth lied calmly, but steam should have been rising from those hot brown eyes. And then she'd contradicted herself by stating, "It doesn't matter what he said. She's just a little girl."

Just a little girl...

That innocent phrase had sent chills up his back, for some reason, still did, but the fact that his wife was standing there lying to his face left Dan so flabbergasted that he'd blurted, "Then I guess I was also *imagining* that giant fucking hand, right?"

She had turned and stared at the wall then, winding even tighter, but she'd answered through clenched teeth: "No. I saw it, too."

Dan should have heeded the warning signs and dropped it, but he was righteously teed-off by that point so he began flinging Q's from the P willy-nilly: "Okay, then—and if I wasn't *imagining* them as well—what the fuck was the deal with McFarlane's twisty new tattoos, or the twin salad bowls? And why was one of them smoking? And what was all that crap there at the end about 'Too late' and 'I win' supposed to mean? And why did Lizzie have a fit when he slung your blood into the—"

And that's when Beth blew sky high.

She began shrieking that Lizzie was *fine*, she was just *fine*, that *they* hadn't gotten what they wanted, that she and Dan had been in time to stop it, and that she didn't want to hear another word about that night ever again or she would take Lizzie and leave him on the spot. She had even pulled that new knife on him!

By that point Dan had been judiciously retreating into the living room and Lizzie was up and crying and Mr. Yoda was raising hell and Abdullah the hotel manager was pounding on the door, saying he'd gotten complaints from the other guests and if they didn't quiet down, he would call the police.

And as for "The Talk"?

That, as they say, was that.

Another Q from the Great Big Fucking P: *What did they say to each other?* It was maybe *the* vital question, but not THE question. *Vital or not, I doubt I'll get an A soon, not with B the way she is now.*

Dan would never accuse his brave, stubborn-to-a-fault wife of running from anything, not after hearing her history, but since that night there had been no more talk of press conferences, or justice for Scandlin and Brennan and Professor Hameed, or any of the missing. She had even deleted Vivian and Chuck from her phone, and then she'd trashed all the pics of the cemetery's headstones. He had watched her do it.

Already gone.

That summed up Beth, now. Already gone to California; already gone from this great state of Tennessee; she had even moved on from Helen. The old woman had tried to call Beth for days and days until finally calling Dan's cell, but Beth refused to talk to her onetime friend even then, or let Lizzie talk to her, and going for a visit was right the fuck out, though Lizzie must have asked two-dozen times if she could go play with Jacob and feed carrots to Butterball and Skipper. Beth just told her that Helen was sick and wasn't up for visitors. Lizzie had been disappointed, but being five, she'd soon found other distractions.

Dan had cautiously asked her if she thought Helen had had something to do with Lizzie's abduction, and her answer had been slow in forming, but Beth eventually said no, she didn't think so, but she *did* think Helen knew more than she'd let on, and she was *sure* the old woman could have warned them about McFarlane, but hadn't.

In Beth's book, that got you a strike, and in a game where kidnapping Lizzie was a move, one strike and you were out.

So Beth was most assuredly shunt of Helen. The only thing she seemed to regret leaving was Takamatsu Sensei and his dojo, but she'd already checked out a new Aikijutsu dojo in Riverside and proclaimed it adequate, so even *that* didn't seem to bother her much. In fact, if his lovely, angry wife wasn't standing there looking up at him, Dan would've said that Beth had left over ten weeks ago.

She's running.

More than that, she's running scared.

What did they say to each other down there?

A horn honked outside. They were still just standing there looking at each other, so Dan hid his unease as best he could and gathered her into his arms, just like he had three days ago when he'd found her crying in the bathroom after she'd tried and failed to dye that silver stripe out of Lizzie's hair for the twelfth time; dye wouldn't touch that thing. It just sloughed right off.

Beth burrowed her face into his chest. Dan said, "She'll be all right. We'll make sure of it."

She nodded, and then pushed away, sniffling and wiping her cheeks before tilting her head back and fixing him with those big, scary eyes: "I want you to promise me you'll be careful out there."

Dan checked a sigh: *Out there.* She wouldn't even joke around and call it the castle anymore; and "home" was out of the fucking question; a few weeks back he'd made the mistake of mentioning her "This is My Home" speech, but he hadn't been dumb enough to bring it up again.

"I'm just boxing our crap for the movers," he said, trying to keep the overt patience out of his voice; she knew all this, but evidently she needed to hear it again. "They'll be there by four, do their thing, and then we're outta there, babe. I'm not going anywhere near…you know."

"I know." She looked away quickly.

Dan watched her, troubled; even a *hint* of that night did this: "I'll be okay," he told her. "Honest injun." He dredged out a grin when she hesitantly looked up at him again: "And besides, I should worry about you guys. Remember that story we saw the other day, the one about America's aging fleet of planes? Seriously, what if some gas jockey is hungover and forgets to fuel the thing, or some wrench monkey doesn't tighten a bolt? Flying is dangerous shit."

Beth gripped his shirt with both small fists: "*Promise me you'll be careful out there!*"

He sighed. "I promise."

"Thank you." Then she pulled him into a kiss, the kind that made Dan wish the cab wasn't waiting and that Lizzie was down for a nap. A long nap. A real Rip-Van-Winkle snoozer. Then their daughter appeared in the doorway. She giggled.

They broke the kiss and looked at her, and she came over without a word and wrapped her arms around their legs. Dan squatted and picked her up, and then they all just stood there holding each other until the horn honked again.

Dan put Lizzie down and turned to get the suitcase from the bed, wiping his eyes and composing himself, then grabbed it and followed them into the tiny living room, where he hoisted the dog's crate by the handle. Mr. Yoda growled. *Nasty little fucker.* Beth picked up her carry-on and Lizzie's suitcase, and Lizzie got her new Dora backpack; all the important stuff was in that canary-yellow backpack, stuff like Mr. Fred and her three favorite horsies and two of her favorite Dora stories and her *Sesame Street* coloring book and her markers, and of course her New New *Star Wars* movie.

Lizzie had received *Return of the Jedi* for her birthday in September, and she'd watched it approximately seventeen thousand four hundred and sixty-three times in the last five weeks. The astounding thing was, Beth had bought it for her. Dan still had trouble wrapping his brain around that; it had also created something of a dilemma in the Sims' household. Pre-*Return*, Lizzie had been set on dressing as Princess Leia for Halloween; now she waffled between Leia and an Ewok. Yesterday it was Ewok; the day before was Leia. Maybe tomorrow she would ditch both and choose Boba Fett, a *mucho* better pick in Dan's humble opinion. Whatever the swings, he was putting a marker down on Leia; Ewoks were cute, sure, but what five-year-old little girl would pass up the chance to be a space princess?

Dan followed his girls out the door and along the second-story railed walk and down the steps and out into the parking lot to the waiting taxi. He shot the guy a look, but the horn-happy fat bastard didn't notice while fiddling with his radio. The trunk popped, and they crammed everything in except the dog.

And then it was time.

Dan received copious smooches topped by a great big juicy hug; he tried to make the hug last, but Lizzie began squirming so he put her down and she opened the back door, snatched up the pet crate—Mr. Yoda sloshing around and whining, Dan was glad to note—and used both hands to muscle it into the middle of the back seat. She scrambled in and shut the door, then turned and smiled at him through the glass; the M-shaped gap in her grille and the silver splash in her hair and the white knife-scar on her little arm were all vivid in the strong October morning sunshine.

"Bye Daddy!" She waved. "Love you!"

Dan fought the enormous lump in his throat that was doing its best to choke him. "Love you too, pumpkin! Be good for your Mommy!"

"I will!"

"Call me and let me know how the plane ride was!"

That grin got bigger, somehow, and she bounced in her seat. "I will! C'mon, Mommy, let's go!"

"I'm coming. Hold your horses, little miss." Then Beth stepped into his arms, and Dan found himself the lucky recipient of premium, Grade-A smooches and another hug. "Remember," she mumbled to his chest. "You promised."

"I remember. And it's only two days. Two days, we'll all be together again."

She looked up at him, heart-shaped face full of fear, then bit her lower lip and nodded and snatched him into another hug; this one made his ribs creak before she released him and went around the back of the taxi and opened the door, then stood there looking at Dan over the roof.

"Two days?"

"Two days."

"Promise?"

"I promise."

"Come *on*, Mommy!"

A nippy breeze that blended diesel fumes from the nearby interstate with the sharp scent of dying leaves blew strands of dark hair across Beth's face, and she used her fingers to tuck them behind an ear; her mahogany eyes were anxious, and intent on his. "We have a three-hour layover in Phoenix. We'll call you then, and you *better* answer."

"Sounds like a plan. We should just be hitting the road by then."

She scowled. "You're driving my car, right? Don't trust some moving goon with it."

"Yes, dear. One of them will drive my truck, and I'll drive your car. Just like we planned."

"Don't take that tone with me! I'm only—"

"*Mommy!*"

The front-passenger window abruptly rolled down, and the cabbie leaned his bulk over the console to peer up at Dan; his spotted pate gleamed in the sun, and that expression said he'd seen a thousand of these touching moments and wasn't impressed with yet another. "Hey, folks, couldya speed it up? I got another—"

Dan bent and thrust his head and shoulders in the window, and the fat man blinked at him from a foot away; the interior was redolent with cigarettes, peanuts, and cheap aftershave. Beth would love it. "We'll be just a minute. I'm saying goodbye to my wife. You don't mind waiting while I say goodbye to my wife, do you?"

From the back came a giggle, and then Lizzie stuck her adorable little mug up between the seats. "Hi Daddy!"

"Hi, baby."

Dan turned back to the cabbie—who had this *look*, you know, like he reeeaaally wanted to say something—but then he took a good, long gander at Dan's smiling face and swallowed whatever it was and wedged his gut back behind the tilted steering wheel. "Sure," he mumbled, not looking at Dan. "I'll wait."

"Thanks, pal." Dan faced his daughter. "Gimme smooches!"

Lizzie giggled again and gave him a kiss.

"Love you, sweet pea."

"Love you too, Daddy."

Dan pulled his head out and was greeted with the full-bore browns across the roof; both barrels.

"What?"

Beth rolled those eyes and shook her head, but then he got a wry smile.
Score one for Dan-o.

"I love you."

"Love you too, beautiful."

Then she climbed in and shut the door and the grimy white four-door Mercury pulled away, both of his girls looking out the wide back glass at him and waving. Lizzie was smiling. Beth wasn't. Dan waved back as they turned out of the parking lot; even then he thought they were still waving, but it was hard to tell through the waterfall that had sheeted his vision.

And then they were gone.

Dan stood there for a time, blinking at the traffic on the feeder road, listening to the steady roar of the interstate beyond, and then he trudged back up to their suite. He needed to hustle out to the castle and get cracking on the packing, but *first* he needed to check out and get his goddamn pet deposit back. *Two hundred motherfucking dollars,* he had *better* get it back, or Abdullah at the front desk was going to have a major fucking problem, and its name was Daniel Terrance Sims.

Up in the room he got a clean piece of sandpaper otherwise known as a hotel washcloth and wet it and scoured his face, then used a wad of toilet paper to blow his nose. He stood straight and looked at himself in the bathroom mirror. *Two days, Danny boy, that's all.* He could handle two days away from his girls. *Barely.* Beth and Lizzie would be safe and sound in their new house in San Berdo by dinnertime today, what with the time flux caused by zipping west across the sky. He and the movers would convoy straight through to Albuquerque tonight and tomorrow morning, crash for a few hours tomorrow afternoon, and then push through tomorrow night into the next day and evening. It would suck, and he would be wiped when Beth wanted him to unpack and arrange her goddamn furniture just so, but it would be worth it.

But first Dan had to go *out there* and get their shit packed, loaded, and on the road.

He took a last careful look around for anything they'd forgotten or stains that would cost him his deposit and then grabbed his keys and loaded his stuff in the Toyota and then walked over to the front office, opened the glass door, and stepped in.

The manager had his back to the door but turned at the ding, the metallic-orange turban piled on his head and the glittery yellow dashiki hanging off his narrow shoulders making him look like an exotic bird that had fallen out of its cage: *Abdullah, my new buddy.* When he saw Dan, brilliant white teeth flashed in a silky black beard as cool black eyes regarded him over the up-swept Mario mustache hovering above the beard; the silly thing looked like it was trying to fly away. It probably was.

"Mr. Sims! Am I to understand that it is checkout time, yes?"

"You bet your turban it is. I want my deposit back."

Abdullah showed him more white teeth; the eyes never changed. "But first I must inspect, yes? Those animals, they are messy. Perhaps there is damage?"

"There's no damage, Mr. Abdullah, but let's get this over with. I've got things to do."

"Ahhhh, of course, I will inspect immediately." The unctuous man came around the counter, hands folded at his waist. "Please make yourself comfortable. Perhaps you will partake of our free continental breakfast and coffee while you wait, yes?"

Dan didn't bother to glance over at the "free" breakfast going stale by the ancient coffee pot; cinnamon rolls as hard as a mortgage broker's heart and bananas more brown than yellow didn't interest him, and you could soak a four-barrel carburetor in that coffee for two minutes and it would come out sparkling.

"No thanks."

"Then please have patience while I—"

"I'm going with you." Dan opened the glass door and held it for the colorful man.

The teeth vanished. "I am fearful that I cannot allow you to—"

"I don't care what you think you can *allow* me to do, Mr. Abdullah, I will be there while you inspect our room. I want *all* of my deposit back." Dan then gifted him with the same smile with which he had blessed the cabbie.

Abdullah was made of sterner stuff, however. "I see." Cold. No teeth. "Very well, then."

Dan followed him up the stairs hanging off the front of the hotel and around the walk to their door, and there the turbaned man paused: "Has anyone ever informed you that you are an extremely rude man, Mr. Sims?"

"They've informed me. Open the fucking door and start inspecting. I don't have time for your bullshit."

Abdullah harrumphed and used his card and swished inside with his chin raised so high the points of his mustache almost poked holes in the ceiling.

Dan was about to follow when he hesitated, then pulled out his phone and woke it up and stared down at the face that filled the screen:

Beth.

When he'd taken this close-up portrait back in March, seven months ago, a lifetime ago, he'd told her it would be the wallpaper on his cool new phone, so she'd issued him her come-fuck-me look, knowing it would torment him every day.

So many questions lying around in the Big Unanswered Question Pile, but there was one that Dan couldn't get out of his mind, one that haunted him more than what Beth was hiding about her conversation with the new and not-so-improved McFarlane or *why* she was hiding it from him or the fact that he was somehow having prescient dreams or hideous booming laughter or nightmare giant smoking hands or glowing-green eyes or just what the hell that weird smelly bitch Keeper would want for helping him or even monstrous nightmare obscenities half-glimpsed behind wavering blue light; one question that kept him from enjoying a good night's sleep for over two months; one question that Dan asked himself over and over as he studied Beth out of the corner of his eye across Lizzie's head as they sat on the cheap hotel couch and watched *Return of the Jedi* for the sixteen thousand four hundred and twenty-second time.

One fucking question:

What in God's name did I marry?

He dragged his eyes away from her and glanced up into the endless October sky, even though he knew his girls weren't up there yet. "Be safe," he whispered, then stuffed his phone back and walked into the suite that had been their home for over ten weeks, determined to go to the mat with this Sikh ass-wipe for every goddamn *bit* of his deposit.

Dan could already tell it was going to be a long fucking day.

Manipulation

DAN WAS brooding on yet another question—the timeless mystery of why women needed so many goddamn shoes—when Artoo blooped and warbled from his pocket.

He grunted as he sat the two-ton cardboard box of footwear at the head of the castle's sweeping staircase, then wiped his face with a sleeve before pulling the phone out; it was the moving company's main office. He checked the time; just after two-thirty. The truck wasn't supposed to arrive until four. *Maybe they've decided to gift me with an early Christmas present and send someone early.*

Sure.

Dan made his voice bright and eager; positive reinforcement, baby. "Hell-ooo!"

"Ah, Mr. Sims?"

"Speaking!"

"This is Mike Rawls with Briscoe Moving. How are you today, sir?"

"I'm fantastic, Mike, how are you?"

"Good, sir. Mr. Sims, I'm calling to—"

"Let me guess, the GPS satellite exploded and your guys need directions?"

"Um, no sir, I'm calling to let you know there's been a mechanical problem with the truck assigned to your move."

"Of course there has."

"Sir?"

Dan sighed and melted down the stairs; the castle's power was off, so no air and no fridge, but Teresa Sims' youngest boy was no fool; he'd stopped on the way and now his big green-and-white Coleman sat on the kitchen island, brim full of ice with a six-pack of Shiner nestled amongst the gleaming cubes. He'd been saving them for a last toast to the castle, but this suddenly seemed like a pretty goddamn good time to crack one. "So assign me another truck, Mike. You do have more than one, right?"

"Yes, sir, but unfortunately they're all engaged with other clients."

"Don't you have backup trucks or something?"

"Yes, sir, but those have also been pressed into service. We're extremely busy at this time, Mr. Sims, but rest assured Briscoe will…"

Dan flung the Coleman open and grabbed a Shiner and twisted the cap and took a long pull; icy water ran down his fist and forearm and dripped from his elbow. A little breeze and a whole lotta sunlight streamed through the chocked-open, triple-pane kitchen windows; outside those drape-less and blind-less windows, small birds twittered and fiddle-farted their way through a warm October afternoon.

Upper sixties Dan's ass—it had to be near eighty out there, and by extension inside. *Forget real estate, I should've been a meteorologist. That way I could be wrong all the time and still keep my fucking job.*

Mike was still blathering about how sorry he was: "Just tell me when you can get a crew here," Dan cut in, and then took another pull. *Damn, that's good.*

He heard taps on a keyboard: "It looks like the soonest is ten o'clock tomorrow morning. Oops, make that eleven."

"Eleven o'clock *tomorrow fucking morning?* Tell me that's not what you just said, Mike."

There was this little silence; when he answered, Mike's voice had mislaid its repentant tone somewhere. "Yes, sir, that's what I said."

"I should've rented a goddamn U-Haul and moved myself!"

"If you would like to cancel service, I am authorized to give you a full refund, Mr. Sims. And once again I would like to apologize on behalf of Briscoe—"

"*Shit!* Hold on, hold on, just let me think a second." Dan downed half the beer, then fought the urge to throw the bottle through a window and into the backyard and freak those cheerful goddamn birds out; it wasn't *his* window anymore—or backyard, for that matter. Steve had sold the castle in just forty-seven days, and no surprise; after Scotty Rison's visit, the place was infamous as well as gorgeous.

"Mr. Sims?"

"I'm still thinking, Mike. Surely you're familiar with the process?"

Mike didn't reply, and Dan got the impression that his RSVP to Mike's next barbecue had just gotten lost in the mail. He downed the rest of the Shiner, set the empty on the island, adjusted the .45 where it hung on his hip, and fished out another beer. *What are my chances of finding another mover this late?* Somewhere between nil and zero, Dan knew; in other words, Briscoe had him over the barrel with his pants tangled around his ankles and the splintery old broom handle poised.

"You can *guarantee* eleven, right Mike? You won't call me at seven and tell me the truck flew off into the blue sky and it'll be five o'clock the next fucking day before I can get another one, will you?"

"I can't guarantee eleven, Mr. Sims." Apologetic be damned; positively frosty now, was Mike. "But as of this moment, my computer is showing that another vehicle in our fleet is scheduled to be returned in the morning, and after an inspection and some minor maintenance for the trip you have planned, we'll send it and a team out there to get you moved."

"Out fucking standing, Mike."

"Mr. Sims, once again let me apologize for—"

"Hey, shit happens, right Mike? I'm not sweating it. In fact, I'm feeling so good about everything I've decided to do you a favor."

"Sir?"

"I know this lady, see, and I'll give her your name and number. You're a lucky guy, Mike. She's a bona fide knockout. Friendly as all get out, too. You'll like her."

"Sir, I—"

"This nice lady expects me to be at our new house in California the day after tomorrow with all her shoes—and she's got a shit-ton of shoes, Mike—and her clothes, and our daughter's clothes, and her furniture, but now that won't happen."

"Sir, on behalf of Briscoe—"

"Save it for her, Mike. You think *I'm* fun? Just wait."

"I—"

"Gotta go, Mike, got packin' ta do. Oh, and one more thing."

"Yes, sir?" Wary.

"You can forget about any goddamn testimonials. Have a great fucking day, Mike." Dan hung up. "*FUUUCK!*" He took a long drink of his fresh beer, pressed the icy bottle to his forehead, and closed his eyes.

Oh, man, Beth's not gonna like this…

A Teensy-Weensy Fib

Beth held Lizzie's hand as they hurried across Terminal Two of Phoenix's Sky Harbor International Airport. Her temper was a live, sparking wire because her carry-on and purse were slung over one shoulder, doubled-up straps cutting a cruel groove into her trap. She also had to pee so bad her tonsils were floating; a favorite maxim of her husband's that made Beth miss him even more and reminded her of the real reason she wanted to bite someone:

Daniel was *out there.*

It wasn't the house that had her upset, but *that place* just down the road. And *those people.* Beth forced herself to stop obsessing about it; someone had to get their stuff, and there was no way she and Lizzie were going anywhere near that place ever again; when Daniel had driven her car out there yesterday and put it in the garage, he had wanted her to come get him in his truck, but she had made him catch a ride back with Steve.

Daniel won't be there long, and he took his precious guns. The movers should already be there, too, busy loading her things into the semi—and they had better be doing it *gently.*

Everything was fine. Daniel was fine. Beth repeated it in her head like a mantra: *Daniel's fine, everything's okay, Daniel's okay…*

She felt naked without even a single knife; stupid airport rules.

Now that they'd landed, Beth itched to call and check on her husband, but first she had complete idiocy to deal with; they'd been informed in Nashville that they would need to claim and then recheck their luggage when they got to Phoenix. She didn't understand why the airline couldn't just switch their stuff onto the new plane, like they would (hopefully) do with Mr. Yoda's crate, but there you go: stupidity at its finest. They weren't changing carriers, so they didn't have to change terminals—although Beth was sure Lizzie would have loved the ride on the tram—but she still had to get her own stupid luggage and make sure it got on the new stupid plane! Beth ground her teeth; she was fast growing a headache to compliment the throbbing in her shoulder and bladder.

"Wow! Look, Mommy!"

"I see, baby."

That was a lie. She had no idea what Lizzie was exclaiming over now; it was the eighth time in five minutes she'd "wowed" about something. Beth tugged her hand to get her to walk faster, but she hung back, rubbernecking with wide blue eyes under the brim of her new pink baseball cap.

"C'mon, kiddo, Mommy's gotta pee. Don't you have to go?" Lizzie didn't answer, still absorbed in the enormous airport's fresh sights. Ahead, Beth caught a blessed glimpse of a woman's restroom sign floating above the throng. "There's the bathroom. We'll go pee and then we can—"

"*Cool!*"

Lizzie slipped her hand out and took off, her new canary-yellow Dora backpack jouncing as she ran to a bank of floor-to-ceiling windows and pressed her face to the glass. The bill of the cap that Beth had bought (for twenty-five dollars!) at the Nashville International Airport hit the window and tumbled off the back of her head. Lizzie either didn't notice or didn't care as one hand joined her face on the glass and the other clutched a tired-looking Mr. Fred by his long neck, pressing him against the front of her neon-orange California Girl tee-shirt.

Beth sighed and joined her, stooping to snatch up the cap; it was hot pink with a pale-blue capital "T" on the front; some Nashville sports team's logo. Daniel would probably know which; Beth couldn't care less if she tried. The hat had been an impulse buy as well as an inspiration, but she hadn't consented to being gouged at the gift shop so her daughter could be turned into the world's cutest walking billboard, and she *especially* hadn't done it so some egotistical billionaire could get free advertising for his stupid team.

The reason she'd bought the hat was simple: camouflage. *I should have thought of this* weeks *ago.* Beth looked down at the top of her daughter's head and grimaced at the silver vein in her dark hair; it shimmered in the strong Arizona sunshine.

Not that my brilliant plan is working out so well…

Lizzie pointed. "Is one of those our new airplane, Mommy?"

A line of planes suckled up to the building like immense, winged piglets. "I don't know, baby." Beth shifted from foot to foot, but standing hurt just as much as walking; maybe if she snuck into that alcove behind those potted ferns over there and just dropped trow, nobody would notice. "Let's go to the bathroom and then we—"

Lizzie pointed again. "What are *those* mountains called?"

Beth raised her gaze beyond the sprawling airport and beheld short, rugged mountains growing like warts out of the middle of the desert city; heat radiating from the tarmac made the dumpy mountains shimmer like a mirage. How hot was it out there, ninety-five? A hundred? Surely not a hundred; even Phoenix wouldn't get that hot during the third week of October.

"I don't know, Lizzie." Beth grabbed her hand and pulled her away from the window. "I have to pee. We'll look at stuff after that, okay? Here, you dropped this." Beth clamped the pink hat onto Lizzie's head with the bill fashionably backwards.

She again didn't seem to notice or care, dragging against Beth's hand as her vivacious five-year-old imagination snagged on something else.

"Wow!"

Somehow Beth made it to the ladies room without soaking her panties and Levi's. She washed her hands and dried them under the blower and then pulled a giggling Lizzie away from playing with the motion-sensor toilets before trekking to the baggage carousel and retrieving their suitcases and rolling them to the ticket counter; it was annoying, but it went smoothly, although not for the lady behind the counter. Beth felt much better after venting, but when they walked away, the woman stared after her, stone-faced.

Too bad, so sad. If she didn't work for such a brainless airline, she wouldn't have these problems.

They rode the people mover, although Beth didn't enjoy the floor shifting under her feet, and she also couldn't help but feel guilty; there was nothing wrong with their legs, and they still had over two hours to kill, but Lizzie's delighted laugh was worth a little guilt and discomfort.

They found their gate and claimed seats in the long rows of connected and supposedly ergonomic dark-blue plastic chairs. Beth dumped her carry-on in one before sitting down next to it and putting her purse on her lap and digging out her phone and powering it up. Lizzie took her backpack off and then her hat, chucked them into a seat without looking, and then skipped to another set of floor-to-ceiling windows, where that silver slash glittered and flashed and gleamed.

Beth grimaced at the abandoned pink hat, then called her husband. It was just after four-thirty Tennessee-time; he was probably busy directing the movers, but she needed to hear his voice.

"Hello?"

"Hey, it's us."

"Hey! How goeth the flight?"

"It went fine. We didn't even run out of gas and crash."

"That's always good."

"Yeah." There was something in Daniel's voice she didn't like. "How's the move coming?"

"Well…"

Lizzie popped up at Beth's knee. "Is that my Daddy? Can I talk to him? I wanna tell him about flying on the airplane!"

"You can tell him when I'm done talking to—"

"*Please!*"

Daniel laughed. "Put her on, we'll catch up in a minute."

"All right." Beth handed the iPhone to her bouncing five-year-old. "Here's your Daddy."

Lizzie began regaling her father with a piping tale about watching out the window as the ground turned into big green and brown and yellow squares like one of Ms. Helen's blankets. She wandered over to the windows again, and Beth kept one eye on her as she stewed. *Maybe I'm imagining things.* Her husband seemed in good spirits, but Beth knew she wouldn't stop worrying until he was safe in California.

A woman directly across the aisle was swiveling her gaze from her to Lizzie and back; Beth kept her head down and prospected in her still-open purse for the Harry Bosh whodunit she'd started on the plane.

"Ma'am?"

She unfolded the corner she'd used to mark her place and began to read; she'd accumulated a drawer-full of bookmarks over the years, but she never remembered to use them. Beth was a page folder; always had been, always would be.

"Ma'am? Excuse me, ma'am?"

Beth scowled and looked up: attractive, fortyish, the bottle blonde wore a gray-and-black plaid skirt and a cream-silk blouse, her makeup a little too heavy and her roots screaming, white-hosed legs crossed and two-inch heels unstrapped and stacked on the floor; her carry-on and purse, both twice as big as Beth's (and five times as expensive) sat on the seat to her left. She held her phone sideways, as if she had been watching a video before deciding to pester Beth; when their eyes met, the woman smiled, but she didn't smile back.

"Hi." Her incredibly cute gold-teardrop earrings swayed as she uncrossed her legs and leaned forward; a matching gold teardrop dangled above her generous tan cleavage. "I'm so sorry to bother you, but…" She looked over at Lizzie. "Your little girl is so *beautiful!*" Her deep-Texas drawl managed to stretch that word into four syllables.

"Thank you."

"How old is she?"

"She's five."

"Five…"

Beth gave the woman credit; Lizzie was the size of a well-fed three-year-old. But that's not what she wanted to talk about, so Beth simply waited.

A line appeared between her teased dark eyebrows as she picked up on Beth's attitude, but she continued to drawl across the aisle gamely: "I *love* what you've done with her hair." *Hay-yer.* "I was a cosmetologist for ten years, and now I co-own four salons back in Dallas, but I've never seen that shade."

"I didn't dye it. It's a birthmark."

"A birthmark?" The woman's light-brown eyes flicked up to Beth's simple dark ponytail and then over to Lizzie. "That's amazing. Does it run in her daddy's family? I've never seen anythi—"

"It's been a long day, and we still have another flight before we're home. I'd like to relax with my book." Beth turned her eyes back down to the Connelly.

She could feel the bottle blonde's astonishment turn to anger, but Beth didn't care; the last thing she wanted to talk about was that stupid silver smudge, but all day long she hadn't gotten her way. It had started with that fat cabbie in his nasty taxicab, then that gaggle of snotty, well-dressed women at the Nashville Airport; after fielding condescending questions from *them,* Beth had been fuming (although Lizzie, for all that she'd never acknowledged the new streak, didn't seem to mind the attention) when she'd spotted the rack of caps in the airport gift shop.

Lizzie was constantly taking it off and forgetting it somewhere, though, so by the time they embarked, the lie about the birthmark had come easy. She'd had to pay for her sins, however; after the attendants had noticed the streak and the inevitable conversation, a garrulous woman spread across two seats in the 747's middle rows had yanked up her pup-tent shirt to reveal a birthmark she bragged was shaped like a running horse. Beth had agreed, although it had looked like nothing more than a disgusting brown blob to her.

If only that dye had taken; *any* of the dyes.

If only Lizzie would keep that stupid hat on...

The print blurred, and Beth knuckled her eyes and marked her place with a folded corner again and stuffed the book back into her purse; her incessant worry made it hard to concentrate. She'd barely managed ten pages on the plane, and normally Connelly kept her up late.

What *did* that streak mean?

No. It didn't matter; they'd taken Lizzie back in time, she was fine and healthy, and that was that.

What did it MEAN?

Unbidden, a dead man's insidious, mad, gleeful voice whispered in her head: *She is the One! The One foretold of in our most ancient and secret prophecies!*

NO!

They'd gone down into that terrible place and brought their daughter out and *nothing else mattered.* The rest of that horrifying night, the absurd things McFarlane had claimed, the impossible things she'd seen...they didn't matter. Beth scratched at the thin white ridge of dead flesh that slanted across her left bicep—the thing still itched abominably—and scrubbed her face again, wearily this time; unlike the bottle blonde, she refused to wear makeup just to impress strangers while she traveled.

I'm so tired of being afraid...

Lizzie turned from the window and headed her way; Beth dropped her hands into her lap with a sigh.

"Okay love you Daddy bye." She held the phone out, but before Beth could even start to reach for it, Lizzie announced, "I'm hungry."

"We'll get something after I talk to your dad, promise."

"Okay." Lizzie moved Mr. Fred to his own blue-plastic ergonomic seat, where he promptly fell over, then climbed up and unzipped her backpack and three plastic horsies joined a prostrate Mr. Fred, then her New New *Star Wars* movie and the *Sesame Street* coloring book and her pack of markers, then finally her Dora adventure books. Beth put the phone to her ear as Lizzie propped Mr. Fred in the crook of her elbow and opened a Dora and began to read to him, sneakers scissoring high above the floor.

"Hello?"

"She's excited, isn't she?" Daniel laughed. "*And* hungry."

"Yes."

"So how did the airplane ride really go?"

"Better than I expected, but of course she slept most of the way; I had to wake her up so she wouldn't miss the landing. There was a little bump when she found out the dog couldn't stay in the cabin..." People around her were listening, including the sulking salon blonde. "Hold on." Beth put the phone on her shoulder and pointed to the bank of windows. "I'm going over there to talk to your daddy. You stay right here."

Lizzie didn't bother to look up. "Okay."

Beth walked to the windows and gratefully slipped into their snug bubble of heat and light; the numbskull running this airport apparently liked the thermostat set to about fifty. Beth was sure that was a fine temperature if you were a two hundred pound man, but she was anything but a two hundred pound man. Outside, a sweltering plane was being connected to their gate by a short accordion walkway; the flight before theirs, a jump to Reno.

"All right," she said when she had some privacy; even so, Beth kept one eye on her daughter. The blonde was watching Lizzie with a smile, then glanced over and saw Beth looking and pouted down at her phone again. "Did you get everything packed in time?"

"Uh, yeah, about that." Daniel cleared his throat. "There's been a slight hitch." He went on to explain, and Beth bit the scarred inside of her cheek to keep from screaming. He finished with, "There's no way I can find another mover this late. I'll just have to wait and deal, I guess."

"I don't like this." *Understatement of the century!*

"I'm not a fan either, but it's really no big thang, beautiful. I'll just be a day or so late getting out there."

"What about tonight?" He didn't answer, and Beth glared out the window at Phoenix; not its fault, with its dumb, lumpy mountains. She glared anyway. "You're going to spend the night…out there?"

"I'll sleep on the couch."

"*No,* Daniel!"

Heads turned, including Lizzie's. Beth faced the window and kept her voice low by pure will: "Get a hotel room—or better yet, crash at Steve and Amy's. You two can hang in his stupid man cave and drink beer and watch sports."

"Not gonna happen."

"Why not?"

"Because Amy's waddling around being a crabby pregnant bitch while Steve's tiptoeing through life until she pops. No thank you. And we've spent enough goddamn money on hotels. I'm *sick* of fucking hotels. You know that prick Abdullah screwed us out of fifty bucks? Fucker claimed there was a new stain in the carpet, right there at the end of the couch before you walk into the kitchenette, but I *know* he did it just to piss me off. You could barely *see* the tiny thing! Fuck him, and fuck hotels. Our couch is comfortable, and free, and right here, and—"

"Daniel, *no!*"

"—I can get up in the morning and have everything ready for those assholes when they finally get here. I'll be *fine,* Beth."

"Go to a hotel. There's room left on the Visa." *Barely.* "Then you can drive back out there early."

"Beth—"

"*Please* get a hotel room. Please." Beth's dread was so strong she wasn't above begging. The fact that he was *making* her beg…oh, he would sooooo pay for that later, but for now… "*Please*, Daniel."

"I don't know what you're so worried about, dear." His voice had turned bright and hard. "McFarlane's dead—or wishes he was—and we took Lizzie back, right? Everything's fine and she's fine and there's absolutely *nothing* to fret about. Isn't that right?"

"Stop it."

Beth took several deep, calming breaths; she didn't want to fight, not on the phone, not here, and a part of her also admitted she deserved that; a *small* part. Her next words felt dredged from the bottom of a wide, muddy river:

"Let's just get this move done." *And get all of us away from that place, those people.* "Then…then you and I will talk."

Silence.

"We'll talk about anything…" Beth gathered her courage. "Anything you want to talk about."

"Anything." Flat. Disbelieving.

Beth's nostrils flared. "Yes. I said so, didn't I?"

"Anything like what you and McFarlane were chumming about down there 'anything'? Even though you *lied* and said you didn't talk about dick 'anything'? *That* kind of anything, Beth?"

She closed her eyes. "Yes."

"And about this…this new thing you've got going on? About 'it'?"

Courage. "Yes, we'll talk about 'it'." Then she laughed; Beth couldn't help herself. "Although I might not have many good answers. I barely understand 'it' myself." *Not at all, really.* "And I'm sorry about lying to you, but…but what McFarlane said…" Her voice dropped to just above a whisper. "What he said was *insane*, Daniel, absolutely, utterly mad! *He* was mad, and what he said just can't be true; especially what he claimed to know about Lizzie. There's no way *that* can be true."

"Oookaaay," he said. But then he brightened: "And don't sweat lying, babe. In fact, I may have told a teensy-weensy fib of my own. But hey, if I can forgive, you can forgive, right?"

Beth was calm. Beth was serene. "What was it?"

"Well, I, uh, I may have lied a bit about…about how I got free from, you know, what you did to stick me in place. I'm still pissed off about that, by the by."

"What do you mean?"

"I said I broke free on my own, right?"

"Right…"

"I didn't. I had help."

"Who—" But then Beth knew. She didn't even hear his answer; she didn't *need* to hear it. Melissa Bane—or whatever her real name was.

The Keeper of Barron Cemetery.

Fear dug hard talons into Beth's heart and squeezed as the pieces clicked into place: Bane had saved Beth. She had also helped Daniel. She had been waiting and watching for them that night, and she had assisted them both.

Used both.

"Hello? Beth? *Hello?*"

"I'm…I'm still here."

"Oh. I thought the call dropped. Did you hear me? I said the Keeper—"

"I heard you. She helped me, too."

"She…*what?* What are you—"

"Remember how you asked about the blood all over me, and I said it wasn't mine, it was Tommy's, but I didn't kill him?"

"You mean *she* killed him? Holy shit. But why would she—"

"Just shut up and listen." Beth ran through Tommy's ambush and Bane saving her; she also relayed a carefully edited version of that bizarre conversation that took place after. Then: "They vanished into these swirling black shadows that came out of nowhere, Daniel. They were just *gone*. I've never seen anything like that. I've never even *imagined* anything like that. And I'm sorry I doubted you about the shadows."

His grunt was wry. "Yeah, well, I guess I would've doubted me, too. Wait, that smelly bitch called me her fucking *tool?*"

"She *used* us, Daniel. She did it to stop McFarlane from accomplishing whatever he had planned for—"

Beth's throat closed down.

Her husband finished grimly for her: "For whatever he had planned for Lizzie."

"Yes," she whispered.

"Then I say jolly good for her. And after what *I* saw, I'd also say she won: game, set, and match."

"Yes."

"Did, uh, did you see her eyes?"

"Yes."

Uneasy silence; then, cautious: "Beth, does…does Lizzie have 'it', like you? Is that what he took her down there for?"

Careful…

"I don't *think* she does. Or at least I haven't…" She'd almost said felt. "I haven't *seen* anything to indicate that she does." She hesitated. "Have you?"

"No, but if it wasn't that, then why did that maniac take her down there?"

Terror surged, squeezing Beth's throat closed again.

Silence, more silence, and then he spoke quietly: "I think I can guess. It had something to do with this 'mad' shit he was spouting when you two were having your cozy little confab, right? And maybe that new chrome hairdo she's sporting?" His voice grew even softer: "And maybe even that…that *thing* we saw, the one behind the blue light? The one attached to the hand? Am I sorta kinda hitting close to the mark here, Beth?"

Before she could respond—if respond she could—Lizzie appeared at her hip. "Mommy, *I'm hungry!*"

Beth managed to answer her daughter through numb lips: "We'll get something in a minute. Let me finish talking to your daddy."

"Ooo*kay.*" Lizzie stamped back to their seats.

Daniel said, "Go. Take her. And forget I asked." Beth rested her forehead against the warm window. "But mark my words, beautiful: One night next week we'll put the Lizmonster to bed early and then you and I are going to sit down and hash all this shit out."

He wasn't asking.

"All right," she sighed.

"So you *promise* you'll talk to me? No more screaming or pulling a fucking knife?"

"I promise."

"Good, because I have questions, Beth."

She'd never heard him sound so serious. "I know you do. I just hope I have answers."

"All right," he said. Then: "Hey, this is good, you know?"

"*Good?*"

"Yeah. I mean we're finally talking about this stuff, right? It would've been a better conversation to have, say, *seven weeks* ago, but better late than never, I guess."

Beth controlled her temper—just. "I suppose I deserve that—"

"You do."

"—and I'm sorry I wouldn't talk to you, but I was so afraid for Lizzie, and I just wanted to focus on getting her far away from that place, and…and *them,* too."

"I know you did," he said gently. "And it's all right. In fact, Lizzie—and everything else—will be all right from now on, I promise. I *more* than promise: I'll make damn sure of it. We'll *both* make sure of it."

Beth dabbed her leaking eyes with the hem of her tee-shirt. "We'll both make sure of it," she said.

"You got it, babe. Damn skippy we will. Okay, you guys go grab some grub and—"

Beth cut in firmly. "You still haven't promised me you'll get a room."

"God damn it, the couch will be *just fine!*"

"No, Daniel, it won't. Promise me you'll get a hotel room. Please."

"Fine," he growled. "I'll go blow more fucking green we can't spare on a goddamn rented room while our comfortable couch just sits here and molders; since that is what my lovely bride wishes, that's the way it will be."

"Promise me."

"Fer chrissakes—"

"*Promise me.*"

"Oh, for the love of—I promise. There, happy?"

"No. I miss you."

He sighed. "I miss you, too. And the Lizmonster."

"She misses you, too." Beth checked on her daughter; she was galloping a plastic horsie in each hand across the empty blue seat next to Beth's. Several of the travelers in the surrounding seats were watching with smiles, including the salon blonde. Beth supposed she should apologize to the woman, especially if she would be sharing their flight to Burbank. *I probably won't, though—and what's wrong with brown hair, anyhow?* "We better go find something to eat before Lizzie wastes away."

He laughed. "Call me when you land in L.A., let me know you guys are safe."

"It's Burbank."

"Same difference."

"No, it's not, and I'll call to make sure *you* remember what you promised." The thought was in the back of her mind that he would stay out there anyway, stubborn moron of a man that he was. He would be thinking: How would she know? Beth didn't need her newfangled awareness to know *that*; she knew him.

"Daniel?"

"Yeah, yeah, I promised. Jeez."

They were quiet, and then they both tried to speak at the same time:

"I love you—"

"I love—"

"You first," she said. "I want to hear it."

"I love you, beautiful."

"And I love you."

"All right, you guys go grab some chow."

"And you're going straight to a hotel? You promised."

"Jesus Christ, yes, I promised! You better remember what *you* promised, too."

Beth frowned, but she only said, "I remember."

And what an interesting conversation it will be...

"Kiss the Lizmonster for me."

"I will."

"Goodbye, my love, mistress of my heart and loins—most especially my loins."

Despite everything, Beth smiled; her Daniel drove her crazy sometimes, and he was irrepressible, but for some reason she loved him for it.

Whoever claims love makes sense is a stone-cold idiot.

"Bye."

And then he was gone.

Beth stared out at the blurry planes taking off and landing and taxiing on the runways, their hard-metal skins glimmering through her tears.

"Be safe," she whispered.

And then she frowned; something about that conversation was bothering her, but she couldn't put her finger on what; she should have been happy at their affectionate goodbyes, and that she'd talked her stubborn husband out of staying the night out there, but for some reason, she wasn't.

So what is it?

After a minute, Beth shook her head; she had more than enough on her plate as it was. She left the bubble of warmth and walked back to where Lizzie was now coloring a picture of Big Bird talking to Oscar the Grouch; Big Bird was turning bright red and had at some point acquired a purple beak; both Oscar and his trash-can had already turned cornflower blue. Between horsies and books and markers and the clear-plastic marker bag and Mr. Fred and the New New *Star Wars* movie and the yellow backpack and the useless pink hat and Beth's carry-on and purse they'd taken up six seats, but even though the place was filling with those about to hop to Reno, no one seemed to mind.

"Hey kid, you still hungry?"

"Yeah!" She stopped defacing Big Bird and looked up; that streak blazed like a silver inferno in the sunlight infusing the boarding gate.

"Then help me gather our crud. And put your hat on."

Lizzie did so, turning the bill around backwards again. "Is there a McDonald's here, Mommy?"

"I don't know, but we'll find something."

"Okay."

They left holding hands. Beth could *feel* the Texas blonde glaring at her back, and when they turned into the long, long hallway that led past all the other gates and eventually back to the concourse, she finally understood what was bothering her about that conversation with Daniel.

I may have told a teensy-weensy fib…

The sudden gust of alarm that blew through Beth made her stumble and stop. Lizzie frowned up at her.

"What's wrong, Mommy?"

"Nothing's wrong, baby."

Lizzie continued to frown while watching her keenly, but Beth didn't notice: He'd concealed from her that Bane had freed him, but *why* had he lied? And what did they say to each other? There had to have been some sort of conversation; the woman had been chatty enough with her, and Beth couldn't imagine her not saying something to Daniel, let alone Daniel (knowing Daniel) not saying something back.

Unfocused dread swirled through her.

What did those two talk about that night?

Beth realized now that her crafty husband had never said.

She let go of Lizzie's hand and shifted her carry-on and purse around and was about to yank her phone out and call him and *demand* that he tell her, then froze when she noticed Lizzie watching her.

It can wait until we have our big sit-down at the new house, she decided. *But he WILL tell me then!*

Beth put her phone back and closed her purse, then stuffed the terror back into the place she had made for it so she could stay sane and attempted to smile reassuringly at her daughter. "I'm all right, sweetie, I'm just hungry."

Lizzie stopped frowning and beamed her gap-toothed smile. "Okay!"

They walked on, holding hands once more.

Why did he lie? What is he hiding?

A Candle to the Sun

L IZZIE WAS staring up at the giant mural when Beth spotted the cafeteria further down the concourse; as a general rule, she didn't like cafeterias—a matter of professional snobbery, she supposed—but since she wasn't about to take her five-year-old into a bar and she wasn't in the mood for fast food, her choices were limited.

Beth glanced back at Lizzie; the desert fresco that so fascinated her daughter took up a rare forty feet of unoccupied wall, and right in front of Lizzie a ten-foot tall cactus loomed, one prickly appendage raised higher than the other. Behind the capitulating cactus, a sun-bleached cow skull rested on the sienna hardpan; the skull was wearing a multi-hued sombrero cocked at a jaunty angle. Beyond the merry skull were fuzzy depictions of live long-horned cattle, and behind them was the elongated horizon and a scarlet smear that was either a setting or rising sun, hard to tell which.

Tasteful. "Hey, you still hungry?"

"Yeah!"

"I see someplace, c'mon."

Lizzie left the painting, and they joined the long line being herded between black ropes strung between short black stanchions. *Popular place.* Beth spotted the prices and almost changed her mind, then reluctantly decided to stay. *Just wish I could get away with charging like that.*

The line shuffled forward, meandering back and forth, and Beth resisted the urge to let out a loud moo. Lizzie shuffled with the rest, holding Beth's hand, her yellow backpack strapped to her back and a natty Mr. Fred pressed to her chest and the hot-pink baseball cap on her head. She looked around big-eyed at the people in line and streaming by out in the concourse, all but a few pulling suitcases on clacking wheels.

But even quiet she attracted attention, especially after she took her cap off; all too soon Beth found herself trapped in an animated discussion about hair dyes and birthmarks with an older couple from Michigan on their way to visit relatives in Palmdale and a woman with a sulking teenage daughter who never looked up from her phone. Beth tried to sweet-talk Lizzie into putting the cap back on but she refused, so she stuffed the stupid pink hat in her purse and did her best to forget about it.

Hat or no hat, Lizzie bore up better than her, answering questions shyly and beaming gap-toothed at comments about what a beautiful and well-mannered little lady she was. Beth got through it by imagining they were customers she had to schmooze; it must've worked, because by the time they'd crept to the register she had somehow managed to not offend anyone. Beth paid the outrageous prices for the pleasure of picking up two plates—she nearly had an apoplectic fit when she saw drinks were separate; at least Lizzie got to eat half-price—and then it was their turn at the trough.

I will kick the next person who wants to talk about hair dye.

A dead-eyed waitress in a horrendous brown and orange uniform led them across the crowded dining room to a tiny two-person booth set hard up against the milky glass partition and took their order for two unsweetened teas and then walked off. Beth glared after her, then cleaned the table herself with a handful of tissue from her purse; at least they had a good view of the courtyard. They dumped their stuff and sat Mr. Fred on the table to guard it, where he promptly slumped over. Beth decided to take her purse with her despite his ferocious diligence.

Over at the trough she filled her plate with salad, and whoever was running the place should've been ashamed at the sad state of the lettuce. Still, the overall quality and selection wasn't bad, just not worth the price. Next time she saw Clint, maybe she should float opening stores in some of the big hubs. They'd make a killing.

Back at their miniature booth, they found not only Mr. Fred and her carry-on and Lizzie's backpack *not* stolen, but—miracle of miracles—two teas, and straws and napkins and silverware to boot. They sat down and dug in. All Lizzie had wanted was chicken fingers and cucumber slices, which she chomped happily; Lizzie loved sliced cucumbers, couldn't get enough of them. The only thing she liked better was McDonald's, which had thankfully disappeared from her radar—for the nonce.

Beth cleaned her plate and went back to the trough; the lettuce wasn't *that* bad, and they might as well try to get their money's worth, although they'd have to snarf six plates apiece to break even. When she turned, there was a strange woman standing by their small booth, speaking to Lizzie.

She didn't exactly run back through the packed dining area, but she didn't walk, that's for sure. The woman was around Beth's age, mid-thirties, with straight, shoulder-length dark hair, dressed in a navy pantsuit and matching pumps. She sported a platinum wedding ring with a glittering boulder Daniel could never afford in this lifetime. She also wore a silver chain around her neck that displayed a silver cross. It swung outside her blouse as she bent down to respond to something Lizzie had said, and Beth noted that the heavy cross came complete with nailed savior hanging. The woman saw her coming and straightened, issuing a smooth smile in response to Beth's glower; despite that smile, Beth thought she looked uneasy.

"I see where she gets her looks," this stranger announced, causing more than a few heads to turn. "Gloria Blaylock." She offered a manicured hand. Beth disregarded it and sat down.

Lizzie piped up around a mouthful of chicken tender. "My name is Lizzie!" She offered her small hand.

Gloria Blaylock shook it gravely. "Nice to meet you, Lizzie." Lizzie giggled and kept chomping. Beth took a deliberate bite of salad. There was an awkward silence, but Gloria Blaylock wasn't knocked off her stride for long: "I'm a talent agent," she told Beth. "With Four Leaves, out of Los Angeles. Perhaps you've heard of us?"

"No."

"Well, I assure you we're known to the studios. The reason I came over and spoke to Lizzie—and let me apologize, I should have approached you first—"

"Yes, you should have. And you can save your breath. We're not interested."

Gloria Blaylock didn't answer; she also didn't take the hint and go away. After three more bites, Beth glanced up, irritated, to find the woman just…standing there, staring down at Lizzie; her right hand had crept up and was clutching the silver cross.

Beth cleared her throat.

Gloria Blaylock started, then glanced down at her hand and frowned before letting the cross go. "I apologize. I…I truly never have done this before, approaching a potential minor client without…without speaking to their guardian first…" Her hand crept up and grasped the cross again; Beth didn't think Gloria knew she was doing it. "It's just that…I'm not sure I've ever seen such a…such a striking child." She gazed raptly at Lizzie.

Suddenly Gloria glanced at Beth again and saw her dire scowl and hastily let go of the cross once more. She faced Beth, and her attempt to marshal her forces and shrug her professional cloak back on was mostly successful: "Yes, truly stunning, and when you factor in that hair adornment—is that natural, by the way?" Beth didn't answer. *Why was she looking at Lizzie like that?* "No matter," the talent agent continued, "because I'll be frank with you: even if she has zero aptitude for acting or singing or dance, she could go far. *Very* far. You can coach talent. You can't instruct beauty." A card appeared and was tucked under the edge of Beth's plate. "If you'd like to discuss your daughter's future, I'm available—"

"We're not interested."

"I see." She cut her eyes toward Lizzie again, but didn't let herself stare; she also didn't leave. Beth had to admire her determination; Gloria was undoubtedly as successful as she appeared. "Perhaps you don't appreciate the opportunities Four Leaves can offer your family. One out of a hundred thousand children receives the chance to—"

"We realize the opportunities you offer. We're still not interested. Thank you for coming over, but we'd like to get back to our meal now." Beth kept her eyes steady on the woman and her temper under control.

Just.

Gloria Blaylock cast a regret-filled yet hunted glance at Lizzie. "If you change your mind, you have my card." She weaved her stiff-backed way to a two-top about thirty feet from their booth and sat down. Gloria was clutching her cross again; she shot one more troubled glance at Beth's daughter, saw Beth watching, and hastily turned away.

"Mommy?"

"What, baby?"

"Are you mad at that lady? She was really nice. She told me I was pretty."

"I'm not mad, sweetheart. I'm just tired and it's been a long day and we still have another flight to get to our new house." She forced a chuckle. *Why was she looking at Lizzie like that?* "I'm just grumpy, I guess."

Lizzie grinned around a mouthful of cucumber. "Daddy says you like being grumpy."

"He does?"

"Yeah."

"I'll have to discuss that with him. *Then* he'll see grumpy."

Lizzie giggled and dipped chicken into a cravat of honey-mustard sauce and Beth tried to go back to her salad but she just moved stuff around with her fork. She snuck a glance at Lizzie; that streak burned like a silver flame, even under the muted lights of the cafeteria. Beth could *feel* Gloria Blaylock's eyes on them again, along with several other travelers who had overheard their conversation, including the couple from Michigan; they were whispering now, whispering. Beth glared, and they all looked away, but several wore uneasy frowns reminiscent of Gloria's.

Beth clenched her fists so hard she almost bent her fork.

I JUST WANT EVERYONE TO LEAVE US ALONE!

Lizzie suddenly looked up at her.

"Okay, Mommy." Her blue eyes narrowed with a peculiar look of concentration that made her seem much older than five.

Beth gaped, astounded. *She heard me!*

And then she felt it.

"No, baby, don't—"

But it was too late.

Everyone sitting in the canteen scraped back their chairs and stood up, all of them at once, and headed for the exit en mass. Murmurs of astonishment swelled, and some people gawked down at their legs as if they couldn't believe what those legs were doing; most had a blank, dreamy look. Someone shouted, several cursed, and then a woman screamed. An employee wearing a green apron dropped a steaming replacement tub on the buffet rail with a clang, then turned and pushed through the swinging double doors that led to the kitchen; the tub teetered for a second and then crashed to the floor, egg-drop soup splashing the back wall. People shouted in confusion and alarm as a hundred patrons at once tried to crowd through the entrance, crushed together like lemmings, and several people screamed as an old man that had to be eighty fell and was trampled.

Lizzie giggled.

"Stop it!" Beth hissed. "*Stop it*, Lizzie!"

There was a jingling crash; the cash register. People became entangled in the ropes and fell, and there were more screams as those pushing behind trod on them. Motion out in the concourse caught Beth's eye, and she watched, stunned, as people who'd been walking toward them suddenly began walking the other way, their astonishment at their change of direction obvious. In seconds the shouting and screaming spread as hundreds of people streamed away from them, like an ocean wave retreating from the beach; their booth had become a tiny island in a sea of chaos.

Lizzie giggled again. Beth stared at her in mute horror.

"I can make them run, Mommy. Watch."

"No! Lizzie, *no!*"

There was a sudden roar as hundreds of shoes started pounding, and more strident screams, and then a crash from the kitchen and a pain-filled shriek from behind the swinging doors. Next to the cafeteria the concourse was now eerily empty, but in both directions a mass of running people packed it from side to side. Beth saw bodies; some of them were bloody and screaming while *still* trying to crawl away. She swallowed; others were motionless. She saw an abandoned baby stroller; the infant's terrified wail punctuated the madness.

Lizzie giggled again. Beth grasped her by the shoulders and leaned over the table and put her face right into her daughter's gleeful little countenance.

"Stop it this instant, young lady! *Stop it!*"

Lizzie got a hurt, confused look. "But Mommy, they left us alone, just like you wanted. Didn't they?"

Beth licked her lips. "Yes, but you can't do this to people. It's not right. Stop making them go away." The shrieks from the kitchen intensified; Beth smelled smoke. "Lizzie, *stop.*"

Lizzie pouted. "Ooo*kay*."

The thunder of the stampede abruptly ceased, but the screaming and shouting only intensified. A smoke alarm began blatting. Beth heard more running footsteps, coming toward them this time, and then a dozen wide-eyed airport police pounded past, guns drawn. Two stopped, speaking into radios, looking around in bafflement. One approached, and Beth realized they stood out because they were the only ones who'd remained seated.

"Ma'am? Are you and your daughter all right? What happened here?" Hard eyes roamed over her shoulder like he expected armed men in masks to pop up from behind the mashed potatoes; times being what they were, Beth had no doubt that's exactly what he expected.

"I…I don't know what happened, officer. Everyone just jumped up and started running." Beth stood, not having to fake terrified as she grabbed her purse and carry-on and Lizzie's backpack and Mr. Fred, then picked up her pouting daughter. Beth handed her Mr. Fred. She took him, but Lizzie kept that ominous scowl as Beth carried her toward the mangled entrance; she also had her little arms crossed stubbornly, and she didn't look scared at all. Beth just had to hope that the airport cop wouldn't notice. She stepped over the bloody body of the old man and past two moaning women trapped in the entrance ropes and then out into the courtyard. "Please help us," she begged the officer, hoping he'd see them as just two more victims.

It worked. They were ushered aside as more airport security arrived and people trickled back along the concourse from both directions. Most were unharmed, but some were bloody and limping, and all appeared shell-shocked. A handful dropped to their knees next to still forms and wailed. Beth tried not to look at those as she stood back against the wall and hugged Lizzie to her while medical personnel flooded in and assisted the wounded; firemen carrying extinguishers rushed past and into the smoking kitchen.

Beth set Lizzie on the floor and squatted so they were face to face.

It was time for a serious talk.

"Are you mad at me, Mommy?" The fuming pout was gone; now she seemed close to tears.

"I'm not mad, baby, but I want you to understand something *very important.*" Beth glanced around to make sure no one was near.

"What?"

She had to work moisture into the wasteland that used to be her mouth: "It's wrong to make people do what you want. Do you understand?"

Lizzie frowned. "You make Daddy and me do stuff all the time. Why is it wrong?"

"That's different, and it just is. I want you to promise me you'll never do that again. *Promise me*, Lizzie."

Lizzie's frown deepened, but she said it: "I promise, Mommy."

Beth stared at her daughter. *She doesn't understand, but she's five…*

She looked around at all the pandemonium.

Lizzie was a five-year-old who had done *this*.

And it had been…effortless.

"Thank you," Beth said, voice faint, then stood and took Lizzie's hand. She wanted to leave, just walk away, but they didn't dare draw any more attention so they stood there and watched the cafeteria patrons come back, some of them bloody, all of them upset, all of them staring at the body of the old man, and at the old woman who wept at his side. No one paid Beth and Lizzie any mind.

No one, that is, except Gloria Blaylock.

The talent agent limped up with pantsuit torn and hair disheveled and makeup smeared and a bruise rising on one cheekbone. She held a navy pump in one hand; the other was missing. She argued stridently with a cop about retrieving her purse and cell phone and carry-on but they weren't letting anyone back there yet. Other diners chimed in, ganging up on the harried officer, but Gloria fell silent as she caught sight of them standing back against the wall.

Beth went cold as her attention lingered on Lizzie; Gloria shook her head, seeming to argue with herself, and then the woman's gaze rose slowly to hers and locked on.

Beth told herself to look away, but she couldn't.

Gloria's eyes widened as far as they would go, and then she put that terrified look back on Lizzie. That's when Beth realized her daughter was watching the woman as well.

Lizzie raised Mr. Fred and waved him. "Hi!"

Gloria's nostrils flared, and she stiffened and stumbled backwards, bumping into several people. She dropped her shoe. Her hand rose to the cross and clutched it so hard her knuckles turned white, and then she limped away as fast as she could limp, abandoning her pump on the concourse. Gloria looked back once. When she met Beth's eyes, she flinched and limped faster. The cop she'd been arguing with watched her go with a bemused scowl.

"Bye!" Lizzie waved Mr. Fred again.

Beth stood there numbly and clutched her daughter's hand. After a bit Lizzie got bored and sat down on the floor and unzipped her backpack and read a Dora adventure. Beth watched her warily, waiting to be told they could go, wondering if their flight would be delayed because of this. She watched the old man's body roll by on a stretcher, mercifully covered; the crying old woman followed on the arm of a young and muscular paramedic.

Lizzie didn't notice. She also didn't notice as two more crushed corpses were wheeled past, distraught loved ones following the creaking gurneys. Beth stared at the top of her daughter's bent head; she seemed oblivious to the terror and destruction and death she'd caused…

Or maybe she just doesn't care.

Beth began to tremble as something McFarlane had said came back to her. It had been on that awful Sunday morning when Lizzie was first kidnapped; the old man had still been pretending to be just your run-of-the-mill megalomaniac farmer, his voice fatherly as he spoke of his regret at not finding Beth sooner. He'd said she would be strong, but nothing compared to her daughter.

He'd said that, next to Lizzie, she was like—

"A candle to the sun," Beth whispered.

Lizzie looked up. She was grinning. The resplendent gap in her upper teeth was still that cute, gummy-pink M it had been since her bike wreck that summer, her daddy's blue eyes were vivid and happy, and the chrome band in her hair shimmered in the terminal's high fluorescents.

"What did you say, Mommy?"

"Nothing, baby." Beth licked her lips. "I love you."

"I love you, too!" Lizzie bent her head over her book again.

What did they do to my little girl?

WHAT IS SHE?

The Last of the Mohicans

The torpid desk clerk at the Murfreesboro La Quinta Inn was wearing a flat-black button-down Hugo Boss and a *sweet* blood-red and royal-purple tartan necktie. Dan admired that eye-catcher of a tie as the sullen young man rang him up for a smoking single; he sighed out the breath he'd been holding when the Visa went through.

Whew.

Dan scribbled his John Hancock and received his key-card along with mumbled directions to his room (the dour lad's name tag said DENNY, and below that GUEST SERVICES, though Dan was disinclined to believe that last part), told Denny he dug the shit out of his tie, went to the second floor and found the new albeit temporary Casa Dan, jogged back downstairs and out the side door to the truck and grabbed his stuff, lugged his crap up and stowed it away, and five minutes later he was bored out of his skull.

He yanked the thick drapes back; his room was at the front of the hotel, thus affording Dan a fabulous view of the parking lot and the lifeless street beyond; there were five vehicles down there, including his truck. *Sure is a hoppin' Thursday night scene.* No wonder Denny looked like he'd just been rousted from a nap.

Dan checked his watch and did the sums: his girls were still in the air somewhere over the desert between Phoenix and L.A., he had eaten nothing but Shiner all damn day, and Thursday Night Football was on. He also had two days of cross-country travel staring at him, with the added joy of shepherding their crap along the way, and then would come unpacking and setting up the new house; Dan was scheduled to start his new job at the San Berdo GMC dealership next Wednesday, as well.

In other words, tonight is my night to decompress. Maybe even have a little fun.

Did they have a bar in this place? Perchance with Shiner on tap and some pub grub and a sixty-inch flat-screen nailed up in the corner? He hadn't glimpsed such an establishment on his way through the lobby, but possibly he'd blinked and missed it. Dan hustled back downstairs to find out.

No luck, though, and no bar, no chow, and no pigskin on the nonexistent flat-screen, either. He walked up to the deserted front desk and looked around for Denny. *Probably ducked into the office to pop another Xanax.* Dan slapped the desk bell.

Ding!

Still no Denny. "Hello?" Dan reached for the bell again and that's when Denny hopped out of the office with a wide, dazzling smile; thin, early twenties, a little taller than Dan, with dark hair and a sporty Van Dyke, he sauntered over and crossed his arms and leaned a jaunty hip against the inside counter. "May I help you, sir?"

Wow. The kid must've downed six fucking Red Bulls in the past five minutes. "Hey, man, you know a good spot to grab a beer and a cheeseburger and watch the game?"

"There's that place over by the campus, Slo Eddie's. They say it's got good food and pool tables, and the waitresses are hot." Denny gave him a slow wink. "If you're into that sort of thing."

Dan said, "Uh, yeah, I've been there once or twice. I was thinking someplace closer. I'm not real familiar with this end of town." Dan decided he liked slug Denny better; this new bubbly, flirty Denny was creeping him out.

The kid shrugged sinuously. "Well, there's a little bar over on North Oak. It's got TV's and an old-timey jukebox and a coupla dart boards and two bar-sized pool tables and about the best cheeseburger around."

"Sounds good. What's it called?"

"My Friend's Place. Hang a left out of the parking lot and go—"

"Whoa, whoa, it's your *friend's* place?" Maybe the kid raked a percentage.

Denny laughed and leaned his elbows on the counter, snazzy tie pooling. "No, man, that's the name of it: My Friend's Place." Again the lithe shrug: "If you don't want Friend's, there's a TGI Friday's over by the movie—"

"Nah, this Friend's Place will work. Tell me how to get there." The kid complied, and Dan thanked him and headed across the lobby; when the double-glass doors slid open, something made him stop and turn. Denny was still leaning on the counter, watching Dan leave with a…certain kind of look, but when he saw Dan glance back, he straightened and strolled into the office.

Dan continued out the doors, shrugging off the prickly feeling he got every time that happened; so the kid was gay, big deal. Each to their own, right? *I probably shouldn't have complimented his tie, though.* He hoped this Friend's Place didn't turn out to be a gay bar. That could be awkward.

He had to swing by a Quick Mart for cigs, so it was about fifteen minutes later when he pulled into the gravel parking lot of My Friend's Place and decided there was zero chance the bar catered to homosexuals; Friend's was long, narrow, comfortably shabby, and three pickups and a battered green Corolla sat in the gravel out front. Friend's reminded Dan of Carmody's, that shithole in Nashville where he'd met Scandlin, but at least there weren't any fucking motorcycles.

A deck spilled out of Friend's at the nearest narrow end, filled with Budweiser and Bud Light umbrellas spread above rough-cut wooden picnic tables and benches. It was a mite chilly for partying on the deck, at least for Dan-o, but twin white floods spotlighted an older couple as they weaved through the umbrellas, dancing to the tinny country music wafting from a speaker mounted below the floods. Another couple sat under a red and white Budweiser umbrella on the far side, laughing as they shared a golden pitcher and what looked like an enormous basket of cheese fries; the crack of pool balls resounded from inside.

"This'll work."

Dan parked and locked the Colt in the glove box and made sure the Smith hadn't slid out from under the passenger seat, then jumped out and beeped the truck and patted his back pocket, where the five-shot American Arms rested; the little burner that Beth had refused to carry was still loaded with .22 Mag hollow points. *Never leave home without it.* Dan crunched across the gravel and clanged up three metal steps and pulled the heavy front door open.

Two young guys clutching plain house cues stopped jawing and eyed him; Dan nodded, but they didn't nod back. *Unsociable little shits.* Short hair, khakis, loafers, pastel Ralph Lauren; they looked like frat boys who'd made a wrong turn. George Jones and David Allan Coe crooned from a jukebox in the corner, as Dan's new amigo Denny had promised; David was commenting on the bottle in his hand, and how he would never have to share it with another man.

The bar was to Dan's right, and he could see three flat-screens hanging back there; the one on the far left was showing a football game, so he motivated that-a-way; the aroma of stale cigarettes made him smile, and the odor of greasy bar food made his tongue hang. A guy sagged on a stool at the opposite end with an empty shot glass and full draught beer in a frosty mug resting on two coasters in front of him; dude had his face pointed up at his very own flat-screen and what looked like a rerun of *Walker, Texas Ranger*, but instead of enjoying Chuck Norris side-kicking a grizzly bear into submission, that expression said he was a zillion miles away; maybe he was with David and his bottle.

Dan took a stool in front of the football…and then he saw the teams playing: The Battle of Ohio, Cincinnati at Cleveland. *You've got to be fucking kidding me.* Even *he* didn't care about this game, and he was an Ohio boy—bred, born, raised, and fled. *Well, fuck it, even bad football is better than no football.* Barely. Dan slid a plastic My Friend's Place ashtray over and was digging for his Zippo when a sign above the back bar caught his eye:

No Non-Smoking Allowed

Dan grinned and lit his cigarette.

Then the bartender stepped out of the walk-in cooler, accompanied by a blast of frigid air: late-twenties, with long, curly dark hair, big, *big* dark eyes, and when she clanged the cooler shut and spotted him sitting at the far end of her bar, she gave him a little smile and swayed over.

"Hi," she said.

"Hi."

She put a Miller Lite coaster down next to the ashtray, and Dan caught a glint from a tiny diamond stud in her nose; normally he wasn't a face jewelry kinda guy, but she pulled it off.

"What can I get for you?"

Someone had sprayed a black My Friend's Place tee-shirt onto her, but they had left most of the top of her breasts uncovered. She folded her arms on the bar. Dan forced himself to look into her eyes. "Do you have Shiner Bock on tap?"

"We have it in the bottle."

"I'll take one of those."

"Comin' up, cutie." She twitched over to a floor cooler and slid it open and dug deep, bottles clanking, then stood back up and used her opener to pop the Shiner. Dan jerked his eyes back up to the bad football as she set his beer on the coaster. "That'll be three bucks. Unless you want to start a tab?"

"A tab would be great." He dug the Visa out and handed it over; her warm brown eyes flickered to his wedding ring as she took it, and Dan waited for the saucy smile to go away, but it just got saucier. "Anything else?"

"Yeah, I heard you guys have the best cheeseburger around."

"You heard right, handsome. What do you want on it?" The arms went back on the bar and the breasts went back on the arms; her light, flowery perfume fought through the reek of beer and cigarettes and bar food to tickle Dan's nose.

He blinked and cleared his throat. Cheeseburger. Want on it. "Uh, tomato and onion and mustard, I guess."

"Any fries with that?"

"Sure."

"You got it." She patted his hand before swaying toward the kitchen. "Reggie, order!"

A short but stocky black guy wearing a My Friend's Place tee-shirt with the sleeves rolled up—the better to display the branded guns—and a backwards orange Volunteer cap came out of the cramped kitchen and yanked one of the buds jammed into his large ears and listened to the brunette relay Dan's order with a scowl. Then he scowled over at Dan, and then he scowled at the three other customers, and then he scowled at the brunette again; Reggie was a first-rate scowler.

"Where the hell'd you disappear to, Sam? I been hollerin' for ten minutes! You go outside 'n check on those folks?"

Sam gave him haughty. "Everyone's fine. Just go cook and shut up."

"Breaks don't take no mutherfuckin' ten minutes, not when we got customers sittin' here. I'm a *cook*, not a goddamn waitress." Reggie jammed the bud in and bopped his way back around the corner; meat sizzled as he slapped Dan's burger on the grill.

Dan rubbed where Sam's silky skin had brushed the back of his hand; for someone who handled cold beer for a living, her hands were incredibly warm. She turned and caught him looking, and that little smile twitched to life. Dan jerked his eyes back up to the game.

I'm here to watch football. And eat a fucking cheeseburger. Dear God, she was sexy.

The brunette appeared in the bottom half of his vision; Dan watched inept football and waited for her to go away. She tapped out a Marlboro Menthol from a pack she picked up from behind the bar and stuck one between glossy pink lips, then stood there. Dan sighed and unlimbered his Zippo and lit her smoke; he somehow kept his eyes on hers even though the Grand Canyon of Cleavage gaped as she leaned into the flame; there was even a smattering of cute little freckles down there. *Good Christ.* She took a drag, then blew smoke toward the ceiling out of the corner of that mouth.

"Thanks."

"Not a problem."

She stuck out a warm little hand. "I'm Samantha, but all my friends call me Sam." A dark twinkle: "You can call me Sam."

"Uh, I'm Dan. Nice to meet you, Sam."

Ho lee crap, maybe I should just abandon the Visa and run.

"Nice to meet you, too, Dan." She blew another stream from the corner of that mouth: "I haven't seen you in here before. I'd remember if I had."

Dan forced a laugh. *Beth-Beth-Beth!* "There's a reason for that, Sam: This is my first time. You could say I'm a My Friend's Place virgin, I guess."

Sam laughed. "We don't get many of those 'round here."

"I bet."

"So, Dan, I see you're married."

"Very."

More smiles and more smoke as she considered that: "That's too bad," she finally said.

"Yeah," he said. "Too bad."

"Where's this lucky wife of yours tonight?"

With a strange mix of relief and disappointment, Dan launched into the story; he figured that saucy smile would vanish when Sam learned he had a family and was going two thousand miles away tomorrow, never to return, but he was wrong.

So wrong.

That freckled wonderland gaped as she leaned close: "So what you're saying, Dan, is that she isn't *here.*"

"Uh, well…"

Sam laughed again and walked away, cigarette smoke trailing over her shoulder like a lariat. Dan pointed his face back up at the football.

Good God, being married is so hard sometimes…

Sam brought his food and another frosty Shiner without asking. Dan mumbled his thanks and dug in and tried not to look at her; she came around the end of the bar and trailed her warm fingers across his shoulders and the nape of his neck; he shivered at the promise in that feathery touch.

Dan ate faster.

Fuck the football, I have to get the hell out of here.

"Grow up, Ricky!"

Dan turned, and he was just in time to watch Sam jerk her arm out of the grasp of one of the lost frat boys. That smile was nowhere to be seen as she stalked back behind the bar and slammed three empty longnecks into the trash so hard they shattered. Dan watched her flounce into the kitchen, gorgeous ass twitching, curls swaying to the middle of her back, and then he looked over his shoulder again and found the kid she'd called Ricky giving him a hard stare.

"What the fuck are *you* looking at?"

Dan sized the punk up, then turned back around and took a bite of his cheeseburger; Steve would have to bail him out of jail, and then he'd have to come all the way back to Tennessee for a fucking court date. *Not worth it.* Besides, he had the .22 in his back pocket, and Dan was pretty sure carrying one inside a bar was a big no-no.

"I said what the fuck are you looking at, faggot?"

Sam reappeared. "Ricky, stop it!"

Dan chewed, swallowed, then slid off the stool and stood up; the Rickster was shorter than him, but heavier, and he oozed arrogance and confidence. Dan smiled, flicked his smile to the Rickster's buddy—a shorter, heavier Rickster clone—and then back to the original and held up his right index finger:

"One."

Ricky frowned. "One what? Get a load of this guy, Philly." Philly smirked and got a load. Rickey added his smirk to Philly's. *It's a bona fide smirk-off.* "What the fuck does 'one' mean, douche bag?"

Dan added a second finger: "Two."

The smirks fell away. Sam screeched, "Ricky, leave him alone!" Everyone ignored her, but Dan saw the guy at the other end of the bar acknowledge the world by turning his head to watch.

Ricky sneered. "Tough guy, huh? Let me guess. Something *baaaaad* happens when you get to three, right?"

Dan's blood was tingling. "Nothing much, Ricky, except that I'll wipe this whole fucking bar with your face. You're little butt-buddy's there, too."

They stared at him. So did Sam. Aerosmith rocked the juke now, Steven crowing about walkin' dis way. Dan loved that song.

Ricky jabbed a finger at Sam. "She's my girlfriend, man, so fuck you."

"I am *not* your girlfriend!"

The Rickster's face fell; Dan almost felt sorry for the dumb-ass. "What do you mean?" he whined. "Hasn't the last three weeks meant anything?"

Sam's tan skin flushed darker, but she wasn't embarrassed. "I'm *supposed* to talk to him, you asshole. It's my *job.*"

Then Reggie pushed past Sam and pulled the buds from his ears and gave all the white people hard stares. "What the fuck goin' on out here?" He looked eager to do something besides cook.

Sam said, "Ricky's being an asshole again."

Reggie put the Reggie Scowl on the Rickster, who didn't look so cocky anymore. Philly decided he had urgent and unfinished business back by the pool tables. "I tole you 'bout dat shit, Ricky. You goan make me come 'round there and kick yo punk ass?" He scowled at Sam. "Why you gotta fuck a pretty boy like dis, girl? You wanna dick-down from a *real* man, jus' let me know." The Scowl shifted to Dan. "What you gotta do wit' dis shit?"

Dan raised both hands, palm out. "I was just eating my cheeseburger, Reggie. It's a goddamn good cheeseburger, by the way."

Flattery would get you nowhere, apparently: "You doan know me." He spun back to the kitchen, barking at Sam, "Git yo pussy-ass boyfriend outta here 'fo I throw 'im out on 'is noodle."

Dan sat down and picked up his cheeseburger and took a bite; he wasn't worried about turning his back on the Rickster. Hell, Dan almost wished the punk would pull something so he could watch Reggie go to work. Show over, the guy propping up the other end of the bar turned his face back up to Chuck's goofy Texas adventures with that same sad detachment.

Dan ate and watched the Bengals score a touchdown just before halftime; it was seven to three. *Woo hoo, a baseball game.* Ricky and Sam held a whispered conversation four stools down from Dan, with Sam doing most of the whispering and Ricky looking like a whipped dog. Dan chewed and watched football and tried not to listen.

"What do you mean you're not my girlfriend? Didn't we agree that—"

"Just go." Judging by that tone—and that cold, cold face—the Rickster had enjoyed his last ride on the coaster known as Wild Sam.

"Sam—"

"*Go*, or do you want Reggie to come back out here?"

"I'll call you later." Sam didn't respond, and Dan looked over as Ricky turned dejectedly away. Their eyes met. Ricky stalked back to the pool table, still holding Dan's eyes, and slammed his cue into the holder next to the jukebox. He whispered something to Philly, then turned back around with his chest puffed and fists clenched, but Philly dragged him toward the front door.

Dan gave the punk a little wave.

"Bye, Ricky!" The door thumped shut. "Man, am I gonna miss him."

Reggie stalked out of the kitchen and gifted Dan with The Scowl. "Doan you start, muthafucka, or you be outta here, too. Got it?"

"Got it."

Reggie chopped a short, satisfied nod, then bee-bopped back into the kitchen. Dan looked at Sam. "Friendly place, My Friend's Place."

"Sorry about that. And Ricky…well, it's a long story—"

"It always is."

The salty smile made a comeback. "The moral of this story, Dan, is don't sleep with the regulars. It just causes problems."

"I picked up on that."

She swayed over and leaned on the bar in front of him. "But you're not a regular, are you, Dan?"

Dan stopped chewing and stared at her. He was saved from coming up with a response when the door to the patio jerked open and a heavyset guy in his fifties with a bushy gray beard and a drunken grin peered in; Dan recognized one half of the dancing couple from the deck.

"Jesus fuck, girl! Wha'dya do, fall in the toilet? Louise'n me are ready for a refill."

Sam favored him with a cool stare. "I'm bringing it, Tom." She moved down the bar and tilted a plastic pitcher under a Budweiser tap.

"N' turn on the goddamn radio if no one's gonna feed the juke. We got dancin' ta do." Tom did an impromptu jig in the doorway.

"*All right*, Tom. You just go back out there and take care of Louise."

He cackled. "You bet your purty little ass I'll take care of her!" Tom danced back out sans music, letting the door clomp shut.

Dan raised an eyebrow at Sam. She shrugged, which did very nice things to the freckles. "It's their thirtieth anniversary. There was this big party outside earlier, but they're the only ones left." Dan enjoyed the view as she dug cold mugs out of a floor cooler. "I'm just glad it's Thursday, or they'd all still be out there."

"I guess they're what you'd call regulars."

She passed in front of him carrying the pitcher and the mugs and then turned and shoved open the door to the deck with her butt. "Yep."

"And I'm not."

Sam paused and gave him the smokiest look he'd ever been graced with: "No, Dan, you're not." She pushed all the way out; the door swung shut with another clomp.

Dan took an unsteady drink of the Shiner. *Now why the hell did I say that?* He sooooo needed to get the fuck out of there before he did something stupid; he checked his watch. Beth and Lizzie should've landed by now, but they still had to claim baggage and pick up the rental car, so it might be a bit before they called.

Sam came back in and turned the radio on and Dan kept his eyes on the football he couldn't give a shit less about while the sad guy down the bar ordered another shot. Sam poured it for him, then came back over and stood in front of Dan. Leonard Skynyrd was singing about giving him three steps as he lit Sam's new smoke.

Her eyes made him sweat.

Damn, this is gonna hurt.

"I can't, Sam."

That smile faded away.

"You're beautiful…I mean, God, you're sexy as hell, but…I just can't do that to Beth. She's my wife." Sam had her warm little hands folded on the bar, and against his better judgment he took the one without her smoke in both of his and stroked it, and just for one tiny fraction of a second he let himself imagine the night they could have, and then he let it go, and her hand. "I love her, and…and I just can't." To soothe her pride—and because it was probably true—he added, "I know I'm giving up the best night of my life."

"You're right about that." Cold. Her smile came back, but a great big dollop of angry had replaced saucy and inviting. "Married men are a dime a dozen, but a married man who's truly faithful to his wife? I didn't know your kind still existed."

Dan put two fingers up behind his head and waggled them. "Last of the Mohicans, baby."

Sam laughed, but it was as hard and as brittle as the new smile. "She's a lucky woman." She turned and swayed toward the kitchen, watching him watch. "It's your loss, Dan."

"I know." He went back to staring at meaningless football.

Shit. Shit. *Shit!*

His mouth had said all the right things, but his cock wanted him to stay. *I really need to get the fuck out of here.* Dan sighed and pushed his uneaten fries away and pulled out his wallet. "What do I owe you?"

She rang him up with this little pout, sexy as all hell. He got his card back and paid cash, tipping way too much, then stood up.

"It was nice to meet you, Sam."

"You too, Dan." She put a hand on her hip, posing, showing him what he was passing up.

He swallowed. "Bye."

"Bye."

Dan walked past the pool tables to the front door, but as he reached for the handle, Lizzie's voice crashed into his mind, freezing him in astonishment.

"*...outside, Daddy. Don't go...*"

Then she was gone.

What the fuck?

Dan looked around wildly; he almost said her name out loud, then caught himself. *Lizzie?* Had he just heard his daughter speaking to him, or had he imagined it?

Then he saw Sam. She was standing behind the bar, watching him with this shocked, almost terrified expression. She saw him looking and scooted into the kitchen.

Dan frowned and shook his head, which suddenly felt like it'd been stuffed with bubble wrap. *The night air will help clear it.*

He yanked open the door and went out.

No Other Light

 ETH STOOD at the Avis counter in the Bob Hope Airport and filled out paperwork. The professionally friendly and attractive blonde woman—Darla, her gold-embossed name tag said—on the other side of the counter had a smile glued on her California-tan face, but the strain beneath it was plain to Beth, even without her new abilities.

Beth didn't care about Darla's problems; she had enough of her own. Without turning around, she checked on her daughter.

Lizzie was still sitting in the red plastic chair in front of the floor-to-ceiling window, Mr. Fred clutched in her lap and yellow backpack resting below her dangling sneakers, their luggage waiting on the floor beside her. Her hair was mussed from the nap she'd taken on the flight, and she was still a little groggy and grouchy; the vast spread of twinkling lights that was Los Angeles filled the darkening window behind her.

Beth sagged in relief. *Groggy is good.* She could live with groggy, because groggy meant Lizzie wasn't doing anything…wrong.

The flight from Phoenix to Burbank had been the tensest hour and fifteen minutes of Beth's life. She'd sat there in her rented chair in the sky, worrying that Lizzie would get it into her five-year-old head to do, well, something, because if she pulled any stunts like the one she'd pulled at the Phoenix airport, they would've been done for, along with everybody trapped with them. So Beth had kept a sharp watch, but Lizzie had done nothing that any other little kid wouldn't do, grinning during the takeoff and looking out the window and exclaiming over everything; she even fell asleep again.

Beth hadn't relaxed a jot, however, because a terrifying thought kept running through her head: If Lizzie *did* do something, could she stop her?

Could I even begin *to stop her?*

Beth licked her lips, which were chapped and raw from a long day of lip-licking. She'd considered what Lizzie had done, and she believed she could do it as well, but only to a handful of people—at the most. The very thought sickened her, however; Beth didn't want to control anyone other than herself, and couldn't even imagine trying, but Lizzie…

Hundreds upon hundreds of people: "*I can make them run, Mommy. Watch.*"

The pen in Beth's hand trembled as she held it poised over the form.

And she wasn't even trying!

What could Lizzie do if she put some effort into it?

That thought twisted her whole being with fear, because Beth couldn't watch her all the time. What if Lizzie woke up in the middle of the night and started doing something? What if she did something to the kids at the new daycare? She wouldn't start kindergarten until next year, now, but what if she....

Cold, greasy sweat broke out all over Beth's body.

How do I manage a five-year-old who possesses the power to get what she wants when she wants it?

Darla reached out a clear fake fingernail and tapped the page twice. "You still need to sign here and here, Mrs. Sims, and then we'll get you on your way."

"Sorry," Beth mumbled, signing. "It's been a long day."

"I understand. I love what you've done with her hair, by the way."

"Thanks."

Beth paid with the MasterCard and said she didn't care what kind of vehicle they got as long as it didn't break down. Darla left in a huff and came back with the keys to a Jeep Grand Cherokee and was frostily explaining the roadside assistance when Beth felt it and stiffened.

The rental agent stopped talking and frowned over Beth's shoulder. "Is there something wrong with your little girl?"

Beth whirled.

Lizzie still sat in the red plastic chair, the sky behind her deepening in colorful smoggy layers, from a smoky yellow on top to burnt orange to purple to black on bottom, the lights of L.A. gleaming like a gazillion fireflies in that spreading darkness, but Mr. Fred had fallen off her lap, and Lizzie had made no move to pick him up. Instead, she stared straight forward, eyes unfocused, just like she did when she grayed-out, except this time her mouth was moving as if she were talking to herself.

Beth darted to her and knelt in front of her and gripped her shoulders. "Lizzie? Baby?" Mind-boggling power pulsed from her daughter; it was so strong Beth was certain everyone in the Los Angeles Basin could feel it, maybe the entire West coast.

What was happening? *What is she doing!?* "Sweetie, can you hear me?"

Lizzie stared straight ahead, mouth moving and moving, whispering something too low for Beth to make out.

"Is she okay?" Darla had come around the counter, and several travelers who'd been waiting in line were staring. Beth ignored them all and shook Lizzie's shoulders as hard as she dared.

"Lizzie? *Lizzie!*" No response. Whatever she was doing, there was no manifestation that Beth could see—or feel or hear or smell or taste, for that matter. *Is that good or bad?* If Beth couldn't tell what her daughter was doing, how could she stop it? She leaned closer, trying to hear what Lizzie was saying:

"...*Daddy. Don't go outside, Daddy. Don't go outside, Daddy. Don't go outside, Daddy. Don't go...*"

Beth stopped breathing.

"*No.*"

"Ma'am?"

Daniel.

"NO!" Beth shook Lizzie harder, shoving her face right into her daughter's blank countenance; she could smell the peanut-butter crackers that the nice flight attendant had brought Lizzie on the plane. "Lizzie! Is it your Daddy? Is he…is he…" Beth couldn't say it. Don't go outside? Damn him! He'd *promised* her, but he was still at that stupid house! "Lizzie, please tell me what's happening! *Please!*"

Just that blank stare and the whispering and that incredible flow of force; wherever Lizzie's mind was, it wasn't where her body sat.

Was she with her father? Somehow, Beth knew that she was.

A tear leaked down Beth's cheek, then another; she stroked Lizzie's face. "Please, baby, help your Daddy. Please."

Darla appeared at Beth's side. "Is she having a seizure? Does she have a medical condition?" Beth didn't answer. "Should I call AMS? They'll be able to—"

"Leave us alone! She's fine!" Darla fell away in shock as Beth went back to stroking Lizzie's smooth, round cheek. She was aware of over a dozen people now watching uneasily, and that at her outburst, Darla's supervisor had picked up a phone to call the airport medics; he also called security. Beth didn't care.

Lizzie went on whispering: *"Don't go outside, Daddy, don't go outside…"*

"Please, baby, help your Daddy. Help him. *Please.*"

Daniel.

Oh, my Daniel…the phone!

Beth dived into her purse and snatched her phone out and frantically called her husband.

Dan stepped out of My Friend's Place and into the crisp October night and shook his head to clear it; he could no longer hear Lizzie's voice. *Boy, I must really be missing her.* He checked his watch; the girls should call any minute. Music throbbed through the door at his back—more Aerosmith; Mr. Tyler was evidently back in the saddle again—and he could hear drunken laughter from around the corner as Tom and Louise boogied on the deck. Sam's inviting brown eyes and fabulous body flashed across his mind, and he had to force himself down the three steps and out into the gravel. *What a great little neighborhood bar, not like Carmody's at all.* Shame he would never see it again. Or Sam.

Dan laughed at himself as he crunched toward the Toyota. Beth was right: he was an idiot, plain and simple, but if she finally got tired of his shit, it was good to know he had options. He'd just have to drive all the way back from California. Dan pictured that body again. *It just might be worth it.* He beeped the truck open and was reaching for the door handle when something caught his eye.

Earlier there had been three pickups in the lot besides his, and the beater Corolla; they were all still there, but the red four-wheel-drive Silverado Z-71—an '08, he was pretty sure—parked furthest from him now held two people. Dan's adrenaline pumped hard as he recognized the Rickster and Philly; for a split second he was sure they were laying for him, but then the way they sat registered.

He squinted. "What the fuck?"

Ricky was behind the wheel of the Chevy with his head thrown back and mouth hanging open; he looked asleep—or dead. Philly slumped in the passenger seat with his head against the side glass.

"Jesus." Well, he sure as fuck didn't want these assholes on the road with him—or anyone else. He would have to go back inside and tell Sam and Reggie.

Let them deal with these lightweights.

Dan started back toward the front door when Lizzie's voice blasted into his head: "*…outside, Daddy, don't…*"

He staggered and fell against the side of the Tundra. "Lizzie?" He could *feel* her presence, as if she were standing right next to him; turns out his daughter *was* speaking to him from thousands of miles away.

But why?

How?

"Baby, I can't understand you," he told the air; he should've felt crazy doing that, but he didn't. "Outside? What does that mean? Lizzie?"

The front door to My Friend's Place suddenly opened and Dan heard Sam's smoker's voice call, "I'll be right back!", and then she stepped out and let the door bang shut and swayed down the three metal steps and undulated over. "I wanted to say a proper goodbye, Dan."

Lizzie was more than halfway across the country, but she was talking to him. Somehow. Dan should've been freaked out by that, but again, for some reason he wasn't; maybe because since those first silver hairs had appeared, he'd been almost expecting something wacky like this.

But why does she sound so scared?

Sam pressed closer, freckled jugs leading the charge, and Dan stifled his irritation; she was hot and all, boy was she, and in a trashy-sorta-fun way he really liked, but he didn't have time for her crap right now. He held up a hand, and she gave him space with a frown.

"Look, Sam, I'm flattered, I really am, but—"

That sexy pout: "I just wanted a hug." Her pink lips twisted, and anger flickered deep inside her eyes, making them a lot less inviting: "I know you're faithful to your *wife*, even though she doesn't deserve or appreciate you!"

Yikes. "One hug." Lizzie's presence seemed to dim as Sam stepped near. That was weird, but then so was thinking he heard his daughter talking to him from over the horizon. "Then I really do have to—"

That's all he got out before she grasped him in a hug that would've shamed Jessie the Body Ventura; Dan grunted and tried to push her away, and she released him and stepped back, letting her warm little strong-ass hand trail across his cheek.

"It could have been so good, Dan."

"Yeah," he gasped. He would be sore for a fucking week. *Bartending must be a better workout than I thought.* Sam was looking at him like she wanted to come back in for another hug, so he backed up…

Or tried to.

Dan gaped down at his feet. They were frozen to the gravel!

"Not this shit again!"

"Dan," Sam said…but it wasn't Sam's voice. His eyeballs almost bugged out of his head as her form *rippled* and became slightly taller as the curly brown hair morphed into shimmering blue-black waves and the warm russet eyes darkened to cold black pits. Sam's face melted away, replaced by features so stunning, so perfect, that they were regal.

Alexandria.

Dan jerked at his foot, and then the other; both stayed put. "Let me go!"

She only smiled, then raised one slender hand. Dan's head jerked around as an engine started, and his mouth dropped open when the red Silverado backed up and drove over and did a K turn before stopping twenty feet away with its grille centered on him. Ricky and Philly were still slumped in the cab, dead to the world, and as Dan looked, he saw Philly fall over in the seat; the Silverado's v-8 revved.

Dan remembered the .22 then, and his right hand crept towards his back pocket as he glared at Alexandria. "Let me go!"

"I was willing to grant you one last night of pleasure, Dan, of bliss you can't even dream of, but you spurned me. Oh, I suppose I could have taken your seed by force, although you would have enjoyed that process much less, but part of the power lies in the conception, and without your…enthusiasm, shall we say, it wouldn't be as special." That icy smile again: "Even my Master must abide by some rules, though it chafes Him." That smile vanished, and now she looked regretful. "It was not meant to be, Dan. You chose *her*." Those exquisite lips pursed. "I wonder, would you have chosen differently had you known it was truly me and not some little serving girl?"

He gripped the butt of the .22, ready to pull it and send this gorgeous bitch down to be with her father. "The answer would be no, sweetheart. Not even on your *best* day. Now turn me loose or I'll—"

"*DADDY!*"

Dan cringed at Lizzie's mental shout, and Alexandria flinched away, as if in pain, but when nothing else happened, she straightened. "She is splendid, is she not? But even *she* is too far away to help you now. So strong, but you and I could have produced a child as powerful, perhaps even *more* powerful." Jealousy twisted that perfect face: "I am infinitely more suited to being the Mother of the One Foretold than *her!*"

One Foretold?

"What the fuck are you talking about?"

"She bears the mark," Alexandria said, awe stealing across that amazing face. "She is the One, Dan. Your daughter is the One our Master has been not-so-patiently waiting for across untold centuries. She is the One that will prepare this world for His triumph."

Dread filled Dan's soul; the mark. She meant the silver streak, the one he'd dreamt of. *No, that's…no. No!* "You're insane, lady." Dan jerked the .22 out and brought it around, but she twisted her fingers sharply; an invisible force yanked the gun from his grip, and it floated to her. She plucked it from the air.

Sonofabitch. Now that shit just wasn't fair. "Give that back!" Dan yanked at his feet to no avail. "Let me go!"

Alexandria examined the little pistol, then murmured, "This could be of some use." She shoved the little burner into her own back pocket.

Artoo abruptly warbled from his pants; Dan fumbled the phone out, then cursed as Alexandria took it away with another twist of her hand.

"Fucking bitch!"

She sneered at the screen and then held it up, just out of his reach: Beth. "She is one of us, you know, even if she does not wish it. Her acceptance means nothing. Your daughter, on the other hand…oh, Dan, the things that we will teach her, and I can hardly imagine what she will teach us once she attains her full potential!" Rapture filled those sable eyes as they stared past him at something wonderful yet to be: "Glorious days are coming, Dan! *Glorious!*"

"You leave them alone! Goddamn you, *leave my family alone!*" With a supreme surge of will, Dan freed one foot and lunged, nearly snatching the iPhone from her hand.

Shock painted that face; she took a hurried step away, holding the phone out of his reach again. "Yes, you are strong," she breathed. "Such a shame that another has claimed you."

"Damn right, and don't you fucking forget it! And you had better stay away from my family or I'll—"

"I wasn't speaking of her." And then she walked away as he fought to follow, but that one step had taken everything he had for the moment. She wasn't talking about Beth? Who, then? Dan panted as he watched her climb the steps, Sam's sexy features oozing back into place as Sam's smoker's voice said, "Goodbye, Dan."

The Silverado's headlights came on, throwing his stark shadow against the Toyota; the v-8 revved again, long and loud. Dan held his hand up, shading his eyes, and looked at it.

Oh shit.

Alex/Sam opened the front door to My Friend's Place and shouted inside: "No, Ricky! Don't do it!"

Dan fought to free himself as the Silverado's lights jumped, gravel flying as it rocketed toward him…and then horror overtook him when he got a good look inside the cab.

Ricky and Philly were gone. Swirling black shadows now filled it, and out of that depthless darkness shone two glowing green eyes; they watched him struggle in the headlights with a gleeful hunger.

"No! NO!"

The front of the Silverado crushed his body into the side of his truck. Strange, globular lights swirled around his face as he vomited dark red blood all over the steaming, crumpled hood. From far away he saw the shadows in the cab vanish and the glowing, gloating eyes wink out, and then a dazed Ricky and Philly sat up and looked at him through the cracked windshield. They screamed in tandem.

I can't breathe. His hands twitched on the hood, and the headlights under his armpits shone a dim scarlet from all the blood, his blood, and then the truck backed up, throwing gravel the other way, and Dan slumped to the ground. He vomited more blood onto the rocks.

"DADDY!"

I can't breathe. Lizzie's love and terror beat around his dimming vision like a storm of butterflies. More lights danced. Dan heard people shouting, more screaming, and then shoes appeared next to him in the bloody gravel.

The lights were growing now, pushing back the shadows, pushing back everything until there was only the light; a light like no other.

That strange, gentle light was all around him now.

Dan's pain vanished, and he laughed as Lizzie's shy, gummy grin appeared; Beth's lips brushed across his. Their love filled him until he thought his heart would burst with joy, and he grasped that love with everything he had, determined to take it with him no matter where he was going.

He would never let them go.

DAAAAADEEEEE!

My girls.

The light was everything.

Freedom

WILLIAM SIMS sat and stared at the orange legal envelope. He was thinking. He wasn't thinking about his little brother Danny; he should have been, but he wasn't.

Will was contemplating freedom.

That hateful, hopeful envelope lurked on the desk in front of him next to a dusty size 11 ½ wide New Balance shoe box crammed full of faded Polaroids, which in turn sat next to a watery Crown mix; the drink had started out as a Crown rocks, but Will had made it over an hour ago and the ice had long since melted. It was just after eleven on a Monday morning, and the nose-to-the-grindstone mentality his dad had hammered into him made it tough for Will to justify imbibing this early, no matter the circumstances.

Circumstances…

Will snatched up the drink and gulped it down and wiped the condensation ring with his sleeve and got up and left his home office and carried the glass downstairs.

He stood behind the wet bar and sipped his new Crown rocks and looked around at his family's home; four bedrooms and three-and-a-half baths and a two-car garage in a nice, safe neighborhood; the picture-perfect suburban life. They'd even installed a twenty-thousand-dollar pool in the backyard three years ago. Will had been in it maybe twice. The kids liked it, though, and he certainly enjoyed it when Tiff brought over her friends to lay out. Will felt no guilt at that; his beloved wife of eighteen years had turned fat and mean and had quit putting out roughly a decade ago.

Yes, they'd had some good years here, raised the kids here, but now Donna was bitching that they needed a bigger one, preferably over in Mist Wood Heights, where all her snotty friends lived. Will snorted; as if living in a fancy new house in a schmancy new neighborhood would make her happy. The fat cunt hadn't been happy in fifteen years.

Will downed his drink and refreshed his ice and poured another, then took it and a Corona coaster back upstairs, his footsteps on the carpeted risers making no sound to disturb the silence. The fat cunt was at work, and the kids were at school—or at least that's where they were all supposed to be; he was supposed to be at work, too. Casey had been busted for skipping last week, and it was Tiffany's senior year, so ditching class was a time-honored tradition; as for Donna, Will didn't give a shit what she did anymore.

His chair creaked when he sat back down behind his desk, and his eyes were immediately drawn to the orange envelope again. Will took a sip and yanked his gaze away and put it on the dusty New Balance shoe box full of memories. He sat the coaster down and the drink on the coaster, then reached in the box and plucked a memory out at random.

There was Will and his brother holding up fly rods, an iridescent trout dangling on each line, proud grins on their skinny faces; they were about ten and eight, Will a good four inches taller than Danny. He vaguely remembered crying over this picture Saturday night after he'd gotten sloshed and yanked down the drop-stairs and crawled up into the attic to find this damn box. Donna had stayed up with him, and he even sorta kinda remembered her being nice. Of course they'd ended up fighting later, but for a time he'd gotten sympathy, even if he and Danny hadn't truly been close in years.

Will stared at the faded picture; there were no tears, now.

He put it to the side and plucked another random, washed-out memory: twelve and ten and mugging for the camera up in the fort they'd cobbled together in that old hickory out back. *I'd damn near forgotten about that fort.* Will thought their mother had been the one down on the ground behind the Instamatic, but couldn't be sure. He put it aside and shuffled through several more, most of him and Danny together, some individual, birthday parties and cookouts and camping and hunting and fishing trips flicking by frame after sepia frame, and then Will pulled out another memory and propped his elbows on the desk and held it in both hands and stared at it for a long time.

It was all four of them together: Mom and Dad and Will and Danny. They were in some backyard he didn't recognize, and he and Danny were about seven and five. He touched the tip of his finger to his mother's face, then his father's; he let go with one hand and explored his own features, which were a near duplicate of Dad's. Danny looked like Mom and Will looked like Dad, and who was whose favorite tracked straight down those same lines; maybe in other families those lines were blurred, but in theirs they'd been hard and clear. His brother had her eyes as well, but Will had gotten nothing from her appearance-wise. Danny had Mom's blonde hair, too.

Had had. Danny *had* had her blonde hair and blue eyes, but he was gone now.

Will had to start thinking of his little brother in the past tense. *How the hell do you make yourself do something like that?* He studied the picture, trying to remember that day, or at least where they had been, but couldn't dredge it up; at least they looked happy.

Or rather, he and Danny looked happy.

Their father was scowling at the camera, as per usual, and their mom had a restless, dissatisfied look on her pretty face and a drink in her hand—also as usual. Will glanced at the highball glass leaving a ring on the cheap cardboard coaster; when he drank, there was a reason Will rarely drank much, and she was staring at him out of the faded Polaroid. On Sunday morning he'd sworn to Christ that he wouldn't touch the shit ever again—one of those hung-over swears he'd thought he might actually keep this time. *It's not like I have any more brothers to lose.* But that was before he'd gone to work this morning and opened the mail.

The mail had changed everything.

The mail…and the phone call.

He picked up the glass and took a drink and swirled the ice as he went back to staring at the picture.

Will snorted. Even at five, Danny had already perfected that shit-eating grin. Then, almost reluctantly, he studied his seven-year-old self; a brash kid with a mop of brown hair and a cocky smile, a kid who didn't have the first goddamn clue how unfair and just plain fucked-up life could be; a stupid kid that didn't know that even when you work hard and do all the right things and play by all their rules and then finally get what you deserve, it *still* wasn't enough. He wanted to shout at the picture, send his grownup voice crashing into the past, tell that smug little shit to do what *he* wanted, not what *they* wanted, because in the end it doesn't matter what you do.

In the end, the darkness eats us all.

Look at Danny; pulped in some shitty little bar parking lot, and for why? Because some frat boy got his panties in a twist when Danny chatted up his girlfriend? He touched his brother's face; there were no guarantees, and life was too short to be miserable. Will wanted to scream it at his seven-year-old smirking self, but Will knew that even if he could somehow time-travel his voice, you couldn't tell kids stuff like that because they wouldn't understand, or believe it if they did; you had to let life crush their dreams in its own sweet, sadistic time, and then hope they gathered what wisdom they could from the pain.

Will laughed, then threw back the Crown; he still couldn't feel the alcohol. He looked at all four of them again, there in the distant past, standing in some stranger's backyard…all four of them together…

And now I'm the last one standing.

He set the Polaroid and the glass down, then got up and walked over to the window and cracked the blinds and peeked out at the winterized swimming pool; Halloween was less than a week away, and yellow and orange leaves had mounded up on the blue cover and around the inside of the privacy fence. He'd tell Casey to rake them and pile them out by the curb, even though his progeny would whine and bitch and put it off until Will stood over him and made him do it; if it wasn't skateboarding or playing video games or smoking weed, Casey didn't want jack shit to do with it.

Will had gone wrong with the boy somewhere. *Should have never listened to that fat cunt tell me I couldn't spank her kids.* They'd turned out to be spoiled, selfish little twats… and God, Donna! They'd been high-school sweethearts, and there was a time, long ago, that Will remembered being madly in love with his wife—a long, *long* time ago.

His phone rang in his pocket: Barbara. She'd called six times this morning, even though after he'd found the envelope with no return address and read the short letter inside—anger stirred in Will; and saw the photographs!—he'd told his secretary to cancel everything for today and that he was going home and not to bother him. Nobody listened to him, though, especially Barbara; he heard the beep as she left him yet another voicemail.

With a bowel-wrenching mixed sense of revulsion, disbelief, and excitement, Will went back to his desk and sat down and picked up the orange envelope and dumped its contents; a typed, single-page letter and three printed digital full-color photographs were all that tumbled out, but they were more than enough.

Will picked up the letter and read it again; there was no salutation:

You are the godfather of Elizabeth Ann Sims. When the time comes that her mother and father can no longer care for her, you will decline the responsibility for her concern. In return, we are prepared to offer you $1,000,000. The money is currently held in a Grand Cayman Island account within an undisclosed banking entity, and if you agree, $500,000 will be wired to any account you choose, in any part of the world, or your name can be put on the current account (at which time the entity will be disclosed). This is just for agreeing. Should you keep your end of the bargain, the remaining balance of $500,000 will be made available. This offer is good until ten p.m. Monday, October 25th, 2010. Call the number provided. The man who answers will present information to verify the existence of the Grand Cayman account, and will supply more details if you indicate your wish to come to an agreement; if you do not call by the deadline, we will assume you decline this generous offer.

Do not contact the authorities.

Do not tell anyone of this communication.

If you do either, we will know.

That was it, except for the number…and the three photographs.

The first was of Tiffany on a sidewalk with two of her yummy friends, backpacks slung over shoulders, gabbing about whatever seventeen-year-old girls gabbed about. It had been taken from what looked like a passing car; her school was in the background. The next was of Casey skateboarding, again taken from a passing car, and the third was of his wife waddling out of her office building while chatting with some guy.

Is he fucking Donna? Will didn't particularly care; he was only curious. *Somebody has to.*

Will fanned out all three photos and felt the anger stir again; they were threatening his family. Oh, they hadn't done so straight out, but the pictures combined with the strange "agreement" they wanted said enough.

He checked the clock: 11:23. His sister-in-law and niece wouldn't be landing in Nashville until four, and they would go straight from the airport to the funeral home and pick up Danny's ashes before they met the movers out at that big house in the country; Beth had to get her car out of the garage and supervise the loading of all their things. Danny was supposed to have done all that last Thursday, but there had been some hitch with the movers, and then…

Beth had told him the whole story in a voice both flat and dead, and when Will asked just why the hell Danny hadn't stayed at the house, he got the first emotion from her when she said she'd asked him not to. Will had started to ask her just why the hell yet again, but she'd cut him off, telling him about the cremation and saying the memorial would be delayed indefinitely because she needed to get her and Lizzie settled into the new house in San Bernardino at the same time that she had to open the new restaurant in Santa Monica. Will said he understood, then asked how Lizzie was doing, and Beth said she wasn't handling the situation well.

Poor thing. Will had only seen his niece three times in her life, but she was a doll, with her mother's looks and Will's own mother's eyes; she was a little sweetie, too, and *smart.* Lizzie had to be taking Danny's death hard…

Will was staring at the letter.

He dashed at his leaking eyes and looked away.

When he'd called the Murfreesboro cop shop Friday morning and told them who he was, he'd been transferred to some assistant DA who'd confidently informed him that first-degree murder charges would shortly be filed against both frat-boy pieces of shit; that had been fine with Will. But then the prime witness had vanished; the bartender, Samantha Gains, the girlfriend of this Ricky Thompson asshole, had not been seen since giving a statement to the cops that night. Her mother had been on television everywhere on Saturday, pleading tearfully with the public for information about her missing daughter. So on Sunday morning a hungover Will had called the Murfreesboro powers-that-be back, but this time they hemmed and hawed and wouldn't tell him shit. Then he'd called Beth once more, hoping *she* would know what the hell was going on, but she had seemed distant, only saying that she had her hands full with Lizzie. She'd given him some guy named Steve's number, saying that he was Danny's friend and probably knew more than her.

Then his sister-in-law had hung up on him.

Will frowned and swiveled his chair, back and forth, back and forth:

Her voice…Beth had sounded angry, yes, furious even, but mostly she'd sounded afraid.

Afraid of what?

He glanced at the letter again, then looked away.

So Will had called this Steve, who turned out to be another real-estate agent and also Danny's best friend, and even though it was weird and a little sad to be talking to a man who knew more about his own brother's life…

Turns out the Murfreesboro fuzz was taking a lot of heat, and not only because of the bartender's disappearance; some kid—Will couldn't remember his name— who'd been working the front desk at the La Quinta Inn the night Danny checked in had also up and vanished, and some rag-head Arabic professor from that state college down there had disappeared around the time that whole fucked-up Rison thing had went down, along with his pal, a math professor with a pregnant wife.

To top it off, some hotshot reporter from Chicago and his investigator had been in town working on a story, and *they* had vanished about the same time.

And, of course, you could now throw in that bizarre murder-suicide, the one that had made Danny's death a footnote: Friday afternoon, the day after Danny's murder, a detective named Jackson had pulled his service weapon and offed his partner, one Detective Frisbee, and then himself—right in the middle of the squad room, no less. Jackson hadn't left a note, just bodies, and a stunned department and two grieving families and a shell-shocked community and about a billion questions with no answers.

Six people disappearing in less than three months and a cop-on-cop murder-suicide had brought loud calls for the Murfreesboro police chief to resign or for the mayor to fire him; local hacks were also calling for the FBI to take over the investigation, and Steve had heard rumors that the feds had already quietly done so.

Will's eyes slipped to the letter and then jerked away; whatever the fuck was going on, none of it brought Danny back, and with the lead witness AWOL, Steve said the two punk frat boys—who'd lawyered up big time, and who'd also been shouting their innocence from the beginning—would likely now get off with second-degree manslaughter charges or some bullshit.

Will stood up and paced between the window and the desk; he should call the feds and give them the photos and the letter. *That's exactly what I should do.* Instead, he changed course to the bookshelf behind his chair and pulled down a photograph of his own family: Will and Donna and Tiff and Case; the kids were about three and five. A pang of nostalgia hit him; back then, everything had still been good. He set the frame back on the shelf and resumed pacing; no, he couldn't risk the kids.

I'll call Beth. That's what I'll do. I'll call her right now.

Will pulled his cell out…and then sank into his chair while staring at the letter. Did not telling anyone include Beth? He had a feeling it did, maybe especially Beth. *If you do either, we will know.* But *how* would they know? And he couldn't just plead ignorance; he'd already called the damn number and talked to that Rickson turd. "Just call me Rick", he says, like they were fucking best buddies or something.

Before that call, he had been *sure* this was all some sick prank, but in the middle of ranting at the guy, Will had sarcastically asked if one mil was all they could go. Don't be cheapskates, he'd said, how 'bout a whole mil up front, *and* on the back end? To Will's utter astonishment, the smarmy bastard had put him on hold and then came back in less than twenty seconds and said that yes, they could modify the agreement for two million dollars.

Will sat and breathed until Rick asked if he was still there. Will said he would call back and hung up; that's when he'd stuffed the letter and the photos back into the envelope and trucked it downstairs to make that first drink.

Two million dollars.

Will slid his phone back in his pocket, leaned and rested his elbows on the desk, put his face in his hands…then cracked his fingers so he could see the letter. Should he have asked for more? Say, two million up front *and* on the back end?

Three? Four? Five? The way they hadn't even quibbled made him think maybe ten million bucks might be chump change to whoever these people were. Will's heart throbbed a little faster; ten million. *What can I do with ten million dollars?*

He had a pretty goddamn good idea. *Should I push for that much?*

Will jerked his face from his hands. *What am I thinking?* He couldn't do that to Beth and Lizzie. They were family. He kept his eyes carefully turned away from the letter. Damn it, he was going to call both the feds *and* Beth; she needed to know about this, and the FBI could haul in this Rickson puke and find out what the hell was going on…of course, then they'd have to provide security for Will's family— even Donna. Will would insist on it. And once the media got wind, it would turn into a three-ring circus. Will and Donna had already fielded calls from two different reporters wanting statements about Danny's death, because of the Rison thing, and they'd given the boilerplate about how he was loved and would be missed and that they needed privacy to grieve. Will doubted these people, whoever they were, would have the gonads to harm his family with all *that* going on.

But what if they just wait?

When time went by and nothing happened, would the cops still protect his family? He grimaced. Y*eah, right.* Then there Will would be, stuck paying for private security, keeping four people safe twenty-four-seven…he did some quick math. *Jesus, I'll go broke in a month.*

Will glanced at the clock; he still had over ten hours to make up his mind. What if he just didn't call back? The letter said they'd take that as a pass…but would they just leave it at that? With a sickening roil of his insides, Will understood the truth:

They would come for them, all of them; they couldn't leave them alive, not now. *They've painted me into a fucking corner.*

Two million dollars…two million, *minimum*; for one moment, Will pushed past the grieving faces of his sister-in-law and little niece…

He'd file on the fat sexless cunt first and then sell the shops; Jiffy Lube had offered to buy him out three times over the last ten years. Will would lose position by going to them, but with his nine Sparky Lubes, they'd dominate the quick-change oil market in Columbus by a mile. He'd then be able to pay off all his debt (and Donna) while keeping the Grand Cayman account secret from whatever mad-dog divorce attorney she'd unleashed. After the dust settled, he'd hop down to one of those Saint islands in the Caribbean, St. Bart's or St. Augustine or St. What the Hell Ever, and live on his own little catamaran and only venture off the water for more bait and more rum and the occasional slice of island poontang; Will could almost smell the salt breeze and hear the gulls calling overhead and feel his schooner rocking on the turquoise waves…

He blinked, considered the letter for a minute, then lifted his hip so he could pull out his wallet; he thumbed through the pictures and slid one out of the little plastic sheath. Danny and Beth and Lizzie smiled up at him from in front of a plum velvet backdrop. Beth had her arms around Lizzie, and Danny had his arms around them both. His little brother seemed to stare at Will accusingly over their shoulders, so he covered him up with a thumb, then touched Beth's face with the tip of his index finger.

Holy crow, is she a looker, or what?

Danny had always been the pretty boy; no surprise he'd landed a hot wife. And not only hot; you could tell after one conversation with Beth that she wouldn't let herself go to pot, not like Donna.

Danny's a lucky little shit…

Was a lucky little shit; Danny's luck had finally run out. Will glanced at the letter again; or maybe it hadn't been luck. Danny had always been the baby, too, the favorite; Mommy's little *darling*, that was Danny.

Will pursed his lips, then threw the wallet-sized picture into the dusty shoe box and dumped the rest of the Polaroids on top of it and jammed the lid on and set the box on the floor. He swung around and picked up the picture of his own family, then turned back and placed it on the desk facing him. Will looked at it for another long stretch, then reached out and gently turned it face down.

Will Sims stared at the letter and thought about freedom.

The Final Payment

J OSEPH WIERLANDER was nearly finished setting up for the Douglas viewing when
the sound of a car outside made him pause and check his stainless-steel Bulova.
That should be them.

He straightened and cinched his tie knot as he quelled a nervous flutter somewhere near his sixty-three-year-old heart.

Everything will be fine.

He left the rack of padded folding chairs and walked to a narrow front window
and was in time to see a diminutive woman slip out of a Black & White Taxi that
had pulled to his curb. A little girl slid out with her, holding her mother's hand. They
were wearing matching blue L.A. Dodgers baseball caps, the woman with her hair
pulled out the back in a short brunette ponytail, the girl's hair tucked up under her
cap, a few dark wisps visible against her pale neck. The woman wore faded jeans
with a hole worn through the left knee and Redwing hiking boots and a hot-pink
Banana Republic tee-shirt tucked into the jeans, and as Joseph watched, she bent
over to speak to the driver. The girl wore a dark-red Dora the Explorer tee-shirt,
and her tiny blue jeans weren't faded.

The Black and White stayed by the curb as they turned up his cobbled walk,
faces expressionless behind the dark sunglasses they both wore despite the gloomy
weather. Joseph eyed that idling taxi with vast relief; they would not be staying long,
praise God. The woman carried a gray gym bag with a white swoosh in addition
to her purse, and what looked like a stuffed giraffe that had seen better days. They
disappeared from view as they neared the long, covered front porch of his elegant
converted Colonial, and Joseph stepped away from the window and slipped into
the mantle of serene respect that had served him so well over the years. He felt
nothing like calm inside, but Joseph had long experience comforting the bereaved
no matter his true feelings; today it was imperative that he maintain the facade.

He smoothed the lapels of his double-breasted charcoal Peter Millar, listening
as they ascended the wide steps, and then there came a loud rap despite the "Please
Ring Bell" sign he'd hung at eye level. *Why did I install a two-thousand-dollar computerized
doorbell that plays everything from a gag funeral dirge to Nirvana to Mozart if no one will ring
the bell?* It was the fourth time this week someone had pounded on his door, and
it was only Monday!

Joseph let none of his irritation show as he crossed the somber foyer, footsteps
falling dead on the woven carpet. "Ah, Mrs. Sims." He stood to the side, holding

the door for them. "Come in, come in, welcome to Wierlander Funeral Home and Crematory. I trust you had a pleasant flight?"

"As pleasant as it could have been under the circumstances."

"Yes, of course, I'm so sorry for your loss, Mrs. Sims, so sorry. I understand Dan was a good man and a good father."

Her full lips trembled, and a tear ran from under the dark glasses; she let go of the girl's hand to wipe it away. "Yes," she said, high voice jagged. "Yes, he was."

Joseph considered the top of the little girl's Dodgers cap; she hadn't looked up at him, nor looked left or right. When her mother had let go of her hand, it had floated down to her side and stayed there.

She just…stood there and breathed.

Joseph felt gooseflesh rise on the back of his arms as he bent to the girl's level. "You must be Lizzie. I'm Joseph. It's nice to meet you."

Nothing. After a moment, Mrs. Sims reached down and took the girl's hand again and moved her away from Joseph.

"Apologies, Mrs. Sims, I only—"

"I need to collect my husband and pay you. The meter is running."

"I understand. Follow me, please. Your loved one is waiting in my office." So much for the pleasantries, though he supposed it was just as well, considering.

Joseph led them past the Family Room and the Viewing Room and the Chapel and then down the hallway with the guest lavatories; at the end of the hall he opened the door to his office. With the low, gray clouds outside and the thick curtains pulled and the walnut paneling, Joseph's office was as murky as the inside of one of his customer's final resting places until he switched on his desk lamp. Even then it was subdued, but when he turned around the woman and girl still wore their sunglasses.

"Please be seated." He motioned to the matching claw-footed chairs that faced his desk, but they stayed standing. The little girl stared straight ahead, as silent and unmoving as ever, but Mrs. Sims had her sunglasses pointed at the blonde-wood urn that sat on his blotter. Joseph picked up the simple rectangular container and placed it on the front edge of the desk, engraved side facing her. "Here he is. I hope this is satisfactory."

Joseph's voice was as comforting and understanding as ever, but inside he grated; she'd requested his basic urn, and she'd also insisted on a simple pine box to ensure even and complete burning. There wouldn't even be a service, and the service was where he padded his profit. Still, Joseph had made more than ten burials already on this deal, though she didn't need to know that, and would make even more when his final payment came later tonight.

Mrs. Sims didn't respond; she seemed to be reading the short inscription. Joseph knew what it said because he'd carved it himself, and once again it was his cheapest option: **Daniel Terrance Sims**, and below that, **Beloved Husband and Father**, and then below that, **August 1st 1977-October 21st 2010.**

Mrs. Sims reached out a shaking hand and touched the urn. She sobbed, then let go of the girl to pick it up and clutch it to her chest. Tears dripped onto the blonde wood as she rocked and wept.

Joseph waited patiently; all in a day's work.

"Oh, my Daniel, what will we do without you?" Her husband didn't answer—they never did—and after a minute Mrs. Sims composed herself enough to set the urn back on Joseph's desk. She wiped her face as she laid her purse and the stuffed giraffe on a chair, then unzipped the gym bag. "Is cash still okay, Mr. Wierlander?"

"Certainly, Mrs. Sims." She'd mentioned that on the phone, but Joseph stared as she counted out hundreds and fifties and twenties until she reached the agreed amount. She looked at him, and he hurried behind the desk and sat down. "I have some additional paperwork for you to read and sign," he told her, "and then I'll print your receipt."

Mrs. Sims didn't respond; she was staring down at the silent girl. Joseph made a show of gathering documents, yet he couldn't help but watch in fascination as she knelt and said, "Baby? Lizzie? Can you say hi to your Daddy?" Mrs. Sims lifted the urn from the desk and held it in front of the girl, placing one of her flaccid little hands on the wood. "Can't you say hi? Your Daddy's in here."

Oh no he's nooooot! Joseph sang in his head; he was giddy with the prospect of receiving the final payment for this sordid job, as well as the eminent departure of these two.

The girl slowly raised her head, those blank, black sunglasses peering at him over the lip of the desk; Joseph froze like a bird before a snake.

Mrs. Sims gasped, then frowned as she followed that dark gaze. She frowned harder at Joseph, then stood up and faced him, holding the urn before her. He trembled, paperwork forgotten; if there'd been a way out of the office besides right past them, he would have bolted, screaming.

"Is there, ah, is there a pro—" He swallowed. "Is there a problem, Mrs. Sims?"

The girl abruptly dropped her head, sunglasses going back to what he assumed was the front of his desk. Her mother watched this with more frown, then put that dire scowl on Joseph again.

Joseph smiled for all he was worth, sweat trickling down his ribs beneath his white cotton Saint Laurent undershirt.

Mrs. Sims finally shook her head and sighed, and Joseph felt the tension leave the room like a massive electric charge bleeding away. She carefully placed her husband's alleged remains on the desk once more. "I apologize, Mr. Wierlander. This has been…difficult…for both of us."

"I understand." He showed her where to sign and she did, Joseph pretending to watch while keeping an eye on the girl; if she looked at him again, he really would run screaming.

Joseph secured the cash in the lock box and then woke the computer up and printed out two copies of her receipt and had her sign them as well. Mrs. Sims gathered the urn and her purse and the gym bag and the stuffed giraffe and her daughter, and he followed as she pulled her silent child through the silent funeral home. In the foyer Joseph hurriedly opened and held the door, and they all trooped down the steps and the cobbled walk to the waiting Black and White. The cabbie fiddled with his iPod and didn't glance up as Joseph opened the back door for them.

"Thank you again, Mr. Wierlander. You've been kind."

"Thank *you*, Mrs. Sims. Once more, I'm terribly sorry for your loss."

"Thank you." She jerked the door out of his grasp and shut it in his face with a thump.

Then the little, silent girl—who had climbed into the back seat without prompting or much ado—turned her head to look up at him, and as she did the bill of the Dodgers cap hit her mother's arm and tumbled into the floorboard.

Joseph stiffened.

Mrs. Sims watched him as the cab pulled away, and when she took her sunglasses off and twisted around to stare at him through the back glass, Joseph's heart just about jumped out of his chest; beneath the bill of the cap her eyes were red-veined and brown and hard with suspicion. She kept that dangerous look pinned to him as the cabbie hit the blinker and turned down Jasmine Street.

And then they were gone.

Joseph pulled an embroidered silk handkerchief from his inside jacket pocket and dabbed cold sweat from his face. His hands trembled. "Christ, oh Christ, Mary Mother of God, please save us," he whispered.

It's true! It's all TRUE!

Joseph stumbled through the manicured grounds and up the steps and inside, then slammed the heavy front door and locked it. He peeked out the etched oval of beveled glass, scanning up and down the street, but saw no returning Black and White.

There's no way she can know, not for sure, Joseph told himself; after two or three minutes and still no cab, he sagged against the door frame. "She's not coming back."

A woman's laugh sounded behind him, and he spun, gripping the knob to stay upright. Joseph's eyes almost fell out of his head as she swayed to his side and peered out the oval.

"She's not coming back," she echoed. "She *does* suspect, however. What would she do if she knew for certain? That's the interesting question, though she's too soft-hearted to do much." Envy filled her voice like poison. "She does not deserve what she has been given!"

Joseph backed away from her, retreating across the foyer. The auburn ringlets spilling down her back swayed as she turned to watch, amused. That shade complemented her dress, which despite the season was a flimsy summer-yellow thing that bared her long legs to mid-thigh. Two yellow straps ran up her back and over her freckled shoulders, holding the delicate material up, her bust more revealed than concealed by that thin barrier; he also noted, somewhat distantly, that she hadn't bothered with a bra.

Despite her beauty, Joseph felt no desire; he knew what this young woman was…mostly, anyway, enough to know he didn't want to know more. What was that quote by Emerson? "There are many things of which a wise man might wish to remain ignorant."

I couldn't agree with old dead Ralph more.

His back hit the paneling next to the Hermle Temple that had ticked and bonged its way through his family for ninety-odd years. "What—what are you doing here? The exchange is scheduled for tonight." She wore Spanish sandals, and she'd painted her toenails a warm yellow; to match the dress, he supposed.

Those eyes were anything but warm. "Do not question me, worm."

Joseph's bladder almost let go; he wanted to run, but even if she hadn't been what she was, she was forty-years younger; running wasn't an option. Groveling would have to do.

He bowed his head. "Yes, Mistress. I apologize, Mistress." Joseph dared to raise his gaze, if not his head. "It's just that I know our Master does not like unexpected changes to His plans."

Her eyes became glittering slits; the grandfather clock beside him ticked.

Joseph swallowed, hard.

She finally deigned to answer: "The timetable has been accelerated, worm, and that is all you need to know. Now take me to the remains." Her tone sharpened to something just short of deadly: "I trust they were prepared and stored under the proscriptions; there had better be no mistakes *this* time."

"There were no mistakes, Mistress."

"Excellent," she purred, then produced a white envelope from under her dress; Joseph's heart fluttered as she replaced the strap on her shoulder. *She doesn't carry a purse,* he mused, dazed, *and that dress doesn't have pockets, so I suppose it's the only place she can store anything…*

She thumbed the envelope open; it was thick with hundred-dollar bills. "Your payment, as agreed." She held it out, then snatched it away when he reached for it, hiding it behind her back coquettishly. "Not until I see that all is as promised."

"Of course." Joseph turned, then faltered as she replaced the envelope. His footsteps were unsteady as he led the way; when he finally received it, that envelope would be deliciously warm.

Without a bra, how does it stay in there?

Joseph quoted Emerson to himself again as he flicked the light hanging over the steep, narrow stairway, and she followed him down to the retort chamber, where he turned on the buzzing fluorescents, brightening the large space in a wash of pale, cold radiance.

Joseph had toured rival crematoriums with as many as four ovens side by side, to service multiple clients at a time, but one was sufficient for his needs; many of his competitors had also upgraded to fancy new computer controls, but Joseph had no need of those, either. His retort was operated manually, almost like a large pizza oven, with a simple on/off switch beside the temperature gage; when it was time to cook you turned it on, waited until the gauge read 2050 degrees Fahrenheit, then slid the client inside. Said client would be surrounded by either a plain pine box or a Custom Oak Cremation Casket (depending on whether said client's family were a bunch of cheapskates or not), and then ninety minutes later or so, determinate upon the mass of the client, you switched the retort off and waited while the client cooled, then used what amounted to an iron yard-rake to crush what bones hadn't powdered from the heat. Then you separated any metal—fillings and hip replacements and whatnot—to be recycled or thrown away before you scraped the dearly departed out and dumped them into the cremulator to further process the bones that were tough enough to survive to that point. Then you bagged 'em and tagged 'em and poured them into their vessel, preferably the Platinum Memorial Urn: "A Guarantee of Comfort and Elegance in your Beloved's Afterlife Time". Joseph made about five-hundred bucks net off those beauties, but there was a range of lesser options to display your dead Beloveds on the bookshelf or on the mantle or wherever you chose—of course, those were all just as good, just not as good for *him*.

This, Joseph thought for the ten-thousandth time, *is* such *a sweet racket...*

He walked over near the dormant retort and pointed into a far, darkened corner; a rolling tray sat there in the shadows. A squat, rectangle shape was on the tray, outlined underneath black velvet, the soft cloth hanging almost to the floor.

"There he is."

She swept past him, the yellow dress swishing on her hips, and twitched aside the cloth. It made a dark puddle on the concrete as she picked up the simple blonde-wood urn; Joseph had seen no reason to waste one of his Platinums. She closed her eyes, and a soft hum filled the retort chamber; her voice seemed to squeeze his eardrums deeper inside his head.

Joseph looked away uneasily. *Emerson.*

Pine boxes were stacked in the far corner, waiting for the cheap patrons alongside a stack of Custom Oaks for the more discerning. A large walk-in freezer occupied the back wall beyond the retort, there to keep the customers as fresh as possible before their rendezvous with the fire or the forever juice. Beyond that was the door to his preparation chamber, and beyond that a chained and padlocked double-steel door that guarded the ramp to the rear grounds; that ramp was how clients were delivered to his loving care, and how those who had a date with the worms departed after his ministrations were complete.

The humming turned to hushed singing, and Joseph broke a sweat; the words were in a harsh, unknowable language he had prayed to Almighty God he would never have to hear again. He put his eyes on the concrete between his burgundy Christian Louboutin's and quivered, wishing he had the courage to flee back up the stairs.

After forever the frightening singing stopped, and Joseph raised his head to see her stride from the shadowy basement corner holding the urn under one slender arm; with her brassy hair and yellow dress and long, tan legs, she seemed out of place in the cold crematorium, a bit of summer plopped into bleakest winter; he glanced at the rune-covered urn, shivered, and looked away.

"You've done well. The glyphs are perfect. Luckily for you."

Joseph had spent ten hours carving those awful symbols; ten tortuous, thirsty hours without pause or restroom break, painstakingly following the diagram in the proscribed order as his bladder throbbed, not understanding why it was imperative he go in order or why he couldn't stop until he finished or what the glyphs meant—not even *wanting* to know that. *God forbid.* He'd thrown away his tools, a brand-new set.

"Yes, Mistress. Thank you, Mistress." They were done down here; Joseph was ready to see sunlight again, even as thin and watery as it was today.

He was three-quarters of the way up the narrow staircase when he ran face-first into a wall. Joseph stumbled back, gaping, touching his aching nose to check for blood, then stretched out a hand and encountered a solid nothing blocking the stairwell. He spider-walked both hands across the nothing, looking for edges, a seam, a crease, anything; his heart pounded in his throat.

Her voice floated up behind him: "Jooooseeeeph, come back down. I haven't delivered your payment yet."

His eyes bulged as he hammered against the nothing; the door to the sun was only scant feet away.

"*Come*, Joseph," as if he were a dog. The solid nothing suddenly battered into him, forcing him back down the stairs. He screamed and kicked and clawed, but it scraped him out of the stairwell and across the floor, where it vanished just before he collapsed in a panting heap. She had set the rune-covered urn down and now had her arms crossed under her breasts like a disappointed schoolmarm; she was even tapping one sandal.

He scrambled to his knees. "Please, Mistress, I've done what you asked!"

"Yes, you've been a good worm, Joseph. A very good worm." A sliver of hot hope inserted itself into his hitching chest, then evaporated at her next words: "However, there have been issues raised."

"I-i-issues, M-Mistress?"

"Yes, worm, *issues*. Some have expressed doubts about your dedication to our Master."

"I…*please*, I—"

"The girl bears the Mark—as you were forewarned. You understand what this means for us?"

"P-please, M-Mistress—"

"Answer me!"

"Y-y-es, M-M-Mistress, I u-understand." *And God help us all…*

"And yet you have declined to take part in our…gatherings…for some time now." She clucked her tongue and shook her head, long, flaming hair swaying: "You pick a poor time to demonstrate a lack of commitment, Joseph."

"M-Mistress, *pleeeaaase*, I—"

"You also insist on charging for services that should be given freely—if not from a sense of friendship, then at least from gratitude at our shared fellowship." She looked away then, and he was wondering what had caught her attention—and also trying to think of a response, *any* response—when the retort's switch flipped to "ON": with a hissing roar, fire bloomed inside the massive oven. Joseph stared at those greedy blue flames through the viewing window and found he couldn't breathe; the temperature gauge climbed swiftly.

Then the iron door ground up, grating and rumbling.

"No," he whispered.

"I'm afraid so, worm." She made an imperious gesture, and to Joseph's utter shock he rose into the air, feet kicking three feet above the concrete. *This can't be happening.* She waved her other hand; wood grated on wood, and a pine box floated over beside him. He gaped at it.

She eyed it critically, then pronounced, "That just won't do", and flicked her fingers; the pine box flew and splintered against the wall with a deafening crash. She waved yet again, and a Special Oak floated up and over. "Nothing but the best for a good worm. I insist."

"You can keep the final payment! I'll give you the other money back as well! I'll give you *all* of it back! *Please!*" The coffin's lid flew off to hover beside him as he thrashed and kicked, but there was nothing to fight against; he simply floated there, helpless.

"Thank you for reminding me." She dropped the strap off her shoulder and re-trieved the envelope; her nipple was large and pink and erect. She rolled it between thumb and index finger, watching him watch, then shrugged the strap back. "That was for being such a good worm." She stuffed the white envelope into his breast pocket, patted it, and stepped back.

"Paid in full."

"*Mistress, PLEEEEEEEAAAAASE!*"

"Goodbye, worm. Say hello to our Master for me."

"NO!" The open coffin came toward him, and he fought, screaming and plead-ing and kicking until something unseen pinned his arms to his sides and his knees together, and then he was shoved in. The lid slammed, and he squirmed in the pitch black, turning face up, then pushed and pushed with all he had but the lid stayed tight. Cruel laughter came hollowly through the oak…and then the double-bump, and then the slide, and that's when Joseph heard something he'd heard hundreds of times over the years, but always from the outside; the low grind and heavy thump as the retort's iron door slid shut.

Gas hissed, flames roared, and Joseph went berserk, brain sloshing in his skull as he punched and pushed and kicked; he could taste smoke in every howling breath. He stopped when he realized he was no longer trapped in total darkness; a small flame licked at the corner above his feet, then more, more.

More.

It's so hot, but at least I can see now, and once the lid burns off, I could…I could…

Billowing smoke had turned his world gray, and Joseph was hacking and hacking and growing blessedly lightheaded, but then his pants caught on fire. He shrieked and thrashed. The lid above his face was a solid sheet of flame now, and Joseph prayed for a mercy he knew wasn't coming…and then something flickered in the bottom of his vision; he broke off the prayer and raised his head and opened his steaming eyelids wide and looked down at his chest, coughing.

The money in his pocket was on fire.

Just Another Flying Cow

They made a mistake. They should have killed me first.

Beth seized a dozen panicked animals and *flexed*, adding them to the three-dozen or so already floating beyond the fence. The ginger and white steers thrashed and bawled, many releasing streams of urine and manure as she swished them past each other in an intricate air-dance, faster, faster. The rest of the herd thundered to the far side of the field and milled, some looking back in bovine astonishment as their friends soared about.

If they're watching, I hope they're afraid.

Nearly fifty heavy animals, and Beth barely felt the strain; this with four days of practice.

Four days!

What would she be able to do in four weeks?

Four *years?*

The thought dried her mouth with equal parts desire and fear as she zipped the terrified creatures over and under and around each other, even flipping several into the air and juggling them until she saw the looks on their faces and had mercy, merely flying them around some more; Beth didn't want any of the smelly things to have a heart attack and die.

Beth was giving notice, showing *them* how strong she had become, but in reality she was at the ragged edge, near exhaustion and running on a fuel of pure rage and determination—a mix as finite as it was toxic. She had only caught snatches of sleep over the past four days, terrified they would come for Lizzie while she was out, that she would wake up and her daughter would be gone forever; she was also worried that Lizzie would snap out of this latest fugue and do something Beth would have to be awake to stop. But even as drained as she was, Beth wanted to seize the entire herd, over a hundred animals, and fill the pasture with mooing, shitting, flying cows, just to see if she could.

No. I must harbor my strength. I'm all alone in this fight, now.

The Murfreesboro PD claimed some college kid and his friend murdered Daniel because he had been flirting with the one kid's bartender girlfriend. *What crap.* The bartender had probably been flirting with *him*, and Daniel may have flirted a little back, but he had been leaving by himself when he was ambushed in the parking lot. *He wouldn't cheat on me, I know it, and I know those young men didn't kill him either, no matter what the stupid cops say.*

They killed him.

Beth had more than suspected it even before she'd learned that the star witness, this Samantha Gains, had up and vanished after her statement at the scene. And when Beth found out that the desk clerk at the La Quinta Inn Daniel had been staying at hadn't been seen since that night either...

They killed him.

"You made a mistake," Beth whispered fiercely as she whisked the petrified animals through the air...but the awful truth was, so had she. *I shouldn't have left him here.* But she had been so ready to get Lizzie away from this place and these people, so convinced that they wanted her and Lizzie and not him, that she'd persuaded herself they would leave him alone and ignored how damaging to her his death would be.

They hadn't ignored it.

Beth didn't even have time to mourn her Daniel; she had a cross-country move to complete and a pristine multi-million dollar restaurant to open and run for a profit (or else) and an amazing little girl to raise and nurture until she grew into the kind and beautiful young lady she was meant to be; all of which would require Beth's utmost concentration and dedication.

I'll just have to paint on a good face during the day and scream into my pillow at night.

Beth checked on Frank and Terry, the Briscoe Moving guys, making sure they were still out front at the truck, then wafted the nearest steer over the fence and let it float in the backyard; the animal bellowed and kicked and twisted its powerful body.

"See the moo cow, baby?"

Lizzie stared straight ahead and didn't respond.

Beth ground her teeth; Lizzie *loved* cows, and she should have been delighted at a hovering version. *She'll look at the stupid funeral director TWICE, but a flying cow gets nothing!*

Before...before everything, before Beth's heart had been crushed and ripped out of her chest, this window's deep recess had been Lizzie's favorite spot to play, so Beth had set Mr. Fred and her *Yertle* book and one of her Dora adventures and two of her favorite horsies on the sill, hoping, always hoping, but Lizzie had paid as much attention to them as she'd paid to the flying cow; only the pulsing of her little tummy gave testament she was breathing, and Beth knew that behind the dark sunglasses her blue eyes would be glazed.

Four DAYS of this, like one of her bad gray-outs, except this one never ends! Although it *was* something less than full catatonia, thankfully; Lizzie would eat mechanically when food was placed before her, and Beth had gotten excited when she'd found her standing in front of the bathroom door that first soul-crushing night at the new house (at least they wouldn't have to resort to pull-ups again), but aside from eating and bathroom functions, Lizzie had only acknowledged the world four times in the last four days that Beth had seen, and two of those were to reach out a dreamy little hand and pat her dog.

Poor Mr. Yoda. He was not happy staying behind at his new veterinarian's shelter, and not happy with Beth *at all* for leaving him there, but he'd been even wilder since

Daniel's murder and the onset of Lizzie's monster gray-out, snarling and snapping at everyone that got near Lizzie; it had only been nine hours since they'd dropped him off on the way to LAX, but Beth had already received a call complaining he'd attacked one of Dr. Johnson's assistants; the woman had needed five stitches in her hand. He was small, true, but those little teeth were sharp, and if he didn't mellow out soon, Beth didn't know *what* the heck they were going to do with him.

She had bigger issues right now besides the crazy dog, however. Beth considered her abnormally still five-year-old again, then sighed and lifted the terrified cow back over the fence and lowered them all to the turf; they stampeded off, bucking and kicking and mooing.

Her daughter hadn't spoken a word in four days.

Not a single word…

Beth squatted and gently turned her so they were face to face and took off Lizzie's cap, letting her hair tumble free, then removed the sunglasses and set them and the hat on the ledge. She brushed Lizzie's bangs back from her forehead, but got no reaction. She stroked her smooth, round cheek and held her hand, just as she'd done a hundred times a day each of the past four days; those eyes only stared through her.

Beth thought she would give anything to hear that sweet, piping voice again.

"Lizzie?" No response. "Baby? It's Mommy." No reply. "Can you hear me? Please talk to me. At least *look* at me." No reaction. "We can watch your New New *Star Wars* movie if you want." Silence. "Lizzie, please, *talk to me*."

Nothing.

Beth kissed her forehead and clutched her, but Lizzie's little arms didn't come up to return the embrace; she had somehow been with her father when he died, and whatever she'd experienced then, she hadn't yet recovered. But there *was* hope: now and then a gush of fearsome power came from Lizzie, and Beth would feel it and go to her and hold her and talk to her, even though Lizzie never changed expression or responded; Beth had also never seen or sensed any manifestations of those power surges, whatever they were, but she took heart that Lizzie was still in there; *something* was going on inside that little head.

Beth pulled back and looked into her daughter's unfocused eyes, feeling a tremor of dread.

Oh, yes, something is definitely happening in there…

She pulled Lizzie against her chest again as fresh tears dripped onto the silver stain; that hateful mark had doubled in length in the last four days; it now trailed almost to Lizzie's shirt collar.

"We'll be okay," she said, clutching, rocking. "Everything will be all right, I won't let them take you, but you need to come back to me, baby. *Please* come back to me."

Don't leave me here alone…

The clump of boots approached, and Beth stood up and hurriedly swiped her cheeks dry as she clamped the Dodgers' hat back on Lizzie before shoving the sunglasses on her blank little face. She turned them toward the window just as the boots stopped, still a long distance behind.

"Ma'am?"

"What is it?"

"Frank and I were, uh…well, we wuz wonderin'…"

"Yes?"

"I know you said to load everythin', but, uh…"

Beth turned. Terry the Briscoe Moving guy was peeking at her through the foyer's entrance to the dining room, and when she looked at him, he flinched and stared at the walnut planks beneath his scuffed boots. Terry the Briscoe Moving guy was a foot taller and a hundred pounds heavier than her at the very least, a brute with no neck and forearms the size of her calves, but he had refused to meet Beth's eyes once in the hour she'd known him.

Maybe it was because she'd ripped into his boss Mike three days ago; whatever the reason, Terry—and the other one, Frank, a wiry black man with a shaved head— refused to meet her eyes, and wouldn't speak to her unless absolutely necessary.

That was fine by her.

"*Spit it out.*"

"There's, ah, there's a mattress and box spring upstairs, with, uh, old bloodstains all over 'em, and—"

"Leave those." *The only set Daniel and I ever bought together.* They would never buy, or make love, on another. Beth fought through the rage and the heartache: "Load everything else, just like I said."

Terry raised his head just enough to glance sidelong at Lizzie.

"Hurry up!" Beth snapped. "I want to be on the road by sunset!" She would not stay here past dark, and if the slugs otherwise known as Frank and Terry couldn't get the job done by then, she'd take Lizzie and wait for them in Nashville.

"Yes, Mistress." Terry scurried upstairs. Frank darted out of the living room, where he'd been hiding; Frank had his head down, and Frank very much didn't look at her as he scampered up after Terry.

Beth patted Lizzie's shoulder, then went into the kitchen and over to the island and picked up her husband and tried to press him into the space where her heart had been.

"They made a mistake," she assured him in a low, savage voice. "And when the time is ripe, I'll make them pay for it!"

The steady rush of cars outside came through the chalked-open front doors as she sat him back down and brushed her palms over his top and traced her fingertips around his sides; the dismal weather was clearing at last, and weak evening sunshine slanted through bare west windows, highlighting the blonde wood under her hands. "I miss you." Hot tears glimmered orange in a sunbeam as they dripped. "I love you." Beth stood there holding her husband, crying and listening to the strange, heavy traffic as she thought about how it wasn't just Frank and Terry the Briscoe Moving guys who were acting strange today:

Mr. Wierlander.

Lizzie had raised her head and looked at the oily funeral director while they were in his office, and then in the taxi she had turned her head to look at him again.

Why?

Beth had seen through Wierlander's counterfeit sympathy, but she'd dismissed him as a callous sycophant who'd witnessed too much death. Besides, Janet and Bill had recommended him, saying they'd used him multiple times over the years, most recently for Bill's mother two summers ago, so Beth had shrugged off her instant distrust…but then Lizzie had raised her head and looked straight at the man. And then, when Lizzie's hat fell off, Beth had seen the raw panic on his thin face; combine that with the terror she'd sensed every time he barely even *glanced* at Lizzie…

It can mean only one thing.

No. Janet and Bill had recommended Mr. Wierlander, and she trusted them. Didn't she?

I have to trust somebody…

Trust or not, Beth resolved to swing by the Wierlander Funeral Home and Crematory on the way out of town; Frank and Terry the Briscoe Moving guys could wait in the truck while she and Lizzie had a little chat with this man who was so afraid of girls with silver in their hair.

Beth glanced outside at the fading light and had a better idea; she doubted Frank and Terry would get everything loaded by dark, so she would leave right now and go chew the fat with Mr. Wierlander while they finished; that got her and Lizzie away from this place faster, and it also had another advantage:

It nixed any possibility of Frank and Terry hearing Mr. Wierlander's screams.

Decision made, Beth picked Daniel up and pulled her keys out of her pocket; it would feel good to drive her car again. She'd missed it.

Then she paused, fatigued brain finally registering the traffic. *What the heck is going on?* There were maybe a handful of times in seven months plus that she could remember multiple cars on Daisy, but now it sounded like a stupid interstate out there.

Beth shook her head irritably; traffic was *way* down there on her list of concerns. She turned toward the dining room. "C'mon kiddo, let's—"

Lizzie was gone.

The Interment

*L*IZZIE!”

Terry yelled from the front yard. “She’s out here, ma’am!”

Beth shoved Daniel back onto the island and darted out of the kitchen and across the foyer to the open front door; Lizzie stood at the edge of the brick porch, facing the road. Beth came up beside her, touched her on the shoulder. “Baby?” Lizzie didn’t respond.

Beth looked at Terry and Frank, but they watched the convoy streaming by on Daisy; the line of cars and pickup trucks and SUVs was crawling east. The end stretched out of sight to Beth’s right, past Helen’s house and over the rise west toward Centerville; every headlight was shining, even though the daylight was just starting to fail and lights were only a judgment call.

Beth looked east again, to where Daisy made the T with McFarlane Farms; everyone was turning right. Just making the turn was a black SUV with darkened windows; American flags flapped from little poles at the front corners of its hood.

“What’s going on?”

Terry said, “It’s some kinda funeral, ma’am.” He and Frank exchanged a glance.

Beth frowned at them, then shoved her keys in her pocket; she saw license plates from every conceivable state except Hawaii and Alaska, and almost every vehicle had multiple people inside, and every single one of those people glanced over as they crept past; not at Terry and Frank, at her and Lizzie. Their faces showed a mix of curiosity and awe.

Frank and Terry looked at each other again, then turned and looked up at her and Lizzie, then put their eyes on the pavers between their boots.

Beth’s heart began to race. She picked Lizzie up and was about to take her back inside when she heard a familiar rumble; Helen’s Silverado appeared around the back of the moving truck, headlights shining. The old lady looked straight at Beth, then grimaced and dropped her eyes to Lizzie; her lined face filled with regret, and more than a touch of dread. Helen at last turned away, slumping behind the wheel as she slow-rolled down Daisy.

Beth trembled all over. Frank and Terry were still just standing there. “Get back to work! You’re not being paid to loaf around!”

“Yes, Mistress!”

“Yes, Mistress!” The ramp clanged and banged as they raced up and into the back of the long trailer; Beth could almost taste their fear.

She was turning with Lizzie to go inside once more when the end of the procession appeared; the car bringing up the rear was the red Mustang with the tinted windows. It detached itself from the line and pulled to a slow stop in front of the mailbox, headlights shining, and Lizzie suddenly pushed away from Beth, sunglasses fixed on the red car. Her legs kicked. She wanted down.

Beth held her tighter.

Lizzie fought her, sweet face empty, glasses pointed at the Mustang; its engine revved, RPMs screaming into the twilight.

Beth hunched and turned her body, shielding her daughter: "*You cannot have her!*"

The Cobra took off again, tires smoking. Lizzie stopped fighting, but her glasses followed it. Brake lights came on as people pulled over to let the red car race by, the line undulating like a flaring ruby snake.

Beth stalked inside and set Lizzie down; she immediately tried to go back out. "No, baby, stay with me." She lifted her again and kicked the rubber stop away and slammed the front door with a crash, then threw both deadbolts.

She put Lizzie down again and watched her walk to the front door, pause for a long moment, then go to one of the narrow windows that flanked it; her face was still vacant, and she was as silent as ever, but there was a new tension in her that was unmistakable.

"Lizzie?"

No response.

Beth watched, fidgeting, breathing in rapid hitches, a ball of ice growing in her core, and then she turned and floated toward the kitchen; she came to a stop next to the rectangle void where their fridge used to clank and hum.

Her husband was where she'd left him, serene and silent on the bare island, the last crimson rays of daylight shining sideways through the empty windows, illuminating the simple epitaph carved into his blonde-wood tomb:

Daniel Terrance Sims
Beloved Husband and Father
August 1, 1977-October 21, 2010

No. No, it can't be.

Her feet moved to him, stopped in front of him. Beth raised her hand…and let it fall back to her side; her soft whisper was barely audible:

"Daniel? Love?"

And then his voice bubbled up from the place where she kept it locked away, treasured and forever safe in her memories:

I may have told you a teensy-weensy fib as well…

A white-hot star bloomed in Beth's brain.

They didn't just want her and Lizzie.

She wanted him, too.

"No. No!" Beth threw back her head and shrieked, *"NOOOOOOOOOOOOOOOOOO!"*

With a coughing roar, the kitchen's windows exploded outward. Deadly shards and slivers blasted into the back and side-yards, glinting in the dying sunlight as little husky gray birds flew off in a panic; two of them didn't move fast enough, vanishing in a puff of feathers and blood. Directly over Beth's head, the floating cabinets dissolved, pieces falling around her, but none of it touched her; without thinking, she whisked it all into a glinting ball and shoved it outside through the jagged hole that was all that remained of the small window over the sink; a crushed cabinet near the oven fell to the counter and then to the tiles with a clatter and crash.

"I WILL NOT LET THIS HAPPEN!"

Beth snatched the urn off the island and dashed out of the destroyed kitchen and found Lizzie where she'd left her, standing motionless and staring out the skinny window; she shifted the urn to her right arm and scooped her daughter up with her left. Lizzie's cap-brim hit Beth's shoulder and the Dodgers' hat fell off; dark hair spilled out, chrome streak gleaming.

"C'mon, kiddo, we're not going to let them do this to your Daddy." Lizzie said nothing, but she raised her arms like a little sleepwalker and hugged Beth's neck. *Right.* They were all on board. She turned and then stopped; the front door was now shut and bolted, but her hands were occupied with carrying what was left of her family.

So who needs hands?

Beth blew the door into the yard. Several jagged pieces sailed across the road into Mr. White's pasture; many more whanged into the side of the moving truck, leaving deep dents before clattering to the driveway. She heard Terry and Frank scream, and then some pathetic whimpering as she ran down the steps and over to the open garage and set Lizzie down long enough to retrieve her keys, then stuck her daughter in the passenger seat, securing her with the lap belt after unhitching the shoulder belt. *No time for the car seat.* She put the urn in the floorboard under Lizzie's dangling Dora sneakers, then climbed in and started the car and revved the engine and backed out of the garage so fast the front end sparked on the lip; she shot backwards onto Daisy without looking. *Daniel.* Beth slapped the transmission into drive and blasted toward the intersection, then braked hard at the sign and made the turn without stopping, tires squealing.

"We won't let them do this, baby. We'll get your Daddy back, I promise."

Lizzie didn't respond.

They were doing a hundred and fifteen when Barron Road appeared. Beth slammed on the brakes, but they still overshot by thirty feet. She threw it into reverse and backed through an acrid cloud of tire smoke, then jammed it into drive, barking the front wheels through the turn, back wheels breaking free, almost sliding into the ditch, flying up and up and up the long incline to the top of the ridge. Beth forced herself to slow as she neared the crest, then brought the ticking Nissan to a halt.

She'd been right about the valley in October; its fiery autumn canopy fluttered in the evening breeze like a giant colony of roosting butterflies, but the cemetery's knoll ruined the view, as usual; the twisted black spike seemed to absorb the last rays of a scarlet sun that was busy sinking below the horizon; beyond the cemetery, the perfect circle of the cenote was a pit of shadow.

Beth strained to see through the canopy and caught headlights moving through the gloom along the cemetery's blacktop; she punched it and shot into the gorge and immediately felt the energy that filled this strange hollow; the pool wasn't near as colossal as the night they'd saved Lizzie, but she embraced it gratefully, letting it wash away her weariness and buttress her rage.

I will not let this happen!

She slowed as she neared the turn, then stamped on the brakes as a Rutherford County Sheriff's patrol car nosed out of the woods at an angle, denying her access; its light-bar came alive, blue flashes strobing the towering trunks and dying foliage.

Beth squinted into the glare and lowered her window as a deputy stepped out; blond, mid-twenties, muscles straining his tan uniform. He keyed a collar microphone and muttered something, listened to the response, then nodded and raised his hand, palm out. A black semi-automatic pistol was holstered on his right; a nightstick and handcuffs and pepper spray balanced it on his left.

"I'm sawrra, ma'am." His Tennessee twang was beyond thick: "This is a praavate service."

Beth vaguely recalled him tromping through her house the evening Scott Rison had died; he'd also obviously just been told not to allow her to interfere.

Taking her silent death-glare for acquiescence, the deputy lowered his hand and hooked his thumb into his utility belt near the pistol. He drawled, "I apologize, ma'am," but he didn't *sound* sorry; he sounded downright *pleased* with himself. He made a shooing motion: "Move along, naow. You're blockin' the road."

Beth had no time for this crap.

Daniel.

She put her car in park and stepped out.

His arrogance slipped as she shut the door, but only a little; Beth knew what he was seeing: a small, unarmed woman in her mid-thirties, wearing a Dodgers' cap and dark sunglasses despite the gloom, but then some base instinct must have kicked in because his face twisted just before he jerked the strap off the holster.

He was quick, Beth gave him that; he had the weapon halfway out before she took it from him. His eyes almost bugged out of his head as it floated to her, and then he yelled in astonishment when she waved her free hand and he jerked into the air. Her control was still iffy, however; there was a dull *thwock*, and orange leaves showered the hood of the cruiser. He groaned. She lowered him out of the tree and let him float over the light-bar. Blood ran out of his scalp to streak his forehead; his legs kicked feebly, and his black boots gleamed purple in the flash.

Beth said, "Sorry. I need more practice."

He fumbled at the microphone so she took that away too, ripping his uniform shirt halfway off. His tan went translucent, but he twisted and reached for his ankle, revealing a smaller holstered pistol. Beth took that away, then emptied both weapons and threw the clips into the meadow behind the rusted sign with the canted arrow that said BARRON CEMETERY and slung the guns into the woods on the opposite side. He didn't make a peep as he watched the toys he'd put all his faith and pride into discarded like impotent trash; in his terror, he seemed even younger than he was.

Beth peered up at him, one hand on a hip and finger tapping her lips; if he was willing to sell himself to *them*, what else had he done, *would* he do? His betrayal of the people he served and protected deserved some punishment, but it wasn't Beth's place to dispense it.

"You're lucky I'm not like them," she told him, then looked at the flashing cruiser and *pushed*. Tires barked, and the entire thing juddered and shuddered before it canted into the ditch; the young cop watched this play out below his polished boots, mouth stretched wide in a silent scream. Beth lifted his cuffs from his belt and dropped him; he yelled one of Daniel's favorite curses before he hit.

"Get up."

He raised wild eyes to her but stayed on hands and knees, swaying, blood dripping onto the asphalt.

"Get *up!*" She didn't have time for this! *Daniel.* Beth glanced back at her daughter; Lizzie sat in the running car, blank glasses turned toward them, watching but not; Beth knew she could also sense the power that was swirling and blowing like a black wind from Barron Woods.

"*Stand UP!* I won't tell you again!"

The young officer staggered to his feet, cocky nowhere in sight.

"Where's the key to your cuffs?" He licked bloody lips and pointed a shaking finger at his belt. "Take it out and throw it away." After two fumbling attempts, he did. "Now go over to your car, lie down on your back, and put your hands on either side of the rear axle." He stared at her. "Do it!" She had no time! "Do it right now, or I'll leave you hanging fifty feet up in a tree!"

He did as he was told. Beth wafted the cuffs over and clamped them on his extended wrists, ratcheting them down tight. He moaned and twisted around to peer at her; she could just see his waxy face strobing beyond the back tire.

"Now stay there; if you somehow manage to get free, and then try to stop us from leaving when we return…well, I just *wouldn't*, if I were you. And scoot your legs out of the road; I don't want to run over them." He complied, sobbing.

She jumped back in her car and turned onto the blacktop, inching by the canted cruiser. Beth had to stop this. *I* WILL *stop this!* A quarter-mile in, the last of the motorcade had pulled to either side, leaving a space wide enough for one vehicle down the middle; far ahead, beyond the bridge, she glimpsed people walking up the cemetery's knoll.

Beth hesitated; if she drove in there, they might use all those cars to trap them. She intended to stop what they planned, get her husband back, *and* get them all out again. She swung the car around and backed it plate-to-plate with the last vehicle, a powder-blue Cadillac Escalade from Kansas.

Time to hoof it, and fast.

Beth shut down the engine, unbuckled Lizzie, took her hat and sunglasses off and Lizzie's glasses as well, threw them all into the glove box, picked her daughter up, exited the car, beeped it locked, and ran down the lane between the twin rows of cars; the shining red and gold tunnel along with the sharp tannin-smell were pungent doses of autumn, but she didn't have time to savor them. *Daniel.* Lizzie didn't say a word, but she hugged Beth's neck tight as she jounced, peering ahead with her vacant blue stare.

They shot past Helen's Silverado and down the slope to the bridge, and Beth paused at its apex to catch her breath. She looked up, panting; people were streaming through the oval high above, backlit by a violet sky streaked by feathery pink and pumpkin clouds; she glimpsed lit cell-phone screens and waving flashlight beams, reminding her of just how dark it must be in here to most people.

Beth took off again, breathing deep; Lizzie was heavier than she looked. A familiar white Tahoe flashed by on her left.

I should've known. I should have KNOWN!

Above, cell screens and flashlights winked out as the last of the people disappeared into that striated oval; rage stretched Bet's stride.

She would *not* be too late!

They reached the oval and emerged into the stark contrast of glowing sky and twilight shadows and stopped.

The three were waiting for them.

They were at the far edge of the lot, blocking the path that cut through the bare thorns; the eldest stood foremost, the blonde and redhead behind and to either side. They wore ornate matching ivory dresses, almost like wedding gowns but without the veils and trains. Behind them, Melissa Bane had just made the turn up toward the cemetery; she was carrying a blonde-wood urn covered in hellish, mind-twisting runes.

Bane met Beth's eyes with her strange glowing ones; her grin was a hateful slash. "Keep her occupied until the ritual is complete!" she shouted. "On your souls, do not harm the girl!" The Keeper rushed up the path and vanished into the cemetery with the urn.

Daniel.

"Hello, sisters," the jet-haired hussy crooned. "So glad you could join us."

Beth glanced around without taking her focus from the three; scattered about the hill, moving gingerly while spreading through the thorns, were close on two hundred people. They were taking their places around the cemetery in some bizarre pattern; even so, quite a few of them peered at the distant cenote wistfully.

Beth saw Janet and Bill, and they saw her; Bill glanced hurriedly away, and Janet dropped her eyes, fear and shame twisting her face. Helen wasn't far beyond them, and behind her Mark and his wife Marcy. Her former kitchen manager spared Beth one triumphant sneer, then turned away. Steve and a very pregnant Amy were on the other side of the parking lot, just below the hedge; Steve supported her by the elbow, and Amy held her bulging belly as they negotiated their way around the mount.

Beth wasn't surprised, not after everything else, but a flash of hatred threatened to consume her; how many other "friends" would she see if she looked? How far back did this go?

And then Beth saw him and had her answer.

He was supposed to be in Santa Monica, but there he was. He was *supposed* to be getting the new store ready to open in two weeks, *her* new store, but there he was; their eyes locked just before the bulk of the cemetery's hill hid Clint Jennings from her, or she might have flared out and ripped her boss to pieces.

I WILL NOT LET THIS HAPPEN!

Beth set her daughter down and stepped forward just as a surge of vile power came from the cemetery; tendrils of shadow gathered from the purpling sky and swirled around the megalith.

Daniel.

"Move out of my way and I'll let you live."

The honey blonde, the youngest, stared at Beth with wide, frightened eyes, then turned her face away sharply. The redhead's gaze held nothing but contempt; she even sneered, but betrayed herself by licking her lips.

The eldest only smirked.

She's the true danger.

"She is confident for one so untrained, is she not, sisters? *Overconfident*, perhaps?" Alexandria shrugged. "It does not matter, for I cannot and *will not* let you interfere; he has already been promised to my Master, you see, and I do not break promises to Him." Black eyes flared. "You could ask the one who dared anoint himself my Father about that particular foolishness, but he is busy learning to grovel and please…and scream." A high, virulent chant suddenly flowed from above, and the raven-hair addressed the people standing in the thorns: "It begins! Sing, thralls, *sing for your pitiful lives! SING!*"

They sang; the terror washing from them was a physical thing, but they sang. Ragged male and female voices blended in a harsh, unknowable language…and the shadows responded, spreading from the megalith like unspeakable storm clouds.

Daniel.

Beth was out of time.

"Beware!" The redhead cried.

"She's so *strong!*" The blonde wailed.

"Join with me, sisters!" The eldest reached behind; all three clasped hands just as Beth let loose with everything she had, combined with all she could draw from the valley…

And was forced back; the four women stood rock still, straining, power shimmering and whirling in the air halfway between. The three were drawing deeply from the vale as well, and eldritch forces battered against each other, then swirled together and shrank, combining, then compressed, becoming something appalling, something that was the innocuous no-color of rain, or dust; the depraved song diminished as those nearest fell back, some screaming, some shouting.

Beth's teeth were vibrating, but she could force the vortex no closer to the three; together, they were stronger than her. Worse, they now realized it. Their frightened looks vanished, replaced by malicious smiles as that whirlpool swung toward Beth; sweat poured down her face and neck and breasts, soaking her bra as she dug deep and somehow stopped it scant inches before it enveloped her, but the three only laughed at her struggles; they knew it was only a matter of time.

Above her, the abysmal chant rose to a crescendo, and the inky shadows boiled, now covering the sky over the entire valley.

Daniel.

She would not let him suffer this!

Beth reached deep inside and found the place where she'd pushed the jack out, dropping their old pickup on her father and stopping the abuse; the place where she'd fled from the chest hairs; the place where she'd found the strength to get a sponsor and go to endless meetings and rid her body, brain, and spirit of the heroin.

Beth found that place and embraced it; pitiless smiles turned to shock as the vortex reversed and sped toward the three.

The blonde fell to her backside, releasing her sisters' hands; the redhead staggered but stayed up, freckled face terror-stricken. The oldest stood firm with a look of fierce concentration, blue-black hair blowing wildly as the compressed cyclone raced toward her, but then the redhead helped the blonde up and they grasped their sister's arms, buttressing her power once more.

The raging vortex stopped.

Beth felt a worm of despair; she couldn't keep this up much longer. Above and behind the three, the cemetery and even the top of the mount had been obliterated by writhing black shadows; thick tendrils stretched from that mass, snaking downhill and into the woods, groping as if they had minds of their own and were seeking something.

More screaming as people tore past her; engines started and tires squealed and fenders crashed as the true believers decided they'd gotten more than they bargained for, but about half still stood in the thorns and sang desperately; the virulent chant rose to that grotesque song and blended, intensifying.

Daniel. Beth was desperate. *I can't stop it by myself!*

There was only one chance.

"Lizzie, help Mommy! *Please*, baby! We have to save your Daddy! *HELP ME!*"

Lizzie walked forward and stopped at Beth's side.

There was a shocked moment as all four women stared at her, and then they were flung to the ground as a force greater than any Beth had ever felt brushed the vortex aside as if it were a dust devil. It collapsed with a low boom, thorns sucking toward the space it had vacated, and then all was still as desiccated maroon petals fluttered to the pavement; even the singing and chanting had stopped.

Beth and the sisters climbed shakily to their feet and found Lizzie's vacant stare gone as if it had never been; stony blue eyes were locked onto the raven-haired sister, and her small voice rolled across the silent hilltop like a sweet thunderclap, echoing over and around and through the hushed woods and the people watching:

"You hurt my Daddy."

Terror bloomed on that perfect face. "Please, M-Mistress, I…I conspired to free you from our Father's influence! You would not have enjoyed living under his thumb, as we have. I *saved* you from that, and you can now lead us to glory without his yoke! Th-that should be worth some thanks, Mistress."

"You hurt my Daddy." Lizzie piped again.

"I only did as commanded! I had no *choice!*" She fell to her knees, white dress tugged tight across her bosom, hands clasped desperately before her. "Forgive me, Mistress! *Please forgive me!*"

"No."

Black lightning struck from everywhere, grounding Alexandria; the thunderclap almost deafened Beth and threw her to the pavement once more, and her hair stood on end, dancing. The blonde and redhead screamed and fell away, hair haloing, and that's when Beth realized she was screaming, too. There was savage howling and barking from the woods, and then the Presidents were there, leaping toward Lizzie, but suddenly all three maddened animals were engulfed in a violent crimson flare, the intense heat making Beth squint; then only the sickening smell of charred pelt gave testament the dogs had ever existed. Lizzie hadn't even looked at them.

There was screeching bedlam then as a wave of people fled into the woods, leaving bloody, ripped clothing in their wake. Beth propped herself up on her elbows and watched, face seared, hair still dancing, eyes wide as they would go.

The eldest jittered amid those sizzling ebon bolts, and suddenly the lightning wound around and around her, forming a sphere, and then the sphere compressed and rotated, slowly at first, and then faster and faster, producing a whirring, whining sound that grated on Beth's brain. Gouts of blood and flesh were thrown wide from that whirling ball of annihilation; then the sizzling roar stopped, the dark lightning vanished, and what was left fell *splat*, now nothing more than a pile of smoking roadkill.

Beth somehow made it back to her feet and wiped blood from her face. The blonde and redhead shot one horrified look at Lizzie, then bolted, thrashing through the thorns; they left pieces of white and red dress behind, but they never slowed or looked back before they vanished between the towering trunks; the reek of ozone, along with roasted meat, fried hair, and burnt blood, was sharp.

Lizzie was untouched by gore as she contemplated what was left of the woman who had hurt her Daddy. Beth's first instinct was to hold her, but she hesitated and hated herself for it; she steeled her nerve and picked her daughter up. Lizzie smelled like green-apple shampoo, and that silver streak blazed in the twilight gloom, as if it possessed its own inner light.

"Hi, Mommy."

"Hi, baby." Beth hugged her as hard as she could.

Lizzie didn't hug her back. "She hurt Daddy."

Beth turned her back on the smoldering pile of goo and hugged Lizzie harder. "I know, sweetie. I know."

Two dozen or so hardy believers still stood in the thorns; they watched Lizzie with wary yet reverent expressions; some had gotten kneebound, and those prayed ecstatically. A man Beth recognized from Daniel's news programs stood a little way off, staring worshipfully at Lizzie. His tailored pinstripe suit was torn and blood-splattered, but his chiseled face and shock of silver hair looked ready for the camera on short notice. Deep in her exhaustion, Beth couldn't summon his name; she'd never been political. Senator Somebody. She couldn't even dredge up any outrage that he was one of *them*; it was all she could do to remain standing.

At Senator Somebody's side were two men dressed in dark, off-the-rack suits; they looked scared, and shocked, and they held shaking pistols pointed at her and Lizzie. One muttered something to Senator Somebody, and the Senator snapped something about "well paid", then with a curt gesture sent the men toward the road. They obeyed while keeping those twitching weapons pointed toward Beth and her daughter; she was glad they didn't shoot; as tired as she was, she wasn't sure she could've done anything about it if they…

Beth remembered why she'd been in such a hurry.

Daniel!

She jerked around and looked up; stars shone clear and bright above that jagged spike; only a faint tinge of orange and red and pink remained above the western rim of the valley.

"No! *NOOOOOOO!*"

Helen stepped from the thorns wearing her red straw hat along with a blood-spattered yellow rain slicker and blue rubber boots; her heavy gardening gloves covered her hands. She folded to her knees and shot a frightened glance at Lizzie, then looked imploringly up at Beth.

"I'm so sorry, dear." Tears dripped from her chins. "I had to help them. I *had* to. They'd a done somethin' ta Jacob or Paul, and I cain't lose them; they're all I have left. Please forgive a foolish old woman." She raised her gloves and covered her face. "Ah, *God forgive me!*"

Beth couldn't be too late. She couldn't! Carrying Lizzie, she staggered past Helen and the pile of hot goop and made the turn and sprinted up toward the cemetery. The lichgate loomed before her, *WELCOME TO BAR-RON CEMETERY* arcing above, climbing white roses snaking through the wrought-iron on the bottom of the curve and partly obscuring the archaic letters; something was wrong about that, but she didn't have the time to dwell on it.

Daniel.

I can't be too late!

Then Beth gasped and halted just before she crossed beneath the lichgate.

The cemetery was full of roses.

It shouldn't be, it *couldn't* be, but white blooms packed Barron Cemetery from hedge to hedge, smothering the black gravestones with their ghastly petals; to Beth's eyes, they shone in the darkness with horrid vitality.

How are these plants still blooming so far out of season?

And then she looked at the top of the mount and forgot about stupid flowers.

The Last Rose

ELISSA BANE stood beside the tall, crooked stone. She still held the rune-covered rectangle Beth had glimpsed earlier, and now it appeared scorched; wisps of smoke ascended from it.

No! I can't be too late!

She passed through the lichgate and marched up the path. Inky shadows writhed over Bane's face and body, obscuring her from even Beth's vision, but those hateful green eyes were clear. Closer, the stone towering over them all now, a black fang eating the stars. Closer. Closer. Lizzie's steady breathing and the scrape of Beth's boot soles were the only sounds.

The stone…

Beth halted.

Muted, blood-red light flashed along its length; a stanza would pulse dull crimson, and then another segment would throb in a different, seemingly random spot. *It looks like some sort of perverted Christmas tree.* She didn't know why it was doing that, but she dare not bring Lizzie any closer. Beth glanced back at Melissa Bane and found a predator's eyes bent on her. Lizzie remained silent, burnished stripe throwing scarlet flashes, reflections from the stone.

Beth spoke two words; her voice was iron.

"Release him."

"Foolish child." Shadows writhed faster: "He is mine now, and through me, my Master's."

"Release him, or I will burn you down where you stand!"

Bane tossed the charred urn away like so much trash; it struck a headstone with a dull crack before it vanished beneath the pallid roses. "The debt has been paid," she announced.

"What debt? We owe you nothing!"

"For all your power, child, you harbor an astonishing amount of ignorance."

"*What are you talking about?*"

"Dan Sims entreated *me* to free him from the hex you had placed upon him."

"No," Beth whispered.

"Yes," the Keeper responded. "I agreed, naturally, although there was a price. There is always a price." Those eyes bore down on Beth, full of mockery: "Dan Sims was as great a fool as you; he was my instrument, and had he exercised but a little patience, I would have freed him without asking, and without cost."

"You tricked him! And you *used* him! You used both of us!"

"John McFarlane had grown much too powerful to confront, or even be disposed of out of hand, yet I knew his way would have led to unmitigated disaster; your daughter must grow into her full power without constraint if she is to fulfill her destiny." A triumphant cackle issued from those crawling shadows: "In the end, John was the greatest fool of all! He dared place his own glory above our Master's!" The shadows swirled away, revealing Bane fully for the first time; she stared at Beth with icy contempt. "The One has come at last, child. The ancient promise has been fulfilled. Those are the essential truths; your husband was only a…sumptuous windfall, if you will."

Beth's heart was being shredded in her chest; she had left him like a goat staked out for the lion. *I just wanted to keep him safe!* She stared up at those gloating, glowing eyes, and pure rage pushed aside her guilt.

She whispered in Lizzie's ear while jabbing one finger up at Bane. "She hurt your Daddy, baby, just like the other one." *But she did worse than hurt him! So much worse!* "Lizzie?" Beth shook her daughter gently—oh-so gently! "Make her release him and then destroy her! She's hurting your Daddy!"

Lizzie just sat there.

"You *are* a foolish child; she will not harm me."

Beth ignored the hateful cunt. "Lizzie! *She's hurting your Daddy!*"

"Do you know *why* she will not harm me, foolish child? Our Master would not be pleased, and His displeasure is to be avoided at all costs." Her smile could have drawn blood: "As John McFarlane has learned. Or, to use one of this era's more distasteful colloquialisms, your daughter and I are on the same team; she is the One Foretold, child. She is the One Destined to tilt the Balance; the One Ordained to scour this Middle Plane in blood and fire and prepare it for our Master's coming." She looked up at the stars with a euphoric expression: "And now that I have fulfilled my task, I will rule at His side when we throw down the Golden Gates of Heaven itself and take back what they stole from us so long ago…"

"Our home."

Beth clutched Lizzie. "She's not…she isn't what you just said! She *can't* be! She's just a little girl! She's *my* little girl, and you can't have her! And you can't have my husband, either!"

Bane lowered her head and looked at Beth; she could have been contemplating a roach. "You are indeed a foolish child, despite your strength; foolish to deny what is plain to your heart; foolish to deny just because you fear. Your husband is my Master's to do with as He will." Lambent eyes shifted to Lizzie. "As is your daughter."

"*Liar!*"

"Am I?"

Beth's soul trembled. "He cannot have them!"

"I have been instructed to make a final offer in His name, child, despite my misgivings; despite you *spurning* His boon once before." A hushed pause, the cemetery, the entire world, utterly still around them. Then: "Give your heart to Him, say the words, and you can serve with your husband and daughter for all time."

Beth stared up at the Keeper of Barron Cemetery; she tried to speak, but her throat had closed down.

Bane sensed her weakness: "He wishes this, child," she almost crooned. "He has told me. Decades of preparation still lie before us, for even with the One's appearance, victory is not assured; the forces of the so-called Good will eventually put forth their own champion." She sneered. "Another weak-kneed sniveler mewling platitudes of love and forgiveness, no doubt, but for all their supposed righteousness, they will seek to harm the One before the true battle is joined, if they can. Your daughter must be taught, sheltered, and protected until she comes into her full power, and then none will dare stand against her. Who better to nurture the One Foretold than the Mother of the One?"

Beth opened her mouth, closed it. "You're lying," she whispered.

Bane turned and half-bowed, then gestured with both hands palm-up toward the pulsing stone; it was a reverent, almost ritualized motion. "Speak the words, and you will hear Him for yourself."

Beth swallowed. Twice. "That…that's just a big, stupid rock!"

The Keeper straightened. "Fool. You continue to deny with your tongue what is plain to your heart. When I sensed the majesty of this node blossoming from half a world away, I knew the Time of the One was approaching at long last. I raised this sliver of earth-bone and embedded it with my Master's essence—and with my Master's aid, of course. One does not attempt such without His acquiescence! Thus I protected this nodule for the One's use in the Last War; as the end grows closer, there will be other, albeit lesser, nodules that must be similarly secured, but that will not be *my* duty." She spread her arms and turned full circle, and for the first time Beth saw her smile not in hateful triumph or contempt, but almost girlish delight. "I will miss this valley! It alone, out of all the wretched places I've dwelt during my long, long search, has felt like home." She fingered a white bloom at the base of the stone. "I will miss my roses most of all, for these will be the last; the world to come will not be…conductive, shall we say, to growing flowers. A pity, but soon I will return to the place where all roses are golden, and they do not wither."

"You grew all these because you *like roses? You?*"

Bane drew herself up proudly. "I've created no St. Germain here, I'll admit, and this isn't a patch on that vainglorious outrage Ultrogote had planted for her own amusement. But unlike *some*…" She glared at Beth, "I like it." She caressed the white bloom again. "Is that so hard for you to comprehend, child? That one such as I could appreciate a unique blossom?" She stared a fiery green challenge down at Beth. "Do you deny this singular locus as well? That will be difficult, considering how I can feel you drawing on its might. I would refuse you that sacred privilege," she gesticulated toward the megalith again, half-bowing, palms up, "but it is not *me* that is permitting it."

Beth stood stock still, staring up at the throbbing megalith, skin crawling. Then she pushed the valley's power away, purging it as fast as she could; it went with an oily reluctance, and she staggered, Lizzie suddenly ten-times heavier.

"That's okay," she panted. "He can keep it."

The Keeper stared at her with narrowed, glowing eyes, then looked at the pulsing lith and cocked her head as if listening; the atmosphere in the cemetery had gained a new and dangerous charge.

Bane bowed to the stone and faced Beth once more. "My Master is not pleased, but He offers one last chance, child. Mother. Speak the words, and you can serve Him and be with your family forever."

"I will never serve Him. Do you hear me? *Never!* Now free my husband, bitch. He doesn't deserve to be in this God-awful, shitty place. If you don't, I will exterminate you!"

There was a long, deadly silence. "So be it." Shadows congealed, thicker than before, and Bane vanished. "Your choice is marked," came from that void. "*Fool!* My Master has no power over the living unless they give themselves to Him; that is the rule, and even some rules must bind Him, or all is chaos." The shadows billowed, and Beth glimpsed a form growing within, black on black; it looked nothing like a stocky woman in her fifties:

"*But His power over the Dead is absolute!*"

There were people in the cemetery, standing all around her.

Bone-cracking cold, pebbling her skin and making her breath steam as she spun this way and that, but they stared fixedly up at the swelling shadow, pale hands hanging, sallow faces still, lurid black eyes intent. There were dozens and dozens, maybe a hundred, men and women and children of all ages and races; their clothing marked eras that varied as greatly as their forms; some wore military uniforms, at least four different wars represented.

Beth convulsed from terror and the cold, but the dead continued to ignore her and Lizzie. Then she watched, dumbfounded, as they bowed their heads.

She turned slowly, dread filling her.

The shadows were gone. So was Melissa Bane. In their place, a being stood next to the megalith, a creature over eight feet tall, a thing with dusky skin and flowing golden hair and midnight wings spread wide against the stars; hooked ebony claws hung from long fingers and toes, and its body, although emaciated, appeared lithe and potent. Hints of withered femininity hung from its gaunt chest, though the rest of it appeared sexless. Green eyes blazed from that sinister face, eyes that now had vertical slashes for pupils.

The wings folded inward with a snap, glossy feathers humping over thin shoulders, mirrored harp silhouettes that Beth had seen in thousands of effigies since she was a little girl.

Horrified, the dead all but forgotten, Beth backed down the path toward the lichgate.

The dark angel watched her go with cruel amusement, then addressed the people standing in the roses. "Rejoice, my children! When our Master enters this world in His triumph, the Army of the Dead will rise to greet him, and you will be their vanguard! *Rejoice! The time of our Master's glory is upon us!*"

The inhabitants of Barron Cemetery stared silently at the winged atrocity, but none expressed the joy she commanded.

Sweating despite the cold, trembling so hard she could barely stand, Beth reached the lichgate just as the fallen launched from the hilltop, wings thrusting again and again, taking her high and then higher still, the backwash blowing Beth and Lizzie's hair around, but only Beth tilted her head to watch as she wheeled threateningly overhead, those dreadful eyes glowing and golden hair streaming, grotesque leftovers of femininity dangling, and then she swooped over the megalith and *screeched* at the sky:

"We are coming, All Father! We are coming, *Old Man!* WE ARE COMING!"

She gathered herself in midair and shot upward, became a shadowy streak and then a black and gold dot and vanished between the stars…but no. With a shriek that pierced Beth's brain, she plunged toward the earth; pure frustration and ultimate rage were in that long scream, and her poison eyes seemed to mark Beth as she fell. Just before she crashed into the top of the lith she became a shadow that was sucked into the stone, and a wave of ruby light rushed down it, bright enough to make Beth squint. The wave spread around the hilltop, jumping from headstone to headstone until all glowed a violent crimson among the white roses, shading them a sickly pink.

The denizens of Barron Cemetery let loose an unearthly moan as the wicked light washed over them; in ecstasy or pain, Beth couldn't tell which. They tilted their heads down and then down again, as if they were standing at the edge of a great cliff and watching something fall away between their feet, down and down and down and down and down and down.

With a silent flash, the megalith went dark. That gloom rippled across the tor as had the red light, engulfing each headstone and leaving it still and black once more. When the last of the gravestones had gone dark, the people in the roses spun as one and surged toward her, a blast of marrow-freezing cold preceding them, misty forms not disturbing a single petal, those with graves on the other side of the cemetery massing and flowing toward the lichgate, a wave of pale, intent faces and insanely angry eyes, flesh withering and drawing in to reveal stark cheekbones and bony brows, gaunt mouths gaping; worst of all were the forked, tubular, blood-red tongues that snaked out between needle teeth to flail about their starving faces…

Beth shrieked, a high, shrill sound that hovered on the brink of madness. They were unbelievably fast, and they would have swarmed her under if it weren't for Lizzie:

"She is not for you," she piped.

That wave of death halted as if crashing into an unseen wall, needle-studded jaws gaping, hollow tongues snapping and flailing, bottomless eyes mad with hunger and fury. They massed beneath the lichgate, churning and hissing in frustration, WELCOME TO BARRON CEMETERY arched over their hairless heads. Beth backed carefully down the path through the thorns, keeping a watch on them just in case, and when she reached the bend, she turned to run… but then something caught her eye:

She stared over the hissing throng at the top of the hill.

There was someone up there, one figure that hadn't joined the others, one form that stood near the tall stone; he wore the blue and white New Balance sneakers she'd bought for him, khaki cargo shorts with deep side pockets, and that ratty Go Buckeyes tee-shirt he loved so much…

No. Please, no.

Beth reluctantly raised her eyes to his face; she screamed so loud she hurt her own ears.

Lizzie was also looking up at the still, sad figure.

"Hi, Daddy."

Still screaming, Beth fled down the path. She hit the parking lot and looked back just before she plunged into the leafy tunnel and caught one last heartbreaking glimpse of the forlorn form standing next to the stone.

He was watching them.

Lizzie waved over Beth's shoulder.

"Bye, Daddy."

A Beautiful Voice

Beth barreled down the yellow and orange tunnel, mind frantic, churning. *I have to repair this!* She had no idea how, but that didn't mean she wouldn't try; there *had* to be a way to free Daniel. She would not leave the love of her life trapped here, trapped and bound to Him.

I WILL NOT!

But first she had to get Lizzie away. They would go back and tell Terry and Frank to meet them in Nashville, then wait somewhere—somewhere well-lighted, with lots of people. *Yes, that's it.* Then, once they'd settled into the new house and Lizzie had fully recovered, once they'd explored what they could do and gained strength, they would be back; together they would free Daniel and then raze that vile cemetery to the ground.

This was just a temporary setback.

I'll return for you, I promise! I love you!

Beth was almost to the bridge when she spotted around thirty people clustered on the uphill bank of the stream between the edge of the trees and the road; several held lit smartphones or flashlights, once again reminding her how dark it must be. They heard her coming, and someone cried out; another shouted a warning as sparkling beams swept through the forest and speared her, making her squint.

Before she could think Beth stopped and lashed out, knocking flashlights from hands, seizing two and flinging them spinning into the woods, people yelling and screaming and sobbing. One suit drew his gun, and Beth snatched it and slammed him back into a tree; he slumped to the loam, out cold. The other suit cursed and fumbled for his weapon, but Senator Somebody shouted, "Leave them be, Jerry! Just let them go!"

An enormous man took a stork stride forward and put his catcher's-mitt hand on the suit named Jerry's arm, bending down and rumbling something; Jerry shook the big man off, but let go of his weapon with another curse. They both stared at her, Jerry with anger and fear and uncertainty, the giant with sublime hate; there was no fear on his weathered and angular face. He wore cowboy boots and jeans and a gray tweed jacket; an old-time string tie hung down the front of his maroon dress shirt; a choker set with a pale blue stone secured the bolo. He looked familiar somehow, but Beth had never seen him before; she would have remembered a man that large.

They were *all* squinting at her, she realized; breathless, fearful, waiting to see what the dark figure on the path would do next…no; most were staring worshipfully at Lizzie. That hated streak was glimmering in the dark. A few dropped to their knees and murmured ecstatic prayers, and then more, more, until only the giant and Jerry and Senator Somebody remained upright.

Sudden rage nearly blinded Beth; why did *they* deserve to live when her Daniel… it would be so easy to send them all down to their Master, let *Him* sort them out…all of them, the whole stinking congregation…she wouldn't even leave bodies. They'd just be…gone, like all the missing Jeff and Daniel told her about…

It would take mere seconds.

No. No, I can't. I won't be like them. I won't!

The giant turned away with a lingering, cold-eyed glare, then went to Senator Somebody and bent and rumbled something; the senator broke off staring at Lizzie to protest: "I can't do—"

The big man seized his shoulder and growled something else while pulling what looked like a clear Ziploc freezer bag from his inside jacket pocket; there was an object sealed in the bag, but when Beth shifted Lizzie to the other arm and moved to see what it was, he turned his body to shield it.

A freezer bag? What is *that?*

The giant was still muttering; Senator Somebody turned his quaffed and Alexandria-splattered head to stare at Jerry, then considered the suit Beth had slammed into the tree. Jerry was now sharing his uncertain squint between his boss and the big man and Beth. The rest of the fools were still praying, and—

Beth took off again; she didn't care what was in the stupid Ziploc bag. They were letting her go, and *she* was letting *them* live; it was enough, for now. She had to get Lizzie away from here. She tossed the gun she'd taken from the comatose suit into the creek as she pounded across the bridge and then sprinted along the fluttering passageway. When the blacktop leveled she saw Helen's Silverado, headlights shining, engine rumbling. The old woman was behind the wheel, staring down at her lap. She raised her head to watch them come, then dropped her face into her palms, shaking as she wept. Beth and Lizzie didn't look at her as they sped past.

Someone had sideswiped her car; the passenger door was dented, the paint scraped. Beth ran around to the driver's side and put Lizzie across the console; as she buckled the lap belt, Beth heard *pow-pow!*

She backed out fast, looking around wildly, ready to defend or destroy—maybe Jerry or the giant had followed them after all—but she saw no one. Another *pow!* She peered down the long tunnel, but glimpsed only fiery autumn foliage.

Why are they shooting back there?

Beth waited, but when there were no more gunshots and the tunnel remained empty, she got in and slammed the door and fastened her seatbelt and cranked the engine and punched the gas, spinning the front tires in the leaves before she shot up onto the blacktop; she didn't bother with headlights.

Lizzie was peering out the side window.

"We'll be okay, baby. Everything will be fine. We'll come back for your Daddy when we're ready."

Lizzie didn't respond.

Up ahead, the police cruiser was still in the ditch, but two more cop cars had joined it, strobing blue lights overlapping; one, a Tennessee State Trooper, had left his door open as he squatted next to the handcuffed deputy. The other recent arrival, another Rutherford County, was just climbing out of his ride.

Their heads came up when they heard her car. The one she'd handcuffed screamed something, and the trooper stood up fast and drew his pistol while the other followed suit.

Beth blasted them.

She tempered herself, though; *no killing. I will not be like them.* The state cop bounced off his car and fell face-forward onto the road, flat-brimmed hat rolling away and black revolver clattering on the asphalt. He immediately pushed to hands and knees, shaking his head. *Good.*

The other flipped over the barbed-wire fence into the field behind Barron Cemetery's canted sign and didn't reappear. Beth hoped he would be okay. She inched by the cruiser in the ditch while listening to the young cop underneath wail piteously and discovered a new problem; the two fresh cruisers were blocking Barron Road to the right, and right was the way back to Frank and Terry and all their stuff. Beth wasn't sure she had the strength to push them out of the way, but she had to try.

Then, out in the field across Barron Road, the Rutherford County deputy she'd blasted stood up. He'd lost his hat, but he still had his gun. There was a pop, and the muzzle flashed as the bullet *thunked* into the front of her car.

Beth floored it, turning left, roaring up the steep incline. She ducked and pushed Lizzie's head down at more pops and more thunks: "Stay low, baby. Everything will be all right, I promise."

Lizzie kept her head down, but didn't reply.

In the rear-view, Beth saw the state cop stand up and stagger over and pick up his pistol, and then his hat. He was listing, but he managed to fall into his car's open door…and then they were over the lip of the corrupted valley.

Beth flew down Barron Road, doing eighty, ninety, a hundred; they had to make it back to the castle to tell Terry and Frank to finish loading, and that she and Lizzie would drive ahead. Everything would be all right once they got to their new house in California.

We'll be fine, everything will be fine, just have to get to California.

They had just blown past an overgrown field with a swaybacked barn straight out of a Mark Adam Webster acrylic when Beth looked in the mirror and saw blue lights. She looked forward again, then punched the brakes, screeching to a cockeyed stop in the four-way intersection she'd nearly gone right through. *Which way to the castle?* She wasn't sure anymore. Those blue flashes were strobing closer. *I have to ditch them.* She took something called Buckhorn Flats Rd., since she was already pointed that way. *I'll lose them on these backwoods roads, then circle around. Frank and Terry should have our things just about loaded by now…* They swerved into the ditch, one tire scraping, and Beth jerked the wheel and brought it back to the middle. She looked in the rear-view; the police made the turn at the intersection and followed.

Beth realized she was talking:

"Everything will be okay, baby, I promise. We'll get our new house set up, and next year you'll start kindergarten, and we'll find other people like us, people that will understand what we are, what we can do, people we can practice with and get better with. Then we'll come back and get your Daddy and we'll all be…we'll all be together again. Everything will be fine, sweetie. I swear to you, everything will be okay."

Lizzie said nothing, chrome streak glimmering.

She had the speedometer north of eighty and was watching the cops gain on them in the mirror when Lizzie turned her head slowly.

Beth glanced over and looked into her daughter's eyes.

Her mouth opened; she was trying to scream, but no sound emerged. Those eyes didn't belong in a little girl's face; they were too knowing, too cunning, and too cold—too *old*. There was gleeful malice dancing in those eyes as well, saying she knew what Beth was thinking, and then Lizzie smiled, showing her missing front teeth, and looked back out the windshield.

She began to sing:

Daddy looked mad, Daddy looked sad.
My Daddy was mad and saaaaad.
Daddy looked mad, Daddy looked sad.
My Daddy was mad and saaaaad.

"Stop it!" Beth screamed, but Lizzie kept singing; her voice, like her eyes, was something Beth no longer recognized; it was still a little girl's voice, but the cute, squeaky, off-key parts had disappeared. This voice was on key and on time, soaring through the ranges; it was a voice the likes of which Beth had never heard.

It was beautiful.

Daddy looked mad, Daddy looked sad.
My Daddy was mad and saaaaad.

"*Stop it!* Your Daddy…your Daddy's right…right here with us, see? There he is, under your feet! Lizzie, I said *stop!*"

Daddy looked mad, Daddy looked sad.
My Daddy was mad and saaaaad.

"*Stop it stop it stop it stop it Lizzie I said STOP!*"

The car lurched and bucked; they'd drifted into the ditch again. Beth attempted to steer out, to bring it back without losing speed or control, and then they hit something, a rock or a piece of debris; whatever it was, it was big. The front passenger tire blew, the air bags deployed, and Beth felt Lizzie do exactly what she did: stop the bag inches from her face, then crumple it up, deflating it in seconds. Lizzie even stuffed hers back and replaced the dash partition, but Beth let hers dangle in her lap.

Lizzie never stopped singing.

The car spun around, giving Beth a glimpse of the cops following; another Smokey had joined the chase. They completed the spin and stopped with a lurch that threw her against her seatbelt. The engine coughed, rattled, and died; steam rose from the hood cracks.

Daddy looked mad, Daddy looked sad...

Beth slammed it into park and turned the key; it cranked reluctantly, then caught. More steam gushed, and there was a new clackety sound she didn't like, but she threw it into gear just as the police caught up. Sparks gushed as the tire shredded and the bare rim ground on pavement, but she got it up to thirty and held there; the cops followed in a little parade, lights flashing.

We can't get away now, Beth realized. *We have to go somewhere public, so there'll be witnesses.* The trooper she'd spared back in the valley tried to pull up beside her, but she yanked the wheel over, cutting him off.

Daddy looked mad, Daddy looked sad.

My Daddy was mad and saaaaad.

There was a two-lane highway in this direction, with a gas station. *A Shell, I think. There'll be people.* Another officer joined the miniature parade behind her, blues strobing. *Surely all these stupid cops can't be with* them, *can they?* An amplified voice boomed, telling her to pull over and exit the vehicle. Beth took the next left without slowing, rim grinding, sparks shooting. She didn't dare go faster than thirty; she had to wrestle the wheel as it was.

Then, up ahead, like a vision in the sky, the red sign with the distinctive yellow scallop; and then a black and white road sign: STATE HIGHWAY 12.

That's it!

Her momentary elation plummeted when two flashing cruisers left the highway and overlapped, blocking her access. The nearest officer jumped out and pointed a shotgun at them, but Beth tossed him back in and slammed the door; the other officer froze halfway out and gaped like a fish, then reversed back onto Highway 12, tires smoking, door flapping.

"Hold on, baby."

Daddy looked mad...

Beth didn't slow as she tried to go around the first car; she almost made it. Metal screeched on metal, and they lurched across the highway and into the ditch and up the other side; there was a crunch and a bang and more sparks as they crashed and bashed into the Shell's lot. People scattered from the pump islands, abandoning their cars as steam poured from under her hood; she sputtered and jerk-rolled into the handicapped spot in front of the electronic glass doors, and then the engine gave a last wheeze and clatter and died.

Lizzie stopped singing.

Cops swarmed them, blocking them in, jumping out to level weapons. They were shouting at Beth to get out and lay on the ground with her fingers laced on the back of her head and ankles crossed.

I don't think so.

"Stay here, baby." Beth would have to hurt them. She would do her best not to kill them, but she would not let them take Lizzie from her. *I will die first.* "Mommy will be right back."

She was reaching to open her door when Lizzie's little hand shot out and grasped her right forearm; a shock went through Beth, and she shrieked screams of scalding agony into the headliner. After an eternity of blistering pain, Lizzie lifted her hand away.

Beth collapsed into the seat, twitching, gasping for breath—and then she felt it; the absence, as if someone had cut off one of her appendages; the blow so swift, so clean, that the knowledge of loss lagged far behind the cut. "What did you do to me? *What did you do?*"

Beth heard a tapping on the window by her head, a deep voice commanding her to exit the vehicle, but she only had eyes for her little girl.

"I'm sorry, Mommy." But she wasn't, Beth could see that. "You must swear to serve my Master, and then I'll give it back."

"I can't let them take you! Please don't do this! *Please!*"

"Pledge yourself to Him, Mommy, and then you can join me and Daddy forever. He promised." That heartless, alien gaze went past Beth's shoulder, then back to her. "They will take you now, Mommy."

"Don't do this to me, baby! I love you!"

"It will be so cool, Mommy, you'll see. It will *aaaall* be *soooo cooool!*"

Beth stared, upper lip curled in unconscious revulsion. Then the door yanked open beside her and rough hands grasped, pulling. She turned into them, punching and kicking, breaking and ripping and tearing and gouging, screaming that they would never take her daughter from her.

NEVER!

Inside the car, Lizzie resumed singing, voice soaring, throbbing with power; stunningly beautiful. It washed over the chaos and didn't sooth, but churned.

Daddy looked mad, Daddy looked sad.

My Daddy was mad and saaaaad.

GOD DAMN it, drive around him!”

Meredith Blake strained forward in the passenger seat of the 5 Live truck, trying to see past the twenty or so cars and pickup trucks and SUVs and one eighteen wheeler between them and the police barricade on State Highway 12 South. *I have to get up there!* “Or fucking run over him, I don’t care which!”

Derrick shot her a look like she was nuts. “You heard the man, they have to make sure it’s safe first. Besides, Dale’s best boy is still splicing the Senator’s grip ‘n grin files for the package. He’ll be ready by the time we are. Chill, you’ll get your big shot.”

Meredith gave her cameraman a withering glare, then focused her ire on the officer blocking their van, a Rutherford County Sheriff’s deputy whose name tag said Cpl. Riggins. At her insistence, Derrick had used the narrow shoulder, sometimes even half-dropping the van into the ditch, and they had made it *this* close before the cops at the barricade had noticed and sent Dudley Do-Right there to stop them.

Riggins returned her scowl, lifting his rover to listen and sometimes murmur a reply as he stood two feet from their bumper. He had cop-style dark hair, and he’d raised his mirrored Aviators to the top of his head now that night had fallen; Riggins was her age, mid-twenties, and their van’s headlights lit up his melting dark eyes. But she didn’t have time for that right now.

I have to get up there!

Frustrated, Meredith turned her glare back on Derrick, but he only stopped ogling her curves and shrugged, grinning. Derrick was past fifty, married with five kids (two of which were older than Meredith), with thinning hair and a sunken chest and a pot belly and one silly earring, but despite being a horny sleazebag, he was the best photog at Channel 5. Derrick was also professional enough to want this story, and would do his best, as always, but it wouldn’t be a career-maker or breaker for him, like it could be for Meredith; Derrick enjoyed where he worked and what he did and wasn’t going anywhere. She, on the other hand, couldn’t *wait* to get out of this misogynistic, shit-heel state and to a bigger market. *And this could be my ticket.*

But she had to get up there and punch it first!

A warbling siren caught her ear, and she watched jealously as two ambulances were let through the north barricade. They pulled into the Shell station, strobing red-and-whites adding to the apocalyptic scene. *There must be ten patrol cars down there, and another twenty out here.*

Excitement pushed through Meredith's aggravation; it all confirmed what she'd been told—not that she doubted her source: her own boss. *God, I have to get in there!* This would go national soon—it would probably even go global! Her work and face could be seen by news directors *across the world!*

And I'm just sitting here!

"Fuck this." *I won't let that blonde cunt from Channel 11 scoop me again!* That willowy bitch was probably already on her way, just itching to interview her pert little ass off while flashing those dimples and thrusting her fake boobs. Meredith dug her phone out of her purse and jerked down the visor to check her curls and makeup before throwing open the door.

Derrick's grin fell into his skinny lap. "What the hell are you doing?"

"You can sit here and pull your little pecker. I'll interview Dudley there, maybe get some landscapes. Dale can put it all in the package later."

"I've got the camera," he reminded her.

She showed him the iPhone. "They can clean it up at the shop." George and Mike in the control room would *love* that, but they'd do it, and listening to engineers piss and moan was preferable to sitting here while Derrick stared at her tits.

"Jesus, Mare, just be patient a minute and they'll—"

Meredith hopped out and slammed the door. *Spineless prick.* She started around the front of the van, but Dudley met her near the big wing mirror with his hand held out.

"Miss, please return to the vehicle." He motioned her back. She ignored him *and* his hand and held her phone up and hit record, then thrust her phallic cordless microphone under his nose, even though right now it was off; Meredith enjoyed watching people recoil and go cross-eyed when she did that.

"Cpl. Riggins, is it true that Senator Thomas Rattling was nearly assassinated while attending a funeral, and that two private security contractors were killed protecting him, and that the police have a suspect cornered at the gas station just ahead, the station you and your fellow officers are keeping us from reaching, denying our viewers' First Amendment rights to a free and unrestricted press?"

"How do you…? We haven't released—"

"Is the Senator otherwise unharmed?" Meredith knew he was, but she would be expected to ask; she had to protect her source. Let those condescending asshole print reporters snicker about broadcast "faces" all they wanted; she never revealed or betrayed a source—and that was of the utmost importance tonight. "Were any others hurt besides the two bodyguards?"

"I can't—"

"Is it true that the suspect is a woman, Elizabeth Marie Sims? The same Elizabeth Sims whose husband Dan Sims was recently killed in Murfreesboro in what the MPD believes was a homicide motivated by jealousy? The same Elizabeth Sims who fought off and killed Scott Duane Rison during a brutal home invasion back in August, stabbing him over forty times? Is it true that her daughter, Elizabeth Ann Sims, age five, is with her, and that the child is endangered?"

Riggins had raised both hands to ward her off by that point. "Wait a second, just…I don't…" He leaned and glanced up toward the barricade, but no cavalry appeared to save him. "Put that thing down, would ya?" Meredith lowered the phone, but didn't stop recording as he walked away, keying the rover and engaging in a low, urgent conversation, but at one point Meredith clearly heard, "She already knows!" Then he came back. "You can go on up." Surly.

She glanced at the remote truck, where Derrick slouched behind the wheel with his mouth hanging open. "Both of us?"

Riggins stepped out of the way, waving them on, impatient. *Sore loser.* "Yeah, yeah, both of you. Go. *Go!*"

She flashed an impish smile, rubbing it in despite how gosh darn cute he was, before climbing back into the van.

Derrick stared at her.

"Don't just sit there! *Drive!*"

He maneuvered by pouting Dudley and down the shoulder. The cops lifted the white-and-black sawhorses to the side; someone in line honked.

Meredith dropped the visor again and pursed her lips in the tiny mirror, wishing she'd worn the cream silk pantsuit that complimented her coloring and figure so well instead of jeans and a blue 5-News tee-shirt and 5-News windbreaker, but this afternoon she'd been shunted off to an unincorporated part of this pus-hole county to do a story about a Rutherford County deputy shooting a vicious dog, and these clothes had seemed apropos.

The hundred and thirty-five pound Rottweiler, named Precious—of course— had made a break from its chain-link dog run yesterday and killed a neighbor's mutt. The neighbor called the police, and the responding deputy, who was probably lurking somewhere around here, had confronted Precious and then felt threatened by Precious (imagine that) and had proceeded to shoot Precious five times with his service weapon.

Bon voyage, Precious.

So there Meredith had been, interviewing some skank with three teeth in her head, trying to project sympathy as the old bag complained that Precious had "neva hut nobody", and that she'd already been contacted by a lawyer, and that she was going to sue the county and the deputy both. Meanwhile, over by the lean-to passing for a house, two other monster Rotties were trying to chew through the chain-link dog run to get at her and Derrick—the chain-link dog run that had already failed to contain Precious. *They'd obviously never harm a soul, either.* The smell of dog shit had been a solid, rank wave, even from fifty feet. Two ragged kids of indeterminate age and gender stood on the hut's sloping porch, watching silently; the dogs had looked better fed.

When her cell rang and Mare had seen it was her big boss, she'd never been so happy to interrupt an interview to take a call. She'd been praying that Jack would laugh at her, that this cellar-dweller shit job that her assignment editor had sprung on her during the afternoon news meeting would turn out to be a practical joke on the new talent, ha ha, but what he'd had to say was way better.

Better?

The best *ever!*

Despite her good fortune, something nagged Meredith: Why didn't Jack want to be known as the source? *He was at the funeral, for God's sake.* He'd instructed her and Derrick to say they'd heard it on the scanner and rushed to the scene, since they were already nearby; an astoundingly lucky break, that.

She shouldn't be grousing, Meredith knew. Jack had given her the chance of a career, a lifetime, but it was puzzling; Jack Elroy Evans, President and General Manager of News Operations, had a lot of faults (a *lot* of faults), but lack of ego wasn't one.

He's never been shy about grabbing a little face-time before; granted, this is no political commentary, but still...

When she'd dug for details—just doing her job, in other words—details like where this Barron Cemetery was, whose funeral it had been, and how did the Senator (or Jack, for that matter) know the deceased, he'd snapped at her, saying if she didn't want it he would call Ann and Billy out even though they would have to race down from the studio in Nashville; so Meredith had shut up, then she and Derrick had rushed off, leaving the three-toothed skank yelling after them, wanting to know if she was going to be on the tae-vae. They'd followed the excitement on the police band, and now they were finally—

Derrick jammed on the brakes; he had been following the officer waving them to a spot on the other side of the pumps, but now...

"Holy shit."

"What?" Meredith slung the visor up and followed his gaze. A herd of cops had gathered around a person on the ground, fists and boots pummeling. The officer guiding them saw where they were looking and ran toward the group, shouting and waving his arms. The herd broke up, many glaring over at them. Meredith covered her mouth with both hands.

"OhmyGod!"

A small, dark haired woman lay face-up on the pavement, and for one horrible second Meredith was sure she was dead, but then the bloody figure moved her arms and attempted to rise. An officer shoved her back down, glancing over at the remote truck again before barking at one of the four paramedics working the scene. A pudgy guy in his thirties with a sick, scared look moved away from the officer he'd been attending and went to the woman and put his back to them, blocking their view. He said something to a fellow paramedic, a woman, and she squatted beside him; before she did, Meredith caught the same repulsed and frightened expression.

Derrick whistled. "She gave as good as she got, though."

"Yeah."

A cop was stretched out on his back, unconscious; as Meredith watched, the two remaining medics carefully attached a neck brace. One officer was just now sitting up and shaking his head; blood covered his lips and chin, his nose but a memory. Another clutched his ruined knee and rocked, crying. Several vertical cops had bloody noses and puffy eyes; one held his neck and bent over, gagging and coughing and spitting. Another cradled his left arm close to his stomach.

Meredith stared at the side of Derrick's head until he glanced at her. "Tell me you got it." Her voice held no hope, however; *we just had a Rodney King in the middle of Tennessee, and WE MISSED IT!* "Tell me you somehow got it."

Derrick only grimaced, thin face conveying his misery.

Meredith firmed her jaw; *she'd* witnessed the aftermath, and that meant the world would—this would be perfect for her follow-up piece! She checked the swarm of cruisers; body cams were the wave of the law-enforcement future, Meredith knew, but she couldn't count on those, not out here in the sticks, and the Rutherford County Sheriff's Department didn't even have dash cams yet—but Tennessee State Troopers did, as of three years ago.

Derrick saw her evil smile. "What?"

"Dash-cams."

He was just starting to grin back when a hand slapped the side of the van, making them jump; an angry face appeared at Derrick's window.

"Move this fucking thing over there *now!*" The officer stabbed his flashlight beam past the islands. When Derrick just looked at him, he backed up and grasped his holstered weapon. "Move it, asshole. They gotta take these officers to the hospital." Over his shoulder, Meredith saw the cop in the neck brace being gently loaded onto a collapsed stretcher; she also noted that nothing was mentioned about the bloody ruin that was the suspect needing attention.

"Okay, okay, Jesus!" Derrick let his foot off the brake and slipped between cars abandoned at the pumps. He gave Meredith a hunted look. "These guys are amped."

"No kidding."

They found clear air near a gated pile of reusable propane tanks; beyond it, on the far side of the building, a small group was being held back by two uniforms: customers, and every single one was jabbering into a cell phone. That lit a fire under her ass; Meredith had the exclusive for now, but—

Derrick knew the pig-fuck was coming, too: "We go live in three!" He slung his door open and ran around to the back.

She piled out. "I'll find whoever's in charge of this mess!"

The mast on top of the remote truck whirred and hummed, stretching toward the bird with their sat-window as two people standing near the station's glass doors caught Meredith's eye; they were civilians, but they hadn't been herded back by the propane tanks with the rest. One was a child, and the other a woman who held her hand; the woman had a clipboard pressed to her chest with her free hand, limp blonde hair, and a pinched face that looked like it smiled only occasionally, and reluctantly at that; she was smiling now as she watched Beth Sims bleed on the pavement.

The girl had to be the daughter, Elizabeth. *Lizzie, they call her.* A vein of silver glittered in her dark hair; it started over her right temple and trailed behind her ear, widening as it went, flashing azure fire in the strobes.

Meredith stared.

She'd never seen anything even remotely like it.

Derrick hustled up with his camera, hand pressed over the lens, nodding as he listened to the producer in his ear: "Your mic is ready when you are, Mare, and Dale says we've got a seven-second delay tonight, for some fucking reason, but follow my—" He did a double-take when he saw Meredith just standing there. "I thought you were in a big hur…" He followed her gaze.

Lizzie Sims noticed them, then; she turned her face their way.

Meredith blanched, then spun, putting her back to the little girl, hunching her shoulders as if she were preparing for a heavy blow.

Her jaw dropped. *Now why did I do that?* Meredith didn't turn around again, though, and she was suddenly sweating despite the cool October evening. Derrick was hunched with his back to the girl as well, clutching the heavy camera with the lens jammed up under his chins.

They looked at each other, trembling and wide-eyed.

What just happened?

"You can't take her! Please don't take her! I'm her mother!" The bloody ruin had been proned, and now her hands were being cuffed behind her back. Beth Sims' eyes were nearly swollen shut, yet she craned her neck and fixed desperate slits on her daughter: "Don't do this to me, baby!" She was jerked to her feet, kicking wildly as two officers hauled her toward the remaining ambulance.

"I love you! *I love you!* DON'T DO THIS TO ME!"

Meredith exchanged another wondering look with Derrick, then risked a glance over her shoulder; Lizzie Sims stood watching this display impassively, chrome band glinting and glimmering.

"Jesus," she whispered.

"Okay," Derrick announced, hoarse but determined, and swung the camera onto his shoulder: "They're about to flash the Breaking-News Elvis, and Annabelle and the meat-puppet are ready to do the lead-in. Annabelle will do the hand-off. Dale also said we gotta nail this, and I agree; we're cutting in on Wheel of Fortune."

"Get her going into the ambulance!"

"On it." The camera's super-bright halogen threw stark shadows as it bathed the scene in its unforgiving light. Derrick touched the IFB in his ear, held up five fingers, counting down, then two; when the last dropped, he gave her thumbs-up.

"Thank you, Reg, thank you, Annabelle. This is Meredith Blake, Channel 5 News Team, coming to you live from Rutherford County with a breaking story: There has been an attempt on Senator Thomas Rattling's life. Thankfully the would-be assassin was foiled, though we're saddened to report that two members of the Senator's private security detail were slain. After a pursuit involving multiple law-enforcement agencies, the police cornered the alleged killer at the gas station behind me, and have just now taken her into custody."

"As to the identity of the suspect, the authorities haven't released it yet, but a source has confirmed to this reporter that she is Elizabeth Marie Sims, age thirty-five. If that name sounds familiar, she is the same Elizabeth Sims who, along with her husband, was the victim of a terrible home-invasion assault in August. Mrs. Sims managed to free herself and then kill her attacker, one Scott Duane Rison, by stabbing him over forty times. Tragically, Dan Sims was also killed last week, a victim of what the Murfreesboro PD is calling a homicide motivated by jealousy. As yet, we don't know whether this evening's events are related to—"

Behind her, Beth Sims began raging. Meredith turned to watch and listen, stepping out of the way so her viewers could do the same.

"I know who you are," the small, bloody figure shrieked. "*I know who all of you are!* You can't have her, do you hear me? *You cannot have her!* I will take her back! *I will destroy you all, and then I'll take*—" Two burly officers threw her into the back of the ambulance and then climbed in after and slammed the door; the boxy vehicle rocked on its springs as muffled screams came from inside.

A man stepped out of the crowd of officers and sauntered their way.

Derrick swung the camera to cover him; tall, six-six or seven, and heavy—not fat, just big, with a barrel chest and long legs. Mid-fifties, he wore jeans and a maroon dress shirt with an open tweed jacket and string tie; Meredith hadn't seen a bolo since her Opa's wake. He wore cowboy boots below the jeans, and he stopped when he got to her and took a white handkerchief from his back pocket and wiped his mouth, grimacing at the blood; his lower lip was just beginning to puff.

Meredith knew him, naturally, even out of uniform; she thought she would have known *what* he was even if she didn't know *who* he was.

"Ma'am." William Jacobson, the Sheriff of Rutherford County, nodded to her before folding the stained cloth and returning it to his pocket.

She shoved her microphone up under his deep chin-cleft. "Sheriff Jacobson, we know that Senator Rattling survived the assassination attempt, but was he injured in the ensuing chaos? And what evidence do you have to connect Elizabeth Sims to the attempt on the Senator's life?"

Sheriff Jacobson shrugged. "The Senator's a little shook up, like anybody would be, but other than that he's just dandy. And as for 'evidence', we've got two-dozen witnesses who saw her ambush Rattling's men and then run away with her little girl. They say she was carryin' on like she was just now, screechin' about knowin' who he was, who everybody was. Evidently she blames him for her husband's murder. And there's this." He reached into the tweed jacket and produced a clear Ziploc freezer bag with a bright-green seal strip and held it up for the camera: "She dropped this little zinger before she ran away, after she did the bodyguards." Derrick focused on the baggie; inside was a small steel revolver with a polished wooden grip. "Multiple firearms were found in her husband's truck after the dustup over the pretty bartender. Dan Sims purchased them from private owners in the wake of that bad Scotty Rison business and gave this baby one to his wife for protection."

Meredith was momentarily speechless; she had never expected him to open up like this, and everything she'd ever learned about evidentiary procedure told her he shouldn't be sharing this with anybody that wasn't part of the prosecution team.

So why is he telling the world?

What she said was, "Shouldn't the murder weapon have been left at the crime scene to be processed by the crime-scene technicians, Sheriff?" Meredith shoved the microphone under his butt-chin.

He tucked the tiny revolver away and rumbled smoothly: "My boys are at the scene now, and it's already been photographed in situ and thoroughly 'processed', as you say." Smooth or not, his face was a rock; he hadn't liked her question much. "The Rutherford County District Attorney, along with the State Police and the FBI, will be holdin' a joint press conference later tonight, or maybe in the mornin'. You're welcome to ask those boys what's goin' on. Even Homeland Security's sendin' someone. All the mukety-mucks. I've got good officers down." He started to turn away.

"Sheriff Jacobson! Mrs. Sims appears to have been beaten to within an inch of her life, beaten by the arresting officers on scene. *Your* good officers, sir. Any comment?"

He glanced at the camera, squinting a little into the bright light. "No."

He turned away again.

"Sheriff! One more question!" She had a hundred more questions, but he could only answer one at a time. "Elizabeth Ann Sims, Mrs. Sims daughter? They call her Lizzie. I see her over there." Meredith pointed, but she didn't follow her own finger; Derrick, she noted, also didn't swing the camera toward the girl in issue. "Was she injured in the pursuit? And what will happen to her now that her father is dead and her mother is in custody?"

"Does she look injured to you? She's as fine as you can be when your Daddy's dead and your Momma's done lost her marbles."

Meredith jumped on that. "Are you saying that the suspect, Elizabeth Sims, is unstable?"

"You heard her yammerin' when my boys were tryin' to get her to the ambulance for treatment. What do *you* think?" He waved away a response. "We done called the Child Services, and Judge Witherspoon's been in contact with her only close relative, the daddy's brother, fella up in O-Hi-O." He shook his head, somber, but his eyes gleamed down at her from their deep sockets: "He's all she's got, but there was bad blood between the brothers. He told the judge he don't want nothin' ta do with her."

Meredith frowned. "You accomplished all that—contacted Children's Services and called Judge Witherspoon, who then got in touch with the uncle in Ohio—in just the last few minutes? That was fast work, Sheriff."

"It was!" he granted cheerfully. "And don't you worry none, missy. We'll take real good care of her," he said.

About the Author

Edward Rand is an American novelist and short-story artist. He wears other hats, such as Dad, zealous reader of great writers, (former) ne'er-do-well, dedicated martial artist, Stoic, dog and cat fanatic, and smarty britches. He loves talking about himself in the third person, too, so he's really getting a kick out of this.

Discover Edward's other work and sign up for his sporadic newsletter, wherein he gives away the short stories he writes just because at bloodchucklespress.com.

Rabid readers and their lovely, oh-so-opinionated opinions are the lifeblood of indie writers and publishers (traditional publishers as well, though they don't like to admit it). So however you felt about this book—love, hate, or meh—please compose an honest review wherever you purchased it.